TOGETHER FOR THE FIRST TIME—
THREE STORIES STARRING ONE OF DICK FRANCIS'S
MOST BELOVED CHARACTERS—
AND ONE OF MYSTERY'S MOST INTRIGUING HEROES . . .

"A rare and magical talent . . .
who never writes the same story twice."
—*San Diego Union-Tribune*

A hard fall took hotshot jockey Sid Halley out of the horse racing game, leaving him with a crippled hand, a broken heart, and a desperate need for a new job. In *Odds Against,* he lands a position with a detective agency. His first case brings him up against a field of thoroughbred criminals, and the odds against him are making it a long shot that he'll even survive . . .

"Among Francis's best."
—*Cincinnati Post*

Whip Hand finds Halley haunted by his glory days, although he still finds a certain satisfaction in solving a case. Hired by the wife of one of England's top racehorse trainers, Halley needs to figure out why her husband's most promising horses have been performing so poorly—and the reason is far more haunting than his memories . . .

"Sid Halley has never been better."
—*The New York Times Book Review*

In *Come to Grief,* Halley becomes convinced that one of his closest friends—and one of the racing world's most beloved figures—is behind a series of shockingly violent acts. No one wants to believe that Ellis Quint could be guilty—so the public and press are turning their wrath against Halley instead. Now he's facing opposition at every turn—and finding danger lies straight ahead . . .

ued . . .

FICTION BY DICK FRANCIS

Shattered	Reflex
Second Wind	Whip Hand
Field of Thirteen	Trial Run
10 lb. Penalty	Risk
To the Hilt	In the Frame
Come to Grief	High Stakes
Wild Horses	Knockdown
Decider	Slay Ride
Driving Force	Smokescreen
Comeback	Bonecrack
Longshot	Rat Race
Straight	Enquiry
The Edge	Forfeit
Hot Money	Blood Sport
Bolt	Flying Finish
Break In	Odds Against
Proof	For Kicks
The Danger	Nerve
Banker	Dead Cert
Twice Shy	

NONFICTION BY DICK FRANCIS

A Jockey's Life
The Sport of Queens

WIN, PLACE, or SHOW

DICK FRANCIS

BERKLEY PRIME CRIME, NEW YORK

THE BERKLEY PUBLISHING GROUP
Published by the Penguin Group
Penguin Group (USA) Inc.
375 Hudson Street, New York, New York 10014, USA

Penguin Group (Canada), 10 Alcorn Avenue, Toronto, Ontario, Canada M4V 3B2, Canada
(a division of Pearson Penguin Canada Inc.)
Penguin Books Ltd, 80 Strand, London WC2R 0RL, England
Penguin Group Ireland, 25 St. Stephen's Green, Dublin 2, Ireland (a division of Penguin Books Ltd.)
Penguin Group (Australia), 250 Camberwell Road, Camberwell, Victoria 3124, Australia
(a division of Pearson Australia Group Pty. Ltd.)
Penguin Books India Pvt. Ltd., 11 Community Centre, Panchsheel Park, New Delhi–110 017, India
Penguin Group (N.Z.), Cnr Airborne and Rosedale Roads, Albany, Auckland 1310, New Zealand
(a division of Pearson New Zealand Ltd.)
Penguin Books (South Africa) (Pty.) Ltd., 24 Sturdee Avenue, Rosebank, Johannesburg 2196, South Africa

Penguin Books Ltd., Registered Offices: 80 Strand, London WC2R 0RL, England

The book is an original publication of The Berkley Publishing Group.

Odds Against and *Whip Hand* reprinted by arrangement with HarperCollins Publishers Inc.
Come to Grief reprinted by arrangement with G.P. Putnam's Sons.

PRINTING HISTORY
Berkley Prime Crime trade paperback edition / October 2004

Library of Congress Cataloging-in-Publication Data

Francis, Dick
Win, place, or show / Dick Francis
p. cm
Contents: Odds against—Whip hand—Come to grief.
ISBN 0-425-19972-X
1. Halley, Sid (Fictitious character)—Fiction. 2. Private investigators—England—Fiction.
3. Detective and mystery stories, English. 4. Horse racing—Fiction. 5. England—Fiction. I. Title
PR6056.R27A6 2004   2004052992
823'.914—dc22

PRINTED IN THE UNITED STATES OF AMERICA

10 9 8 7 6 5 4 3 2 1

CONTENTS

WIN, PLACE, or SHOW

ODDS AGAINST

CHAPTER 1

I WAS NEVER particularly keen on my job before the day I got shot and nearly lost it, along with my life. But the .38 slug of lead that made a pepper shaker out of my intestines left me with fire in my belly in more ways than one. Otherwise I should never have met Zanna Martin, and would still be held fast in the spider threads of departed joys, of no use to anyone, least of all myself.

It was the first step to liberation, that bullet, though I wouldn't have said so at the time. I stopped it because I was careless. Careless because bored.

I woke gradually in the hospital, in a private room for which I got a whacking great bill a few days later. Even before I opened my eyes I began to regret I had not left the world completely. Someone had lit a bonfire under my navel.

A fierce conversation was being conducted in unhushed voices over my head. With woolly wits, the anesthetic still drifting inside my skull like puff-ball clouds in a summer sky, I tried unenthusiastically to make sense of what was being said.

"Can't you give him something to wake him more quickly?"

"No."

"We can't do much until we have his story, you must see that. It's nearly seven hours since you finished operating. Surely—"

"And he was all of four hours on the table before that. Do you want to finish off what the shooting started?"

"Doctor—"

"I am sorry, but you'll have to wait."

There's my pal, I thought. They'll have to wait. Who wants to hurry back into the dreary world? Why not go to sleep for a month and take things up again after they've put the bonfire out? I opened my eyes reluctantly.

It was night. A globe of electric light shone in the center of the ceiling. That figured. It had been morning when Jones-boy found me still seeping gently onto the office linoleum and went to telephone, and it appeared that about twelve hours had passed since they stuck the first blessed needle into my arm. Would a twenty-four-hour start, I wondered, be enough for a panic-stricken ineffectual little crook to get himself undetectably out of the country?

There were two policemen on my left, one in uniform, one not. They were both sweating, because the room was hot. The doctor stood on the right, fiddling with a tube which ran from a bottle into my elbow. Various other tubes sprouted disgustingly from my abdomen, partly covered by a light sheet. Drip and drainage, I thought sardonically. How absolutely charming.

Radnor was watching me from the foot of the bed, taking no part in the argument still in progress between medicine and the law. I wouldn't have thought I rated the boss himself attendant at the bedside, but then I suppose it wasn't every day that one of his employees got himself into such a spectacular mess.

He said, "He's conscious again, and his eyes aren't so hazy. We might get some sense out of him this time." He looked at his watch.

The doctor bent over me, felt my pulse, and nodded. "Five minutes, then. Not a second more."

The plainclothes policeman beat Radnor to it by a fraction of a second. "Can you tell us who shot you?"

I still found it surprisingly difficult to speak, but not as impossible as it had been when they asked me the same question that morning. Then, I had been too far gone. Now, I was apparently on the way back. Even so, the policeman had plenty of time to repeat his question, and to wait some more, before I managed to answer.

"Andrews."

It meant nothing to the policeman, but Radnor looked astonished and also disappointed.

"Thomas Andrews?" he asked.

"Yes."

Radnor explained to the police. "I told you that Halley here and another of my operatives set some sort of a trap intending to clear up an intimidation case we are investigating. I understand they were hoping for a big fish, but it seems now they caught a tiddler. Andrews is small stuff, a weak sort of youth used for running errands. I would never have thought he would carry a gun, much less that he would use it."

Me neither. He had dragged the revolver clumsily out of his jacket pocket, pointed it shakily in my direction, and used both hands to pull the trigger. If I hadn't seen that it was only Andrews who had come to nibble at the bait I wouldn't have ambled unwarily out of the darkness of the washroom to tax him with breaking into the Cromwell Road premises of Hunt Radnor Associates at one o'clock in the morning. It simply hadn't occurred to me that he would attack me in any way.

By the time I realized that he really meant to use the gun and was not waving it about for effect, it was far too late. I had barely begun to turn to flip off the light switch when the bullet hit, in and out diagonally through my body. The force of it spun me onto my knees and then forward onto the floor.

As I went down he ran for the door, stiff-legged, crying out, with circles of white showing wild round his eyes. He was almost as horrified as I was at what he had done.

"At what time did the shooting take place?" asked the policeman formally.

After another pause I said, "One o'clock, about."

The doctor drew in a breath. He didn't need to say it; I knew I was lucky to be alive. In a progressively feeble state I'd lain on the floor through a chilly September night looking disgustedly at a telephone on which I couldn't summon help. The office telephones all worked through a switchboard. This might have been on the moon as far as I was concerned, instead of along the passage, down the curving stairs and through the door to the reception desk, with the girl who worked the switches fast asleep in bed.

The policeman wrote in his notebook. "Now sir, I can get a description of Thomas Andrews from someone else so as not to trouble you too much now, but I'd be glad if you can tell me what he was wearing."

"Black jeans, very tight. Olive-green jersey. Loose black jacket." I paused. "Black fur collar, black and white checked lining. All shabby . . . dirty." I tried again. "He had gun in jacket pocket right side . . . took it with him . . . no gloves . . . can't have a record."

"Shoes?"

"Didn't see. Silent, though."

"Anything else?"

I thought. "He had some badges . . . place names, skull and crossbones, things like that . . . sewn on his jacket, left sleeve."

"I see. Right. We'll get on with it then." He snapped shut his notebook, smiled briefly, turned, and walked to the door, followed by his uniformed ally, and by Radnor, presumably for Andrews' description.

The doctor took my pulse again, and slowly checked all the tubes. His face showed satisfaction.

He said cheerfully, "You must have the constitution of a horse."

"No," said Radnor, coming in again and hearing him. "Horses are really quite delicate creatures. Halley has the constitution of a jockey. A steeplechase jockey. He used to be one. He's got a body like a shock absorber . . . had to have to deal with all the fractures and injuries he got racing."

"Is that what happened to his hand? A fall in a steeplechase?"

Radnor's glance flicked to my face and away again, uncomfortably. They never mentioned my hand to me in the office if they could help it. None of them, that is, except my fellow trap-setter Chico Barnes, who didn't care what he said to anyone.

"Yes," Radnor said tersely. "That's right." He changed the subject. "Well, Sid, come and see me when you are better. Take your time." He nodded uncertainly to me, and he and the doctor, with a joint backward glance, ushered each other out of the door.

So Radnor was in no hurry to have me back. I would have smiled if I'd had the energy. When he first offered me the job I guessed that somewhere in the background my father-in-law was pulling strings; but I had been in a why-not mood at the time. Nothing mattered very much.

"Why not?" I said to Radnor, and he put me on his payroll as an investigator, racing section, ignoring my complete lack of experience, and explained to the rest of the staff that I was there in an advisory capacity, owing to my intimate knowledge of the game. They had taken it very well, on the whole. Perhaps they realized, as I did, that my employment was an act of pity. Perhaps they thought I should be too proud to accept that sort of pity. I wasn't, I didn't care one way or the other.

Radnor's agency ran Missing Persons, Guard, and Divorce departments, and also a section called Bona Fides, which was nearly as big as the others put together. Most of the work was routine painstaking inquiry stuff, sometimes leading to civil or divorce action, but oftener merely to a discreet report sent to the client. Criminal cases, though accepted, were rare. The Andrews business was the first for three months.

The Racing section was Radnor's special baby. It hadn't existed, I'd been told, when he bought the agency with an army gratuity after the war and developed it from a dingy three-roomed affair into something like a national institution. Radnor printed "Speed, Results, and Secrecy" across the top of his stationery; promised them, and delivered them. A lifelong addiction to racing, allied to six youthful rides in point-to-points, had led him not so much to ply for hire from the Jockey Club and the National Hunt Committee as to indicate that his agency was at their disposal. The Jockey Club and the National Hunt Committee tentatively wet their feet, found the water beneficial, and plunged right in. The Racing section blossomed. Eventually private business outstripped the official, especially when Radnor began supplying pre-race guards for fancied horses.

By the time I joined the firm, "Bona Fides: Racing" had proved so successful that it had spread from its own big office into the room next door. For a reasonable fee a trainer could check on the character and background of a prospective owner, a bookmaker on a client, a client on a bookmaker, anybody on anybody. The phrase "OK'd by Radnor" had passed into racing slang. Genuine, it meant. Trustworthy. I had even heard it applied to a horse.

They had never given me a Bona Fides assignment. This work was done by a bunch of inconspicuous middle-aged retired policemen who took minimum time to get results. I'd never been sent to sit all night outside the box of a hot favorite, though I would have done it willingly. I had never been put on a racecourse security patrol. If the stewards asked for operators to keep tabs on undesirables at race meetings, I didn't go. If anyone had to watch for pickpockets in Tattersalls, it wasn't me. Radnor's two unvarying excuses for giving me nothing to do were first that I was too well known to the whole racing world to be inconspicuous, and second, that even if I didn't seem to care, he was not going to be the one to give an ex-champion jockey tasks which meant a great loss of face.

As a result I spent most of my time kicking around the office reading other people's reports. When anyone asked me for the informed advice I was supposedly there to give, I gave it; if anyone asked what I would do in a certain set of circumstances, I told them. I got to know all the operators and gossiped with them when they came into the office. I always had the time. If I took a day off and went to the races nobody complained. I sometimes wondered whether they even noticed.

At intervals I remarked to Radnor that he didn't have to keep me, as I so obviously did nothing to earn my salary. He replied each time that he was satisfied with the arrangement, if I was. I had the impression that he was waiting for something, but if it wasn't for me to leave, I didn't know what. On the day I walked into Andrews' bullet I had been with the agency in this fashion for exactly two years.

A nurse came in to check the tubes and take my blood pressure. She was starched and efficient. She smiled, but didn't speak. I waited for her to say that my wife was outside asking about me anxiously. She didn't say it. My wife hadn't come. Wouldn't come. If I couldn't hold her when I was properly alive, why should my near-death bring her running? Jenny. My wife. Still my wife in spite of three years' separation. Regret, I think, held both of us back from the final step of divorce: we had been through passion, delight, dissension, anger and explosion. Only regret was left, and it wouldn't be strong enough to bring her to the hospital. She'd seen me in too many hospitals before. There was no more drama, no more impact, in my form recumbent, even with tubes. She wouldn't come. Wouldn't telephone. Wouldn't write. It was stupid of me to want her to.

Time passed slowly and I didn't enjoy it, but eventually all the tubes except the one in my arm were removed and I began to heal. The police didn't find Andrews, Jenny didn't come, Radnor's typists sent me a get-well card, and the hospital sent the bill.

Chico slouched in one evening, his hands in his pockets and the usual derisive grin on his face. He looked me over without haste and the grin, if anything, widened.

"Rather you than me, mate," he said.

"Go to bloody hell."

He laughed. And well he might. I had been doing his job for him because he had a date with a girl, and Andrews' bullet should have been his bellyache, not mine.

"Andrews," he said musingly. "Who'd have thought it? Sodding little weasel. All the same, if you'd done what I said and stayed in the washroom, and taken his photo quietlike on the old infrared, we'd have picked him up later nice and easy and you'd have been lolling on your arse around the office as usual instead of sweating away in here."

"You needn't rub it in," I said. "What would you have done?"

He grinned. "The same as you, I expect. I'd have reckoned it would only take the old one-two for that little worm to come across with who sent him."

"And now we don't know."

"No." He sighed. "And the old man ain't too sweet about the whole thing. He did know I was using the office as a trap, but he didn't think it would work, and now this has happened he doesn't like it. He's leaning over backwards, hushing the whole thing up. They might have sent a bomb, not a sneak thief, he said. And of course Andrews bust a window getting in, which I've probably got to pay for. Trust the little sod not to know how to pick a lock."

"I'll pay for the window," I said.

"Yeah," he grinned. "I reckoned you would if I told you."

He wandered round the room, looking at things. There wasn't much to see.

"What's in that bottle dripping into your arm?"

"Food of some sort, as far as I can gather. They never give me anything to eat."

"Afraid you might bust out again, I expect."

"I guess so," I agreed.

He wandered on. "Haven't you got a telly then? Cheer you up a bit, wouldn't it, to see some other silly buggers getting shot?" He looked at the chart on the bottom of the bed. "Your temperature was one hundred and two this morning, did they tell you? Do you reckon you're going to kick it?"

"No."

"Near thing, from what I've heard. Jones-boy said there was enough of your life's blood dirtying up the office floor to make a tidy few black puddings."

I didn't appreciate Jones-boy's sense of humor.

Chico said, "Are you coming back?"

"Perhaps."

He began tying knots in the cord of the window blind. I watched him, a thin figure imbued with so much energy that it was difficult for him to keep still. He had spent two fruitless nights watching in the washroom before I took his place, and I knew that if he hadn't been dedicated to his job he couldn't have borne such inactivity. He was the youngest of Radnor's team. About twenty-four, he believed, though as he had been abandoned as a child on the steps of a police station in a push-chair, no one knew for certain.

If the police hadn't been so kind to him, Chico sometimes said, he would have taken advantage of his later opportunities and turned delinquent. He never grew tall enough to be a copper. Radnor's was the best he could do. And he did very well by Radnor. He put two and two together quickly and no one on the staff had faster physical reactions. Judo and wrestling were his hobbies, and along with the regular throws and holds he had been taught some strikingly dirty tricks. His smallness bore no relation whatever to his effectiveness in his job.

"How are you getting on with the case?" I asked.

"What case? Oh . . . that. Well, since you got shot the heat's off, it seems. Brinton's had no threatening calls or letters since the other night. Whoever was leaning on him must have got the wind up. Anyway, he's feeling a bit safer all of a sudden and he's carping a lot to the old man about fees. Another day or two, I give it, and there won't be no one holding his hand at night. Anyway, I've been pulled off it. I'm flying from Newmarket to Ireland tomorrow, sharing a stall with a hundred thousand pounds' worth of stallion."

Escort duty was another little job I never did. Chico liked it, and went often. As he had once thrown a fifteen-stone would-be nobbler over a seven-foot wall, he was always much in demand.

"You ought to come back," he said suddenly.

"Why?" I was surprised.

"I don't know . . ." He grinned. "Silly, really, when you do sweet off all, but everybody seems to have got used to you being around. You're missed, kiddo, you'd be surprised."

"You're joking, of course."

"Yeah . . ." He undid the knots in the window cord, shrugged, and thrust his hands into his trouser pockets. "God, this place gives you the willies. It reeks of warm disinfectant. Creepy. How much longer are you going to lie here rotting?"

"Days," I said mildly. "Have a good trip."

"See you." He nodded, drifting in relief to the door. "Do you want anything? I mean books or anything?"

"Nothing, thanks."

"Nothing . . . that's just your form, Sid, mate. You don't want nothing." He grinned and went.

I wanted nothing. My form. My trouble. I'd had what I wanted most in the world and lost it irrevocably. I'd found nothing else to want. I stared at the ceiling, waiting for time to pass. All I wanted was to get back onto my feet and stop feeling as though I had eaten a hundredweight of green apples.

Three weeks after the shooting I had a visit from my father-in-law. He came in the late afternoon, bringing with him a small parcel which he put without comment on the table beside the bed.

"Well, Sid, how are you?" He settled himself into an easy chair, crossed his legs and lit a cigar.

"Cured, more or less. I'll be out of here soon."

"Good. Good. And your plans are . . . ?"

"I haven't any."

"You can't go back to the agency without some . . . er, convalescence," he remarked.

"I suppose not."

"You might prefer somewhere in the sun," he said, studying the cigar. "But I would like it if you could spend some time with me at Aynsford."

I didn't answer immediately.

"Will . . . ?" I began and stopped, wavering.

"No," he said. "She won't be there. She's gone out to Athens to stay with Jill and Tony. I saw her off yesterday. She sent you her regards."

"Thanks," I said dryly. As usual I did not know whether to be glad or sorry that I was not going to meet my wife. Nor was I sure that this trip to see her sister Jill was not as diplomatic as Tony's job in the Corps.

"You'll come, then? Mrs. Cross will look after you splendidly."

"Yes, Charles, thank you. I'd like to come for a little while."

He gripped the cigar in his teeth, squinted through the smoke, and took out his diary.

"Let's see, suppose you leave here in, say, another week. . . . No point in hurrying out before you're fit to go. That brings us to the twenty-sixth . . . hm . . . now, suppose you come down a week on Sunday, I'll be at home all that day. Will that suit you?"

"Yes, fine, if the doctors agree."

"Right, then." He wrote in the diary, put it away and took the cigar carefully out of his mouth, smiling at me with the usual inscrutable blankness in his eyes. He sat easily in his dark city suit, Rear Admiral Charles Roland, R.N., retired, a man carrying his sixty-six years lightly. War photographs showed him tall, straight, bony almost, with a high forehead and thick dark hair. Time had grayed the hair, which in receding left his forehead higher than ever, and had added weight where it did no harm. His manner was ordinarily extremely charming and occasionally patronizingly offensive. I had been on the receiving end of both.

He relaxed in the armchair, talking unhurriedly about steeplechasing.

"What do you think of that new race at Sandown? I don't know about you, but I think it's framed rather awkwardly. They're bound to get a tiny field with those conditions, and if Devil's Dyke doesn't run after all the whole thing will be a non-crowd puller par excellence."

His interest in this game only dated back a few years, but recently to his pleasure he had been invited by one or two courses to act as a Steward. Listening to his easy familiarity with racing problems and racing jargon, I was in a quiet inward way amused. It was impossible to forget his reaction long ago to Jenny's engagement to a jockey, his unfriendly rejection of me as a future son-in-law, his absence from our wedding, the months afterward of frigid disapproval, the way he had seldom spoken to or even looked at me.

I believed at the time that it was sheer snobbery, but it wasn't as simple as that. Certainly he didn't think me good enough, but not only, or even mainly, on a class distinction level; and probably we would never have understood each other, or come eventually to like each other, had it not been for a wet afternoon and a game of chess.

Jenny and I went to Aynsford for one of our rare, painful Sunday visits.

We ate our roast beef in near silence, Jenny's father staring rudely out of the window and drumming his fingers on the table. I made up my mind that we wouldn't go again. I'd had enough. Jenny could visit him alone.

After lunch she said she wanted to sort out some of her books now that we had a new bookcase, and disappeared upstairs. Charles Roland and I looked at each other in dislike, the afternoon stretching drearily ahead and the downpour outside barring retreat into the garden and park beyond.

"Do you play chess?" he asked in a bored, expecting-the-answer-no-voice.

"I know the moves," I said.

He shrugged (it was more like a squirm), but clearly thinking that it would be less trouble than making conversation, he brought a chess set out and gestured to me to sit opposite him. He was normally a good player, but that afternoon he was bored and irritated and inattentive, and I beat him quite early in the game. He couldn't believe it. He sat staring at the board, fingering the bishop with which I'd got him in a classic discovered check.

"Where did you learn?" he said eventually, still looking down.

"Out of a book."

"Have you played a great deal?"

"No, not much. Here and there." But I'd played with some good players.

"Hm." He paused. "Will you play again?"

"Yes, if you like."

We played. It was a long game and ended in a draw, with practically every piece off the board. A fortnight later he rang up and asked us, next time we came, to stay overnight. It was the first twig of the olive branch. We went more often and more willingly to Aynsford after that. Charles and I played chess occasionally and won a roughly equal number of games, and he began rather tentatively to go to the races. Ironically from then on our mutual respect grew strong enough to survive even the crash of Jenny's and my marriage, and Charles's interest in racing expanded and deepened with every passing year.

"I went to Ascot yesterday," he was saying, tapping off his cigar. "It wasn't a bad crowd, considering the weather. I had a drink with that handicap fellow, John Pagan. Nice chap. He was very pleased with himself because he got six abreast over the last in the handicap hurdle. There was an objection after the three-mile chase—flagrant bit of crossing on the run-in. Carter swore blind he was leaning and couldn't help it, but you can never believe a word he says. Anyway, the Stewards took it away from him. The only thing they could do. Wally Gibbons rode a brilliant finish in the handicap hurdle and then made an almighty hash of the novice chase.

"He's heavy-handed with novices," I agreed.

"Wonderful course, that."

"The tops." A wave of weakness flowed outward from my stomach. My legs trembled under the bedclothes. It was always happening. Infuriating.

"Good job it belongs to the Queen and is safe from the land-grabbers." He smiled.

"Yes, I suppose so. . . ."

"You're tired," he said abruptly. "I've stayed too long."

"No," I protested. "Really, I'm fine."

He put out the cigar, however, and stood up. "I know you too well, Sid. Your idea of fine is not the same as anyone else's. If you're not well enough to come to Aynsford a week on Sunday you'll let me know. Otherwise I'll see you then."

"Yes, OK."

He went away, leaving me to reflect that I did still tire infernally easily. Must be old age, I grinned to myself, old age at thirty-one. Old tired battered Sid Halley, poor old chap. I grimaced at the ceiling.

A nurse came in for the evening jobs.

"You've got a parcel," she said brightly, as if speaking to a retarded child. "Aren't you going to open it?"

I had forgotten about Charles's parcel.

"Would you like me to open it for you? I mean, you can't find things like opening parcels very easy with a hand like yours."

She was only being kind. "Yes," I said. "Thank you."

She snipped through the wrappings with scissors from her pocket and looked dubiously at the slim dark book she found inside.

"I suppose it is meant for you? I mean somehow it doesn't seem like things people usually give patients."

She put the book into my right hand and I read the title embossed in gold on the cover. *Outline of Company Law.*

"My father-in-law left it on purpose. He meant it for me."

"Oh well, I suppose it's difficult to think of things for people who can't eat grapes and such." She bustled around, efficient and slightly bullying, and finally left me alone again.

Outline of Company Law. I riffled through the pages. It was certainly a book about company law. Solidly legal. Not light entertainment for an invalid. I put the book on the table.

Charles Roland was a man of subtle mind, and subtlety gave him plea-sure. It hadn't been my parentage that he had objected to so much as what he took to be Jenny's rejection of his mental standards in choosing a jockey for a husband. He'd never met a jockey before, disliked the idea of racing, and took it for granted that everyone engaged in it was either a rogue or a moron. He'd wanted both his daughters to marry clever men, clever more than handsome or well-born or rich, so that he could enjoy their company. Jill had obliged him with Tony, Jenny disappointed him with me: that was how he saw it, until he found that at least I could play chess with him now and then.

Knowing his subtle habits, I took it for granted that he had not idly brought such a book and hadn't chosen it or left it by mistake. He meant me to read it for a purpose. Intended it to be useful to me—or to him—later on. Did he think he could maneuver me into business, now that I hadn't distinguished myself at the agency? A nudge, that book was. A nudge in some specific direction.

I thought back over what he had said, looking for a clue. He'd been insistent that I should go to Aynsford. He'd sent Jenny to Athens. He'd talked about racing, about the new race at Sandown, about Ascot, John Pagan, Carter, Wally Gibbons . . . nothing there that I could see had the remotest connection with company law.

I sighed, shutting my eyes. I didn't feel too well. I didn't have to read the book, or go wherever Charles pointed. And yet . . . why not? There was nothing I urgently wanted to do instead. I decided to do my stodgy homework. Tomorrow.

Perhaps.

CHAPTER 2

FOUR DAYS AFTER my arrival at Aynsford I came downstairs from an afternoon's rest to find Charles delving into a large packing case in the center of the hall. Strewn round on the half-acre of parquet was a vast amount of wood shavings, white and curly, and arranged carefully on a low table beside him were the first trophies out of the lucky dip, appearing to me to be dull chunks of rock.

I picked one of them up. One side had been ground into a smooth face and across the bottom of this was stuck a neat label. "Porphyry" it read, and beneath, "Carver Mineralogy Foundation."

"I didn't know you had an obsessive interest in quartz."

He gave me one of his blank stares which I knew didn't mean that he hadn't heard or understood what I'd said, but that he didn't intend to explain.

"I'm going fishing," he said, plunging his arms back into the box.

So the quartz was bait. I put down the porphyry and picked up another piece. It was small, the size of a squared-off egg, and beautiful, as clear and translucent as glass. The label read simply "Rock Crystal."

"If you want something useful to do," said Charles, "you can write out what sort they all are on the plain labels you will find on my desk, and then soak the Foundation's labels off and put the new ones on. Keep the old ones, though. We'll have to replace them when all this stuff goes back."

"All right," I agreed.

The next chunk I picked up was heavy with gold. "Are these valuable?" I asked.

"Some are. There's a booklet somewhere. But I told the Foundation they'd be safe enough. I said I'd have a private detective in the house all the time guarding them."

I laughed and began writing the new labels, working from the inventory. The lumps of quartz overflowed from the table onto the floor before the box was empty.

"There's another box outside," Charles observed.

"Oh no!"

"I collect quartz," said Charles with dignity, "and don't you forget it. I've collected it for years. Years. Haven't I?"

"Years," I agreed. "You're an authority. Who wouldn't be an authority on rocks, after a life at sea?"

"I've got exactly one day to learn them in," said Charles, smiling. "They've come later than I asked. I'll have to be word-perfect by tomorrow night."

He fetched the second lot, which was smaller and was fastened with important-looking seals. Inside were uncut gem quartz crystals, mounted on small individual black plinths. Their collective value was staggering. The Carver Foundation must have taken the private detective bit seriously. They'd have held tight to their rocks if they'd seen my state of health.

We worked for some time changing the labels while Charles muttered their names like incantations under his breath. "Chrysoprase, aventurine, agate, onyx, chalcedony, tiger's-eye, carnelian, citrine, rose, plasma, basanite, bloodstone, chert. Why the hell did I start this?"

"Well, why?"

I got the blank stare again. He wasn't telling. "You can test me on them," he said.

We carried them piece by piece into the dining room, where I found the glass-doored bookshelves on each side of the fire had been cleared of their yards of leather-bound classics.

"They can go up there later," said Charles, coveting the huge dining-room table with a thick felt. "Put them on the table for now."

When they were all arranged he walked slowly round learning them. There were about fifty altogether. I tested him after a while, at his request, and he muddled up and forgot about half of them. They were difficult, because so many looked alike.

He sighed. "It's time we had a noggin and you went back to bed." He led the way into the little sitting room he occasionally referred to as the ward-room, and poured a couple of stiffish brandies. He raised his glass to me and appreciatively took a mouthful. There was a suppressed excitement in his expression, a glint in the unfathomable eyes. I sipped the brandy, wondering with more interest what he was up to.

"I have a few people coming for the weekend," he said casually, squinting at his glass. "A Mr. and Mrs. Rex van Dysart, a Mr. and Mrs. Howard Kraye, and my cousin Viola, who will act as hostess."

"Old friends?" I murmured, having ever heard only of Viola.

"Not very," he said smoothly. "They'll be here in time for dinner tomorrow night. You'll meet them then."

"But I'll make it an odd number. . . . I'll go up before they come and stay out of your way for most of the weekend."

"No," he said sharply. Much too vehemently. I was surprised. Then it came to me suddenly that all he had been doing with his rocks and his offer of a place for my convalescence was to engineer a meeting between me and the weekend guests. He offered me rest. He offered Mr. van Dysart, or perhaps Mr. Kraye, rocks. Both of us had swallowed the hook. I decided to give the line a tug, to see just how determined was the fisherman.

"I'd be better upstairs. You know I can't eat normal meals." My diet at that time consisted of brandy, beef juice, and some vacuum-packed pots of stuff which had been developed for feeding astronauts. Apparently none of these things affected the worst-shot-up bits of my digestive tract.

"People loosen up over the dinner table . . . they talk more, and you get to know them better." He was carefully unpersuasive.

"They'll talk to you just as well if I'm not there—better in fact. And I couldn't stand watching you all tuck into steaks."

He said musingly, "You can stand anything, Sid. But I think you'd be interested. Not bored, I promise you. More brandy?"

I shook my head, and relented. "All right, I'll be there at dinner, if you want it."

He relaxed only a fraction. A controlled and subtle man. I smiled at him, and he guessed that I'd been playing him along.

"You're a bastard," he said.

From him, it was a compliment.

THE TRANSISTOR BESIDE my bed was busy with the morning news as I slowly ate my breakfast pot of astronaut paste.

"The race meeting scheduled for today and tomorrow at Seabury," the announcer said, "has had to be abandoned. A tanker carrying liquid chemical crashed and overturned at dusk yesterday afternoon on a road crossing the racecourse. There was considerable damage to the turf, and after an examination this morning, the Stewards regretfully decided that it was not fit to be raced on. It is hoped to replace the affected turf in time for the next meeting in a fortnight's time, but an announcement will be made about this at a later date. And here is the weather forecast. . . ."

Poor Seabury, I thought, always in the wars. It was only a year since their stable block had been burned down on the eve of a meeting. They had had to cancel then too, because temporary stables could not be erected overnight and the National Hunt Committee in consultation with Radnor had decided that indiscriminate stabling in the surrounding district was too much of a security risk.

It was a nice track to ride on, a long circuit with no sharp bends, but there had been trouble with the surface in the spring, a drain of some sort had collapsed during a hurdle race: the forefeet of one unfortunate horse had gone right through into it to a depth of about eighteen inches and he had broken a leg. In the resulting pile-up two more horses had been injured and one jockey badly concussed. Maps of the course didn't even warn that the drain existed, and I'd heard trainers wondering whether there were any more antique waterways ready to collapse with as little notice. The executive, on their side, naturally swore there weren't.

For some time I lay daydreaming, racing round Seabury again in my mind, and wishing uselessly, hopelessly, achingly, that I could do it again in fact.

Mrs. Cross tapped on the door and came in. She was a quiet, unobtrusive mouse of a woman with soft brown hair and a slight outward cast in her gray-green eyes. Although she seemed to have no spirit whatever and seldom spoke, she ran the place like oiled machinery, helped by a largely invisible squad of "dailies." She had the great virtue to me of being fairly new in the job and impartial on the subject of Jenny and me. I wouldn't have trusted her predecessor, who had been frantically fond of Jenny, not to have added cascara to my beef juice.

"The Admiral would like to know if you are feeling well today, Mr. Halley," said Mrs. Cross primly, picking up my breakfast tray.

"Yes, I am, thank you." More or less.

"He said, then, when you're ready would you join him in the dining room?"

"The rocks?"

She gave me a small smile. "He was up before me this morning, and had his breakfast on a tray in there. Shall I tell him you'll come down?"

"Please."

When she had gone, and while I was slowly dressing, the telephone bell rang. Not long afterward, Charles himself came upstairs.

"That was the police," he said abruptly with a frown. "Apparently they've found a body and they want you to go and identify it."

"Whose body, for heaven's sake?"

"They didn't say. They said they would send a car for you immediately though. I gathered they really rang here to locate you."

"I haven't any relatives. It must be a mistake."

He shrugged. "We'll know soon, anyway. Come down now and test me on the quartz. I think I've got it taped at last."

We went down to the dining room, where I found he was right. He went round the whole lot without a mistake. I changed the order in which they stood, but it didn't throw him. He smiled, very pleased with himself.

"Word-perfect," he said. "Let's put them up on the shelves now. At least, we'll put all the least valuable ones up there, and the gemstones in the bookcase in the drawing room—that one with the curtains inside the glass doors."

"They ought to be in a safe." I had said it yesterday evening as well.

"They were quite all right on the dining-room table last night, in spite of your fears."

"As the consultant private detective in the case I still advise a safe."

He laughed. "You know bloody well I haven't got a safe. But as consultant private detective you can guard the things properly tonight. You can put them under your pillow. How's that?"

"OK," I nodded.

"You're not serious?"

"Well, no . . . they'd be too hard under the pillow."

"Damn it. . . ."

"But upstairs, either with you or me, yes. Some of those stones really are valuable. You must have had to pay a big insurance premium on them."

"Er . . . no," admitted Charles. "I guaranteed to replace anything which was damaged or lost."

I goggled. "I know you're rich, but . . . you're an absolute nut. Get them insured at once. Have you any idea what each specimen is worth?"

"No, as a matter of fact . . . no. I didn't ask."

"Well, if you've got a collector coming to stay, he'll expect you to remember how much you paid for each."

"I thought of that," he interrupted. I inherited them all from a distant cousin. That covers a lot of ignorance, not only cost and values but about crystallography and distribution and rarity, and everything specialized. I found I couldn't possibly learn enough in one day. Just to be able to show some familiarity with the collection should be enough."

"That's fair enough. But you ring the Carver Foundation at once and find out what the stones are worth just the same, and then get straight onto your broker. The trouble with you, Charles, is that you are too honest. Other people aren't. This is the bad, rough world you're in now, not the navy."

"Very well," he said amicably. "I'll do as you say. Hand me that inventory."

He went to telephone and I began putting the chunks of quartz on the empty bookshelves, but before I had done much the front doorbell rang. Mrs. Cross went to answer it and presently came to tell me that a policeman was asking for me.

I put my useless, deformed left hand into my pocket, as I always did with strangers, and went into the hall. A tall, heavy young man in uniform stood there, giving the impression of trying not to be overawed by his rather grand surroundings. I remembered how it felt.

"Is it about this body?" I asked.

"Yes, sir, I believe you are expecting us."

"Whose body is it?"

"I don't know, sir. I was just asked to take you."

"Well . . . where to?"

"Epping Forest, sir."

"But that's miles away," I protested.

"Yes, sir," he agreed, with a touch of gloom.

"Are you sure it's me that's wanted?"

"Oh, positive, sir."

"Well, all right. Sit down a minute while I get my coat and say where I am going."

The policeman drove on his gears, which I found tiring. It took two hours to go from Aynsford, west of Oxford, to Epping Forest, and it was much too long. Finally, however, we were met at a crossroads by another policeman on a motorcycle, and followed him down a twisting secondary road. The forest stretched away all round, bare-branched and mournful in the gray, damp day.

Round the bend we came on a row of two cars and a van, parked. The motorcyclist stopped and dismounted, and the policeman and I got out.

"ETA 12:15," said the motorcyclist, looking at his watch. "You're late. The brass has been waiting here twenty minutes."

"Traffic like caterpillars on the A.40," said my driver defensively.

"You should have used your bell," the motorcyclist grinned. "Come on. It's over this way."

He led us down a barely perceptible track into the wood. We walked on dead brown leaves, rustling. After about half a mile we came to a group of men standing round a screen made of hessian. They were stamping their feet to keep warm and talking in quiet voices.

"Mr. Halley?" One of them shook hands, a pleasant, capable-looking man in middle age who introduced himself as Chief Inspector Cornish. "We're sorry to bring you here all this way, but we want you to see the er . . . remains . . . before we move them. I'd better warn you, it's a perfectly horrible sight." He gave a very human shudder.

"Who is it?" I asked.

"We're hoping you can tell us that, for sure. We think . . . but we'd like you to tell us without us putting it into your head. All right? Now?"

I nodded. He showed me round the screen.

It was Andrews. What was left of him. He had been dead a long time, and the Epping Forest scavengers seemed to have found him tasty. I could see why the police had wanted me to see him *in situ*. He was going to fall to pieces as soon as they moved him.

"Well?"

"Thomas Andrews," I said.

They relaxed. "Are you sure? Positive?"

"Yes."

"It's not just the clothes?"

"No. The shape of the hairline. Protruding ears. Exceptionally rounded helix, vestigial lobes. Very short eyebrows, thick near the nose. Spatulate thumbs, white marks across nails. Hair growing on backs of phalanges."

"Good," said Cornish. "That's conclusive, I'd say. We made a preliminary identification fairly early because of the clothes—they were detailed on the wanted-for-questioning list, of course. But our first inquiries were negative. He seems to have no family, and no one could remember that he had any distinguished marks—no tattoos, no scars, no operations, and as far as we could find out he hadn't been to a dentist all his life."

"It was intelligent of you to check all that before you gave him to the pathologist," I remarked.

"It was the pathologist's idea, actually." He smiled.

"Who found him?" I asked.

"Some boys. It's usually boys who find bodies."

"When?"

"Three days ago. But obviously he's been here weeks, probably from very soon after he took a pot at you."

"Yes. Is the gun still in his pocket?"

Cornish shook his head. "No sign of it."

"You don't know yet how he died?" I asked.

"No, not yet. But now you've identified him we can get on with it."

We went out from behind the screen and some of the other men went in with a stretcher. I didn't envy them.

Cornish turned to walk back to the road with me, the driver following at a short distance. We went fairly slowly, talking about Andrews, but it seemed more like eight miles than eight hundred yards. I wasn't quite ready for jolly country rambles.

As we reached the cars he asked me to lunch with him. I shook my head, explained about the diet, and suggested a drink instead.

"Fine," he said. "We could both do with one after that." He jerked his head in the direction of Andrews. "There's a good pub down the road this way. Your driver can follow us."

He climbed into his car and we drove after him.

In the bar, equipped with a large brandy and water for me and a whisky and sandwiches for him, we sat at a black oak table, on chintzy chairs, surrounded by horse brasses, hunting horns, warming pans and pewter pots.

"It's funny, meeting you like this," said Cornish, in between bites. "I've watched you so often racing. You've won a tidy bit for me in your time. I hardly missed a meeting on the old Dunstable course, before they sold it for building. I don't get so much racing now, it's so far to a course. Nowhere now to slip along to for a couple of hours in an afternoon." He grinned cheerfully and went on, "You gave us some rare treats at Dunstable. Remember the day you rode that dingdong finish on Brushwood?"

"I remember," I said.

"You literally picked that horse up and carried him home." He took another bite. "I never heard such cheering. There's no mistake about it, you were something special. Pity you had to give it up."

"Yes. . . ."

"Still, I suppose that's a risk you run steeplechasing. There is always one crash too many."

"That's right."

"Where was it you finally bought it?"

"At Stratford-on-Avon, two years ago last May."

He shook his head sympathetically. "Rotten bad luck."

I smiled. "I'd had a pretty good run, though, before that."

"I'll say you did." He smacked his palm on the table. "I took the Missus down to Kempton on Boxing Day, three or four years ago. . . ." He went on talking with enjoyment about races he had watched, revealing himself as a true enthusiast, one of the people without whose interest all racing would collapse. Finally, regretfully, he finished his whisky and looked at his watch. "I'll have to get back. I've enjoyed meeting you. It's odd how things turn out, isn't it? I don't suppose you ever thought when you were riding that you would be good at this sort of work."

"What do you mean, good?" I asked, surprised.

"Hm? Oh, Andrews of course. That description of his clothes you gave after he had shot you. And identifying him today. Most professional. Very efficient." He grinned.

"Getting shot wasn't very efficient," I pointed out.

He shrugged. "That could happen to anyone, believe me. I shouldn't worry about that."

I smiled, as the driver drove me back to Aynsford, at the thought that anyone could believe me good at detective work. There was a simple explanation of my being able to describe and identify—I had read so many of the Missing Persons and Divorce files. The band of ex-policemen who compiled them knew what to base identification on, the unchanging things like ears and hands, not hair color or the wearing of spectacles or a mustache. One of them had told me without pride that wigs, beards, face-padding, and the wearing of or omission of cosmetics made no impression on him, because they were not what he looked at. "Ears and fingers," he said, "they can't disguise those. They never think of trying. Stick to ears and fingers, and you don't go far wrong."

Ears and fingers were just about all there was left of Andrews to identify. The unappetizing gristly bits.

The driver decanted me at Charles's back door and I walked along the passage to the hall. When I had one foot on the bottom tread of the staircase Charles himself appeared at the drawing-room door.

"Oh, hullo, I thought it might be you. Come in here and look at these."

Reluctantly leaving the support of the bannisters I followed him into the drawing room.

"There," he said, pointing. He had fixed up a strip of light inside his bookcase and it shone down onto the quartz gems, bringing them to sparkling life. The open doors with their red silk curtains made a softly glowing frame. It was an eye-catching and effective arrangement, and I told him so.

"Good. The light goes on automatically when the doors are open. Nifty, don't you think?" He laughed. "And you can set your mind at rest. They are now insured."

"That's good."

He shut the doors of the bookcase and the light inside went out. The red curtains discreetly hid their treasure. Turning to me, more seriously he said, "Whose body?"

"Andrews'."

"The man who shot you? How extraordinary. Suicide?"

"No, I don't think so. The gun wasn't there, anyway."

He made a quick gesture toward the chair. "My dear Sid, sit down, sit down. You look like d . . . er . . . a bit worn out. You shouldn't have gone all that way. Put your feet up, I'll get you a drink." He fussed over me like a mother hen, fetching me first water, then brandy, and finally a cup of warm beef juice from Mrs. Cross, and sat opposite me watching while I dispatched it.

"Do you like that stuff?" he asked.

"Yes, luckily." I grinned.

"We used to have it when we were children. A ritual once a week. My father used to drain it out of the Sunday joint, propping the dish on the carving fork. We all loved it, but I haven't had any for years."

"Try some?" I offered him the cup.

He took it and tasted it. "Yes, it's good. Takes me back sixty years. . . ." He smiled companionably, relaxing in his chair, and I told him about Andrews and the long-dead state he was in.

"It sounds," he said slowly, "as if he might have been murdered."

"I wouldn't be surprised. He was young and healthy. He wouldn't just lie down and die of exposure in Hertfordshire."

Charles laughed.

"What time are your guests expected?" I asked, glancing at the clock. It was just after five.

"About six."

"I think I'll go up and lie on my bed for a while, then."

"You are all right, Sid, aren't you? I mean, really all right?"

"Oh yes. Just tired."

"Will you come down to dinner?" There was the faintest undercurrent of disappointment in his casual voice. I thought of all his hard work with the rocks and the amount of maneuvering he had done. Besides, I was getting definitely curious myself about his intentions.

"Yes," I nodded, getting up. "Lay me a teaspoon."

I made it upstairs and lay on my bed, sweating. And cursing. Although the bullet had missed everything vital in tearing holes through my gut, it had singed and upset a couple of nerves. They had warned me in the hospital that it would be some time before I felt well. It didn't please me that so far they were right.

I heard the visitors arrive, heard their loud cheerful voices as they were shown up to their rooms, the doors shutting, the bathwaters running, the various bumps and murmurs from the adjoining rooms; and eventually the diminishing chatter as they finished changing and went downstairs past my door. I heaved myself off the bed, took off the loose-waisted slacks and jersey shirt I felt most comfortable in, and put on a white cotton shirt and dark gray suit.

My face looked back at me, pale, gaunt and dark-eyed, as I brushed my hair. A bit of a death's-head at the feast. I grinned nastily at my reflection. It was only a slight improvement.

CHAPTER 3

BY THE TIME I got to the foot of the stairs, Charles and his guests were coming across the hall from the drawing room to the dining room. The men all wore dinner jackets and the women, long dresses. Charles deliberately hadn't warned me, I reflected. He knew my convalescent kit didn't include a black tie.

He didn't stop and introduce me to his guests, but nodded slightly and went straight on into the dining room, talking with charm to the rounded, fluffy little woman who walked beside him. Behind came Viola and a tall dark girl of striking good looks. Viola, Charles's elderly widowed cousin, gave me a passing half smile, embarrassed and worried. I wondered what was the matter: normally she greeted me with affection, and it was only a short time since she had written warm wishes for my recovery. The girl beside her barely glanced in my direction, and the two men bringing up the rear didn't look at me at all.

Shrugging, I followed them into the dining room. There was no mistaking the place laid for me: it consisted, in actual fact, of a spoon, a mat, a glass, and a fork, and it was situated in the center of one of the sides. Opposite me was an empty gap. Charles seated his guests, himself in his usual place at the end of the table with fluffy Mrs. van Dysart on his right, and the striking Mrs. Kraye on his left. I sat between Mrs. Kraye and Rex van Dysart. It was only gradually that I sorted everyone out. Charles made no introductions whatever.

The groups at each end of the table fell into animated chat and paid me as much attention as a speed limit. I began to think I would go back to bed.

The manservant whom Charles engaged on these occasions served small individual tureens of turtle soup. My tureen, I found, contained more beef juice. Bread was passed, spoons clinked, salt and pepper were shaken and the meal began. Still no one spoke to me, though the visitors were growing slightly curious. Mrs. van Dysart flicked her sharp china-blue eyes from Charles to me and back again, inviting an introduction. None came. He went on talking to the two women with almost overpowering charm, apparently oblivious.

Rex vain Dysart on my left offered me bread, with lifted eyebrows and a faint noncommittal smile. He was a large man with a flat white face, heavy black rimmed spectacles and a domineering manner. When I refused the bread he put the basket down on the table, gave me the briefest of nods, and turned back to Viola.

Even before he brought quartz into his conversation I guessed it was for Howard Kraye that the show was being put on; and I disliked him on sight with a hackle-raising antipathy that disconcerted me. If Charles was planning that I should ever work for, or with, or near Mr. Kraye, I thought, he could think again.

He was a substantial man of about forty-eight to fifty, with shoulders, waist and hips all knocking forty-four. The dinner jacket sat on him with the ease of a second skin, and when he shot his cuffs occasionally he did so without affectation, showing off noticeably well-manicured hands.

He had tidy gray-brown hair, straight eyebrows, narrow nose, small firm mouth, rounded freshly shaven chin, and very high unwrinkled lower eyelids, which gave him a secret, shuttered look.

A neat enclosed face like a mask, with perhaps something rotten underneath. You could almost smell it across the dinner table. I guessed, rather fancifully, that he knew too much about too many vices. But on top he was smooth. Much too smooth. In my book, a nasty type of phony. I listened to him talking to Viola.

". . . So when Doria and I got to New York I looked up those fellows in that fancy crystal palace on First Avenue and got them moving. You have to give the clotheshorse diplomats a lead, you know, they've absolutely no initiative of their own. Look, I told them, unilateral action is not only inadvisable, it's impracticable. But they are so steeped in their own brand of pragmatism that informed opinion has as much chance of osmosing as mercury through rhyolite. . . ."

Viola was nodding wisely while not understanding a word. The pretentious rigmarole floated comfortably over her sensible head and left her unmoved. But its flashiness seemed to me to be part of a gigantic confidence trick: one was meant to be enormously impressed. I couldn't believe that Charles had fallen under his spell; it was impossible. Not my subtle, clever, coolheaded father-in-law. Mr. van Dysart, however, hung on every word.

By the end of the soup his wife at the other end of the table could contain her curiosity no longer. She put down her spoon and with her eyes on me, said to Charles in a low but clearly audible voice, "Who is that?"

All the heads turned toward him, as if they had been waiting for the question. Charles lifted his chin and spoke distinctly, so that they should all hear the answer.

"That," he said, "is my son-in-law." His tone was light, amused, and infinitely contemptuous; and it jabbed raw on a nerve I had thought long-dead. I looked at him sharply, and his eyes met mine, blank and expressionless.

My gaze slid up over and past his head to the wall behind him. There, for some years, and certainly that morning, had hung an oil painting of me on a horse going over a fence at Cheltenham. In its place there was now an old-fashioned seascape, brown with Victorian varnish.

Charles was watching me. I looked back at him briefly and said nothing. I suppose he knew I wouldn't. My only defense against his insults long ago had been silence, and he was counting on my instant reaction being the same again.

Mrs. van Dysart leaned forward a little, and with waking malice murmured, "Do go on, Admiral."

Without hesitation Charles obeyed her, in the same flaying voice. "He was fathered, as far as he knows, by a window cleaner on a nineteen-year-old unmarried girl from the Liverpool slums. She later worked, I believe, as a packer in a biscuit factory."

"Admiral, no!" exclaimed Mrs. van Dysart breathlessly.

"Indeed yes," nodded Charles. "As you might guess, I did my best to stop my daughter making such an unsuitable match. He is small, as you see, and he has a crippled hand. Working class and undersized . . . but my daughter was determined. You know what girls are." He sighed.

"Perhaps she was sorry for him," suggested Mrs. van Dysart.

"Maybe," said Charles. He hadn't finished, and wasn't to be deflected. "If she had met him as a student of some sort, one might have understood it . . . but he isn't even educated. He finished school at fifteen to be apprenticed to a trade. He has been unemployed now for some time. My daughter, I may say, has left him."

I sat like stone, looking down at the congealed puddle at the bottom of my soup dish, trying to loosen the clamped muscles in my jaw, and to think straight. Not four hours ago he'd shown concern for me and had drunk from my cup. As far as I could ever be certain of anything, his affection for me was genuine and unchanged. So he must have a good reason for what he was doing to me now. At least I hoped so.

I glanced at Viola. She hadn't protested. She was looking unhappily down at her place. I remembered her embarrassment out in the hall, and I guessed that Charles had warned her what to expect. He might have warned me too, I thought grimly.

Not unexpectedly, they were all looking at me. The dark and beautiful Doria Kraye raised her lovely eyebrows and in a flat, slightly nasal voice, remarked, "You don't take offense, then." It was halfway to a sneer. Clearly she thought I ought to take offense, if I had any guts.

"He is not offended," said Charles easily. "Why should the truth offend?"

"Is it true then," asked Doria down her flawless nose, "that you are illegitimate, and all the rest?"

I took a deep breath and eased my muscles.

"Yes."

There was an uncomfortable short silence. Doria said, "Oh," blankly, and began to crumble her bread.

On cue, and no doubt summoned by Charles's foot on the bell, the manservant came in to remove the plates, and conversation trickled back to the party like cigarette smoke after a cancer scare.

I sat thinking of the details Charles had left out: the fact that my twenty-year-old father, working overtime for extra cash, had fallen from a high ladder and been killed three days before his wedding day, and that I had been born eight months later. The fact that my young mother, finding that she was dying from some obscure kidney ailment, had taken me from grammar school at fifteen, and because I was small for my age had apprenticed me to a racehorse trainer in Newmarket, so that I should have a home and someone to turn to when she had gone. They had been good enough people, both of them, and Charles knew that I thought so.

The next course was some sort of fish smothered in mushroom-colored sauce. My astronauts' delight, coming at the same time, didn't took noticeably different, as it was not in its pot, but out on a plate. Dear Mrs. Cross, I thought fervently, I could kiss you. I could eat it this way with a fork, single-handed. The pots needed to be held—in my case inelegantly hugged between forearm and chest—and at that moment I would have starved rather than taken my left hand out of my pocket.

Fluffy Mrs. van Dysart was having a ball. Clearly she relished the idea of me sitting there practically isolated, dressed in the wrong clothes, and an object of open derision to her host. With her fair frizzy hair, her baby-blue eyes and her rose-pink silk dress embroidered with silver, she looked as sweet as sugar icing. What she said showed that she thoroughly understood the pleasures of keeping a whipping boy.

"Poor relations are such a problem, aren't they?" she said to Charles sympathetically, and intentionally loud enough for me to hear. "You can't neglect them in our position, in case the Sunday papers get hold of them and pay them to make a smear. And it's especially difficult if one has to keep them in one's own house. One can't, I suppose, put them to eat in the kitchen, but there are so many occasions when one could do without them. Perhaps a tray upstairs is the best thing."

"Ah, yes," nodded Charles smoothly, "but they won't always agree to that."

I half choked on a mouthful, remembering the pressure he had exerted to get me downstairs. And immediately I felt not only reassured but deeply interested. This, then, was what he had been so industriously planning, the destruction of me as a man in the eyes of his guests. He would no doubt explain why in his own good time. Meanwhile I felt slightly less inclined to go back to bed.

I glanced at Kraye, and found his greenish-amber eyes steady on my face. It wasn't as overt as in Mrs. van Dysart's case, but it was there: pleasure. My toes curled inside my shoes. Interested or not, it went hard to sit tight before that loathsome, taunting half smile. I looked down, away, blotting him out.

He gave a sound halfway between a cough and a laugh, turned his head, and began talking down the table to Charles about the collection of quartz.

"So sensible of you, my dear chap, to keep them all behind glass, though most tantalizing to me from here. Is that a geode, on the middle shelf? The reflection, you know . . . I can't quite see."

"Er . . ." said Charles, not knowing any more than I did what a geode was. "I'm looking forward to showing them to you. After dinner, perhaps? Or tomorrow?"

"Oh, tonight, I'd hate to postpone such a treat. Did you say that you had any felspar in your collection?"

"No," said Charles uncertainly.

"No, well, I can see it is a small specialized collection. Perhaps you are wise in sticking to silicon dioxide."

Charles glibly launched into the cousinly-bequest alibi for ignorance, which Kraye accepted with courtesy and disappointment.

"A fascinating subject, though, my dear Roland. It repays study. The earth beneath our feet, the fundamental sediment from the Triassic and Jurassic epochs, is our priceless inheritance, the source of all our life and power. . . . There is nothing which interests me so much as land."

Doria on my right gave the tiniest of snorts, which her husband didn't hear. He was busy constructing another long, polysyllabic and largely unintelligible chat on the nature of the universe.

I sat unoccupied through the steaks, the meringue pudding, the cheese and the fruit. Conversations went on on either side of me and occasionally past me, but a deaf-mute could have taken as much part as I did. Mrs. van Dysart commented on the difficulties of feeding poor relations with delicate stomachs and choosy appetites. Charles neglected to tell her that I had been shot and wasn't poor, but agreed that a weak digestion in dependents was a moral fault. Mrs. van Dysart loved it. Doria occasionally looked at me as if I were an interesting specimen of low life. Rex van Dysart again offered me the bread; and that was that. Finally Viola shepherded Doria and Mrs. van Dysart out to have coffee in the drawing room and Charles offered his guests port and brandy. He passed me the brandy bottle with an air of irritation and compressed his lips in disapproval when I took some. It wasn't lost on his guests.

After a while he rose, opened the glass bookcase doors, and showed the quartzes to Kraye. Piece by piece the two discussed their way along the rows, with van Dysart standing beside them exhibiting polite interest and hiding his yawns of boredom. I stayed sitting down. I also helped myself to some more brandy.

Charles kept his end up very well and went through the whole lot without a mistake. He then transferred to the drawing room, where his gem cabinet proved a great success. I tagged along, sat in an unobtrusive chair and listened to them all talking, but I came to no conclusions except that if I didn't soon go upstairs I wouldn't get there under my own steam. It was eleven o'clock and I had had a long day. Charles didn't look round when I left the room.

Half an hour later, when the guests had come murmuring up to their rooms, he came quietly through my door and over to the bed. I was still lying on top of it in my shirt and trousers, trying to summon some energy to finish undressing.

He stood looking down at me, smiling.

"Well?" he said.

"It is you," I said, "who is the dyed-in-the-wool, twenty-four-carat, unmitigated bastard."

He laughed. "I thought you were going to spoil the whole thing when you saw your picture had gone." He began taking off my shoes and socks. "You looked as bleak as the Bering Strait in December. Pajamas?"

"Under the pillow."

He helped me undress in his quick neat naval fashion.

"Why did you do it?" I said.

He waited until I was lying between the sheets, then he perched on the edge of the bed.

"Did you mind?"

"Hell, Charles . . . of course. At first anyway."

"I'm afraid it came out beastlier than I expected, but I'll tell you why I did it. Do you remember that first game of chess we had? When you beat me out of sight? You know why you won so easily?"

"You weren't paying enough attention."

"Exactly. I wasn't paying enough attention, because I didn't think you were an opponent worth bothering about. A bad tactical error." He grinned. "An admiral should know better. If you underrate a strong opponent you are at a disadvantage. If you grossly underrate him, if you are convinced he is absolutely no account, you prepare no defense and are certain to be defeated." He paused for a moment, and went on. "It is therefore good strategy to delude the enemy into believing you are too weak to be considered. And that is what I was doing tonight on your behalf."

He looked at me gravely. After some seconds I said, "At what game, exactly, do you expect me to play Howard Kraye?"

He sighed contentedly, and smiled. "Do you remember what he said interested him most?"

I thought back. "Land."

Charles nodded. "Land. That's right. He collects it. Chunks of it, yards of it, acres of it. . . ." He hesitated.

"Well?"

"You can play him," he said slowly, "for Seabury Racecourse."

The enormity of it took my breath away.

"What?" I said incredulously. "Don't be silly. I'm only—"

"Shut up," he interrupted. "I don't want to hear what you think you are only. You're intelligent, aren't you? You work for a detective agency? You wouldn't want Seabury to close down? Why shouldn't you do something about it?"

"But I imagine he's after some sort of take-over bid, from what you say. You want some powerful city chap or other to oppose him, not . . . me."

"He is very much on his guard against powerful chaps in the city, but wide open to you."

I stopped arguing because the implications were pushing into the background my inadequacy for such a task.

"Are you sure he is after Seabury?" I asked.

"Someone is," said Charles. "There has been a lot of buying and selling of the shares lately, and the price per share is up although they haven't paid a dividend this year. The clerk of the course told me about it. He said that the directors are very worried. On paper, there is no great concentration of shares in any one name, but there wasn't at Dunstable either. There, when it came to a vote on selling out to a land developer, they found that about twenty various nominees were in fact all agents for Kraye. He carried enough of the other shareholders with him, and the racecourse was lost to housing."

"It was all legal, though?"

"A wangle; but legal, yes. And it looks like it's happening again."

"But what's to stop him, if it's legal?"

"You might try."

I stared at him in silence. He stood up and straightened the bedcover neatly. "It would be a pity if Seabury went the way of Dunstable." He went toward the door.

"Where does van Dysart fit in?" I asked.

"Oh," he said, turning, "Nowhere. It was Mrs. van Dysart I wanted. She has a tongue like a rattlesnake. I knew she would help me tear you to pieces." He grinned. "She'll give you a terrible weekend, I'm glad to say."

"Thanks very much," I said sarcastically. "Why didn't you tell me of this before? When you so carefully left me that book on company law for instance? Or at least this evening when I came back from seeing Andrews, so that I could have been prepared, at dinner?"

He opened the door and smiled across the room, his eyes blank again.

"Sleep well," he said. "Good night, Sid."

CHARLES TOOK THE two men out shooting the following morning and Viola drove their wives into Oxford to do some shopping and visit an exhibition of Venetian glass. I took the opportunity of having a good look round the Krayes' bedroom.

It wasn't until I'd been there for more than ten minutes that it struck me that two years earlier I wouldn't have dreamed of doing such a thing. Now I had done it as a matter of course, without thinking twice. I grinned sardonically. Evidently even in just sitting around in a detective agency one caught an attitude of mind. I realized, moreover, that I had instinctively gone about my search methodically and with a careful touch. In an odd way it was extremely disconcerting.

I wasn't of course looking for anything special: just digging a little into the Krayes' characters. I wouldn't even concede in my own mind that I was interested in the challenge Charles had so elaborately thrown down. But all the same I searched, and thoroughly.

Howard Kraye slept in crimson pajamas with his initials embroidered in white on the pocket. His dressing gown was of crimson brocade with a black quilted collar and black tassels on the belt. His washing things, neatly arranged

in a large fitted toilet case in the adjoining bathroom, were numerous and or-
nate. He used pine-scented aftershave lotion, cologne friction rub, lemon
hand cream, and an oily hair dressing, all from gold-topped cut-glass bottles.
There were also medicated soap tablets, special formula toothpaste, talcum
powder in a gilt container, a deodorant, and a supersonic-looking electric razor. He wore false teeth and had a spare set. He had brought a half-full tin of
laxatives, some fruit salts, a bottle of mouthwash, some antiseptic foot powder,
penicillin throat lozenges, a spot-sealing stick, digestive tablets and an eye
bath. The body beautiful, in and out.

All his clothes, down to his vests and pants, had been made to measure,
and he had brought enough to cover every possibility of a country weekend. I
went through the pockets of his dinner jacket and the three suits hanging beside it, but he was a tidy man and they were all empty, except for a nail file in
each breast pocket. His six various pairs of shoes were handmade and nearly
new. I looked into each shoe separately, but except for trees they were all
empty.

In a drawer I found neatly arranged his stock of ties, handkerchiefs, and
socks: all expensive. A heavy chased silver box contained cuff links, studs, and
tiepins; mostly of gold. He had avoided jewels, but one attractive pair of cuff
links was made from pieces of what I now knew enough to identify as tiger's-
eye. The backs of his hairbrushes were beautiful slabs of the gemstone, smoky
quartz. A few brown and gray hairs were lodged in between the bristles.

There remained only his luggage, four lavish suitcases standing in a neat
row beside the wardrobe. I opened each one. They were all empty except for
the smallest, which contained a brown calf attaché case. I looked at it carefully before I touched it, but as Kraye didn't seem to have left any telltales
like hairs or pieces of cotton attached, I lifted it out and put it on one of the
beds. It was locked, but I had learned how to deal with such drawbacks. A
lugubrious ex–police sergeant on Radnor's payroll gave me progressively harder
lessons in lock-picking every time he came into the office between jobs,
moaning all the while about the damage London soot did to his chrysanthemums. My one-handedness he had seen only as a challenge, and had invented
a couple of new techniques and instruments entirely for my benefit. Recently
he had presented me with a collection of fine delicate keys which he had once
removed from a burglar, and had bullied me until I carried them with me
everywhere. They were in my room. I went and fetched them and without
much trouble opened the case.

It was as meticulous as everything else, and I was particularly careful not
to alter the position or order of any of the papers. There were several letters

from a stockbroker, a bunch of share transfer certificates, various oddments, and a series of typed sheets, headed with the previous day's date, which were apparently an up-to-the-minute analysis of his investments. He seemed to be a rich man and to do a good deal of buying and selling. He had money in oils, mines, property and industrial stocks. There was also a sheet headed simply S.R., on which every transaction was a purchase. Against each entry was a name and the address of a bank. Some names occurred three or four times, some only once.

Underneath the papers lay a large thick brown envelope inside which were two packets of new ten-pound notes. I didn't count, but there couldn't have been fewer than a hundred of them. The envelope was at the bottom of the case except for a writing board with slightly used white blotting paper held by crocodile and gold corners. I pulled up the board and found underneath it two more sheets of paper, both covered with dates, initials, and sums of money.

I let the whole lot fall back into place, made sure that everything looked exactly as I had found it, relocked the case, and put it back into its covering suitcase.

The divine Doria, I found, was far from being as tidy as her husband. All her things were in a glorious jumble, which made leaving them undisturbed a difficult job, but also meant that she would be less likely than her husband to notice if anything were slightly out of place.

Her clothes, though they looked and felt expensive, were bought ready-made and casually treated. Her washing things consisted of a plastic zipped case, a flannel, a toothbrush, bath essence, and a puffing bottle of talc. Almost stark beside Howard's collection. No medicine. She appeared to wear nothing in bed, but a pretty white quilted dressing gown hung half off a hanger behind the bathroom door.

She had not completely unpacked. Suitcases propped on chairs and stools still held stirred-up underclothes and various ultra-feminine equipment which I hadn't seen since Jenny left.

The top of the dressing table, though the daily seemed to have done her best to dust it, was an expensive chaos. Pots of cosmetics, bottles of scent and hair spray stood on one side, a box of tissues, a scarf, and the cluttered tray out of the top of a dressing case filled the other. The dressing case itself, of crocodile with gold clips, stood on the floor. I picked it up and put it on the bed. It was locked. I unlocked it, and looked inside.

Doria was quite a girl. She possessed two sets of false eyelashes, spare fingernails, and a hairpiece on a tortoiseshell headband. Her big jewel case, the only tidy thing in her whole luggage, contained on the top layer the sapphire and diamond earrings she had worn the previous evening, along with a diamond sunburst brooch and a sapphire ring; and on the lower layer a second necklace, bracelet, earrings, brooch and ring all of gold, platinum, and citrine. The yellow jewels were uncommon, barbaric in design, and had no doubt been made especially for her.

Under the jewel case were four paperback novels so pornographic in content as to raise doubts about Kraye's ability as a lover. Jenny had held that a truly satisfied woman didn't need to read dirty sex. Doria clearly did.

Alongside the books was a thick leather-covered diary to which the beautiful Mrs. Kraye had confided the oddest thoughts. Her life seemed to be as untidy as her clothes, a mixture of ordinary social behavior, dream fantasy and a perverted marriage relationship. If the diary were to be believed, she and Howard obtained deeper pleasure, both of them, from his beating her than from the normal act of love. Well, I reflected, at least they were well matched. Some of the divorces that Hunt Radnor Associates dealt with arose because one partner alone was pain-fixated, the other being revolted.

At the bottom of the case were two other objects of interest. First, coiled in a brown velvet bag, the sort of leather strap used by schoolmasters, at whose purpose, in view of the diary, it was easy to guess; and second, in a chocolate box, a gun.

CHAPTER 4

TELEPHONING FOR THE local taxi to come and fetch me, I went to Oxford and bought a camera. Although the shop was starting a busy Saturday afternoon, the boy who served me tackled the problem of a one-handed photographer with enthusiasm and as if he had all the time in the world. Between us we sorted out a miniature German 16 mm camera, three inches long by one and a half wide, which I could hold, set, snap and wind with one hand with the greatest ease.

He gave me a thorough lesson in how to work it, added an inch to its length in the shape of a screwed-on photoelectric light meter, loaded it with film, and slid it into a black case so small that it made no bulge in my trouser pocket. He also offered to change the film later if I couldn't manage it. We parted on the best of terms.

When I got back everyone was sitting round a cozy fire in the fitting room, eating crumpets. Very tantalizing. I loved crumpets.

No one took much notice when I went in and sat down on the fringe of the circle except Mrs. van Dysart, who began sharpening her claws. She got in a couple of quick digs about spongers marrying girls for their money, and Charles didn't say that I hadn't. Viola looked at me searchingly, worry opening her mouth. I winked, and she shut it again in relief.

I gathered that the morning's bag had been the usual mixture (two brace of pheasant, five wild duck and a hare), because Charles preferred a rough shoot over his own land to organized affairs with beaters. The women had collected a poor opinion of Oxford shop assistants and a booklet on the manufacture of fifteenth-century Italian glass. All very normal for a country weekend. It was my snooping that seemed unreal. That, and the false position Charles had steered me into.

Kraye's gaze, and finally his hands, strayed back to the gem bookshelves. Again the door was opened, Charles's trick lighting working effectively, and one by one the gems were brought out, passed round and closely admired. Mrs. van Dysart seemed much attached to a spectacular piece of rose quartz, playing with it to make light strike sparks from it, and smoothing her fingers over the glossy surface.

"Rex, you must collect some of this for me!" she ordered, her will showing like iron inside the fluff; and masterful-looking Rex nodded his meek agreement.

Kraye was saying, "You know, Roland, these are really remarkably fine specimens. Among the best I've ever seen. Your cousin must have been extremely fortunate and influential to acquire so many fine crystals."

"Oh, indeed he was," agreed Charles equably.

"I should be interested if you ever think of realizing on them . . . a first option, perhaps?"

"You can have a first option by all means," smiled Charles. "But I shan't be selling them, I assure you."

"Ah well, so you say now. But I don't give up easily. . . . I shall try you later. But don't forget, my first option?"

"Certainly," said Charles. "My word on it."

Kraye smiled at the stone he held in his hands, a magnificent raw amethyst like a cluster of petrified violets.

"Don't let this fall into the fire," he said. "It would turn yellow." He then treated everyone to a lecture on amethysts which would have been interesting had he made any attempt at simplicity: but blinding by words was with him either a habit or a policy. I wasn't certain which.

". . . Manganese, of course, occurring in geodes or agate nodules in South America or Russia, but with such a worldwide distribution it was only to be expected that elementary societies should ascribe to its supra rational inherencies and attributes . . ."

I suddenly found him looking straight at me, and I knew my expression had not been one of impressed admiration. More like quizzical sarcasm. He didn't like it. There was a quick flash in his eyes.

"It is symptomatic of the slum mentality," he remarked, "to scoff at what it can't comprehend."

"Sid," said Charles sharply. "I'm sure you must have something else to do. We can let you go until dinner."

I stood up. The natural anger rose quickly, but only as far as my teeth. I swallowed. "Very well," I muttered.

"Before you go, Sid," said Mrs. van Dysart from the depths of a sofa, ". . . Sid, what a deliciously plebeian name, so suitable. . . . Put these down on the table for me."

She held out both hands, one stone in each and another balanced between them. I couldn't manage them all, and dropped them.

"Oh dear," said Mrs. van Dysart, acidly sweet, as I knelt and picked them up, putting them one by one on the table, "I forgot you were disabled, so silly of me." She hadn't forgotten. "Are you sure you can't get treatment for whatever is wrong with you? You ought to try some exercises, they'd do you the world of good. All you need is a little perseverance. You owe it to the Admiral, don't you think, to *try*?"

I didn't answer, and Charles at least had the grace to keep quiet.

"I know a very good man," went on Mrs. van Dysart. "He used to work for the army. . . . excellent at getting malingerers back into service. Now he's the sort of man who'd do you good. What do you think, Admiral, shall I fix it up for your son-in-law to see him?"

"Er . . . ," said Charles, "I don't think it would work."

"Nonsense." She was brisk and full of smiles. "You can't let him lounge about doing nothing for the rest of his life. A good bracing course of treatment, that's what he needs. Now," she said turning to me, "so that I know exactly what I'm talking about when I make an appointment, let's see this precious crippled hand of yours."

There was a tiny pause. I could feel their probing eyes, their unfriendly curiosity.

"No," I said calmly. "Excuse me, but no."

As I walked across the room and out of the door her voice floated after me. "There you are, Admiral, he doesn't *want* to get better. They're all the same. . . ."

I lay on my bed for a couple of hours rereading the book on company law, especially, now, the section on takeovers. It was no easier going than it had been in the hospital, and now that I knew why I was reading it, it seemed more involved, not less. If the directors of Seabury were worried, they would surely have called in their own investigator. Someone who knew his way round the stock markets like I knew my way round the track. An expert. I wasn't at all the right sort of person to stop Kraye, even if indeed anyone could stop him. And yet . . . I stared at the ceiling, taking my lower lip between my teeth. And yet . . . I did have a wild idea. . . .

Viola came in, knocking as she opened the door.

"Sid, dear, are you all right? Can I do anything for you?" She shut the door, gentle, generous, and worried.

I sat up and swung my legs over the side of the bed. "No, thanks, I'm fine."

She perched on the arm of an easy chair, looked at me with her kind, slightly mournful brown eyes, and said a little breathlessly, "Sid, why are you letting Charles say such terrible things about you? It isn't only when you are there in the room; they've been, oh, almost sniggering about you behind your back. Charles and that frightful Mrs. van Dysart. . . . What has happened between you and him? When you nearly died he couldn't have been more worried if you'd been his own son . . . but now he is so cruel, and terribly unfair."

"Dear Viola, don't worry. It's only some game that Charles is playing, and I go along with him."

"Yes," she said, nodding. "He warned me. He said that you were both going to lay a smoke screen and that I was on no account to say a single word in your defense the whole weekend. But it wasn't true, was it? When I saw your face, when Charles said that about your poor mother, I knew you didn't know what he was going to do."

"Was it so obvious?" I said ruefully. "Well, I promise you I haven't quarreled with him. Will you just be a dear and do exactly as he asked? Don't say a single word to any of them about . . . um . . . the more successful bits of my life history, or about my job at the agency, or about the shooting. You didn't today, did you, on the trip to Oxford?" I finished with some anxiety.

She shook her head. "I thought I'd talk to you first."

"Good." I grinned.

"Oh dear," she cried, partly in relief, partly in puzzlement. "Well, in that case, Charles asked me to pop in and make sure you would come down to dinner."

"Oh he did, did he? Afraid I'll throw a boot at him, I should think, after sending me out of the room like that. Well, you just pop back to Charles and say that I'll come down to dinner on condition that he organizes some chemmy afterwards, and includes me out."

Dinner was a bit of a trial: with their smoked salmon and pheasant the guests enjoyed another round of Sid-baiting. Both the Krayes, egged on by Charles and the fluffy harpy beside him, had developed a pricking skill for this novel weekend parlor game, and I heartily wished Charles had never thought of it. However, he kept his side of the bargain by digging out the chemin-de-fer shoe, and after the coffee, the brandy, and another inspection of the dining-room quartzes, he settled his guests firmly round the table in the drawing room.

Upstairs, once the shoe was clicking regularly and the players were well involved, I went and collected Kraye's attaché case and took it along to my room.

Because I was never going to get another chance and did not want to miss something I might regret later, I photographed every single paper in the case. All the stockbroker's letters and all the investment reports. All the share certificates, and also the two separate sheets under the writing board.

Although I had an ultra-bright lightbulb and the exposure meter to help me get the right setting, I took several pictures at different light values of the paper I considered the most important in order to be sure of getting the sharpest possible result. The little camera handled beautifully, and I found I could change the films in their tiny casettes without much difficulty. By the time I had finished I had used three whole films of twenty exposures on each. It took me a long time, as I had to put the camera down between each shot to move the next paper into my pool of light, and also had to be very careful not to alter the orders in which the papers had lain in the case.

The envelope of ten-pound notes kept me hoping like crazy that Howard Kraye would not lose heavily and come upstairs for replacements. It seemed to me at the time a ridiculous thing to do, but I took the two flat blocks of tenners out of the envelope, and photographed them as well. Putting them back I flipped through them: the notes were new, consecutive, fifty to a packet. One thousand pounds to a penny.

When everything was back in the case I sat looking at the contents for a minute, checking their position against my visual memory of how they looked when I first saw them. At last satisfied, I shut the case, locked it, rubbed it over to remove any finger marks I might have left, and put it back where I had found it.

After that I went downstairs to the dining room for the brandy I had refused at dinner. I needed it. Carrying the glass, I listened briefly outside the drawing-room door to the murmurs and clicks from within and went upstairs again, to bed.

Lying in the dark I reviewed the situation. Howard Kraye, drawn by the bait of a quartz collection, had accepted an invitation to a quiet weekend in the country with a retired admiral. With him he had brought a selection of private papers. As he had no possible reason to imagine that anyone in such innocent surroundings would spy on him, the papers might be very private indeed. So private that he felt safest when they were with him? Too private to leave at home? It would be nice to think so.

At that point, imperceptibly, I fell asleep.

THE NERVES IN my abdomen wouldn't give up. After about five hours of fighting them unsuccessfully I decided that staying in bed all morning thinking about it was doing no good, and got up and dressed.

Drawn partly against my will, I walked along the passage to Jenny's room, and went in. It was the small sunny room she had had as a child. She had gone back to it when she left me and it was all hers alone. I had never slept there. The single bed, the relics of childhood, girlish muslin frills on curtains and dressing table, everything shut me out. The photographs round the room were of her father, her dead mother, her sister, brother-in-law, dogs and horses, but not of me. As far as she could, she had blotted out her marriage.

I walked slowly round touching her things, remembering how much I had loved her. Knowing, too, that there was no going back, and that if she walked through the door at that instant we would not fall into each other's arms in tearful reconciliation.

Removing a one-eyed teddy bear I sat down for a while on her pink armchair. It's difficult to say just where a marriage goes wrong, because the accepted reason often isn't the real one. The rows Jenny and I had had were all ostensibly caused by the same thing: my ambition. Grown finally too heavy for flat racing, I had switched entirely to steeplechasing the season before we married, and I wanted to be champion jumping jockey. To this end I was prepared to eat little, drink less, go to bed early, and not make love if I were racing the next day. It was unfortunate that she liked late-night parties and dancing more than anything else. At first she gave them up willingly, then less willingly, and finally in fury. After that, she started going on her own.

In the end she told me to choose between her and racing. But by then I was indeed champion jockey, and had been for some time, and I couldn't give it up. So Jenny left. It was just life's little irony that six months later I lost the racing as well. Gradually since then I had come to realize that a marriage didn't break up just because one half liked parties and the other didn't. I thought now that Jenny's insistence on a gay time was the result of my having failed her in some basic, deeply necessary way. Which did nothing whatsoever for my self-respect or my self-confidence.

I sighed, stood up, replaced the teddy bear, and went downstairs to the drawing room. Eleven o'clock on a windy autumn morning.

Doria was alone in the big comfortable room, sitting on the window seat and reading the Sunday papers, which lay around her on the floor in a haphazard mess.

"Hello," she said, looking up. "What hole did you crawl out of?"

I walked over to the fire and didn't answer.

"Poor little man, are his feelings hurt then?"

"I do have feelings, the same as anyone else."

"So you actually can talk?" she said mockingly. "I'd begun to wonder."

"Yes, I can talk."

"Well, now, tell me all your troubles, little man."

"Life is just a bowl of cherries."

She uncurled herself from the window seat and came across to the fire, looking remarkably out of place in skintight leopard-printed pants and a black silk shirt.

She was the same height as Jenny, the same height as me, just touching five foot six. As my smallness had always been an asset for racing, I never looked on it as a handicap for life in general, either physical or social. Neither had I ever really understood why so many people thought that height for its own sake was important. But it would have been naïve not to take note of the widespread extraordinary assumption that the mind and heart could be measured by tallness. The little man with the big emotion was a stock comic figure. It was utterly irrational. What difference did three or four inches of leg bone make to a man's essential nature? Perhaps I had been fortunate in coming to terms early with the effect of poor nutrition in a difficult childhood; but it did not stop me understanding why other short men struck back in defensive aggression. There were the pinpricks, for instance, of girls like Doria calling one "little" and intending it as an insult.

"You've dug yourself into a cushy berth here, haven't you?" she said, taking a cigarette from the silver box on the mantelpiece.

"I suppose so."

"If I were the Admiral I'd kick you out."

"Thank you," I said, neglecting to offer her a light. With a mean look she found a box of matches and struck one for herself.

"Are you ill, or something?"

"No. Why?"

"You eat those faddy health foods, and you look such a sickly little creature. . . . I just wondered." She blew the smoke down her nose. "The Admiral's daughter must have been pretty desperate for a wedding ring."

"Give her her due," I said mildly. "At least she didn't pick a rich father figure twice her age."

I thought for a moment she meant to go into the corny routine of smacking my face, but as it happened she was holding the cigarette in the hand she needed.

"You little shit," she said instead. A charming girl, altogether.

"I get along."

"Not with me, you don't." Her face was tight. I had struck very deep, it seemed.

"Where is everyone else?" I asked, gesturing around the empty room.

"Out with the Admiral somewhere. And you can take yourself off again too. You're not wanted in here."

"I'm not going. I live here, remember?"

"You went quick enough last night," she sneered. "When the Admiral says jump, you jump. But fast, little man. And that I like to see."

"The Admiral," I pointed out, "is the hand that feeds. I don't bite it."

"Bootlicking little creep."

I grinned at her nastily and sat down in an armchair. I still didn't feel too good. Pea green and clammy, to be exact. Nothing to be done though, but wait for it to clear off.

Doria tapped ash off her cigarette and looked at me down her nose, thinking up her next attack. Before she could launch it, however, the door opened and her husband came in.

"Doria," he said happily, not immediately seeing me in the armchair, "where have you hidden my cigarette case? I shall punish you for it."

She made a quick movement toward me with her hand and Howard saw me and stopped dead.

"What are you doing here?" he said brusquely, the fun-and-games dying abruptly out of his face and voice.

"Passing the time."

"Clear out, then. I want to talk to my wife."

I shook my head and stayed out.

"Short of picking him up and throwing him out bodily," said Doria, "you won't get rid of him. I've tried."

Kraye shrugged. "Roland puts up with him. I suppose we can too." He picked up one of the newspapers and sat down in an armchair facing me. Doria wandered back to the window seat, pouting. Kraye straightened up the paper and began to read the front page. Across the back page, the racing page, facing me across the fireplace, the black, bold headlines jumped out.

"ANOTHER HALLEY?"

Underneath, side by side, were two photographs: one of me, and the other of a boy who had won a big race the day before.

It was by then essential that Kraye should not discover how Charles had misrepresented me; it had gone much too far to be explained away as a joke. The photograph was clearly printed for once. I knew it well. It was an old one which the papers had used several times before, chiefly because it was a good likeness. Even if none of the guests read the racing column, as Doria obviously hadn't, it might catch their eye in passing, through being in such a conspicuous place.

Kraye finished reading the front page and began to turn the paper over.

"Mr. Kraye," I said. "Do you have a very big quartz collection yourself?"

He lowered the paper a little and gave me an unenthusiastic glance.

"Yes, I have," he said briefly.

"Then could you please tell me what would be a good thing to give the Admiral to add to his collection? And where would I get it, and how much would it cost?"

The paper folded over, hiding my picture. He cleared his throat and with strained politeness started to tell me about some obscure form of crystal which the Admiral didn't have. Press the right button, I thought . . . Doria spoiled it. She walked jerkily over to Kraye and said crossly, "Howard, for God's sake. The little creep is buttering you up. I bet he wants something. You're a sucker for anyone who will talk about rocks."

"People don't make a fool of me," said Kraye flatly, his eyes narrowing in irritation.

"No. I only want to please the Admiral," I explained.

"He's a sly little beast," said Doria. "I don't like him."

Kraye shrugged, looked down at the newspaper and began to unfold it again.

"It's mutual," I said casually. "You daddy's doll."

Kraye stood up slowly and the paper slid to the floor, front page up.

"What did you say?"

"I said I didn't think much of your wife."

He was outraged, as well as he might be. He took a single step across the rug, and there was suddenly something more in the room than three guests sparring round a Sunday-morning fire.

Even though I was as far as he knew an insignificant fly to swat, a clear quality of menace flowed out of him like a radio signal. The calm social mask had disappeared along with the wordy, phony, surface personality. The vague suspicion I had gained from reading his papers, together with the antipathy I had felt for him all along, clarified into belated recognition: this was not just a smooth speculator operating near the legal border line, but a full-blown, powerful, dangerous big-time crook.

Trust me, I thought, to prod an anthill and find a hornets' nest. Twist the tail of a grass snake and find a boa constrictor. What on earth would he be like, I wondered, if one did more to cross him than disparage his choice of wife?

"He's sweating," said Doria, pleased. "He's afraid of you."

"Get up," he said.

As I was sure that if I stood up he would simply knock me down again, I stayed where I was.

"I'll apologize," I said.

"Oh, no," said Doria, "that's much too easy."

"Something subtle," suggested Kraye, staring down.

"I know!" Doria was delighted with her idea. "Let's get that hand out of his pocket."

They both saw from my face that I would hate that more than anything. They both smiled. I thought of bolting, but it meant leaving the paper behind.

"That will do very nicely," said Kraye. He leaned down, twined one hand into the front of my jersey shirt and the other into my hair, and pulled me to my feet. The top of my head reached about to his chin. I wasn't in much physical shape for resisting, but I took a halfhearted swipe at him as I came up.

Doria caught my swinging arm and twisted it up behind my back, using both of hers and an uncomfortable amount of pressure. She was a strong, healthy girl with no inhibitions about hurting people.

"That'll teach you to be rude to me," she said with satisfaction.

I thought of kicking her shins, but it would only have brought more retaliation. I also wished Charles would come back at once from wherever he was.

He didn't.

Kraye transferred his grip from my hair to my left forearm and began to pull. That arm was no longer much good, but I did my best. I tucked my elbow tight against my side, and my hand stayed in my pocket.

"Hold him harder," he said to Doria. "He's stronger than he looks." She levered my arm up another inch and I started to roll round to get out of it. But Kraye still had his grasp on the front of my jersey, with his forearm leaning across under my throat, and between the two of them I was properly stuck. All the same, I found I couldn't just stand still and let them do what I so much didn't want them to.

"He squirms, doesn't he?" said Doria cheerfully.

I squirmed and struggled a good deal more—until they began getting savage with frustration, and I was panting. It was my wretched stomach which finished it. I began to feel too ill to go on. With a terrific jerk Kraye dragged my hand out.

"Now," he said triumphantly.

He gripped my elbow fiercely and pulled the jersey sleeve up from my wrist. Doria let go of my right arm and came to look at their prize. I was shaking with rage, pain, humiliation . . . heaven knows what.

"Oh," said Doria blankly. "Oh."

She was no longer smiling, nor was her husband. They looked steadily at the wasted, flabby, twisted hand, and at the scars on my forearm, wrist and palms, not only the terrible jagged marks of the original injury but the several tidier ones of the operations I had had since. It was a mess, a right and proper mess.

"So that's why the Admiral lets him stay, the nasty little beast," said Doria, screwing up her face in distaste.

"It doesn't excuse his behavior," said Kraye. "I'll make sure he keeps that tongue of his still, in future."

He stiffened his free hand and chopped the edge of it down across the worst part, the inside of my wrist. I jerked in his grasp.

"Ah . . . ," I said. "Don't."

"He'll tell tales to the Admiral," said Doria warningly, "if you hurt him too much. It's a pity, but I should think that's about enough."

"I don't agree, but—"

There was a scrunch on the gravel outside, and Charles's car swept past the window, coming back.

Kraye let go of my elbow with a shake. I went weakly down on my knees on the rug, and it wasn't all pretense.

"If you tell the Admiral about this, I'll deny it," said Kraye, "and we know who he'll believe."

I did know who he'd believe, but I didn't say so. The newspaper which had caused the whole rumpus lay close beside me on the rug. The car doors slammed distantly. The Krayes turned away from me toward the window, listening. I picked up the paper, got to my feet, and set off for the door. They didn't try to stop me in any way. They didn't mention the newspaper either. I opened the door, went through, shut it, and steered a slightly crooked course across the hall to the wardroom. Upstairs was too far. I shut the wardroom door behind me, hid the newspaper, slid into Charles's favorite armchair, and waited for my various miseries, mental and physical, to subside.

Some time later Charles came in to fetch some fresh packages of cigarettes.

"Hullo," he said over his shoulder, opening the cupboard. "I thought you were still in bed. Mrs. Cross said you weren't very well this morning. It isn't at all warm in here. Why don't you come into the drawing room?"

"The Krayes . . ." I stopped.

"They won't bite you." He turned round, cigarette in hand. He looked at my face. "What's so funny?" and then more sharply, looking closer. "What's the matter?"

"Oh, nothing. Have you seen today's Sunday *Hemisphere*?"

"No, not yet. Do you want it? I thought it was in the drawing room with the other papers."

"No, it's in the top drawer of your desk. Take a look."

Puzzled, he opened the drawer, took out the paper, and unfolded it. He went to the racing section unerringly.

"My God!" he said, aghast. "Today of all days." His eyes skimmed down the page and he smiled. "You've read this, of course?"

I shook my head. "I just took it to hide it."

He handed me the paper. "Read it then. It'll be good for your ego. They

won't let you die! 'Young Finch,'" he quoted, "'showed much of the judgment and miraculous precision of the great Sid.' How about that? And that's
just the start."

"Yeah, how about it?" I grinned. "Count me out for lunch, if you don't
mind, Charles. You don't need me there anymore."

"All right, if you don't feel like it. They'll be gone by six at the latest,
you'll be glad to hear." He smiled and went back to his guests.

I read the newspaper before putting it away again. As Charles had said, it
was good for the ego. I thought the columnist, whom I'd known for years, had
somewhat exaggerated my erstwhile powers. A case of the myth growing bigger than the reality. But still, it was nice. Particularly in view of the galling,
ignominious end to the roughhouse in which the great Sid had so recently
landed himself.

ON THE FOLLOWING morning Charles and I changed back the labels on
the chunks of quartz and packed them up ready to return to the Carver Foundation. When we had finished we had one label left over.

"Are you sure we haven't put one stone in the box without changing the
label?" said Charles.

"Positive."

"I suppose we'd better check. I'm afraid that's what we've done."

We took all the chunks out of the big box again. The gem collection,
which Charles under protest had taken to bed with him each night, was complete; but we looked through them again too to make sure the missing rock
had not got among them by mistake. It was nowhere to be found.

"St. Luke's stone," I read from the label. "I remember where that was, up
on the top shelf on the right-hand side."

"Yes," agreed Charles, "a dull-looking lump about the size of a fist. I do
hope we haven't lost it."

"We have lost it," I remarked. "Kraye's pinched it."

"Oh no," Charles exclaimed. "You can't be right."

"Go and ring up the Foundation, and ask them what the stone is worth."

He shook his head doubtfully, but went to the telephone and came back
frowning.

"They say it hasn't any intrinsic value, but it's an extremely rare form of
meteorite. It never turns up in mines or quarrying of course. You have to wait
for it to fall from the heavens, and then find it. Very tricky."

"A quartz which friend Kraye didn't have."

"But he surely must know I'd suspect him?" Charles protested.

"You'd never have missed it, if it had really been part of your cousin's passed-on collection. There wasn't any gap on the shelf just now. He'd moved the others along. He couldn't know you would check carefully almost as soon as he had gone."

Charles sighed. "There isn't a chance of getting it back."

"No," I agreed.

"Well, it's a good thing you insisted on the insurance," he said. "Carver's valued that boring-looking lump more than all the rest together. Only one other meteorite like it has ever been found: the St. Mark's stone." He smiled suddenly. "We seem to have mislaid the equivalent of the penny black."

CHAPTER 5

TWO DAYS LATER I went back through the porticoed, columned doorway of Hunt Radnor Associates a lot more alive than when I last came out.

I got a big hullo from the girl on the switchboard, went up the curving staircase very nearly whistling, and was greeted by a barrage of ribald remarks from the Racing Section. What most surprised me was the feeling I had of coming home: I had never thought of myself as really belonging to the agency before, even though down at Aynsford I had realized that I very much didn't want to leave it. A bit late, that discovery. The skids were probably under me already.

Chico grinned widely. "So you made it."

"Well . . . yes."

I mean, back here to the grindstone."

"Yeah."

"But," he cast a rolling eye at the clock, "late as usual."

"Go stuff yourself," I said.

Chico threw out an arm to the smiling department. "Our Sid is back, his normal charming bloody self. Work in the agency can now begin."

"I see I still haven't got a desk," I observed, looking round. No desk. No roots. No real job. As ever.

"Sit on Dolly's, she's kept it dusted for you."

Dolly looked at Chico, smiling, the mother-hunger showing too vividly in her great blue eyes. She might be the second-best head of department the agency possessed, with a cross-referencing filing-index mind like a computer, she might be a powerful, large, self-assured woman of forty-odd with a couple of marriages behind her and an ever hopeful old bachelor at her heels, but she still counted her life a wasteland because her body couldn't produce children. Dolly was a terrific worker, overflowing with intensely female vitality, excellent drinking company, and very, very sad.

Chico didn't want to be mothered. He was prickly about mothers. All of them in general, not just those who abandoned their tots in push-chairs at police stations near Barnes Bridge. He jollied Dolly along and deftly avoided her tentative maternal invitations.

I hitched a hip onto a long-accustomed spot on the edge of Dolly's desk, and swung my leg.

"Well, Dolly, my love, how's the sleuthing trade?" I said.

"What we need," she said with mock tartness, "is a bit more work from you and a lot less lip."

"Give me a job, then."

"Ah, now." She pondered. "You could . . . ," she began, then stopped. "Well, on . . . perhaps not. And it had better be Chico who goes to Lambourn; some trainer there wants a doubtful lad checked on. . . ."

"So there's nothing for me?"

"Er . . . well . . . ," said Dolly. "No." She had said no a hundred times before. She had never once said yes.

I made a face at her, picked up her telephone, pressed the right button, and got through to Radnor's secretary.

"Joanie? This is Sid Halley. Yes . . . back from Beyond, that's right. Is the old man busy? I'd like a word with him."

"Big deal," said Chico.

Joanie's prim voice said, "He's got a client with him just now. When she's gone I'll ask him, and ring you back."

"OK," I put down the receiver.

Dolly raised her eyebrows. As head of the department she was my immediate boss, and in asking direct for a session with Radnor I was blowing agency protocol a raspberry. But I was certain that her constant refusal to give me anything useful to do was a direct order from Radnor. If I wanted the drain unblocked I would have to go and pull out the plug. Or go on my knees to stay at all.

"Dolly, love, I'm tired of kicking my heels. Even against your well-worn desk, though the view from here is ravishing." She was wearing, as she often did, a crossover cream silk shirt: it crossed over at a point, which on a young girl, would have caused a riot. On Dolly it still looked pretty potent, owing to the generosity of nature and the disposal of her arrangements.

"Are you chucking it in?" said Chico, coming to the point.

"It depends on the old man," I said. "He may be chucking me out."

There was a brief, thoughtful silence in the department. They all knew very well how little I did. How little I had been content to do. Dolly looked blank, which wasn't helpful.

Jones-boy clattered in with a tray of impeccable unchipped tea mugs. He was sixteen; noisy, rude, anarchistic, callous, and probably the most efficient office boy in London. His hair grew robustly heavy down to his shoulders, wavy and fanatically clean, dipping slightly in an expensive styling at the back. From behind he looked like a girl, which never disconcerted him. From in front his bony, acned face proclaimed him an unprepossessing male. He spent half his pay packet and his Sundays in Carnaby Street and the other half on weeknights chasing girls. According to him, he caught them. No girls had so far appeared in the office to corroborate his story.

Under the pink shirt beat a stony heart; inside the sprouting head hung a big "So what?" Yet it was because this amusing, ambitious, unsocial creature invariably arrived well before his due hour to get his office arrangements ready for the day that he had found me before I died. There was a moral there, somewhere.

He gave me a look. "The corpse has returned, I see."

"Thanks to you," I said idly, but he knew I meant it. He didn't care, though.

He said, "Your blood and stuff ran through a crack in the linoleum and soaked the wood underneath. The old man was wondering if it would start dry rot or something."

"Jones-boy," protested Dolly, looking sick. "Get the hell out of here, and shut up."

The telephone rang on her desk. She picked it up and listened, said, "All right," and disconnected.

"The old man wants to see you. Right away."

"Thanks." I stood up.

"The flipping boot?" asked Jones-boy interestedly.

"Keep your snotty nose out," said Chico.

"And balls to you. . . ."

I went out smiling, hearing Dolly start to deal once again with the running dogfight Chico and Jones-boy never tired of. Downstairs, across the hall, into Joanie's little office and through into Radnor's.

He was standing by the window, watching the traffic doing its nut in Cromwell Road. This room, where the clients poured out their troubles, was restfully painted a quiet gray, carpeted and curtained in crimson and furnished with comfortable armchairs, handy little tables with ashtrays, pictures on the walls, ornaments, and vases of flowers. Apart from Radnor's small desk in the corner, it looked like an ordinary sitting room, and indeed everyone believed that he had bought the room intact with the lease, so much was it what one would expect to find in a graceful, six-storied, late Victorian town house. Radnor had a theory that people exaggerated and distorted facts less in such peaceful surroundings than in the formality of a more orthodox office.

"Come in, Sid," he said. He didn't move from the window, so I joined him there. He shook hands.

"Are you sure you're fit enough to be here? You haven't been as long as I expected. Even knowing you . . ." He smiled slightly, with watching eyes.

I said I was all right. He remarked on the weather, the rush hour and the political situation, and finally worked round to the point we both knew was at issue.

"So, Sid, I suppose you'll be looking around a bit now?"

Laid on the line, I thought.

"If I wanted to stay here . . ."

"If? Hm, I don't know." He shook his head very slightly.

"Not on the same terms, I agree."

"I'm sorry it hasn't worked out." He sounded genuinely regretful, but he wasn't making it easy.

I said with careful calm, "You've paid me for nothing for two years. Well, give me a chance now to earn what I've had. I don't really want to leave."

He lifted his head slightly like a pointer to a scent, but he said nothing. I ploughed on.

"I'll work for you for nothing, to make up for it. But only if it's real, decent work. No more sitting around. It would drive me mad."

He gave me a hard stare and let out a long breath like a sigh.

"Good God. At last," he said. "And it took a bullet to do it."

"What do you mean?"

"Sid, have you ever seen a zombie wake up?"

"No," I said ruefully, understanding him. "It hasn't been as bad as that?"

He shrugged one shoulder. "I saw you racing, don't forget. You notice when a fire goes out. We've had the pleasant, flippant ashes drifting round this office, that's all." He smiled deprecatingly at his flight of fancy: he enjoyed making pictures of words. It wasted a lot of office time, on the whole.

"Consider me alight again, then." I grinned. "And I've brought a puzzle back with me. I want very much to sort it out."

"A long story?"

"Fairly, yes."

"We'd better sit down, then."

He waved me to an armchair, sank into one himself, and prepared to listen with the stillness and concentration which sent him time and time again to the core of a problem.

I told him about Kraye's dealing in racecourses. Both what I knew and what I guessed. When at length I finished he said calmly, "Where did you get hold of this?"

"My father-in-law, Charles Roland, tossed it at me while I was staying with him last weekend. He had Kraye as a houseguest." The subtle old fox, I thought, throwing me in at the deep end: making me wake up and swim.

"And Roland got it from where?"

"The clerk of the course at Seabury told him that the directors were worried about too much share movement, that it was Kraye who got control of Dunstable, and they were afraid he was at it again."

"But the rest, what you've just told me, is your own supposition?"

"Yes."

"Based on your appraisal of Kraye over one weekend?"

"Partly on what he showed me of his character, yes. Partly on what I read of his papers. . . ." With some hesitation I told him about my snooping and the photography. ". . . The rest, I suppose, a hunch."

"Hmm. It needs checking. . . . Have you brought the films with you?"

I nodded, took them out of my pocket, and put them on the little table beside me.

"I'll get them developed." He drummed his fingers lightly on the arm of the chair, thinking. Then, as if having made a decision, said more briskly, "Well, the first thing we need is a client."

"A client?" I echoed absentmindedly.

"Of course. What else? We are not the police. We work strictly for profit. Ratepayers don't pay the overheads and salaries in this agency. The clients do."

"Oh . . . , yes, of course."

"The most likely client in this case is either the Seabury Racecourse executive, or perhaps the National Hunt Committee. I think I should sound out the Senior Steward first, in either case. No harm in starting at the top."

"He might prefer to try the police," I said, "free."

"My dear Sid, one thing people want when they employ private investigators is privacy. They pay for privacy. When the police investigate something, everyone knows about it. When we do, they don't. That's why we sometimes get criminal cases when it would undoubtedly be cheaper to go to the police."

"I see. So you'll try the Senior Steward—"

"No," he interrupted. "You will."

"I?"

"Naturally. It's your case."

"But it's your agency—he is used to negotiating with you."

"You know him too," he pointed out.

"I used to ride for him, and that puts me on a bad footing for this sort of thing. I'm a jockey to him, an ex-jockey. He won't take me seriously."

Radnor shrugged a shoulder. "If you want to take on Kraye, you need a client. Go and get one."

I knew very well that he never sent even senior operatives, let alone inexperienced ones, to arrange or angle for an assignment, so that for several moments I couldn't really believe that he intended me to go. But he said nothing else, and eventually I stood up and went toward the door.

"Sandown races are on today," I said tentatively. "He's sure to be there."

"A good opportunity." He looked straight ahead, not at me.

"I'll try it, then."

"Right."

He wasn't letting me off. But then he hadn't kicked me out either. I went through the door and shut it behind me, and while I was still hesitating in disbelief I heard him inside the room give a sudden guffaw, a short, sharp, loud, triumphant snort of laughter.

I WALKED BACK to my flat, collected the car, and drove down to Sandown. It was a pleasant day, dry, sunny, and warm for November, just right for drawing a good crowd for steeplechasing.

I turned in through the racecourse gates, spirits lifting, parked the car (a Mercedes 230 SL with automatic gears, power-assisted steering, and a strip on the back saying NO HAND SIGNALS), and walked round to join the crowd outside the weighing-room door. I could no longer go through it. It had been one of the hardest things to get used to, the fact that all the changing rooms and weighing rooms which had been my second homes for fourteen years were completely barred to me from the day I rode my last race. You didn't lose just a job when you handed in your jockey's license, you lost a way of life.

There were a lot of people to talk to at Sandown, and as I hadn't been racing for six weeks I had a good deal of gossip to catch up on. No one seemed to know about the shooting, which was fine by me, and I didn't tell them. I immersed myself very happily in the racecourse atmosphere and for an hour Kraye retreated slightly into the background.

Not that I didn't keep an eye on my purpose, but until the third race the Senior Steward, Viscount Hagbourne, was never out of a conversation long enough for me to catch him.

Although I had ridden for him for years and had found him undemanding and fair, he was in most respects still a stranger. An aloof, distant man, he seemed to find it difficult to make ordinary human contacts, and unfortunately he had not proved a great success as Senior Steward. He gave the impression, not of power in himself, but of looking over his shoulder at power behind: I'd have said he was afraid of incurring the disapproval of the little knot of rigidly determined men who in fact ruled racing themselves, regardless of who might be in office at the time. Lord Hagbourne postponed making decisions until it was almost too late to make them, and there was still a danger after that that he would change his mind. But all the same he was the front man until his year of office ended, and with him I had to deal.

At length I fielded him neatly as he turned away from the clerk of the course and forestalled a trainer who was advancing upon him with a grievance. Lord Hagbourne, with one of his rare moments of humor, deliberately turned his back on the grievance and consequently greeted me with more warmth than usual.

"Sid, nice to see you. Where have you been lately?"

"Holidays," I explained succinctly. "Look, sir, can I have a talk with you after the races? There's something I want to discuss urgently."

"No time like the present," he said, one eye on the grievance. "Fire away."

"No, sir. It needs time and all your attention."

"Hm?"

The grievance was turning away. "Not today, Sid, I have to get home. What is it? Tell me now."

"I want to talk to you about the take-over bid for Seabury racecourse."

He looked at me, startled. "You want . . . ?"

"That's right. It can't be said out here where you will be needed at any moment by someone else. If you could just manage twenty minutes at the end of the afternoon . . . ?"

"Er . . . what is your connection with Seabury?"

"None in particular, sir. I don't know if you remember, but I've been connected" (a precise way of putting it) "with Hunt Radnor Associates for the last two years. Various . . . er . . . facts about Seabury have come our way and Mr. Radnor thought you might be interested. I am here as his representative."

"Oh, I see. Very well, Sid, come up to the Stewards' tearoom after the last. If I'm not there, wait for me. Right?"

"Yes. Thank you."

I walked down the slope and then up the iron staircase to the jockeys' box in the stand, smiling at myself. Representative. A nice big important word. It covered anything from an ambassador down. Commercial travelers had rechristened themselves with its rolling syllables years ago; they had done it because of the jokes, of course. It didn't sound the same, somehow, starting off with "Did you hear the one about the representative who stopped at a lonely farmhouse?. . . ."

Rodent officers, garbage disposal and sanitary staff: pretty new names for rat catchers, dustmen and road sweepers. So why not for me?

"Only idiots laugh at nothing," said a voice in my ear. "What the hell are you looking so pleased about all of a sudden? And where the blazes have you been this last month?"

"Don't tell me you've missed me?" I grinned, not needing to look round. We went together through the door of the high-up jockeys' box, two of a kind, and stood looking out over the splendid racecourse.

"Best view in Europe." He sighed. Mark Witney, thirty-eight years old, racehorse trainer. He had a face battered like a boxer's from too many racing falls, and in the two years since he hung up his boots and stopped wasting he had put on all of forty pounds. A fat, ugly man. We had a host of memories in common, a host of hard-ridden races. I liked him a lot.

"How's things?" I said.

"Oh, fair, fair. They'll be a damn sight better if that animal of mine wins the fifth."

"He must have a good chance."

"He's a damn certainty, boy. A certainty. If he doesn't fall over his goddamned legs. Clumsiest sod this side of Hades." He lifted his race glasses and looked at the number board. "I see poor old Charlie can't do the weight again on that thing of Bob's. . . . That boy of Plumtree's is getting a lot of riding just now. What do you think of him?"

"He takes too many risks," I said. "He'll break his neck."

"Look who's talking. No, seriously, I'm considering taking him on. What do you think?" He lowered his glasses. "I need someone available regularly from now on and all the ones I'd choose are already tied up."

"Well, you could do better, you could do worse, I suppose. He's a bit flashy for me, but he can ride, obviously. Will he do as he's told?"

He made a face. "You've hit the bull's-eye. That's the snag. He always knows best."

"Pity."

"Can you think of anyone else?"

"Um . . . what about that boy Cotton? He's too young really. But he's got the makings. . . ." We drifted out in amiable chat, discussing his problem, while the box filled up around us and the horses went down to the start.

It was a three-mile chase, and one of my ex-mounts was favorite. I watched the man who had my old job ride a very pretty race, and with half my mind thought about housing estates. Sandown itself had survived, some years ago, a bid to cover its green tempting acres with little boxes. Sandown had powerful friends. But Hurst Park, Manchester and Birmingham racecourses had all gone under the rolling tide of bricks and mortar, lost to the double-barreled persuasive arguments that shareholders liked capital gains and people needed houses. To defend itself from such a fate Cheltenham Racecourse had transformed itself from a private, dividend-paying company into a non-profit-making holdings trust, and other racecourses had followed their lead.

But not Seabury. And Seabury was deep in a nasty situation. Not Dunstable, and Dunstable Racecourse was now a tidy dormitory for the Vauxhall workers of Luton.

Most British racecourses were, or had been, private companies, in which it was virtually impossible for an outsider to acquire shares against the will of the members. But four—Dunstable, Seabury, Sandown and Chepstow—were public companies, and their shares could be bought in open market, through the stock exchange.

Sandown had been played for in a straightforward and perfectly honorable way, and plans to turn it into suburban housing had been turned down by the local and county councils. Sandown flourished, made a good profit, paid a 10 per cent dividend, and was probably now impregnable. Chepstow was surrounded by so much other open land that it was in little danger from developers. But little Dunstable had been an oasis inside a growing industrial area.

Seabury was on the flat part of the south coast, flanked on every side by miles of warm little bungalows representing the dreams and savings of people in retirement. At twelve bungalows to the acre—elderly people liked tiny gardens—there must be room on the spacious racecourse for over three thousand more. Add six or seven hundred pounds to the building price of each bungalow for the plot it stood on, and you scooped something in the region of two million.

The favorite won and was duly cheered, I clattered down the iron staircase with Mark, and we went and had a drink together.

"Are you sending anything to Seabury next week?" I asked. Seabury was one of his nearest meetings.

"Perhaps. I don't know. It depends if they hold it at all, of course. But I've got mine entered at Lingfield as well, and I think I'll send them there instead. It's a much more prosperous-looking place, and the owners like it better. Good lunch and all that. Seabury's so dingy these days. I had a hard job getting old Carmichael to agree to me running his horse there at the last meeting— and look what happened. The meeting was off and we'd missed the other engagement at Worcester too. It wasn't my fault, but I'd persuaded him that he stood more chance at Seabury, and he blamed me because in the end the horse stayed at home eating his head off for nothing. He says there's a jinx on Seabury, and I've a couple more owners who don't like me entering their horses there. I've told them that it's a super track from the horses' point of view, but it doesn't make much difference, they don't know it like we do."

We finished our drinks and walked back toward the weighing room. His horse scrambled home in the fifth by a whisker and I saw him afterward in the unsaddling enclosure beaming like a Halloween pumpkin.

After the last race I went to the Stewards' tearoom. There were several Stewards with their wives and friends having tea, but no Lord Hagbourne. The Stewards pulled out a chair, gave me a welcome, and talked, as ever, about the racing. Most of them had ridden as amateurs in their day, one against me in the not too distant past, and I knew them all well.

"Sid, what do you think of the new-type hurdles?"

"Oh, much better. Far easier for a young horse to see."

"Do you know of a good young chaser I could buy?"

"Didn't you think Hayward rode a splendid race?"

"I watched the third down at the Pond, and believe me that chestnut took off outside the wings. . . ."

". . . do you think we ought to have had him in, George?"

". . . heard that Green bust his ribs again yesterday . . ."

"Don't like that breed, never did, not genuine. . . ."

"Miffy can't seem to go wrong, he'd win with a cart horse. . . ."

"Can you come and give a talk to our local pony club, Sid? I'll write you the details. What date would suit you?"

Gradually they finished their tea, said good-bye, and left for home. I waited. Eventually he came, hurrying, apologizing, explaining what had kept him.

"Now," he said, biting into a sandwich. "What's it all about, eh?"

"Seabury."

"Ah yes, Seabury. Very worrying. Very worrying indeed."

"A Mr. Howard Kraye has acquired a large number of shares—"

"Now hold on a minute, Sid. That's only a guess, because of Dunstable. We've been trying to trace the buyer of Seabury shares through the stock exchange, and we can find no definite lead to Kraye."

"Hunt Radnor Associates do have that lead."

He stared. "Proof?"

"Yes."

"What sort?"

"Photographs of share transfer certificates." And heaven help me, I thought, if I've messed them up.

"Oh," he said somberly. "While we weren't sure, there was some hope we were wrong. Where did you get these photographs?"

"I'm not at liberty to say, sir. But Hunt Radnor Associates would be prepared to make an attempt to forestall the takeover of Seabury."

"For a fat fee, I suppose," he said dubiously.

"I'm afraid so, sir, yes."

"I don't connect you with this sort of thing, Sid." He moved restlessly and looked at his watch.

"If you would forget about me being a jockey, and think of me as having come from Mr. Radnor, it would make things a lot easier. How much is Seabury worth to National Hunt racing?"

He looked at me in surprise, but he answered the question, though not in the way I meant.

"Er . . . well, you know it's an excellent course, good for horses and so on."

"It didn't show a profit this year, though."

"There was a great deal of bad luck."

"Yes. Too much to be true, don't you think?"

"What do you mean?"

"Has it ever occurred to the National Hunt Committee that bad luck can be . . . well, arranged?"

"You aren't seriously suggesting that Kraye. . . . I mean that anyone would damage Seabury on purpose? In order to make it show a loss?"

"I am suggesting that it is a possibility. Yes."

"Good God." He sat down rather abruptly.

"Malicious damage," I said. "Sabotage, if you like. There's a great deal of industrial precedent. Hunt Radnor Associates investigated a case of it only last year in a small provincial brewery where the fermentation process kept going wrong. A prosecution resulted, and the brewery was able to remain in business."

He shook his head. "It is quite ridiculous to think that Kraye would be implicated in anything like that. He belongs to one of my clubs. He's a wealthy, respected man."

"I know, I've met him," I said.

"Well then, you must be aware of what sort of person he is."

"Yes." Only too well.

"You can't seriously suggest—" he began.

"There would be no harm in finding out," I interrupted. "You'll have studied the figures. Seabury's quite a prize."

"How do you see the figures, then?" It seemed he genuinely wanted to know, so I told him.

"Seabury Racecourse has an issued share capital of eighty thousand pounds in fully paid-up one-pound shares. The land was bought when that part of the coast was more or less uninhabited, so that this sum bears absolutely no relation to the present value of the place. Any company in that position is just asking for a takeover.

"A buyer would in theory need fifty-one per cent of the shares to be certain of gaining control, but in practice, as was found at Dunstable, forty would be plenty. It could probably be swung on a good deal less, but from the point of view of the buyer, the more he got his hands on before declaring his intentions, the bigger would be his profit.

"The main difficulty in taking over a racecourse company—its only natural safeguard, in fact—is that the shares seldom come on the market. I understand that it isn't always by any means possible to buy even a few on the stock exchange, as people who own them tend to be fond of them, and as long as the shares pay any dividend, however small, they won't sell. But it's obvious that not everyone can afford to have bits of capital lying around unproductively, and once the racecourse starts showing a loss, the temptation grows to transfer to something else.

"Today's price of Seabury shares is thirty shillings, which is about four shillings higher than it was two years ago. If Kraye can manage to get hold of a forty per cent holding at an average price of thirty shillings, it will cost him only about forty-eight thousand pounds.

"With a holding that size, aided by other shareholders tempted by a very large capital gain, he can outvote any opposition, and sell the whole company to a land developer. Planning permission would almost certainly be granted, as the land is not beautiful, and is surrounded already by houses. I estimate that a developer would pay roughly a million for it, as he could double that by selling off all those acres in tiny plots. There's the capital gains tax, of course, but Seabury shareholders stand to make eight hundred per cent on their original investment, if the scheme goes through. Four hundred thousand gross for Mr. Kraye, perhaps. Did you ever find out how much he cleared at Dunstable?"

He didn't answer.

I went on, "Seabury used to be a busy, lively, successful place, and now it isn't. It's a suspicious coincidence that as soon as a big buyer comes along the place goes downhill fast. They paid a dividend of only sixpence per share last year, a gross yield of under one and three-quarters per cent at today's price, and this year they showed a loss of three thousand, seven hundred and fourteen pounds. Unless something is done soon, there won't be a next year."

He didn't reply at once. He stared at the floor for a long time with the half-eaten sandwich immobile in his hand.

Finally he said, "Who did the arithmetic? Radnor?"

"No . . . I did. It's very simple. I went to Company House in the city yesterday and looked up the Seabury balance sheets for the last few years, and I rang for a quotation of today's share price from a stockbroker this morning. You can easily check it."

"Oh, I don't doubt you. I remember now, there was a rumor that you made a fortune on the stock exchange by the time you were twenty."

"People exaggerate so." I smiled. "My old governor, where I was apprenticed, started me off investing, and I was a bit lucky."

"Hm."

There was another pause while he hesitated over his decision. I didn't interrupt him, but I was much relieved when finally he said, "You have Radnor's authority for seeing me, and he knows what you have told me?"

"Yes."

"Very well." He got up stiffly and put down the unfinished sandwich. "You can tell Radnor that I agree to an investigation being made, and I think I can vouch for my colleagues agreeing. You'll want to start at once, I suppose."

I nodded.

"The usual terms?"

"I don't know," I said. "Perhaps you would get onto Mr. Radnor about that."

As I didn't know what the usual terms were, I didn't want to discuss them.

"Yes, all right. And Sid . . . it's understood that there is to be no leak about this? We can't afford to have Kraye slapping a libel or slander action on us."

"The agency is always discreet," I said, with an outward and an inward smile. Radnor was right. People paid for privacy. And why not?

CHAPTER 6

THE RACING SECTION was quiet when I went in the next morning, mostly because Chico was out on an escort job. All the other heads, including Dolly's, were bent studiously over their desks.

She looked up and said with a sigh, "You're late again." It was ten to ten. "The old man wants to see you."

I made a face at her and retraced my way down the staircase. Joanie looked pointedly at her watch.

"He's been asking for you for half an hour."

I knocked and went in. Radnor was sitting behind his desk, reading some papers, pencil in hand. He looked at me and frowned.

"Why are you so late?"

"I had a pain in me tum," I said flippantly.

"Don't be funny," he said sharply, and then, more reasonably, "Oh . . . I suppose you're not being funny."

"No. But I'm sorry about being late." I wasn't a bit sorry, however, that it had been noticed; before, no one would have said a thing if I hadn't turned up all day.

"How did you get on with Lord Hagbourne?" Radnor asked. "Was he interested?"

"Yes. He agreed to an investigation. I said he should discuss terms with you."

"I see." He flicked a switch on the small box on his desk. "Joanie, see if you can get hold of Lord Hagbourne. Try the London flat number first."

"Yes, sir," her voice came tinnily out of the speaker.

"Here," said Radnor, picking up a shallow brown cardboard box. "Look at these."

The box contained a thick wad of large glossy photographs. I looked at them one by one and heaved a sigh of relief. They had all come out sharp and clear, except some of the ones I had duplicated at varying exposures.

The telephone on Radnor's desk rang once, quietly. He lifted the receiver.

"Oh, good morning, Lord Hagbourne. Radnor here. Yes, that's right. . . ." He gestured to me to sit down, and I stayed there listening while he negotiated terms in a smooth, civilized, deceptively casual voice.

"And of course in a case like this, Lord Hagbourne, there's one other thing: we make a small surcharge if our operatives have to take out-of-the-ordinary risks. . . . Yes, as in the Canlas case, exactly. Right then, you shall have a preliminary report from us in a few days. Yes . . . good-bye."

He put down the receiver, bit his thumbnail thoughtfully for a few seconds, and said finally, "Right, then, Sid. Get on with it."

"But—" I began.

"But nothing," he said. "It's your case. Get on with it."

I stood up, holding the packet of photographs. "Can I . . . can I use Bona Fides and so on?"

He waved his hand permissively. "Sid, use every resource in the agency you need. Keep an eye on expenses though, we don't want to price ourselves out of business. And if you want legwork done, arrange it through Dolly or the other department heads. Right?"

"Won't they think it odd? I mean . . . I don't amount to much around here."

"And whose fault is that? If they won't do what you ask, refer them to me." He looked at me expressionlessly.

"All right." I walked to the door. "Er . . . who . . . ," I said, turning the knob, "gets the danger money? The operative or the agency?"

"You said you would work for nothing," he observed dryly.

I laughed. "Just so. Do I get expenses?"

"That car of yours drinks petrol."

"It does twenty," I protested.

"The agency rate is based on thirty. You can have that. And other expenses, yes. Put in a chit to accounts."

"Thanks."

He smiled suddenly, the rare sweet smile so incongruous to his military bearing, and launched into another elaborate metaphor.

"The tapes are up," he said. "What you do with the race depends on your skill and timing, just as it always used to. I've backed you with the agency's reputation for getting results, and I can't afford to lose my stake. Remember that."

"Yes," I said soberly. "I will."

I thought, as I took my stupidly aching stomach up two stories to Bona Fides, that it was time Radnor had a lift installed; and was glad I wasn't bound for Missing Persons away in the rarefied air of the fifth floor. There was a lot more character, I supposed, in the splendidly proportioned, solidly built town house that Radnor had chosen on a corner site on Cromwell Road, but a flat half acre of modern office block would have been easier on his staff. And about ten times as expensive, no doubt.

The basement, to start at the bottom, was—except for the kitchen—given over entirely to files and records. On the ground floor, besides Radnor himself and Joanie there were two interview-cum-waiting rooms, and also the Divorce Section. On the first floor, the Racing Section, Accounts, another interview room and the general secretarial department. Up one was Bona Fides, and above that, on the two smaller top floors, Guard and Missing Persons. Missing Persons alone had room to spare. Bona Fides, splitting at the seams, was encroaching on Guard. Guard was sticking in its toes.

Jones-boy, who acted as general messenger, must have had legs like iron from pounding up and down the stairs, though thanks to a tiny service lift used long ago to take nursery food to top-floor children, he could haul his ten trays up from landing to landing instead of carrying them.

In Bona Fides there was the usual chatter of six people talking on the telephone all at once. The department head, receiver glued to one ear and finger stuck in the other, was a large bald-headed man with half-moon spectacles sitting halfway down a prominent nose. As always, he was in his shirtsleeves, teamed with a frayed pullover and baggy gray flannels. No tie. He seemed to have an inexhaustible supply of old clothes but never any new ones, and Jones-boy had a theory that his wife dressed him from jumble sales.

I waited until he had finished a long conversation with a managing director about the character of the proposed production manager of a glass factory. The invaluable thing about Jack Copeland was his quick and comprehensive grasp of what dozens of jobs entailed. He was speaking to the glass manufacturer as if he had grown up in the industry; and in five minutes, I knew, he might be advising just as knowledgeably on the suitability of a town clerk. His summing up of a man went far beyond the basic list of honesty, conscientiousness, normality and prudence, which was all that many employers wanted. He liked to discover his subject's reaction under stress, to find out what he disliked doing, and what he often forgot. The resulting footnotes to his reports were usually the most valuable part of them, and the faith large numbers of industrial firms had in him bore witness to his accuracy.

He wielded enormous power but did not seem conscious of it, which made him much liked. After Radnor, he was the most important person in the agency.

"Jack," I said, as he put down the receiver. "Can you check a man for me, please?"

"What's wrong with the Racing Section, pal?" he said, jerking his thumb toward the floor.

"He isn't a racing person."

"Oh? Who is it?"

"A Howard Kraye. I don't know if he has a profession. He speculates on the stock market. He is a rabid collector of quartz." I added Kraye's London address.

He scribbled it all down fast.

"OK, Sid. I'll put one of the boys on to it and let you have a prelim. Is it urgent?"

"Fairly."

"Right." He tore the sheet off the pad. "George? You still doing that knitting-wool client's report? When you've finished, here's your next one."

"George," I said. "Be careful."

They both looked at me, suddenly still.

"An unexploded bomb," I observed. "Don't set him off."

George said cheerfully, "Makes a nice change from knitting wool. Don't worry, Sid. I'll walk on eggs."

Jack Copeland peered at me closely through the half specs.

"You've cleared it with the old man, I suppose?"

"Yes." I nodded. "It's a query fraud. He said to check with him if you wanted to."

He smiled briefly. "No need, I guess. Is that all then?"

"For the moment, yes, thanks."

"Just for the record, is this your own show, or Dolly's, or whose?"

"I suppose . . . mine."

"Uh-huh," he said accenting the second syllable. "The winds of change, if I read it right?"

I laughed. "You never know."

Down in the Racing Section I found Dolly supervising the reshuffling of the furniture. I asked what was going on, and she gave me a flashing smile.

"It seems you're in, not out. The old man just rang to say you needed somewhere to work, and I've sent Jones-boy upstairs to pinch a table from Missing Persons. That'll do for now, won't it? There isn't a spare desk in the place."

A series of bangs from outside heralded the return of Jones-boy, complete with a spindly plywood affair in a sickly lemon color. "How that lot ever find a missing person I'll never know. I bet they don't even find their missing junk."

He disappeared and came back shortly with a chair.

"The things I do for you!" he said, setting it down in front of me. "A dim little bird in the typing pool is now squatting on a stool. I chatted her up a bit."

"What this place needs is some more equipment," I murmured.

"Don't be funny," said Dolly. "Every time the old man buys one desk he takes on two assistants. When I first came here fifteen years ago we had a whole room each, believe it or not."

The rearranged office settled down again, with my table wedged into a corner next to Dolly's desk. I sat behind it and spread out the photographs to sort them. The people who developed and printed all the agency's work had come up with their usual excellent job, and it amazed me that they had been able to enlarge the tiny negatives up to nine-by-seven-inch prints and get a clearly readable result.

I picked out all the fuzzy ones, the duplicates at the wrong exposures, tore them up, and put the pieces in Dolly's wastepaper basket. That left me with fifty-one pictures of the contents of Kraye's attaché case. Innocent enough to the casual eye, but they turned out to be dynamite.

The two largest piles, when I had sorted them out, were Seabury share transfer certificates, and letters from Kraye's stockbroker. The paper headed S.R. revealed itself to be a summary in simple form of the share certificates, so I added it to that pile. I was left with the photographs of the bank notes, of share dealings which had nothing to do with Seabury, and the two sheets of figures I had found under the writing board at the bottom of the case.

I read through all the letters from the stockbroker, a man called Ellis Bolt, who belonged to a firm known as Charing, Street and King. Bolt and Kraye were on friendly terms; the letters referred sometimes to social occasions on which they had met; but for the most part the typewritten sheets dealt with the availability and prospects of various shares (including Seabury), purchases made or proposed, and references to tax, stamp duty, and commission.

Two letters had been written in Bolt's own hand. The first, dated ten days ago, said briefly:

> *Dear H.*
>   *Shall wait with interest for the news on Friday.*
>   *E.*

The second, which Kraye must have received on the morning he went to Aynsford, read:

> *Dear H.*
>   *I have put the final draft in the hands of the printers, and the leaflets should be out by the end of next week, or the Tuesday following at the latest. Two or three days before the next meeting, anyway. That should do it, I think. There would be a lot of unrest should there be another hitch, but surely you will see to that.*
>   *E.*

"Dolly," I said. "May I borrow your phone?"

"Help yourself."

I rang upstairs to Bona Fides. "Jack? Can I have a rundown on another man as well? Ellis Bolt, stockbroker, works for a firm called Charing, Street and King." I gave him the address. "He's a friend of Kraye's. Same care needed, I'm afraid."

"Right. I'll let you know."

I sat staring down at the two harmless-looking letters.

"Shall wait with interest for the news on Friday." It could mean any news, anything at all. It also could mean the News; and on the radio on Friday I had heard that Seabury Races were off because a lorry carrying chemicals had over-turned and burned the turf.

The second letter was just as tricky. It could easily refer to a shareholder's meeting at which a hitch should be avoided at all costs. Or it could refer to a race meeting—at Seabury—where another hitch could affect the sale of shares yet again.

It was like looking at a conjuring trick: from one side you saw a normal object, but from the other, a sham.

If it were a sham, Mr. Ellis Bolt was in a criminal career up to his eyebrows. If it was just my suspicious mind jumping to hasty conclusions I was doing an old-established respectable stockbroker a shocking injustice.

I picked up Dolly's telephone again and got an outside line.

"Charing, Street and King, good morning," said a quiet female voice.

"Oh, good morning. I would like to make an appointment to see Mr. Bolt and discuss some investments. Would that be possible?"

"Certainly, yes. This is Mr. Bolt's secretary speaking. Could I have your name?"

"Halley. John Halley."

"You would be a new client, Mr. Halley?"

"That's right."

"I see. Well, now, Mr. Bolt will be in the office tomorrow afternoon, and I could fit you in at three-thirty. Would that suit you?"

"Thank you. That's fine. I'll be there."

I put down the receiver and looked tentatively at Dolly.

"Would it be all right with you if I go out for the rest of the day?"

She smiled. "Sid, dear, you're very sweet, but you don't have to ask my permission. The old man made it very clear that you're on your own now. You're not accountable to me or anyone else in the agency, except the old man himself. I'll grant you I've never known him give anyone quite such a free hand before, but there you are, my love, you can do what you like. I'm your boss no longer."

"You don't mind?" I asked.

"No," she said thoughtfully. "Come to think of it, I don't. I've a notion that what the old man has always wanted of you in this agency is a partner."

"Dolly!" I was astounded. "Don't be ridiculous."

"He's not getting any younger," she pointed out.

I laughed. "So he picked on a broken-down jockey to help him out."

"He picks on someone with enough capital to buy a partnership, someone who's been to the top of one profession and has the time in years to get to the top of another."

"You're raving, Dolly, dear. He nearly chucked me out yesterday morning."

"But you're still here, aren't you? More here than ever before. And Joanie said he was in a fantastically good mood all day yesterday, after you'd been in to see him."

I shook my head, laughing. "You're too romantic. Jockeys don't turn into investigators any more than they turn into . . ."

"Well, what?" she prompted.

"Into auctioneers, then . . . or accountants."

She shook her head. "You've already turned into an investigator, whether you know it or not. I've been watching you these two years, remember? You look as if you're doing nothing, but you've soaked up everything the blood-hounds have taught you like a hungry sponge. I'd say, Sid love, if you don't watch out, you'll be part of the fixtures and fittings for the rest of your life."

But I didn't believe her, and I paid no attention to what she had said.

I grinned. "I'm going down to take a look at Seabury Racecourse this afternoon. Like to come?"

"Are you kidding?" she sighed. Her in-tray was six inches deep. "I could have just done with a ride in that rocket car of yours, and a breath of sea air."

I stacked the photographs together and returned them to the box, along with the negatives. There was a drawer in the table, and I pulled it open to put the photographs away. It wasn't empty. Inside lay a packet of sandwiches, some cigarettes, and a flat half bottle of whisky.

I began to laugh. "Someone," I said, "will shortly come rampaging down from Missing Persons looking for his missing lunch."

SEABURY RACECOURSE LAY about half a mile inland, just off a trunk road to the sea. Looking backward from the top of the stands one could see the wide silver sweep of the English Channel. Between and on both sides the crowded rows of little houses seemed to be rushing toward the coast like Gadarene swine. In each little unit a retired schoolmaster or civil servant or clergyman—or their widows—thought about the roots they had pulled up from wherever it had been too cold or too dingy for their old age, and sniffed the warm south salt-laden air.

They had made it. Done what they'd always wanted. Retired to a bungalow by the sea.

I drove straight in through the open racecourse gate and stopped outside the weighing room. Climbing out, I stretched, and walked over to knock on the door of the racecourse manager's office.

There was no reply. I tried the handle. It was locked. So was the weighing-room door, and everything else.

Hands in pockets, I strolled round the end of the stands to look at the course. Seabury was officially classified in Group Three: that is to say, lower than Doncaster and higher than Windsor when it came to receiving aid from the Betting Levy Board.

It had less than Grade Three stands: wooden steps with corrugated tin roofs for the most part, and drafts from all parts of the compass. But the track itself was a joy to ride on, and it had always seemed a pity to me that the rest of the amenities didn't match it.

There was no one about near the stands. Down at one end of the course, however, I could see some men and a tractor, and I set off toward them, walking down inside the rails, on the grass. The going was just about perfect for November racing, soft but springy underfoot, exactly right for tempting trainers to send their horses to the course in droves. In ordinary circumstances, that was. But as things stood at present, more trainers than Mark Witney were sending their horses elsewhere. A course which didn't attract runners didn't attract crowds to watch them. Seabury's gate receipts had been falling off for some time, but its expenses had risen; and therein lay its loss.

Thinking about the sad tale I had read in the balance sheets, I reached the men working on the course. They were digging up a great section of it and loading it onto a trailer behind the tractor. There was a pervasive unpleasant smell in the air.

An irregular patch about thirty yards deep, stretching nearly the whole width of the course, had been burned brown and killed. Less than half of the affected turf had already been removed, showing the grayish chalky mud underneath, and there was still an enormous amount to be shifted. I didn't think there were enough men working on it for there to be a hope of its being returfed and ready to race on in only eight days' time.

"Good afternoon," I said to the men in general. "What a horrible mess."

One of them thrust his spade into the earth and came over, rubbing his hands on the sides of his trousers.

"Anything you want?" he said, with fair politeness.

"The racecourse manager. Captain Oxon."

His manner shifted perceptibly toward the civil. "He's not here today, sir. Hey! Aren't you Sid Halley?"

"That's right."

He grinned, doing another quick change, this time toward brotherhood. "I'm the foreman. Ted Wilkins." I shook his outstretched hand. "Captain Oxon's gone up to London. He said he wouldn't be back until tomorrow."

"Never mind," I said. "I was just down in this part of the world and I thought I'd drop in and have a look at the poor old course."

He turned with me to look at the devastation. "Shame, isn't it?"

"What happened, exactly?"

"The tanker overturned on the road over there." He pointed, and we began to walk toward the spot, edging round the dug-up area. The road, a narrow secondary one, ran across near the end of the racecourse, with a wide semicircle of track on the far side of it. During the races the hard road surface was covered thickly with tan or peat, or with thick green matting, which the horses galloped over without any trouble. Although not ideal, it was an arrangement to be found on many courses throughout the country, most famously with the Melling Road at Aintree, and reaching a maximum with five road crossings at Ludlow.

"Just here," said Ted Wilkins, pointing. "Worst place it could possibly have happened, right in the middle of the track. The stuff just poured out of the tanker. It turned right over, see, and the hatch thing was torn open in the crash."

"How did it happen?" I asked. "The crash, I mean?"

"No one knows, really."

"But the driver? He wasn't killed, was he?"

"No, he wasn't even hurt much. Just shook up a bit. But he couldn't remember what happened. Some people in a car came driving along after dark and nearly ran into the tanker. They found the driver sitting at the side of the road, holding his head and moaning. Concussion, it was, they say. They reckon he hit his head somehow when his lorry went over. Staggers me how he got out of it so lightly, the cab was fair crushed, and there was glass everywhere."

"Do tankers often drive across here? Lucky it's never happened before, if they do."

"They used not to," he said, scratching his head. "But they've been over here quite regularly now for a year or two. The traffic on the London road's getting chronic, see?"

"Oh . . . did it come from a local firm, then?"

"Down the coast a bit. Intersouth Chemicals, that's the firm it belonged to."

"How soon do you think we'll be racing here again?" I asked, turning back to look at the track. "Will you make it by next week?"

He frowned. "Strictly between you and me, I don't think there's a bleeding hope. What we needed, as I said to the captain, was a couple of bulldozers, not six men with spades."

"I would have thought so too."

He sighed. "He just told me we couldn't afford them and to shut up and get on with it. And that's what we've done. We'll just about have cut out all the dead turf by next Wednesday, at this rate of going on."

"That doesn't leave any time for new turf to settle," I remarked.

"It'll be a miracle if it's laid, let alone settled," he agreed gloomily.

I bent down and ran my hand over a patch of brown grass. It was decomposing and felt slimy. I made a face, and the foreman laughed.

"Horrible, isn't it? It stinks, too."

I put my fingers to my nose and wished I hadn't. "Was it slippery like this right from the beginning?"

"Yes, that's right. Hopeless."

"Well, I won't take up any more of your time," I said, smiling.

"I'll tell Captain Oxon you came. Pity you missed him."

"Don't bother him. He must have a lot to worry about just now."

"One bloody crisis after another." He nodded. "So long, then." He went back to his spade and his heartbreaking task, and I retraced the quarter mile up the straight to the deserted stands.

I hesitated for a while outside the weighing room, wondering whether to pick the lock and go in, and knowing it was mainly nostalgia that urged me to do it, not any conviction that it would be a useful piece of investigation. There would always be the temptation, I supposed, to use dubious professional skills for one's own pleasure. Like doctors sniffing ether. I contented myself with looking through the windows.

The deserted weighing room looked the same as ever: a large bare expanse of wooden board floor, with a table and some upright chairs in one corner, and the weighing machine itself on the left. Racecourse weighing machines were not all of one universal design. There weren't any left of the old type where the jockeys stood on a platform while weights were added to the balancing arm. That whole process was much too slow. Now there were either seats slung from above, in which one felt much like a bag of sugar, or chairs bolted to a base plate on springs: in both these cases the weight was quickly indicated by a pointer which swung round a gigantic clock face. In essence, modern kitchen scales vastly magnified.

The scales at Seabury were the chair-on-base-plate type, which I'd always found simplest to use. I recalled a few of the before-and-after occasions when I had sat on that particular spot. Some good, some bad, as always with racing.

Shrugging, I turned away. I wouldn't, I thought, ever be sitting there again. And no one walked over my grave.

Climbing into the car, I drove to the nearest town, looked up the whereabouts of Intersouth Chemicals, and an hour later was speaking to the personnel manager. I explained that on behalf of the National Hunt Committee I had just called in passing to find out if the driver of the tanker had fully recovered, or had remembered anything else about the accident.

The manager, fat and fiftyish, was affable but unhelpful. "Smith's left," he said briefly. "We gave him a few days off to get over the accident, and then he came back yesterday and said his wife didn't fancy him driving chemicals anymore, and he was packing it in." His voice held a grievance.

"Had he been with you long?" I asked sympathetically.

"About a year."

"A good driver, I suppose?"

"Yes, about average for the job. They have to be good drivers, or we don't use them, you see. Smith was all right, but nothing special."

"And you still don't really know what happened?"

"No," he sighed. "It takes a lot to tip one of our tankers over. There was nothing to learn from the road. It was covered with oil and petrol and chemical. If there had ever been any marks, skid marks I mean, they weren't there after the breakdown cranes had lifted the tanker up again, and the road was cleared."

"Do your tankers use that road often?"

"They have done recently, but not anymore after this. As a matter of fact, I seem to remember it was Smith himself who found that way round. Going over the racecourse missed out some bottleneck at a junction, I believe. I know some of the drivers thought it a good idea."

"They go through Seabury regularly, then?"

"Sure, often. Straight line to Southampton and round to the oil refinery at Fawley."

"Oh? What exactly was Smith's tanker carrying?"

"Sulfuric acid. It's used in refining petrol, among other things."

Sulfuric acid. Dense, oily, corrosive to the point of charring. Nothing more instantly lethal could have poured out over Seabury's turf. They could have raced had it been a milder chemical, put sand or tan on the dying grass and raced over the top. But no one would risk a horse on ground soaked with sulfuric acid.

I said, "Could you give me Smith's address? I'll call round and see if his memory has come back."

"Sure." He searched in a file and found it for me. "Tell him he can have his job back if he's interested. Another of the men gave notice this morning."

I said I would, thanked him, and went to Smith's address, which proved to be two rooms upstairs in a suburban house. But Smith and his wife no longer lived there. Packed up and gone yesterday, I was told by a young woman in curlers. No, she didn't know where they went. No, they didn't leave a forwarding address, and if I was her I wouldn't worry about his health as he'd been laughing and drinking and playing records till all hours the day after the crash, his concussion having cured itself pretty quick. Reaction, he'd said when she complained of the noise, against not being killed.

It was dark by then, and I drove slowly back into London against the stream of headlights pouring out. Back to my flat in a modern block, a short walk from the office, down the ramp into the basement garage, and up in the lift to the fifth floor, home.

There were two rooms facing south, bedroom and sitting room, and two behind them, bathroom and kitchen, with windows into an inner well. A pleasant place, furnished in blond wood and cool colors, centrally heated, cleaning included in the rent. A regular order of groceries arrived week by week directly into the kitchen through a hatch, and rubbish disappeared down a chute. Instant living. No fuss, no mess, no strings. And damnably lonely, after Jenny.

Not that she had ever been in the place; she hadn't. The house in the Berkshire village where we had mostly lived had been too much of a battle-ground, and when she walked out I sold it, with relief. I'd moved into the new flat shortly after going to the agency, because it was close. It was also expensive, but I had no fares to pay.

I mixed myself a brandy with ice and water, sat down in an armchair, put my feet up, and thought about Seabury. Seabury, Captain Oxon, Ted Wilkins, Intersouth Chemicals, and a driver called Smith.

After that I thought about Kraye. Nothing pleasant about him, nothing at all. A smooth, phony crust of sophistication hiding ruthless greed; a seething passion for crystals, ditto for land; an obsession with the cleanliness of his body to compensate for the murk in his mind; unconventional sexual pleasures; and the abnormal quality of being able to look carefully at a crippled hand and *then hit it*.

No, I didn't care for Howard Kraye one little bit.

CHAPTER 7

"CHICO," I SAID. "How would you overturn a lorry on a predeter-
mined spot?"

"Huh? That's easy. All you'd need would be some heavy lifting gear. A
big hydraulic jack. A crane. Anything like that."

"How long would it take?"

"You mean, supposing the lorry and the crane were both in position?"

"Yes."

"Only a minute or two. What sort of lorry?"

"A tanker."

"A petrol job?"

"A bit smaller than the petrol tankers. More the size of milk ones."

"Easy as kiss your hand. They've got a low center of gravity, mind. It'd
need a good strong lift. But dead easy, all the same."

I turned to Dolly. "Is Chico busy today, or could you spare him?"

Dolly leaned forward, chewing the end of a pencil and looking at her
day's chart. The crossover blouse did its stuff.

I could send someone else to Kempton. . . ." She caught the direction of
my eyes and laughed, and retreated a whole half inch. "Yes, you can have
him." She gave him a fond glance.

"Chico," I said. "Go down to Seabury and see if you can find any trace of
heavy lifting gear having been seen near the racecourse last Friday . . . those
little bungalows are full of people with nothing to do but watch the world go
by. You might check whether anything was hired locally, but I suppose that's
a bit much to hope for. The road would have to have been closed for a few
minutes before the tanker went over, I should think. See if you can find anyone who noticed anything like that . . . detour signs, for instance. And after
that, go to the council offices and see what you can dig up among their old
maps on the matter of drains." I told him the rough position of the subsiding
trench which had made a slaughterhouse of the hurdle race, so that he should
know what to look for on the maps. "And be discreet."

"Teach your grandmother to suck eggs." He grinned.

"Our quarry is rough."

"And you don't want him to hear us creep up behind him?"

"Quite right."

"Little Chico," he said truthfully, "can take care of himself."

After he had gone I telephoned Lord Hagbourne and described to him in no uncertain terms the state of Seabury's turf.

"What they need is some proper earth-moving equipment, fast, and apparently there's nothing in the kitty to pay for it. Couldn't the Levy Board . . . ?"

"The Levy Board is no fairy godmother," he interrupted. "But I'll see what can be done. Less than half cleared, you say? Hmm. However, I understand that Captain Oxon assured Weatherbys that the course would be ready for the next meeting. Has he changed his mind?"

"I didn't see him, sir. He was away for the day."

"Oh." Lord Hagbourne's voice grew a shade cooler. "Then he didn't ask you to enlist my help?"

"No."

"I don't see that I can interfere then. As racecourse manager it is his responsibility to decide what can be done and what can't, and I think it must be left like that. Mm, yes. And of course he will consult the clerk of the course if he needs advice."

"The clerk of the course is Mr. Fotherton, who lives in Bristol. He is clerk of the course there, too, and he's busy with the meetings there tomorrow and Monday."

"Er, yes, so he is."

"You could ring Captain Oxon up in an informal way and just ask how the work is getting on," I suggested.

"I don't know—"

"Well, sir, you can take my word for it that if things dawdle on at the same rate down there, there won't be any racing at Seabury next weekend. I don't think Captain Oxon can realize just how slowly those men are digging."

"He must," he protested. "He assured Weatherbys—"

"Another last-minute cancellation will kill Seabury off," I said with some force.

There was a moment's pause. Then he said reluctantly, "Yes, I suppose it might. All right then. I'll ask Captain Oxon and Mr. Fotherton if they are both satisfied with the way things are going."

And I couldn't pin him down to any more direct action than that, which was certainly not going to be enough. Protocol would be the death of Seabury, I thought.

Monopolizing Dolly's telephone, I next rang up the Epping police and spoke to Chief Inspector Cornish.

"Any more news about Andrews?" I asked.

"I suppose you have a reasonable personal interest." His chuckle came down the wire. "We found he did have a sister after all. We called her at the inquest yesterday for identification purposes as she is a relative, but if you ask me she didn't really know. She took one look at the bits in the mortuary and was sick on the floor."

"Poor girl, you couldn't blame her."

"No. She didn't look long enough to identify anyone. But we had your identification for sure, so we hadn't the heart to make her go in again."

"How did he die? Did you find out?"

"Indeed we did. He was shot in the back. The bullet ricocheted off a rib and lodged in the sternum. We got the experts to compare it with the one they dug out of the wall of your office. Your bullet was a bit squashed by the hard plaster, but there's no doubt that they are the same. He was killed with the gun he used on you."

"And was it there, underneath him?"

"Not a sign of it. They brought in 'murder by persons unknown.' And between you and me, that's how it's likely to stay. We haven't a lead to speak of."

"What lead do you have?" I asked.

His voice had a smile in it. "Only something his sister told us. She has a bed-sitter in Islington, and he spent the evening there before breaking into your place. He showed her the gun. She says he was proud of having it; apparently he was a bit simple. All he told her was that a big chap had lent it to him to go out and fetch something, and he was to shoot anyone who got in his way. She didn't believe him. She said he was always making things up, always had, all his life. So she didn't ask him anything about the big chap, or about where he was going, or anything at all."

"A bit casual," I said. "With a loaded gun under her nose."

"According to the neighbors she was more interested in a stream of men friends than in anything her brother did."

"Sweet people, neighbors."

"You bet. Anyway we checked with anyone we could find who had seen Andrews the week he shot you, and he hadn't said a word to any of them about a gun or a 'big chap,' or an errand in Cromwell Road."

"He didn't go back to his sister afterwards?"

"No, she'd told him she had a guest coming."

"At one in the morning? The neighbors must be right. You tried racecourses, of course? Andrews is quite well known there, as a sort of spivvy odd-job messenger boy."

"Yes, we mainly tried the racecourses. No results. Everyone seemed surprised that such a harmless person should have been murdered."

"Harmless!"

He laughed. "If you hadn't thought him harmless, you'd have kept out of his way."

"You're so right," I said with feeling. "But now I see a villain in every respectable citizen. It's very disturbing."

"Most of them are villains, in one way or another," he said cheerfully. "Keeps us busy. By the way, what do you think of Sparkle's chances this year in the Henessy? . . ."

When eventually I put the telephone down Dolly grabbed it with a sarcastic, "Do you mind?" and asked the switchboard girl to get her three numbers in a row, "without interruptions from Halley." I grinned, got the packet of photographs out of the plywood table drawer, and looked through them again. They didn't tell me any more than before. Ellis Bolt's letters to Kraye. Now you see it, now you don't. A villain in every respectable citizen. Play it secretly, I thought, close to the chest, in case the eyes looking over your shoulder give you away. I wondered why I was so oppressed by a vague feeling of apprehension, and decided in irritation that a bullet in the stomach had made me nervous.

When Dolly finished her calls I took the receiver out of her hand and got through to my bank manager.

"Mr. Harper? This is Sid Halley . . . yes, fine thanks, and you? Good. Now, would you tell me just how much I have in both my accounts, deposit and current?"

"They're quite healthy, actually," he said in his gravelly base voice. "You've had several dividends in lately. Hang on a minute, and I'll send for the exact figures." He spoke to someone in the background and then came back. "It's time you reinvested some of it."

"I do have some investments in mind," I agreed. "That's what I want to discuss with you. I'm planning to buy some shares this time from another stockbroker, not through the bank. Er . . . please don't think that I'm dissatisfied; how could I be, when you've done so well for me. It's something to do with my work at the agency."

"Say no more. What exactly do you want?"

"Well, to give you as a reference," I said. "He's sure to want one, but I would be very grateful if you would make it as impersonal and as strictly financial as possible. Don't mention either my past occupation or my present one. That's very important."

"I won't, then. Anything else?"

"Nothing . . . oh, yes. I've introduced myself to him as John Halley. Would you refer to me like that if he gets in touch with you?"

"Right. I'll look forward to hearing from you one day what it's all about. Why don't you come in and see me? I've some very good cigars." The deep voice was amused. "Ah, here are the figures. . . ." He told me the total, which for once was bigger than I expected. That happy state of affairs wouldn't last very long, I reflected, if I had to live for two years without any salary from Radnor. And no one's fault but my own.

Giving Dolly back her telephone with an ironic bow, I went upstairs to Bona Fides. Jack Copeland's mud-colored jersey had a dark blue darn on the chest and a fraying stretch of ribbing on the hip. He was picking at a loose thread and making it worse.

"Anything on Kraye yet?" I asked. "Or is it too early?"

"George has got something on the prelim, I think," he answered. "Anybody got any scissors?" A large area of jersey disintegrated into ladders. "Blast."

Laughing, I went over to George's desk. The prelim was a sheet of handwritten notes in George's style. "Leg mat, 2 yrs. 2 prev, 1 div, 1 sui dec.," it began, followed by a list of names and dates.

"Oh, yeah?" I said.

"Yeah." He grinned. "Kraye was legally married to Doria Dawn, nee Easterman, two years ago. Before that he had two other wives. One killed herself; the other divorced him for cruelty." He pointed to the names and dates.

"So clear," I agreed. "When you know how."

"If you weren't so impatient you'd have had a legible typed report. But as you're here . . ." He went on down the page pointing. "Geologists think him a bit eccentric . . . quartz has no intrinsic value, most of it's much too common, except for the gemstones, but Kraye goes round trying to buy chunks of it if they take his fancy. They know him quite well along the road at the Geology Museum. But not a breath of any dirty work. Clubs: he belongs to these three, not overliked, but most members think he's a brilliant fellow, talks very well. He gambles at Crockfords, ends up about all square over the months. He travels, always first class, usually by boat, not air. No job or profession, can't trace him on any professional or university lists. Thought to live on investments, playing the stork market, etc. Not much liked, but considered by most a clever, cultured man, by one or two a hypocritical gasbag."

"No talk of him being crooked in any way?"

"Not a word. You want him dug deeper?"

"If you can do it without him finding out."

George nodded. "Do you want him tailed?"

"No, I don't think so. Not at present." A twenty-four-hour tail was heavy on man power, and expensive to the client, quite apart from the risk of the quarry noticing and being warned of the hunt. "Anything of his early life?" I asked.

George shook his head. "Nothing. Nobody who knows him now has known him longer than about ten years. He either wasn't born in Britain, or his name at birth wasn't Kraye. No known relatives."

"You've done marvels, George. All this in one day."

"Contacts, chum, contacts. A lot of phoning, a bit of pubbing, a touch of gossip with the local tradesmen—nothing to it."

Jack, moodily poking his fingers through the cobweb remains of his jersey, looked at me over the half-moon specs and said that there wasn't a prelim on Bolt yet because ex-sergeant Lamar, who was working on it, hadn't phoned in.

"If he does," I said, "let me know? I've an appointment with Bolt at three-thirty. It would be handy to know the setup before I go."

"OK."

After that I went down and looked out of the windows of the Racing Section for half an hour, idly watching life go by in Cromwell Road and wondering just what sort of mess I was making of the Kraye investigation. A novice chaser in the Grand National, I thought wryly; that was me. Though, come to think of it, I had once ridden a novice in the National, and got round, too. Slightly cheered, I took Dolly out to a drink and a sandwich in the snack bar at the Air Terminal, where we sat and envied the people starting off on their travels. So much expectation in the faces, as if they could fly away and leave their troubles on the ground. An illusion, I thought sourly. Your troubles flew with you; a drag in the mind . . . a deformity in the pocket.

I laughed and joked with Dolly, as usual. What else can you do?

THE FIRM OF Charing, Street and King occupied two rooms in a large block of offices belonging to a bigger firm, and consisted entirely of Bolt, his clerk and a secretary.

I was shown the door of the secretary's office, and went into a dull, tidy, fog-colored box of a room with cold fluorescent lighting and a close-up view of the fire escape through the grimy window. A woman sat at a desk by the right-hand wall, facing the window, with her back toward me. A yard behind her chair was a door with ELLIS BOLT painted on a frosted glass panel. It occurred to me that she was most awkwardly placed in the room, but that perhaps she liked sitting in a potential draft and having to turn around every time someone came in.

She didn't turn round, however. She merely moved her head round a fraction toward me and said, "Yes?"

"I have an appointment with Mr. Bolt," I said. "At three-thirty."

"Oh, yes, you must be Mr. Halley. Do sit down. I'll see if Mr. Bolt is free now."

She pointed to an easy chair a step ahead of me, and flipped a switch on her desk. While I listened to her telling Mr. Bolt I was there, in the quiet voice I had heard on the telephone, I had time to see she was in her late thirties, slender, upright in her chair, with a smooth wing of straight, dark hair falling down her cheek. If anything, it was too young a hairstyle for her. There were no rings on her fingers, and no nail varnish either. Her clothes were dark and uninteresting. It seemed as though she were making a deliberate attempt to be unattractive, yet her profile, when she half turned and told me Mr. Bolt would see me, was pleasant enough. I had a glimpse of one brown eye quickly cast down, the beginning of a smile on pale lips, and she presented me again squarely with the back of her head.

Puzzled, I opened Ellis Bolt's door and walked in. The inner office wasn't much more inspiring than the outer; it was larger and there was a new green square of carpet on the linoleum, but the grayish walls prevailed, along with the tidy dullness. Through the two windows was a more distant view of the fire escape of the building across the alley. If a drab conventional setting equaled respectability, Bolt was an honest stockbroker; and Lamar, who had phoned in just before I left, had found nothing to suggest otherwise.

Bolt was on his feet behind his desk, hand outstretched. I shook it, he gestured me to a chair with arms, and offered me a cigarette.

"No, thank you, I don't smoke."

"Lucky man," he said benignly, tapping ash off one he was half through and settling his pin-striped bulk back into his chair.

His face was rounded at every point, large round nose, round cheeks, round heavy chin; no planes, no impression of bone structure underneath. He had exceptionally heavy eyebrows, a full, mobile mouth, and a smug, self-satisfied expression.

"Now, Mr. Halley, I believe in coming straight to the point. What can I do for you?"

He had a mellifluous voice, and he spoke as if he enjoyed the sound of it.

I said, "An aunt has given me some money now rather than leave it to me in her will, and I want to invest it."

"I see. And what made you come to me? Did someone recommend . . . ?" He tailed off, watching me with eyes that told me he was no fool.

"I'm afraid . . ." I hesitated, smiling apologetically to take the offense out of the words, "that I literally picked you with a pin. I don't know any stock-brokers. I didn't know how to get to know one, so I picked up a classified directory and stuck a pin into the list of names, and it was yours."

"Ah," he said paternally, observing the bad fit of Chico's second-best suit, which I had borrowed for the occasion, and listening to me reverting to the accent of my childhood.

"Can you help me?" I asked.

"I expect so, I expect so. How much is this, er, gift?" His voice was minutely patronizing, his manner infinitesimally bored. His time, he suspected, was being wasted.

"Fifteen hundred pounds."

He brightened a very little. "Oh, yes, definitely, we can do something with that. Now, do you want growth stock or a high rate of yield?"

I looked vague. He told me quite fairly the difference between the two and offered no advice.

"Growth, then," I said, tentatively. "Turn it into a fortune in time for my old age."

He smiled without much mirth, and drew a sheet of paper toward him.

"Could I have your full name?"

"John Halley . . . John Sidney Halley," I said truthfully. He wrote it down.

"Address?" I gave it.

"And your bank?" I told him that too.

"And I'll need a reference, I'm afraid."

"Would the bank manager do?" I asked. "I've had an account there for two years. He knows me quite well."

"Excellent." He screwed up his pen. "Now, do you have any idea what companies you'd like shares in, or will you leave it to me?"

"Oh, I'll leave it to you. If you don't mind, that is. I don't know anything about it, you see, not really. Only it seems silly to leave all that money around doing nothing."

"Quite, quite." He was bored with me. I thought with amusement that Charles would appreciate my continuing his strategy of the weak front. "Tell me, Mr. Halley, what do you do for a living?"

"Oh . . . um . . . I work in a shop," I said. "In the men's wear. Very interesting, it is."

"I'm sure it is." There was a yawn stuck in his throat.

"I'm hoping to be made an assistant buyer next year," I said eagerly.

"Splendid. Well done." He'd had enough. He got cumbrously to his feet and ushered me to the door. "All right, Mr. Halley, I'll invest your money safely for you in good long-term growth stock, and send you the papers to sign in due course. You'll hear from me in a week or ten days. All right?"

"Yes, Mr. Bolt, thank you very much indeed," I said. He shut the door gently behind me.

There were now two people in the outer office. The woman with her back still turned, and a spare, middle-aged man with a primly folded mouth, and tough stringy tendons pushing his collar away from his neck. He was quite at home, and with an incurious, unhurried glance at me he went past into Bolt's office. The clerk, I presumed.

The woman was typing addresses on envelopes. The twenty or so that she had done lay in a slithery stack on her left; on her right an open file provided a list of names. I looked over her shoulder casually, and then with quickened interest. She was working down the first page of a list of Seabury shareholders.

"Do you want something, Mr. Halley?" she asked politely, pulling one envelope from the typewriter and inserting another with a minimum of flourish.

"Well, er, yes," I said diffidently. I walked round to the side of her desk and found that one couldn't go on round to the front of it: a large old-fashioned table with bulbous legs filled all the space between the desk and the end of the room. I looked at this arrangement with some sort of understanding and with compassion.

"I wondered," I said, "if you could be very kind and tell me something about investing money, and so on. I didn't like to ask Mr. Bolt too much, he's a busy man. And I'd like to know a bit about it."

"I'm sorry, Mr. Halley." Her head was turned away from me, bent over the Seabury investors. "I've a job to do, as you see. Why don't you read the financial columns in the papers, or get a book on the subject?"

I had a book all right. *Outline of Company Law.* One thing I had learned from it was that only stockbrokers—apart from the company involved—could send circulars to shareholders. It was illegal if private citizens did it. Illegal for Kraye to send letters to Seabury shareholders offering to buy them out: legal for Bolt.

"Books aren't as good as people at explaining things," I said. "If you are busy now, could I come back when you're finished work and take you out for a meal? I'd be so grateful if you would, if you possibly could."

A sort of shudder shook her. "I'm sorry, Mr. Halley, but I'm afraid I can't."

"If you will look at me, so that I can see all of your face," I said, "I will ask you again."

Her head went up with a jerk at that, but finally she turned round and looked at me.

I smiled. "That's better. Now, how about coming out with me this evening?"

"You guessed?"

I nodded. "The way you've got your furniture organized. Will you come?"

"You still want to?"

"Well, of course. What time do you finish?"

"About six, tonight."

"I'll come back. I'll meet you at the door, down in the street."

"All right," she said. "If you really mean it, thank you. I'm not doing anything else tonight. . . ."

Years of hopeless loneliness showed raw in the simple words. Not doing anything else, tonight or most nights. Yet her face wasn't horrific; not anything as bad as I had been prepared for. She had lost an eye, and wore a false one. There had been some extensive burns and undoubtedly some severe fracture of the facial bones, but plastic surgery had repaired the damage to a great extent, and it had all been a long time ago. The scars were old. It was the inner wound which hadn't healed. Well . . . I knew a bit about that myself, on a smaller scale.

CHAPTER 8

SHE CAME OUT of the door at ten past six wearing a neat well-cut dark overcoat and with a plain silk scarf covering her hair, tied under her chin. It hid only a small part of the disaster to her face, and seeing her like that, defenseless, away from the shelter she had made in her office, I had an uncomfortably vivid vision of the purgatory she suffered day in and day out on the journeys to work.

She hadn't expected me to be there. She didn't look round for me when she came out, but turned directly up the road toward the tube station. I walked after her and touched her arm. Even in low heels she was taller than I.

"Mr. Halley!" she said. "I didn't think—"

"How about a drink first?" I said. "The pubs are open."

"Oh no—"

"Oh yes. Why not?" I took her arm and steered her firmly across the road into the nearest bar. Dark oak, gentle lighting, brass pump handles, and the lingering smell of lunchtime cigars: a warm beckoning stop for city gents on their way home. There were already half a dozen of them, prosperous and dark-suited, adding fizz to their spirits.

"Not here," she protested.

"Here." I held a chair for her to sit on at a small table in a corner, and asked her what she would like to drink.

"Sherry, then . . . dry."

I took the two glasses over one at a time, sherry for her, brandy for me. She was sitting on the edge of the chair, uncomfortably, and it was not the one I had put her in. She had moved round so that she had her back to everyone except me.

"Good luck, Miss . . . ?" I said, lifting my glass.

"Martin. Zanna Martin."

"Good luck, Miss Martin." I smiled.

Tentatively she smiled back. It made her face much worse: half the muscles on the disfigured right side didn't work or could do nothing about lifting the corner of her mouth or crinkling the skin round the socket of her eye. Had life been even ordinarily kind she would have been a pleasant-looking, assured woman in her late thirties with a loving husband and a growing family: years of heartbreak had left her a shy, lonely spinster who dressed and moved as though she would like to be invisible. Yet, looking at the sad travesty of her face, one could neither blame the young men who hadn't married her nor condemn her own efforts at effacement.

"Have you worked for Mr. Bolt long?" I asked peaceably, settling back lazily into my chair and watching her gradually relax into her own.

"Only a few months. . . ." She talked for some time about her job in answer to my interested questions, but unless she was supremely artful, she was not aware of anything shady going on in Charing, Street and King. I mentioned the envelopes she had been addressing, and asked what was going into them.

"I don't know yet," she said. "The leaflets haven't come from the printers."

"But I expect you typed the leaflet anyway," I said idly.

"No, actually I think Mr. Bolt did that one himself. He's quite helpful in that way, you know. If I'm busy he'll often do letters himself."

Will he, I thought. Will he, indeed. Miss Martin, as far as I was concerned, was in the clear. I bought her another drink and extracted her opinion about Bolt as a stockbroker. Sound, she said, but not busy. She had worked for other stockbrokers, it appeared, and knew enough to judge.

"There aren't many stockbrokers working on their own anymore," she explained, "and . . . well, I don't like working in a big office, you see . . . and it's getting more difficult to find a job which suits me. So many stockbrokers have joined up into partnerships of three or more; it reduces overheads terrifically, of course, and it means that they can spend more time in the House. . . ."

"Where are Mr. Charing, Mr. Street, and Mr. King?" I asked.

Charing and Street were dead, she understood, and King had retired some years ago. The firm now consisted simply and solely of Ellis Bolt. She didn't really like Mr. Bolt's offices being contained inside of those of another firm. It wasn't private enough, but it was the usual arrangement nowadays. It reduced overhead so much. . . .

When the city gents had mostly departed to the bosoms of their families, Miss Martin and I left the pub and walked through the empty city streets toward the Tower. We found a quiet little restaurant where she agreed to have dinner. As before, she made a straight line for a corner table and sat with her back to the room.

"I'm paying my share," she announced firmly when she had seen the prices on the menu. "I had no idea this place was so expensive or I wouldn't have let you choose it. Mr. Bolt mentioned that you worked in a shop."

"There's Aunty's legacy," I pointed out. "The dinner's on Aunty."

She laughed. It was a happy sound if you didn't look at her, but I found I was already able to talk to her without continually, consciously thinking about her face. One got used to it after a very short while. Sometime, I thought, I would tell her so.

I was still on a restricted diet, which made social eating difficult enough without one-handedness thrown in, but did very well on clear soup and Dover sole, expertly removed from the bone by a waiter. Miss Martin, shedding inhibitions visibly, ordered lobster cocktail, fillet steak, and peaches in kirsch. We drank wine, coffee and brandy, and took our time.

"Oh!" she said ecstatically at one point. "It is so long since I had anything like this. My father used to take me out now and then, but since he died . . . well, I can't go to places like this by myself. I sometimes eat in a café round the corner from my rooms, they know me there . . . it's very good food really, chops, eggs and chips . . . you know . . . things like that." I could picture her there, sitting alone with her ravaged head turned to the wall. Lonely unhappy Miss Martin. I wished I could do something—anything—to help her.

Eventually, when she was stirring her coffee, she said simply, "It was a rocket, this." She touched her face. "A firework. The bottle it was standing in tipped over just as it went off and it came straight at me. It hit me on the cheekbone and exploded. It wasn't anybody's fault. I was sixteen."

"They made a good job of it," I said.

She shook her head, smiling the crooked tragic smile. "A good job from what it was, I suppose, but . . . they said if the rocket had struck an inch higher it would have gone through my eye into my brain and killed me. I often wish it had."

She meant it. Her voice was calm. She was stating a fact.

"Yes," I said.

"It's strange, but I've almost forgotten about it this evening, and that doesn't often happen when I'm with anyone."

"I'm honored."

She drank her coffee, put down her cup, and looked at me thoughtfully.

She said, "Why do you keep your hand in your pocket all the time?"

I owed it to her, after all. I put my hand palm upward on the table, wishing I didn't have to.

She said "Oh!" in surprise, and then, looking back at my face, "So you do know. That's why I feel so . . . so easy with you. You do understand."

I shook my head. "Only a little. I have a pocket; you haven't. I can hide." I rolled my hand over (the back of it was less off-putting) and finally retreated it onto my lap.

"But you can't do the simplest things," she exclaimed. Her voice was full of pity. "You can't tie your shoelaces, for instance. You can't even eat steak in a restaurant without asking someone else to cut it up for you—"

"Shut up," I said abruptly. "Shut up, Miss Martin. Don't you dare do to me what you can't bear yourself."

"Pity . . . ," she said, biting her lip and staring at me unhappily. "Yes, it's so easy to give—"

"And embarrassing to receive." I grinned at her. "And my shoes don't have shoelaces. They're out of date, for a start."

"You can know as well as I do what it feels like, and yet do it to someone else . . ." She was very upset.

"Stop being miserable. It was kindness. Sympathy."

"Do you think," she said hesitantly, "that pity and sympathy are the same thing?"

"Very often, yes. But sympathy is discreet and pity is tactless. Oh . . . I'm so sorry." I laughed. "Well, it was sympathetic of you to feel sorry I can't cut up my own food, and tactless to say so. The perfect example."

"It wouldn't be so hard to forgive people for just being tactless," she said thoughtfully.

"No," I agreed, surprised. "I suppose it wouldn't."

"It might not hurt so much . . . just tactlessness?"

"It mightn't."

"And curiosity—that might be easier, too, if I just thought of it as bad manners, don't you think? I mean tactlessness and bad manners wouldn't be so hard to stand. In fact *I* could be sorry for *them*, for not knowing better how to behave. Oh why, why didn't I think of that years ago, when it seems so simple now. So sensible."

"Miss Martin," I said with gratitude. "Have some more brandy. You're a liberator."

"How do you mean?"

"Pity is bad manners and can be taken in one's stride, as you said."

"You said it," she protested.

"Indeed I didn't, not like that."

"All right," she said with gaiety, "we'll drink to a new era. A bold front to the world. I will put my desk back to where it was before I joined the office, facing the door. I'll let every caller see me. I'll—" Her brave voice nearly cracked. "I'll just think poorly of their manners if they pity me too openly. That's settled."

We had some more brandy. I wondered inwardly whether she would have the same resolve in the morning, and doubted it. There had been so many years of hiding. She too, it seemed, was thinking along the same lines.

"I don't know that I can do it alone. But if you will promise me something, then I can."

"Very well," I said incautiously. "What?"

"Don't put your hand in your pocket tomorrow. Let everyone see it."

I couldn't. Tomorrow I would be going to the races. I looked at her, appalled, and really understood only then what she had to bear, and what it would cost her to move her desk. She saw the refusal in my face, and some sort of light died in her own. The gaiety collapsed, the defeated, defenseless look came back, the liberation was over.

"Miss Martin . . ." I swallowed.

"It doesn't matter," she said tiredly. "It doesn't matter. And anyway, it's Saturday tomorrow. I only go in for a short while to see to the mail and anything urgent from today's transactions. There wouldn't be any point in changing the desk."

"And on Monday?"

"Perhaps." It meant no.

"If you'll change it tomorrow and do it all next week, I'll do what you ask," I said, quaking at the thought of it.

"You can't," she said sadly, "I can see that you can't."

"If you can, I must."

"But I shouldn't have asked you . . . you work in a shop."

"Oh." That I had forgotten. "It won't matter."

An echo of her former excitement crept back.

"Do you really mean it?"

I nodded. I had wanted to do something—anything—to help her. Anything. My God.

"Promise?" she said doubtfully.

"Yes. And you?"

"All right," she said, with returning resolution. "But I can only do it if I know you are in the same boat. I couldn't let you down then, you see."

I paid the bill, and although she said there was no need, I took her home. We went on the underground to Finchley. She made straight for the least conspicuous seat and sat presenting the good side of her face to the carriage. Then, laughing at herself, she apologized for doing it.

"Never mind," I said, "the new era doesn't start until tomorrow," and hid my hand like a proper coward.

Her room was close to the station (a deliberately short walk, I guessed) in a large, prosperous-looking suburban house. At the gate she stopped.

"Will . . . er . . . I mean, would you like to come in? It's not very late . . . but perhaps you are tired."

She wasn't eager, but when I accepted she seemed pleased.

"This way, then."

We went through a bare tidy garden to a black-painted front door adorned with horrible stained-glass panels. Miss Martin fumbled endlessly in her bag for her key and I reflected idly that I could have picked that particular lock as quickly as she opened it legally. Inside there was a warm hall smelling healthily of air freshener, and at the end of a passage off it, a door with a card saying "Martin."

Miss Martin's room was a surprise. Comfortable, large, close carpeted, newly decorated, and alive with color. She switched on a standard lamp and a rosy table lamp, and drew burnt orange curtains over the black expanse of French windows. With satisfaction she showed me the recently built tiny bathroom leading out of her room, and the suitcase-sized kitchen beside it, both of which additions she had paid for herself. The people who owned the house were very understanding, she said. Very kind. She had lived there for eleven years. It was home.

Miss Martin had no mirrors in her home. Not one.

She bustled in her little kitchen, making more coffee: for something to do, I thought. I sat relaxed on her long comfortable modern sofa and watched how, from long habit, she leaned forward most of the time so that the heavy shoulder-length dark hair swung down to hide her face. She brought the tray and set it down, and sat on the sofa carefully on my right. One couldn't blame her.

"Do you ever cry?" she said suddenly.

"No."

"Not . . . from frustration?"

"No." I smiled. "Swear."

She sighed. "I used to cry often. I don't anymore, though. Getting older, of course. I'm nearly forty. I've got resigned now to not getting married. I knew I was resigned to it when I had the bathroom and kitchen built. Up to then, you see, I'd always pretended to myself that one day . . . one day, perhaps . . . but I don't expect it anymore, not anymore."

"Men are fools," I said inadequately.

"I hope you don't mind me talking like this? It's so seldom that I have anyone in here, and practically never anyone I can really talk to. . . ."

I stayed for an hour, listening to her memories, her experiences, her whole shadowed life. What, I chided myself, had ever happened to me that was one tenth as bad? I had had far more ups than downs.

At length, she said, "How did it happen with you? Your hand. . . ."

"Oh, an accident. A sharp bit of metal." A razor-sharp racing horseshoe attached to the foot of a horse galloping at thirty miles an hour, to be exact. A hard kicking slash as I rolled on the ground from an easy fall. One of those things.

Horses race in thin light shoes called plates, not the heavy ones they normally wear; blacksmiths change them before and after, every time a horse runs. Some trainers save a few shillings by using the same racing plates over and over again, so that the leading edge gradually wears down to the thickness of a knife. But jagged knives, not smooth. They can cut you open like a hatchet.

I'd really known at once when I saw my stripped wrist, with the blood spurting out in a jet and the broken bones showing white, that I was finished as a jockey. But I wouldn't give up hope, and insisted on the surgeons' sewing it all up, even though they wanted to take my hand off there and then. It would never be any good, they said; and they were right. Too many of the tendons and nerves were severed. I persuaded them to try twice later on to rejoin and graft some of them and both times it had been a useless agony. They had refused to consider it again.

Miss Martin hesitated on the brink of asking for details, and fortunately didn't. Instead she said, "Are you married? Do you know, I've talked so much about myself that I don't know a thing about you."

"My wife's in Athens, visiting her sister."

"How lovely," Miss Martin sighed. "I wish . . ."

"You'll go one day," I said firmly. "Save up, and go in a year or two. On a bus tour or something. With people anyway. Not alone."

I looked at my watch, and stood up. "I've enjoyed this evening a great deal. Thank you so much for coming out with me."

She stood and formally shook hands, not suggesting another meeting. So much humility, I thought, so little expectation. Poor, poor Miss Martin.

"Tomorrow morning . . ." she said tentatively, at the door.

"Tomorrow," I nodded. "Move that desk. And I . . . I promise I won't forget."

I went home cursing that fate had sent me someone like Miss Martin. I had expected Charing, Street and King's secretary to be young, perhaps pretty, a girl I could take to a café and the pictures and flirt with, with no great involvement on either side. Instead it looked as if I should have to pay more than I'd meant to for my inside information on Ellis Bolt.

CHAPTER 9

"NOW LOOK," SAID Lord Hagbourne, amid the bustle of Kempton races, "I've had a word with Captain Oxon and he's satisfied with the way things are going. I really can't interfere any more. Surely you understand that."

"No, sir, I don't. I don't think Captain Oxon's feelings are more important than Seabury Racecourse. The course should be put right quickly, even if it means overruling him."

"Captain Oxon," he said with a touch of sarcasm, "knows more about his job than you do. I give more weight to his assurance than to your quick look at the track."

"Then couldn't you go and see for yourself? While there is still time."

He didn't like being pushed. His expression said so, plainly. There was no more I could say, either, without risking his ringing up Radnor to cancel the whole investigation.

"I may . . . er . . . I may find time on Monday," he said at last, grudgingly. "I'll see. Have you found anything concrete to support your idea that Seabury's troubles were caused maliciously?"

"Not yet, sir."

"A bit farfetched, if you ask me," he said crossly. "I said so to begin with, as you remember. If you don't turn something up pretty soon . . . it's all expense, you know."

He was intercepted by a passing Steward who took him off to another problem, leaving me grimly to reflect that so far there was a horrid lack of evidence of any sort. What there was was negative.

George had still found no chink in Kraye's respectability, ex-sergeant Lamar had given Bolt clearance, and Chico had come back from Seabury with no results all along the line.

We'd met in the office that morning before I went to Kempton.

"Nothing," said Chico. "I wagged my tongue off, knocking at every front door along that road. Not a soggy flicker. The bit that crosses the racecourse wasn't closed by diversion notices, that's for sure. There isn't much traffic along there, of course. I counted it. Only forty to the hour, average. Still, that's too much for at least some of the neighbors not to notice if there'd been anything out of the ordinary."

"Did anyone see the tanker before it overturned?"

"They're always seeing tankers nowadays. Several complaints about it, I got. No one noticed that one, especially."

"It can't be coincidence. Just at that spot at that time where it would do most harm. And the driver packing up and moving a day or two afterwards, with no forwarding address."

"Well . . ." Chico scratched his ear reflectively. "I got no dice with the hiring of lifting gear either. There isn't much to be had, and what there was was accounted for. None of the little bungalows saw anything in that line, except the breakdown cranes coming to lift the tanker up again."

"How about the drains?"

"No drains," he said. "A blank back to doomsday."

"Good."

"Come again?"

"If you'd found them on a map the hurdle race accident would have been a genuine accident. This way, they reek of tiger traps."

"A spot of spadework after dark? Dodgy stuff."

I frowned. "Yes. And it had to be done long enough before the race meeting for the ground to settle, so that the line of the trench didn't show."

"And strong enough for a tractor to roll over it."

"Tractor?"

"There was one on the course yesterday, pulling a trailer of dug-up turf."

"Oh yes, of course. Yes, strong enough to hold a tractor . . . but wheels wouldn't pierce the ground like a horse's legs. The weight is more spread."

"True enough."

"How fast was the turf-digging going?" I asked.

"Fast? You're joking."

It was depressing. So was Lord Hagbourne's shilly-shallying. So, acutely, was the whole day, because I kept my promise to Miss Martin. Pity, curiosity, surprise, embarrassment and revulsion, I encountered the lot. I tried hard to look on some of the things that were said as tactlessness or bad manners, but it didn't really work. Telling myself it was idiotic to be so sensitive didn't help either. If Miss Martin hadn't kept her side of the bargain, I thought miserably, I would throttle her.

Halfway through the afternoon I had a drink in the big upstairs bar with Mark Witney.

"So that's what you've been hiding all this time in pockets and gloves," he said.

"Yes."

"Bit of a mess," he commented.

"I'm afraid so."

"Does it hurt still?"

"No, only if I knock it. And it aches sometimes."

"Mm," he said sympathetically. "My ankle still aches too. Joints are always like that; they mend, but they never forgive you." He grinned. "The other half? There's time; I haven't a runner until the fifth."

We had another drink, talking about horses, and I reflected that it would be easy if they were all like him.

"Mark," I said as we walked back to the weighing room, "do you remember whether Dunstable ran into any sort of trouble before it packed up?"

"That's going back a bit." He pondered. "Well, it certainly wasn't doing so well during the last year or two, was it? The attendances had fallen off, and they weren't spending any money on paint."

"But no specific disasters?"

"The clerk of the course took an overdose, if you call that a disaster. Yes, I remember now, the collapse of the place's prosperity was put down to the clerk's mental illness. Brinton, I think his name was. He'd been quietly going loco and making hopeless decisions all over the place."

"I'd forgotten," I said glumly. Mark went into the weighing room and I leaned against the rails outside. A suicidal clerk of the course could hardly have been the work of Kraye, I thought. It might have given him the idea of accelerating the demise of Seabury, though. He'd had plenty of time over Dunstable, but owing to a recent political threat of nationalization of building land, he might well be in a hurry to clinch Seabury. I sighed, disregarded as best I could a stare of fascinated horror from the teenage daughter of a man I used to ride for, and drifted over to look at the horses in the parade ring.

At the end of the too-long afternoon I drove back to my flat, mixed a bigger drink than usual, and spent the evening thinking, without any world-shattering results. Late the next morning, when I was similarly engaged, the doorbell rang, and I found Charles outside.

"Come in," I said with surprise: he rarely visited the flat, and was seldom in London at weekends. "Like some lunch? The restaurant downstairs is quite good."

"Perhaps. In a minute." He took off his overcoat and gloves and accepted some whisky. There was something unsettled in his manner, a ruffling of the smooth, urbane exterior, a suggestion of a troubled frown on the high domed forehead.

"OK," I said. "What's the matter?"

"Er . . . I've just driven up from Aynsford. No traffic at all, for once. Such a lovely morning, I thought the drive would be . . . oh damn it," he finished explosively, putting down his glass with a bang. "To get it over quickly, Jenny telephoned from Athens last night. She's met some man there. She asked me to tell you she wants a divorce."

"Oh," I said. How like her, I thought, to get Charles to wield the ax. Practical Jenny, eager for a new fire, hacking away the deadwood. And if some of the wood was still alive, too bad.

"I must say," said Charles, relaxing, "you make a thorough job of it."

"Of what?"

"Of not caring what happens to you."

"I do care."

"No one would suspect it," he sighed. "When I tell you your wife wants to divorce you, you just say, 'Oh.' When that happened"—he nodded to my arm—"the first thing you said to me afterwards when I arrived full of sorrow and sympathy was, if I remember correctly, and I do, 'Cheer up, Charles. I had a good run for my money.'"

"Well, so I did." Always, from my earliest childhood, I had instinctively shied away from too much sympathy. I didn't want it. I distrusted it. It made you soft inside, and an illegitimate child couldn't afford to be soft. One might weep at school, and one's spirit would never recover from so dire a disgrace. So the poverty and the snickers, and later the lost wife and the smashed career, had to be passed off with a shrug, and what one really felt about it had to be locked up tightly inside, out of view. Silly, really, but there it was.

We lunched companionably together downstairs, discussing in civilized tones the mechanics of divorce. Jenny, it appeared, did not want me to use the justified grounds of desertion. I, she said, should "arrange things" instead. I must know how to do it, working for the agency. Charles was apologetic: Jenny's prospective husband was in the diplomatic service like Tony, and would prefer her not to be the guilty party.

Had I, Charles inquired, delicately, already been . . . er . . . unfaithful to Jenny? No, I replied, watching him light his cigar, I was afraid I hadn't. For much of the time, owing to one thing and another, I hadn't felt well enough. That, he agreed with amusement, was a reasonable excuse.

I indicated that I would fix things as Jenny wanted, because it didn't affect my future as it did hers. She would be grateful, Charles said. I thought, knowing her, she would very likely take it for granted.

When there was little else to say on that subject, we switched to Kraye. I asked Charles if he had seen him again during the week.

"Yes, I was going to tell you. I had lunch with him in the Club on Thursday. Quite accidentally. We both just happened to be there alone."

"That's where you met him first, in your club?"

"That's right. Of course he thanked me for the weekend and so on. Talked about the quartz. Very interesting collection, he said. But not a murmur about the St. Luke's stone. I would have liked to have asked him straight out, just to see his reaction." He tapped off the ash, smiling. "I did mention you, though, in passing, and he switched on all the charm and said you had been extremely insulting to him and his wife, but that of course you hadn't spoiled his enjoyment. Very nasty, I thought it. He was causing bad trouble for you. Or at least, he intended to."

"Yes," I said cheerfully. "But I did insult him, and I also spied on him. Anything he says of me is fully merited." I told Charles how I had taken the photographs, and all that I had discovered or guessed during the past week. His cigar went out. He looked stunned.

"Well, you wanted me to, didn't you?" I said. "You started it. What did you expect?"

"It's only that I had almost forgotten . . . this is what you used to be like, always. Determined. Ruthless, even." He smiled. "My game for convalescence has turned out better than I expected."

"God help your other patients," I said, "if Kraye is standard medicine."

We walked along the road toward where Charles had left his car. He was going straight home again.

I said, "I hope that in spite of the divorce I shall see something of you? I should be sorry not to. As your ex-son-in-law, I can hardly come to Aynsford anymore."

He looked startled. "I'll be annoyed if you don't, Sid. Jenny will be living all round the world, like Jill. Come to Aynsford whenever you want."

"Thank you," I said. I meant it, and it sounded like it.

He stood beside his car, looking down at me from his straight six feet.

"Jenny," he said casually, "is a fool."

I shook my head. Jenny was no fool. Jenny knew what she wanted, and it wasn't me.

WHEN I WENT into the office (on time) the following morning, the girl on the switchboard caught me and said Radnor wanted me straightaway.

"Good morning," he said. "I've just had Lord Hagbourne on the telephone telling me it's time we got results and that he can't go to Seabury today because his car is being serviced. Before you explode, Sid . . . I told him that you would take him down there now, at once, in your own car. So get a move on."

I grinned. "I bet he didn't like that."

"He couldn't think of an excuse fast enough. Get round and collect him before he comes up with one."

"Right."

I made a quick detour up to the Racing Section where Dolly was adjusting her lipstick. No crossover blouse today. A disappointment.

I told her where I was going and asked if I could use Chico.

"Help yourself," she said resignedly. "If you can get a word in edgeways. He's along in Accounts arguing with Jones-boy."

Chico, however, listened attentively and repeated what I had asked him. "I'm to find out exactly what mistakes the clerk of the course at Dunstable made, and make sure that they and nothing else were the cause of the course losing money."

"That's right. And dig out the file on Andrews and the case you were working on when I got shot."

"But that's all dead," he protested, "the file's down in records in the basement."

"Send Jones-boy down for it," I suggested, grinning. "It's probably only a coincidence, but there is something I want to check. I'll do it tomorrow morning. OK?"

"If you say so, chum."

Back at my flat, I filled up with Extra and made all speed round to Beauchamp Place. Lord Hagbourne, with a civil but cool good morning, lowered himself into the passenger seat, and we set off for Seabury. It took him about a quarter of an hour to get over having been maneuvered into something he didn't want to do, but at the end of that time he sighed and moved in his seat and offered me a cigarette.

"No, thank you, sir. I don't smoke."

"You don't mind if I do?" He took one out.

"Of course not."

"This is a nice car," he remarked, looking round.

"It's nearly three years old now. I bought it the last season I was riding. It's the best I've ever had, I think."

"I must say," he said inoffensively, "that you manage extremely well. I wouldn't have thought that you could drive a car like this with only one effective hand."

"Its power makes it easier, actually. I took it across Europe last spring . . . good roads, there."

We talked on about cars and holidays, then about theaters and books, and he seemed for once quite human. The subject of Seabury we carefully bypassed. I wanted to get him down there in a good mood—the arguments, if any, could take place on the way back—and it seemed as if he was of the same mind.

The state of Seabury's track reduced him to silent gloom. We walked down to the burnt piece with Captain Oxon, who was bearing himself stiffly and being pointedly polite. I thought he was a fool: he should have fallen on the Senior Steward and begged for instant help.

Captain Oxon, whom I had not met before, though he said he knew me by sight, was a slender, pleasant-looking man of about fifty, with a long pointed chin and a slight tendency to watery eyes. The present offended obstinacy of his expression looked more like childishness than real strength. A colonel *manqué*, I thought uncharitably, and no wonder.

"I know it's not really my business," I said, "but surely a bulldozer would shift what's left of the burnt bit in a couple of hours? There isn't time to settle new turf, but you could cover the whole area with some tons of tan and race over it quite easily, like that. You must be getting tan anyway, to cover the road surface. Surely you could just increase the order?"

Oxon looked at me with irritation. "We can't afford it."

"You can't afford another cancellation at the last minute," I corrected.

"We are insured against cancellations."

"I doubt whether an insurance company would stand this one," I said. "They'd say you could have raced if you'd tried hard enough."

"It's Monday now," remarked Lord Hagbourne thoughtfully. "Racing's due on Friday. Suppose we call in a bulldozer tomorrow; the tan can be unloaded and spread on Wednesday and Thursday. Yes, that seems sound enough."

"But the cost—" began Oxon.

"I think the money must be found," said Lord Hagbourne. "Tell Mr. Fotherton when he comes over that I have authorized the expenditure. The bills will be met, in one way or another. But I do think there is no case for not making an effort."

It was on the tip of my tongue to point out that if Oxon had arranged for the bulldozer on the first day he could have saved the price of casual labor from six hand-diggers for a week, but as the battle was already won, I nobly refrained. I continued to think, however, that Oxon was a fool. Usually the odd custom of giving the managerships of racecourses to ex-army officers worked out well, but conspicuously not in this case.

The three of us walked back up to the stands, Lord Hagbourne pausing and pursing his lips at their dingy appearance. I reflected that it was a pity Seabury had a clerk of the course whose heart and home were far away on the thriving course at Bristol. If I'd been arranging things, I'd have seen to it a year ago, when the profits turned to loss, that Seabury had a new clerk entirely devoted to its own interests, someone moreover whose livelihood depended

on its staying open. The bungle, delay, muddle, too much politeness and failure to take action showed by the Seabury executive had been of inestimable
value to the quietly burrowing Kraye.

Mr. Fotherton might have been worried, as he said, but he had done little except mention it in passing to Charles in his capacity as Steward at some
other meeting. Charles, looking for something to divert my mind from my
stomach, and perhaps genuinely anxious about Seabury, had tossed the facts
to me. In his own peculiar way, naturally.

The casualness of the whole situation was horrifying. I basely wondered
whether Fotherton himself had a large holding in Seabury shares and therefore a vested interest in its demise. Planning a much closer scrutiny of the list
of shareholders, I followed Lord Hagbourne and Captain Oxon round the end
of the stands, and we walked the three hundred yards or so through the racecourse gates and down the road to where Captain Oxon's flat was situated
above the canteen in the stable block.

On Lord Hagbourne's suggestion he rang up a firm of local contractors
while we were still there, and arranged for the urgent earth-moving to be
done the following morning. His manner was still ruffled, and it didn't improve things when I declined the well-filled ham and chutney sandwiches he
offered, though I would have adored to have eaten them, had he but known.
I had been out of hospital for a fortnight, but I had another fornight to go before things like new bread, ham, mustard and chutney were due back on the
agenda. Very boring.

After the sandwiches Lord Hagbourne decided on a tour of inspection, so
we all three went first round the stable block, into the lads' hostel, through
the canteen to the kitchen, and into all the stable administrative offices.
Everywhere the story was the same. Except for the rows of wooden boxes
which had been thrown up cheaply after the old ones burned down, there was
no recent maintenance and no new paint.

Then we retraced our steps up the road, through the main gate, and across
to the long line of stands with the weighing room dining rooms, bars and
cloakrooms built into the back. At one end were the secretary's office, the
press room and the Stewards' room; at the other, the first-aid room and a
store. A wide tunnel like a passage ran centrally through the whole length of
the building, giving secondary access on one side to many of the rooms, and
on the other to the steps of the stands themselves. We painstakingly covered
the lot, even down to the boiler room and the oil bunkers, so I had my nos-
talgic look inside the weighing room and changing room after all.

The whole huge block was dankly cold, very drafty, and smelled of dust.

Nothing looked new, not even the dirt. For inducing depression it was hard to beat, but the dreary buildings along in the cheaper rings did a good job of trying.

Captain Oxon said the general dilapidation was mostly due to the sea air, the racecourse being barely half a mile from the shore, and no doubt in essence he was right. The sea air had had a free hand for far too long.

Eventually we returned to where my car was parked inside the gate, and looked back to the row of stands: forlorn, deserted, decaying on a chilly early November afternoon, with a salt-laden drizzle just beginning to blur the outlines.

"What's to be done?" said Lord Hagbourne glumly, as we drove through the rows of bungalows on our way home.

"I don't know." I shook my head.

"The place is dead."

I couldn't argue. Seabury had suddenly seemed to me to be past saving. The Friday and Saturday fixtures could be held now, but as things stood the gate money would hardly cover expenses. No company could go on taking a loss indefinitely. Seabury could plug the gap at present by drawing on their reserve funds, but as I'd seen from their balance sheets at Company House, the reserves only amounted to a few thousands. Matters were bound to get worse. Insolvency waited round a close corner. It might be more realistic to admit that Seabury had no future and to sell the land at the highest price offered as soon as possible. People were, after all, crying out for flat land at the seaside. And there was no real reason why the shareholders shouldn't be rewarded for their long loyalty and recent poor dividends and receive eight pounds for each one they had invested. Many would gain if Seabury came under the hammer, and no one would lose. Seabury was past saving: best to think only of the people who would benefit.

My thoughts stopped with a jerk. This, I realized, must be the attitude of the clerk, Mr. Fotherton, and of the manager, Oxon, and of all the executives. This explained why they had made surprisingly little attempt to save the place. They had accepted defeat easily and seen it to be not only harmless but, to many, usefully profitable. As it had been with other courses, big courses like Hurst Park and Birmingham, so it should be with Seabury.

What did it matter that yet another joined the century's ghost ranks of Cardiff, Derby, Bournemouth, Newport? What did it matter if busy people like inspector Cornish of Dunstable couldn't go racing much because their local course had vanished? What did it matter if Seabury's holidaymakers went to the bingo halls instead?

Chasing owners, I thought, should rise up in a body and demand that

Seabury should be preserved, because no racecourse was better for their horses. But of course they wouldn't. You could tell owners how good it was, but unless they were horsemen themselves, it didn't register. They only saw the rotten amenities of the stands, not the splendidly sited well-built fences that positively invited their horses to jump. They didn't know how their horses relished the short springy turf underfoot, or found the arc and cambers of the bends perfect for maintaining an even speed. Corners at many other racecourses threw horses wide and broke up their stride, but not those at Seabury. The original course builder had been brilliant, and regular visits from the inspector of courses had kept his work fairly intact. Fast, true-run, unhazardous racing, that's what Seabury gave.

Or had given, before Kraye.

Kraye and the executive's inertia between them. . . . I stamped on the accelerator in a surge of anger and the car swooped up the side of the South Downs like a bird. I didn't often drive fast anymore: I did still miss having two hands on the wheel. At the top, out of consideration for my passenger's nerves, I let the speedometer ribbon slide back to fifty.

He said, "I feel like that about it too."

I glanced at him in surprise.

"The whole situation is infuriating," he said. "Such a good course basically, and nothing to be done."

"It could be saved," I said.

"How?"

"A new attitude of mind. . . ." I trailed off.

"Go on," he said. But I couldn't find the words to tell him politely that he ought to chuck out all the people in power at Seabury; too many of them were probably his ex–school chums or personal friends.

"Suppose," he said after a few minutes, "that you had a free hand, what would you do?"

"One would never get a free hand. That's half the trouble. Someone makes a good suggestion, and someone else squashes it. They end up, often as not, by doing nothing."

"No, Sid, I mean you personally. What would you do?"

"I?" I grinned. "What I'd do would have the National Hunt Committee swooning like Victorian maidens."

"I'd like to know."

"Seriously?"

He nodded. As if he could ever be anything else but serious.

I sighed. "Very well, then. I'd pinch every good crowd-pulling idea that any other course has thought of and put them all into operation on the same day."

"What, for instance?"

"I'd take the whole of the reserve fund and offer it as a prize for a big race. I'd make sure the race was framed to attract the really top chasers. Then I'd go round to their trainers personally and explain the situation, and beg for their support. I'd go to some of the people who sponsor Gold Cup races and cajole them into giving five-hundred-pound prizes for all the other races on that day. I'd make the whole thing into a campaign. I'd get Save Seabury discussed on television, and in the sports columns of newspapers. I'd get people interested and involved. I'd make helping Seabury the smart thing to do. I'd get someone like the Beatles to come and present the trophies. I'd advertise free car-parking and free race cards, and on the day I'd have the whole place bright with flags and bunting and tubs of flowers to hide the lack of paint. I'd make sure everyone on the staff understood that a friendly welcome must be given to the customers. And I'd insist that the catering firm use its imagination. I'd fix the meeting for the beginning of April, and pray for a sunny spring day. That," I said, running down, "would do for a start."

"And afterwards?" He was noncommittal.

"A loan, I suppose. Either from a bank or from private individuals. But the executive would have to show first that Seabury could be a success again, like it used to be. No one falls over himself to lend to a dying business. The revival has to come before the money, if you see what I mean."

"I do see," he agreed slowly, "but . . ."

"Yes. But. It always comes to 'but.' But no one at Seabury is going to bother."

We were silent for a long way.

Finally I said, "This meeting on Friday and Saturday—it would be a pity to risk another last-minute disaster. Hunt Radnor Associates could arrange for some sort of guard on the course. Security patrols, that kind of thing."

"Too expensive," he said promptly. "And you've not yet proved that it is really needed. Seabury's troubles still look like plain bad luck to me."

"Well, a security patrol might prevent any more of it."

"I don't know. I'll have to see." He changed the subject then, and talked firmly about other races on other courses all the way back to London.

CHAPTER 10

DOLLY LENT ME her telephone with resignation on Tuesday morning, and I buzzed the switchboard for an internal call to Missing Persons.

"Sammy?" I said. "Sid Halley, down in Racing. Are you busy?"

"The last teenager has just been retrieved from Gretna. Fire away. Who's lost?"

"A man called Smith."

Some mild blasphemy sped three stories down the wire.

I laughed. "I think his name really is Smith. He's a driver by trade. He's been driving a tanker for Intersouth Chemicals for the last year. He left his job and his digs last Wednesday; no forwarding address." I told him about the crash, the suspected concussion and the revelry by night.

"You don't think he was planted on purpose on the job a year ago? His name likely wouldn't be Smith in that case . . . make it harder."

"I don't know. But I think it's more likely he was a bona fide Intersouth driver who was offered a cash payment for exceptional services rendered."

"OK, I'll try that first. He might give Intersouth as a reference, in which case they'll know if he applies for another job somewhere, or I might trace him through his union. The wife might have worked, too. I'll let you know."

"Thanks."

"Don't forget, when the old man buys you a gold-plated executive desk I want my table back."

"You'll want forever," I said, smiling. It had been Sammy's lunch.

On the table in question lay the slim file on the Andrews case that Jones-boy had unearthed from the basement. I looked round the room.

"Where's Chico?" I asked.

Dolly answered. "Helping a bookmaker to move house."

"He's doing *what*?" I goggled.

"That's right. Long-standing date. The bookmaker is taking his safe with him and wants Chico to sit on it in the furniture van. It had to be Chico, he said. No one else would do. The paying customer is always right, so Chico's gone."

"Damn."

She reached into a drawer. "He left you a tape," she said.

"Undamn, then."

She grinned and handed it to me, and I took it over to the recorder, fed it through onto the spare reel, and listened to it in the routine office way, through the earphones.

"After wearing my plates down to the ankles," said Chico's cheerful voice, "I found out that the worst things your clerk of the course did at Dunstable were to frame a lot of races that did the opposite of attract any decent runners, and be stinking rude to all and sundry. He was quite well liked up to the year before he killed himself. Then everyone says he gradually got more and more crazy. He was so rude to people who worked at the course that half of them wouldn't put up with it and left. And the local tradesmen practically spat when I mentioned his name. I'll fill you in when I see you, but there wasn't anything like Seabury—no accidents or damage or anything like that."

Sighing, I wiped the tape clean and gave it back to Dolly. Then I opened the file on my table and studied its contents.

A Mr. Mervyn Brinton of Reading, Berkshire, had applied to the agency for personal protection, having had reason to believe that he was in danger of being attacked. He had been unwilling to say why he might be attacked, and refused to have the agency make inquiries. All he wanted was a bodyguard. There was a strong possibility, said the report, that Brinton had tried a little amateurish blackmail, which had backfired. He had at length revealed that he possessed a certain letter, and was afraid of being attacked and having it stolen. After much persuasion by Chico Barnes, who pointed out that Brinton could hardly be guarded for the rest of his life, Brinton had agreed to inform a certain party that the letter in question was lodged in a particular desk drawer in the Racing Section of Hunt Radnor Associates. In fact it was not; and had not at any time been seen by anyone working for the agency. However, Thomas Andrews came, or was sent, to remove the letter, was interrupted by J. S. Halley (whom he wounded by shooting), and subsequently made his escape. Two days later Brinton telephoned to say he no longer required a bodyguard, and as far as the agency was concerned the case was then closed.

The foregoing information had been made available to the police in their investigation into the shooting of Halley.

I shut the file. A drab little story, I thought, of a pathetic little man playing out of his league.

Brinton.

The clerk of the course at Dunstable had also been called Brinton.

I sat gazing at the short file. Brinton wasn't an uncommon name. There was probably no connection at all. Brinton of Dunstable had died a good two years before Brinton of Reading had asked for protection. The only visible connection was that at different ends of the scale both the Dunstable Brinton and Thomas Andrews had earned their living on the racecourse. It wasn't much. Probably nothing. But it nagged.

I went home, collected the car, and drove to Reading.

A nervous, gray-haired elderly man opened the front door on a safety chain, and peered through the gap.

"Yes?"

"Mr. Brinton?"

"What is it?"

"I'm from Hunt Radnor Associates. I'd be most grateful for a word with you."

He hesitated, chewing an upper lip adorned with an untidy pepper-and-salt mustache. Anxious brown eyes looked me up and down and went past me to the white car parked by the curb.

"I sent a check," he said finally.

"It was quite in order," I assured him.

"I don't want any trouble . . . it wasn't my fault that that man was shot." He didn't sound convinced.

"Oh, no one blames you for that," I said. "He's perfectly all right now. Back at work, in fact."

His relief showed, even through the crack. "Very well," he said, and pushed the door shut to take off the chain.

I followed him into the front room of his tall terrace house. The air smelled stale and felt still, as if it had been hanging in the same spot for days. The furniture was of the hard-stuffed and brown shellacked substantial type that in my plywood childhood I had thought the peak of living, unobtainable; and there were cases of tropical butterflies on the walls, and carved ornaments from somewhere like Java or Borneo on several small tables. A life abroad, retirement at home, I thought. From color and heat to suburban respectability in Reading.

"My wife has gone out shopping," he said, still nervously. "She'll be back soon." He looked hopefully out of the lace-curtained window, but Mrs. Brinton didn't oblige him by coming to his support.

I said, "I just wanted to ask you, Mr. Brinton, if you were by any chance related to a Mr. William Brinton, one-time clerk of Dunstable racecourse."

He gave me a long agonized stare, and to my consternation sat down on his sofa and began to cry, his shaking hands covering his eyes and the tears splashing down onto his tweed-clad knees.

"Please . . . Mr. Brinton . . . I'm so sorry," I said awkwardly.

He snuffled and coughed, and dragged a handkerchief out to wipe his eyes. Gradually the paroxysm passed, and he said indistinctly, "How did you find out? I told you I didn't want anyone asking questions."

"It was quite accidental. Nobody asked any questions, I promise you. Would you like to tell me about it? Then I don't think any questions will need to be asked at all, from anyone else."

"The police . . . ," he said doubtfully, on a sob. "They came before. I refused to say anything, and they went away."

"Whatever you tell me will be in confidence."

"I've been such a fool. I'd like to tell someone, really."

I pictured the strung-up, guilt-ridden weeks he'd endured, and the crying fit became not only understandable but inevitable.

"It was the letter, you see," he said, sniffling softly. "The letter William began to write to me, though he never sent it. I found it in a whole trunk of stuff that was left when he . . . killed himself. I was in Sarawak then, you know, and they sent me a cable. It was a shock . . . one's only brother doing such a . . . a terrible thing. He was younger than me. Seven years. We weren't very close, except when we were children. I wish . . . but it's too late now. Anyway, when I came home I fetched all his stuff round from where it had been stored and put it up in the attic here, all his racing books and things. I didn't know what to do with them, you see. I wasn't interested in them, but it seemed . . . I don't know . . . I couldn't just burn them. It was months before I bothered to sort them out, and then I found the letter. . . ." His voice faltered and he looked at me appealingly, wanting to be forgiven.

"Kitty and I had found my pension didn't go anywhere near as far as we'd expected. Everything is so terribly expensive. The rates . . . we decided we'd have to sell the house again though we'd only just bought it, and Kitty's family are all close. And then . . . I thought . . . perhaps I could sell the letter instead."

"And you got threats instead of money," I said.

"Yes. It was the letter itself which gave me the idea." He chewed his mustache.

"And now you no longer have it," I said matter-of-factly, as if I knew for certain and wasn't guessing. "When you were first threatened you thought you could still sell the letter if Hunt Radnor kept you safe, and then you got more frightened and gave up the letter, and then canceled the protection because the threats had stopped."

He nodded unhappily. "I gave them the letter because that man was shot. . . . I didn't realize anything like that would happen. I was horrified. It

was terrible. I hadn't thought it could be so dangerous, just selling a letter. . . . I wish I'd never found it. I wish William had never written it."

So did I, as it happened.

"What did the letter say?" I asked.

He hesitated, his fear showing. "It might cause more trouble. They might
come back."

"They won't know you've told me," I pointed out. "How could they?"

"I suppose not." He looked at me, making up his mind. There's one thing
about being small: no one is ever afraid of you. If I'd been big and command-
ing I don't think he'd have risked it. As it was, his face softened and relaxed
and he threw off the last threads of reticence.

"I know it by heart," he said. "I'll write it down for you, if you like. It's
easier than saying it."

I sat and waited while he fetched a ballpoint pen and a pad of large writing paper and got on with his task. The sight of the letter materializing again
in front of his eyes affected him visibly, but whether to fear or remorse or sorrow, I couldn't tell. He covered one side of the page, then tore it off the pad
and shakily handed it over.

I read what he had written. I read it twice. Because of these short desperate sentences, I reflected unemotionally, I had come within spitting distance
of St. Peter.

"That's fine," I said. "Thank you very much."

"I wish I'd never found it," he said again. "Poor William."

"Did you go to see this man?" I asked, indicating the letter as I put it
away in my wallet.

"No, I wrote to him . . . he wasn't hard to find."

"And how much did you ask for?"

Shamefaced, he muttered, "Five thousand pounds."

Five thousand pounds had been wrong, I thought. If he'd asked fifty
thousand, he might have had a chance. But five thousand didn't put him
among the big-power boys, it just revealed his mediocrity. No wonder he had
been stamped on, fast.

"What happened next?" I asked.

"A big man came for the letter, about four o'clock one afternoon. It was
awful. I asked him for the money and he just laughed in my face and pushed
me into a chair. No money, he said, but if I didn't hand over the letter at once
he'd . . . he'd teach me a thing or two. That's what he said, teach me a thing
or two. I explained that I had put the letter in my box at the bank and that
the bank was closed and that I couldn't get it until the next morning. He said

that he would come to the bank with me the next day, and then he went away."

"And you rang up the agency almost at once? Yes. What made you choose Hunt Radnor?"

He looked surprised. "It was the only one I knew about. Are there any others? I mean, most people have heard of Hunt Radnor, I should think."

"I see. So Hunt Radnor sent you a bodyguard, but the big man wouldn't give up."

"He kept telephoning . . . then your man suggested setting a trap in his office, and in the end I agreed. Oh, I shouldn't have let him, I was such a fool. I knew all the time, you see, who was threatening me, but I couldn't tell your agency because I would have had to admit I'd tried to get money . . . illegally."

"Yes. Well, there's only one more thing. What was he like, the man who came and threatened you?"

Brinton didn't like even the memory of him. "He was very strong. Hard. When he pushed me it was like a wall. I'm not . . . I mean, I've never been good with my fists, or anything like that. If he'd started hitting me I couldn't have stopped him."

"I'm not blaming you for not standing up to him," I pointed out. "I just want to know what he looked like."

"Very big," he said vaguely. "Huge."

"I know it's several weeks ago now, but can't you possibly remember more than that? How about his hair? Anything odd about his face? How old? What class?"

He smiled for the first time, the sad wrinkles folding for a moment into some semblance of faded charm. If he'd never taken his first useless step into crime, I thought, he might still have been a nice gentle innocuous man, fading without rancor toward old age, troubled only by how to make a little pension go a long way. No tearing, destructive guilt.

"It's certainly easier when you ask questions like that. He was beginning to go bald, I remember now. And he had big blotchy freckles on the backs of his hands. It's difficult to know about his age. Not a youth, though; more than thirty, I think. What else did you ask? Oh yes, class. Working class, then."

"English?"

"Oh yes, not foreign. Sort of cockney, I suppose."

I stood up, thanked him, and began to take my leave. He said, begging me still for reassurance, "There won't be any more trouble?"

"Not from me or the agency."

"And the man who was shot?"

"Not from him either."

"I tried to tell myself it wasn't my fault . . . but I haven't been able to sleep. How could I have been such a fool? I shouldn't have let that young man set any trap. . . . I shouldn't have called in your agency . . . and it cost another chunk of our savings. . . . I ought never to have tried to get money for that letter."

"That's true, Mr. Brinton, you shouldn't. But what's done is done, and I don't suppose you'll start anything like that again."

"No, no," he said with pain. "I wouldn't. Ever. These last few weeks have been . . ." His voice died. Then he said more strongly, "We'll have to sell the house now. Kitty likes it here, of course. But what I've always wanted myself is a little bungalow by the sea."

WHEN I REACHED the office I took out the disastrous letter and read it again, before adding it to the file. Being neither the original nor a photocopy, but only a reproduction from memory, it wasn't of the slightest use as evidence. In the elder Brinton's small tidy script, the weird contrast to the heartbroken contents, it ran:

> *Dear Mervy, dear big brother,*
>
> *I wish you could help me, as you did when I was little. I have spent fifteen years building up Dunstable Racecourse, and a man called Howard Kraye is making me destroy it. I have to frame races which nobody likes. Very few horses come now, and the gate receipts are falling fast. This week I must see that the racecard goes to the printers too late, and the pressroom telephones will all be out of order. There will be a terrible muddle. People must think I am mad. I can't escape him. He is paying me as well, but I must do as he says. I can't help my nature, you know that. He has found out about a boy I was living with, and I could be prosecuted. He wants the racecourse to sell for housing. Nothing can stop him getting it. My racecourse, I love it.*
>
> *I know I shan't send this letter. Mervy, I wish you were here. I haven't anyone else. Oh dear God, I can't go on much longer, I really can't.*

At five to six that afternoon I opened the door of Zanna Martin's office. Her desk was facing me and so was she. She raised her head, recognized me, and looked back at me in a mixture of pride and embarrassment.

"I did it," she said. "If you didn't, I'll kill you."

She had combed her hair even further forward, so that it hung close round her face, but all the same one could see the disfigurement at first glance. I had forgotten, in the days since Friday, just how bad it was.

"I felt the same about you," I said, grinning.

"You really did keep your promise?"

"Yes, I did. All day Saturday and Sunday, most of yesterday and most of today, and very nasty it is, too."

She sighed with relief. "I'm glad you've come. I nearly gave it up this morning. I thought you wouldn't do it, and you'd never come back to see if I had, and that I was being a proper idiot."

"Well, I'm here," I said. "Is Mr. Bolt in?"

She shook her head. "He's gone home. I'm just packing up."

"Finished the envelopes?" I said.

"Envelopes? Oh, those I was doing when you were here before? Yes, they're all done."

"And filled and sent?"

"No, the leaflets haven't come back from the printers yet, much to Mr. Bolt's disgust. I expect I'll be doing them tomorrow."

She stood up, tall and thin, put on her coat and tied the scarf over her hair.

"Are you going anywhere this evening?" I asked.

"Home," she said decisively.

"Come out to dinner," I suggested.

"Aunty's legacy won't last long, the way you spend. I think Mr. Bolt has already invested your money. You'd better save every penny until after settlement day."

"Coffee, then, and the flicks?"

"Look," she said hesitantly, "I sometimes buy a hot chicken on my way home. There's a fish-and-chips shop next to the station that sells them. Would you . . . would you like to come and help me eat it? In return, I mean, for Friday night."

"I'd enjoy that," I said, and was rewarded by a pleased, half-incredulous laugh.

"Really?"

"Really."

As before, we went to Finchley by underground, but this time Miss Martin sat boldly where her whole face showed. To try to match her fortitude, I rested my elbow on the seat arm between us. She looked at my hand and then at my face, gratefully, almost as if we were sharing an adventure.

As we emerged from the tube station she said, "You know, it makes a great deal of difference if one is accompanied by a man, even—" she stopped abruptly.

"Even," I finished, smiling, "if he is smaller than you and also damaged."

"Oh dear . . . and much younger, as well." Her real eye looked at me with rueful amusement. The glass one stared stonily ahead. I was getting used to it again.

"Let me buy the chicken," I said, as we stopped outside the shop. The smell of hot chips mingled with diesel fumes from a passing lorry. Civilization, I thought. Delightful.

"Certainly not." Miss Martin was firm and bought the chicken herself. She came out with it wrapped in newspaper. "I got a few chips and a packet of peas," she said.

"And I," I said firmly, as we came to an off-license, "am getting some brandy." What chips and peas would do to my digestion I dared not think.

We walked round to the house with the parcels and went through into her room. She moved with a light step.

"In that cupboard over there," she said, pointing, as she peeled off her coat and scarf, "there are some glasses and a bottle of sherry. Will you pour me some? I expect you prefer brandy, but have some sherry if you'd like. I'll just take these things into the kitchen and put them to keep hot."

While I unscrewed the bottles and poured the drinks I heard her lighting her gas stove and unwrapping the parcels. There was dead quiet as I walked across the room with her sherry, and when I reached the door I saw why. She held the chicken in its piece of greaseproof paper absently in one hand; the bag of chips lay open on the table with the box of peas beside it; and she was reading the newspaper they had all been wrapped in.

She looked up at me in bewilderment.

"You," she said. "It's you. This is you."

I looked down where her finger pointed. The fish-and-chips shop had wrapped up her chicken in the Sunday *Hemisphere.*

"Here's your sherry," I said, holding it out to her.

She put down the chicken and took the glass without appearing to notice it.

"Another Halley," she said. "It caught my eye. Of course I read it. And it's your picture, and it even refers to your hand. You are Sid Halley."

"That's right." There was no chance of denying it.

"Good heavens. I've known about you for years. Read about you. I saw you on television, often. My father loved watching the racing, we always had it on when he was alive—" She broke off and then said with increased puzzlement, "Why on earth did you say your name was John and that you worked in a shop? Why did you come to see Mr. Bolt? I don't understand."

"Drink your sherry, put your chicken in the oven before it freezes and I'll tell you." There was nothing else to do: I didn't want to risk her brightly passing on the interesting tidbit of news to her employer.

Without demur she put the dinner to heat, came to sit on the sofa, opposite to where I apprehensively waited in an armchair, and raised her eyebrows in expectation.

"I don't work in a shop," I admitted. "I am employed by a firm called Hunt Radnor Associates."

Like Brinton, she had heard of the agency. She stiffened her whole body and began to frown. As casually as I could, I told her about Kraye and the Seabury shares; but she was no fool and she went straight to the heart of things.

"You suspect Mr. Bolt too. That's why you went to see him."

"Yes, I'm afraid so."

"And me? You took me out simply and solely to find out about him?" Her voice was bitter.

I didn't answer at once. She waited, and somehow her calmness was more piercing than tears or temper could have been. She asked so little of life.

At last I said, "I went to Bolt's office as much to take out his secretary as to see Bolt himself, yes."

The peas boiled over, hissing loudly. She stood up slowly. "At least that's honest."

She went into the tiny kitchen and turned out the gas under the saucepan.

I said, "I came to your office this afternoon because I wanted to look at those leaflets Bolt is sending to Seabury shareholders. You told me at once that they hadn't come from the printers. I didn't need to accept your invitation to supper after that. But I'm here."

She stood in the kitchen doorway, holding herself straight with an all too apparent effort.

"I suppose you lied about that too," she said in a quiet rigidly controlled voice, pointing to my arm. "Why? Why did you play such a cruel game with me? Surely you could have got your information without that. Why did you make me change my desk round? I suppose you were laughing yourself sick all day Saturday thinking about it."

I stood up. Her hurt was dreadful.

I said, "I went to Kempton races on Saturday."

She didn't move.

"I kept my promise."

She made a slight gesture of disbelief.

"I'm sorry," I said helplessly.

"Yes. Good night, Mr. Halley. Good night."

I went.

CHAPTER 11

RADNOR HELD A Seabury conference the next morning, Wednesday, consisting of himself, Dolly, Chico and me; the result, chiefly, of my having the previous afternoon finally wrung grudging permission from Lord Hagbourne to arrange a twenty-four-hour guard at Seabury for the coming Thursday, Friday and Saturday.

The bulldozing had been accomplished without trouble, and a call to the course that morning had established that the tan was arriving in regular lorry loads and was being spread. Racing, bar any last-minute accidents, was now certain. Even the weather was cooperating. The glass was rising; the forecast was dry, cold and sunny.

Dolly proposed a straight patrol system, and Radnor was inclined to agree. Chico and I had other ideas.

"If anyone intended to sabotage the track," Dolly pointed out, "they would be frightened off by a patrol. Same thing if they were planning something in the stands themselves."

Radnor nodded. "Safest way of making sure racing takes place. I suppose we'll need at least four men to do it properly."

I said, "I agree that we need a patrol tonight, tomorrow night and Friday night, just to play safe. But tomorrow, when the course will be more or less deserted . . . what we need is to pinch them at it, not frighten them off. There's no evidence yet that could be used in a court of law. If we could catch them in mid-sabotage, so to speak, we'd be much better off."

"That's right," said Chico. "Hide and pounce. Much better than scaring them away."

"I seem to remember," said Dolly with a grin, "that the last time you two set a trap the mouse shot the cheese."

"Oh God, Dolly, you slay me," said Chico, laughing warmly and for once accepting her affection.

Even Radnor laughed. "Seriously, though," he said, "I don't see how you can. A racecourse is too big. If you are hiding you can only see a small part of it. And surely if you show yourself your presence would act like any other patrol to stop anything plainly suspicious being done? I don't think it's possible."

"Um," I said. "But there's one thing I can still do better than anyone else in this agency."

"And what's that?" said Chico, ready to argue.

"Ride a horse."

"Oh," said Chico. "I'll give you that, chum."

"A horse," said Radnor thoughtfully. "Well, that's certainly an idea. Nobody's going to look suspiciously at a horse on a racecourse, I suppose. Mobile, too. Where would you get one?"

"From Mark Witney. I could borrow his hack. Seabury's his local course. His stables aren't many miles away."

"But can you still——?" began Dolly, and broke off. "Well, don't glare at me like that, all of you. I can't ride with two hands, let alone one."

"A man called Gregory Philips had his arm amputated very high up," I said, "and went on racing in point-to-points for years."

"Enough said," said Dolly. "How about Chico?"

"He can wear a pair of my jodhpurs. Protective coloring. And lean nonchalantly on the rails."

"Stick insects," said Chico cheerfully.

"That's what you want, Sid?" said Radnor.

I nodded. "Look at it from the worst angle: we haven't anything on Kraye that will stand up. We might not find Smith, the tanker driver, and even if we do, he has everything to lose by talking and nothing to gain. When the racecourse stables burned down a year ago, we couldn't prove it wasn't an accident; an illicit cigarette end. Stable lads do smoke, regardless of bans.

"The so-called drain which collapsed—we don't know if it was dug a day, a week, or six weeks before it did its work. That letter William Brinton of Dunstable wrote to his brother, it's only a copy from memory that we've got, no good at all for evidence. All it proves, to our own satisfaction, is that Kraye is capable of anything. We can't show it to Lord Hagbourne, because I obtained it in confidence, and he still isn't a hundred percent convinced that Kraye has done more than buy shares. As I see it, we've just got to give the enemy a chance to get on with their campaign."

"You think they will, then?"

"It's awfully likely, isn't it? This year there isn't another Seabury meeting until February. A three months' gap. And if I read it right, Kraye is in a hurry now because of the political situation. He won't want to spend fifty thousand buying Seabury and then find building land has been nationalized overnight. If I were him, I'd want to clinch the deal and sell to a developer as quickly as possible. According to the photographs of the share transfers, he already holds twenty-three percent of the shares. This is almost certainly enough to swing the sale of the company if it comes to a vote. But he's greedy. He'll want more. But he'll only want more if he can get it soon. Waiting for February is too risky. So yes, I do think if we give him a chance that he will organize some more damage this week."

"It's a risk," said Dolly. "Suppose something dreadful happens and we neither prevent it nor catch anyone doing it?"

They kicked it round among the three of them for several more minutes, the pros and cons of the straight patrols versus cat and mouse. Finally Radnor turned back to me and said, "Sid?"

"It's your agency," I said seriously. "It's your risk."

"But it's your case. It's still your case. You must decide."

I couldn't understand him. It was all very well for him to have given me a free hand so far, but this wasn't the sort of decision I would have ever expected him to pass on.

Still . . . "Chico and I, then," I said. "We'll go alone tonight and stay all day tomorrow. I don't think we'll let even Captain Oxon know we're there. Certainly not the foreman, Ted Wilkins, or any of the other men. We'll come in from the other side from the stands, and I'll borrow the horse for mobility. Dolly can arrange official patrol guards with Oxon for tomorrow night— suggest he gives them a warm room, Dolly. He ought to have the central heating on by then."

"Friday and Saturday?" asked Radnor, noncommittally.

"Full guards, I guess. As many as Lord Hagbourne will sub for. The race-going crowds make cat-and-mouse impossible."

"Right," said Radnor, decisively. "That's it, then."

When Dolly, Chico and I had got as far as the door he said, "Sid, you wouldn't mind if I had another look at those photographs? Send Jones-boy down with them if you're not needing them."

"Sure," I agreed. "I've pored over them till I know them by heart. I bet you'll spot something at once that I've missed."

"It often works that way," he said, nodding.

The three of us went back to the Racing Section, and via the switchboard I traced Jones-boy, who happened to be in Missing Persons. While he was on his way down I flipped through the packet of photographs yet again. The share transfers, the summary with the list of bank accounts, the letters from Bolt, the ten-pound notes, and the two sheets of dates, initials and figures from the very bottom of the attaché case. It had been clear all along that these last were lists either of receipts or expenditures, but by now I was certain they were the latter. A certain W.L.B. had received regular sums of fifty pounds a month for twelve months, and the last date for W.L.B. was four days before William Leslie Brinton, clerk of Dunstable Racecourse, had taken the quickest way out. Six hundred pounds and a threat; the price of a man's soul.

Most of the other initials meant nothing to me, except the last one, J.R.S., which looked as if they could be the tanker driver's. The first entry for J.R.S., for one hundred pounds, was dated the day before the tanker overturned at Seabury, the day before Kraye went to Aynsford for the weekend.

In the next line, the last of the whole list, a further sum of one hundred and fifty pounds was entered against J.R.S. The date of this was that of the following Tuesday, three days after I had taken the photographs. Smith had packed up and vanished from his job and his digs on that Tuesday.

Constantly recurring among the other varying initials were two Christian names, Leo and Fred. Each of these was on the regular payroll, it seemed. Either Leo or Fred, I guessed, had been the big man who had visited and frightened Mervyn Brinton. Either Leo or Fred was the "big chap" who had sent Andrews with a gun to Cromwell Road.

I had a score to settle with either Leo or Fred.

Jones-boy came in for the photographs. I tapped them together back into their box and gave them to him.

"Where, you snotty-nosed little coot, is our coffee?" said Chico rudely. We had been downstairs when Jones-boy did his rounds.

"Coots are bald," observed Dolly coyly, eyeing Jones-boy's luxuriant locks.

Jones-boy unprintably told Chico where he could find his coffee.

Chico advanced a step, saying, "You remind me of the people sitting on the walls of Jerusalem." He had been raised in a church orphanage, after all.

Jones-boy also knew the more basic bits of Isaiah. He said callously, "You did it on the doorstep of Barnes cop shop, I believe."

Chico furiously lashed out a fist to Jones-boy's head. Jones-boy jumped back, laughed insultingly, and the box he was holding flew high out of his hand, opening as it went.

"Stop it you two, damn you," shouted Dolly, as the big photographs floated down onto her desk and onto the floor.

"Babes in the wood," remarked Jones-boy, in great good humor from having got the best of the slinging match. He helped Dolly and me pick up the photographs, shuffled them back into the box in no sort of order, and departed grinning.

"Chico," said Dolly severely, "you ought to know better."

"The bossy-mother routine bores me sick," said Chico violently.

Dolly bit her lip and looked away. Chico stared at me defiantly, knowing very well he had started the row and was in the wrong.

"As one bastard to another," I said mildly, "pipe down."

Not being able to think of a sufficiently withering reply fast enough Chico merely scowled and walked out of the room. The show was over. The office returned to normal. Typewriters clattered, someone used the tape recorder, someone else the telephone. Dolly sighed and began to draw up her list for Seabury. I sat and thought about Leo. Or Fred. Unproductively.

After a while I ambled upstairs to Bona Fides, where the usual amount of telephone shouting filled the air. George, deep in a mysterious conversation about mothballs, saw me and shook his head. Jack Copeland, freshly attired in a patchily faded green sleeveless pullover, took time out between calls to say that they were sorry, but they'd made no progress with Kraye. He had, Jack said, very craftily covered his tracks about ten years back. They would keep digging, if I liked. I liked.

Up in Missing Persons Sammy said it was too soon for results on Smith.

When I judged that Mark Witney would be back in his house after exercising his second lot of horses, I rang him up and asked him to lend me his hack, a pensioned-off old steeplechaser of the first water.

"Sure," he said. "What for?"

I explained what for.

"You'd better have my horse box as well," he commented. "Suppose it pours with rain all night? Give you somewhere to keep dry, if you have the box."

"But won't you be needing it? The forecast says clear and dry anyway."

"I won't need it until Friday morning. I haven't any runners until Seabury. And only one there, I may say, in spite of it being so close. The owners just won't have it. I have to go all the way to Banbury on Saturday. Damn silly with another much better course on my doorstep."

"What are you running at Seabury?"

He told me, at great and uncomplimentary length, about a half-blind, utterly stupid, one-paced habitual non-jumper with which he proposed to win the novice chase. Knowing him, I guessed he would. We agreed that Chico and I should arrive at his place at about eight that evening, and I rang off.

After that I left the office, went across London by underground to Company House in the city, and asked for the files of Seabury Racecourse. In a numbered chair at a long table, surrounded by earnest men and women clerks poring over similar files and making copious notes, I studied the latest list of investors. Apart from Kraye and his various aliases, which I now recognized on sight from long familiarity with the share-transfer photographs, there were no large blocks in single ownership. No one else held more than 3 per cent of the total: and as 3 per cent meant that roughly £2500 was lying idle and not bringing in a penny in dividends, it was easy to see why no one wanted a larger holding.

Fotherton's name was not on the list. Although this was not conclusive, because a nominee name like "Mayday Investments" could be anyone at all, I was more or less satisfied that Seabury's clerk was not gambling on Seabury's death. All the big share movements during the past year had been to Kraye, and no one else.

A few of the small investors, holding two hundred or so shares each, were people I knew personally. I wrote down their names and addresses, intending to ask them to let me see Bolt's circular letter when it arrived. Slower than via Zanna Martin, but surer.

My mind shied away from Miss Martin. I'd had a bad night thinking about her. Her and Jenny, both.

Back in the office I found it was the tail end of the lunch hour, with nearly all the desks still empty. Chico alone was sitting behind his, biting his nails.

"If we're going to be up all night," I suggested, "we'd better take the afternoon off for sleep."

"No need."

"Every need. I'm not as young as you."

"Poor old grandpa." He grinned suddenly, apologizing for the morning. "I can't help it. That Jones-boy gets on my wick."

"Jones-boy can look after himself. It's Dolly—"

"It's not my bloody fault she can't have kids."

"She wants kids like you want a mother."

"But I don't—" he began indignantly.

"Your own," I said flatly. "Like you want your own mother to have kept you and loved you. Like mine did."

"You had every advantage, of course."

"That's right."

He laughed. "Funny thing is I like old Dolly, really. Except for the hen bit."

"Who wouldn't?" I said amicably. "You can sleep on my sofa."

He sighed. "You're going to be less easy than Dolly to work for, I can see that."

"Eh?"

"Don't kid yourself, mate. Sir, I mean." He was lightly ironic.

The other inmates of the office drifted back, including Dolly, with whom I fixed for Chico to have the afternoon free. She was cool to him and unforgiving, which I privately thought would do them both good.

She said, "The first official patrol will start on the racecourse tomorrow at six P.M. Shall I tell them to find you and report?"

"No," I said defiantly. "I don't know where I'll be."

"It had better be the usual then," she said. "They can report to the old man at his home number when they start the job, and again at six A.M. when they go off and the next lot take over."

"And they'll ring him in between if anything happens?" I said.

"Yes. As usual."

"It's as bad as being a doctor," I said, smiling.

Dolly nodded, and half to herself she murmured, "You'll find out."

Chico and I walked round to my flat, pulled the curtains, and did our best to sleep. I didn't find it easy at two-thirty in the afternoon: it was the time for racing, not rest. It seemed to me that I had barely drifted off when the telephone rang. I looked at my watch on my way to answer it in the sitting room and found it was only ten to five. I had asked for a call at six.

It was not the telephone exchange, however, but Dolly.

"A message has come for you by hand, marked 'very urgent.' I thought you might want it before you go to Seabury."

"Who brought it?"

"A taxi driver."

"Shunt him round here, then."

"He's gone, I'm afraid."

"Who's the message from?"

"I've no idea. It's a plain brown envelope, the size we use for interim reports."

"Oh. All right, I'll come back."

Chico had drowsily propped himself up on one elbow on the sofa.

"Go to sleep again," I said. "I've got to go and see something in the office. Won't be long."

When I reached the Racing Section again I found that whatever had come for me, something else had gone. The shaky lemon-colored table. I was desk-less again.

"Sammy said he was sorry," explained Dolly, "but he has a new assistant and nowhere to park him."

"I had things in the drawer," I complained. Shades of Sammy's lunch, I thought.

"They're here," Dolly said, pointing to a corner of her desk. "There was only the Brinton file, a half bottle of brandy, and some pills. Also I found this on the floor." She held out a flat, crackly cellophane packet.

"The negatives of those photographs are in here," I said, taking it from her. "They were in the box, though."

"Until Jones-boy dropped it."

"Oh yes." I put the packet of negatives inside the Brinton file and pinched a large rubber band from Dolly to snap round the outside.

"How about that mysterious very urgent message?" I asked.

Dolly silently and considerately slit open the envelope in question, drew out the single sheet of paper it contained and handed it to me. I unfolded it and stared at it in disbelief.

It was a circular, headed Charing, Street and King, Stockbrokers, dated with the following day's date, and it ran:

> *Dear Sir or Madam,*
> *We have various clients wishing to purchase small parcels of shares in the following lists of minor companies. If you are considering selling your interests in any of these, we would be grateful if you would get in touch with us. We would assure you of a good fair price, based on today's quotation.*

There followed a list of about thirty companies, of which I had heard of only one. Tucked in about three-quarters of the way down was Seabury Race-course.

I turned the page over. Zanna Martin had written on the back in a hurried hand.

> *This is only going to Seabury shareholders. Not to anyone owning shares in the other companies. The leaflets came from the printer's this morning, and*

*are to be posted tomorrow. I hope it is what you want. I'm sorry about last
night.*

Z. M.

"What is it?" asked Dolly.

"A free pardon," I said lightheartedly, slipping the circular inside the
Brinton file along with the negatives. "Also confirmation that Ellis Bolt is not
on the side of the angels."

"You're a nut," she said. "And take these things off my desk. I haven't
room for them."

I put the pills and brandy in my pocket and picked up the Brinton file.

"Is that better?"

"Thank you, yes."

"So long, then, my love. See you on Friday."

On the walk back to the flat I decided suddenly to go and see Miss Martin. I went straight down to the garage for my car without going up and waking Chico again, and made my way eastward to the city for the second time
that day. The rush-hour traffic was so bad that I was afraid I would miss her,
but in fact she was ten minutes late leaving the office and I caught her up just
before she reached the underground station.

"Miss Martin," I called. "Would you like a lift home?"

She turned round in surprise.

"Mr. Halley!"

"Hop in."

She hopped. That is to say, she opened the door, picked up the Brinton
file, which was lying on the passenger seat, sat down, tidily folded her coat
over her knees, and pulled the door shut again. The bad side of her face was
toward me, and she was very conscious of it. The scarf and the hair were
gently pulled forward.

I took a pound and a ten-shilling note out of my pocket and gave them to
her. She took them smiling.

"The taxi man told our switchboard girl you gave him that for bringing
the leaflet. Thank you very much." I swung out through the traffic and headed
for Finchley.

She answered obliquely. "That wretched chicken is still in the oven, stone
cold. I just turned the gas out yesterday, after you'd gone."

"I wish I could stay this evening instead," I said, "but I've got a job on for
the agency."

"Another time," she said tranquilly. "Another time, perhaps. I understand that you couldn't tell me at first who you worked for, because you didn't know whether I was an . . . er, an accomplice of Mr. Bolt's, and afterwards you didn't tell me for fear of what actually happened, that I would be upset. So that's that."

"You are generous."

"Realistic, even if a bit late."

We went a little way in silence. Then I asked, "What would happen to the shares Kraye owns if it were proved he was sabotaging the company? If he were convicted, I mean. Would his shares be confiscated, or would he still own them when he came out of jail?"

"I've never heard of anyone's shares being confiscated," she said, sounding interested. "But surely that's a long way in the future?"

"I wish I knew. It makes a good deal of difference to what I should do now."

"How do you mean?"

"Well . . . an easy way to stop Kraye buying too many more shares would be to tell the racing press and the financial press that a takeover is being attempted. The price would rocket. But Kraye already holds twenty-three percent, and if the law couldn't take it away from him, he would either stick to that and vote for a sellout, or if he got cold feet he could unload his shares at the higher price and still make a fat profit. Either way, he'd be sitting pretty financially, in jail or out. And either way Seabury would be built on."

"I suppose this sort of thing's happened before?"

"Takeovers, yes, several. But only one other case of sabotage. At Dunstable. Kraye again."

"Haven't any courses survived a takeover bid?"

"Only Sandown, publicly. I don't know of any others, but they may have managed it in secrecy."

"How did Sandown do it?"

"The local council did it for them. Stated loudly that planning permission would not be given for building. Of course the bid collapsed then."

"It looks as though the only hope for Seabury, in that case, is that the council there will act in this same way. I'd try a strong lobby, if I were you."

"You're quite a girl, Miss Martin," I said, smiling. "That's a very good idea. I'll go and dip a toe into the climate of opinion at the Town Hall."

She nodded approvingly. "No good lobbying against the grain. Much better to find out which way people are likely to move before you start pushing!"

Finchley came into sight. I said, "You do realize, Miss Martin, that if I am successful at my job, you will lose yours?"

She laughed. "Poor Mr. Bolt. He's not at all bad to work for. But don't worry about my job. It's easy for an experienced stockbroker's secretary to get a good one, I assure you."

I stopped at her gate, looking at my watch. "I'm afraid I can't come in. I'm already going to be a bit late."

She opened the door without ado and climbed out. "Thank you for coming at all." She smiled, shut the door crisply, and waved me away.

I drove back to my flat as fast as I could, fuming slightly at the traffic. It wasn't until I switched off the engine down in the garage and leaned over to pick it up that I discovered the Brinton file wasn't there. And then remembered Miss Martin holding it on her lap during the journey, and me hustling her out of the car. Miss Martin still had Brinton's file. I hadn't time to go back for it, and I couldn't ring her up because I didn't know the name of the owner of the house she lived in. But surely, I reassured myself, surely the file would be safe enough where it was until Friday.

CHAPTER 12

CHICO AND I sat huddled together for warmth in some gorse bushes and watched the sunrise over Seabury Racecourse. It had been a cold clear night with a tingle of naught degrees centigrade about it, and we were both shivering.

Behind us, among the bushes and out of sight, Revelation, one-time winner of the Cheltenham Gold Cup, was breakfasting on meager patches of grass. We could hear the scrunch when he bit down close to the roots, and the faint chink of the bridle as he ate. For some time Chico and I had been resisting the temptation to relieve him of his nice warm rug.

"They might try something now," said Chico hopefully. "First light, before anyone's up."

Nothing had moved in the night, we were certain of that. Every hour I had ridden Revelation at a careful walk round the whole of the track itself, and Chico had made a plimsoll-shod inspection of the stands at one with the shadows. There had been no one about. Not a sound but the stirring breeze, not a glimmer of light but from the stars and a waning moon.

Our present spot, chosen as the sky lightened and some concealment became necessary, lay at the furthest spot from the stands, at the bottom of the semicircle of track cut off by the road which ran across the course. Scattered bushes and scrub filled the space between the track and boundary fence, enough to shield us from all but closely prying eyes. Behind the boundary fence were the little back gardens of the first row of bungalows. The sun rose bright and yellow away to our left and the birds sang around us. It was half past seven.

"It's going to be a lovely day," said Chico.

At ten past nine there was some activity up by the stands and the tractor rolled onto the course pulling a trailer. I unshipped my race glasses, balanced them on my bent-up knees, and took a look. The trailer was loaded with what I guessed were hurdles, and was accompanied by three men on foot.

I handed the glasses to Chico without comment, and yawned.

"Lawful occasions," he remarked, bored.

We watched the tractor and trailer lumber slowly round the far end of the course, pause to unload, and return for a refill. On its second trip it came close enough for us to confirm that it was in fact the spare hurdles that were being dumped in position, four or five at each flight, ready to be used if any were splintered in the races. We watched for a while in silence. Then I said slowly, "Chico, I've been blind."

"Huh?"

"The tractor," I said. "The tractor. Under our noses all the time."

"So?"

"So the sulfuric acid tanker was pulled over by a tractor. No complicated lifting gear necessary. Just a couple of ropes or chains slung over the top of the tanker and fastened round the axles. Then you unscrew the hatches and stand well clear. Someone drives the tractor at full power up the course, over goes the tanker and out pours the juice. And Bob's your uncle!"

"Every racecourse has a tractor," said Chico thoughtfully.

"That's right."

"So no one would look twice at a tractor on a racecourse. Quite. No one would remark on any tracks it left. No one would mention seeing one on the road. So if you're right, and I'd say you certainly are, it wouldn't necessarily have been that tractor, the racecourse tractor, which was used."

"I'll bet it was, though." I told Chico about the photographed initials and payments. "Tomorrow I'll check the initials of all the workmen here from Ted Wilkins downwards against that list. Any one of them might have been paid just to leave the tractor on the course, lying handy. The tanker went over on the evening before the meeting, like today. The tractor would have been in use then too. Warm and full of fuel. Nothing easier. And afterwards, straight on up the racecourse, and out of sight."

"It was dusk," agreed Chico. "As long as no one came along the road in the minutes it took to unhitch the ropes or chains afterwards, they were clear. No traffic diversions, no detours, nothing."

We sat watching the tractor lumbering about, gloomily realizing we couldn't prove a word of it.

"We'll have to move," I said presently. "There's a hurdle just along there, about fifty yards away, where those wings are. They'll be down here over the road soon."

We adjourned with Revelation back to the horse box half a mile away down the road to the west and took the opportunity to eat our own breakfast. When we had finished Chico went back first, strolling along confidently in my jodhpurs, boots and polo-necked jersey, the complete horseman from head to foot. He had never actually sat on a horse in his life.

After a while I followed on Revelation. The men had brought the hurdles down into the semicircular piece of track and had laid them in place. They were now moving further away up the course, unloading the next lot. Unremarked, I rode back to the bushes and dismounted. Of Chico there was no sign for another half hour, and then he came whistling across from the road with his hands in his pockets.

When he reached me he said, "I had another look round the stands. Rotten security, here. No one asked me what I was doing. There are some women cleaning here and there, and some are working in the stable block, getting the lads' hostel ready, things like that. I said good morning to them, and they said good morning back." He was disgusted.

"Not much scope for saboteurs," I said morosely. "Cleaners in the stands and workmen on the course."

"Dusk tonight," nodded Chico. "That's the most likely time now."

The morning ticked slowly away. The sun rose to its low November zenith and shone straight into our eyes. I passed the time by taking a photograph of Revelation and another of Chico. He was fascinated by the tiny camera and said he couldn't wait to get one like it. Eventually I put it back into my breeches pocket, and shading my eyes against the sun took my hundredth look up the course.

Nothing. No men, no tractor. I looked at my watch. One o'clock. Lunch hour. More time passed.

Chico picked up the race glasses and swept the course.

"Be careful," I said idly. "Don't look at the sun with those. You'll hurt your eyes."

"Do me a favor."

I yawned, feeling the sleepless night catch up.

"There's a man on the course," he said. "One. Just walking."

He handed me the glasses and I took a look. He was right. One man was walking alone across the racecourse; not round the track but straight across the rough grass in the middle. He was too far away for his features to be distinguishable and in any case he was wearing a fawn duffel coat with the hood up. I shrugged and lowered the glasses. He looked harmless enough.

With nothing better to do we watched him reach the far side, duck under the rails, and move along until he was standing behind one of the fences with only his head and shoulders in our sight.

Chico remarked that he should have attended to nature in the gents' before he left the stands. I yawned again, smiling at the same time. The man went on standing behind the fence.

"What on earth is he doing?" said Chico, after about five minutes.

"He isn't doing anything," I said, watching through the glasses. "He's just standing there looking this way."

"Do you think he's spotted us?"

"No, he couldn't. He hasn't any binocs, and we are in the bushes."

Another five minutes passed in inactivity.

"He must be doing *something*," said Chico, exasperated.

"Well, he isn't," I said.

Chico took a turn with the glasses. "You can't see a damn thing against the sun," he complained. "We should have camped up the other end."

"In the car park?" I suggested mildly. "The road to the stables and the main gates runs along the other end. There isn't a scrap of cover."

"He's got a flag," said Chico suddenly. "Two flags. One in each hand. White on the left, orange on the right. He seems to be waving them alternately. He's just some silly nit of a racecourse attendant practicing calling up the ambulance and the vet." He was disappointed.

I watched the flags waving, first white, then orange, then white, then orange, with a gap of a second or two between each wave. It certainly wasn't any form of recognizable signaling: nothing like semaphore. They were, as Chico had said, quite simply the flags used after a fall in a race: white to summon the ambulance for the jockey, orange to get attention for a horse. He didn't keep it up very long. After about eight waves altogether he stopped, and in a moment or two began to walk back across the course to the stands.

"Now what," said Chico, "do you think all that was in aid of?"

He swept the glasses all round the whole racecourse yet again. "There isn't a soul about except him and us."

"He's probably been standing by a fence for months waiting for a chance to wave his flags, and no one has been injured anywhere near him. In the end, the temptation proved too much."

I stood up and stretched, went through the bushes to Revelation, undid the halter with which he was tethered to the bushes, unbuckled the surcingle and pulled off his rug.

"What are you doing?" said Chico.

"The same as the man with the flags. Succumbing to an intolerable temptation. Give me a leg up." He did what I asked, but hung on to the reins.

"You're mad. You said in the night that they might let you do it after this meeting, but they'd never agree to it before. Suppose you smash the fences?"

"Then I'll be in almighty trouble," I agreed. "But here I am on a super jumper looking at a heavenly course on a perfect day, with everyone away at lunch." I grinned. "Leave go."

Chico took his hand away, "It's not like you," he said doubtfully.

"Don't take it to heart," I said flippantly, and touched Revelation into a walk.

At this innocuous pace the horse and I went out onto the track and proceeded in the direction of the stands. Counterclockwise, the way the races were run. Still at a walk we reached the road and went across its uncovered Tarmac surface. On the far side of the road lay the enormous dark brown patch of tan, spread thick and firm where the burnt turf had been bulldozed away. Horses would have no difficulty in racing over it.

Once on the other side, on the turf again, Revelation broke into a trot. He knew where he was. Even with no crowds and no noise the fact of being on a familiar racecourse was exciting him. His ears were pricked, his step springy. At fourteen he had been already a year in retirement, but he moved beneath me like a four-year-old. He too, I guessed fancifully, was feeling the satanic tug of a pleasure about to be illicitly snatched.

Chico was right, of course. I had no business at all to be riding on the course so soon before a meeting. It was indefensible. I ought to know better. I did know better. I eased Revelation gently into a canter.

There were three flights of hurdles and three fences more or less side-by-side up the straight, and the water jump beyond that. As I wasn't sure that Revelation would jump the fences in cold blood on his own (many horses won't), I set him at the hurdles.

Once he had seen these and guessed my intention I doubt if I could have stopped him, even if I'd wanted to. He fairly ate up the first flight and stretched out eagerly for the second. After that I gave him a choice, and of the two obstacles lying ahead, he opted for the fence. It didn't seem to bother him that he was on his own. They were excellent fences and he was a Gold Cup winner, born and bred for the job and being given an unexpected, much-missed treat. He flew the fence with all his former dash and skill.

As for me, my feelings were indescribable. I'd sat on a horse a few times since I'd given up racing, but never found an opportunity of doing more than riding out quietly at morning exercise with Mark's string. And here I was, back in my old place, doing again what I'd ached for in the two and a half years. I grinned with irrepressible joy and got Revelation to lengthen his stride for the water jump.

He took it with feet to spare. Perfect. There were no irate shouts from the stands on my right, and we swept away on round the top bend of the course, fast and free. Another fence at the end of the bend—Revelation floated it—and five more stretching away down the far side. It was at the third of these, the open ditch, that the man had been standing and waving the flags.

It's an undoubted fact that emotions pass from rider to horse, and Revelation was behaving with the same reckless exhilaration which gripped me, so after two spectacular leaps over the next two fences we both sped onward with arms open to fate. There ahead was the guardrail, the four-foot-wide open ditch and the four-foot-six fence rising on the far side of it. Revelation, knowing all about it, automatically put himself right to jump.

It came, the blinding flash in the eyes, as we soared into the air. White, dazzling, brain-shattering light, splintering the day into a million fragments and blotting out the world in a blaze as searing as the sun.

I felt Revelation falling beneath me and rolled instinctively, my eyes open and quite unable to see. Then there was the rough crash on the turf and the return of vision from light to blackness and up through gray to normal sight.

I was on my feet before Revelation, and I still had hold of the reins. He struggled up, bewildered and staggering, but apparently unhurt. I pulled him forward into an unwilling trot to make sure of his legs, and was relieved to find them whole and sound. It only remained to remount as quickly as possible, and this was infuriatingly difficult. With two hands I could have jumped up easily; as it was I scrambled untidily back into the saddle at the third attempt, having lost the reins altogether and bashed my stomach on the pommel of the saddle into the bargain. Revelation behaved very well, all things considered. He trotted only fifty yards or so in the wrong direction before I collected myself and the reins into a working position and turned him round. This time we bypassed the fence and all subsequent ones: I cantered him first down the side of the track, slowed to a trot to cross the road, and steered then not on round the bottom semicircle but off to the right, heading for where the boundary fence met the main London road.

Out of the corner of my eye I saw Chico running in my direction across the rough grass. I waved him toward me with a sweep of the arm and reined in and waited for him where our paths converged.

"I thought you said you could bloody well ride," he said, scarcely out of breath from the run.

"Yeah," I said. "I thought so once."

He looked at me sharply. "You fell off. I was watching. You fell off like a baby."

"If you were watching . . . the horse fell, if you don't mind. There's a distinction. Very important to jockeys."

"Nuts," he said. "You fell off."

"Come on," I said, walking Revelation toward the boundary fence. "There's something to find." I told Chico what. "In one of those bungalows, I should think. At a window or on the roof, or in a garden."

"Sods," said Chico forcefully. "The dirty sods."

I agreed with him.

It wasn't very difficult, because it had to be within a stretch of only a hundred yards or so. We went methodically along the boundary fence toward the London road, stopping to look carefully into every separate little garden, and at every separate little house. A fair number of inquisitive faces looked back.

Chico saw it first, propped into a high leafless branch of a tree growing well back in the second-to-last garden. Traffic whizzed along the London road only ten yards ahead, and Revelation showed signs of wanting to retreat.

"Look," said Chico, pointing upward.

I looked, fighting a mild battle against the horse. It was five feet high, three feet wide, and polished to a spotless brilliance. A mirror.

"Sods," said Chico again.

I nodded, dismounted, led Revelation back to where the traffic no longer fretted him, and tied the reins to the fence. Then Chico and I walked along to the London road and round into the road of bungalows. Napoleon Close, it said. Napoleon wasn't *that* close, I reflected, amused.

We rang the door of the second bungalow. A man and a woman both came to the door to open it, elderly, gentle, inoffensive and inquiring.

I came straight to the point, courteously. "Do you know you have a mirror in your tree?"

"Don't be silly," said the woman, smiling as if at an idiot. She had flat wavy gray hair and was wearing a sloppy black cardigan over a brown wool dress. No color sense, I thought.

"You'd better take a look," I suggested.

"It's not a mirror, you know," said the husband, puzzled. "It's a placard. One of those advertisement things."

"That's right," said his wife contrapuntally. "A placard."

"We agreed to lend our tree—"

"For a small sum, really . . . only our pension—"

"A man put up the framework—"

"He said he would be back soon with the poster—"

"A religious one, I believe. A good cause—"

"We wouldn't have done it otherwise—"

Chico interrupted. "I wouldn't have thought it was a good place for a poster. Your tree stands further back than the others. It isn't conspicuous."

"I did think—" began the man doubtfully, shuffling in his checked, woolly bedroom slippers.

"But if he was willing to pay rent for your particular tree, you didn't want to put him off," I finished. "An extra quid or two isn't something you want to pass on next door."

They wouldn't have put it so bluntly, but they didn't demur.

"Come and look," I said.

They followed me round along the narrow path beside their bungalow wall and into their own back garden. The tree stood halfway to the racecourse boundary fence, the sun slanting down through the leafless branches. We could see the wooden back of the mirror, and the ropes which fastened it to the tree trunk. The man and his wife walked round to the front, and their puzzlement increased.

"He said it was for a poster," repeated the man.

"Well," I said as matter-of-factly as I could, "I expect it is for a poster, as he said. But at the moment, you see, it is a mirror. And it's pointing straight out over the racecourse; and you know how mirrors reflect the sunlight? We just thought it might not be too safe, you know, if anyone got dazzled, so we wondered if you would mind us moving it?"

"Why, goodness," agreed the woman, looking with more awareness at our riding clothes, "no one could see the racing with light shining in their eyes."

"Quite. So would you mind if we turned the mirror round a bit?"

"I can't see that it would hurt, Dad," she said doubtfully.

He made a nondescript assenting movement with his hand, and Chico asked how the mirror had been put up in the tree in the first place. The man had brought a ladder with him, they said, and no, they hadn't one themselves. Chico shrugged, placed me beside the tree, put one foot on my thigh, one on my shoulder, and was up in the bare branches like a squirrel. The elderly couple's mouths sagged open.

"How long ago?" I asked. "When did the man put up the mirror?"

"This morning," said the woman, getting over the shock. "He came back just now, too, with another rope or something. That's when he said he'd be back with the poster."

So the mirror had been hauled up into the tree while Chico and I had been obliviously sitting in the bushes, and adjusted later when the sun was at the right angle in the sky. At two o'clock. The time, the next day, of the third race, the handicap steeplechase. Some handicap, I thought, a smash of light in the eyes.

White flag: a little bit to the left. Orange flag: a little bit to the right. No flag: dead on target.

Come back tomorrow afternoon and clap a religious poster over the glass as soon as the damage was done, so that even the most thorough search wouldn't reveal a mirror. Just another jinx on Seabury Racecourse. Dead horses, crushed and trampled jockeys. A jinx. Send my horses somewhere else, Mr. Witney, something always goes wrong at Seabury.

I was way out in one respect. The religious poster was not due to be put in place the following day.

CHAPTER 13

"I THINK," I said gently to the elderly couple, "that it might be better if you went indoors. We will explain to the man who is coming what we are doing to his mirror."

Dad glanced up the path toward the road, put his arm protectively round his wife's woolly shoulders, and said gratefully, "Er . . . yes . . . yes."

They shuffled rapidly through the back door into the bungalow just as a large man carrying an aluminum folding ladder and a large rolled-up paper came barging through their front gate. There had been the squeak of his large, plain, dark blue van stopping, the hollow crunch of the handbrake being forcibly applied, the slam of the door and the scrape of the ladder being unloaded. Chico in the tree crouched quite still, watching.

I was standing with my back to the sun, but it fell full on the big man's face when he came into the garden. It wasn't the sort of face one would naturally associate with religious posters. He was a cross between a heavyweight wrestler and Mount Vesuvius. Craggy, brutally strong and not far off erupting.

He came straight toward me across the grass, dropped the ladder beside him, and said inquiringly, "What goes on?"

"The mirror," I said, "comes down."

His eyes narrowed in sudden awareness and his body stiffened. "There's a poster going over it," he began quite reasonably, lifting the paper roll. Then with a rush the lava burst out, the paper flew wide, and the muscles bunched into action.

It wasn't much of a fight. He started out to hit my face, changed his mind, and ploughed both fists in below the belt. It was quite a long way down for him. Doubling over in pain onto the lawn, I picked up the ladder, and gave him a swinging swipe behind the knees.

The ground shook with the impact. He fell on his side, his coat swinging open. I lunged forward, snatching at the pistol showing in the holster beside his ribs. It came loose, but he brushed me aside with an arm like a telegraph pole. I fell, sprawling. He rolled over into a crouch, picked up the gun from the grass and sneered down into my face. Then he stood up like a released spring and on the way with force and deliberation booted his toecap into my navel. He also clicked back the catch on his gun.

Up in the tree Chico yelled. The big man turned and took three steps toward him, seeing him for the first time. With a choice of targets, he favored the one still in a state to resist. The hand with the pistol pointed at Chico.

"Leo," I shouted. Nothing happened. I tried again.

"Fred!"

The big man turned his head a fraction back to me and Chico jumped down onto him from ten feet up.

The gun went off with a double crash and again the day flew apart in shining splintering fragments. I sat on the ground with my knees bent up, groaning quietly, cursing fluently, and getting on with my business.

Drawn by the noise, the inhabitants of the bungalows down the line came out into their back gardens and looked in astonishment over the fences. The elderly couple stood palely at their window, their mouths again open. The big man had too big an audience now for murder.

Chico was overmatched for size and nearly equaled in skill. He and the big man threw each other round a bit while I crept doubled up along the path into the front garden as far as the gate, but the battle was a foregone conclusion, bar the retreat.

He came alone, crashing up the path, saw me hanging on to the gate and half raised the gun. But there were people in the road now, and more people peering out of opposite windows. In scorching fury he whipped at my head with the barrel, and I avoided it by letting go of the gate and collapsing on the ground again. Behind the gate, with the bars nice and comfortingly between me and his boot.

He crunched across the pavement, slammed into the van, cut his cogs to ribbons and disappeared out onto the London road in a cloud of dust.

Chico came down the garden path staggering, with blood sloshing out of a cut eyebrow. He looked anxious and shaken.

"I thought you said you could bloody well fight," I mocked him.

He came to a halt beside me on his knees. "Blast you." He put his fingers to his forehead and winced at the result.

I grinned at him.

"You were running away," he said.

"Naturally."

"What have you got here?" He took the little camera out of my hand. "Don't tell me," he said, his face splitting into an unholy smile. "Don't tell me."

"It's what we came for, after all."

"How many?"

"Four of him. Two of the van."

"Sid, you slay me, you really do."

"Well," I said, "I feel sick." I rolled over and retched what was left of my breakfast onto the roots of the privet hedge. There wasn't any blood. I felt a lot better.

"I'll go and get the horse box," said Chico, "and pick you up."

"You'll do nothing of the sort," I said, wiping my mouth on a handkerchief. "We're going back into the garden. I want that bullet."

"It's halfway to Seabury," he protested, borrowing my handkerchief to mop the blood off his eyebrow.

"What will you bet?" I said. I used the gate again to get up, and after a moment or two was fairly straight. We presented a couple of reassuring grins to the audience, and retraced our way down the path into the back garden.

The mirror lay in sparkling pointed fragments all over the lawn.

"Pop up the tree and see if the bullet is there, in the wood. It smashed the mirror. It might be stuck up there. If not, we'll have to comb the grass."

Chico went up the aluminum ladder that time.

"Of all the luck," he called. "It's here." I watched him take a penknife out of his pocket and carefully cut away at a section just off-center of the back-board of the ex-mirror. He came down and held the little misshapen lump out to me on the palm of his hand. I put it carefully away in the small waist pocket of my breeches.

The elderly couple had emerged like tortoises from their bungalow. They were scared and puzzled, understandably. Chico offered to cut down the remains of the mirror, and did, but we left them to clear up the resulting firewood.

As an afterthought, however, Chico went across the garden and retrieved the poster from a soggy winter rosebed. He unrolled it and showed it to us, laughing.

BLESSED ARE THE MEEK, FOR THEY SHALL INHERIT THE EARTH.

"One of them," said Chico, "has a sense of humor."

MUCH AGAINST HIS wishes, we returned to our observation post in the scrubby gorse.

"Haven't you had enough?" he said crossly.

"The patrols don't get here till six," I reminded him. "And you yourself said that dusk would be the likely time for them to try something."

"But they've already done it."

"There's nothing to stop them from rigging up more than one booby trap," I pointed out. "Especially as that mirror thing wouldn't have been one hundred per cent reliable, even if we hadn't spotted it. It depended on the sun. Good weather forecast, I know, but weather forecasts are as reliable as a perished hot-water bottle. A passing cloud would have wrecked it. I would think they have something else in mind."

"Cheerful," he said resignedly. He led Revelation away along the road to stow him in the horse box, and was gone a long time.

When he came back he sat down beside me and said, "I went all round the stables. No one stopped me or asked what I was doing. Don't they have *any* security here? The cleaners have all gone home, but there's a woman cooking in the canteen. She said I was too early, to come back at half past six. There wasn't anyone about in the stands block except an old geezer with snuffles mucking about with the boiler."

The sun was lower in the sky and the November afternoon grew colder. We shivered a little and huddled inside our jerseys.

Chico said, "You guessed about the mirror before you set off round the course."

"It was a possibility, that's all."

"You could have ridden along the boundary fence, looking into the gardens like we did afterwards, instead of haring off over all those jumps."

I grinned faintly. "Yes. As I told you, I was giving in to temptation."

"Screwy. You must have known you'd fall."

"Of course I didn't. The mirror mightn't have worked very effectively. Anyway, it's better to test a theory in a practical way. And I just wanted to ride round there. I had a good excuse if I were hauled up for it. So I went. And it was grand. So shut up."

He laughed. "All right." Restlessly he stood up again and said he would make another tour. While he was gone I watched the racecourse with and without the binoculars, but not a thing moved on it.

He came back quietly and dropped down beside me.

"As before," he said.

"Nothing here, either."

He looked at me sideways. "Do you feel as bad as you look?"

"I shouldn't be surprised," I said. "Do you?"

He tenderly touched the area round his cut eyebrow. "Worse. Much worse. Soggy bad luck, him slugging away at your belly like that."

"He did it on purpose," I said idly, "and it was very informative."

"Huh?"

"It showed he knew who I was. He wouldn't have needed to have attacked us like that if we'd just been people come over from the racecourse to see if we could shift the mirror. But when he spoke to me he recognized me, and he knew I wouldn't be put off by any poster eyewash. And his sort don't mildly back down and retreat without paying you off for getting in their way. He just hit where he knew it would have most effect. I actually saw him think it."

"But how did he know?"

"It was he who sent Andrews to the office," I said. "He was the man Mervyn Brinton described: big, going a bit bald, freckles on the back of his hands, cockney accent. He was strong-arming Brinton, and he sent Andrews to get the letter that was supposed to be in the office. Well, Andrews knew me, and I knew him. He must have gone back and told our big friend Fred that he had shot me in the stomach. My death wasn't reported in the papers, so Fred knew I was still alive and would put the finger on Andrews at once. Andrews wasn't exactly a good risk to Fred, just a silly spiv with no sense, so Fred, I guess, marched him straight off to Epping Forest and left him for the birds. Who did a fair job, I'll give them that."

"Do you think," said Chico slowly, "that the gun Fred had today . . . is that why you wanted the bullet?"

I nodded. "That's right. I tried for the gun too, but no dice. If I'm going on with this sort of work, pal, you'll have to teach me a spot of judo."

He looked down doubtfully. "With that hand?"

"Invent a new sport," I said. "One-armed combat."

"I'll take you to the club," he said, smiling. "There's an old Jap there who'll find a way if anyone can."

"Good."

Up at the far end of the racecourse a horse box turned in off the main road and trundled along toward the stables. The first of the next day's runners had apparently arrived.

Chico went to have a look.

I sat on in fading daylight, watching nothing happen, hugging myself against the cold and the reawakened grinding ache in my gut, and thinking evil thoughts about Fred. Not Leo. Fred.

There were four of them, I thought. Kraye, Bolt, Fred and Leo.

I had met Kraye: he knew me only as Sid, a despised hanger-on in the home of a retired admiral he had met at his club and had spent a weekend with.

I had met Bolt: he knew me as John Halley, a shop assistant wanting to invest a gift from an aunt.

I had met Fred: he knew my whole name, and that I worked for the agency, and that I had turned up at Seabury.

I did not know if I had met Leo. But Leo might know *me*. If he had anything to do with racing, he definitely did.

It would be all right, I thought, as long as they did not connect all the Halleys and Sids too soon. But there was my wretched hand, which Kraye had pulled out of my pocket, which Fred could have seen in the garden, and which Leo, whoever he was, might have noticed almost anywhere in the last six days, thanks to my promise to Miss Martin. Miss Martin, who worked for Bolt. A proper merry-go-round, I thought wryly.

Chico materialized out of the dusk. "It was Ping Pong, running in the first tomorrow. All aboveboard," he said. "And nothing doing anywhere, stands or course. We might as well go."

It was well after five. I agreed, and got up stiffly.

"That Fred," said Chico, casually giving me a hand, "I've been thinking. I've seen him before, I'm certain. At race meetings. He's not a regular. Doesn't work for a bookie, or anything like that. But he's about. Cheap rings, mostly."

"Let's hope he doesn't burrow," I said.

"I don't see why he should," he said seriously. "He can't possibly think you'd connect him with Andrews, or with Kraye. All you caught him doing was fixing a poster in a tree. If I were him, I'd be sleeping easy."

"I called him Fred," I said.

"Oh," said Chico glumly. "So you did."

We reached the road and started along it toward the horse box.

"Fred must be the one who does all the jobs," said Chico. "Digs the false drains, sets fire to stables, and drives tractors to pull over tankers. He's big enough for anything."

"He didn't wave the flags. He was up the tree at the time."

"Um. Yes. Who did?"

"Not Bolt," I said. "It wasn't fat enough for Bolt, even in a duffel coat. Possibly Kraye. More likely Leo, whoever he is."

"One of the workmen, or the foreman. Yes. Well, that makes two of them for overturning tankers and so on."

"It would be easier for two," I agreed.

Chico drove the horse box back to Mark's, and then, to his obvious delight, my Mere back to London.

CHAPTER 14

CHIEF INSPECTOR CORNISH was pleased but trying to hide it.

"I suppose you can chalk it up to your agency," he said as if it were debatable.

"He walked slap into us, to be fair."

"And slap out again," he said dryly.

I grimaced. "You haven't met him."

"You want to leave that sort to us," he said automatically.

"Where were you, then?"

"That's a point," he admitted, smiling.

He picked up the matchbox again and looked at the bullet. "Little beauty. Good clear markings. Pity he has a revolver, though, and not an automatic. It would have been nice to have had cartridge cases as well."

"You're greedy," I said.

He looked at the aluminum ladder standing against his wall, and at the poster on his desk, and at the rush-job photographs. Two clear prints of the van showing its number plates and four of Fred in action against Chico. Not exactly posed portraits, these, but four different, characteristic and recognizable angles taken in full sunlight.

"With all this lot to go on, we'll trace him before he draws breath."

"Fine," I said. And the sooner Fred was immobilized the better, I thought. Before he did any more damage to Seabury. "You'll need a tiger net to catch him. He's a very tough baby, and he knows judo. And unless he has the sense to throw it away, he'll still have that gun."

"I'll remember," he said. "And thanks." We shook hands amicably as I left.

IT WAS RESULTS day at Radnor's, too. As soon as I got back Dolly said Jack Copeland wanted me up in Bona Fides. I made the journey.

Jack gleamed at me over the half-moons, pleased with his department. "George's got him. Kraye. He'll tell you."

I went over to George's desk. George was fairly smirking but after he'd talked for two minutes, I allowed he'd earned it.

"On the off-chance," he said, "I borrowed a bit of smooth quartz Kraye recently handled in the Geology Museum and got Sammy to do the prints on it. Two or three different sets of fingers came out, so we photographed the lot. None of them were on the British files, but I've given them the runaround with the odd pal in Interpol and so on, just in case. And brother, have we hit pay dirt or have we."

"We have?" I prompted, grinning.

"And how. Your friend Kraye is in the ex-con library of the state of New York."

"What for?"

"Assault."

"Of a girl?" I asked.

George raised his eyebrows. "A girl's father. Kraye had beaten the girl, apparently with her permission. She didn't complain. But her father saw the bruises and raised the roof. He said he'd get Kraye on a rape charge, though it seems the girl had been perfectly willing on that count too. But it looked bad for Kraye, so he picked up a chair and smashed it over the father's head and scampered. They caught him boarding a plane for South America and hauled him back. The father's brain was damaged. There are long medical details, but what it all boils down to is that he couldn't coordinate properly afterwards. Kraye got off on the rape charge, but served four years for attacking the father.

"Three years after that he turned up in England with some money and a new name, and soon acquired a wife. The one who divorced him for cruelty. Nice chap."

"Yes indeed," I said. "What was his real name?"

"Wilbur Potter," said George sardonically. "And you'll never guess. He was a geologist by profession. He worked for a construction firm, surveying. Always moving about. Character assessment: slick, a pusher, a good talker. Cut a few corners, always had more money than his salary, threw his weight about, but nothing indictable. The assault on the father was his first brush with the law. He was thirty-four at that time."

"Messy," I said. "The whole thing."

"Very," George agreed.

"But sex, violence, and fraudulent takeovers aren't much related," I complained.

"You might as well say it is impossible to have boils and cancer at the same time. Something drastically wrong with the constitution, and two separate symptoms."

"I'll take your word for it," I said.

SAMMY UP IN Missing Persons had done more than photograph Kraye's fingerprints, he had almost found Smith.

"Intersouth rang us this morning," he purred. "Smith gave them as a reference. He's applied for a driving job in Birmingham."

"Good," I said.

"We should have his address by this afternoon."

DOWNSTAIRS IN RACING I reached for Dolly's telephone and got through to Charing, Street and King.

"Mr. Bolt's secretary speaking," said the quiet voice.

"Is Mr. Bolt in?" I asked.

"I'm afraid not . . . er, who is that speaking, please?"

"Did you find you had a file of mine?"

"Oh. . . ." She laughed. "Yes, I picked it up in your car. I'm so sorry."

"Do you have it with you?"

"No," she said, "I didn't bring it here. I thought it might be better not to risk Mr. Bolt seeing it, as it's got Hunt Radnor Associates printed on the outside along with a red sticker saying 'Ex Records, care of Sid Halley.'"

"Yes, it would have been a disaster," I agreed with feeling.

"I left it at home. Do you want it in a hurry?"

"No, not really. As long as it's safe, that's the main thing. How would it be if I came over to fetch it the day after tomorrow—Sunday morning? We could go for a drive, perhaps, and have some lunch."

There was a tiny pause. Then she said strongly, "Yes, please. Yes."

"Have the leaflets gone out?" I asked.

"They went yesterday."

"See you on Sunday, Miss Martin."

I put down Dolly's telephone to find her looking at me quizzically. I was again squatting on the corner of her desk, the girl from the typing pool having in my absence reclaimed her chair.

"The mouse got away again, I understand," she said.

"Some mouse."

Chico came into the office. The cut on his eyebrow looked red and sore, and all the side of his face showed grayish bruising.

"Two of you," said Dolly disgustedly, "and he knocked you about like kids."

Chico took this a lot better than if she had fussed maternally over his injury.

"It took more than two Lilliputians to peg down Gulliver," he said with good humor. (They had a large library in the children's orphanage.)

"But only one David to slay Goliath."

Chico made a face at her, and I laughed.

"And how are our collywobbles today?" he asked me ironically.

"Better than your looks."

"You know why Sid's best friends won't tell him?" said Chico.

"Why?" said Dolly, seriously.

"He suffers from halley-tosis."

"Oh God," said Dolly. "Take him away, someone. Take him away. I can't stand it."

ON THE GROUND floor I sat in a padded maroon armchair in Radnor's drawing-room office and listened to him saying there were no out-of-the-ordinary reports from the patrols at Seabury.

"Fison has just been on the telephone. Everything is normal for a race day, he says. The public will start arriving very shortly. He and Thom walked all round the course just now with Captain Oxon for a thorough check. There's nothing wrong with it, that they can see."

There might be something wrong with it that they couldn't see. I was uneasy.

"I might stay down there tonight, if I can find a room," I said.

"If you do, give me a ring again at home, during the evening."

"Sure." I had disturbed his dinner, the day before, to tell him about Fred and the mirror.

"Could I have those photographs back, if you've finished with them?" I asked. "I want to check that list of initials against the racecourse workmen at Seabury."

"I'm sorry, Sid, I haven't got them."

"Are they back upstairs?"

"No, no, they aren't here at all. Lord Hagbourne has them."

"But why?" I sat up straight, disturbed.

"He came here yesterday afternoon. I'd say on balance he is almost down on our side of the fence. I didn't get the usual caution about expenses, which is a good sign. Anyway, what he wanted was to see the proofs you told him we held which show it is Kraye who is buying the shares. Photographs of share transfer certificates. He knew about them. He said you'd told him."

"Yes, I did."

"He wanted to see them. That was reasonable, and I didn't want to risk tipping him back into indecision, so I showed them to him. He asked me very courteously if he could take them to show them to the Seabury executive. They held a meeting this morning, I believe. He thought they might be roused to some effective action if they could see for themselves how big Kraye's holding is."

"What about the other photographs? The others that were in the box."

"He took them all. They were all jumbled up, and he was in a hurry. He said he'd sort them out himself later."

"He took them to Seabury?" I said uneasily.

"That's right. For the executive meeting this morning."

He looked at his watch. "The meeting must be on at this moment, I should think. If you want them you can ask him for them as soon as you get there. He should have finished with them by then."

"I wish you hadn't let him take them," I said.

"It can't do any harm. Even if he lost them we'd still have the negatives. You could get another print done tomorrow, of your list."

The negatives, did he but know it, were inaccessibly tucked into a mislaid file in Finchley. I didn't confess. Instead I said, unconvinced, "All right. I suppose it won't matter. I'll get on down there, then."

I PACKED AN overnight bag in the flat. The sun was pouring in through the windows, making the blues and greens and blond wood furniture look warm and friendly. After two years the place was at last beginning to feel like home. A home without Jenny. Happiness without Jenny. Both were possible, it seemed. I certainly felt more myself than at any time since she left.

The sun was still shining, too, at Seabury. But not on a very large crowd. The poor quality of the racing was so obvious as to be pathetic: and it was in order that such a rotten gaggle of weedy quadrupeds could stumble and scratch their way round to the winning post, I reflected philosophically, that I had tried to pit my inadequate wits against Lord Hagbourne, Captain Oxon, the Seabury executive, Kraye, Bolt, Fred, Leo, and Uncle Tom Cobley and all.

There were no mishaps all day. The horses raced nonchalantly over the tan patch at their speedy crawl, and no light flashed in their eyes as they knocked hell out of the fences on the far side. Round One to Chico and me.

As the fine weather put everyone in a good mood, a shred of Seabury's former vitality temporarily returned to the place: enough, anyway, for people to notice the dinginess of the stands and remark that it was time something was done about it. If they felt like that, I thought, a revival shouldn't be impossible.

The Senior Steward listened attentively while I passed on Miss Martin's suggestion that Seabury council should be canvassed, and surprisingly said that he would see it was promptly done.

In spite of these small headways, however, my spine wouldn't stop tingling. Lord Hagbourne didn't have the photographs.

"They are only mislaid, Sid," he said soothingly. "Don't make such a fuss. They'll turn up."

He had put them down on the table round which the meeting had been held, he said. After the official business was over, he had chatted, standing up. When he turned back to pick up the box, it was no longer there. The whole table had been cleared. The ashtrays were being emptied. The table was required for lunch. A white cloth was being spread over it.

What, I asked, had been the verdict of the meeting, anyway? Er, um, it appeared the whole subject had been shelved for a week or two: no urgency was felt. Shares changed hands slowly, very slowly. But they had agreed that Hunt Radnor could carry on for a bit.

I hesitated to go barging into the executive's private room just to look for a packet of photographs, so I asked the caterers instead. They hadn't seen it, they said, rushing round me. I tracked down the man and woman who had cleared the table after the meeting and laid it for lunch.

Any amount of doodling on bits of paper, said the waitress, but no box of photographs, and excuse me love, they're waiting for these sandwiches. She agreed to look for it, looked, and came back shaking her head. It wasn't there, as far as she could see. It was quite big, I said despairingly.

I asked Mr. Fotherton, clerk of the course; I asked Captain Oxon; I asked the secretary and anyone else I could think of who had been at the meeting. None of them knew where the photographs were. All of them, busy with their racing jobs, said much the same as Lord Hagbourne.

"Don't worry, Sid, they're bound to turn up."

But they didn't.

I STAYED ON the racecourse until after the security patrols changed over at six o'clock. The in-comers were the same men who had been on watch the night before, four experienced and sensible ex-policemen, all middle-aged. They entrenched themselves comfortably in the press room, which had windows facing back and front, effective central heating, and four telephones; better headquarters than usual on their night jobs, they said.

Between the last race (three-thirty) and six o'clock, apart from hunting without success for the photographs and driving Lord Hagbourne round to Napoleon Close for a horrified firsthand look at the smashed-up mirror, I persuaded Captain Oxon to accompany me on a thorough nook-and-cranny checkup of all the racecourse buildings.

He came willingly enough, his stiffness of earlier in the week having been thawed, I supposed, by the comparative success of the day; but we found nothing and no one that shouldn't have been there.

I drove into Seabury and booked into the Seafront Hotel, where I had often stayed in the past. It was only half full. Formerly, on racing nights, it had been crammed. Over a brandy in the bar the manager lamented with me the state of trade.

"Race meetings used to give us a boost every three weeks nearly all the winter. Now hardly anyone comes, and I hear they didn't even ask for the January fixtures this year. I tell you, I'd like to see that place blooming again, we need it."

"Ah," I said. "Then write to the Town Council and say so."

"That wouldn't help," he said gloomily.

"You never know. It might. Do write."

"All right, Sid. Just to please you then. For old time's sake. Let's have another brandy on the house."

I had an early dinner with him and his wife and afterward went for a walk along the seashore. The night was dry and cold and the onshore breeze smelled of seaweed. The banked pebbles scrunched into trickling hollows under my shoes and the winter sand was as hard-packed as rock. Thinking about Kraye and his machinations, I had strolled quite a long way eastward, away from the racecourse, before I remembered I had said I would ring Radnor at his home during the evening.

There was nothing much to tell him. I didn't hurry, and it was nearly ten o'clock when I got back to Seabury. The modernizations didn't yet run to telephones in all the bedrooms at the hotel, so I used the kiosk outside on the promenade, because I came to it first.

It wasn't Radnor who answered, but Chico, and I knew at once from his voice that things had gone terribly wrong.

"Sid . . . ," he said. "Sid . . . look, pal, I don't know how to tell you. You'll have to have it straight. We've been trying to reach you all the evening."

"What . . . ?" I swallowed.

"Someone bombed your flat."

"*Bombed*," I said stupidly.

"A plastic bomb. It blew the street wall right out. All the flats round yours were badly damaged, but yours . . . well, there's nothing there. Just a big hole with disgusting black sort of cobwebs. That's how they knew it was a plastic bomb. The sort the French terrorists used. . . . Sid, are you there?"

"Yes."

"I'm sorry, pal. I'm sorry. But that's not all. They've done it to the office, too." His voice was anguished. "It went off in the Racing Section. But the whole place is cracked open. It's . . . it's bloody ghastly."

"Chico."

"I know. I know. The old man's round there now, just staring at it. He made me stay here because you said you'd ring, and in case the racecourse patrols want anything. No one was badly hurt, that's the only good thing. Half a dozen people were bruised and cut, at your flats. And the office was empty, of course."

"What time . . . ?"

"The bomb in the office went off about an hour and a half ago, and the one in your flat was just after seven. The old man and I were round there with the police when they got the radio message about the office. The police seem to think that whoever did it was looking for something. The people who live underneath you heard someone moving about upstairs for about two hours shortly before the bomb went off, but they just thought it was you making more noise than usual. And it seems everything in your flat was moved into one pile in the sitting room and the bomb put in the middle. The police said it meant that they hadn't found what they were looking for and were destroying everything in case they had missed it."

"Everything . . . ," I said.

"Not a thing was left. God, Sid, I wish I didn't have to . . . but there it is. Nothing that was there exists anymore."

The letters from Jenny when she loved me. The only photograph of my mother and father. The trophies I won racing. The lot. I leaned numbly against the wall.

"Sid, are you still there?"

"Yes."

"It was the same thing at the office. People across the road saw lights on and someone moving about inside, and just thought we were working late. The old man said we must assume they still haven't found what they were looking for. He wants to know what it is."

"I don't know," I said.

"You must."

"No. I don't."

"You can think on the way back."

"I'm not coming back, not tonight. It can't do any good. I think I'll go out to the racecourse again, just to make sure nothing happens there too."

"All right. I'll tell him when he calls. He said he'd be over in Cromwell Road all night, very likely."

We rang off and I went out of the kiosk into the cold night air. I thought that Radnor was right. It was important to know what it was that the bomb merchants had been looking for. I leaned against the outside of the box, thinking about it. Deliberately not thinking about the flat, the place that had begun to be home, and all that was lost. That had happened before in one way or another. The night my mother died, for instance. And I'd ridden my first winner the next day.

To look for something, you had to know it existed. If you used bombs, destroying it was more important than finding it. What did I have, which I hadn't had long (or they would have searched before) which Kraye wanted obliterated.

There was the bullet which Fred had accidentally fired into the mirror. They wouldn't find that, because it was somewhere in a police ballistics laboratory. And if they had thought I had it, they would have looked for it the night before.

There was the leaflet Bolt had sent out, but there were hundreds of those, and he wouldn't want the one I had, even if he knew I had it.

There was the letter Mervyn Brinton had rewritten for me, but if it were that it meant . . .

I went back into the telephone box, obtained Mervyn Brinton's number from directory inquiries, and rang him up.

To my relief, he answered.

"You are all right, Mr. Brinton?"

"Yes, yes. What's the matter?"

"You haven't had a call from the big man? You haven't told anyone about my visit to you, or that you know your brother's letter by heart?"

He sounded scared. "No. Nothing's happened. I wouldn't tell anyone. I never would."

"Fine," I reassured him. "That's just fine. I was only checking."

So it was not Brinton's letter.

The photographs, I thought. They had been in the office all the time until Radnor gave them to Lord Hagbourne yesterday afternoon. No one outside the agency, except Lord Hagbourne and Charles, had known they existed. Not until this morning, when Lord Hagbourne took them to the Seabury executive meeting, and lost them.

Suppose they weren't lost, but stolen. By someone who knew Kraye, and thought he ought to have them. From the dates on all those documents Kraye would know exactly when the photographs had been taken. And where.

My scalp contracted. I must assume, I thought, that they had now connected all the Halleys and Sids.

Suddenly fearful, I rang up Aynsford. Charles himself answered, calm and sensible.

"Charles, please will you do as I ask, at once, and no questions? Grab Mrs. Cross, go out and get in the car and drive well away from the house, and ring me back at Seabury 79411. Got that? Seabury 79411."

"Yes," he said, and put down the telephone. Thank God, I thought, for a naval training. There might not be much time. The office bomb had exploded an hour and a half ago; London to Aynsford took the same.

Ten minutes later the phone began to ring. I picked up the receiver.

"They say you're in a call box," Charles said.

"That's right. Are you?"

"No, the pub down in the village. Now, what's it all about?"

I told him about the bombs, which horrified him, and about the missing photographs.

"I can't think what else it can be that they are looking for."

"But you said that they've got them."

"The negatives," I said.

"Oh. Yes. And they weren't in your flat or the office?"

"No. Quite by chance, they weren't."

"And you think if they're still looking, that they'll come to Aynsford?"

"If they are desperate enough, they might. They might think you would know where I keep things. . . . And even have a go at making you tell them. I asked you to come out quick because I didn't want to risk it. If they are going to Aynsford, they could be there at any minute now. It's horribly likely they'll think of you. They'll know I took the photos in your house."

"From the dates. Yes. Right. I'll get on to the local police and ask for a guard on the house at once."

"Charles, one of them . . . well, if he's the one with the bombs, you'll need a squad." I described Fred and his van, together with its number.

"Right." He was still calm. "Why would the photographs be so important to them? Enough to use bombs, I mean?"

"I wish I knew."

"Take care."

"Yes," I said.

I did take care. Instead of going back into the hotel, I rang it up.

The manager said, "Sid, where on earth are you, people have been trying to reach you all the evening—the police too."

"Yes, Joe, I know. It's all right. I've talked to the police in London. Now, has anyone actually called at the hotel, wanting me?"

"There's someone up in your room, yes. Your father-in-law, Admiral Roland."

"Oh really? Does he look like an admiral?"

"I suppose so." He sounded puzzled.

"A gentleman?"

"Yes, of course." Not Fred, then.

"Well, he isn't my father-in-law. I've just been talking to him in his house in Oxfordshire. You collect a couple of helpers and chuck my visitor out."

I put down the receiver sighing. A man up in my room meant everything

I'd brought to Seabury would very likely be ripped to bits. That left me with just the clothes I stood in, and the car—

I fairly sprinted round to where I'd left the car. It was locked, silent and safe. No damage. I patted it thankfully, climbed in, and drove out to the race-course.

CHAPTER 15

ALL WAS QUIET as I drove through the gates and switched off the engine. There were lights on—one shining through the windows of the press room, one outside the weighing-room door, one high up somewhere on the stands. The shadows in between were densely black. It was a clear night with no moon.

I walked across to the press room, to see if the security patrols had anything to report.

They hadn't.

All four of them were fast asleep.

Furious, I shook the nearest. His head lolled like a pendulum, but he didn't wake up. He was sitting slumped into his chair. One of them had his arms on the table and his head on his arms. One of them sat on the floor, his head on the seat of the chair and his arms hanging down. The fourth lay flat, face downward, near the opposite wall.

The stupid fools, I thought. Ex-policemen letting themselves be put to sleep like infants. It shouldn't have been possible. One of the first rules in guard work was to take their own food and drink with them and not accept sweets from strangers.

I stepped round their heavily breathing hulks and picked up one of the press telephones to ring Chico for reinforcements. The line was dead. I tried the three other instruments. No contact with the exchange on any of them.

I would have to go back and ring up from Seabury, I thought. I went out of the press room but in the light pouring out before I shut the door I saw a dim figure walking toward me from the direction of the gate.

"Who's that?" he called imperiously, and I recognized his voice. Captain Oxon.

"It's only me, Sid Halley," I shouted back. "Come and look at this."

He came on into the light, and I stood aside for him to go into the press room.

"Good heavens. What on earth's the matter with them?"

"Sleeping pills. And the telephones don't work. You haven't seen anyone about who ought not to be?"

"No. I haven't heard anything except your car. I came down to see who had come."

"How many lads are there staying overnight in the hostel? Could we use some of those to patrol the place while I ring the agency to get some more men?"

"I should think they'd love it," he said. "There are about five of them. They shouldn't be in bed yet. We'll go over and ask them, and you can use the telephone from my flat to ring your agency."

"Thanks," I said. "That's fine."

I looked round the room at the sleeping men. "I think perhaps I ought to see if any of them tried to write a message. I won't be a minute."

He waited patiently while I looked under the head and folded arms of the man at the table and under the man on the floor, and all round the one with his head on the chair seat, but none of them had even reached for a pencil. Shrugging, I looked at the remains of their supper, lying on the table. Half-eaten sandwiches on greaseproof paper, dregs of coffee in cups and thermos flasks, a couple of apple cores, some cheese sections and empty wrappings, and an unpeeled banana.

"Found anything?" asked Oxon.

I shook my head in disgust. "Not a thing. They'll have terrible headaches when they wake up, and serve them right."

"I can understand you being annoyed . . ." he began. But I was no longer really listening. Over the back of the chair occupied by the first man I had shaken was hanging a brown leather binoculars case, and on its lid were stamped three black initials: L. E. O. Leo. *Leo.*

"Something the matter?" asked Oxon.

"No." I smiled at him and touched the strap of the binoculars. "Are these yours?"

"Yes. The men asked if I could lend them some. For the dawn, they said."

"It was very kind of you."

"Oh. Nothing." He shrugged, moving out into the night. "You'd better make that phone call first. We'll tackle the boys afterwards."

I had absolutely no intention of walking into his flat.

"Right," I said.

We went out of the door, and I closed it behind us.

A familiar voice, loaded with satisfaction, spoke from barely a yard away. "So you've got him, Oxon. Good."

"He was coming—" began Oxon in anxious anger, knowing that "got him" was an exaggeration.

"No," I said, and turned and ran for the car.

When I was barely ten yards from it someone turned the lights on. The headlights of my own car. I stopped dead.

Behind me one of the men shouted and I heard their feet running. I wasn't directly in the beam, but silhouetted against it. I swerved off to the right, toward the gate. Three steps in that direction, and the headlights of a car turning in through it caught me straight in the eyes.

There were more shouts, much closer, from Oxon and Kraye. I turned, half-dazzled, and saw them closing in. Behind me now the incoming car rolled forward. And the engine of my Mercedes purred separately into life.

I ran for the dark. The two cars, moving, caught me again in their beams. Kraye and Oxon ran where they pointed.

I was driven across and back toward the stands like a coursed hare, the two cars behind inexorably finding me with their lights and the two men running with reaching, clutching hands. Like a nightmare game of "He," I thought wildly, with more than a child's forfeit if I were caught.

Across the parade ring, across the flat Tarmac stretch beyond it, under the rails of the unsaddling enclosure and along the inside of the door into the trainers' luncheon room and through there without stopping into the kitchen. And weaving on from there out into the members' lunchroom, round acres of tables with upturned chairs, through the far door into the wide passage which cut like a tunnel along the length of the huge building, across it, and up a steep stone staircase emerging halfway up the open steps of the stands, and sideways along them as far as I could go. The pursuit was left behind.

I sank down, sitting with one leg bent to run, in the black shadow where the low wooden wall dividing the members from Tattersalls cut straight down the steps separating the stands into two halves. On top of the wall wire netting stretched up too high to climb: high enough to keep out the poorer customers from gate crashing the expensive ring.

At the bottom of the steps lay a large expanse of members' lawn stretching to another metal mesh fence, chest high, and beyond that lay the whole expanse of racecourse. Half a mile across it to the London road to Seabury, with yet another barrier, the boundary fence, to negotiate.

It was too far. I knew I couldn't do it. Perhaps once, with two hands for vaulting, with a stomach which didn't already feel as if it were tearing into more holes inside. But not now. Although I always mended fast, it was only two weeks since I had found the short walk to Andrews' body very nearly too much; and Fred's well-aimed attentions on the previous day had not been therapeutic.

Looking at it straight: if I ran, it had to be successful. My kingdom for a horse, I thought. Any reasonable cowboy would have had Revelation hitched to the rails, ready for a flying leap into the saddle and a thundering exit. I had a hundred-and-fifty-mile-an-hour little white Mercedes, and someone else was sitting in it.

To run and be caught running would achieve nothing and be utterly pointless.

Which left just one alternative.

The security patrol hadn't been drugged for nothing. Kraye wasn't at Seabury for his health. Some more damage had been planned for this night. Might already have been done. There was just a chance, if I stayed to look, that I could find out what it was. Before they found *me*. Naturally.

If I ever have any children, they won't get me playing hide-and-seek.

Half an hour later the grim game was still in progress. My own car was now parked on the racecourse side of the stands, on the Tarmac in Tattersalls where the bookies had called that afternoon. It was facing the stands with the headlights full on. Every inch of the steps was lit by them, and since the car had arrived there I had not been able to use that side of the building at all.

The other car was similarly parked inside the racecourse gates, its headlights shining on the fronts of the weighing room, bars, dining rooms, cloakrooms, and offices.

Presuming that each car still had a watching occupant, that left only Kraye and Oxon, as far as I could guess, to run me to ground; but I became gradually sure that there were three, not two, after me in the stands. Perhaps one of the cars was empty. But which? And it would be unlikely to have its ignition key in place.

Bit by bit I covered the whole enormous block. I didn't know what I was looking for, that was the trouble. It could have been anything from a plastic bomb downward, but if past form was anything to go by, it was something which could appear accidental. Bad luck. A jinx. Open, recognizable sabotage would be ruinous to the scheme.

Without a surveyor, I couldn't be certain that part of the steps would not collapse the following day under the weight of the crowd, but I could find no trace of any structural damage at all, and there hadn't been much time, only five or six hours since the day's meeting ended.

There were no large quantities of food in the kitchen: the caterers appeared to have removed what had been left over ready to bring fresh the next day. A large double-doored refrigerator was securely locked. I discounted the possibility that Kraye could have thought of large-scale food poisoning.

All the fire extinguishers seemed to be in their places, and there were no smoldering cigarette ends near tins of paraffin. Nothing capable of spontaneous combustion. I suppose another fire, so soon after the stables, might have been too suspicious.

I went cautiously, carefully, every nerve-racking step of the way, peering round corners, easing through doors, fearing that at any moment one of them would pounce on me from behind.

They knew I was still there, because everywhere they went they turned on lights, and everywhere I went I turned them off. Opening a door from a lighted room onto a dark passage made one far too easy to spot; I turned off the lights before I opened any door. There had been three lights in the passage itself, but I had broken them early on with a broom from the kitchen.

Once when I was in the passage, creeping from the men's lavatories to the Tattersalls bar, Kraye himself appeared at the far end, the members' end, and began walking my way. He came in through the faint glow from the car's headlights, and he hadn't seen me. One stride took me across the passage, one jump and a wriggle into the only cover available, the heap of equipment the bookmakers had left there out of the weather, overnight.

These were only their metal stands, their folded umbrellas, the boxes and stools they stood on: a thin, spiky, precarious heap. I crouched down beside them, praying I wouldn't dislodge anything.

Kraye's footsteps scraped hollowly as he trod toward my ineffective hiding place. He stopped twice, opening doors and looking into the storerooms which were in places built back under the steps of the stands. They were mostly empty or nearly so, and offered nothing to me. They were too small, and all dead ends: if I were found in one of them I couldn't get out.

The door of the bar I had been making for suddenly opened, spilling bright light into the passage between me and Kraye.

Oxon's voice said anxiously, "He can't have got away."

"Of course not, you fool," said Kraye furiously. "But if you'd had the sense to bring your keys over with you we'd have had him long ago." Their voices echoed up and down the passage.

"It was your idea to leave so much unlocked. I could go back and fetch them."

"He'd have too much chance of giving us the slip. But we're not getting anywhere with all this dodging about. We'll start methodically from this end and move down."

"We did that to start with," complained Oxon. "And we missed him. Let me go back for the keys. Then as you said before, we can lock all the doors behind us and stop him doubling back."

"No," said Kraye decisively. "There aren't enough of us. You stay here. We'll go back to the weighing room and start all together."

They began to walk away. The bar door was still open, lighting up the passage, which I didn't like. If anyone came in from the other end, he would see me for sure.

I shifted my position to crawl away along the wall for better concealment, and one of the bookmakers' metal tripods slid down and clattered off the side of the pile with an echoing noise like a dozen demented machine guns.

There were shouts from the two men down the passage.

"There he is."

"Get him."

I stood up and ran.

The nearest opening in the wall was a staircase up to a suite of rooms above the changing room and members' dining room. I hesitated a fraction of a second and then passed it. Up those steps were the executive's rooms and offices. I didn't know my way round up them, but Oxon did. He had a big enough advantage already in his knowledge of the building without my giving him a bonus.

I ran on, past the gents' cloaks, and finally in through the last possible door, that of a long, bare, dirty room smelling of beer. It was a sort of extra, subsidiary bar, and all it now contained was a bare counter backed by empty shelves. I nearly fell over a bucket full of crinkled metal bottle tops which someone had carelessly left in my way, and then wasted precious seconds to dart back to put the bucket just inside the door I'd come in by.

Kraye and Oxon were running. I snapped off the lights, and with no time to get clear through the far door out into the paddock, where anyway I would be lit by car headlights, I scrambled down behind the bar counter.

The door jerked open. There was a clatter of the bucket and a yell, and the sound of someone falling. Then the light snapped on again, showing me just how tiny my hiding place really was, and two bottle tops rolled across the floor into my sight.

"For God's sake," yelled Kraye in anger. "You clumsy, stupid fool. Get up. Get up." He charged down the room to the far door, the board floor bouncing slightly under his weight. From the clanking, cursing, and clattering of bottle tops I imagined that Oxon was extricating himself from the bucket and following. If it hadn't been so dangerous it would have been funny.

Kraye yanked the outside door open, stepped outside and yelled across to the stationary car to ask where I had gone. I felt rather than saw Oxon run down the room to join him. I crawled round the end of the counter, sprinted for the door I had come in by, flipped off the light again, slammed the door, and ran back up the passage. There was a roar from Kraye as he fumbled back into the darkened room; and long before they had emerged into the passage again, kicking bottle tops in all directions, I was safe in the opening of a little offshoot lobby to the kitchen.

The kitchens were safest for me because there were so many good hiding places and so many exits, but it wasn't much good staying there because I had searched them already.

I was fast running out of places to look. The boiler room had given me an anxious two minutes as its only secondary exit was into a dead-end storeroom containing, as far as I could see, nothing but vast oil tanks with pipes and gauges. They were hard against the walls: nowhere to hide. The boiler itself roared, keeping the central heating going all through the night.

The weighing room was even worse, because it was big and entirely without cover. It contained nothing it shouldn't have, just tables, chairs, notices pinned on the walls, and the weighing machine itself. Beyond, in the changing room, there were rows of pegs with saddles on, the warm, banked-up coke stove in the corner, and a big wicker basket full of helmets, boots, weight cloths and other equipment left by the valets overnight. A dirty cup and saucer. A copy of *Playboy*. Several raincoats. Racing colors on pegs. A row of washed breeches hanging up to dry. It was the most occupied-looking part of the stands, the place I felt most at home in and where I wanted to go to ground, like an ostrich in familiar sand. But on the far side of the changing room lay only the washroom, another dead end.

Opening out of the weighing room on the opposite side of the changing room was the Stewards' room, where in the past like all jockeys I'd been involved in cases of objections-to-the-winner. It was a bare room: large table, chairs round it, sporting pictures, small threadbare carpet. A few of the Stewards' personal possessions lay scattered about, but there was no concealment.

A few doors here and there were locked, in spite of Oxon's having left the keys in his flat. As usual I had the bunch of lock pickers in my pocket; and with shortened breath I spent several sticky minutes letting myself into one well-secured room off the members' bar. It proved to be the liquor store: crates of spirits, champagne, wine and beer. Beer from floor to ceiling, and a porter's trolley to transport it. It was a temptation to lock myself in there, and wait for the caterers to rescue me in the morning. This was one door that Oxon would not expect to find me on the far side of.

In the liquor store I might be safe. On the other hand, if I were safe the racecourse might not be. Reluctantly I left again; but I didn't waste time locking up. With the pursuit out of sight, I risked a look upstairs. It was warm and quiet, and all the lights were on. I left them on, figuring that if the watchers in the car saw them go out they would know too accurately where I was.

Nothing seemed to be wrong. On one side of a central lobby there was the big room where the executives held their meetings and ate their lunch. On the other side there was a sort of drawing room furnished with light armchairs, with two cloakrooms leading off it at the back. At the front, through double glass doors, it led out into a box high up on the stands. The private box for directors and distinguished guests, and with a superb view over the whole course.

I didn't go out there. Sabotage in the royal box wouldn't stop a race meeting to which royalty weren't going anyway. And besides, whoever was in my car would see me opening the door.

Retreating, I went back, right through the dining-board room and out into the service room on the far side. There I found a storeroom with plates, glass and cutlery, and in the storeroom also a second exit. A small service lift down to the kitchens. It worked with ropes, like the one in the office on Cromwell Road . . . like the office lift *had* worked, before the bomb.

Kraye and Oxon were down in the kitchen. Their angry voices floated up the shaft, mingled with a softer murmuring voice which seemed to be arguing with them. Since for once I knew where they all were, I returned with some boldness to the ground again. But I was worried. There seemed to be nothing at all going wrong in the main building. If they were organizing yet more damage somewhere out on the course itself, I didn't see how I could stop it.

While I was still dithering rather aimlessly along the passage the kitchen door opened, the light flooded on, and I could hear Kraye still talking. I dived yet again for the nearest door and put it between myself and them.

I was, I discovered, in the ladies' room, where I hadn't been before, and there was no second way out. Only a double row of cubicles, all with doors open, a range of washbasins, mirrors on the walls with a wide shelf beneath them, a few chairs, and a counter like that in the bar. Behind the counter there was a rail with coat hangers.

There were heavy steps in the passage outside. I slid instantly behind and under the counter and pressed myself into a corner. The door opened.

"He won't be in here," said Kraye. "The light's still on."

"I looked in here not five minutes ago, anyway," agreed Oxon.

The door closed behind them and their footsteps went away. I began to breathe again and my thudding heart slowed down. But for a couple of seconds only. Across the room, someone coughed.

I froze. I couldn't believe it. The room had been empty when I came in, I was certain. And neither Kraye nor Oxon had stayed . . . I stretched my ears, tense, horrified.

Another cough. A soft, single cough.

Try as I could I could hear nothing else. No breathing. No rustle of clothing, no movement. It didn't make sense. If someone in the room knew I was behind the counter, why didn't they do something about it? If they didn't know, why were they so unnaturally quiet?

In the end, taking a conscious grip on my nerves, I slowly stood up.

The room was empty.

Almost immediately there was another cough. Now that my ears were no longer obstructed by the counter, I got a clearer idea of its direction. I swung toward it. There was no one there.

I walked across the room and stared down at the washbasin. Water was trickling from one of the taps. Even while I looked at it the tap coughed. Almost laughing with relief I stretched out my hand and turned it off.

The metal was very hot. Surprised, I turned the water on again. It came spluttering out of the tap, full of air bubbles and very hot indeed. Steaming. How stupid, I thought, turning it off again, to have the water so hot at this time of night . . .

Christ, I thought. The boiler.

CHAPTER 16

KRAYE AND OXON'S so-called methodical end-to-end search, which had just failed to find me in the ladies', was proceeding from the members' end of the stands toward Tattersalls. The boiler, like myself, was in the part they had already put behind them. I switched out the ladies'-room lights, carefully eased into the passage, and via the kitchen, the members' dining room, the gentlemen's cloaks and another short strip of passage returned to the boiler room.

Although there was no door through, I knew that on the far side of the inside wall lay to the left the weighing room and to the right the changing room, with the dividing wall between. From both those rooms, when it was quiet, as it was that night, one could quite clearly hear the boiler's muffled roar.

The light that I had switched off was on again in the boiler room. I looked round. It all looked as normal as it had before, except . . . except that away to the right there was a very small pool of water on the floor.

Boilers. We had had a lesson on them at school. Sixteen or seventeen years ago, I thought hopelessly. But I remembered very well the way the master had begun the lesson.

"The first thing to learn about boilers," he said, "is that they explode."

He was an excellent teacher: the whole class of forty boys listened from then on with avid interest. But since then the only acquaintance I'd had with boilers were down in the basement of the flats, where I sometimes drank a cup of orange tea with the caretaker. A tough ex–naval stoker, he was, and a confirmed student of racing form. Mostly we'd talked about horses, but sometimes about his job. There were strict regulations for boilers, he'd said, and regular official inspections every three months, and he was glad of it, working alongside them every day.

The first thing to learn about boilers is that they explode.

It's no good saying I wasn't frightened, because I was. If the boiler burst it wasn't simply going to make large new entrances into the weighing room and changing room, it was going to fill every cranny near it with scalding tornadoes of steam. Not a death I looked on with much favor.

I stood with my back against the door and tried desperately to remember that long-ago lesson, and to work out what was going wrong.

It was a big steam boiler. An enormous cylinder nine feet high and five feet in diameter. Thick steel, with dark red antirust paint peeling off. Fired at the bottom not by coke, which it had been built for, but by the more modern roaring jet of burning oil. If I opened the fire door I would feel the blast of its tremendous heat.

The body of the cylinder would be filled almost to the top with water. The flame boiled the water. The resulting steam went out of the top under its own fierce pressure in a pipe which—I followed it with my eye—led into a large yellow-painted round-ended cylinder slung horizontally near the ceiling. This tank looked rather like a zeppelin. It was, if I remembered right, a calorifier. Inside it, the steampipe ran in a spiral, like an immobile spring. The tank itself was supplied from the mains with the water which was to be heated, the water going to the central heating radiators, and to the hot taps in the kitchen, the cloakrooms and the jockeys' washrooms. The scorching heat from the spiral steampipe instantly passed into the water touching it, so that the cold water entering the calorifier was made very hot in the short time before it left at the other end.

The steam, however, losing its heat in the process, gradually condensed back into water. A pipe led down the wall from the calorifier into a much smaller tank, an ordinary square one, standing on the floor. From the bottom of this, yet another pipe tracked right back across the room and up near the boiler itself to a bulbous metal contraption just higher than my head. An electric pump. It finished the circuit by pumping the condensed water up from the tank on the floor and returning it to the boiler, to be boiled, steamed and condensed all over again. Round and round, continuously.

So far, so good. But if you interfered with the circuit so that the water didn't get back into the boiler, and at the same time kept the heat full on at the bottom, all the water inside the cylinder gradually turned to steam. Steam, which was strong enough to drive a liner, or pull a twelve-coach train, but could in this case only get out at all through a narrow, closely spiraled pipe.

This type of boiler, built not for driving an engine but only for heating water, wasn't constructed to withstand enormous pressures. It was a toss-up, I thought, whether when all the water had gone the fast-expanding air and steam found a weak spot to break out of before the flames burned through the bottom. In either case, the boiler would blow up.

On the outside of the boiler there was a water gauge, a foot-long vertical glass tube held in brackets. The level of water in the tube indicated the level of water in the boiler. Near the top of the gauge a black line showed what the water level ought to be. Two thirds of the way down a broad red line obviously acted as a warning. The water in the gauge was higher than the red line by half an inch.

To put it mildly, I was relieved. The boiler wasn't bulging. The explosion lay in the future, which gave me more time to work out how to prevent it. As long as it would take Oxon and Kraye to decide on a repeat search, perhaps.

I could simply have turned out the flame, but Kraye and Oxon would notice that the noise had stopped, and merely light it again. Nothing would have been gained. On the other hand, I was sure that the flame was higher than it should have been at night, because the water in the ladies' tap was nearly boiling.

Gingerly I turned the adjusting wheel on the oil line. Half a turn. A full turn. The roaring seemed just as loud. Another turn, and that time there was a definite change. Half a turn more. It was perceptibly quieter. Slowly I inched the wheel around more, until quite suddenly the roar turned to a murmur. Too far. Hastily I reversed. At the point where the murmur was again a roar, I left it.

I looked consideringly at the square tank of condensed water on the floor. It was this, overflowing, which was making the pool of water; and it was overflowing because the contents were not being pumped back into the boiler. If they've broken the pump, I thought despairingly, I'm done. I didn't know the first thing about electric pumps.

Another sentence from that faraway school lesson floated usefully through my mind. *For safety's sake, every boiler must have two sources of water.*

I chewed my lower lip, watching the water trickle down the side of the tank onto the floor. Even in the few minutes I had been there the pool had spread. One source of water was obviously knocked out. Where and what was the other?

There were dozens of pipes in the boiler room; not only oil pipes and water pipes, but all the electric cables were installed inside tubes as well. There were about six separate pipes with stopcocks on them. It seemed to me that all the water for the entire building came in through the boiler room.

Two pipes, apparently rising mains, led from the floor up the wall and into the calorifier. Both had stopcocks, which I tested. Both were safely open. There was no rising main leading directly into the boiler.

By sheer luck I was halfway round the huge cylinder looking for an inlet pipe when I saw the lever-type door handle move down. I leaped for the only vestige of cover, the space between the boiler and the wall. It was scorching hot there: pretty well unbearable.

Kraye had to raise his voice to make himself heard over the roaring flame. "You're sure it's still safe?"

"Yes, I told you, it won't blow up for three hours yet. At least three hours."

"The water's running out already," Kraye objected.

"There's a lot in there." Oxon's voice came nearer. I could feel my heart thumping and hear the pulse in my ears. "The level's not down to the caution mark on the gauge yet," he said. "It won't blow for a long time after it goes below that."

"We've got to find Halley," Kraye said. "Got to." If Oxon moved another step he would see me. "I'll work from this end; you start again from the other. Look in every cupboard. The little rat has gone to ground somewhere."

Oxon didn't answer audibly. I had a sudden glimpse of his sleeve as he turned, and I shrank back into my hiding place.

Because of the noise of the boiler I couldn't hear them go away through the door, but eventually I had to risk that they had. The heat where I stood was too appalling. Moving out into the ordinarily hot air in the middle of the room was like diving into a cold bath. And Oxon and Kraye had gone.

I slipped off my jacket and wiped the sweat off my face with my shirt-sleeves. Back to the problem: water supply.

The pump *looked* all right. There were no loose wires, and it had an undisturbed, slightly greasy, slightly dirty appearance. With luck, I thought, they hadn't damaged the pump, they'd blocked the pipe where it left the tank. I took off my tie and shirt as well, and put them with my jacket on the grimy floor.

The lid of the tank came off easily enough, and the water, when I tested it, proved to be no more than uncomfortably hot. I drank some in my cupped palm. The running and the heat had made me very thirsty, and although I would have preferred it iced, no water could have been purer, or more taste-less, though I was not inclined to be fussy on that point.

I stretched my arm down into the water, kneeling beside the tank. As it was only about two feet deep, I could touch the bottom quite easily, and al-most at once my searching fingers found and gripped a loose object. I pulled it out.

It was a fine mesh filter, which should no doubt have been in place over the opening of the outlet pipe.

Convinced now that the pipe was blocked from this end, I reached down again into the water. I found the edge of the outlet, and felt carefully into it. I could reach no obstruction. Bending over further, so that my shoulder was half in the water, I put two fingers as far as they would go into the outlet. I could feel nothing solid, but there did seem to be a piece of string. It was difficult to get it between two fingers firmly enough to pull as hard as was necessary, but gradually with a series of little jerks I managed to move the plug backward into the tank.

It came away finally so suddenly that I nearly overbalanced. There was a burp from the outer pipe of the tank and on the other side of the room a sharp click from the pump.

I lifted my hand out of the water to see what had blocked the pipe, and stared in amazement. It was a large mouse. I had been pulling its tail.

Accidental sabotage, I thought. The same old pattern. However unlikely it was that a mouse should dive into a tank, find the filter conveniently out of place, and get stuck just inside the outlet pipe, one would have a hard job proving that it was impossible.

I carefully put the sodden little body out of sight in the small gap between the tank and the wall. With relief I noticed that the water level was already going down slightly, which meant that the pump was working properly and the boiler would soon be more or less back to normal.

I splashed some more water out of the tank to make a larger pool should Kraye or Oxon glance in again, and replaced the lid. Putting on my shirt and jacket I followed with my eyes the various pipes in and out of the boiler. The lagged steam exit pipe to the calorifier. The vast chimney flue for the hot gases from the burning oil. There had to be another water inlet somewhere, partly for safety, partly to keep the steam circuit topped up.

I found it in the end running alongside and behind the inlet pipe from the pump. It was a gravity feed from a stepped series of three small unobtrusive tanks fixed high on the wall. Filters, I reckoned, so that the main's water didn't carry its mineral salts into the boiler and fur it up. The filter tanks were fed by a pipe, which branched off one of the rising mains and had its own stopcock.

Reaching up, I tried to turn it clockwise. It didn't move. The main's water was cut off. With satisfaction, I turned it on again.

Finally, with the boiler once more working exactly as it should, I took a look at the water gauge. The level had already risen to nearly halfway between the red and black marks. Hoping fervently Oxon wouldn't come back for another check on it, I went over to the door and switched off the light.

There was no one in the passage. I slipped through the door, and in the last three inches before shutting it behind me stretched my hand back and put the light on again. I didn't want Kraye knowing I'd been in there.

Keeping close to the wall I walked softly down the passage toward the

Tattersalls end. If I could get clear of the stands there were other buildings out that way to give cover. The barn, cloakrooms and tote buildings in the silver ring. Beyond these lay the finishing straight, the way down to the tan patch and the bisecting road. Along that, bungalows, people and telephones.

That was when my luck ran out.

CHAPTER 17

I WAS BARELY two steps past the door of the Tattersalls bar when it opened and the lights blazed out onto my tiptoeing figure. In the two seconds it took Oxon to realize what he was seeing I was six running paces down toward the way out.

His shouts echoed in the passage mingled with others further back, and I still thought that if Kraye too were behind me I might have a chance. But when I was within ten steps of the end another figure appeared there, hurrying, called by the noise.

I skidded nearly to a stop, sliding on one of the scattered bottle tops, and crashed through the only possible door, into the same empty bar as before. I raced across the board floor, kicking bottle tops in all directions, but I never got to the far door. It opened before I reached it, and that was the end.

Doria Kraye stood there, maliciously triumphant. She was dressed theatrically in white slender trousers and a shiny short white jacket. Her dark hair fell smoothly, her face was as flawlessly beautiful as ever, and she held rock-steady in one elegantly long-fingered hand the little .22 automatic I had last seen in a chocolate box at the bottom of her dressing case.

"The end of the line, buddy boy," she said. "You stay just where you are."

I hesitated on the brink of trying to rush her.

"Don't risk it," she said. "I'm a splendid shot. I wouldn't miss. Do you want a kneecap smashed?"

There was little I wanted less. I turned round slowly. There were three men coming forward into the long room. Kraye, Oxon and Ellis Bolt. All three of them looked as if they had long ago tired of the chase and were going to take it out on the quarry.

"Will you walk," said Doria behind me, "or be dragged?"

I shrugged. "Walk."

All the same, Kraye couldn't keep his hands off me. When, following Doria's instructions, I walked past him to go back out through the passage he caught hold of my jacket at the back of my neck and kicked my legs. I kicked back, which wasn't too sensible, as I presently ended up on the floor. There was nothing like little metal bottle tops for giving you a feeling of falling on little metal bottle tops, I thought, with apologies to Michael Flanders and Donald Swan.

"Get up," said Kraye. Doria stood beside him, pointing at me with the gun.

I did as he said.

"Right," said Doria. "Now, walk down the passage and go into the weighing room. And Howard, for God's sake wait till we get there, or we'll lose him again. Walk, buddy boy. Walk straight down the middle of the passage. If you try anything, I'll shoot you in the leg."

I saw no reason not to believe her. I walked down the center of the passage with her too close behind for escape, and with the two men bringing up the rear.

"Stop a minute," said Kraye, outside the boiler room.

I stopped. I didn't look round.

Kraye opened the door and looked inside. The light spilled out, adding to that already coming from the other open doors along the way.

"Well?" said Oxon.

"There's more water on the floor." He sounded pleased, and shut the door without going in for a further look. Not all of my luck had departed, it seemed.

"Move," he said. I obeyed.

The weighing room was as big and bare as ever. I stopped in the middle of it and turned round. The four of them stood in a row, looking at me, and I didn't at all like what I read in their faces.

"Go and sit there," said Doria, pointing.

I went on across the floor and sat where she said, on the chair of the weighing machine. The pointer immediately swung round the clock face to show my weight. Nine stone seven. It was, I was remotely interested to see, exactly ten pounds less than when I had last raced. Bullets would solve any jockey's weight problem, I thought.

The four of them came closer. It was some relief to find that Fred wasn't among them, but only some. Kraye was emitting the same livid fury as he had twelve days ago at Aynsford. And then, I had merely mildly insulted his wife.

"Hold his arms," he said to Oxon. Oxon was one of those thin wiry men of seemingly limitless strength. He came round behind me, clamped his fingers round my elbows and pulled them back. With concentration Kraye hit me several times in the face.

"Now," he said. "Where are they?"

"What?" I said indistinctly.

"The negatives."

"What negatives?"

He hit me again and hurt his own hand. Shaking it out and rubbing his knuckles, he said, "You know what negatives. The films you took of my papers."

"Oh, those."

"Those." He hit me again, but less hard.

"In the office," I mumbled.

He tried a slap to save his knuckles. "Office," I said.

He tried with his left hand, but it was clumsy. After that he sucked his knuckles and kept his hands to himself.

Bolt spoke for the first time, in his consciously beautiful voice. "Fred wouldn't have missed them, especially as there was no reason for them to be concealed. He's too thorough."

If Fred wouldn't have missed them, the bombs had been pure spite. I licked the inside of a split lip and thought about what I would like to do to Fred.

"Where in the office?" said Kraye.

"Desk."

"Hit him," said Kraye. "My hand hurts."

Bolt had a go, but it wasn't his sort of thing.

"Try with this," said Doria, offering Bolt the gun, but it was luckily so small he couldn't hold it effectively.

Oxon let go of my elbows, came round to the front, and looked at my face.

"If he's decided not to tell you, you won't get it out of him like that," he said.

"I told you," I said.

"Why not?" said Bolt.

"You're hurting yourselves more than him. And if you want my opinion, you won't get anything out of him at all."

"Don't be silly," said Doria scornfully. "He's so small."

Oxon laughed without mirth.

"If Fred said so, the negatives weren't at his office," asserted Bolt again. "Nor in his flat. And he didn't bring them with him. Or at least, they weren't in his luggage at the hotel."

I looked at him sideways, out of an eye which was beginning to swell. And if I hadn't been so quick to have him flung out of my hotel room, I thought sourly, he wouldn't have driven in through the racecourse gate at exactly the wrong moment. But I couldn't have foreseen it, and it was too late to help.

"They weren't in his car either," said Doria. "But this was." She put her hand into her shining white pocket and brought out my baby camera. Kraye took it from her, opened the case, and saw what was inside. The veins in his neck and temples became congested with blood. In a paroxysm of fury he threw the little black toy across the room so that it hit the wall with a disintegrating crash.

"Sixteen millimeter," he said savagely. "Fred must have missed them."

Bolt said obstinately, "Fred would find a needle in a haystack. And those films wouldn't have been hidden."

"He might have them in his pocket," suggested Doria.

"Take your coat off," Kraye said. "Stand up."

I stood up, and the base plate of the weighing machine wobbled under my feet. Oxon pulled my coat down over the back of my shoulders, gave a tug to get the sleeves off, and passed the jacket to Kraye. His own hand he thrust into my trouser pocket. In the right one, under my tie, he found the bunch of lock pickers.

"Sit down," he said. I did so, exploring with the back of my hand some of the damage to my face. It could have been worse, I thought resignedly, much worse. I would be lucky if that were all.

"What are those?" said Doria curiously, taking the jingling collection from Oxon.

Kraye snatched them from her and slung them after the camera. "Skeleton keys," he said furiously. "What he used to unlock my cases."

"I don't see how he could," said Doria, "with that . . . that . . . *claw*." She looked down where it lay on my lap.

A nice line in taunts, I thought, but a week too late. Thanks to Miss Martin, I was at least learning to live with the claw. I left it where it was.

"Doria," said Bolt calmly, "would you be kind enough to go over to the flat and wait for Fred to ring? He may already have found what we want at Aynsford."

I turned my head and found him looking straight at me, assessingly.

There was a detachment in the eyes, an unmoved quality in the rounded features; and I began to wonder whether his stolid coolness might not in the end prove even more difficult to deal with than Kraye's rage.

"Aynsford," I repeated thickly. I looked at my watch. If Fred had really taken his bombs to Aynsford, he should by now be safely in the bag. One down, four to go. Five of them altogether, not four. I hadn't thought of Doria being an active equal colleague of the others. My mistake.

"I don't want to," said Doria, staying put.

Bolt shrugged. "It doesn't matter. I see that the negatives aren't at Aynsford, because the thought of Fred looking for them there doesn't worry Halley one little bit."

The thought of what Fred might be doing at Aynsford or to Charles himself didn't worry any of them either. But more than that I didn't like the way Bolt was reasoning. In the circumstances, a clear-thinking opponent was something I could well have done without.

"We must have them," said Kraye intensely. "We must. Or be certain beyond doubt that they were destroyed." To Oxon he said, "Hold his arms again."

"No," I said, shrinking back.

"Ah, that's better. Well?"

"They were in the office." My mouth felt stiff.

"Where?"

"In Mr. Radnor's desk, I think."

He stared at me, eyes narrowed, anger half under control, weighing up whether I were telling the truth or not. He certainly couldn't go to the office and make sure.

"Were," said Bolt suddenly.

"What?" asked Kraye, impatiently.

"Were," said Bolt. "Halley said were. The negatives *were* in the office. Now that's very interesting indeed, don't you think?"

Oxon said, "I don't see why."

Bolt came close to me and peered into my face. I didn't meet his eyes, and anything he could read from my bruised features he was welcome to.

"I think he knows about the bombs," he said finally.

"How?" said Doria.

"I should think he was told at the hotel. People in London must have been trying to contact him. Yes, I think we can take it for granted he knows about the bombs."

"What difference does that make?" said Oxon.

Kraye knew. "It means he thinks he is safe saying the negatives were in the office, because we can't prove they weren't."

"They were," I insisted, showing anxiety.

Bolt pursed his full moist lips. "Just how clever is Halley?" he said.

"He was a jockey," said Oxon flatly, as if that automatically meant an I.Q. of 70.

Bolt said, "But they took him on at Hunt Radnor's."

"I told you before," said Oxon patiently, "I asked various people about that. Radnor took him on as an advisor, but never gave him anything special to do, and if that doesn't show that he wasn't capable of much, I don't know what does. Everyone knows that his job is only a face-saver. It sounds all right, but it means nothing really. Jobs are quite often given in that way to top jockeys when they retire. No one expects them to *do* much, it's just their name that's useful for a while. When their news value has gone, they get the sack."

This all-too-true summing up of affairs depressed me almost as deeply as my immediate prospects.

"Howard?" said Bolt.

"I don't know," said Kraye slowly. "He doesn't strike me as being in the least clever. Very much the opposite. I agree he did take those photographs, but I think you are quite right in believing he doesn't know why we want them destroyed."

That, too, was shatteringly correct. As far as I had been able to see, the photographs proved nothing conclusively except that Kraye had been buying Seabury shares under various names with Bolt's help. Kraye and Bolt could not be prosecuted for that. Moreover the whole of Seabury executives had seen the photographs at the meeting that morning, so their contents were no secret.

"Doria?" Bolt said.

"He's a slimy, spying little creep, but if he was clever he wouldn't be sitting where he is."

You couldn't argue with that, either. It had been fairly certain all along that Kraye was getting help from somebody working at Seabury, but even after knowing about clerk of the course Brinton's unwilling collaboration at Dunstable, I had gone on assuming that the helper at Seabury was one of the laborers. I hadn't given more than a second's flicker of thought to Oxon, because it didn't seem reasonable that it should be him. In destroying the racecourse he was working himself out of a job, and good jobs for forty-year-old ex–army captains weren't plentiful enough to be lost lightly. As he certainly wasn't mentally affected like Brinton, he wasn't being blackmailed into doing it against his will. I had thought him silly and self-important, but not a rogue. As Doria said, had I been clever enough to suspect him, I wouldn't be sitting where I was.

Bolt went on discussing me as if I weren't there, and as if the decision they would come to would have ordinary everyday consequences.

He said, "You may all be right, but I don't think so, because since Halley has been on the scene everything's gone wrong. It was he who persuaded Hagbourne to get the course put right, and he who found the mirror as soon as it was up. I took him without question for what he said he was when he came to see me—a shop assistant. You two took him for a wretched little hanger-on of no account. All that, together with the fact that he opened your locked cases and took good clear photographs on a miniature camera, adds up to just one thing to me. Professionalism. Even the way he sits there saying nothing is professional. Amateurs call you names and try to impress you with how much they know. All he has said is that the negatives were in the office. I consider we ought to forget every previous impression we have of him and think of him only as coming from Hunt Radnor."

They thought about this for five seconds. Then Kraye said, "We'll have to make sure about the negatives."

Bolt nodded. If reason hadn't told me what Kraye meant, his wife's smile would have. My skin crawled.

"How?" she said interestedly.

Kraye inspected his grazed knuckles. "You won't beat it out of him," said Oxon. "Not like that. You haven't a hope."

"Why not?" said Bolt.

Instead of replying, Oxon turned to me. "How many races did you ride with broken bones?"

I didn't answer. I couldn't remember anyway.

"That's ridiculous," said Doria scornfully. "How could he?"

"A lot of them do," said Oxon. "And I'm sure he was no exception."

"Nonsense," said Kraye.

Oxon shook his head. "Collarbones, ribs, forearms, they'll ride with cracks in any of those if they can keep the owners and trainers from finding out."

Why couldn't he shut up, I thought savagely. He was making things much worse; as if they weren't appalling enough already.

"You mean," said Doria with sickening pleasure, "that he can stand a great deal?"

"No," I said. "No." It sounded like the plea it was. "You can only ride with cracked bones if they don't hurt."

"They must hurt," said Bolt reasonably.

"No," I said. "Not always." It was true, but they didn't believe it.

"The negatives were in the office," I said despairingly. "In the office."

"He's scared," said Doria delightedly. And that too was true.

It struck a chord with Kraye. He remembered Aynsford. "We know where he's most easily hurt," he said. "That hand."

"No," I said in real horror.

They all smiled.

My whole body flushed with uncontrollable fear. Racing injuries were one thing: they were quick, one didn't expect them, and they were part of the job.

To sit and wait and know that a part of one's self which had already proved a burden was about to be hurt as much as ever was quite something else. Instinctively I put my arm up across my face to hide from them that I was afraid, but it must have been obvious.

Kraye laughed insultingly. "So there's your brave clever Mr. Halley for you. It won't take much to get the truth."

"What a pity," said Doria.

THEY LEFT HER standing in front of me holding the little pistol in an unswerving pink-nailed hand while they went out and rummaged for what they needed. I judged the distance to the door, which was all of thirty feet, and wondered whether the chance of a bullet on the way wasn't preferable to what was going to happen if I stayed where I was.

Doria watched my indecision with amusement.

"Just try it, buddy boy. Just try it."

I had read that to shoot accurately with an automatic pistol took a great deal of skill and practice. It was possible that all Doria had wanted was the power feeling of owning a gun and that she couldn't aim it. On the other hand she was holding it high and with a nearly straight arm, close to where she could see along the sights. On balance, I thought her claim to be a splendid shot had too much probability to be risked.

It was a pity Doria had such a vicious soul inside her beautiful body. She looked gay and dashing in her white Courréges clothes, smiling a smile which seemed warm and friendly and was as safe as the yawn of a python. She was the perfect mate for Kraye, I thought. Fourth, fifth, sixth time lucky, he'd found a complete complement to himself. If Kraye could do it, perhaps one day I would too . . . but I didn't know if I would even see tomorrow.

I put the back of my hand up over my eyes. My whole face hurt, swollen and stiff, and I was developing a headache. I decided that if I ever got out of this I wouldn't try any more detecting. I had made a proper mess of it.

The men came back, Oxon from the Stewards' room lugging a wooden spoked-backed chair with arms, Kraye and Bolt from the changing room with the yard-long poker from the stove and the rope the wet breeches had been hung on to dry. There were still a couple of pegs clinging to it.

Oxon put the chair down a yard or two away and Doria waved the gun a fraction to indicate I should sit in it. I didn't move.

"God," she said disappointedly, "you really are a little worm, just like at Aynsford. Scared to a standstill."

"He isn't a shop assistant," said Bolt sharply. "And don't forget it."

I didn't look at him. But for him and his rejection of Charles's usefully feeble Halley image, I might not have been faced with quite the present situation.

Oxon punched me on the shoulder. "Move," he said.

I stood up wearily and stepped off the weighing machine. They stood close round me. Kraye thrust out a hand, twisted it into my shirt, and pushed me into the chair. He, Bolt and Oxon had a fine old time tying my arms and legs to the equivalent wooden ones with the washing line. Doria watched, fascinated.

I remembered her rather unusual pleasures.

"Like to change places?" I said tiredly.

It didn't make her angry. She smiled slowly, put her gun in a pocket, and leaned down and kissed me long and hard on the mouth. I loathed it. When at length she straightened up she had a smear of my blood on her lip. She wiped it off onto her hand, and thoughtfully licked it. She looked misty-eyed and languorous, as if she had had a profound sexual experience. It made me want to vomit.

"Now," said Kraye. "Where are they?" He didn't seem to mind his wife kissing me. He understood her, of course.

I looked at the way they had tied the rope tightly round and round my left forearm, leaving the wrist bare, palm downward. A hand, I thought. What good, anyway, was a hand that didn't work?

I looked at their faces, one by one. Doria, rapt. Oxon, faintly surprised. Kraye confident, flexing his muscles. And Bolt, calculating and suspicious. None of them within a mile of relenting.

"Where are they?" Kraye repeated, lifting his arm.

"In the office," I said helplessly.

He hit my wrist with the poker. I'd hoped he might at least try to be subtle, but instead he used all his strength and with that one first blow smashed the whole shooting match to smithereens. The poker broke through the skin. The bones cracked audibly like sticks.

I didn't scream only because I couldn't get enough breath to do it. Before that moment I would have said I knew everything there was to know about pain, but it seems one can always learn. Behind my shut eyes the world turned yellow and gray, like sun shining through mist, and every inch of my skin began to sweat. There had never been anything like it. It was too much, too much. And I couldn't manage any more.

"Where are they?" said Kraye again.

"Don't," I said. "Don't do it." I could hardly speak.

Doria sighed deeply.

I opened my eyes a slit, my head lolling weakly back, too heavy to hold up. Kraye was smiling, pleased with his efforts. Oxon looked sick.

"Well?" said Kraye.

I swallowed, hesitating still.

He put the tip of the poker on my shattered bleeding wrist and gave a violent jerk. Among other things it felt like a fizzing electric shock, up my arm into my head and down to my toes. Sweat started sticking my shirt to my chest and my trousers to my legs.

"Don't," I said. "Don't." It was a croak, a capitulation, a prayer.

"Come on, then," said Kraye, and jolted the poker again.

I told them. I told them where to go.

CHAPTER 18

THEY DECIDED IT should be Bolt who went to fetch the negatives.

"What is this place?" he said. He hadn't recognized the address.

"The home of . . . a . . . girlfriend."

He dispassionately watched the sweat run in trickles down my face. My mouth was dry. I was very thirsty.

"Say . . . I sent you," I said, between jagged breaths. "I . . . asked her . . . to keep them safe. . . . They . . . are with . . . several other things. . . . The package . . . you want . . . has a name on it . . . a make of film . . . Jigoro . . . Kano."

"Jigoro Kano. Right," Bolt said briskly.

"Give me . . . ," I said, "some morphine."

Bolt laughed. "After all the trouble you've caused us? Even if I had any, I wouldn't. You can sit there and sweat it out."

I moaned. Bolt smiled in satisfaction and turned away.

"I'll ring you as soon as I have the negatives," he said to Kraye. "Then we can decide what to do with Halley. I'll give it some thought on the way up." From his tone he might have been discussing the disposal of a block of worthless stocks.

"Good," said Kraye. "We'll wait for your call over in the flat."

They began to walk toward the door. Oxon and Doria hung back, Doria because she couldn't tear her fascinated, dilated eyes away from watching me, and Oxon for more practical reasons.

"Are you just going to leave him here?" he asked in surprise.

"Yes. Why not?" said Kraye. "Come on, Doria darling. The best is over." Unwillingly she followed him, and Oxon also.

"Some water," I said. "Please."

"No," said Kraye.

They filed past him out of the door. Just before he shut it he gave me a last look compounded of triumph, contempt and satisfied cruelty. Then he switched off all the lights and went away.

I heard the sound of a car starting up and driving off. Bolt was on his way. Outside the windows the night was black. Darkness folded round me like a fourth dimension. As the silence deepened I listened to the low hum of the boiler roaring safely on the far side of the wall. At least, I thought, I don't have to worry about that as well. Small, small consolation.

The back of the chair came only as high as my shoulders and gave no support to my head. I felt deathly tired. I couldn't bear to move: every muscle in my body seemed to have a private line direct to my left wrist, and merely flexing my right foot had me panting. I wanted to lie down flat. I wanted a long cold drink. I wanted to faint. I went on sitting in the chair, wide awake, with a head that ached and weighed a ton, and an arm which wasn't worth the trouble.

I thought about Bolt going to Zanna Martin's front door, and finding that his own secretary had been helping me. I wondered for the hundredth time what he would do about that: whether he would harm her. Poor Miss Martin, whom life had already hurt too much.

Not only her, I thought. In the same file was the letter Mervyn Brinton had written out for me. If Bolt should see that, Mervyn Brinton would be needing a bodyguard for life.

I thought about the people who had borne the beatings and brutalities of the Nazis and of the Japanese and had often died without betraying their secrets. I thought about the atrocities still going on throughout the world, and the ease with which man could break man. In Algeria, they said, unbelievable things had been done. Behind the Iron Curtain, brainwashing wasn't all. In African jails, who knew?

Too young for World War Two, safe in a tolerant society, I had no thought that I should ever come to such a test. To suffer or to talk. The dilemma that stretched back to antiquity. Thanks to Kraye, I now knew what it was like at first hand. Thanks to Kraye, I didn't understand how anyone could keep silent unto death.

I thought: I wanted to ride round Seabury Racecourse again, and to go back into the weighing room, and to sit on the scales; and I've done all those things.

I thought: a fortnight ago I couldn't let go of the past. I was clinging to too many ruins, the ruins of my marriage and my racing career and my useless hand. They were gone for good now, all of them. There was nothing left to cling to. And every tangible memory of my life had blown away with a plastic bomb. I was rootless and homeless: and liberated.

What I refused to think about was what Kraye might still do during the next few hours.

BOLT HAD BEEN gone for a good long time when at last Kraye came back. It had seemed half eternity to me, but even so I was in no hurry for it to end.

Kraye put the lights on. He and Doria stood just inside the doorway, staring across at me.

"You're sure there's time?" said Doria.

Kraye nodded, looking at his watch. "If we're quick."

"Don't you think we ought to wait until Ellis rings?" she said. "He might have thought of something better."

"He's late already," said Kraye impatiently. They had clearly been arguing for some time. "He should have rung by now. If we're going to do this, we can't wait any longer."

"All right," she shrugged. "I'll go and take a look."

"Be careful. Don't go in."

"No," she said. "Don't fuss."

They both came over to where I sat. Doria looked at me with interest, and liked what she saw.

"He looks ghastly, doesn't he? Serves him right."

"Are you human?" I said.

A flicker of awareness crossed her lovely face, as if deep down she did indeed know that everything she had enjoyed that night was sinful and obscene, but she was too thoroughly addicted to turn back. "Shall I help you?" she said to Kraye, not answering me.

"No. I can manage. He's not very heavy."

She watched me with a smile while her husband gripped the back of the chair I was sitting in and began to tug it across the floor toward the wall. The jerks were almost past bearing. I grew dizzy with the effort of not yelling my head off. There was no one close enough to hear me if I did. Not the few overnight stable lads fast asleep three hundred yards away. Only the Krayes, who would find it sweet.

Doria licked her lips, as if at a feast.

"Go on," said Kraye. "Hurry."

"Oh, all right," she agreed crossly, and went out through the door into the passage.

Kraye finished pulling me across the room, turned the chair round so that I was facing the wall with my knees nearly touching it and stood back, breathing deeply from the exertion.

On the other side of the wall the boiler gently roared. One could hear it more clearly at such close quarters. I knew I had no crashing explosion, no flying bricks, no killing steam to worry about. But the sands were running out fast, all the same.

Doria came back and said in a puzzled voice, "I thought you said there would be water all down the passage."

"That's right."

"Well, there isn't. Not a drop. I looked into the boiler room and it's as dry as a bone."

"It can't be. It's nearly three hours since it started overflowing. Oxon warned us it must be nearly ready to blow. You must be wrong."

"I'm not," she insisted. "The whole thing looks perfectly normal to me."

"It can't be." Kraye's voice was sharp. He went off in a hurry to see for himself, and came back even faster.

"You're right. I'll go and get Oxon. I don't know how the confounded thing works." He went straight on out of the main door, and I heard his foot-steps running. There was no urgency except his own anger. I shivered.

Doria wasn't certain enough of the boiler's safety to spend any time near me, which was about the first really good thing which had happened the whole night. Nor did she find the back of my head worth speaking to: she liked to see her worms squirm. Perhaps she had even lost her appetite, now things had gone wrong. She waited uneasily near the door for Kraye to come back, fiddling with the catch.

Oxon came with him, and they were both running. They charged across the weighing room and out into the passage.

I hadn't much left anyway, I thought. A few tatters of pride, perhaps. Time to nail them to the mast.

The two men walked softly into the room and down to where I sat. Kraye grasped the chair and swung it violently round. The weighing room was quiet, undisturbed. There was only blackness through the window. So that was that.

I looked at Kraye's face, and wished on the whole that I hadn't. It was white and rigid with fury. His eyes were two black pits.

Oxon held the mouse in his hand. "It must have been Halley," he said, as if he'd said it before. "There's no one else."

Kraye put his right hand down on my left, and systematically began to take his revenge. After three long minutes I passed out.

I CLUNG TO the dark, trying to hug it round me like a blanket, and it ob-stinately got thinner and thinner, lighter and lighter, noisier and noisier, more and more painful, until I could no longer deny that I was back in the world.

My eyes unstuck themselves against my will.

The weighing room was full of people. People in dark uniforms. Police-men. Policemen coming through every door. Bright yellow lights at long last shining outside the window. Policemen carefully cutting the rope away from my leaden limbs.

Kraye and Doria and Oxon looked smaller, surrounded by the dark blue men. Doria in her brave white suit instinctively and unsuccessfully tried to flirt with her captors. Oxon, disconcerted to his roots, faced the facts of life for the first time.

Kraye's fury wasn't spent. His eyes stared in hatred across the room.

He shouted, struggling in strong restraining arms, "Where did you send him? Bolt. Where did you send him?"

"Ah, Mr. Potter," I said into a sudden oasis of silence. "Mr. Wilbur Pot-ter. Find out. But not from me."

CHAPTER 19

OF COURSE I ended up where I had begun, flat on my back in a hospital. But not for so long, that time. I had a pleasant sunny room with a distant view of the sea, some exceedingly pretty nurses and a whole stream of visitors. Chico came first, as soon as they would let him, on the Sunday afternoon.

He grinned down at me.

"You look bloody awful."

"Thanks very much."

"Two black eyes, a scabby lip, a purple-and-yellow complexion and a three-day beard. Glamorous."

"It sounds it."

"Do you want to look?" he asked, picking up a hand mirror from a chest of drawers.

I took the mirror and looked. He hadn't exaggerated. I would have faded into the background in a horror movie.

Sighing, I said, "X certificate, definitely."

He laughed, and put the mirror back. His own face still bore the marks of battle. The eyebrow was healing, but the bruise showed dark right down his cheek.

"This is a better room than you had in London," he remarked, strolling over to the window. "And it smells OK. For a hospital, that is."

"Pack in the small talk and tell me what happened," I said.

"They told me not to tire you."

"Don't be an ass."

"Well, all right. You're a bloody rollicking nit in many ways, aren't you?"

"It depends how you look at it," I agreed peaceably.

"Oh sure, sure."

"Chico, give," I pleaded. "Come on."

"Well, there I was harmlessly snoozing away in Radnor's armchair with the telephone on one side and some rather good chicken sandwiches on the other, dreaming about a willing blonde and having a ball, when the front doorbell rang." He grinned. "I got up, stretched and went to answer it. I thought it might be you, come back after all and with nowhere to sleep. I knew it wouldn't be Radnor, unless he'd forgotten his key. And who else would be knocking on his door at two o'clock in the morning? But there was this fat geezer standing on the doorstep in his city pinstripes, saying you'd sent him. 'Come in, then,' I said, yawning my head off. He came in, and I showed him into Radnor's sort of study place, where I'd been sitting.

" 'Sid sent you?' I asked him. 'What for?' He said he understood your girl-friend lived here. God, mate, don't ever try snapping your mouth shut at the top of a yawn. I nearly dislocated my jaw. Could he see her, he said. Sorry it was so late, but it was extremely important.

" 'She isn't here,' I said. 'She's gone away for a few days. Can I help you?'

" 'Who are you?' he said, looking me up and down.

"I said I was her brother. He took a sharpish look at the sandwiches and the book I'd been reading, which had fallen on the floor, and he could see I'd been asleep, so he seemed to think everything was OK, and he said, 'Sid asked me to fetch something she is keeping for him. Do you think you could help me find it?'

" 'Sure,' I said. 'What is it?'

"He hesitated a bit but he could see that it would look too weird if he refused to tell me, so he said, 'It's a packet of negatives. Sid said your sister had several things of his, but the packet I want has a name on it, a make of films. Jigoro Kano.'

" 'Oh?' I said innocently. 'Sid sent you for a packet marked Jigoro Kano?'

" 'That's right,' he said, looking round the room. 'Would it be in here?'

" 'It certainly would,' I said."

Chico stopped, came over beside the bed, and sat on the edge of it, by my right toe.

"How come you know about Jigoro Kano?" he said seriously.

"He invented judo," I said. "I read it somewhere."

Chico shook his head. "He didn't really invent it. In 1882 he took all the best bits of hundreds of versions of jujitsu and put them into a formal sort of order, and called it judo."

"I was sure you would know," I said, grinning at him.

"You took a very sticky risk."

"You had to know. After all, you're an expert. And there were all those years at your club. No risk. I knew you'd know. As long as I'd got the name right, that is. Anyway what happened next?"

Chico smiled faintly.

"I tied him into a couple of knots. Armlocks and so on. He was absolutely flabbergasted. It was really rather funny. Then I put a bit of pressure on. You know. The odd thumb screwing down onto a nerve. God, you should have heard him yell. I suppose he thought he'd wake the neighbors, but you know what London is. No one took a blind bit of notice. So then I asked him where you were, when you sent him. He didn't show very willing, I must say, so I gave him a bit more. Poetic justice, wasn't it, considering what they'd just been doing to you? I told him I could keep it up all night, I'd hardly begun. There was a whole bookful I hadn't touched on. It shook him, it shook him bad."

Chico stood up restlessly and walked about the room.

"You know?" he said wryly. "He must have had a lot to lose. He was a pretty tough cookie, I'll give him that. If I hadn't been sure that you'd sent him to me as a sort of SOS, I don't think I'd have had the nerve to hurt him enough to bust him."

"I'm sorry," I said.

He looked at me thoughtfully. "We both learned about it, didn't we? You on the receiving end, and me. . . . I didn't like it. Doing it, I mean. I mean, the odd swipe or two and a few threats, that's usually enough, and it doesn't worry you a bit, you don't give it a second thought. But I've never hurt anyone like that before. Not seriously, on purpose, beyond bearing. He was crying, you see. . . ."

Chico turned his back to me, looking out of the window.

There was a long pause. The moral problems of being on the receiving end were not so great, I thought. It was easier on the conscience altogether.

At last Chico said, "He told me, of course. In the end."

"Yes."

"I didn't leave a mark on him, you know. Not a scratch. . . . He said you were at Seabury Racecourse. Well, I knew that was probably right, and that he wasn't trying the same sort of misdirection you had, because you'd told me yourself that you were going there. He said that you were in the weighing room and that the boiler would soon blow up. He said that he hoped it would kill you. He seemed half out of his mind with rage about you. How he should have known better than to believe you, he should have realized that you were as slippery as a snake, he'd been fooled once before. . . . He said he'd taken it for granted you were telling the truth when you broke down and changed your story about the negatives being in the office, because you . . . because you were begging for mercy and morphine and God knows what."

"Yes," I said. "I know all about that."

Chico turned away from the window, his face lightening into a near grin. "You don't say," he said.

"He wouldn't have believed it if I'd given in sooner or less thoroughly. Kraye would have, but not him. It was very annoying."

"Annoying," said Chico. "I like that word." He paused, considering. "At what moment exactly did you think of sending Bolt to me?"

"About half an hour before they caught me," I admitted. "Go on. What happened next?"

"There was a ball of string on Radnor's writing desk, so I tied old Fatso up with that in an uncomfortable position. Then there was the dicey problem of who to ring up to get the rescue squads on the way. I mean, the Seabury police might think I was some sort of a nut, ringing up at that hour and telling such an odd sort of story. At the best, they might send a bobby or two out to have a look, and the Krayes would easily get away. And I reckoned you'd want them rounded up red-handed, so to speak. I couldn't get hold of Radnor on account of the office phones being plasticated. So, well, I rang Lord Hag-bourne."

"You didn't!"

"Well, yes. He was OK, he really was. He listened to what I told him about you and the boiler and the Krayes and so on, and then he said, 'Right,' he'd see that half the Sussex police force turned up at Seabury Racecourse as soon as possible."

"Which they did."

"Which they did," agreed Chico. "To find my old pal Sid had dealt with the boiler himself, but was otherwise in a fairly ropey state."

"Thanks," I said. "For everything."

"Be my guest."

"Will you do me another favor?"

"Yes, what?"

"I was supposed to take someone out to lunch today. She'll be wondering why I didn't turn up. I'd have got one of the nurses to ring her, but I still don't know her telephone number."

"Are you talking about Miss Zanna Martin? The poor old duck with the disaster area of a face?"

"Yes," I said, surprised.

"Then don't worry. She wasn't expecting you. She knows you're here."

"How?"

"She turned up at Bolt's office yesterday morning, to deal with the mail apparently, and found a policeman waiting on the doorstep with a search war-rant. When he had gone she put two and two together smartly and trailed over to Cromwell Road to find out what was going on. Radnor had gone down to Seabury with Lord Hagbourne, but I was there poking about in the ruins, and we sort of swapped info. She was a bit upset about you, mate, in a quiet sort of way. Anyhow, she won't be expecting you to take her out to lunch."

"Did she say anything about having one of our files?"

"Yes. I told her to hang on to it for a day or two. There frankly isn't anywhere in the office to put it."

"All the same, you go over to where she lives as soon as you get back, and collect it. It's the Brinton file. And take great care of it. The negatives Kraye wanted are inside it."

Chico stared. "You're not serious."

"Why not?"

"But everyone—Radnor, Lord Hagbourne, even Kraye and Bolt, and the police—everyone has taken it for granted that what you said first was right, that they were in the office and were blown up."

"It's lucky they weren't," I said. "Get some more prints made. We've still got to find out why they were so hellishly important. And don't tell Miss Martin they were what Kraye wanted."

The door opened and one of the pretty nurses came in.

"I'm afraid you'll have to go now," she said to Chico. She came close beside the bed and took my pulse. "Haven't you any sense?" she exclaimed, looking at him angrily. "A few quiet minutes was what we said. Don't talk too much, and don't let Mr. Halley talk at all."

"You try giving *him* orders," said Chico cheerfully, "and see where it gets you."

"Miss Martin's address," I began.

"No," said the nurse severely. "No more talking."

I told Chico the address.

"See what I mean?" he said to the nurse. She looked down at me and laughed. A nice girl behind the starch.

Chico went across the room and opened the door.

"So long, then, Sid. Oh, by the way, I brought this for you to read. I thought you might be interested."

He pulled a glossy booklet folded lengthwise out of an inner pocket and threw it over onto the bed. It fell just out of my reach, and the nurse picked it up to give it to me. Then suddenly she held on to it tight.

"Oh no," she said. "You can't give him that!"

"Why not?" said Chico. "What do you think he is, a baby?"

He went out and shut the door. The nurse clung to the booklet, looking very troubled. I held out my hand for it.

"Come on."

"I think I ought to ask the doctors. . . ."

"In that case," I said, "I can guess what it is. Knowing Chico. So be a dear and hand it over. It's quite all right."

She gave it to me hesitantly, waiting to see my reaction when I caught sight of the bold words on the cover: *Artificial limbs. The Modern Development.*

I laughed. "He's a realist," I said. "You wouldn't expect him to bring fairy stories."

CHAPTER 20

WHEN RADNOR CAME the next day he looked tired, dispirited and ten years older. The military jauntiness had gone from his bearing, there were deep lines around his eyes and mouth, and his voice was lifeless.

For some moments he stared in obvious distress at the white-wrapped arm which stopped abruptly four inches below the elbow.

"I'm sorry about the office," I said.

"For God's sake—"

"Can it be rebuilt? How bad is it?"

"Sid—"

"Are the outside walls still solid, or is the whole place a write-off?"

"I'm too old," he said, giving in, "to start again."

"It's only bricks and mortar that are damaged. You haven't got to start again. The agency is you, not the building. Everyone can work for you just as easily somewhere else."

He sat down in an armchair, rested his head back, and closed his eyes.

"I'm tired," he said.

"I don't suppose you've had much sleep since it happened."

"I am seventy-one," he said flatly.

I was utterly astounded. Until that day I would have put him in the late fifties.

"You can't be."

"Time passes," he said. "Seventy-one."

"If I hadn't suggested going after Kraye it wouldn't have happened," I said with remorse. "I'm so sorry . . . so sorry. . . ."

He opened his eyes. "It wasn't your fault. If it was anyone's it was my own. You wouldn't have let Hagbourne take those photographs to Seabury, if it had been left to you. I know you didn't like it, that I'd given them to him. Letting the photographs go to Seabury was the direct cause of the bombs, and it was my mistake, not yours."

"You couldn't possibly tell," I protested.

"I should have known better, after all these years. I think . . . perhaps I may not see so clearly . . . consequences, things like that." His voice died to a low, miserable murmur. "Because I gave the photographs to Hagbourne, you lost your hand."

"No," I said decisively. "It's ridiculous to start blaming yourself for that. For heaven's sake snap out of it. No one in the agency can afford to have you in this frame of mind. What are Dolly and Jack Copeland and Sammy and Chico and all the others to do if you don't pick up the pieces?"

He didn't answer.

"My hand was useless anyway," I said. "And if I'd been willing to give in to Kraye I needn't have lost it. It had nothing whatever to do with you."

He stood up.

"You told Kraye a lot of lies," he said.

"That's right."

"But you wouldn't lie to me."

"Naturally not."

"I don't believe you."

"Concentrate on it. It'll come in time."

"You don't show much respect for your elders."

"Not when they behave like bloody fools," I agreed dryly.

He blew down his nostrils, smoldering inwardly. But all he said was, "And you? Will you still work for me?"

"It depends on you. I might kill us all next time."

"I'll take the risk."

"All right then. Yes. But we haven't finished this time, yet. Did Chico get the negatives?"

"Yes. He had two sets of prints done this morning. One for him, and he gave me one to bring to you. He said you'd want them, but I didn't think—"

"But you did bring them?" I urged.

"Yes, they're outside in my car. Are you sure——?"

"For heaven's sake," I said in exasperation. "I can hardly wait."

BY THE FOLLOWING day I had acquired several more pillows, a bedside telephone and a reputation for being a difficult patient.

The agency restarted work that morning, squeezing into Radnor's own small house. Dolly rang to say it was absolute hell, there was only one telephone instead of thirty, the blitz spirit was fortunately in operation, not to worry about a thing, there was a new word going round the office, it was Halley-lujah, and good-bye, someone else's turn now.

Chico rang a little later from a call box.

"Sammy found that driver, Smith," he said. "He went to see him in Birmingham yesterday. Now that Kraye's in jug Smith is willing to turn Queen's evidence. He agreed that he did take two hundred and fifty quid, just for getting out of his cab, unclipping the chains when the tanker had gone over, and sitting on the side of the road moaning and putting on an act. Nice easy money."

"Good," I said.

"But that's not all. The peach of it is he still has the money, most of it, in a tin box, saving it for a deposit on a house. That's what tempted him, apparently, needing money for a house. Anyway, Kraye paid him the second installment in tenners, from one of the blocks you photographed in his case. Smith still has one of the actual tenners in the pictures. He agreed to part with that for evidence, but I can't see anyone making him give the rest back, can you?"

"Not exactly!"

"So we've got Kraye nicely tied up on malicious damage."

"That's terrific," I said. "What are they holding him on now?"

"Gross bodily harm. And the others for aiding and abetting."

"Consecutive sentences, I trust."

"You'll be lucky."

I sighed. "All the same, he still owns twenty-three percent of Seabury's shares."

"So he does," agreed Chico gloomily.

"How bad exactly is the office?" I asked.

"They're surveying it still. The outside walls look all right, it's just a case of making sure. The inside was pretty well gutted."

"We could have a better layout," I said. "And a lift."

"So we could," he said happily. "And I'll tell you something else which might interest you."

"What?"

"The house next door is up for sale."

I WAS ASLEEP when Charles came in the afternoon, and he watched me wake up, which was a pity. The first few seconds of consciousness, were always the worst: I had the usual hellish time, and when I opened my eyes, there he was.

"Good God, Sid," he said in alarm. "Don't they give you anything?"

I nodded, getting a firmer grip on things.

"But with modern drugs, surely . . . I'm going to complain."

"No."

"But Sid—"

"They do what they can, I promise you. Don't look so upset. It'll get better in a few days. Just now it's a bore, that's all. Tell me about Fred."

Fred had already been at the house when the police guard arrived at Aynsford. Four policemen had gone there, and it took all four to hold him, with Charles going back and helping as well.

"Did he do much damage?" I asked. "Before the police got there?"

"He was very methodical, and very quick. He had been right through my desk, and all the wardroom. Every envelope, folder and notebook had been ripped apart, and the debris was all in a heap, ready to be destroyed. He'd started on the dining room when the police arrived. He was very violent. And they found a box of plastic explosive lying on the hall table, and some more out in the van." He paused. "What made you think he would come?"

"They knew I took the photographs at Aynsford, but how would they know I got them developed in London? I was afraid they might think I'd had them done locally, and that they'd think you'd know where the negatives were, as it was you who inveigled Kraye down there in the first place."

He smiled mischievously. "Will you come to Aynsford for a few days when you get out of here?"

"I've heard that somewhere before," I said. "No thanks."

"No more Krayes," he promised. "Just a rest."

"I'd like to, but there won't be time. The agency is in a dicky state. And I've just been doing to my boss what you did to me at Aynsford."

"What's that?"

"Kicking him out of depression into action."

His smile twisted in amusement.

"Do you know how old he is?" I said.

"About seventy, why?"

I was surprised. "I'd no idea he was that age, until he told me yesterday."

Charles squinted at the tip of his cigar. He said, "You always thought I asked him to give you a job, didn't you? And guaranteed your wages."

I made a face at him, embarrassed.

"You may care to know it wasn't like that at all. I didn't know him personally, only by name. He sought me out one day in the club and asked me if I thought you'd be any good at working with him. I said yes, I thought you would. Given time."

"I don't believe it."

He smiled. "I told him you played a fair game of chess. Also that you had become a jockey simply through circumstances, because you were small and your mother died, and that you could probably succeed at something else just as easily. He said that from what he'd seen of you racing you were the sort of chap he needed. He told me then how old he was. That's all. Nothing else. Just how old he was. But we both understood what he was saying."

"I nearly threw it away," I said. "If it hadn't been for you—"

"Oh yes," he said wryly. "You have a lot to thank me for. A lot."

Before he went I asked him to look at the photographs, but he studied them one by one and handed them back shaking his head.

CHIEF INSPECTOR CORNISH rang up to tell me Fred was not only in the bag but sewn up.

"The bullets match all right. He drew the same gun on the men who arrested him, but one of them fortunately threw a vase at him and knocked it out of his hand before he could shoot."

"He was a fool to keep that gun after he had shot Andrews."

"Stupid. Crooks often are, or we'd never catch them. And he didn't mention his little murder to Kraye and the others, so they can't be pinched as accessories to that. Pity. But it's quite clear he kept it quiet. The Sussex force said that Kraye went berserk when he found out. Apparently he mostly regretted not having known about your stomach while he had you in his cluthces."

"Thank God he didn't!" I exclaimed with feeling.

Cornish's chuckle came down the wire. "Fred was supposed to look for Brinton's letter at your agency himself, but he wanted to go to a football match up north or something, and sent Andrews instead. He said he didn't think there'd be a trap, or anything subtle like that. Just an errand, about on

Andrews' level. He said he only lent him the gun for a lark, he didn't mean Andrews to use it, didn't think he'd be so silly. But then Andrews went back to him scared stiff and said he'd shot you, so Fred says he suggested a country ramble in Epping Forest and the gun went off by accident. I ask you, try that on a jury! Fred says he didn't tell Kraye because he was afraid of him."

"What! Fred afraid?"

"Kraye seems to have made an adverse impression on him."

"Yes, he's apt to do that," I said.

I READ CHICO'S booklet from cover to cover. One had to thank the thalidomide children, it appeared, for the speedup of modern techniques. As soon as my arm had properly healed I could have a versatile gas-powered tool-hand with a swiveling wrist, activated by small pistons and controlled by valves, and operated by my shoulder muscles. The main snag to that, as far as I could gather, was that one always had to carry the small gas cylinders about, strapped on, like a permanent skin diver.

Much more promising, almost fantastic, was the latest invention of British and Russian scientists, the myo-electric arm. This worked entirely by harnessing the tiny electric currents generated in one's own remaining muscles, and the booklet cheerfully said it was easiest to fit on someone whose amputation was recent. The less one had lost of a limb, the better were one's chances of success. That put me straight in the guinea seats.

Finally, said the booklet with a justifiable flourish of trumpets, at St. Thomas' Hospital they had invented a miraculous new myo-electric hand which could do practically everything a real one could except grow nails.

I missed my real hand, there was no denying it. Even in its deformed state it had had its uses, and I suppose that any loss of so integral a part of oneself must prove a radical disturbance. My unconscious mind did its best to reject the facts: I dreamed each night that I was whole, riding races, tying knots, clapping—anything which required two hands. I awoke to the frustrating stump.

The doctors agreed to inquire from St. Thomas' how soon I could go there.

ON WEDNESDAY MORNING I rang up my accountant and asked when he had a free day. Owing to an unexpected cancellation of plans, he said, he would be free on Friday. I explained where I was and roughly what had happened. He said that he would come to see me, he didn't mind the journey, a breath of sea air would do him good.

As I put the telephone down my door opened and Lord Hagbourne and Mr. Fotherton came tentatively through it. I was sitting on the edge of the bed in a dark blue dressing gown, my feet in slippers, my arm in a cradle inside a sling, chin freshly shaved, hair brushed, and the marks of Kraye's fists fading from my face. My visitors were clearly relieved at these encouraging signs of revival, and relaxed comfortably into the armchairs.

"You're getting on well, then, Sid?" said Lord Hagbourne.

"Yes, thank you."

"Good, good."

"How did the meeting go?" I asked. "On Saturday?"

Both of them seemed faintly surprised at the question.

"Well, you did hold it, didn't you?" I said anxiously.

"Why, yes," said Fotherton. "We did. There was a moderately good gate, thanks to the fine weather." He was a thin, dry man with a long face molded into drooping lines of melancholy, and on that morning he kept smoothing three fingers down his cheek as if he were nervous.

Lord Hagbourne said, "It wasn't only your security men who were drugged. The stable lads all woke up feeling muzzy, and the old man who was supposed to look after the boiler was asleep on the floor in the canteen. Oxon had given them all a glass of beer. Naturally, your men trusted him."

I sighed. One couldn't blame them too much. I might have drunk with him myself.

"We had the inspector in yesterday to go over the boiler thoroughly," said Lord Hagbourne. "It was nearly due for its regular check anyway. They said it was too old to stand much interference with its normal working, and that it was just as well it hadn't been put to the test. Also that they thought that it wouldn't have taken as long as three hours to blow up. Oxon was only guessing."

"Charming," I said.

"I sounded out Seabury council," said Lord Hagbourne. "They're putting the racecourse down on their agenda for next month. Apparently a friend of yours, the manager of the Seafront Hotel, has started a petition in the town urging the council to take an interest in the racecourse on the grounds that it gives a seaside town prestige and free advertising and is good for trade."

"That's wonderful," I said, very pleased.

Fotherton cleared his throat, looked hesitantly at Lord Hagbourne, and then at me.

"It has been discussed . . . ," he began. "It has been decided to ask you if you . . . er . . . would be interested in taking on . . . in becoming clerk of the course at Seabury."

"Me?" I exclaimed, my mouth falling open in astonishment.

"It's getting too much for me, being clerk of two courses," he said, admitting it a year too late.

"You saved the place on the brink of the grave," said Lord Hagbourne with rare decisiveness. "We all know it's an unusual step to offer a clerkship to a professional jockey so soon after he's retired, but Seabury executives are unanimous. They want you to finish the job."

They were doing me an exceptional honor. I thanked them, and hesitated, and asked if I could think it over.

"Of course, think it over," said Lord Hagbourne. "But say yes."

I asked them to have a look at the box of photographs, which they did. They both scrutinized each print carefully one by one, but they could suggest nothing at the end.

MISS MARTIN CAME to see me the next afternoon, carrying some enormous, sweet-smelling bronze chrysanthemums. A transformed Miss Martin, in a smart dark-green tweed suit and shoes chosen for looks more than sturdy walking. Her hair had been restyled so that it was shorter and curved in a bouncy curl onto her cheek. She had even tried a little lipstick and powder, and had tidied her eyebrows into a shapely line. The scars were just as visible, the facial muscles as wasted as ever, but Miss Martin had come to terms with them at last.

"How super you look," I said truthfully.

She was embarrassed, but very pleased. "I've got a new job. I had an interview yesterday, and they didn't even seem to notice my face. Or at least they didn't say anything. In a bigger office, this time. A good bit more than I've earned before, too."

"How splendid," I congratulated her sincerely.

"I feel new," she said.

"I too."

"I'm glad we met." She smiled, saying it lightly. "Did you get that file back all right? Your young Mr. Barnes came to fetch it."

"Yes, thank you."

"Was it important?"

"Why?"

"He seemed very odd when I gave it to him. I thought he was going to tell me something about it. He kept starting to, and then he didn't."

I would have words with Chico, I thought.

"It was only an ordinary file," I said. "Nothing to tell."

On the off-chance, I got her to look at the photographs. Apart from commenting on the many examples of her own typing, and expressing surprise that anybody should have bothered to photograph such ordinary papers, she had nothing to say.

She rose to go, pulling on her gloves. She still automatically leaned forward slightly, so that the curl swung down over her cheek.

"Good-bye, Mr. Halley. And thank you for changing everything for me. I'll never forget how much I owe you."

"We didn't have that lunch," I said.

"No." She smiled, not needing me anymore. "Never mind. Some other time." She shook hands. "Good-bye."

She went serenely out of the door.

"Good-bye, Miss Martin," I said to the empty room. "Good-bye, good-bye, good-bye." I sighed sardonically at myself, and went to sleep.

NOEL WAYNE CAME loaded on Friday morning with a bulging briefcase of papers. He had been my accountant ever since I began earning big money at eighteen, and he probably knew more about me than anyone else on earth. Nearly sixty, bald except for a gray fringe over the ears, he was a small, round man with alert black eyes and a slow-moving mills-of-God mind. It was his advice more than my knowledge which had turned my earnings into a modest fortune via the stockmarkets, and I seldom did anything of any importance financially without consulting him first.

"What's up?" he said, coming straight to the point as soon as he had taken off his overcoat and scarf.

I walked over to the window and looked out. The weather had broken. It was drizzling, and a fine mist lay over the distant sea.

"I've been offered a job," I said. "Clerk of the course at Seabury."

"No!" he said, as astonished as I had been. "Are you going to accept?"

"It's tempting," I said. "And safe."

He chuckled behind me. "Good. So you'll take it."

"A week ago I definitely decided not to do any more detecting."

"Ah."

"So I want to know what you think about me buying a partnership in Radnor's agency."

He checked.

"I didn't think you even liked the place."

"That was a month ago. I've changed since then. And I won't be changing back. The agency is what I want."

"But has Radnor *offered* a partnership?"

"No. I think he might have eventually, but not since someone let a bomb off in the office. He's hardly likely to ask me to buy a half share of the ruins. And he blames himself for this." I pointed to the sling.

"With reason?"

"No," I said rather gloomily. "I took a risk which didn't come off."

"Which was?"

"Well, if you need it spelled out, that Kraye would only hit hard enough to hurt, not to damage beyond repair."

"I see." He said it calmly, but he looked horrified. "And do you intend to take similar risks in future?"

"Only if necessary."

"You always said the agency didn't do much crime work," he protested.

"It will from now on, if I have anything to do with it. Crooks make too much misery in the world." I thought of the poor Dunstable Brinton. "And listen, the house next door is for sale. We could knock the two into one. Radnor's is bursting at the seams. The agency has expanded a lot even in the two years I've been there. There seems more and more demands for his sort of service. Then the head of Bona Fides, that's one of the departments, is a natural to expand as an employment consultant on the management level. He has a gift for it. And insurance—Radnor's always neglected that. We don't have an insurance investigation department. I'd like to start one. Suspect insurance claims, you know. There's a lot of work in that."

"You're sure Radnor will agree, if you suggest a partnership?"

"He may kick me out. I'd risk it though. What do you think?"

"I think you've gone back to how you used to be," he said thoughtfully. "Which is good. Nothing but good. But . . . well, tell me what you really think about that." He nodded at my chopped-off arm. "None of your flippant lies, either. The truth."

I looked at him and didn't answer.

"It's only a week since it happened," he said, "and as you still look the color of a grubby sheet I suppose it's hardly fair to ask. But I want to know."

I swallowed. There were some truths which really couldn't be told. I said instead, "It's gone. Gone, like a lot of other things I used to have. I'll live without it."

"Live, or exist?"

"Oh live, definitely. Live." I reached for the booklet Chico had brought, and flicked it at him. "Look."

He glanced at the cover and I saw the faint shock in his face. He didn't have Chico's astringent brutality. He looked up and saw me smiling.

"All right," he said soberly. "Yes. Invest your money in yourself."

"In the agency," I said.

"That's what I mean," he said. "In the agency. In yourself."

He said he'd need to see the agency's books before a definite figure could be reached, but we spent an hour discussing the maximum he thought I should prudently offer Radnor, what return I could hope for in salary and dividends, and what I should best sell to raise the sum once it was agreed.

When we had finished I trotted out once more the infuriating photographs.

"Look them over, will you?" I said. "I've shown them to everyone else without result. These photographs were the direct cause of the bombs in my flat and the office, and of me losing my hand, and I can't see why. It's driving me ruddy well mad."

"The police . . . ," he suggested.

"The police are only interested in the one photograph of a ten-pound note. They looked at the others, said they could see nothing significant, and gave them back to Chico. But Kraye couldn't have been worried about that bank note, it was ten thousand to one we'd come across it again. No, it's something else. Something not obviously criminal, something Kraye was prepared to go to any lengths to obliterate immediately. Look at the time factor. Oxon only pinched the photographs just before lunch, down at Seabury. Kraye lived in London. Say Oxon rang him and told him to come and look: Oxon couldn't leave Seabury, it was a race day. Kraye had to go to Seabury himself. Well, he went down and looked at the photographs and saw . . . what? What? My flat was being searched by five o'clock."

Noel nodded in agreement. "Kraye was desperate. Therefore there was something to be desperate about." He took the photographs and studied them one by one.

Half an hour later he looked up and stared blankly out the window at the wet, gray skies. For several minutes he stayed completely still, as if in a state of suspended animation: it was his way of concentrated thinking. Finally he stirred and sighed. He moved his short neck as if it were stiff, and lifted the top photograph off the pile.

"This must be the one," he said.

I nearly snatched it out of his hand.

"But it's only the summary of the share transfers," I said in disappointment. It was the sheet headed S.R., Seabury Racecourse, which listed in summary form all Kraye's purchases of Seabury shares. The only noticeable factor in what had seemed to me merely a useful at-a-glance view of his total holding, was that it had been typed on a different typewriter, and not by Miss Martin. This hardly seemed enough reason for Kraye's hysteria.

"Look at it carefully," said Noel. "The three left-hand columns you can disregard, because I agree they are simply a tabulation of the share transfers, and I can't see any discrepancies."

"There aren't," I said. "I checked that."

"How about the last column, the small one on the right?"

"The banks?"

"The banks."

"What about them?" I said.

"How many different ones are there?"

I looked down at the long list, counting. "Five. Barclays, Picadilly. Westminster, Birmingham. British Linen Bank, Glasgow. Lloyds, Doncaster. National Provincial, Liverpool."

"Five bank accounts, in five different towns. Perfectly respectable. A very sensible arrangement in many ways. He can move round the country and always have easy access to his money. I myself have accounts in three different banks: it avoids muddling my clients' affairs with my own."

"I know all that. I didn't see any significance in his having several accounts. I still don't."

"Hm," said Noel. "I think it's very likely that he has been evading income tax."

"Is that all?" I said disgustedly.

Noel looked at me in amusement, pursing his lips. "You don't understand in the least, I see."

"Well, for heaven's sake, you wouldn't expect a man like Kraye to pay up every penny he was liable for like a good little citizen."

"You wouldn't," agreed Noel, grinning broadly.

"I'll agree he might be worried. After all, they sent Al Capone to jug in the end for tax evasion. But over here, what's the maximum sentence?"

"He'd only get a year, at the most," he said, "but—"

"And he would have been sure to get off with a fine. Which he won't do now, after attacking me. Even so, for that he'll only get three or four years, I should think, and less for the malicious damage. He'll be out and operating again far too soon. Bolt, I suppose, will be stuck off, or whatever it is with stockbrokers."

"Stop talking," he said, "and listen. While it's quite normal to have more than one bank account, an inspector of taxes, having agreed to your tax liability, may ask you to sign a document stating that you have disclosed to him *all* your bank accounts. If you fail to mention one or two, it constitutes a fraud, and if you are discovered you can then be prosecuted. So, suppose Kraye has signed such a document, omitting one or two or even three of the five accounts? And then he finds a photograph in existence of his most private papers, listing all five accounts as undeniably his?"

"But no one would have noticed," I protested.

"Quite. Probably not. But to him it must have seemed glaringly dangerous. Guilty people constantly fear their guilt will be visible to others. They're vibratingly sensitive to anything which can give them away. I see quite a lot of it in my job."

"Even so, bombs are pretty drastic."

"It would entirely depend on the sum involved," he said primly.

"Huh?"

"The maximum fine for income tax evasion is twice the tax you didn't pay. If, for example, you amassed ten thousand pounds but declared only two, you could be fined a sum equal to twice the tax on eight thousand pounds. With a surtax and so on, you might be left with almost nothing. A nasty setback."

"To put it mildly," I said in awe.

"I wonder," Noel said thoughtfully, putting the tips of his fingers together, "just how much undeclared loot Kraye has got stacked away in his five bank accounts?"

"It must be a lot," I said, "for bombs."

"Quite so."

There was a long silence. Finally I said, "One isn't required either legally or morally to report people to the Inland Revenue."

He shook his head.

"But we could make a note of those five banks, just in case?"

"If you like," he agreed.

"Then I think I might let Kraye have the negatives of the new sets of prints," I said. "Without telling him I know why he wants them."

Noel looked at me inquiringly, but didn't speak.

I grinned faintly. "On condition that he makes a free, complete and outright gift to Seabury Racecourse Company of his twenty-three percent holding."

WHIP HAND

PROLOGUE

I DREAMED I was riding in a race.

Nothing odd in that. I'd ridden in thousands.

There were fences to jump. There were horses, and jockeys in a rainbow of colors, and miles of green grass. There were massed banks of people, with pink oval faces, undistinguishable pink blobs from where I crouched in the stirrups, galloping past, straining with speed.

Their mouths were open, and although I could hear no sound, I knew they were shouting.

Shouting my name, to make me win.

Winning was all. Winning was my function. What I was there for. What I wanted. What I was born for.

In the dream, I won the race. The shouting turned to cheering, and the cheering lifted me up on its wings, like a wave. But the winning was all; not the cheering.

I woke in the dark, as I often did, at four in the morning.

There was silence. No cheering. Just silence.

I could still feel the way I'd moved with the horse, the ripple of muscle through both the striving bodies, uniting in one. I could still feel the irons round my feet, the calves of my legs gripping, the balance, the nearness to my head of the stretching brown neck, the mane blowing in my mouth, my hands on the reins.

There came, at that point, the second awakening. The real one. The moment in which I first moved, and opened my eyes, and remembered that I wouldn't ride any more races, ever. The wrench of loss came again as a fresh grief. The dream was a dream for whole men.

I dreamed it quite often.

Damned senseless thing to do.

Living, of course, was quite different. One discarded dreams, and got dressed, and made what one could of the day.

CHAPTER 1

I TOOK THE battery out of my arm and fed it into the recharger, and only realized I'd done it when ten seconds later the fingers wouldn't work.

How odd, I thought. Recharging the battery, and the maneuver needed to accomplish it, had become such second nature that I had done them instinctively, without conscious decision, like brushing my teeth. And I realized for the first time that I had finally squared my subconscious, at least when I was awake, to the fact that what I now had as a left hand was a matter of metal and plastic, not muscle and bone and blood.

I pulled my tie off and flung it haphazardly onto my jacket, which lay over the leather arm of the sofa; stretched and sighed with the ease of homecoming; listened to the familiar silences of the flat; and as usual felt the welcoming peace unlock the gritty tensions of the outside world.

I suppose that that flat was more of a haven than a home. Comfortable certainly, but not slowly and lovingly put together. Furnished, rather, on one brisk unemotional afternoon in one store: "I'll have that, that, that, and that . . . and send them as soon as possible." The collection had jelled, more or less, but I now owned nothing whose loss I would ache over; and if that was a defense mechanism, at least I knew it.

Contentedly padding around in shirtsleeves and socks, I switched on the warm pools of table lights, encouraged the television with a practiced slap, poured a soothing Scotch, and decided not to do yesterday's washing up. There was steak in the fridge and money in the bank, and who needed an aim in life, anyway?

I tended nowadays to do most things one-handed, because it was quicker. My ingenious false hand, which worked via solenoids from electrical impulses in what was left of my forearm, would open and close in a fairly viselike grip, but at its own pace. It did *look* like a real hand, though, to the extent that people sometimes didn't notice. There were shapes like fingernails, and ridges for tendons, and blue lines for veins. When I was alone I seemed to use it less and less, but it pleased me better to see it on than off.

I shaped up to that evening as to many another—on the sofa, feet up, knees bent, in contact with a chunky tumbler, and happy to live vicariously via the small screen—and I was mildly irritated when halfway through a decent comedy the doorbell rang.

With more reluctance than curiosity I stood up, parked the glass, fumbled through my jacket pockets for the spare battery I'd been carrying there, and snapped it into the socket in my arm. Then, buttoning the shirt cuff down over the plastic wrist, I went out into the small hall and took a look through the spyhole in the door.

There was no trouble on the mat, unless trouble had taken the shape of a middle-aged lady in a blue head scarf. I opened the door and said politely, "Good evening, can I help you?"

"Sid," she said. "Can I come in?"

I looked at her, thinking that I didn't know her. But then a good many people whom I didn't know called me Sid, and I'd always taken it as a compliment.

Coarse dark curls showed under the head scarf, a pair of tinted glasses hid her eyes, and heavy crimson lipstick focused attention on her mouth. There was embarrassment in her manner and she seemed to be trembling inside her loose fawn raincoat. She still appeared to expect me to recognize her, but it was not until she looked nervously over her shoulder, and I saw her profile against the light, that I actually did.

Even then I said incredulously, tentatively, "Rosemary?"

"Look," she said, brushing past me as I opened the door wider. "I simply must talk to you."

"Well . . . come in."

While I closed the door behind us, she stopped in front of the looking glass in the hall and started to untie the head scarf.

"My God, whatever do I look like?"

I saw that her fingers were shaking too much to undo the knot, and finally, with a frustrated little moan, she stretched over her head, grasped the points of the scarf, and forcefully pulled the whole thing forward. Off with the scarf came all the black curls, and out shook the more familiar chestnut mane of Rosemary Caspar, who had called me Sid for fifteen years.

"My God," she said again, putting the tinted glasses away in her handbag and fetching out a tissue to wipe off the worst of the gleaming lipstick. "I had to come. I had to come."

I watched the tremors in her hands and listened to the jerkiness in her voice, and reflected that I'd seen a whole procession of people in this state since I'd drifted into the trade of sorting out trouble and disaster.

"Come on in and have a drink," I said, knowing it was what she both needed and expected, and sighing internally over the ruins of my quiet evening. "Whisky or gin?"

"Gin . . . tonic . . . anything."

Still wearing the raincoat, she followed me into the sitting room and sat abruptly on the sofa as if her knees had given way beneath her. I looked briefly at the vague eyes, switched off the laughter on the television, and poured her a tranquilizing dose of mothers' ruin.

"Here," I said, handing her the tumbler. "So what's the problem?"

"Problem!" She was transitorily indignant. "It's more than that."

I picked up my own drink and carried it round to sit in an armchair opposite her.

"I saw you in the distance at the races today," I said. "Did the problem exist at that point?"

She took a large gulp from her glass. "Yes, it damn well did. And why do you think I came creeping around at night searching for your damn flat in this ropy wig if I could have walked straight up to you at the races?"

"Well . . . why?"

. "Because the last person I can be seen talking to on a racecourse or off it is Sid Halley."

I had ridden a few times for her husband way back in the past. In the days when I was a jockey. When I was still light enough for flat racing and hadn't taken to steeplechasing. In the days before success and glory and falls and smashed hands . . . and all that. To Sid Halley, ex-jockey, she could have talked publicly forever. To Sid Halley, recently changed into a sort of all-purpose investigator, she had come in darkness and fright.

Forty-fivish, I supposed, thinking about it for the first time, and realizing that although I had known her casually for years, I had never before looked long enough or closely enough at her face to see it feature by feature. The general impression of thin elegance had always been strong. The drooping lines of eyebrow and eyelid, the small scar on the chin, the fine noticeable down on the sides of the jaw, these were new territory.

She raised her eyes suddenly and gave me the same sort of inspection, as if she'd never really seen me before: and I guessed that for her it was a much more radical reassessment. I was no longer the boy she'd once rather brusquely issued with riding instructions, but a man she had come to in trouble. I was accustomed, by now, to seeing this new view of me supplant older and easier relationships, and although I might often regret it, there seemed no way of going back.

"Everyone says . . ." she began doubtfully. "I mean . . . over this past year,

I keep hearing . . ." She cleared her throat. "They say you're good . . . very good . . . at this sort of thing. But I don't know. . . . Now I'm here, it doesn't seem . . . I mean, . . . you're a jockey."

"Was," I said succinctly.

She glanced vaguely at my left hand, but made no other comment. She knew all about that. As racing gossip goes, it was last year's news.

"Why don't you tell me what you want done?" I said. "If I can't help, I'll say so."

The idea that I couldn't help after all reawoke her alarm and set her shivering again inside the raincoat.

"There's no one else," she said. "I can't go to anyone else. I have to believe . . . I have to . . . that you can do . . . all they say."

"I'm no superman," I protested. "I just snoop around a bit."

"Well . . . Oh, God . . ." The glass rattled against her teeth as she emptied it to the dregs. "I hope to God . . ."

"Take your coat off," I said persuasively. "Have another gin. Sit back on the sofa, and start at the beginning."

As if dazed, she stood up, undid the buttons, shed the coat, and sat down again.

"There isn't a beginning."

She took the refilled glass and hugged it to her chest. The newly revealed clothes were a cream silk shirt under a rust-colored cashmere-looking sweater, a heavy gold chain, and a well-cut black skirt: the everyday expression of no financial anxieties.

"George is at dinner," she said. "We're staying here in London overnight. . . . He thinks I've gone to a film."

George, her husband, ranked in the top three of British race horse trainers and probably in the top ten internationally. On racecourses from Hong Kong to Kentucky he was revered as one of the greats. At Newmarket, where he lived, he was king. If his horses won the Derby, the Arc de Triomphe, the Washington International, no one was surprised. Some of the cream of the world's bloodstock floated year by year to his stable, and even having a horse in his yard gave the owner a certain standing. George Caspar could afford to turn down any horse or any man. Rumor said he rarely turned down any woman; and if that was Rosemary's problem, it was one I couldn't solve.

"He mustn't know," she said nervously. "You'll have to promise not to tell him I came here."

"I'll promise provisionally," I said.

"That's not enough."

"It'll have to be."

"You'll see," she said. "You'll see why. . . ." She took a drink. "He may not like it, but he's worried to death."

"Who . . . George?"

"Of course George. Who else? Don't be so damned stupid. For who else would I risk coming here on this damn charade?" The brittleness shrilled in her voice and seemed to surprise her. She took some deep breaths, and started again. "What did you think of Gleaner?"

"Er . . ." I said. "Disappointing."

"A damned disaster," she said. "You know it was."

"One of those things," I said.

"No, it was *not* one of those things. One of the best two-year-olds George ever had. Won three brilliant two-year-old races. Then all that winter, favorite for the Guineas and the Derby. Going to be the tops, everyone said. Going to be marvelous."

"Yes," I said. "I remember."

"And then what? Last spring he ran in the Guineas. Fizzled out. Total flop. And he never even got within sight of the Derby."

"It happens," I said.

She looked at me impatiently, compressing her lips. "And Zingaloo?" she said. "Was that, too, just one of those things? The two best colts in the country, both brilliant at two, both in our yard. And neither of them won a damn penny last year as three-year-olds. They just stood there in their boxes, looking well, eating their heads off, and totally damn bloody useless."

"It was a puzzler," I agreed, but without much conviction. Horses that didn't come up to expectations were as normal as rain on Sundays.

"And what about Bethesda, the year before?" She glared at me vehemently. "Top two-year-old filly. Favorite for months for the One Thousand and the Oaks. Terrific. She went down to the start of the One Thousand looking a million dollars, and she finished tenth. *Tenth*, I ask you!"

"George must have had them all *checked*," I said mildly.

"Of course he did. Damn vets crawling all round the place for weeks on end. Dope tests. Everything. All negative. Three brilliant horses all gone useless. And no damned explanation. Nothing!"

I sighed slightly. It sounded to me more like the story of most trainers' lives, not a matter for melodramatic visits in false wigs.

"And now," she said, casually dropping the bomb, "there is Tri-Nitro."

I let out an involuntarily audible breath, halfway to a grunt. Tri-Nitro filled columns just then on every racing page, hailed as the best colt for a decade. His two-year-old career the previous autumn had eclipsed all competitors, and his supremacy in the approaching summer was mostly taken for granted. I had seen him win the Middle Park at Newmarket in September at a record-breaking pace, and had a vivid memory of the slashing stride that covered the turf at almost incredible speed.

"The Guineas is only a fortnight away," Rosemary said. "Two weeks today, in fact. Suppose something happens . . . suppose it's just as bad? What if he fails, like the others . . . ?"

She was trembling again, but when I opened my mouth to speak, she rushed on at a higher pitch. "Tonight was the only chance . . . the only night I could come here . . . and George would be livid. He says nothing can happen to the horse, no one can get at him, the security's too good. But he's scared, I know he is. Strung up. Screwed up tight. I suggested he call you in to guard the horse and he nearly went berserk. I don't know why. I've never seen him in such a fury."

"Rosemary," I began, shaking my head.

"Listen," she interrupted. "I want you to make sure nothing happens to Tri-Nitro before the Guineas. That's all."

"All . . ."

"It's no good wishing afterwards . . . if somebody tries something . . . that I'd asked you. I couldn't stand that. So I had to come. I had to. So say you'll do it. Say how much you want, and I'll pay it."

"It's not the money," I said. "Look . . . There's no way I can guard Tri-Nitro without George knowing and approving. It's impossible."

"You can do it. I'm sure you can. You've done things before that people said couldn't be done. I had to come. I can't face it . . . George can't face it. Not three years in a row. Tri-Nitro has got to win. You've got to make sure nothing happens. You've got to."

She was suddenly shaking worse than ever and looked well down the road to hysteria. More to calm her than from any thought of being able in fact to do what she wanted, I said, "Rosemary . . . all right. I'll try to do something."

"He's got to win," she said.

I said soothingly, "I don't see why he shouldn't."

She picked up unerringly the undertone I hadn't known would creep into my voice: the skepticism, the easy complacent tendency to discount her urgency as the fantasies of an excitable woman. I heard the nuances myself, and saw them uncomfortably through her eyes.

"My God, I've wasted my time coming here, haven't I?" she said bitterly, standing up. "You're like all bloody men. You've got menopause on the brain."

"That's not true. And I said I'd try."

"Yes." The word was a sneer. She was stoking up her own anger, indulging an inner need to explode. She practically threw her empty glass at me instead of handing it. I missed catching it, and it fell against the side of the coffee table and broke.

She looked down at the glittering pieces and stuffed the jagged rage halfway back into its box.

"Sorry," she said shortly.

"It doesn't matter."

"Put it down to strain."

"Yes."

"I'll have to go and see that film. George will ask." She slid into her raincoat and moved jerkily toward the door, her whole body still trembling with tension. "I shouldn't have come here. But I thought . . ."

"Rosemary," I said flatly. "I've said I'll try, and I will."

"Nobody knows what it's like."

I followed her into the hall, feeling her jangling desperation almost as if it were making actual disturbances in the air. She picked the black wig off the small table there and put it back on her head, tucking her own brown hair underneath with fierce unfriendly jabs, hating herself, her disguise, and me; hating the visit, the lies to George, the seedy furtiveness of her actions. She painted on a fresh layer of the dark lipstick with unnecessary force, as if assaulting herself; tied the knot on the scarf with a savage jerk, and fumbled in her handbag for the tinted glasses.

"I changed in the lavatories at the tube station," she said. "It's all revolting. But I'm not having anyone see me leaving here. There are things going on. I know there are. And George is scared. . . ."

She stood by my front door, waiting for me to open it; a thin elegant woman looking determinedly ugly. It came to me that no woman did that to herself without a need that made esteem an irrelevance. I'd done nothing to relieve her distress, and it was no good realizing that it was because of knowing her too long in a different capacity. It was she who was subtly used to being in control, and I, from sixteen, who had respectfully followed her wishes. I thought that if tonight I had made her cry and given her warmth and contact and even a kiss, I could have done her more service; but the block was there, and couldn't be lightly dismantled.

"I shouldn't have come here," she said. "I see that now."

"Do you want me . . . to take any action?"

A spasm twisted her face. "Oh, God . . . Yes, I do. But I was stupid. Fooling myself. You're only a jockey after all."

I opened the door.

"I wish," I said lightly, "that I were."

She looked at me unseeingly, her mind already on her return journey, on her film, on her report of it to George.

"I'm not crazy," she said.

She turned abruptly and walked away without a backward glance. I watched her turn toward the stairs and go unhesitatingly out of sight. With a continuing feeling of having been inadequate, I shut the door and went back into the sitting room; and it seemed that the very air there too was restless from her intensity.

I bent down and picked up the larger pieces of broken glass, but there were too many sharp little splinters for total laziness, so I fetched dustpan and brush from the kitchen.

Holding the dustpan could usefully be done left-handed. If I simply tried to bend backward the real hand that wasn't there, the false fingers opened away from the thumb. If I sent the old message to bend my hand inward, they closed. There was always about two seconds' delay between mental instruction and electrical reaction, and taking that interval into account had been the most difficult thing to learn.

The fingers could not of course feel when their grip was tight enough. The people who had fitted the arm had told me that success was picking up eggs: and I'd broken a dozen or two in practicing, at the beginning. Absent-mindedness had since resulted in an exploding light bulb and crushed-flat cigarette packets and explained why I used the marvels of science less than I might.

I emptied the bits of glass into the dustbin and switched on the television again; but the comedy was over, and Rosemary came between me and a cops-and-robbers. With a sigh I switched off, and cooked my steak, and after I'd eaten it, picked up the telephone to talk to Bobby Unwin, who worked for the *Daily Planet*.

"Information will cost you," he said immediately, when he found who was on the line.

"Cost me what?"

"A sport of quid pro quo."

"All right," I said.

"What are you after, then?"

"Um," I said. "You wrote a long piece about George Caspar in your Saturday color supplement a couple of months ago. Pages and pages of it."

"That's right. Special feature. In-depth analysis of success. The *Planet's* doing a once-a-month series on high-fliers, tycoons, pop stars, you name it. Putting them under the cliché microscope and coming up with a big yawn-yawn exposé of bugger all."

"Are you horizontal?" I said.

There was a short silence, followed by a stifled girlish giggle.

"You just take your intuitions to Siberia," Bobby said. "What made you think so?"

"Envy, I daresay." But I'd really only been asking if he was alone, without making it sound important. "Will you be at Kempton tomorrow?"

"I reckon."

"Could you bring a copy of that magazine, and I'll buy you a bottle of your choice."

"Oh, boy, oh boy. You're on."

His receiver went down without more ado, and I spent the rest of the evening reading the flat-racing form books of recent years, tracing the careers of Bethesda, Gleaner, Zingaloo, and Tri-Nitro, and coming up with nothing at all.

CHAPTER 2

I HAD FALLEN into a recent habit of lunching on Thursdays with my father-in-law. To be accurate, with my *ex*-father-in-law; Admiral (retired) Charles Roland, parent of my worst failure. To his daughter Jenny I had given whatever devotion I was capable of, and had withheld the only thing she eventually said she wanted, which was that I should stop riding in races. We had been married for five years: two in happiness, two in discord, and one in bitterness; and now only the itching half-mended wounds remained. Those, and the friendship of her father, which I had come by with difficulty and now prized as the only treasure saved from the wreck.

We met most weeks at noon in the upstairs bar of the Cavendish Hotel, where a pink gin for him and a whisky and water for me now stood on prim little mats beside a bowl of peanuts.

"Jenny will be at Aynsford this weekend," he said.

Aynsford was his house in Oxfordshire. London on Thursdays was his business. He made the journey between the two in a Rolls.

"I'd be glad if you would come down," he said.

I looked at the fine distinguished face and listened to the drawling non-committal voice. A man of subtlety and charm who could blast through you like a laser if he felt the need. A man whose integrity I would trust to the gates of hell, and whose mercy, not an inch.

I said carefully, without rancor, "I am not coming to be sniped at."

"She agreed that I should invite you."

"I don't believe it."

He looked with suspicious concentration at his glass. I knew from long experience that when he wanted me to do something he knew I wouldn't like, he didn't look at me. And there would be a pause, like this, while he found it in him to light the fuse. From the length of the pause, I drew no comfort of any sort. He said finally, "I'm afraid she's in some sort of trouble."

I stared at him, but he wouldn't raise his eyes.

"Charles," I said despairingly. "you *can't* . . . you can't ask me. You know how she speaks to me these days."

"You give as good as you get, as I recall."

"No one in their senses walks into a tiger's cage."

He gave me a brief flashing upward glance, and there was a small twitch to his mouth. And perhaps it was not the best way of referring to a man's beautiful daughter.

"I have known you, Sid," he said, "to walk into tigers' cages more than once."

"A tigress, then," I amended with a touch of humor.

He pounced on it. "So you'll come?"

"No. Some things, honestly, are too much."

He sighed and sat back in his chair, looking at me over the gin. I didn't care for the blank look in his eyes, because it meant he was still plotting.

"Dover sole?" he suggested smoothly. "Shall I call the waiter? We might eat soon, don't you think?"

He ordered sole for both of us, and off the bone, out of habit. I could eat perfectly well in public now, but there had been a long and embarrassing period when my natural hand had been a wasted, useless deformity, which I'd self-consciously hidden in pockets. At about the time I finally got used to it, it had been smashed up again, and I'd lost it altogether. I guessed life was like that. You gained and you lost, and if you saved anything from the ruins, even if only a shred of self-respect, it was enough to take you through the next bit.

The waiter told us our table would be ready in ten minutes and went quietly away, hugging menus and order pad to his dinner jacket and gray silk tie. Charles glanced at his watch and then gazed expansively round the big, light, quiet room, where other couples, like us, sat in beige armchairs and sorted out the world.

"Are you going to Kempton this afternoon?" he said.

I nodded. "The first race is at two-thirty."

"Are you working on a job?" As an inquiry, it was a shade too bland.

"I'm not coming to Aynsford," I said. "Not while Jenny is there."

After a pause, he said, "I wish you would, Sid."

I merely looked at him. His eyes were following the track of a bar waiter delivering drinks to distant customers; and he was taking a great deal too much time thinking out his next sentence.

He cleared his throat and addressed himself to nowhere in particular. "Jenny has lent some money . . . and her name, I'm afraid . . . to a business enterprise which would appear to be fraudulent."

"She's done *what?*" I said.

His gaze switched back to me with suspicious speed, but I interrupted him as he opened his mouth.

"No," I said. "If she's done that, it's well within your province to sort it out."

"It's your name she's used, of course," Charles said. "Jennifer Halley."

I could feel the trap closing round me. Charles studied my silent face and with a tiny sigh of relief let go of some distinct inner anxiety. He was a great deal too adept, I thought bitterly, at hooking me.

"She was attracted to a man," he said dispassionately. "I didn't especially like him, but then I didn't like you either, to begin with . . . and I have found that error of judgment inhibiting, as a matter of fact, because I no longer always trust my first instincts."

I ate a peanut. He had disliked me because I was a jockey, which he saw as no sort of husband for his well-bred daughter; and I had disliked him right back as an intellectual and social snob. It was odd to reflect that he was now probably the individual I valued most in the world.

He went on, "This man persuaded her to go in for some sort of mail order business . . . all frightfully up-market and respectable, at least on the surface. A worthy way of raising money for charity . . . you know the sort of thing. Like Christmas cards, only in this case I think it was a sort of wax polish for antique furniture. One was invited to buy expensive wax, knowing that much of the profits would go to a good cause."

He looked at me somberly. I simply waited, without much hope.

"The orders rolled in," he said. "And the money with them, of course. Jenny and a girlfriend were kept busy sending off the wax."

"Which Jenny," I guessed, "had bought ready, in advance?"

Charles sighed. "You don't need to be told, do you?"

"And Jenny paid for the postage and packing and advertisements and general literature?"

He nodded. "She banked all the receipts into a specially opened account in the name of the charity. Those receipts have all been drawn out, the man has disappeared, and the charity, as such, has been found not to exist."

I regarded him in dismay.

"And Jenny's position?" I said.

"Very bad, I'm afraid. There may be a prosecution. And her name is on everything, and the man's nowhere."

My reaction was beyond blasphemy. Charles observed my blank silence and nodded slowly in sympathy.

"She has been exceedingly foolish," he said.

"Couldn't you have stopped her? Warned her?"

He shook his head regretfully. "I didn't know about it until she came to Aynsford yesterday in a panic. She has done it all from that flat she's taken in Oxford."

We went in to lunch, and I couldn't remember, afterward, the taste of the sole.

"The man's name is Nicholas Ashe," Charles said, over the coffee. "At least that's what he said." He paused briefly. "My solicitor chap thinks it would be a good idea if you could find him."

I DROVE TO Kempton with visual and muscular responses on autopilot and my thoughts uncomfortably on Jenny.

Divorce itself, it seemed, had changed nothing. The recent antiseptic drawing of the line, the impersonal court to which neither of us had gone (no children, no maintenance disputes, no flicker of reconciliation, petition granted, next case please), seemed to have punctuated our lives not with a full stop but with hardly a comma. The legal position had not proved a great liberating open door. The recovery from emotional cataclysm seemed a long, slow process, and the certificate was barely an aspirin.

Where once we had clung together with delight and passion, we now, if

we chanced to meet, ripped with claws. I had spent eight years in loving, losing, and mourning Jenny, and although I could wish my feelings were dead,
they weren't. The days of indifference still seemed a weary way off.

If I helped her out of the mess she was in, she would give me a rotten
time. If I didn't help her, I would give it to myself. *Why,* I thought violently,
in impotent irritation, had the silly bitch been so *stupid*?

THERE WAS A fair attendance at Kempton for a weekday in April, though
as often before, I regretted that in Britain, the nearer a racecourse was to London, the more vulnerable it became to stay-away crowds. City dwellers might
be addicted to gambling, but not to fresh air and horses. Birmingham and
Manchester, in days gone by, had lost their racecourses to indifference, and
Liverpool had survived only through the Grand National. Most times it took
a course in the country to burst at the seams and run out of race cards: the
thriving plants still growing from the oldest roots.

Outside the weighing room there was the same old bunch of familiar
faces carrying on chats that had been basically unchanged for centuries: who
was going to ride what, and who was going to win, and there should be a
change in the rules, and what so-and-so had said about his horse losing, and
wasn't the general outlook grim, and did you know young-fella-me-lad has
left his wife? There were the scurrilous stories and the slight exaggerations
and the downright lies. The same mingling of honor and corruption, of principle and expediency. People ready to bribe, people with the ready palm. Anguished little hopefuls and arrogant big guns. The failures making brave
excuses, and the successful hiding the anxieties behind their eyes. All as it had
been, and was, and would be, as long as racing lasted.

I had no real right any longer to wander in the space outside the weighing room, although no one ever turned me out. I belonged in the gray area of
ex-jockeys: barred from the weighing room itself but tolerantly given the run
of much else. The cozy inner sanctum had gone down the drain the day half a
ton of horse landed feet first on my metacarpals. Since then I had come to be
glad simply to be still part of the brotherhood, and the ache to be riding was
just part of the general regret. Another ex-champion had told me it took him
twenty years before he no longer yearned to be out there on the horses, and I'd
said thanks very much.

George Caspar was there, talking to his jockey, with three runners scheduled that afternoon; and also Rosemary, who reacted with a violent jerk when
she saw me at ten paces, and promptly turned her back. I could imagine the
waves of alarm quivering through her, although that day she looked her usual

well-groomed elegant self: mink coat for the chilly wind, glossy boots, velvet hat. If she feared I would talk about her visit, she was wrong.

There was a light grasp on my elbow and a pleasant voice saying, "A word in your ear, Sid."

I was smiling before I turned to him, because Lord Friarly, earl, land-owner, and frightfully decent fellow, had been one of the people for whom I'd ridden a lot of races. He was of the old school of aristocrats: sixtyish, beautifully mannered, genuinely compassionate, slightly eccentric, and more intelligent than people expected. A slight stammer had nothing to do with speech impediment but all to do with not wanting to seem to throw his rank about in an egalitarian world.

Over the years I had stayed several times in his house in Shropshire, mostly on the way to northern race meetings, and had traveled countless miles with him in a succession of elderly cars. The age of cars was not an extension of the low profile, but rather a disinclination to waste money on nonessentials. Essentials, in terms of the earl's income, were keeping up Friarly Hall and owning as many race horses as possible.

"Great to see you, sir," I said.

"I've told you to call me Philip."

"Yes . . . sorry."

"Look," he said, "I want you to do something for me. I hear you're damned good at looking into things. Doesn't surprise me, of course; I've always valued your opinion, you know that."

"Of course I'll help if I can," I said.

"I've an uncomfortable feeling I'm being *used*," he said. "You know that I'm a sucker for seeing my horses run, the more the merrier, and all that. Well, during the past year I have agreed to be one of the registered owners in a syndicate . . . you know, sharing the costs with eight or ten people, though the horses run in my name, and my colors."

"Yeah," I said, nodding. "I've noticed."

"Well . . . I don't know all the other people, personally. The syndicates were formed by a chap who does just that—gets people together and sells them a horse. You know?"

I nodded. There had been cases of syndicate formers buying horses for a smallish sum and selling them to the members of the syndicate for up to four times as much. A healthy little racket, so far legal.

"Those horses don't run true to form, Sid," he said bluntly. "I've a nasty feeling that somewhere in the syndicate we've got someone fixing the way the horses run. So will you find out for me? Nice and quietly?"

"I'll certainly try," I said.

"Good," he said, with satisfaction. "Thought you would. So I brought the names for you, of the people in the syndicates." He pulled a folded paper out of his inner pocket. "There you are," he said, opening it and pointing. "Four horses. The syndicates are all registered with the Jockey Club, everything aboveboard, audited accounts, and so on. It all looks all right on paper, but frankly, Sid, I'm not *happy*."

"I'll look into it," I promised, and he thanked me profusely, and also genuinely, and moved away, after a minute or two, to talk to Rosemary and George.

Farther away, Bobby Unwin, notebook and pencil in evidence, was apparently giving a middle-rank trainer a hard time. His voice floated over, sharp with northern aggression and tinged with an inquisitorial tone caught from teleinterviewers. "Can you say, then, that you are perfectly satisfied with the way your horses are running?" The trainer looked around for escape and shifted from foot to foot. It was amazing, I thought, that he put up with it, even though Bobby Unwin's printed barbs tended to be worse if he hadn't had the personal pleasure of intimidating his victim face to face. He wrote well, was avidly read, and among most of the racing fraternity was heartily disliked. Between him and me there had been for many years a sort of sparring truce, which in practice had meant a diminution of words like "blind" and "cretinous" to two per paragraph when he was describing any race I'd lost. Since I'd stopped riding I was no longer a target, and in consequence we had developed a perverse satisfaction in talking to each other, like scratching an itch.

Seeing me out of the corner of his eye, he presently released the miserable trainer and steered his beaky nose in my direction. Tall, forty, and forever making copy out of having been born in a back-to-back terrace in Bradford: a fighter, come up the hard way, and letting no one ever forget it. We ought to have had much in common, since I too was the product of a dingy back street, but temperament had nothing to do with environment. He tended to meet fate with fury and I with silence, which meant that he talked a lot and I listened.

"The color mag's in my briefcase in the press room," he said. "What do you want it for?"

"Just general interest."

"Oh, come off it," he said. "What are you working on?"

"And would you," I said, "give me advance notice of your next scoop?"

"All right," he said. "Point taken. And I'll have a bottle of the best vintage bubbly in the members' bar. After the first race. O.K.?"

"And for smoked salmon sandwiches extra, would I acquire some background info that never saw the light of print?"

He grinned nastily and said he didn't see why not; and in due course, after the first race, he kept his bargain.

"You can afford it, Sid, lad," he said, munching a pink-filled sandwich and laying a protective hand on the gold-foiled bottle standing beside us on the bar counter. "So what do you want to know?"

"You went to Newmarket . . . to George Caspar's yard . . . to do this article?" I indicated the color magazine, which lay, folded lengthwise, beside the bottle.

"Yeah. Sure."

"So tell me what you didn't write."

He stopped in midmunch. "In what area?"

"What do you privately think of George as a person?"

He spoke round bits of brown bread. "I said most of it in that." He looked at the magazine. "He knows more about when a horse is ready to race and what race to run him in than any other trainer on the turf. And he's got as much feeling for people as a block of stone. He knows the name and the breeding back to the flood of every one of the hundred and twenty plus horses in his yard, and he can recognize them walking away from him in a downpour, which is practically impossible, but as for the forty lads he's got there working for him, he calls them all Tommy, because he doesn't know tother from which."

"Lads come and go," I said neutrally.

"So do horses. It's in his mind. He doesn't give a bugger's damn for people."

"Women?" I suggested.

"Uses them, poor sods. I bet when he's at it he's got his mind on his next day's runners."

"And Rosemary . . . what does she think about things?"

I poured a refill into his glass, and sipped at my own. Bobby finished his sandwich with a gulp and licked the crumbs off his fingers.

"Rosemary? She's halfway off her rocker."

"She looked all right yesterday at the races," I said. "And she's here today, as well."

"Yeah, well, she can hold on to the grande dame act in public still, I grant you, but I was in and out of the house for three days, and I'm telling you, mate, the going on there had to be heard to be believed."

"Such as?"

"Such as Rosemary screaming all over the place that they hadn't enough security and George telling her to belt up. Rosemary's got some screwy idea that some of their horses have been got at in the past, and I daresay she's right, at that, because you don't have a yard that size and that successful that hasn't had its share of villains trying to alter the odds. But anyway"—he drank deep and tipped the bottle generously to replenish his supplies—"she seized me by the coat in their hall one day—and that hall's as big as a fair-sized barn—literally seized me by the coat and said what I should be writing was some stuff about Gleaner and Zingaloo being got at—you remember, those two spanking two-year-olds who never developed—and George came out of his office and said she was neurotic and suffering from the change of life, and right then and there in front of me they had a proper slanging match." He took a breath and a mouthful. "Funny thing is, in a way I'd say they were fond of each other. As much as he could be fond of anybody."

I ran my tongue round my teeth and looked only marginally interested, as if my mind was on something else. "What did George say about her ideas on Gleaner and Zingaloo?" I said.

"He took it for granted I wouldn't take her seriously, but anyway, he said it was just that she had the heebie-jeebies that someone would nobble Tri-Nitro, and she was getting everything out of proportion. Her age, he said. Women always went very odd, he said, at that age. He said the security round Tri-Nitro was already double what he considered really necessary, because of her nagging, and when the new season began he'd have night patrols with dogs, and suchlike. Which is now, of course. He told me that Rosemary was quite wrong, anyway, about Gleaner and Zingaloo being got at, but that she had this obsession on the subject, and he was ready to humor her to some degree to stop her going completely bonkers. It seems that both of them—the horses, that is—proved to have a heart murmur, which of course accounted for their rotten performances as they matured and grew heavier. So that was that. No story." He emptied his glass and refilled it. "Well, Sid, mate, what is it you *really* want to know about George Caspar?"

"Um," I said, "do you think there's anything he is afraid of?"

"George?" he said disbelievingly. "What sort of thing?"

"Anything."

"When I was there, I'd say he was about as frightened as a ton of bricks."

"He didn't seem worried?"

"Not a bit."

"Or edgy?"

He shrugged. "Only with his wife."

"How long ago was it that you went there?"

"Oh . . ." He considered, thinking. "After Christmas. Yes . . . second week in January. We have to do those color mags such a long time in advance."

"You don't think, then," I said slowly, sounding disappointed, "that he'd be wanting any extra protection for Tri-Nitro?"

"Is that what you're after?" He gave the leering grin. "No, dice, then, Sid, mate. Try someone smaller. George has got his whole ruddy yard sewn up tight. For a start, see, it's one of those old ones enclosed inside a high wall, like a fortress. Then there's ten-foot-high double gates across the entrance, with spikes on top."

I nodded. "Yes . . . I've seen them."

"Well, then." He shrugged, as if that settled things.

There were closed-circuit televisions in all the bars at Kempton to keep serious drinkers abreast of the races going on outside, and on the nearest of these sets Bobby Unwin and I watched the second race. The horse that won by six lengths was the one trained by George Caspar, and while Bobby was still thoughtfully eyeing the two inches of fizz still left in the bottle, George himself came into the bar. Behind him, in a camel-colored overcoat, came a substantial man bearing all the stigmata of a satisfied winning owner. Cat-with-the-cream smile, big gestures, have this one on me.

"Finish the bottle, Bobby," I said.

"Don't you want any?"

"It's yours."

He made no objections. Poured, drank, and comfortably belched. "Better go," he said. "Got to write up these effing colts in the third. Don't you go telling my editor I watched the second in the bar. I'd get the sack." He didn't mean it. He saw many a race in the bar. "See you, Sid. Thanks for the drink."

He turned with a nod and made a sure passage to the door, showing not a sign of having dispatched seven eighths of a bottle of champagne within half an hour. Merely laying the foundations, no doubt. His capacity was phenomenal.

I tucked his magazine inside my jacket and made my own way slowly in his wake, thinking about what he'd said. Passing George Caspar, I said, "Well done," in the customary politeness of such occasions, and he nodded briefly and said, "Sid," and, transaction completed, I continued toward the door.

"Sid . . ." he called after me, his voice rising.

I turned. He beckoned. I went back.

"Want you to meet Trevor Deansgate," he said.

I shook the hand offered: snow-white cuff, gold links, smooth pale skin, faintly moist; well-tended nails, onyx-and-gold signet ring on little finger.

"Your winner?" I said. "Congratulations."

"Do you know who I am?"

"Trevor Deansgate?"

"Apart from that."

It was the first time I'd seen him at close quarters. There was often, in powerful men, a giveaway droop of the eyelids which proclaimed an inner sense of superiority, and he had it. Also dark grey eyes, black controlled hair, and the tight mouth which goes with well-exercised decision-making muscles.

"Go on, Sid," George said into my tiny hesitation. "If you know, say. I told Trevor you knew everything."

I glanced at George, but all that was to be read on his tough, weathered countenance was a sort of teasing expectancy. For many people, I knew, my new profession was a kind of game. There seemed to be no harm, on this occasion, of jumping obligingly through his offered hoop.

"Bookmaker?" I said tentatively; and to Trevor Deansgate directly, added, "Billy Bones?"

"There you are," said George, pleased. "I told you so."

Trevor Deansgate took it philosophically. I didn't try for a further reaction, which might not have been so friendly. His name at birth was reputed to be Shummuck. Trevor Shummuck from Manchester, who'd been born with a razor mind in a slum and changed his name, accent, and chosen company on the way up. As Bobby Unwin might have said, hadn't we all, and why not?

Trevor Deansgate's climb to the big league had been all but completed by buying out the old but ailing firm of "Billy Bones," in itself a blanket pseudonym for some brothers called Rubenstein and their uncle Solly. In the past few years "Billy Bones" had become big business. One could scarcely open a sports paper or go to the races without seeing the blinding fluorescent pink advertising, and slogans like "Make no Bones about it, Billy's best" tended to assault one's peace on Sundays. If the business was as vigorous as its sales campaign, Trevor Deansgate was doing all right.

We civilly discussed his winner until it was time to adjourn outside to watch the colts.

"How's Tri-Nitro?" I said to George, as we moved toward the door.

"Great," he said. "In great heart."

"No problems?"

"None at all."

We passed outside, and I spent the rest of the afternoon in the usual desultory way, watching the races, talking to people, and thinking unimportant thoughts. I didn't see Rosemary again, and calculated she was avoiding me, and after the fifth race I decided to go.

A racecourse official at the exit gate stopped me with an air of relief, as if he'd been waiting for me a shade too long.

"Note for you, Mr. Halley."

"Oh? Thanks."

He gave me an unobtrusive brown envelope. I put it in my pocket and walked on, out to my car. Climbed in. Took out, opened, and read the letter.

Sid, I've been busy all afternoon but I want to see you. Please can you meet me in the tearoom? After the last?

Lucas Wainwright

Cursing slightly, I walked back across the car park, through the gate, and along to the restaurant, where lunch had given place to sandwiches and cake. The last race being just finished, the tea customers were trickling in in small thirsty bunches, but there was no sign of Commander Lucas Wainwright, Director of Security of the Jockey Club.

I hung around, and he came in the end, hurrying, anxious, apologizing, and harassed.

"Do you want some tea?" He was out of breath.

"Not much."

"Never mind. Have some. We can sit here without being interrupted, and there are always too many people in the bar." He led the way to a table and gestured to me to sit down.

"Look, Sid. How do you feel about doing a job for us?" No waster of time, Commander Wainwright.

"Does 'us' mean the Security Service?"

"Yes."

"Official?" I said, surprised. The racecourse security people knew in moderate detail what I'd recently been doing and had raised no objections, but I hadn't imagined they actually approved. In some respects, I'd been working in their territory, and stepping on their toes.

Lucas drummed his fingers on the tablecloth.

"Unofficial," he said. "My own private show."

As Lucas Wainwright was himself the top brass of the Security Service, the investigative, policing arm of the Jockey Club, even unofficial requests from him could be considered to be respectably well-founded. Or at least until proved otherwise.

"What sort of job?" I said.

The thought of what sort of job slowed him up for the first time. He hummed and hahed and drummed his fingers some more, but finally shaped up to what proved to be a brute of a problem.

"Look, Sid, this is in strictest confidence."

"Yes."

"I've no higher authority for approaching you like this."

"Well," I said, "never mind. Go on."

"As I've no authority, I can't promise you any pay."

I sighed.

"All I could offer is . . . well . . . help if you should ever need it. And if it was within my power to give it, of course."

"That could be worth more than pay," I said.

He looked relieved. "Good. Now . . . this is very awkward. Very delicate." He still hesitated, but at last, with a sigh like a groan, he said, "I'm asking you to make . . . er . . . discreet inquiries into the . . . er . . . background of one of our people."

There was an instant's silence. Then I said, "Do you mean one of *you*? One of the Security Service?"

"I'm afraid that's right."

"Inquiries into exactly what?" I said.

He looked unhappy. "Bribery. Backhanders. That sort of thing."

"Um," I said. "Have I got this straight? You believe one of your chaps may be collecting payoffs from villains, and you want me to find out?"

"That's it," he said. "Exactly."

I thought it over. "Why don't you do the investigating yourselves? Just detail another of your chaps."

"Ah. Yes." He cleared his throat. "But there are difficulties. If I am wrong, I cannot afford to have it known that I was suspicious. It would cause a great, a very great, deal of trouble. And if I am right, which I fear I am, we—that is, the Jockey Club—would want to be able to deal with things quietly. A public scandal involving the Security Service would be very damaging to racing."

I thought he was perhaps putting it a bit high, but he wasn't.

"The man in question," he said miserably, "is Eddy Keith."

There was another countable silence. In the hierarchy of the Security Service then existing, there was Lucas Wainwright at the top, with two equal deputies one step down. Both of the deputies were retired senior-rank policemen. One of them was ex-Superintendent Eddison Keith.

I had a clear mental picture of him, as I had talked with him often. A big bluffy breezy man with a heavy hand for clapping one on the shoulder. More than a trace of Suffolk accent in a naturally loud voice. A large flourishing straw-colored mustache, fluffy light brown hair through which one could see the pink scalp shining, and fleshy-lidded eyes which seemed always to be twinkling with good humor, and often weren't.

I had glimpsed there occasionally a glint as cold and unmerciful as a crevasse. Very much a matter of sun on ice: pretty, but full of traps. One for applying the handcuffs with a cheery smile; that was Eddy Keith.

But crooked . . . ? I would never have thought so.

"What are the indications?" I said at last.

Lucas Wainwright chewed his lower lip for a while and then said, "Four of his inquiries over the past year have come up with incorrect results."

I blinked. "That's not very conclusive."

"No. Precisely. If I were sure, I wouldn't be here talking to you."

"I guess not." I thought a bit. "What sort of inquiries were they?"

"They were all syndicates. Inquiries into the suitability of people wanting to form syndicates to own horses. Making sure there weren't any undesirables sneaking into racing through the back door. Eddy gave all-clear reports on four proposed syndicates which do in fact all contain one or more people who would not be allowed through the gates."

"How do you know?" I said. "How did you find out?"

He made a face. "I was interviewing someone last week in connection with a dope charge. He was loaded with spite against a group of people he said had let him down, and he crowed over me that those people all owned horses under false names. He told me the names, and I checked, and the four syndicates which contain them were all passed by Eddy."

"I suppose," I said slowly, "they couldn't possibly be syndicates headed by Lord Friarly?"

He looked depressed. "Yes, I'm afraid so. Lord Friarly mentioned to me earlier this afternoon that he'd asked you to take a look-see. Told me out of politeness. It just reinforced the idea I'd already had of asking you myself. But I want it kept quiet."

"So does he," I said reassuringly. "Can you let me have Eddy's reports? Or copies of them? And the false and true names of the undesirables?"

He nodded. "I'll see you get them." He looked at his watch and stood up, the briskness returning to his manner like an accustomed coat. "I don't need to tell you . . . but do be discreet."

I joined him on his quick march to the door, where he left me at an even faster pace, sketching the merest wave of farewell. His back view vanished uprightly through the weighing room door, and I took myself out again to my car, reflecting that if I went on collecting jobs at the present rate, I would need to call up the troops.

CHAPTER 3

I TELEPHONED THE North London Comprehensive School and asked to speak to Chico Barnes.

"He's teaching judo," a voice said repressively.

"His class usually ends about now."

"Wait a minute."

I waited, driving toward London with my right hand on the wheel and my left round the receiver and a spatter of rain on the windshield. The car had been adapted for one-handed steering by the addition of a knob on the front face of the wheel's rim: very simple, very effective, and no objections from the police.

"Hullo?"

Chico's voice, cheerful, full even in one single word of his general irreverent view of the world.

"Want a job?" I said.

"Yeah." His grin traveled distinctly down the line. "It's been too dead quiet this past week."

"Can you go to the flat? I'll meet you there."

"I've got an extra class. They lumbered me. Some other guy's evening class of stout ladies. He's ill. I don't blame him. Where are you phoning from?"

"The car. From Kempton to London. I'm calling in at Roehampton, at the limb center, as it's on the way, but I could be outside your school in, say, an hour and a half. I'll pick you up. O.K.?"

"Sure," he said. "What are you going to the limb center for?"

"To see Alan Stephenson."

"He'll have gone home."

"He said he'd be there, working late."

"Your arm hurting again?"

"No. Matter of screws and such."

"Yeah," he said. "O.K. See you."

I put the phone down with the feeling of satisfaction that Chico nearly always engendered. There was no doubt that as a working companion I found him great: funny, inventive, persistent, and deceptively strong. Many a rogue had discovered too late that young slender Chico with his boyish grin could throw a two-hundred-fifty-pound man over his shoulder with the greatest ease.

When I first got to know him he was working, as I was, in the Radnor Detective Agency, where I had learned my new trade. At one point there had been a chance that I would become first a partner and eventually the owner of that agency, but although Radnor and I had come to an agreement, and had even changed the agency's name to Radnor-Halley, life had delivered an earthquake upheaval and decided things otherwise. It must have been only a day before the partnership agreements were ready to be signed, with finances arranged and the champagne approaching the ice, that Radnor himself sat down for a quiet snooze in his armchair at home and never woke up.

Back from Canada, as if on stretched elastic, had immediately snapped an unsuspected nephew, brandishing a will in his favor and demanding his rights. He did not, he said forthrightly, want to sell half his inheritance to a one-handed ex-jockey, especially at the price agreed. He himself would be taking over and breathing new life into the whole works. He himself would be setting it all up in new modern offices, not the old crummy bomb-damaged joint in the Cromwell Road, and anyone who didn't like the transfer could vote with his feet.

Most of the old bunch had stayed on into the new order, but Chico had had a blazing row with the nephew and opted for the dole. Without much trouble he had then found the part-time job teaching judo, and the first time I'd asked for his help he joined up with enthusiasm. Since then I myself seemed to have become the most regularly employed investigator working in racing, and if Radnor's nephew didn't like it (and he was reputed to be furious), it was just too bad.

CHICO BOUNCED OUT through the glass swinging doors of the school, the lights behind him making a halo round his curly hair. Any resemblance to sainthood stopped precisely there, since the person under the curls was in no way long-suffering, God-fearing, or chaste.

He slid into the car, gave me a wide grin, and said, "There's a pub round the corner with a great set of bristols."

Resignedly I pulled into the pub's car park and followed him into the bar. The girl dispensing drinks was, as he'd said, nicely endowed, and moreover, she greeted Chico with telling warmth. I listened to the flirting chitchat and paid for the drinks.

We sat on a bench by the wall, and Chico approached his pint with the thirst brought on by too much healthy exercise.

"Ah," he said, putting down the tankard temporarily. "That's better." Eyed my glass. "Is that straight orange juice?"

I nodded. "Been drinking on and off all day."

"Don't know how you bear it, all that high life and luxury."

"Easily."

"Yeah." He finished the pint, went back for a refill and another close encounter with the girl, and finally retracked to the bench. "Where do I go then, Sid? And what do I do?"

"Newmarket. Spot of pub crawling."

"Can't be bad."

"You're looking for a head lad called Paddy Young. He's George Caspar's head lad. Find out where he drinks, and sort of drift into conversation."

"Right."

"We want to know the present whereabouts of three horses which used to be in his yard."

"We do?"

"He shouldn't have any reason for not telling you, or at least I don't think so."

Chico eyed me. "Why don't you ask George Caspar right out? Be simpler, wouldn't it?"

"At that moment we don't want George Caspar to know we're asking questions about his horses."

"Like that, is it?"

"I don't know, really." I sighed. "Anyway, the three horses are Bethesda, Gleaner, and Zingaloo."

"O.K. I'll go up there tomorrow. Shouldn't be too difficult. You want me to ring you?"

"Soon as you can."

He glanced at me sideways. "What did the limb man say?"

"Hello, Sid, nice to see you."

He made a resigned noise with his mouth. "Might as well ask questions of a brick wall."

"He said the ship wasn't leaking and the voyage could go on."

"Better than nothing."

"As you say."

I went to Aynsford, as Charles had known I would, driving down on Saturday afternoon and feeling the apprehensive gloom deepen with every mile. For distraction I concentrated on Chico's news from Newmarket, telephoned through at lunchtime.

"I found him," he said. "He's a much-married man who has to take his pay packet home like a good boy on Friday evenings, but he sneaked out for a quick jar just now. The pub's nearly next door to the yard; very handy. Anyway, if you can understand what he says, and he's so Irish it's like talking to a foreigner, what it boils down to is that all three of those horses have gone to stud."

"Did he know where?"

"Sure. Bethesda went to someplace called Garvey's in Gloucestershire, and the other two are at a place just outside Newmarket, which Paddy Young called Traces, or at least I think that's what he said, although as I told you, he chews his words up something horrible."

"Thrace," I said. "Henry Thrace."

"Yeah? Well, maybe you can make sense of some other things he said, which were that Gleaner had a tritus and Zingaloo had the virus and Bruttersmit gave them both the turns down as quick as Concorde."

"Gleaner had a what?"

"Tritus."

I tried turning "Gleaner had a tritus" into an Irish accent in my head and came up with Gleaner had arthritis, which sounded a lot more likely. I said to Chico, ". . . and Brothersmith gave them the thumbs down . . ."

"Yeah," he said. "You got it."

"Where are you phoning from?"

"Box in the street."

"There's a bit of boozing time left," I said. "Would you see if you can find out if this Brothersmith is George Caspar's vet, and if so, look him up in the phone book and bring back his address and number."

"O.K. Anything else?"

"No." I paused. "Chico, did Paddy Young give you any impression that there was anything odd in these three horses going wrong?"

"Can't say he did. He didn't seem to care much, one way or the other. I just asked him casual like where they'd gone, and he told me, and threw in the rest for good measure. Philosophical, you could say he was."

"Right, then," I said. "Thanks."

We disconnected, but he rang again an hour later to tell me that Brothersmith was indeed George Caspar's vet, and to give me his address.

"If that's all then, Sid, there's a train leaving in half an hour, and I've a nice little dolly waiting for me round Wembley way who'll have her Saturday night ruined if I don't get back."

The more I thought about Chico's report and Bobby Unwin's comments, the less I believed in Rosemary's suspicions; but I'd promised her I would try, and try I still would, for a little while longer. For as long as it took me, anyway, to check up on Bethesda, Zingaloo, and Gleaner, and talk to Brothersmith the vet.

AYNSFORD STILL LOOKED its mellow stone self, but the daffodil-studded tranquillity applied to the exterior only. I stopped the car gently in front of the house and sat there wishing I didn't have to go in.

Charles, as if sensing that even then I might back off and drive away, came purposefully out of his front door and strode across the gravel. Watching for me, I thought. Waiting. Wanting me to come.

"Sid," he said, opening my door and stooping down to smile. "I knew you would."

"You hoped," I said.

I climbed out onto my feet.

"All right." The smile stayed in his eyes. "Hoped. But I know you."

I looked up at the front of the house, seeing only blank windows reflecting the grayish sky.

"Is she here?" I said.

He nodded. I turned away, went round to the back of the car, and lugged out my suitcase.

"Come on, then," I said. "Let's get it over."

"She's upset," he said, walking beside me. "She needs your understanding."

I glanced at him and said, "Mm." We finished the short journey in silence, and went through the door.

Jenny was standing there, in the hall.

I had never got used to the pang of seeing her on the rare occasions we had met since she left. I saw her as I had when I first loved her, a girl not of great classical beauty, but very pretty, with brown curling hair and a neat figure, and a way of holding her head high, like a bird on the alert. The old curving smile and the warmth in her eyes were gone, but I tended to expect them, with hopeless nostalgia.

"So you came," she said. "I said you wouldn't."

I put down the suitcase and took the usual deep breath. "Charles wanted me to," I said. I walked the steps toward her, and as always, we gave each other a brief kiss on the cheek. We had maintained the habit as the outward and public mark of a civilized divorce; but privately, I often thought, it was more like the ritual salute before a duel.

Charles shook his head impatiently at the lack of real affection, and walked ahead of us into the drawing room. He had tried in the past to keep us together, but the glue for any marriage had to come from the inside, and ours had dried to dust.

Jenny said, "I don't want any lectures from you, Sid, about this beastly affair."

"No."

"You're not perfect yourself, even though you like to think so."

"Give it a rest, Jenny," I said.

She walked abruptly away into the drawing room, and I more slowly followed. She would use me, I thought, and discard me again, and because of Charles I would let her. I was surprised that I felt no tremendous desire to offer comfort. It seemed that irritation was still well in the ascendancy over compassion.

She and Charles were not alone. When I went in she had crossed the room to stand at the side of a tall blond man whom I'd met before; and beside Charles stood a stranger, a stocky young-old man whose austere eyes were disconcertingly surrounded by a rosy country face.

Charles said in his most uncivilized voice, "You know Toby, don't you, Sid?" and Jenny's shield and supporter and I nodded to each other and gave the faint smiles of an acquaintanceship we would each have been happier without. "And this, Sid, is my solicitor, Oliver Quayle. Gave up his golf to be here. Very good of him."

"So you're Sid Halley," the young-old man said, shaking hands. There was nothing in his voice either way, but his gaze slid down and sideways, seeking to see the half-hidden hand that he wouldn't have looked at if he hadn't known. It often happened that way. He brought his gaze back to my face and saw that I knew what he'd been doing. There was the smallest flicker in his lower eyelids, but no other remark. Judgment suspended, I thought, on either side.

Charles's mouth twitched, and he said smoothly, "I warned you, Oliver. If you don't want him to read your thoughts, you mustn't move your eyes."

"Yours don't move," I said to him.

"I learned that lesson years ago."

He made courteous sit-down motions with his hands, and the five of us sank into comfort and pale gold brocade.

"I've told Oliver," Charles said, "that if anyone can find this Nicholas Ashe person, you will."

"Frightfully useful, don't you know," drawled Toby, "having a plumber in the family when the pipes burst."

It was a fraction short of offensiveness. I gave him the benefit of a doubt I didn't have, and asked nobody in particular whether the police wouldn't do the job more quickly.

"The trouble is," Quayle said, "that technically it is Jenny alone who is guilty of obtaining money by false pretenses. The police have listened to her, of course, and the man in charge seems to be remarkably sympathetic, but"— he slowly shrugged the heavy shoulders in a way that skillfully combined sympathy and resignation—"one feels they might choose to settle for the case they have."

"But I say," protested Toby. "It was that Ashe's idea, all of it."

"Can you prove it?" Quayle said.

"Jenny says so," Toby said, as if that were proof enough.

Quayle shook his head. "As I've told Charles, it would appear from all documents she signed that she did know the scheme was fraudulent. And ignorance, even if genuine, is always a poor, if not impossible, defense."

I said, "If there's no evidence against him, what would you do, even if I did find him?"

Quayle looked my way attentively. "I'm hoping that if you find him, you'll find evidence as well."

Jenny sat up exceedingly straight and spoke in a voice sharp with perhaps anxiety but certainly anger.

"This is all rubbish, Sid. Why don't you say straight out that the job's beyond you?"

"I don't know if it is."

"It's pathetic," she said to Quayle, "how he longs to prove he's clever, now he's disabled."

The flicking sneer in her voice shocked Quayle and Charles into visible discomfort, and I thought dejectedly that this was what I'd caused in her, this compulsive need to hurt. I didn't just mind what she'd said; I minded bitterly that because of me she was not showing to Quayle the sunny-tempered person she would still be if I weren't there.

"If I find Nicholas Ashe," I said grimly, "I'll give him to Jenny. Poor fellow."

None of the men liked it. Quayle looked disillusioned, Toby showed he despised me, and Charles sorrowfully shook his head. Jenny alone, behind her anger, looked secretly pleased. She seldom managed nowadays to goad me into a reply to her insults, and counted it a victory that I'd done it and earned such general disapproval. My own silly fault. There was only one way not to let her see when her barbs went in, and that was to smile . . . and the matter in hand was not very funny.

I said, more moderately, "There might be ways . . . if I can find him. At any rate, I'll do my best. If there's anything I can do, I'll do it."

Jenny looked unplacated, and no one else said anything. I sighed internally. "What did he look like?" I asked.

After a pause Charles said, "I saw him once only, for about thirty minutes, four months ago. I have a general impression, but that's all. Young, personable, dark-haired, clean-shaven. Something too ingratiating in his manner to me. I would not have welcomed him as a junior officer aboard my ship."

Jenny compressed her lips and looked away from him, but could not protest against this judgment. I felt the first faint stirrings of sympathy for her and tried to stamp on them: they would only make me more vulnerable, which was something I could do without.

I said to Toby, "Did you meet him?"

"No," he said loftily. "Actually, I didn't."

"Toby has been in Australia," Charles said, explaining.

They all waited. It couldn't be shirked. I said directly to her, neutrally, "Jenny?"

"He was *fun*," she said vehemently, unexpectedly. "My God, he was fun. And after you . . ." She stopped. Her head swung around my way with bitter eyes. "He was full of life and jokes. He made me laugh. He was terrific. He lit things up. It was like . . . it was like . . ." She suddenly faltered and stopped, and I knew she was thinking, Like us when we first met. Jenny, I thought desperately, don't say it, please don't.

Perhaps it was too much, even for her. How could people, I wondered for the ten thousandth useless time, how could people who had loved so dearly come to such a wilderness; and yet the change in us was irreversible, and neither of us would even search for a way back. It was impossible. The fire was out. Only a few live coals lurked in the ashes, searing unexpectedly at the incautious touch.

I swallowed. "How tall was he?" I said.

"Taller than you."

"Age?"

"Twenty-nine."

The same age as Jenny. Two years younger than I. If he had told the truth, that was. A confidence trickster might lie about absolutely everything as a matter of prudence.

"Where did he stay, while he was . . . er . . . operating?"

Jenny looked unhelpful, and it was Charles who answered. "He told Jenny he was staying with an aunt, but after he had gone, Oliver and I checked up. The aunt, unfortunately, proved to be a landlady who lets rooms to students in north Oxford. And in any case"—he cleared his throat—"it seems that fairly soon he left the lodgings and moved into the flat Jenny is sharing in Oxford with another girl."

"He lived in your flat?" I said to Jenny.

"So what of it?" She was defiant. And something else . . .

"So when he left, did he leave anything behind?"

"No."

"Nothing at all?"

"No."

"Do you want him found?" I said.

To Charles and Quayle and Toby the answer to that question was an automatic yes, but Jenny didn't answer, and the blush that started at her throat rose fast to two bright spots on her cheekbones.

"He's done you great harm," I said.

With stubbornness stiffening her neck, she said, "Oliver says I won't go to prison."

"Jenny!" I was exasperated. "A conviction for fraud will affect your whole life in all sorts of horrible ways. I see that you liked him. Maybe you even loved him. But he's not just a naughty boy who pinched the jam pot for a lark. He has callously arranged for you to be punished in his stead. *That's* the crime for which I'll catch him if I damned well can, even if you don't want me to."

Charles protested vigorously. "Sid, that's ridiculous. Of course she wants to see him punished. She agreed that you should try to find him. She wants you to, of course she does."

I sighed and shrugged. "She agreed, to please you. And because she doesn't think I'll succeed; and she's very likely right. But even *talk* of my succeeding is putting her in a turmoil and making her angry . . . and it's by no means unknown for women to go on loving scoundrels who've ruined them."

Jenny rose to her feet, stared at me blindly, and walked out of the room. Toby took a step after her and Charles too got to his feet, but I said with some force, "Mr. Quayle, please will you go after her and tell her the consequences if she's convicted. Tell her brutally, make her understand, make it shock."

He had taken the decision and was on his way after her before I'd finished.

"It's hardly kind," Charles said. "We've been trying to spare her."

"You can't expect Halley to show her any sympathy," Toby said waspishly.

I eyed him. Not the brightest of men, but Jenny's choice of undemanding escort, the calm sea after the hurricane. A few months earlier she had been thinking of marrying him but whether she would do it post-Ashe was to my mind doubtful. He gave me his usual lofty look of noncomprehension and decided Jenny needed him at once.

Charles watched his departing back and said, with a tired note of despair, "I simply don't understand her. And it took you about ten minutes to see . . . what I wouldn't have seen at all." He looked at me gloomily. "It was pointless, then, to try to reassure her, as I've been doing?"

"Oh, Charles, what a bloody muddle . . . It won't have done any harm. It's just given her a way of excusing him—Ashe—and putting off the time when she'll have to admit to herself that she's made a shattering . . . shaming mistake."

The lines in his face had deepened with distress. He said somberly, "It's worse. Worse than I thought."

"Sadder," I said. "Not worse."

"Do you think you can find him?" he said. "How on earth do you start?"

CHAPTER 4

I STARTED IN the morning, having not seen Jenny again, as she'd driven off the previous evening with Toby at high speed to Oxford, leaving Charles and me to dine alone, a relief to us both; and they had returned late and not appeared for breakfast by the time I left.

I went to Jenny's flat in Oxford, following directions from Charles, and rang the doorbell. The lock, I thought, looking at it, would give me no trouble if there was no one in, but in fact, after my second ring, the door opened a few inches, on a chain.

"Louise McInnes?" I said, seeing an eye, some tangled fair hair, a bare foot, and a slice of dark blue dressing gown.

"That's right."

"Would you mind if I talked to you? I'm Jenny's . . . er . . . ex-husband. Her father asked me to see if I could help her."

"You're Sid?" she said, sounding surprised. "Sid Halley?"

"Yes."

"Well . . . wait a minute." The door closed and stayed closed for a good long time. Finally it opened again, this time wide, and the whole girl was revealed. This time she wore jeans, a checked shirt, baggy blue sweater, and slippers. The hair was brushed, and there was lipstick: a gentle pink, unaggressive.

"Come in."

I went in and closed the door behind me. Jenny's flat, as I would have guessed, was not constructed of plasterboard and held together with drawing pins. The general address was a large Victorian house in a prosperous side street, with a semicircular driveway and parking room at the back. Jenny's section, reached by its own enclosed, latterly added staircase, was the whole of the spacious first floor. Bought, Charles had told me, with some of her divorce settlement. It was nice to see that on the whole my money had been well spent.

Switching on lights, the girl led the way into a low bow-fronted sitting room which still had its curtains drawn and the day before's clutter slipping haphazardly off tables and chairs. Newspapers, a coat, some kicked-off boots, coffee cups, an empty yogurt carton in a fruit bowl, with spoon, some dying daffodils, a typewriter with its cover off, some scrunched-up pages that had missed the wastepaper basket.

Louise McInnes drew back the curtains, letting in the gray morning to dilute the electricity.

"I wasn't up," she said unnecessarily.

"I'm sorry."

The mess was the girl's. Jenny was always tidy, clearing up before bed. But the room itself was Jenny's. One or two pieces from Aynsford, and an overall similarity to the sitting room of our own house, the one we'd shared. Love might change, but taste endured. I felt a stranger, and at home.

"Want some coffee?" she said.

"Only if . . ."

"Sure. I'd have some anyway."

"Can I help you?"

"If you like."

She led the way through the hall and into a bare-looking kitchen. There was nothing precisely prickly in her manner, but all the same it was cool. Not surprising, really. What Jenny thought of me, she would say, and there wouldn't be much that was good.

"Like some toast?" She was busy producing a packet of white sliced bread and a jar of powdered coffee.

"Yes, I would."

"Then stick a couple of pieces in the toaster. Over there."

I did as she said, while she ran some water into an electric kettle and dug into a cupboard for butter and marmalade. The butter was a half-used packet still in its torn greaseproof wrapping, the center scooped out and the whole thing messy: exactly like my own butter packet in my own flat. Jenny had put butter into dishes automatically. I wondered if she did when she was alone.

"Milk and sugar?"

"No sugar."

When the toast popped up she spread the slices with butter and marmalade and put them on two plates. Boiling water went onto the brown powder in mugs, and milk followed straight from the bottle.

"You bring the coffee," she said, "and I'll take the toast." She picked up the plates and out of the corner of her eye saw my left hand closing round one of the mugs. "Look out," she said urgently. "That's hot."

I gripped the mug carefully with the fingers that couldn't feel.

She blinked.

"One of the advantages," I said, and picked up the other mug more gingerly by the handle.

She looked at my face, but said nothing; merely turned away and went back to the sitting room.

"I'd forgotten," she said, as I put down the mugs on the space she had cleared for them on the low table in front of the sofa.

"False teeth are more common," I said politely.

She came very near to a laugh, and although it ended up as a doubtful frown, the passing warmth was a glimpse of the true person living behind the slightly brusque façade. She scrunched into the toast and looked thoughtful, and after a chew and a swallow, she said, "What can you do to help Jenny?"

"Try to find Nicholas Ashe."

"Oh . . ." There was another spontaneous flicker of smile, again quickly stifled by subsequent thought.

"You liked him?" I said.

She nodded ruefully. "I'm afraid so. He is . . . was . . . such tremendous fun. Fantastic company. I find it terribly hard to believe he's just gone off and left Jenny in this mess. I mean . . . he lived here, here in this flat . . . and we had so many laughs. What he's done . . . it's incredible."

"Look," I said, "would you mind starting at the beginning and telling me all about it?"

"But hasn't Jenny . . . ?"

"No."

"I suppose," she said slowly, "that she wouldn't like admitting to you that he made such a fool of us."

"How much," I said, "did she love him?"

"Love? What's love? I can't tell you. She was *in* love with him." She licked her fingers. "All fizzy. Bright and bubbly. Up in the clouds."

"Have you been there? Up in the clouds?"

She looked at me straightly. "Do you mean, do I know what it's like? Yes, I do. If you mean, was I in love with Nicky, then no, I wasn't. He was fun, but he didn't turn me on like he did Jenny. And in any case, it was she who attracted him. Or at least," she finished doubtfully, "it seemed like it." She wagged her licked fingers. "Would you give me that box of tissues that's just behind you?"

I gave her the box and watched her as she wiped off the rest of the stickiness. She had fair eyelashes and English-rose skin, and a face that had left shyness behind. Too soon for life to have printed unmistakable signposts; but there did seem, in her natural expression, to be little in the way of cynicism or intolerance. A practical girl, with sense.

"I don't really know where they met," she said, "except that it was some-where here in Oxford. I came back one day, and he was *here*, if you see what I mean? They were already . . . well . . . interested in each other."

"Er," I said, "have you always shared this flat with Jenny?"

"More or less. We were at school together . . . didn't you know? Well, we met one day and I told her I was going to be living in Oxford for two years while I wrote a thesis, and she said had I anywhere to stay, because she'd seen this flat, but she'd like some company. . . . So I came. Like a shot. We've got on fine, on the whole."

I looked at the typewriter and the signs of effort. "Do you work here all the time?"

"Here or in the Sheldonian—er, the library, that is—or out doing other research. I pay rent to Jenny for my room . . . and I don't know why I'm telling you all this."

"It's very helpful."

She got to her feet. "It might be as well for you to see all the stuff. I've put it in his room—Nicky's room—to get it out of sight. It's all too boringly painful, as a matter of fact."

Again I followed her through the hall, and this time to farther down the wide passage, which was recognizably the first-floor landing of the old house.

"That room," she said, pointing at doors, "is Jenny's. That's the bath-room. That's my room. And this one at the end was Nicky's."

"When exactly did he go?" I said, walking behind her.

"Exactly? Who knows? Sometime on Wednesday. Two weeks last Wednes-day." She opened the white-painted door and walked into the end room. "He was here at breakfast, same as usual. I went off to the library, and Jenny caught the train to London to go shopping, and when we both got back, he was gone. Just gone. Everything. Jenny was terribly shocked. Wept all over the place. But of course, we didn't know then that he hadn't just left her, he'd cleared out with all the money as well."

"How did you find out?"

"Jenny went to the bank on the Friday to pay in the checks and draw out some cash for postage, and they told her the account was closed."

I looked round the room. It had thick carpet, Georgian dressing chest, big comfort-promising bed, upholstered armchair, pretty, Jenny-like cur-tains, fresh white paint. Six large brown boxes of thick cardboard stood in a double stack in the biggest available space; and none of it looked as if it had ever been lived in.

I went over to the chest and pulled out a drawer. It was totally empty. I put my fingers inside and drew them along, and they came out without a speck of dust or grit.

Louise nodded. "He had dusted. And vacuumed too. You could see the marks on the carpet. He cleaned the bathroom, as well. It was all sparkling. Jenny thought it was nice of him . . . until she found out just why he didn't want to leave any trace."

"I should think it was symbolic," I said absently.

"What do you mean?"

"Well . . . not so much that he was afraid of being traced through hair and fingerprints, but just that he wanted to feel that he'd wiped himself out of this place. So that he didn't feel he'd left anything of himself here. I mean . . . if you want to go back to a place, you subconsciously leave things there, you 'forget' them. Well-known phenomenon. So if you subconsciously, as well as consciously, don't want to go back to a place, you may feel impelled to remove even your dust." I stopped. "Sorry. Didn't mean to bore you."

"I'm not bored."

I said matter-of-factly, "Where did they sleep?"

"Here." She looked carefully at my face and judged it safe to proceed. "She used to come along here. Well . . . I couldn't help but know. Most nights. Not always."

"He never went to her?"

"Funny thing, I never ever saw him go into her room, even in the day-time. If he wanted her, he'd stand outside and call."

"It figures."

"More symbolism?" She went to the pile of boxes and opened the top-most. "The stuff in here will tell you the whole story. I'll leave you to read it . . . I can't stand the sight of it. And anyway, I'd better clean the place up a bit, in case Jenny comes back."

"You don't expect her, do you?"

She tilted her head slightly, hearing the faint alarm in my voice. "Are you frightened of her?"

"Should I be?"

"She says you're a worm." A hint of amusement softened the words.

"Yes, she would," I said. "And no, I'm not frightened of her. She just . . . distracts me."

With sudden vehemence she said, "Jenny's a super girl." Genuine friendship, I thought. A statement of loyalties. The merest whiff of challenge. But Jenny, the super girl, was the one I'd married.

I said, "Yes," without inflection, and after a second or two she turned and went out of the room. With a sigh I started on the boxes, shifting them clumsily and being glad neither Jenny nor Louise was watching. They were large, and although one or two were not as heavy as the others, their proportions were all wrong for gripping electrically.

The top one contained two foot-deep stacks of office-size paper, white, good quality, and printed with what looked like a typewritten letter. At the top of each sheet there was an impressive array of headings, including, in the center, an embossed and gilded coat of arms. I lifted out one of the letters, and began to understand how Jenny had fallen for the trick.

"Research into Coronary Disability," it said, in engraved lettering above the coat of arms, with, beneath it, the words "Registered Charity." To the left of the gold embossing there was a list of patrons, mostly with titles, and to the right a list of the charity's employees, one of whom was listed as Jennifer Halley, Executive Assistant. Below her name, in small capital letters, was the address of the Oxford flat.

The letter bore no date and no salutation. It began about a third of the way down the paper, and said:

So many families nowadays have had sorrowful first-hand knowledge of the seriousness of coronary artery disease, which even where it does not kill can leave a man unable to continue with a full, strenuous working life.

Much work has already been done in the field of investigation into the causes and possible prevention of this scourge of modern man, but much more remains still to be done. Research funded by government money being of necessity limited in today's financial climate, it is of the utmost importance that the public should be asked to support directly the essential programs now in hand in privately run facilities.

We do know, however, that many people resent receiving straightforward fund-raising letters, however worthy the cause, so to aid Research into Coronary Disability we ask you to buy something, along the same principle as Christmas cards, the sale of which does so much good work in so many fields. Accordingly the patrons, after much discussion, have decided to offer for sale a supply of exceptionally fine wax polish, which has been especially formulated for the care of antique furniture.

The wax is packed in quarter-kilo tins, and is of the quality used by expert restorers and museum curators. If you should wish to buy, we are offering the wax at five pounds a tin; and you may be sure that at least three quarters of all revenue goes straight to research.

*The wax will be good for your furniture, your contribution will be good
for the cause, and with your help there may soon be significant advances in the
understanding and control of this killing disease.*

*If you should wish to, please send a donation to the address printed above.
(Checks should be made out to Research into Coronary Disability.) You will
receive a supply of wax immediately, and the gratitude of future heart patients
everywhere.*

*Yours sincerely,
Executive Assistant*

I said "Phew" to myself, and folded the letter and tucked it into my
jacket. Sob stuff; the offer of something tangible in return; and the veiled hint
that if you didn't cough up, it could one day happen to you. And, according
to Charles, the mixture had worked.

The second big box contained several thousand white envelopes, unad-
dressed. The third was half full of mostly hand-written letters on every con-
ceivable type of writing paper; orders for wax, all saying, among other things,
"Check enclosed."

The fourth contained printed Compliments slips, saying that Research
into Coronary Disability acknowledged the contribution with gratitude and
had pleasure herewith in sending a supply of wax.

The fifth brown box, half empty, and the sixth, unopened and full, contained numbers of flat white boxes about six inches square by two inches
deep. I lifted out a white box and looked inside. Contents, one flat round unprinted tin with a firmly screwed-on lid. The lid put up a fight, but I got it
off in the end, and found underneath it a soft mid-brown mixture that certainly smelled of polish. I shut it up, returned the tin to its package, and left
it out, ready to take.

There seemed to be nothing else. I looked into every cranny in the room
and down the sides of the armchair, but there wasn't as much as a pin.

I picked up the square white box and went back slowly and quietly
toward the sitting room, opening the closed doors one by one, and looking at
what they concealed. There had been two that Louise had not identified: one
proved to be a linen cupboard, and the other a small unfurnished room containing suitcases and assorted junk.

Jenny's room was decisively feminine: pink and white, frothy with net
and frills. Her scent lay lightly in the air, the violet scene of Mille. No use remembering the first bottle I'd given her, long ago in Paris. Too much time

had passed. I shut the door on the fragrance and the memory and went into the bathroom.

A white bathroom. Huge fluffy towels. Green carpet, green plants. Looking glass on two walls, light and bright. No visible toothbrushes: everything in cupboards. Very tidy. Very Jenny. Roger & Gallet soap.

The snooping habit had ousted too many scruples. With hardly a hesitation, I opened Louise's door and put my eyes round, trusting to luck she wouldn't come out into the hall and find me.

Organized mess, I thought. Heaps of papers, and books everywhere. Clothes on chairs. Unmade bed; not surprising, since I'd sprung her out of it.

A washbasin in a corner, no cap on the toothpaste, pair of tights hung to dry. An open box of chocolates. A haphazard scatter on the dressing table. A tall vase with horse chestnut buds bursting. No smell at all. No long-term dirt, just surface clutter. The blue dressing gown on the floor. Basically the room was furnished much like Ashe's: and one could clearly see where Jenny ended and Louise began.

I pulled my head out and closed the door, undetected. Louise, in the sitting room, had been easily sidetracked in her tidying, and was sitting on the floor intently reading a book.

"Oh, hello," she said, looking up vaguely as if she had forgotten I was there. "Have you finished?"

"There must be other papers," I said. "Letters, bills, cash books, that sort of thing."

"The police took them."

I sat on the sofa, facing her. "Who called the police in?" I said. "Was it Jenny?"

She wrinkled her forehead. "No. Someone complained to them that the charity wasn't registered."

"Who?"

"I don't know. Someone who received one of the letters, and checked up. Half those patrons on the letterhead don't exist, and the others didn't know their names were being used."

I thought and said, "What made Ashe bolt just when he did?"

"We don't know. Maybe someone telephoned here to complain, as well. So he went while he could. He'd been gone for a week when the police turned up."

I put the square white box on the coffee table. "Where did the wax come from?" I said.

"Some firm or other. Jenny wrote to order it, and it was delivered here. Nicky knew where to get it."

"Invoices?"

"The police took them."

"These begging letters . . . who got them printed?"

She sighed. "Jenny, of course. Nicky had some others, just like them, except that they had his name in the space where they put Jenny's. He explained that it was no use sending any more letters with his name and address on, as he'd moved. He was keen, you see, to keep on working for the cause. . . ."

"You bet he was," I said.

She was half irritated. "It's all very well to jeer, but you didn't meet him. You'd have believed him, same as we did."

I left it. Maybe I would have. "These letters," I said. "Who were they sent to?"

"Nicky had lists of names and addresses. Thousands of them."

"Have you got them? The lists?"

She looked resigned. "He took them with him."

"What sort of people were on them?"

"The sort of people who would own antique furniture and cough up a fiver without missing it."

"Did he say where he'd got them from?"

"Yes," she said. "From the charity's headquarters."

"And who addressed the letters and sent them out?"

"Nicky typed the envelopes. Yes—don't ask—on my typewriter. He was very fast. He could do hundreds in a day. Jenny signed her name at the bottom of the letters, and I usually folded them and put them in the envelopes. She used to get writer's cramp doing it and Nicky would often help her."

"Signing her name?"

"That's right. He copied her signature. He did it hundreds of times. You couldn't really tell the difference."

I looked at her in silence.

"I know," she said. "Asking for trouble. But you see, he made all that hard work with the letter seem such fun. Like a game. He was full of jokes. You don't understand. And then, when the checks started rolling in, it was obviously worth the effort."

"Who sent off the wax?" I said gloomily.

"Nicky typed the addresses on labels. I used to help Jenny stick them on the boxes and seal the boxes with sticky tape, and take them to the post office."

"Ashe never went?"

"Too busy typing. We used to wheel them round to the post office in those shopping bags on wheels."

"And the checks . . . I suppose Jenny herself paid them in?"

"That's right."

"How long did all this go on?" I said.

"A couple of months, once the letters were printed and the wax had arrived."

"How much wax?"

"Oh, we had stacks of it, all over the place. It came in those big brown boxes . . . sixty tins in each, ready packed. They practically filled the flat. Actually, in the end Jenny wanted to order some more, as we were running very low, but Nicky said no, we'd finish what we had and take a breather before starting again."

"He meant to stop, anyway," I said.

Reluctantly, she said, "Yes."

"How much money," I said, "did Jenny bank?"

She looked at me somberly. "In the region of ten thousand pounds. Maybe a bit more. Some people sent much more than a fiver. One or two sent a hundred, and didn't want the wax."

"It's incredible."

"The money just came pouring in. It still does, every day. But it goes direct to the police from the post office. They'll have a hell of a job sending it all back."

"What about that box of letters in Ashe's room saying 'Check enclosed'?"

"Those," she said, "are people whose money was banked, and who've been sent the wax."

"Didn't the police want those letters?"

She shrugged. "They didn't take them, anyway."

"Do you mind if I do?"

"Help yourself."

After I'd fetched the box of letters and dumped it by the front door, I went back into the sitting room to ask her another question. Deep in the book again, she looked up without enthusiasm.

"How did Ashe get the money out of the bank?"

"He took a typewritten letter signed by Jenny saying she wanted to withdraw the balance so as to be able to give it to the charity in cash at its annual gala dinner, and also a check signed by Jenny for every penny."

"But she didn't . . ."

"No. He did. But I've seen the letter and the check. The bank gave them to the police. You can't tell it isn't Jenny's writing. Even Jenny can't tell the difference."

She got gracefully to her feet, leaving the book on the floor. "Are you go-ing?" she said hopefully. "I've got so much to do. I'm way behind, because of Nicky." She went past me into the hall, but when I followed her she delivered another chunk of dismay.

"The bank clerks can't remember Nicky. They pay out cash in thousands for wages every day, because there's so much industry in Oxford. They were used to Jenny in connection with that account, and it was ten days or more before the police asked questions. No one can remember Nicky there at all."

"He's professional," I said flatly.

"Every pointer to it, I'm afraid." She opened the door while I bent down and awkwardly picked up the brown cardboard box, balancing the small white one on top.

"Thank you," I said, "for your help."

"Let me carry that box downstairs."

"I can do it," I said.

She looked briefly into my eyes. "I'm sure you can. You're too damned proud." She took the box straight out of my arms and walked purposefully away. I followed her, feeling a fool, down the stairs and out onto the tarmac.

"Car?" she said.

"Round the back, but . . ."

As well talk to the tide. I went with her, weakly gestured to the Scimitar, and opened the boot. She dumped the boxes inside, and I shut them in.

"Thank you," I said again. "For everything."

The faintest of smiles came back into her eyes.

"If you think of anything that could help Jenny," I said, "will you let me know?"

"If you give me your address."

I forked a card out of an inner pocket and gave it to her. "It's on there."

"All right." She stood still for a moment with an expression I couldn't read. "I'll tell you one thing," she said. "From what Jenny's said . . . you're not a bit what I expected."

CHAPTER 5

FROM OXFORD I drove west to Gloucestershire and arrived at Garvey's stud farm at the respectable visiting hour of eleven-thirty, Sunday morning.

Tom Garvey, standing in his stable yard talking to his stud groom, came striding across as I braked to a halt.

"Sid Halley!" he said. "What a surprise. What do you want?"

I grimaced through the open car window. "Does everyone think I want something, when they see me?"

"Of course, lad. Best snooper in the business now, so they say. We hear things, you know, even us dim country bumpkins; we hear things."

Smiling, I climbed out of the car and shook hands with a sixty-year-old near rogue who was about as far from a dim country bumpkin as Cape Horn from Alaska: a big strong bull of a man, with unshakable confidence, a loud domineering voice, and the wily mind of a gypsy. His hand in mine was as hard as his business methods and as dry as his manner. Tough with men, gentle with horses. Year after year he prospered, and if I would have had every foal on the place exhaustively blood-typed before I believed its alleged breeding, I was probably in the minority.

"What are you after, then, Sid?" he said.

"I came to see a mare, Tom. One that you've got here. Just general interest."

"Oh, yes? Which one?"

"Bethesda."

There was an abrupt change in his expression from half amusement to no amusement at all. He narrowed his eyes and said brusquely, "What about her?"

"Well . . . has she foaled, for instance?"

"She's dead."

"*Dead?*"

"You heard, lad. She's dead. You'd better come in the house."

He turned and scrunched away, and I followed. His house was old and dark and full of stale air. All the life of the place was outside, in fields and foaling boxes and the breeding shed. Inside, a heavy clock ticked loudly into silence, and there was no aroma of Sunday roast.

"In here."

It was a cross between a dining room and an office: heavy old table and chairs at one end, filing cabinets and sagging armchairs at the other. No attempts at cosmetic décor to please the customers. Sales went on outside, on the hoof.

Tom perched against his desk and I on the arm of one of the chairs: not the sort of conversation for relaxing in comfort.

"Now then," he said. "Why are you asking about Bethesda?"

"I just wondered what had become of her."

"Don't fence with me, lad. You don't drive all the way here out of general interest. What do you want to know for?"

"A client wants to know," I said.

"What client?"

"If I was working for you," I said, "and you'd told me to keep quiet about it, would you expect me to tell?"

He considered me with sour concentration.

"No, lad. Guess I wouldn't. And I don't suppose there's much secret about Bethesda. She died foaling. The foal died with her. A colt, it would have been. Small, though."

"I'm sorry," I said.

He shrugged. "It happens sometimes. Not often, mind. Her heart packed up."

"Heart?"

"Aye. The foal was lying wrong, see, and the mare, she'd been straining longer than was good for her. We got the foal turned inside her once we found she was in trouble, but she just packed it in, sudden like. Nothing we could do. Middle of the night, of course, like it nearly always is."

"Did you have a vet to her?"

"Aye, he was there, right enough. I called him when we found she'd started, because there was a chance it would be dicey. First foal, and the heart murmur, and all."

I frowned slightly. "Did she have a heart murmur when she came to you?"

"Of course she did, lad. That's why she stopped racing. You don't know much about her, do you?"

"No," I said. "Tell me."

He shrugged. "She came from George Caspar's yard, of course. Her owner wanted to breed from her on account of her two-year-old form, so we bred her to Timberley, which should have given us a sprinter, but there you are, best-laid plans, and all that."

"When did she die?"

"Month ago, maybe."

"Well, thanks, Tom." I stood up. "Thanks for your time."

He shoved himself off his desk. "Bit of a tame turn-up for you, asking questions, isn't it? I can't square it with the old Sid Halley, all speed and guts over the fences."

"Times change, Tom."

"Aye, I suppose so. I'll bet you miss it, though, that roar from the stands when you'd come to the last and bloody well lift your horse over it." His face echoed remembered excitements. "By God, lad, that was a sight. Not a nerve in your body . . . Don't know how you did it."

I supposed it was generous of him, but I wished he would stop.

"Bit of bad luck, losing your hand. Still, with steeplechasing it's always something. Broken backs and such." We began to walk to the door. "If you go jump racing you've got to accept the risks."

"That's right," I said.

We went outside and across to my car.

"You don't do too badly with that contraption, though, do you, lad? Drive a car, and such."

"It's fine."

"Aye, lad." He knew it wasn't. He wanted me to know he was sorry, and he'd done his best. I smiled at him, got into the car, sketched a thank-you salute, and drove away.

AT AYNSFORD THEY were in the drawing room, drinking sherry before lunch: Charles, Toby, and Jenny.

Charles gave me a glass of fino, Toby looked me up and down as if I'd come straight from a pigsty, and Jenny said she had been talking to Louise on the telephone.

"We thought you had run away. You left the flat two hours ago."

"Sid doesn't run away," Charles said, as if stating a fact.

"Limps, then," Jenny said.

Toby sneered at me over his glass: the male in possession enjoying his small gloat over the dispossessed. I wondered if he really understood the extent of Jenny's attachment to Nicholas Ashe, or, if knowing, he didn't care.

I sipped the sherry: a thin dry taste, suitable to the occasion. Vinegar might have been better.

"Where did you buy all that polish from?" I said.

"I don't remember." She spoke distinctly, spacing out the syllables, willfully obstructive.

"Jenny!" Charles protested.

I sighed. "Charles, the police have the invoices, which will have the name and address of the polish firm on them. Can you ask your friend Oliver Quayle to ask the police for the information, and send it to me?"

"Certainly," he said.

"I cannot see," Jenny said in the same sort of voice, "that knowing who supplied the wax will make the slightest difference one way or the other."

It appeared that Charles privately agreed with her. I didn't explain. There was a good chance, anyway, that they were right.

"Louise said you were prying for ages."

"I liked her," I said mildly.

Jenny's nose, as always, gave away her displeasure. "She's out of your class, Sid," she said.

"In what way?"

"Brains, darling."

Charles said smoothly, "More sherry, anyone?" and, decanter in hand, began refilling glasses. To me, he said, "I believe Louise took a first at Cambridge in mathematics. I have played her at chess. . . . You would beat her with ease."

"A grand master," Jenny said, "can be obsessional and stupid and have a persecution complex."

Lunch came and went in the same sort of atmosphere, and afterward I went upstairs to put my few things into my suitcase. While I was doing it, Jenny came into the room and stood watching me.

"You don't use that hand much," she said.

I didn't answer.

"I don't know why you bother with it."

"Stop it, Jenny."

"If you'd done as I asked, and given up racing, you wouldn't have lost it."

"Probably not."

"You'd have a hand, not half an arm . . . not a stump."

I threw my spongebag with too much force into the suitcase.

"Racing first. Always racing. Dedication and winning and glory. And me nowhere. It serves you right. We'd still have been married . . . you'd still have your hand . . . if you'd have given up your precious racing when I wanted you to. Being champion jockey meant more to you than I did."

"We've said all this a dozen times," I said.

"Now you've got nothing. Nothing at all. I hope you're satisfied."

The battery charger stood on a chest of drawers, with two batteries in it.

She pulled the plug out of the main socket and threw the whole thing on the bed. The batteries fell out and lay on the bedspread haphazardly with the charger and its cord.

"It's disgusting," she said, looking at it. "It revolts me."

"I've got used to it." More or less, anyway.

"You don't seem to care."

I said nothing. I cared all right.

"Do you enjoy being crippled, Sid?"

Enjoy . . . Jesus Christ.

She walked to the door and left me looking down at the charger. I felt more than saw her pause there, and wondered numbly what else there was left that she could say.

Her voice reached me quite clearly across the room.

"Nicky has a knife in his sock."

I turned my head fast. She looked both defiant and expectant. "Is that true?" I asked.

"Sometimes."

"Adolescent," I said.

She was annoyed. "And what's so mature about hurtling around on horses and knowing . . . *knowing* . . . that pain and broken bones are going to happen?"

"You never think they will."

"And you're always wrong."

"I don't do it any more."

"But you would if you could."

There was no answer to that, because we both knew it was true.

"And look at you," Jenny said. "When you have to stop racing, do you look around for a nice quiet job in stockbroking, which you know about, and start to lead a normal life? No, you damned well don't. You go straight into something which lands you up in fights and beatings and hectic scrambles. You can't live without danger, Sid. You're addicted. You may think you aren't, but it's like a drug. If you just imagine yourself working in an office, nine to five, and commuting like any sensible man, you'll see what I mean."

I thought about it, silently.

"Exactly," she said. "In an office, you'd die."

"And what's so safe about a knife in the sock?" I said. "I was a jockey when we met. You knew what it entailed."

"Not from the inside. Not all those terrible bruises, and no food and no drink, and no damned sex life half the time."

"Did he show you the knife, or did you just see it?"

"What does it matter?"

"Is it adolescent . . . or truly dangerous?"

"There you are," she said. "You'd prefer him dangerous."

"Not for your sake."

"Well . . . I saw it. In a little sheath, snapped to his leg. And he made a joke about it."

"But you told me," I said. "So was it a warning?"

She seemed suddenly unsure and disconcerted, and after a moment or two simply frowned and walked away down the passage.

If it marked the first crack in her indulgence toward her precious Nicky, so much the better.

I PICKED CHICO up on Tuesday morning and drove north to Newmarket. A windy day, bright, showery, rather cold.

"How did you get on with the wife, then?"

He had met her once and had described her as unforgettable, the overtones in his voice giving the word several meanings.

"She's in trouble," I said.

"Pregnant?"

"There are other forms of trouble, you know."

"Really?"

I told him about the fraud, and about Ashe, and his knife.

"Gone and landed herself in a whoopsy," Chico said.

"Face down."

"And for dusting her off, do we get a fee?"

I looked at him sideways.

"Yeah," he said. "I thought so. Working for nothing again, aren't we? Good job you're well oiled, Sid, mate, when it comes to my wages. What is it this year? You made a fortune in anything since Christmas?"

"Silver, mostly. And cocoa. Bought and sold."

"Cocoa?" He was incredulous.

"Beans," I said. "Chocolate."

"Nutty bars?"

"No, not the nuts. They're risky."

"I don't know how you find the time."

"It takes as long as chatting up barmaids."

"What do you want with all that money, anyway?"

"It's a habit," I said. "Like eating."

Amicably we drew nearer to Newmarket, consulted the map, asked a couple of locals, and finally arrived at the incredibly well kept stud farm of Henry Thrace.

"Sound out the lads," I said, and Chico said, "Sure," and we stepped out of the car onto weedless gravel. I left him to it and went in search of Henry Thrace, who was reported by a cleaning lady at the front door of the house to be "down there on the right, in his office." Down there he was, in an armchair, fast asleep.

My arrival woke him, and he came alive with the instant awareness of people used to broken nights. A youngish man, very smooth, a world away from rough, tough, wily Tom Garvey. With Thrace, according to predigested opinion, breeding was strictly big business; handling the mares could be left to lower mortals. His first words, however, didn't match the image.

"Sorry. Been up half the night. . . . Er . . . who are you, exactly? Do we have an appointment?"

"No." I shook my head. "I just hoped to see you. My name's Sid Halley."

"Is it? Any relation to . . . Good Lord. You're him."

"I'm him."

"What can I do for you? Want some coffee?" He rubbed his eyes. "Mrs. Evans will get us some."

"Don't bother, unless . . ."

"No. Fire away." He looked at his watch. "Ten minutes do? I've got a meeting in Newmarket."

"It's very vague, really," I said. "I just came to inquire into the general health and so on of two of the stallions you've got here."

"Oh. Which two?"

"Gleaner," I said. "And Zingaloo."

We went through the business of why did I want to know, and why should he tell me, but finally, like Tom Garvey, he shrugged and said I might as well know.

"I suppose I shouldn't say it, but you wouldn't want to advise a client to buy shares in either of them," he said, taking for granted this was really the purpose of my visit. "They might have difficulty in covering their full quota of mares, both of them, although they're only four."

"Why's that?"

"They've both got bad hearts. They get exhausted with too much exercise."

"Both?"

"That's right. That's what stopped them racing as three-year-olds. And I reckon they've got worse since then."

"Somebody mentioned Gleaner was lame," I said.

Henry Thrace looked resigned. "He's developed arthritis recently. You can't keep a damn thing to yourself in this town." An alarm clock made a clamor on his desk. He reached over and switched it off. "Time to go, I'm afraid." He yawned. "I hardly take my clothes off at this time of the year." He took a battery razor out of his desk drawer, and attacked his beard. "Is that everything then, Sid?"

"Yes," I said. "Thanks."

CHICO PULLED THE car door shut, and we drove away toward the town.

"Bad hearts," he said.

"Bad hearts."

"Proper epidemic, isn't it?"

"Let's ask Brothersmith the vet."

Chico read out the address, in Middleton Road.

"Yes, I know it. It was old Follett's place. He was our old vet, still alive when I was here."

Chico grinned. "Funny somehow to think of you being a snotty little apprentice with the head lad chasing you."

"And chilblains."

"Makes you seem almost human."

I had spent five years in Newmarket, from sixteen to twenty-one. Learning to ride, learning to race, learning to live. My old guvnor had been a good one, and because every day I saw his wife, his life style, and his administrative ability, I'd slowly changed from a boy from the back streets into something more cosmopolitan. He had shown me how to manage the money I'd begun earning in large quantities, and how not to be corrupted by it; and when he turned me loose I found he'd given me the status that went with having been taught in his stable. I'd been lucky in my guvnor, and lucky to be for a long time at the top of the career I loved; and if one day the luck had run out, it was too damned bad.

"Takes you back, does it?" Chico said.

"Yeah."

We drove across the wide heath and past the racecourse toward the town. There weren't many horses about: a late morning string, in the distance, going home. I swung the car round familiar corners and pulled up outside the vet's.

Mr. Brothersmith was out.

If it was urgent, Mr. Brothersmith could be found seeing to a horse in a stable along Bury Road. Otherwise he would be home to his lunch, probably in half an hour. We said thank you, and sat in the car, and waited.

"We've got another job," I said. "Checking on syndicates."

"I thought the Jockey Club always did it themselves."

"Yes, they do. The job we've got is to check on the man from the Jockey Club who checks on the syndicates."

Chico digested it. "Tricky, that."

"Without him knowing."

"Oh, yes?"

I nodded. "Ex-Superintendent Eddy Keith."

Chico's mouth fell open. "You're joking."

"No."

"But he's the fuzz. The Jockey Club fuzz."

I passed on Lucas Wainwright's doubts, and Chico said Lucas Wainwright must have got it wrong. The job, I pointed out mildly, was to find out whether he had or not.

"And how do we do that?"

"I don't know. What do you think?"

"It's you that's supposed to be the brains of this outfit."

A muddy Range-Rover came along Middleton Road and turned into Brothersmith's entrance. As one, Chico and I removed ourselves from the Scimitar and went toward the tweed-jacketed man jumping down from his buggy.

"Mr. Brothersmith?"

"Yes? What's the trouble?"

He was young and harassed, and kept looking over his shoulder, as if something was chasing him. Time, perhaps, I thought. Or lack of it.

"Could you spare us a few minutes?" I said. "This is Chico Barnes, and I'm Sid Halley. It's just a few questions. . . ."

His brain took in my name and his gaze switched immediately toward my hands, fastening finally on the left.

"Aren't you the man with the myoelectric prosthesis?"

"Er . . . yes." I said.

"Come in, then. Can I look at it?"

He turned away and strode purposefully toward the side door of the house. I stood still and wished we were anywhere else.

"Come on, Sid," Chico said, following him. He looked back and stopped. "Give the man what he wants, Sid, and maybe he'll do the same for us."

Payment in kind, I thought; and I didn't like the price. Unwillingly I followed Chico into what turned out to be Brothersmith's surgery.

He asked a lot of questions in a fairly clinical manner, and I answered him in impersonal tones learned from the limb center.

"Can you rotate the wrist?" he said at length.

"Yes, a little." I showed him. "There's a sort of cup inside there which fits over the end of my arm, with another electrode to pick up the impulses for turning."

I knew he wanted me to take the hand off and show him properly, but I wouldn't have done it, and perhaps he saw there was no point in asking.

"It fits very tightly over your elbow," he said, delicately feeling round the gripping edges.

"So as not to fall off."

He nodded intently. "Is it easy to put on and remove?"

"Talcum powder," I said economically.

Chico's mouth opened, and shut again as he caught my don't-say-it stare, and he didn't tell Brothersmith that removal was often a distinct bore.

"Thinking of fitting one to a horse?" Chico said.

Brothersmith raised his still-harassed face and answered him seriously. "Technically it looks perfectly possible, but it's doubtful if one could train a horse to activate the electrodes, and it would be difficult to justify the expense."

"It was only a joke," Chico said faintly.

"Oh? Oh, I see. But it isn't unknown, you know, for a horse to have a false foot fitted. I was reading the other day about a successful prosthesis fitted to the forelimb of a valuable broodmare. She was subsequently covered, and produced a live foal."

"Ah," Chico said. "Now that's what we've come about. A broodmare. Only this one died."

Brothersmith detached his attention reluctantly from false limbs and transferred it to horses with bad hearts.

"Bethesda," I said, rolling down my sleeve and buttoning the cuff.

"Bethesda?" He wrinkled his forehead and turned the harassed look into one of anxiety. "I'm sorry. I can't recall . . ."

"She was a filly with George Caspar," I said. "Beat everything as a two-year-old, and couldn't run at three because of a heart murmur. She was sent to stud, but her heart packed up when she was foaling."

"Oh, dear," he said, adding sorrow to the anxiety. "What a pity. But I say, I'm so sorry: I treat so many horses, and I often don't know their names. Is there a question of insurance in this, or negligence, even? Because I assure you . . ."

"No," I said amiably. "Nothing like that. Can you remember, then, treating Gleaner and Zingaloo?"

"Yes, of course. Those two. Wretched shame for George Caspar. So disappointing."

"Tell us about them."

"Nothing much to tell, really. Nothing out of the ordinary, except that they were both so good as two-year-olds. Probably that was the cause of their troubles, if the truth were told."

"How do you mean?" I said.

His nervous tensions escaped in small jerks of his head as he brought forth some unflattering opinions. "Well, one hesitates to say so, of course, to top trainers like Caspar, but it is all too easy to strain a two-year-old's heart, and if they are good two-year-olds they run in top races, and the pressure to win may be terrific, because of stud values and everything, and a jockey, riding strictly to orders, mind you, may press a game youngster so hard that although it wins it is also more or less ruined for the future."

"Gleaner won the Doncaster Futurity in the mud," I said thoughtfully. "I saw it. It was a very hard race."

"That's right," Brothersmith said. "I checked him thoroughly afterwards, though. The trouble didn't start at once. In fact, it didn't show at all, until he ran in the Guineas. He came in from that in a state of complete exhaustion. First of all we thought it was the virus, but then after a few days we got this very irregular heartbeat, and then it was obvious what was the matter."

"What virus?" I said.

"Let's see. . . . The evening of the Guineas he had a very slight fever, as if he were in for equine flu, or some such. But it didn't develop. So it wasn't that. It was his heart, all right. But we couldn't have foreseen it."

"What percentage of horses develop bad hearts?" I said.

Some of the chronic anxiety state diminished as he moved confidently on neutral ground.

"Perhaps ten percent have irregular heartbeats. It doesn't always mean anything. Owners don't like to buy horses that have them, but look at Night Nurse, which won the Champion Hurdle, and had a heart murmur."

"But how often do you get horses having to stop racing because of bad hearts?"

He shrugged. "Perhaps two or three in a hundred."

George Caspar, I reflected, trained upward of a hundred and thirty horses, year after year.

"On average," I said, "are George Caspar's horses more prone to bad hearts than other trainers?"

The anxiety state returned in full force. "I don't know if I should answer that."

"If it's 'no'," I said, "what's the hassle?"

"But your purpose in asking . . ."

"A client," I said, lying with regrettable ease, "wants to know if he should send George Caspar a sparkling yearling. He asked me to check on Gleaner and Zingaloo."

"Oh, I see. Well, no, I don't suppose he has more. Nothing significant. Caspar's an excellent trainer, of course. If your client isn't too greedy when his horse is two, there shouldn't be any risk at all."

"Thanks, then." I stood up and shook hands with him. "I suppose there's no heart trouble with Tri-Nitro?"

"None at all. Sound, through and through. His heart bangs away like a gong, loud and clear."

CHAPTER 6

"THAT'S THAT, THEN," Chico said over a pint and pie in the White Hart Hotel. "End of case. Mrs. Casper's off her tiny rocker, and no one's been getting at George Caspar's youngsters except George Caspar himself."

"She won't be pleased to hear it," I said.

"Will you tell her?"

"Straight away. If she's convinced, she might calm down."

So I telephoned to George Caspar's house and asked for Rosemary, saying I was a Mr. Barnes. She came on the line and said hello in the questioning voice one uses to unknown callers.

"Mr. . . . Barnes?"

"It's Sid Halley."

The alarm came instantly. "I can't talk to you."

"Can you meet me, then?"

"Of course not. I've no reason for going to London."

"I'm just down the road, in the town," I said. "I've things to tell you. And I don't honestly think there's any need for disguises and so on."

"I'm not being seen with you in Newmarket."

She agreed, however, to drive out in her car, pick up Chico, and go where he directed; and Chico and I worked out a place on the map which looked a tranquilizing spot for paranoiacs. The churchyard at Barton Mills, eight miles toward Norwich.

We parked the cars side by side at the gate, and Rosemary walked with me among the graves. She was wearing again the fawn raincoat and a scarf, but not this time the false curls. The wind blew wisps of her own chestnut hair across her eyes, and she pulled them away impatiently: not with quite as much tension as when she had come to my flat, but still with more force than was needed.

I told her I had been to see Tom Garvey and Henry Thrace at their stud farms. I told her I had talked to Brothersmith; and I told her what they'd all said. She listened, and shook her head.

"The horses were nobbled," she said obstinately. "I'm sure they were."

"How?"

"I don't know how." Her voice rose sharply, the agitation showing in spasms of the muscles round her mouth. "But I told you. I told you, they'll get at Tri-Nitro. A week tomorrow, it's the Guineas. You've got to keep him safe for a week."

We walked along the path beside the quiet mounds and the gray weather-beaten headstones. The grass was mown, but there were no flowers, and no mourners. The dead there were long gone, long forgotten. Raw grief and tears now in the municipal plot outside the town: brown heaps of earth and brilliant wreaths and desolation in tidy rows.

"George has doubled the security on Tri-Nitro," I said.

"I know that. Don't be stupid."

I said reluctantly, "In the normal course of events he'll be giving Tri-Nitro some strong work before the Guineas. Probably on Saturday morning."

"I suppose so. What do you mean? Why do you ask?"

"Well . . ." I paused, wondering if indeed it would be sensible to suggest a way-out theory without testing it, and thinking that there was no way of testing it, anyway.

"Go on," she said sharply. "What do you mean?"

"You could . . . er . . . make sure he takes all sorts of precautions when he gives Tri-Nitro that last gallop." I paused. "Inspect the saddle. . . . That sort of thing."

Rosemary said fiercely, "What are you saying? Spell it out, for God's sake. Don't pussyfoot round it."

"Lots of races have been lost because of too hard training gallops too soon beforehand."

"Of course," she said impatiently. "Everyone knows that. But George would never do it."

"What if the saddle was packed with lead? What if a three-year-old was given a strong gallop carrying fifty pounds dead weight? And then ran under severe pressure a few days later in the Guineas? And strained his heart?"

"My God," she said. "My God."

"I'm not saying that it did happen to Zingaloo and Gleaner, or anything like it. Only that it's a distant possibility. And if it's something like that . . . it must involve someone inside the stable."

She had begun trembling again.

"You must go on," she said. "Please go on trying. I brought some money for you." She plunged a hand into her raincoat pocket and brought out a smallish brown envelope. "It's cash. I can't give you a check."

"I haven't earned it," I said.

"Yes, yes. Take it." She was insistent, and finally I put it in my pocket, unopened.

"Let me consult George," I said.

"No. He'd be furious. I'll do it . . . I mean, I'll warn him about the gallops. He thinks I'm crazy, but if I go on about it long enough he'll take notice." She looked at her watch and her agitation increased. "I'll have to go back now. I said I was going for a walk on the heath. I never do that. I'll have to get back, or they'll be wondering."

"Who'll be wondering?"

"George, of course."

"Does he know where you are every minute of the day?"

We were retracing our steps with some speed toward the churchyard gates. Rosemary looked as if she would soon be running.

"We always talk. He asks where I've been. He's not suspicious . . . it's just a habit. We're always together. Well, you know what it's like in a racing household. Owners come at odd times. George likes me to be there."

We reached the cars. She said goodbye uncertainly, and drove off homeward in a great hurry. Chico, waiting in the Scimitar, said, "Quiet here, isn't it? Even the ghosts must find it boring."

I got into the car and tossed Rosemary's envelope onto his lap. "Count that," I said, starting the engine, "See how we're doing."

He tore it open, pulled out a neat wad of expensive-colored bank notes, and licked his fingers.

"Phew," he said, coming to the end. "She's bonkers."

"She wants us to go on."

"Then you know what this is, Sid," he said, flicking the stack. "Guilt money. To spur you on when you want to stop."

"Well, it works."

WE SPENT SOME of Rosemary's incentive in staying overnight in Newmarket and going round the bars, Chico where the lads hung out and me with the trainers. It was Tuesday evening and very quiet everywhere. I heard nothing of any interest and drank more than enough whisky, and Chico came back with hiccups and not much else.

"Ever heard of Inky Poole?" he said.

"Is that a song?"

"No, it's a work jockey. What's a work jockey? Chico, my son, a work jockey is a lad who rides work on the gallops."

"You're drunk," I said.

"Certainly not. What's a work jockey?"

"What you just said. Not much good in races but can gallop the best at home."

"Inky Poole," he said, "is George Caspar's work jockey. Inky Poole rides Tri-Nitro his strong work at home in the gallops. Did you ask me to find out who rides Tri-Nitro's gallops?"

"Yes, I did," I said. "And you're drunk."

"Inky Poole, Inky Poole," he said.

"Did you talk to him?"

"Never met him. Bunch of the lads, they told me. George Caspar's work jockey. Inky Poole."

ARMED WITH RACE glasses on a strap round my neck, I walked along to Warren Hill at seven-thirty in the morning to watch the strings out at morning exercise. A long time, it seemed, since I'd been one of the tucked-up figures in sweaters and skullcap, with three horses to muck out and care for, and a bed in a hostel with rain-soaked breeches forever drying out on an airer in the kitchen. Frozen fingers and not enough baths, ears full of four-letter words and no chance of being alone.

I had enjoyed it well enough when I was sixteen, on account of the horses. Beautiful, marvelous creatures whose responses and instincts worked on a plane as different from humans' as water and oil, not mingling even where they touched. Insight into their senses and consciousness had been like an opening door, a foreign language glimpsed and half learned, full comprehension maddeningly balked by not having the right sort of hearing or sense of smell, nor sufficient skill in telepathy.

The feeling of oneness with horses I'd sometimes had in the heat of a race had been their gift to an inferior being; and maybe my passion for winning had been my gift to them. The urge to get to the front was born in them; all they needed was to be shown where and when to go. It could fairly be said that like most jump jockeys, I had aided and abetted horses beyond the bounds of common sense.

The smell and sight of them on the Heath was like a sea breeze to a sailor. I filled my lungs and eyes, and felt content.

Each exercise string was accompanied and shepherded by its watchful trainer, some of them arriving in cars, some on horseback, some on foot. I collected a lot of "Good morning, Sid"s. Several smiling faces seemed genuinely pleased to see me; and some that weren't in a hurry stopped to talk.

"Sid!" exclaimed one I'd ridden on the flat for in the years before my weight caught up with my height. "Sid, we don't see you up here much these days."

"My loss," I said, smiling.

"Why don't you come and ride out for me? Next time you're here, give me a ring, and we'll fix it."

"Do you mean it?"

"Of course I mean it. If you'd like to, that is."

"I'd love it."

"Right. That's great. Don't forget, now." He wheeled away, waving, to shout to a lad earning his disfavor by slopping in the saddle like a disorganized jellyfish. "How the bloody hell d'you expect your horse to pay attention if you don't?" The boy sat decently for all of twenty seconds. He'd go far, I thought, starting from Newmarket station.

Wednesday being a morning for full training gallops, there was the usual scattering of interested watchers: owners, pressmen, and assorted bookmakers' touts. Binoculars sprouted like an extra growth of eyes, and notes went down in private shorthand. Though the morning was cold, the new season was warming up. There was a feeling overall of purpose, and the bustle of things happening. An industry flexing its muscles. Money, profit, and tax revenue making their proper circles under the wide Suffolk sky. I was still a part of it, even if not in the old way. And Jenny was right; I'd die in an office.

"Morning, Sid."

I looked around. George Caspar, on a horse, his eyes on a distant string walking down the side of the Heath from his stable in Bury Road.

"Morning, George."

"You staying up here?"

"Just for a night or two."

"You should've let us know. We've always a bed. Give Rosemary a ring." His eyes were on his string; the invitation a politeness, not meant to be accepted. Rosemary, I thought, would have fainted if she'd heard.

"Is Tri-Nitro in that lot?" I said.

"Yes, he is. Sixth from the front." He glanced at the interested spectators. "Have you seen Trevor Deansgate anywhere? He said he was coming up here this morning from London. Setting off early."

"Haven't seen him." I shook my head.

"He's got two in the string. He was coming to see them work." He shrugged. "He'll miss them if he isn't here soon."

I smiled to myself. Some trainers might delay working the horses until the owner did arrive, but not George. Owners queued up for his favors and treasured his comments, and Trevor Deansgate for all his power was just one of a crowd. I lifted my race glasses and watched while the string, forty strong, approached and began circling, waiting for their turn on the uphill gallop. The stable before George's had nearly finished, and George would be next.

The lad on Tri-Nitro wore a red scarf in the neck of his olive-green Husky jacket. I lowered the glasses and kept my eye on him as he circled, and looked at his mount with the same curiosity as everyone else. A good-looking bay colt, well grown, with strong shoulders and a lot of heart room; but nothing about him to shout from the housetops that here was the wildly backed winter favorite for the Guineas and the Derby. If you hadn't known, you wouldn't have known, as they say.

"Do you mind photographs, George?" I said.

"Help yourself, Sid."

"Thanks."

I seldom went anywhere these days without a camera in my pocket. Sixteen-millimeter, automatic light meter, all the expense in its lens. I brought it out and showed it to him, and he nodded. "Take what you like."

He shook up his patient hack and went away, across to his string, to begin the morning's business. The lad who rode a horse down from the stables wasn't necessarily the same one who rode it in fast work, and as usual there was a good deal of swapping around, to put the best lads up where it mattered.

The boy with the red scarf dismounted from Tri-Nitro and held him, and presently a much older lad swung up onto his back.

I walked across to be close to the string, and took three or four photographs of the wonder horse and a couple of closer shots of his rider.

"Inky Poole?" I said to him at one point, as he rode by six feet away.

"That's right," he said. "Mind your back. You're in the way."

A right touch of surliness. If he hadn't seen me talking to George first, he would have objected to my being there at all. I wondered if his grudging against-the-world manner was the cause or the result of his not getting on as a jockey, and felt sympathy for him, on the whole.

George began detailing his lads into the small bunches that would go up the gallops together, and I walked back to the fringes of things, to watch.

A car arrived very fast and pulled up with a jerk, alarming some horses alongside and sending them skittering, with the lads' voices rising high in alarm and protest.

Trevor Deansgate climbed out of his Jaguar and for good measure slammed the door. He was dressed in a city suit, in contrast to everyone else there, and looked ready for the board room. Black hair rigorously brushed, chin smoothly shaven, shoes polished like glass. Not the sort of man I would have sought as a friend, because I didn't on the whole like to sit at the feet of power, picking up crumbs of patronage with nervous laughter; but a force to be reckoned with on the racing scene.

Big-scale bookmakers could be and often were a positive influence for good, a stance, I thought sardonically, that they had been pushed into, to survive the lobby that knew a Tote monopoly (and a less greedy tax climate) would put back into racing what bookmakers took out. Trevor Deansgate personified the new breed: urbane, a man of the world, seeking top company, becoming a name in the City, the sycophant of earls.

"Hello," he said, seeing me. "I met you at Kempton. . . . Do you know where George's horses are?"

"Right there," I said, pointing. "You're just in time."

"Bloody traffic."

He strode across the grass toward George, race glasses swinging from his hand, and George said hello briefly and apparently told him to watch the gallops with me, because he came straight back, heavy and confident, and stopped at my side.

"George says my two both go in the first bunch. He said you'd tell me how they're doing, insolent bugger. Got eyes, haven't I? He's going on up the hill."

I nodded. Trainers often went up halfway and watched from there, the better to see their horses' action as they galloped past.

Four horses were wheeling into position at the starting point. Trevor Deansgate applied his binoculars, twisting them to focus. Navy suiting with faint red pin stripes. The well-kept hands, gold cuff links, onyx ring, as before.

"Which are yours?" I said.

"The two chestnuts. That one with the white socks is Pinafore. The other's nothing much."

The nothing much had short cannon bones and a rounded rump. Might make a 'chaser one day, I thought. I liked the look of him better than the whippet-shaped Pinafore. They set off together up the gallop at George's signal, and the sprinting blood showed all the way to the top. Pinafore romped it and the nothing much lived up to his owner's assessment. Trevor Deansgate lowered his binoculars with a sigh.

"That's that, then. Are you coming to George's for breakfast?"

"No. Not today."

He raised the glasses again and focused them on the much nearer target of the circling horses, and, from the angle, he was looking at the riders, not the horses. The search came to an end on Inky Poole: he lowered his glasses and followed Tri-Nitro with the naked eye.

"A week today," I said.

"Looks a picture."

I supposed that he, like all bookmakers, would be happy to see the hot favorite lose the Guineas, but there was nothing in his voice except admiration for a great horse. Tri-Nitro lined up in his turn and at a signal from George set off with two companions at a deceptively fast pace. Inky Poole, I was interested to see, sat as quiet as patience and rode with a skill worth ten times what he would be paid. Good work jockeys were undervalued. Bad ones could ruin a horse's mouth and temperament and whole career. It figured that for the stableful he had, George Caspar would employ only the best.

Poole was not riding the flat-out searching gallop the horse would be given the following Saturday morning over a long smooth surface like the Limekilns. Up the incline of Warren Hill a fast canter was testing enough. Tri-Nitro took the whole thing without a hint of effort, and breasted the top as if he could go up there six times more without noticing.

Impressive, I thought. The press, clearly agreeing, were scribbling in their notebooks. Trevor Deansgate looked thoughtful, as well he might, and George Caspar, coming down the hill and reining in near us, looked almost smugly satisfied. The Guineas, one felt, were in the bag.

After they had done their work, the horses walked down the hill to join the still circling string, where the work riders changed onto fresh mounts and set off again up to the top. Tri-Nitro got back his lad with the olive-green Husky and the red scarf, and eventually the whole lot of them set off home.

"That's that, then," George said. "All set, Trevor? Breakfast?"

They nodded farewells to me and set off, one in the car, one on the horse. I had eyes mostly, however, for Inky Poole, who had been four times up the hill and was walking off a shade morosely to a parked car.

"Inky," I said, coming up behind him. "The gallop on Tri-Nitro . . . that was great."

He looked at me sourly. "I've got nothing to say."

"I'm not from the press."

"I know who you are. Saw you racing. Who hasn't?" Unfriendly: almost a sneer. "What do you want?"

"How does Tri-Nitro compare with Gleaner, this time last year?"

He fished the car keys out of a zipper pocket in his parka, and fitted one into the lock. What I could see of his face looked obstinately unhelpful.

"Did Gleaner, a week before Christmas, give you the same sort of feel?" I said.

"I'm not talking to you."

"How about Zingaloo?" I said. "Or Bethesda?"

He opened his car door and slid down into the driving seat, taking out time to give me a hostile glare.

"Piss off," he said. Slammed the door. Stabbed the ignition key into the dashboard and forcefully drove away.

CHICO HAD ARISEN to breakfast but was sitting in the pub's dining room, holding his head.

"Don't look so healthy," he said when I joined him.

"Bacon and eggs," I said. "That's what I'll have. Or kippers, perhaps. And strawberry jam."

He groaned.

"I'm going back to London," I said. "But would you mind staying here?" I pulled the camera from my pocket. "Take the film out of that and get it developed. Overnight if possible. There's some pictures of Tri-Nitro and Inky Poole on there. We might find them helpful; you never know."

"O.K., then," he said. "But you'll have to ring up the Comprehensive and tell them that my black belt's at the cleaners."

I laughed. "There were some girls riding in George Caspar's string this morning," I said. "See what you can do."

"That's beyond the call of duty." But his eyes seemed suddenly brighter. "What am I asking?"

"Things like who saddles Tri-Nitro for exercise gallops, and what's the routine from now until next Wednesday, and whether anything nasty is stirring in the jungle."

"What about you, then?"

"I'll be back Friday night," I said. "In time for the gallops on Saturday. They're bound to gallop Tri-Nitro on Saturday. A strong workout, to bring him to a peak."

"Do you really think anything dodgy's going on?" Chico asked.

"A tossup. I just don't know. I'd better ring Rosemary."

I went through the Mr. Barnes routine again and Rosemary came on the line sounding as agitated as ever.

"I can't talk. We've people here for breakfast."

"Just listen, then," I said. "Try to persuade George to vary his routine when he gallops Tri-Nitro on Saturday. Put up a different jockey, for instance. Not Inky Poole."

"You don't think . . ." Her voice was high, and broke off.

"I don't know at all," I said. "But if George changed everything about, there'd be less chance of skullduggery. Routine is the robber's best friend."

"What? Oh, yes. All right. I'll try. What about you?"

"I'll be out watching the gallop. After that I'll stick around, until after the Guineas is safely over. But I wish you'd let me talk to George."

"No. He'd be livid. I'll have to go now." The receiver went down with a rattle which spoke of still unsteady hands, and I feared that George might be right about his wife's being neurotic.

CHARLES AND I met as usual at the Cavendish the following day, and ate in the upstairs bar's armchairs.

"You look happier," he said, "than I've seen you since . . ." He gestured to my arm with his glass. "Released in spirit. Not your usual stoic self."

"I've been in Newmarket," I said. "Watched the gallops yesterday morning."

"I would have thought . . ." He stopped.

"That I'd be eaten by jealousy?" I said. "So would I. But I enjoyed it."

"Good."

"I'm going up again tomorrow night and staying until after the Guineas next Wednesday."

"And lunch next Thursday?"

I smiled and bought him a large pink gin. "I'll be back for that."

In due course we ate scallops in a wine and cheese sauce, and he gave me the news of Jenny.

"Oliver Quayle sent the address you asked for, for the polish." He took a paper from his breast pocket and handed it over. "Oliver is worried. He says the police are actively pursuing their inquiries, and Jenny is almost certain to be charged."

"When?"

"I don't know. Oliver doesn't know. Sometimes these things take weeks, but not always. And when they charge her, Oliver says, she will have to appear in a magistrates' court, and they are certain to refer the case to the Crown Court, as so much money is involved. They'll give her bail, of course."

"Bail!"

"Oliver says she is unfortunately very likely to be convicted, but that if it is stressed that she acted as she did under the influence of Nicholas Ashe, she'll probably get some sympathy from the judge and a conditional discharge."

"Even if he isn't found?"

"Yes. But of course if he *is* found, and charged, and found guilty, Jenny would with luck escape a conviction altogether."

I took a deep breath that was half a sigh.

"Have to find him then, won't we?" I said.

"How?"

"Well . . . I spent a lot of Monday, and all of this morning, looking through a box of letters. They came from the people who sent money, and ordered wax. Eighteen hundred of them, or thereabouts."

"How do they help?"

"I've started sorting them into alphabetical order, and making a list." He frowned skeptically, but I went on. "The interesting thing is that all the surnames start with the letters *L*, *M*, *N*, and *O*. None from *A* to *K*, and none from *P* to *Z*."

"I don't see . . ."

"They might be part of a mailing list," I said. "Like for a catalogue. Or even for a charity. There must be thousands of mailing lists, but this one certainly did produce the required results, so it wasn't a mailing list for dog license reminders, for example."

"That seems reasonable," he said dryly.

"I thought I'd get all the names into order and then see if anyone, like Christie's or Southeby's, say—because of the polish angle—has a mailing list which matches. A long shot, I know, but there's a chance."

"I could help you," he said.

"It's a boring job."

"She's my daughter."

"All right, then. I'd like it."

I finished the scallops and sat back in my chair, and drank Charles's good cold white wine.

He said he would stay overnight in his club and come to my flat in the morning to help with the sorting, and I gave him a spare key to get in with, in case I should be out for a newspaper or cigarettes when he came. He lit a cigar and watched me through the smoke. "What did Jenny say to you upstairs after lunch on Sunday?"

I looked at him briefly. "Nothing much."

"She was moody all day afterwards. She even snapped at Toby." He smiled. "Toby protested, and Jenny said, 'At least Sid didn't whine.'" He paused. "I gathered that she'd been giving you a particularly rough mauling and was feeling guilty."

"It wouldn't be guilt. With luck, it was misgivings about Ashe."

"And not before time."

FROM THE CAVENDISH I went to the Portman Square headquarters of the Jockey Club, to keep an appointment made that morning on the telephone by Lucas Wainwright. Unofficial my task for him might be, but official enough for him to ask me to his office. Ex-Superintendent Eddy Keith, it transpired, had gone to Yorkshire to look into a positive doping test, and no one else was going to wonder much at my visit.

"I've got all the files for you," Lucas said. "Eddy's reports on the syndicates, and some notes on the rogues he O.K.'d."

"I'll make a start, then," I said. "Can I take them away, or do you want me to look at them here?"

"Here, if you would," he said. "I don't want to draw my secretary's attention to them by letting them out or getting Xerox copies, as she works for Eddy too, and I know she admires him. She would tell him. You'd better copy down what you need."

"Right," I said.

He gave me a table to one side of his room, and a comfortable chair, and a bright light, and for an hour or so I read and made notes. At his own desk he did some desultory pen-pushing and rustled a few papers, but in the end it was clear it was only a pretense of being busy. He wasn't so much waiting for me to finish as generally uneasy.

I looked up from my writing. "What's the matter?" I said.

"The . . . matter?"

"Something's troubling you."

He hesitated. "Have you done all you want?" he said, nodding at my work.

"Only about half," I said. "Can you give me another hour?"

"Yes, but . . . Look, I'll have to be fair with you. There's something you'll have to know."

"What sort of thing?"

Lucas, who was normally urbane even when in a hurry, and whose naval habits of thought I understood from long practice with my admiral father-in-law, was showing signs of embarrassment. The things that acutely embarrassed naval officers were collisions between warships and quaysides, ladies visiting the crew's mess deck with the crew present and at ease, and dishonorable conduct among gentlemen. It couldn't be the first two, so where were we with the third?

"I have not perhaps given you all the facts," he said.

"Go on, then."

"I did send someone else to check on two of the syndicates, some time ago. Six months ago." He fiddled with some paper clips, no longer looking in my direction. "Before Eddy checked them."

"With what result?"

"Ah. Yes." He cleared his throat. "The man I sent . . . his name's Mason . . . We never received his report because he was attacked in the street before he could write it."

Attacked in the street . . . "What sort of attack?" I asked. "And who attacked him?"

He shook his head. "Nobody knows who attacked him. He was found on the pavement by some passers-by, who called the police."

"Well . . . have you asked him—Mason?" But I guessed at something of the answer, if not all of it.

"He's . . . er . . . never really recovered," Lucas said regretfully. "His head, it seemed, had been repeatedly kicked, as well as his body. There was a good deal of brain damage. He's still in an institution. He always will be. He's a vegetable . . . and he's blind."

I bit the end of the pencil with which I'd been making notes. "Was he robbed?" I said.

"His wallet was missing. But not his watch." His face was worried.

"So it might have been a straightforward mugging?"

"Yes . . . except that the police treated it as intended homicide, because of the number and target of the boot marks."

He sat back in his chair as if he'd got rid of an unwelcome burden. Honor among gentlemen . . . Honor satisfied.

"All right," I said. "Which two syndicates was he checking?"

"The first two that you have there."

"And do you think any of the people on them—the undesirables—are the sort to kick their way out of trouble?"

He said unhappily, "They might be."

"And am I," I said carefully, "investigating the possible corruption of Eddy Keith, or Mason's semimurder?"

After a pause, he said, "Perhaps both."

There was a long silence. Finally I said, "You do realize that by sending me notes at the races and meeting me in the tearoom and bringing me here, you haven't left much doubt that I'm working for you?"

"But it could be about anything."

I said gloomily, "Not when I turn up on the syndicates' doorsteps."

"I'd quite understand," he said, "if, in view of what I've said, you wanted to . . . er . . ."

So would I, I thought. I would understand that I didn't want my head kicked in. But then what I'd told Jenny was true: one never thought it would happen. And you're always wrong, she'd said.

I sighed. "You'd better tell me about Mason. Where he went and who he saw. Anything you can think of."

"It's practically nothing. He went off in the ordinary way and the next we heard was he'd been attacked. The police couldn't trace where he'd been, and all the syndicate people swore they'd never seen him. The case isn't closed, of course, but after six months it's got no sort of priority."

We talked it over for a while, and I spent another hour after that writing notes. I left the Jockey Club premises at a quarter to six, to go back to the flat; and I didn't get there.

CHAPTER 7

I WENT HOME in a taxi and paid it off outside the entrance to the flats, yet not exactly outside, because a dark car was squarely parked there on the double yellow lines, which was a towaway zone.

I scarcely looked at the car, which was my mistake, because as I reached it and turned away toward the entrance, its curbside doors opened and spilled out the worst sort of trouble.

Two men in dark clothes grabbed me. One hit me dizzyingly on the head with something hard and the other flung what I later found was a kind of lasso of thick rope over my arms and chest and pulled it tight. They both bundled me into the back of the car, where one of them for good measure tied a dark piece of cloth over my dazed halfshut eyes.

"Keys," a voice said. "Quick. No one saw us."

I felt them fumbling in my pockets. There was a clink as they found what they were looking for. I began to come back into focus, so to speak, and to struggle, which was a reflex action but all the same another mistake.

The cloth over my eyes was reinforced by a sickly-smelling wad over my nose and mouth. Anesthetic fumes made a nonsense of consciousness, and the last thing I thought was that if I was going the way of Mason, they hadn't wasted any time.

I WAS AWARE, first of all, that I was lying on straw.

Straw, as in a stable. Rustling when I tried to move. Hearing, as always, had returned first.

I had been concussed a few times over the years, in racing falls. I thought for a while that I must have come off a horse, though I couldn't remember which, or where I'd been riding.

Funny.

The unwelcome news came back with a rush. I had not been racing. I had one hand. I had been abducted in daylight from a London street. I was lying on my back on some straw, blindfolded, with a rope tied round my chest, above the elbows, fastening my upper arms against my body. I was lying on the knot. I didn't know why I was there . . . and had no great faith in the future.

Damn, damn, *damn*.

My feet were tethered to some immovable object. It was black dark, even round the edges of the blindfold. I sat up and tried to get some part of me disentangled: a lot of effort and no results.

Ages later there was a tramp of footsteps outside on a gritty surface, and the creak of a wooden door, and sudden light on the sides of my nose.

"Stop trying, Mr. Halley," a voice said. "You won't undo those knots with one hand."

I stopped trying. There was no point in going on.

"A spot of overkill," he said, enjoying himself. "Ropes *and* anesthetic *and* blackjack *and* blindfold. Well, I did tell them, of course, to be careful, and not to get within distance of that tin arm. A villain I know has very nasty things to say about you hitting him with what he didn't expect."

I knew the voice. Undertones of Manchester, overtones of all the way up the social ladder. The confidence of power.

Trevor Deansgate.

Last seen on the gallops at Newmarket, looking for Tri-Nitro in the string, and identifying him because he knew the work jockey, which most people didn't. Deansgate, going to George Caspar's for breakfast. Bookmaker Trevor Deansgate had been a question mark, a possibility, someone to be assessed, looked into. Something I would have done, and hadn't done yet.

"Take the blindfold off," he said. "I want him to see me."

Fingers took their time over untying the tight piece of cloth. When it fell away, the light was temporarily dazzling; but the first thing I saw was the double barrel of a shotgun pointing my way.

"Guns too," I said sourly.

It was a storage barn, not a stable. There was a stack of several tons of straw bales to my left, and on the right, a few yards away, a tractor. My feet were fastened to the trailer bar of a farm roller. The barn had a high roof, with beams; and one meager electric light, which shone on Trevor Deansgate.

"You're too bloody clever for your own good," he said. "You know what they say? If Halley's after you, watch out. He'll sneak up on you when you think he doesn't know you exist, and they'll be slamming the cell doors on you before you've worked it out."

I didn't say anything. What could one say? Especially sitting trussed up like a fool at the wrong end of a shotgun.

"Well, I'm not waiting for you, do you see?" he said. "I know how bloody close you are to getting me nicked. Just laying your snares, weren't you? Just waiting for me to fall into your hands, like you've caught so many others." He stopped and reconsidered what he'd said. "Into your hand," he said, "and that fancy hook."

He had a way of speaking to me that acknowledged mutual origins, that we'd both come a long way from where we'd started. It was not a matter of accent, but of manner. There was no need for social pretense. The message was raw, and between equals, and would be understood.

He was dressed, as before, in a city suit. Navy; chalk pin stripe this time; Gucci tie. The well-manicured hands held the shotgun with the expertise of many a weekend on country estates. What did it matter, I thought, if the finger that pulled the trigger was clean and cared for? What did it matter if his shoes were polished? . . . I looked at the silly details because I didn't want to think about death.

He stood for a while without speaking; simply watching. I sat without moving, as best I could, and thought about a nice safe job in a stockbroker's office.

"No bloody nerves, have you?" he said. "None at all."

I didn't answer.

The other two men were behind me to the right, out of my sight. I could hear their feet as they occasionally shuffled on the straw. Far too far away for me to reach.

I was wearing what I had put on for lunch with Charles. Gray trousers, socks, dark brown shoes; rope extra. Shirt, tie, and a recently bought blazer, quite expensive. What did that matter? If he killed me, Jenny would get the rest. I hadn't changed my will.

Trevor Deansgate switched his attention to the man behind me.

"Now listen," he said, "and don't snarl it up. Get these two pieces of rope and tie one to his left arm, and one to the right. And watch out for any tricks."

He lifted the gun a fraction until I could see down the barrels. If he shot from there, I thought, he would hit his chums. It didn't after all look like straight execution. The chums were busy tying bits of rope to both my wrists.

"Not the left wrist, you stupid bugger," Trevor Deansgate said. "That one comes right off. Use your bloody head. Tie it high, above his elbow."

The chum in question did as he said and pulled the knots tight, and almost casually picked up a stout metal bar, like a crowbar, and stood there gripping it as if he thought that somehow I could liberate myself like Superman and still attack him.

Crowbar . . . Nasty shivers of apprehension suddenly crawled all over my scalp. There had been another villain, before, who had known where to hurt me most, the one who had hit my already useless left hand with a poker, and turned it from a ruin into a total loss. I had had regrets enough since, and all sorts of private agonies, but I hadn't realized, until that sickening moment, how much I valued what remained. The muscles that worked the electrodes, they at least gave me the semblance of a working hand. If they were injured again I wouldn't have even that. As for the elbow itself . . . If he wanted to put me out of effective action for a long time, he had only to use that crowbar.

"You don't like that, do you, Mr. Halley?" Trevor Deansgate said.

I turned my head back to him. His voice and face were suddenly full of a mixture of triumph and satisfaction, and what seemed like relief.

I said nothing.

"You're sweating," he said.

He had another order for the chums. "Untie that rope round his chest. And do it carefully. Hold on to the ropes on his arms."

They untied the knot, and pulled the constricting rope away from my chest. It didn't make much difference to my chances of escape. They were wildly exaggerating my ability in a fight.

"Lie down," he said to me; and when I didn't at once comply, he said, "Push him down," to the chums. One way or another, I ended on my back.

"I don't want to kill you," he said. "I could dump your body somewhere, but there would be too many questions. I can't risk it. But if I don't kill you, I've got to shut you up. Once and for all. Permanently."

Short of killing me, I didn't see how he could do it; and I was stupid.

"Pull his arm sideways, away from his body," he said.

The pull on my left arm had a man's weight behind it and was stronger than I was. I rolled my head that way and tried not to beg, not to weep.

"Not that one, you bloody fool," Trevor Deansgate said. "The other one. The right one. Pull it out, to this side."

The chum on my right used all his strength on the rope and hauled so that my arm finished straight out sideways, at right angles to my body, palm upward.

Trevor Deansgate stepped toward me and lowered the gun until the black holes of the barrel were pointing straight at my stretched right wrist. Then he carefully lowered the barrel another inch, making direct contact on my skin, pressing down against the straw-covered floor. I could feel the metal rims hard across the bones and nerves and sinews. Across the bridge to a healthy hand.

I heard the click as he cocked the firing mechanism. One blast from a twelve-bore would take off most of my arm.

A dizzy wave of faintness drenched all my limbs with sweat.

Whatever anyone said, I intimately knew about fear. Not fear of any horse, or of racing or falling, or of ordinary physical pain. But of humiliation and rejection and helplessness and failure . . . all of those.

All the fear I'd ever felt in all my life was as nothing compared with the liquefying, mind-shattering disintegration of that appalling minute. It broke me in pieces. Swamped me. Brought me down to a morass of terror, to a whimper in the soul. And instinctively, hopelessly, I tried not to let it show.

He watched motionlessly through uncountable intensifying silent seconds. Making me wait. Making it worse.

At length he took a deep breath and said, "As you see, I could shoot off your hand. Nothing easier. But I'm probably not going to. Not today." He paused. "Are you listening?"

I nodded the merest fraction. My eyes were full of gun.

His voice came quietly, seriously, giving weight to every sentence. "You can give me your assurance that you'll back off. You'll do nothing more which is directed against me, in any way, ever. You'll go to France tomorrow morning, and you'll stay there until after the Two Thousand Guineas. After that, you can do what you like. But if you break your assurance . . . well, you're easy to find. I'll find you, and I'll blow your right hand off. I mean it, and you'd better believe it. Sometime or other. You'd never escape it. Do you understand?"

I nodded, as before. I could feel the gun as if it were hot. Don't let him, I thought. Dear God, don't let him.

"Give me your assurance. Say it."

I swallowed painfully. Dredged up a voice. Low and hoarse. "I give it."

"You'll back off."

"Yes."

"You'll not come after me again, ever."

"No."

"You'll go to France and stay there until after the Guineas."

"Yes."

Another silence lengthened for what seemed a hundred years, while I stared beyond my undamaged wrist to the dark side of the moon.

He took the gun away in the end. Broke it open. Removed the cartridges. I felt physically, almost uncontrollably, sick.

He knelt on his pin-striped knees beside me and looked closely at whatever defense I could put into an unmoving face and expressionless eye. I could feel the treacherous sweat trickling down my cheek. He nodded, with grim satisfaction.

"I knew you couldn't face that. Not the other one as well. No one could. There's no need to kill you."

He stood up again and stretched his body, as if relaxing a wound-up inner tension. Then he put his hands into various pockets, and produced things.

"Here are your keys. Your passport. Your checkbook. Credit cards." He put them on a straw bale. To the chums, he said, "Untie him, and drive him to the airport. To Heathrow."

CHAPTER 8

I FLEW TO Paris and stayed right there where I landed, in an airport hotel, with no impetus or heart to go farther. I stayed for six days, not leaving my room, spending most of the time by the window, watching the airplanes come and go.

I felt stunned. I felt ill. Disoriented and overthrown and severed from my own roots. Crushed into an abject state of mental misery, knowing that this time I really had run away.

It was easy to convince myself that logically I had had no choice but to give Deansgate his assurance when he asked for it. If I hadn't, he would have killed me. I could tell myself, as I continually did, that sticking to his instructions had been merely common sense; but the fact remained that when the chums decanted me at Heathrow they had driven off at once, and it had been of my own free will that I'd bought my ticket, waited in the departure lounge, and walked to the aircraft.

There had been no one there with guns to make me do it. Only the fact that as Deansgate had truly said, I couldn't face losing the other hand. I couldn't face even the risk of it. The thought of it, like a conditioned response, brought out the sweat.

As the days passed, the feeling I had had of disintegration seemed not to fade but to deepen.

The automatic part of me still went on working: walking, talking, ordering coffee, going to the bathroom. In the part that mattered there was turmoil and anguish and a feeling that my whole self had been literally smashed in those few cataclysmic minutes on the straw.

Part of the trouble was that I knew my own weaknesses too well. Knew that if I hadn't had so much pride, it wouldn't have destroyed me so much to have lost it.

To have been forced to realize that my basic view of myself had been an illusion was proving a psychic upheaval like an earthquake, and perhaps it wasn't surprising that I felt I had, I really had, come to pieces.

I didn't know that I could face that, either.

I wished I could sleep properly, and get some peace.

WHEN WEDNESDAY CAME I thought of Newmarket and of all the brave hopes for the Guineas.

Thought of George Caspar, taking Tri-Nitro to the test, producing him proudly in peak condition and swearing to himself that this time nothing could go wrong. Thought of Rosemary, jangling with nerves, willing the horse to win and knowing it wouldn't. Thought of Trevor Deansgate, unsuspected, moving like a mole to vandalize, somehow, the best colt in the kingdom.

I could have stopped him if I'd tried.

Wednesday for me was the worst day of all, the day I learned about despair and desolation and guilt.

ON THE SIXTH day, Thursday morning, I went down to the lobby and bought an English newspaper.

They had run the Two Thousand Guineas, as scheduled.

Tri-Nitro had started as a hot favorite at even money; and he had finished last.

I paid my bill and went to the airport. There were airplanes to everywhere, to escape in. The urge to escape was very strong. But wherever one went, one took oneself along. From oneself there was no escape. Wherever I went, in the end I would have to go back.

If I went back in my split-apart state I'd have to live all the time on two levels. I'd have to behave in the old way, which everyone would expect. Have to think and drive and talk and get on with life. Going back meant all that. It also meant doing all that, and proving to myself that I could do it, when I wasn't the same inside.

I thought that what I had lost might be worse than a hand. For a hand there were substitutes which could grip and look passable. But if the core of oneself had crumbled, how could one manage at all?

If I went back, I would have to try.

If I couldn't try, why go back?

It took me a long lonely time to buy a ticket to Heathrow.

I LANDED AT midday, made a brief telephone call to the Cavendish, to ask them to apologize to the Admiral because I couldn't keep our date, and took a taxi home.

Everything in the lobby, on the stairs, and along the landing looked the same, and yet completely different. It was I who was different. I put the key in the lock and turned it, and went into the flat.

I had expected it to be empty, but before I'd even shut the door I heard a rustle in the sitting room, and then Chico's voice. "Is that you, Admiral?"

I simply didn't answer. In a brief moment his head appeared, questioning, and after that, his whole self.

"About time, too," he said. He looked, on the whole, relieved to see me.

"I sent you a telegram."

"Oh, sure. I've got it here, propped on the shelf. 'Leave Newmarket, and go home, shall be away for a few days, will telephone.' What sort of telegram's that? Sent from Heathrow, early Friday. You been on holiday?"

"Yeah."

I walked past him, into the sitting room. In there, it didn't look at all the same. There were files and papers everywhere, on every surface, with coffee-marked cups and saucers holding them down.

"You went away without the charger," Chico said. "You never do that, even overnight. The spare batteries are all here. You haven't been able to move that hand for six days."

"Let's have some coffee."

"You didn't take any clothes, or your razor."

"I stayed in a hotel. They had throwaway razors, if you asked. What's all this mess?"

"The polish letters."

"What?"

"You know. The polish letters. Your wife's spot of trouble."

"Oh . . ."

I stared at it blankly.

"Look," Chico said. "Cheese on toast? I'm starving."

"That would be nice." It was unreal. It was all unreal.

He went into the kitchen and started banging about. I took the dead battery out of my arm and put in a charged one. The fingers opened and closed, like old times. I had missed them more than I would have imagined.

Chico brought the cheese on toast. He ate his, and I looked at mine. I'd better eat it, I thought, and didn't have the energy. There was the sound of the door of the flat being opened with a key, and after that, my father-in-law's voice from the hall.

"He didn't turn up at the Cavendish, but he did at least leave a message." He came into the room from behind where I sat and saw Chico nodding his head in my direction.

"He's back," said Chico. "The boy himself."

"Hello, Charles," I said.

He took a long slow look. Very controlled, very civilized. "We have, you know, been worried." It was a reproach.

"I'm sorry."

"Where have you been?" he said.

I found I couldn't tell him. If I told him where, I would have to tell him why; and I shrank from why. I just didn't say anything at all.

Chico gave him a cheerful grin. "Sid's got a bad attack of the brick walls." He looked at his watch. "Seeing that you're here, Admiral, I might as well get along and teach the little bleeders at the Comprehensive how to throw their grannies over their shoulders. And, Sid, before I go, there's about fifty messages on the phone pad. There's two new insurance investigations waiting to be done, and a guard job. Lucas Wainwright wants you; he's rung four times. And Rosemary Casper has been screeching fit to blast the eardrums. It's all there, written down. See you, then. I'll come back here later."

I almost asked him not to, but he'd gone.

"You've lost weight," Charles said.

It wasn't surprising. I looked again at the toasted cheese and decided that coming back also had to include things like eating.

"Want some?" I asked.

He eyed the congealing square. "No, thank you."

Nor did I. I pushed it away. Sat and stared into space.

"What's happened to you?" he asked.

"Nothing."

"Last week you came into the Cavendish like a spring," he said. "Bursting with life. Eyes actually sparkling. And now look at you."

"Well, don't," I said. "Don't look at me. How are you doing with the letters?"

"Sid . . ."

"Admiral." I stood up restlessly, to escape his probing gaze. "Leave me alone."

He paused, considering, then said, "You've been speculating in commodities recently. Have you lost your money, is that it?"

I was surprised almost to the point of amusement.

"No," I said.

He said, "You went dead like this before, when you lost your career and my daughter. So what have you lost this time, if it isn't money? What could be as bad . . . or worse?"

I knew the answer. I'd learned it in Paris, in torment and shame. My whole mind formed the word "courage" with such violent intensity that I was afraid it would leap of its own accord from my brain to his.

He showed no sign of receiving it. He was still waiting for a reply.

I swallowed. "Six days," I said neutrally. "I've lost six days. Let's get on with tracing Nicholas Ashe."

He shook his head in disapproval and frustration, but began to explain what he'd been doing.

"This thick pile is from people with names beginning with *M*. I've put them into strictly alphabetical order, and typed out a list. It seems to me that we might get results from one letter only . . . Are you paying attention?"

"Yes."

"I took the list to Christie's and Sotheby's, as you suggested, and persuaded them to help. But the *M* section of their catalogue mailing list is not the same as this one. And I found that there may be difficulties with this matching, as so many envelopes are addressed nowadays by computers."

"You've worked hard," I said.

"Chico and I have been sitting here in shifts, answering your telephone and trying to find out where you'd gone. Your car was still here, in the garage, and Chico said you would never have gone anywhere of your own accord without the battery charger for your arm."

"Well . . . I did."

"Sid . . ."

"No," I said. "What we need now is a list of periodicals and magazines dealing with antique furniture. We'll try those first with the *M* people."

"It's an awfully big project," Charles said doubtfully. "And even if we do find it, what then? I mean, as the man at Christie's pointed out, even if we find whose waiting list was being used, where does it get us? The firm or magazine wouldn't be able to tell us which of the many people who had access to the list was Nicholas Ashe, particularly as he is almost certain not to have used that name if he had any dealings with them."

"Mm," I said. "But there's a chance he's started operating again somewhere else, and is still using the same list. He took it with him, when he went. If we can find out whose list it is, we might go and call on some people who are on it, whose names start with *A* to *K*, and *P* to *Z*, and find out if they've received any of those begging letters very recently. Because if they have, the letters will have the address to which the money is to be sent. And there, at that address, we might find Mr. Ashe."

Charles put his mouth into the shape of a whistle, but what came out was more like a sigh.

"You've come back with your brains intact, anyway," he said.

Oh, God, I thought, I'm making myself think to shut out the abyss. I'm in splinters. . . . I'm never going to be right again. The analytical reasoning part of my mind might be marching straight on, but what had to be called the soul was sick and dying.

"And there's the polish," I said. I still had in my pocket the paper he'd given me the week before. I took it out and put it on the table. "If the idea of special polish is closely geared to the mailing list, then to get maximum results the polish is necessary. There can't be many private individuals ordering so much wax in unprinted tins packed in little white boxes. We could ask the polish firm to let us know if another lot is ordered. It's just faintly possible that Ashe will use the same firm again, even if not at once. He ought to see the danger . . . but he might be a fool."

I turned away wearily. Thought about whisky. Went over and poured myself a large one.

"Drinking heavily, are you?" Charles said from behind me, in his most offensive drawl.

I shut my teeth hard, and said, "No." Apart from coffee and water, it was my first drink for a week.

"Your first alcoholic blackout, was it, these last few days?"

I left the glass untouched on the drinks tray and turned round. His eyes were at their coldest, as unkind as in the days when we'd first met.

"Don't be so bloody stupid," I said.

He lifted his chin a fraction. "A spark," he said sarcastically. "Still got your pride, I see."

I compressed my lips and turned my back on him, and drank a lot of the Scotch. After a bit, I deliberately loosened a few tensed-up muscles, and said, "You won't find out that way. I know you too well. You use insults as a lever, to sting people into opening up. You've done it to me in the past. But not this time."

"If I find the right sting," he said, "I'll use it."

"Do you want a drink?" I said.

"Since you ask, yes."

We sat opposite each other in armchairs in unchanged companionship, and I thought vaguely of this and that and shied away from the crucifying bits.

"You know," I said. "We don't have to go trailing that mailing list around to see whose it is. All we do is ask the people themselves. Those . . ." I nodded toward the *M* stack. "We just ask some of them what mailing lists they themselves are on. We'd only need to ask a few. . . . The common denominator would be certain to turn up."

WHEN CHARLES HAD gone home to Aynsford I wandered aimlessly round the flat, tie off and in shirtsleeves, trying to be sensible. I told myself that nothing much had happened, only that Trevor Deansgate had used a lot of horrible threats to get me to stop doing something that I hadn't yet started. But I couldn't dodge the guilt. Once he'd revealed himself, once I knew he would do *something*, I could have stopped him, and I hadn't.

If he hadn't got me so effectively out of Newmarket, I would very likely have still been prodding unproductively away, unsure even if there was anything to discover, right up to the moment in the Guineas when Tri-Nitro tottered in last. But I would also be up there now, I thought, certain and inquisitive; and because of his threat, I wasn't.

I could call my absence prudence, common sense, the only possible course in the circumstances. I could rationalize and excuse. I could say I wouldn't have been doing anything that wasn't already being done by the Jockey Club. I returned all the time, to the swinging truth, that I wasn't there now because I was afraid to be.

Chico came back from his judo class and set to again to find out where I'd been; and for the same reasons I didn't tell him, even though I knew he wouldn't despise me as I despised myself.

"All right," he said finally. "You just keep it all bottled up and see where it gets you. Wherever you've been, it was bad. You've only got to look at you. It's not going to do you any good to shut it all up inside."

Shutting it all up inside, however, was a lifelong habit, a defense learned in childhood, a wall against the world, impossible to change.

I raised at least half a smile. "You setting up in Harley Street?"

"That's better," he said. "You missed all the fun, did you know? Tri-Nitro got stuffed after all in the Guineas yesterday, and they're turning George Caspar's yard inside out. It's all here, somewhere, in the *Sporting Life*. The Admiral brought it. Have you read it?"

I shook my head.

"Our Rosemary, she wasn't bonkers after all, was she? How do you think they managed it?"

"They?"

"Whoever did it."

"I don't know."

"I went along to see the gallop on Saturday morning," he said. "Yeah, yeah, I know you sent the telegram about leaving, but I'd got a real little dolly lined up for a bit of the other on Friday night, so I stayed. One more night wasn't going to make any difference, and besides, she was George Caspar's typist."

"She was . . ."

"Does the typing. Rides the horses sometimes. Into everything, she is, and talkative with it."

The new scared Sid Halley didn't even want to listen.

"There was a right old rumpus all day Wednesday in George Caspar's house," Chico said. "It started at breakfast when that Inky Poole turned up and said Sid Halley had been asking questions that he, Inky Poole, didn't like."

He paused for effect. I simply stared.

"Are you listening?" he said.

"Yes."

"You got your stone face act on again."

"Sorry."

"Then Brothersmith the vet turned up and heard Inky Poole letting off, and he said funny, Sid Halley had been around him asking questions too. About bad hearts, he said. Same horses as Inky Poole was talking about. Bethesda, Gleaner, and Zingaloo. And how was Tri-Nitro's heart, for good measure. My little dolly typist said you could've heard George Caspar blowing all the way to Cambridge. He's real touchy about those horses."

Trevor Deansgate, I thought coldly, had been at George Caspar's breakfast, and had heard every word.

"Of course," Chico said, "sometime, later they checked the studs, Garvey's and Thrace's, and found you'd been there too. My dolly says your name is mud."

I rubbed my hand over my face. "Does your dolly know you were working with me?"

"Do us a favor. Of course not."

"Did she say anything else?" What the hell am I asking for? I thought.

"Yeah. Well, she said Rosemary got on to George Caspar to change all the routine for the Saturday morning gallop, nagged him all day Thursday and all day Friday, and George Caspar was climbing the walls. And at the yard they had so much security they were tripping over their own alarm bells." He paused for breath. "After that she didn't say much else on account of three martinis and time for tickle."

I sat on the arm of the sofa and stared at the carpet.

"Next morning," Chico said, "I watched the gallop, like I said. Your photos came in very handy. Hundreds of ruddy horses . . . Someone told me which were Caspar's, and there was Inky Poole, scowling like in the pictures, so I just zeroed in on him and hung about. There was a lot of fuss when it came to Tri-Nitro. They took the saddle off and put a little one on, and Inky Poole rode on that."

"It was Inky Poole, then, who rode Tri-Nitro, same as usual?"

"They looked just like your pictures," Chico said. "Can't swear to it more than that."

I stared some more at the carpet.

"So what do we do next?" he said.

"Nothing . . . We give Rosemary her money back and draw a line."

"But hey," Chico said in protest. "Someone got at the horse. You know they did."

"Not our business any more."

I wished that he, too, would stop looking at me. I felt a distinct need to crawl into a hole and hide.

The doorbell rang with the long peal of a determined thumb. "We're out," I said; but Chico went and answered it.

Rosemary Caspar swept past him, through the hall and into the sitting room, advancing in the old fawn raincoat and a fulminating rage. No scarf, no false curls, and no loving kindness.

"So there you are," she said forcefully. "I knew you'd be here, skulking out of sight. Your friend kept telling me when I telephoned that you weren't here, but I knew he was lying."

"I wasn't here," I said. As well try damming the St. Lawrence with a twig.

"You weren't where I paid you to be, which was up in Newmarket. And I told you from the beginning that George wasn't to find out you were asking questions, and he did, and we've been having one God-awful bloody row ever since, and now Tri-Nitro has disgraced us unbearably and it's all your bloody fault."

Chico raised his eyebrows comically. "Sid didn't ride it . . . or train it."

She glared at him with transferred hatred. "And he didn't keep him safe, either."

"Er . . . no," Chico said. "Granted."

"As for you," she said, swinging back to me. "You're a useless bloody humbug. It's all rubbish, this detecting. Why don't you grow up and stop playing games? All you did was stir up trouble, and I want my money back."

"Will a check do?" I said.

"You're not arguing, then?"

"No," I said.

"Do you mean you admit that you failed?"

After a small pause, I said, "Yes."

"Oh." She sounded as if I had unexpectedly deprived her of a good deal of what she had come to say, but while I wrote out a check for her she went on complaining sharply enough.

"All your ideas about changing the routine, they were useless. I've been on and on at George about security and taking care, and he says he couldn't have done any more, no one could, and he's in absolute despair; and I'd hoped, I'd really hoped—what a laugh—that somehow or other you would work a miracle, and that Tri-Nitro would win, because I was so sure, so sure . . . and I was right."

I finished writing. "Why were you always so sure?" I said.

"I don't know. I just *knew*. I've been afraid of it for weeks . . . otherwise I would not have been so desperate as to try you in the first place. And I might as well not have bothered. . . . It's caused so much trouble, and I can't bear it. I can't bear it. Yesterday was terrible. He should have won . . . I knew he wouldn't. I felt ill. I still feel ill."

She was trembling again. The pain in her face was acute. So many hopes, so much work had gone into Tri-Nitro, such anxiety and such care. Winning races was to a trainer like a film to a film-maker. If you got it right, they applauded; wrong, and they booed. And either way you'd poured your soul into it, and your thoughts and your skill and weeks of worry. I understood what the lost race meant to George, and to Rosemary equally, because she cared so much.

"Rosemary . . ." I said, in useless sympathy.

"It's pointless Brothersmith saying he must have had an infection," she said. "He's always saying things like that. He's so wet, I can't stand him; always looking over his shoulder. I've never liked him. And it was his job anyway to check Tri-Nitro and he did, over and over, and there was nothing wrong with him, nothing. He went down to the post looking beautiful, and in the parade ring before that there was nothing wrong, nothing. And then in the race, he just went backward, and he finished . . . he came back . . . exhausted." There was a glitter of tears for a moment, but she visibly willed them away from overwhelming her.

"They've done dope tests, I suppose," Chico said.

It angered her again. "Dope tests! Of course they have. What do you expect? Blood tests, urine tests, saliva tests, dozens of bloody tests. They gave George duplicate samples, and that's why we're down here; he's trying to fix up with some private lab . . . but they won't be positive. It will be like before . . . absolutely nothing."

I tore out the check and gave it to her, and she glanced at it blindly.

"I wish I'd never come here. My God, I wish I hadn't. You're only a jockey. I should have known better. I don't want to talk to you again. Don't talk to me at the races, do you understand?"

I nodded. I did understand. She turned abruptly, to go away. "And for God's sake don't speak to George, either." She went alone out of the room, and out of the flat, and slammed the door.

Chico clicked his tongue, and shrugged. "You can't win them all," he said. "What could you do that her husband couldn't, not to mention a private police force and half a dozen guard dogs?" He was excusing me, and we both knew it.

I didn't answer.

"Sid?"

"I don't know that I'm going on with it," I said. "This sort of job."

"You don't want to take any notice of what she said," he protested. "You can't give it up. You're too good at it. Look at all the awful messes you've put right. Just because of one that's gone wrong . . ."

I stared hollowly at a lot of unseen things.

"You're a big boy now," he said. And he was seven years younger than I, near enough. "You want to cry on Daddy's shoulder?" He paused. "Look, Sid, mate, you've got to snap out of it. Whatever's happened, it can't be as bad as when that horse sliced your hand up; nothing could. This is no time to die inside: we've got about five other jobs lined up. The insurance, and the guard job, and Lucas Wainwright's syndicates . . ."

"No," I said. I felt leaden and useless. "Not now, honestly, Chico."

I got up and went into the bedroom. Shut the door. Went purposelessly to the window and looked out at the scenery of roofs and chimney pots, glistening in the beginnings of rain. The pots were still there, though the chimneys underneath were blocked off and the fires long dead. I felt at one with the chimney pots. When fires went out, one froze.

The door opened.

"Sid," Chico said.

I said resignedly, "Remind me to put a lock on that door."

"You've got another visitor."

"Tell him to go away."

"It's a girl. Louise somebody."

I rubbed my hand over my face and head and down to the back of my neck. Eased the muscles. Turned from the window.

"Louise McInnes?"

"That's right."

"She shares the flat with Jenny," I said.

"Oh, that one. Well, then, Sid, if that's all for today, I'll be off. And . . . er . . . be here tomorrow, won't you?"

"Yeah."

He nodded. We left everything else unsaid. The amusement, mockery, friendship, and stifled anxiety were all there in his face and his voice . . . Maybe he read the same in mine. At any rate, he gave me a widening grin as he departed, and I went into the sitting room thinking that some debts couldn't be paid.

Louise was standing in the middle of things, looking around her as I had in Jenny's flat. Through her eyes I saw my own room afresh: its irregular shape, high-ceilinged, not modern; and the tan leather sofa, the table with drinks by the window, the shelves with books, the prints framed and hung, and on the floor, leaning against the wall, the big painting of race horses which I'd somehow never bothered to hang up. There were coffee cups and glasses scattered about, and full ashtrays, and the piles of letters on the coffee table and everywhere else.

Louise herself looked different: the full production, not the Sunday morning tumble out of bed. A brown velvet jacket, a blazing white sweater, a soft mottled brown skirt with a wide leather belt round an untroubled waist. Fair hair washed and shining, rose petal make-up on the English-rose skin. A detachment in the eyes which said that all this honey was not chiefly there for the attracting of bees.

"Mr. Halley."

"You could try Sid," I said. "You know me quite well, by proxy."

Her smile reached halfway. "Sid."

"Louise."

"Jenny says Sid is a plumber's mate's sort of name."

"Very good people, plumber's mates."

"Did you know," she said, looking away and continuing the visual tour of inspection, "that in Arabic 'Sid' means 'lord'?"

"No, I didn't."

"Well, it does."

"You could tell Jenny," I said.

Her gaze came back fast to my face. "She gets to you, doesn't she?"

I smiled. "Like some coffee? Or a drink?"

"Tea?"

"Sure."

She came into the kitchen with me and watched me make it, and made no funny remarks about bionic hands, which was a nice change from most new acquaintances, who tended to be fascinated, and to say so, at length. Instead she looked around with inoffensive curiosity, and finally fastened her attention on the calendar which hung from the knob on the pine cupboard door. Photographs of horses, a Christmas handout from a book-making firm. She flipped up the pages, looking at the pictures of the future months, and stopped at December, where a horse and jockey jumping the Chair at Aintree was silhouetted spectacularly against the sky.

"That's good," she said, and then, in surprise, reading the caption, "That's *you*."

"He's a good photographer."

"Did you win that race?"

"Yes," I said mildly. "Do you take sugar?"

"No, thanks." She let the pages fall back. "How odd to find oneself on a calendar."

To me, it wasn't odd. How odd, I thought, to have seen one's picture in print so much that one scarcely noticed.

I carried the tray into the sitting room and put it on top of the letters on the coffee table. "Sit down," I said, and we sat.

"All these," I said, nodding to them, "are the letters which came with the checks for the wax."

She looked doubtful. "Are they of any use?"

"I hope so," I said, and explained about the mailing list.

"Good heavens." She hesitated, "Well, perhaps you won't need what I brought." She picked up her brown leather handbag and opened it. "I didn't come all this way specially," she said. "I've an aunt near here whom I visit. Anyway, I thought you might like to have this, as I was here, near your flat."

She pulled out a paperback book. She could have posted it, I thought, but I was quite glad that she hadn't.

"I was trying to put a bit of order into the chaos in my bedroom," she said. "I've a lot of books. They tend to pile up."

I didn't tell her I'd seen them. "Books do," I said.

"Well, this was among them. It's Nicky's."

She gave me the paperback. I glanced at the cover and put it down, in order to pour out the tea. *Navigation for Beginners.* I handed her the cup and saucer. "Was he interested in navigation?"

"I've no idea. But I was. I borrowed it out of his room. I don't think he even knew I'd borrowed it. He had a box with some things in—like a tuck box that boys take to public school—and one day when I went into his room the things were all on the chest of drawers, as if he was tidying. Anyway, he was out, and I borrowed the book—he wouldn't have minded; he was terribly easygoing—and I suppose I put it down in my room, and put something else on top, and just forgot it."

"Did you read it?" I said.

"No. Never got round to it. It was weeks ago."

I picked up the book and opened it. On the flyleaf someone had written "John Viking" in a firm legible signature in black felt-tip.

"I don't know," Louise said, anticipating my question, "whether that is Nicky's writing or not."

"Does Jenny know?"

"She hasn't seen this. She's staying with Toby in Yorkshire."

Jenny with Toby. Jenny with Ashe. For God's sake, I thought, what do you expect? She's gone, she's not yours, you're divorced. And I hadn't been alone, not entirely.

"You look very tired," Louise said doubtfully.

I was disconcerted. "Of course not." I turned the pages, letting them flick over from under my thumb. It was, as it promised to be, a book about navigation, sea and air, with line drawings and diagrams. Dead reckoning, sextants, magnetism, and drift. Nothing of any note except a single line of letters and figures, written with the same black ink, on the inside of the back cover.

$$\text{Lift} = 22 \cdot 024 \times V \times P \times \left(\frac{1}{T1} - \frac{1}{T2} \right)$$

I handed it over to Louise.

"Does this mean anything to you? Charles said you've a degree in mathematics."

She frowned at it faintly. "Nicky needed a calculator for two plus two."

He had done all right at two plus ten thousand, I thought.

"Um," she said. "Lift equals $22 \cdot 024$ times volume times pressure, times . . . I should think this is something to do with temperature change. Not my subject, really. This is physics."

"Something to do with navigation?" I asked.

She concentrated. I watched the way her face grew taut while she did the internal scan. A fast brain, I thought, under the pretty hair.

"It's funny," she said finally, "but I think it's just possibly something to do with how much you can lift with a gasbag."

"Airship?" I said, thinking.

"It depends what $22 \cdot 024$ is," she said. "That's a constant. Which means," she added, "it is special to whatever this equation is all about."

"I'm better at what's likely to win the three-thirty."

She looked at her watch. "You're three hours too late."

"It'll come round again tomorrow."

She relaxed into the armchair, handing back the book. "I don't suppose it will help," she said, "but you seemed to want anything of Nicky's."

"It might help a lot. You never know."

"But how?"

"It's John Viking's book. John Viking might know Nicky Ashe."

"But . . . you don't know John Viking."

"No," I said. "But he knows gasbags. And I know someone who knows gasbags. And I bet gasbags are a small world, like racing."

She looked at the heaps of letters, and then at the book. She said slowly, "I guess you'll find him, one way or another."

I looked away from her, and at nothing in particular.

"Jenny says you never give up."

I smiled faintly. "Her exact words?"

"No." I felt her amusement. " 'Obstinate, selfish, and determined to get his own way.' "

"Not far off." I tapped the book. "Can I keep this?"

"Of course."

"Thanks."

We looked at each other as people do, especially if they're youngish and male and female, and sitting in a quiet flat at the end of an April day.

She read my expression and answered the unspoken thought. "Some other time," she said dryly.

"How long will you be staying with Jenny?"

"Would that matter to you?" she asked.

"Mm."

"She says you're as hard as flint. She says steel's a pushover beside you."

I thought of terror and misery and self-loathing. I shook my head.

"What I see," she said slowly, "is a man who looks ill being polite to an unwanted visitor."

"You're wanted," I said. "And I'm fine."

She stood up, however, and I also, after her.

"I hope," I said, "that you're fond of your aunt?"

"Devoted."

She gave me a cool, half-ironic smile in which there was also surprise.

"Goodbye . . . Sid."

"Goodbye, Louise."

WHEN SHE'D GONE I switched on a table light or two against the slow dusk, and poured a whisky, and looked at a pale bunch of sausages in the fridge and didn't cook them.

No one else would come, I thought. They had all in their way held off the shadows, particularly Louise. No one else real would come, but he would be with me, as he'd been in Paris . . . Trevor Deansgate. Inescapable. Reminding me inexorably of what I would rather forget.

After a while I stepped out of trousers and shirt and put on a short blue bathrobe, and took off the arm. It was one of the times when taking it off really hurt. It didn't seem to matter, after the rest.

I went back to the sitting room to do something about the clutter, but there was simply too much to bother with, so I stood looking at it, and held my weaker upper arm with my strong, whole, agile right hand, as I often did, for support, and I wondered which crippled one worse, amputation without or within.

Humiliation and rejection and helplessness and failure . . .

After all these years I would *not*, I thought wretchedly, I would damned well *not* be defeated by fear.

CHAPTER 9

LUCAS WAINWRIGHT TELEPHONED the next morning while I was stacking cups in the dishwasher.

"Any progress?" he asked, sounding very commanderish.

"I'm afraid," I said regretfully, "that I've lost all those notes. I'll have to do them again."

"For heaven's sake." He wasn't pleased. I didn't tell him that I'd lost the notes on account of being bashed on the head and dropping in the gutter the large brown envelope that contained them. "Come right away, then. Eddy won't be in until this afternoon."

Slowly, absent-mindedly, I finished tidying up, while I thought about Lucas Wainwright, and what he could do for me, if he would. Then I sat at the table and wrote down what I wanted. Then I looked at what I'd written, and at my fingers holding the pen, and shivered. Then I folded the paper and put it in my pocket, and went to Portman Square, deciding not to give it to Lucas after all.

He had the files ready in his office, and I sat at the same table as before and recopied all I needed.

"You won't let it drag on much longer, will you, Sid?"

"Full attention," I said. "Starting tomorrow. I'll go to. Kent tomorrow afternoon."

"Good." He stood up as I put the new notes into a fresh envelope and waited for me to go, not through impatience with me particularly, but because he was that sort of man. Brisk. One task finished, get on with the next, don't hang about.

I hesitated cravenly and found myself speaking before I had consciously decided whether to or not. "Commander. Do you remember that you said you might pay me for this job not with money but with help, if I should want it?"

I got a reasonable smile and a postponement of the goodbyes.

"Of course I remember. You haven't done the job yet. What help?"

"Er . . . it's nothing much. Very little." I took the paper out and handed it to him. Waited while he read the brief contents. Felt as if I had planted a land mine and would presently step on it.

"I don't see why not," he said. "If that's what you want. But are you on to something that we should know about?"

I gestured to the paper. "You'll know about it as soon as I do, if you do that." It wasn't a satisfactory answer, but he didn't press it. "The only thing I beg of you, though, is that you won't mention my name at all. Don't say it was my idea, not to *anyone*. I . . . er . . . you might get me killed, Commander, and I'm not being funny."

He looked from me to the paper and back again, and frowned. "This doesn't look like a killing matter, Sid."

"You never know what is until you're dead."

He smiled. "All right. I'll write the letter as from the Jockey Club, and I'll take you seriously about the death risk. Will that do?"

"It will indeed."

We shook hands, and I left his office carrying the brown envelope, and at the Portman Square entrance, going out, I met Eddy Keith coming in. We both paused, as one does. I hoped he couldn't see the dismay on my face at his early return, or guess that I was perhaps carrying the seeds of his downfall.

"Eddy," I said, smiling and feeling a traitor.

"Hello, Sid," he said cheerfully, twinkling at me from above rounded cheeks. "What are you doing here?" A good-natured, normal inquiry. No suspicions. No tremor.

"Looking for crumbs," I said.

He chuckled fatly. "From what I hear, it's us picking up yours. Have us all out of work, you will, soon."

"Not a chance."

"Don't step on our toes, Sid."

The smile was still there, the voice devoid of threat. The fuzzy hair, the big mustache, the big broad fleshy face, still exuded good will; but the arctic had briefly come and gone in his eyes, and I was in no doubt that I'd received a serious warning off.

"Never, Eddy," I said insincerely.

"See you, fella," he said, preparing to go indoors, nodding, smiling widely, and giving me the usual hearty buffet on the shoulder. "Take care."

"You too, Eddy," I said to his departing back; and under my breath, again, in a sort of sorrow, "You too."

I CARRIED THE notes safely back to the flat, and thought a bit, and telephoned to my man in gasbags.

He said hello and great to hear from you and how about a jar sometime, and no, he had never heard of anyone called John Viking. I read out the equation and asked if it meant anything to him, and he laughed and said it sounded like a formula for taking a hot air balloon to the moon.

"Thanks very much," I said sarcastically.

"No, seriously, Sid. It's a calculation for maximum height. Try a balloonist. They're always after records . . . the highest, the farthest, that sort of thing."

I asked if he knew any balloonists, but he said sorry, no, he didn't, he was only into airships, and we disconnected with another vague resolution to meet somewhere, sometime, one of these days. Idly, and certain it was useless, I leafed through the telephone directory, and there, incredibly, the words stood out bold and clear: The Hot Air Balloon Company, offices in London, number provided.

I got through. A pleasant male voice at the other end said that of course he knew John Viking, everyone in ballooning knew John Viking, he was a madman of the first order.

Madman?

John Viking, the voice explained, took risks which no sensible balloonist would dream of. If I wanted to talk to him, the voice said, I would undoubtedly find him at the balloon race on Monday afternoon.

Where was the balloon race on Monday afternoon?

Horse show, balloon race, swings and roundabouts, you name it: all part of the May Day holiday junketings at Highalane Park in Wiltshire. John Viking would be there. Sure to be.

I thanked the voice for his help and rang off, reflecting that I had forgotten about the May Day holiday. National holidays had always been workdays for me, as for everyone in racing: providing the entertainment for the public's leisure. I tended not to notice them come and go.

Chico arrived with fish and chips for two in the sort of hygienic grease-proof wrappings that kept the steam in and made the chips go soggy.

"Did you know it's the May Day holiday on Monday?" I said.

"Running a judo tournament for the little bleeders, aren't I?"

He tipped the lunch onto two plates, and we ate it, mostly with fingers.

"You've come to life again, I see," he said.

"It's temporary."

"We'd better get some work done, then, while you're still with us."

"The syndicates," I said; and told him about the luckless Mason having been sent out on the same errand and having his brains kicked to destruction.

Chico shook salt on his chips. "Have to be careful then, won't we?"

"Start this afternoon?"

"Sure." He paused reflectively, licking his fingers. "We're not getting paid for this, didn't you say?"

"Not directly."

"Why don't we do these insurance inquiries, then? Nice quiet questions with a guaranteed fee."

"I promised Lucas Wainwright I'd do the syndicates first."

He shrugged. "You're the boss. But that makes three in a row, counting your wife and Rosemary getting her cash back, that we've worked on for nothing."

"We'll make up for it later."

"You are going on, then?"

I didn't answer at once. Apart from not knowing whether I wanted to, I didn't know if I could. Over the past months Chico and I had tended to get somewhat battered by bully boys trying to stop us in our tracks. We didn't have the protection of being either in the Racecourse Security Service or the police. No one to defend us but ourselves. We had looked upon the bruises as part of the job, as racing falls had been to me and bad judo falls to Chico. What if Trevor Deansgate had changed all that . . . not just for one terrible week, but for much longer: for always?

"Sid," Chico said sharply, "Come back."

I swallowed. "Well . . . er . . . we'll do the syndicates. Then we'll see." Then I'll know, I thought. I'll know inside me, one way or the other. If I couldn't walk into tigers' cages any more, we were done. One of us wasn't enough: it had to be both.

If I couldn't . . . I'd as soon be dead.

THE FIRST SYNDICATES on Lucas's list had been formed by eight people, of whom three were registered owners, headed by Philip Friarly. Registered owners were those acceptable to the racing authorities, owners who paid their dues and kept the rules, were no trouble to anybody, and represented the source and mainspring of the whole industry.

Syndicates were a way of involving more people directly in racing, which was good for the sport, and dividing the training costs into smaller fractions, which was good for the owners. There were syndicates of millionaires, coal miners, groups of rock guitarists, the clientele of pubs. Anyone from Auntie Flo to the undertaker could join a syndicate, and all Eddy Keith should have done was check that all those on the list were who they said they were.

"It's not the registered owners we're looking at," I said. "It's all the others."

We were driving through Kent on our way to Tunbridge Wells. Ultra-respectable place, Tunbridge Wells. Resort of retired colonels and ladies who played bridge. Low on the national crime league. Hometown, all the same, of a certain Peter Rammileese, who was, so Lucas Wainwright's informant had said, in fact the instigating member of all four of the doubtful syndicates, although his own name nowhere appeared.

"Mason," I said, conversationally, "was attacked and left for dead in the streets of Tunbridge Wells."

"Now he tells me."

"Chico," I said, "do you want to turn back?"

"You got a premonition or something?"

After a pause, I said, "No," and drove a shade too fast round a sharpish bend.

"Look, Sid," he said. "We don't have to go to Tunbridge Wells. We're on a hiding to nothing, with this lark."

"What do you think, then?"

He was silent.

"We do have to go," I said.

"Yeah."

"So we have to work out what it was that Mason asked, and not ask it."

"This Rammileese," Chico said. "What's he like?"

"I haven't met him myself, but I've heard of him. He's a farmer who's made a packet out of crooked dealings in horses. The Jockey Club won't have him as a registered owner, and most racecourses don't let him through the gates. He'll try to bribe anyone from the senior steward to the scrubbers, and where he can't bribe, he threatens."

"Oh, jolly."

"Two jockeys and a trainer, not so long ago, lost their licenses for taking his bribes. One of the jockeys got the sack from his stable and he's so broke he's hanging around outside the racecourse gates begging for handouts."

"Is that the one I saw you talking to a while ago?"

"That's right."

"And how much did you give him?"

"Never you mind."

"You're a pushover, Sid."

"A case of 'but for the grace of God,'" I said.

"Oh, sure. I could just see you taking bribes from a crooked horse dealer. Most likely thing on earth."

"Anyway," I said, "what we're trying to find out is not whether Peter Rammileese is manipulating four race horses, which he is, but whether Eddy Keith knows it and is keeping quiet."

"Right." We sped deeper into rural Kent, and then he said, "You know why we've had such good results, on the whole, since we've been together on this job?"

"Why, then?"

"It's because all the villains know you. I mean, they know you by sight, most of them. So when they see you poking around on their patch, they set the heebies and start doing silly things like setting the heavies on us, and then we see them loud and clear, and what they're up to, which we wouldn't have done if they'd sat tight."

I sighed and said, "I guess so," and thought about Trevor Deansgate; thought and tried not to. Without any hands one couldn't drive a car. . . . Just don't think about it, I told myself. Just keep your mind off it; it's a one-way trip into jellyfish.

I swung round another corner too fast and collected a sideways look from Chico, but no comment.

"Look at the map," I said. "Do something useful."

We found the house of Peter Rammileese without much trouble, and pulled into the yard of a small farm that looked as if the outskirts of Tunbridge Wells had rolled round it like a sea, leaving it isolated and incongruous. There was a large white farmhouse, three stories high, and a modern wooden stable block, and a long, extra-large barn. Nothing significantly prosperous about the place, but no nettles, either.

No one around. I put the brake on as we rolled to stop, and we got out of the car.

"Front door?" Chico said.

"Back door, for farms."

We had taken only five or six steps in that direction, however, when a small boy ran into the yard from a doorway in the barn and came over to us breathlessly.

"Did you bring the ambulance?"

His eyes looked past me, to my car, and his face puckered into agitation and disappointment. He was about seven, dressed in jodhpurs and T-shirt, and he had been crying.

"What's the matter?" I said.

"I rang for the ambulance . . . a long time ago."

"We might help," I said.

"It's Mum," he said. "She's lying in there, and she won't wake up."

"Come on; you show us."

He was a sturdy little boy, brown-haired and brown-eyed and very frightened. He ran ahead toward the barn, and we followed without wasting time.
Once through the door we could see that it wasn't an ordinary barn, but an
indoor riding school, a totally enclosed area of about twenty meters wide by
thirty-five long, lit by windows in the roof. The floor, wall to wall, was covered with a thick layer of tan-colored wood chips, springy and quiet for horses
to work on.

There were a pony and a horse careering about; and, in danger from their
hoofs, a crumpled female figure lying on the ground.

Chico and I went over to her, fast. She was young, on her side, face half
downward; unconscious, but not, I thought, deeply. Her breathing was shallow and her skin had whitened in a mottle fashion under her make-up, but
the pulse in her wrist was strong and regular. The crash helmet which hadn't
saved her lay several feet away on the floor.

"Go and ring again," I said to Chico.

"Shouldn't we move her?"

"No . . . in case she's broken anything. You can do a lot of damage moving people too much when they're unconscious."

"You should know." He turned away and run off toward the house.

"Is she all right?" the boy said anxiously. "Bingo started bucking and she
fell off, and I think he kicked her head."

"Bingo is the horse?"

"His saddle slipped," he said; and Bingo, with the saddle down under his
belly, was still bucking and kicking like a rodeo.

"What's your name?" I said.

"Mark."

"Well, Mark, as far as I can see, your mum is going to be all right, and
you're a brave little boy."

"I'm six," he said, as if that wasn't so little.

The worst of the fright had died out of his eyes, now that he had help. I
knelt on the ground beside his mother and smoothed the brown hair away
from her forehead. She made a small moaning sound, and her eyelids flut-
tered. She was perceptibly nearer the surface, even in the short time we'd been
there.

"I thought she was dying," the boy said. "We had a rabbit a little time
ago. . . . He panted and shut his eyes, and we couldn't wake him up again,
and he died."

"Your mum will wake up again."

"Are you sure?"

"Yes, Mark. I'm sure."

He seemed deeply reassured, and told me readily that the pony was called Sooty, and was his own, and that his dad was away until tomorrow morning, and there was only his mum there, and him, and she'd been schooling Bingo because she was selling him to a girl for show jumping.

Chico came back and said the ambulance was on its way. The boy, cheering up enormously, said we ought to catch the horses because they were cantering about and the reins were all loose, and if the saddles and bridles got broken his dad would be bloody angry.

Both Chico and I laughed at the adult words, seriously spoken. While he and Mark stood guard over the patient, I caught the horses one by one, with the aid of a few horse nuts that Mark produced from his pockets, and tied their reins to tethering rings in the walls. Bingo, once the agitating girths were undone and the saddle safely off, stood quietly enough, and Mark darted briefly away from his mother to give his own pony some brisk encouraging slaps and some more horse nuts.

Chico said the emergency service had indeed had a call from a child fifteen minutes earlier, but he'd hung up before they could ask him where he lived.

"Don't tell him," I said.

"You're a softie."

"He's a brave little kid."

"Not bad for a little bleeder. While you were catching the bucking bronco, he told me his dad gets bloody angry pretty often." He looked down at the still unconscious girl. "You really reckon she's O.K., do you?"

"She'll come out of it. It's a matter of waiting."

The ambulance came in due course, but Mark's anxiety reappeared, strongly, when the men loaded his mother into the van and prepared to depart. He wanted to go with her, and the men wouldn't take him on his own. She was stirring and mumbling, and it distressed him.

I said to Chico, "Drive him to the hospital . . . follow the ambulance. He needs to see her wide awake and speaking to him. I'll take a look round in the house. His dad's away until tomorrow."

"Convenient," he said sardonically. He collected Mark into the Scimitar and drove away down the road, and through the rear window I could see their heads talking to each other.

I went through the open back door with the confidence of the invited. Nothing difficult about entering a tiger's cage while the tiger was out.

It was an old house filled with brash new opulent furnishings, which I found overpowering. Lush loud carpets, huge stereo equipment, a lamp standard of a golden nymph, and deep armchairs covered in black and khaki zigzags. Sitting and dining rooms shining and tidy, with no sign that a small boy lived there. Kitchen uncluttered, hygienic surfaces wiped clean. Study . . .

The positively aggressive tidiness of the study made me pause and consider. No horse trader that I'd ever come across had kept his books and papers in such neat rectangular stacks; and the ledgers themselves, when I opened them, contained up-to-the-minute entries.

I looked into drawers and filing cabinets, being extremely careful to leave everything squared up after me, but there was nothing there except the outward show of honesty. Not a single drawer or cupboard was locked. It was almost, I thought with cynicism, as if the whole thing were stage dressing, orchestrated to confound any invasion of tax snoopers. The real records, if he kept any, were probably somewhere inside, in a biscuit tin, in a hole in the ground.

I went upstairs. Mark's room was unmistakable, but all the toys were in boxes, and all the clothes in drawers. There were three unoccupied bedrooms with the outlines of folded blankets showing under covers, and a suite of bedroom, dressing room, and bathroom furnished with the same expanse and tidiness as downstairs.

An oval dark red bath with taps like gilt dolphins. A huge bed with a bright brocade cover clashing with wall-to-wall jazz on the floor. No clutter on the curvaceous cream-and-gold dressing table, no brushes on any surface in the dressing room.

Mark's mum's clothes were fur and glitter and breeches and jackets. Mark's dad's clothes, thornproof tweeds, vicuna overcoat, a dozen or more suits, none of them handmade, all seemingly bought because they were expensive. Handfuls of illicit cash, I thought, and nothing much to do with it. Peter Rammileese, it seemed, was crooked by nature and not by necessity.

The same incredible tidiness extended through every drawer and every shelf, and even into the soiled-linen basket, where a pair of pajamas were neatly folded.

I went through the pockets of his suits, but he had left nothing at all in them. There were no pieces of paper of any sort anywhere in the dressing room.

Frustrated, I went up to the third floor, where there were six rooms, one containing a variety of empty suitcases, and the others, nothing at all.

No one, I thought on the way down again, lived so excessively carefully if he had nothing to hide; which was scarcely evidence to offer in court. The present life of the Rammileese family was an expensive vacuum, and of the past there was no sign at all. No souvenirs, no old books, not even any photographs, except a recent one of Mark on his pony, taken outside in the yard.

I was looking round the outbuildings when Chico came back. There were no animals except seven horses in the stable and the two in the covered school. No sign of farming in progress. No rosettes in the tack room, just a lot more tidiness and the smell of saddle soap. I went out to meet Chico and ask what he had done with Mark.

"The nurses are stuffing him with jam butties and trying to ring his dad. Mum is awake and talking. How did you get on? Do you want to drive?"

"No, you drive." I sat in beside him. "That house is the most suspicious case of no history I've ever seen."

"Like that, eh?"

"Mm. And not a chance of finding any link with Eddy Keith."

"Wasted journey, then," he said.

"Lucky for Mark."

"Yeah. Good little bleeder, that. Told me he's going to be a furniture moving man when he grows up." Chico looked across at me and grinned. "Seems he's moved house three times that he can remember."

CHAPTER 10

CHICO AND I spent most of Saturday separately traipsing around all the London addresses on the M list of wax names, and met at six o'clock, footsore and thirsty, at a pub we both knew in Fulham.

"We never ought to have done it on a Saturday, and a holiday weekend at that," Chico said.

"No," I agreed.

Chico watched the beer sliding mouth-wateringly into the glass. "More than half of them were out."

"Mine too. Nearly all."

"And the ones that were in were watching the racing or the wrestling or groping their girlfriends, and didn't want to know."

We carried his beer and my whisky over to a small table, drank deeply, and compared notes. Chico had finally pinned down four people, and I only two, but the results were there, all the same.

All six, whatever other mailing lists they had confessed to, had been in regular happy receipt of *Antiques for All.*

"That's it, then," Chico said. "Conclusive." He leaned back against the wall, luxuriously relaxing. "We can't do any more until Tuesday. Everything's shut."

"Are you busy tomorrow?"

"Have a heart. The girl in Wembley." He looked at his watch and swallowed the rest of the beer. "And so long, Sid, boy, or I'll be late. She doesn't like me sweaty."

He grinned and departed, and I more slowly finished my drink and went home.

Wandered about. Changed the batteries. Ate some cornflakes. Got out the form books and looked up the syndicated horses. Highly variable form: races lost at short odds and won at long. All the signs of steady and expert fixing. I yawned. It went on all the time.

I puttered some more, restlessly, sorely missing the peace that usually filled me in that place when I was alone. Undressed, put on a bathrobe, pulled off the arm. Tried to watch the television; couldn't concentrate. Switched it off.

I usually pulled the arm off after I'd put the bathrobe on, because that way I didn't have to look at the bit of me that remained below the left elbow. I could come to terms with the fact of it but still not really the sight, though it was neat enough and not horrific, as the messed-up hand had been. I daresay it was senseless to be faintly repelled, but I was. I hated anyone except the limb man to see it; even Chico. I was ashamed of it, and that too was illogical. People without handicaps never understood that ashamed feeling, nor had I, until the day soon after the original injury when I'd blushed crimson because I'd had to ask someone to cut up my food. There had been many times after that when I'd gone hungry rather than ask. Not having to ask, ever, since I'd had the electronic hand, had been a psychological release of soul-saving proportions.

The new hand had meant, too, a return to full normal human status. No one treated me as an idiot, or with the pity which in the past had made me cringe. No one made allowances any more, or got themselves tongue-tied with trying not to say the wrong thing. The days of the useless deformity seemed in retrospect an unbearable nightmare. I was often quite grateful to the villain who had set me free.

With one hand, I was a self-sufficient man.

Without any . . .

Oh, God, I thought. Don't think about it. "There is nothing either good or bad, but thinking makes it so." Hamlet, however, didn't have the same problems.

I got through the night, and the next morning, and the afternoon, but at around six I gave up and got in the car, and drove to Aynsford.

If Jenny was there, I thought, easing up the back drive and stopping quietly in the yard outside the kitchen, I would just turn right around and go back to London, and at least the driving would have occupied the time. But no one seemed to be about, and I walked into the house from the side door, which had a long passage into the hall.

Charles was in the small sitting room that he called the wardroom, sitting alone, sorting out his much-loved collection of fly hooks for fishing.

He looked up. No surprise. No effusive welcome. No fuss. Yet I'd never gone there before without invitation.

"Hello," he said.

"Hello."

I stood there, and he looked at me, and waited.

"I wanted some company," I said.

He squinted at a dry fly. "Did you bring an overnight bag?"

I nodded.

He pointed to the drinks tray. "Help yourself. And pour me a pink gin, will you? Ice in the kitchen."

I fetched him his drink, and my own, and sat in an armchair.

"Come to tell me?" he said.

"No."

He smiled. "Supper, then? And chess."

We ate, and played two games. He won the first, easily, and told me to pay attention. The second, after an hour and a half, was a draw. "That's better," he said.

The peace I hadn't been able to find on my own came slowly back with Charles, even though I knew it had more to do with the ease I felt with him personally, and the timelessness of his vast old house, than with a real resolution of the destruction within. In any case, for the first time in ten days, I slept soundly for hours.

At breakfast we discussed the day ahead. He himself was going to the steeplechase meeting at Towcester, forty-five minutes northward, to act as a steward, an honorary job that he enjoyed. I told him about John Viking and the balloon race, and also about the visits to the M people, and *Antiques for All*, and he smiled with his own familiar mixture of satisfaction and amusement, as if I were some creation of his that was coming up to his expectations. It was he who had originally driven me to becoming an investigator. Whenever I got anything right, he took the credit for it to himself.

"Did Mrs. Cross tell you about the telephone call?" he said, buttering toast. Mrs. Cross was his housekeeper, quiet, efficient, and kind.

"What telephone call?"

"Someone rang here about seven this morning, asking if you were here. Mrs. Cross said you were asleep and could she take a message, but whoever it was said he would ring later."

"Was it Chico? He might guess I'd come here, if he couldn't get me in the flat."

"Mrs. Cross said he didn't give a name."

I shrugged and reached for the coffeepot. "It can't have been urgent, or he'd have told her to wake me up."

Charles smiled. "Mrs. Cross sleeps in curlers and face cream. She'd never have let you see her at seven o'clock in the morning, short of an earthquake. She thinks you're a lovely young man. She tells me so, every time you come."

"For God's sake."

"Will you be back here tonight?" he said.

"I don't know yet."

He folded his napkin, looking down at it. "I'm glad that you came yesterday."

I looked at him. "Yeah," I said. "Well, you want me to say it, so I'll say it. And I mean it." I paused a fraction, searching for the simplest words that would tell him what I felt for him. Found some. Said them. "This is my home."

He looked up quickly, and I smiled twistedly, mocking myself, mocking him, mocking the whole damned world.

HIGHLANE PARK WAS a stately home uneasily coming to terms with the plastic age. The house itself opened to the public like an agitated virgin only half a dozen times a year, but the parkland was always out for rent for game fair and circuses, and things like the May Day jamboree.

They had made little enough effort on the roadside to attract the passing crowd. No bunting, no razzmatazz, no posters with print large enough to read at ten paces; everything slightly coy and apologetic. Considering a'l that, the numbers pouring onto the showground were impressive. I paid at the gate in my turn and bumped over some grass to park the car obediently in a row in the roped-off parking area. Other cars followed, neatly alongside.

There were a few people on horses cantering busily about in haphazard directions, but the roundabouts on the fairground to one side were silent and motionless, and there was no sight of any balloons.

I stood up out of the car and locked the door, and thought that one-thirty was probably too early for much in the way of action.

One can be so wrong.

A voice behind me said, "Is this the man?"

I turned and found two people advancing into the small space between my car and the one next to it: a man I didn't know, and a little boy, whom I did.

"Yes," the boy said, pleased. "Hello."

"Hello, Mark," I said. "How's your mum?"

"I told Dad about you coming." He looked up at the man beside him.

"Did you, now." I thought his being at Highalane was only an extraordinary coincidence, but it wasn't.

"He described you," the man said. "That hand, and the way you could handle horses . . . I knew who he meant, right enough." His face and voice were hard and wary, with a quality that I by now recognized on sight: guilty knowledge faced by trouble. "I don't take kindly to you poking your nose around my place."

"You were out," I said mildly.

"Aye, I was out. And this nipper here, he left you there all alone."

He was about forty, a wiry, watchful fox of a man, with evil intentions stamped clearly all over him.

"I knew your car too," Mark said proudly. "Dad says I'm clever."

"Kids are observant," his father said, with nasty relish.

"We waited for you to come out of a big house," Mark said. "And then we followed you all the way here." He beamed, inviting me to enjoy the game. "This is our car, next to yours." He patted the maroon Daimler alongside.

The telephone call, I thought fleetingly. Not Chico. Peter Rammileese, checking around.

"Dad says," Mark chatted on happily, "that he'll take me to see those roundabouts while our friends take you for a ride in our car."

His father looked down at him sharply, not having expected so much repeated truth, but Mark, oblivious, was looking at a point behind my back.

I glanced around. Between the Scimitar and the Daimler stood two more people. Large unsmiling men from a muscular brotherhood. Brass knuckles and toecaps.

"Get into the car," Rammileese said, nodding to his, not to mine. "Rear door."

Oh, sure, I thought. Did he think I was mad? I stooped slightly as if to obey and then instead of opening the door scooped Mark up bodily, with my right arm, and ran.

Rammileese turned with a shout. Mark's face, next to mine, was astonished but laughing. I ran about twenty paces with him, and set him down in the path of his furiously advancing father, and then kept on going, away from the cars and toward the crowds in the center of the showground.

Bloody hell, I thought. Chico was right. These days we had only to twitch an eyelid for them to wheel out the heavies. It was getting too much.

It had been the sort of ambush that might have worked if Mark hadn't been there: one kidney punch and into the car before I'd got my breath. But they'd needed Mark, I supposed, to identify me, because although they knew me by name, they hadn't by sight. They weren't going to catch me on the open showground, that was for sure, and when I went back to my car it would be with a load of protectors. Maybe, I thought hopefully, they would see it was useless, and just go away.

I reached the outskirts of the show-jumping arena, and looked back from over the head of a small girl licking an ice cream cone. No one had called off the heavies. They were still doggedly in pursuit. I decided not to see what would happen if I simply stood my ground and requested the assorted families round about to save me from being frog-marched to oblivion and waking with my head kicked in in the streets of Tunbridge Wells. The assorted families, with dogs and grannies and prams and picnics, were more likely to dither with their mouths open and wonder, once it was over, what it had all been about.

I went on, deeper in the show, circling the ring, bumping into children as I looked over my shoulder, and seeing the two men always behind me.

The arena itself was on my left, with show jumping in progress inside, and ringside cars encircling it outside. Behind the cars there was the broad grass walkway along which I was going, and on my right, the outer ring of the stalls one always gets at horse shows. Tented shops selling saddlery, riding clothes, pictures, toys, hot dogs, fruit, more saddles, hardware, tweeds, sheepskin slippers . . . an endless circle of small traders.

Among the tents, the vans: ice cream vans, riding associations', trailers, a display of crafts, a fortune-teller, a charity jumble stall, a mobile cinema showing films of sheep dogs, a drop-sided caravan spilling out kitchen equipment in orange and yellow and green. Crowds along the fronts of all of them and no depth of shelter inside.

"Do you know where the balloons are?" I asked someone, and he pointed, and it was to a stall selling small gas balloons of brilliant colors, children buying them and tying them to their wrists.

Not those, I thought. Surely not those. I didn't stop to explain, but asked again, farther on.

"The balloon race? In the next field, I think, but it isn't time yet."

"Thanks," I said. The posters had announced a three o'clock start, but I'd have to talk to John Viking well before that, while he was willing to listen.

What was a balloon race? I wondered. Surely all balloons went at the same speed, the speed of the wind.

My trackers wouldn't give up. They weren't running, nor was I. They just followed me steadily, as if locked onto a target by a radio beam; minds taking literally an order to stick to my heels. I'd have to get lost, I thought, and stay lost until after I'd found John Viking, and maybe then I'd go in search of helpful defenses like show secretaries and first aid ladies, and the single policeman out on the road directing traffic.

I was on the far side of the arena by that time, crossing the collecting ring area, with children on ponies buzzing around like bees, looking strained as they went in to jump, and tearful or triumphant as they came out.

Past them, past the commentators' box—"Jane Smith had a clear round; the next to jump is Robin Daly on Traddles"—past the little private grandstand for the organizers and bigwigs—rows of empty folding seats—past an open-sided refreshment tent, and so back to the stalls.

I did a bit of dodging in and out of those, and round the backs, ducking under guy ropes and round dumps of cardboard boxes. From the inside depths of a stall hung thickly outside with riding jackets I watched the two of them go past, hurrying, looking about them, distinctly anxious.

They weren't like the two Trevor Deansgate had sent, I thought. His had been clumsier, smaller, and less professional. These two looked as if this sort of work was their daily bread; and for all the comparative safety of the showground, where as a last resort I could get into the arena itself and scream for help, there was something daunting about them. Rent-a-thugs usually came at so much per hour. These two looked salaried, if not actually on the board.

I left the riding jackets and dodged into the film about sheep dogs, which I daresay would have been riveting but for the shepherding going on outside, with me as the sheep.

I looked at my watch. After two o'clock. Too much time was passing. I had to try another sortie outside and find my way to the balloons.

I couldn't see them. I slithered among the crowd, asking for directions.

"Up at the end, mate," a decisive man told me, pointing. "Past the hot dogs, turn right, there's a gate in the fence. You can't miss it."

I nodded my thanks and turned to go that way, and saw one of my trackers coming toward me, searching the stalls with his eyes and looking worried.

In a second he would see me . . . I looked around in a hurry and found I was outside the caravan of the fortune-teller. There was a curtain of plastic streamers, black and white, over the open doorway, and behind that a shadowy figure. I took four quick strides, brushed through the plastic strips, and stepped up into the van.

It was quieter inside, and darker, with daylight filtering dimly through lace-hung windows. A Victorian sort of décor: mock oil lamps and chenille tablecloths. Outside, the tracker went past, giving the fortune-teller no more than a flickering glance. His attention lay ahead. He hadn't seen me come in.

The fortune-teller, however, had, and to her I represented business.

"Do you want your whole life, dear, the past and everything, or just the future?"

"Er . . ." I said. "I don't really know. How long does it take?"

"A quarter of an hour, dear, for the whole thing."

"Let's just have the future."

I looked out the window. A part of my future was searching among the ringside cars, asking questions and getting a lot of shaken heads.

"Sit on the sofa beside me—here, dear—and give me your left hand."

"It'll have to be my right," I said absently.

"No, dear." Her voice was quite sharp. "Always the left."

Amused, I sat down and gave her the left. She felt it, and looked at it, and raised her eyes to mine. She was short and plump, dark-haired, middle-aged, and in no way remarkable.

"Well, dear," she said after a pause, "it will have to be the right, though I'm not used to it, and we may not get such good results."

"I'll risk it," I said; so we changed places on the sofa, and she held my right hand firmly in her two warm ones, and I watched the tracker move along the row of cars.

"You have suffered," she said.

As she knew about my left hand, I didn't think much of that for a guess, and she seemed to sense it. She coughed apologetically.

"Do you mind if I use a crystal?" she said.

"Go ahead."

I had vague visions of her peering into a large ball on a table, but she took a small one, the size of a tennis ball, and put it on the palm of my hand.

"You are a kind person," she said. "Gentle. People like you. People smile at you wherever you go."

Outside, twenty yards away, the two heavies had met to consult. Not a smile, there, of any sort.

"You are respected by everyone."

Regulation stuff, designed to please the customers.

Chico should hear it, I thought. Gentle, kind, respected . . . he'd laugh his head off.

She said doubtfully. "I see a great many people, cheering and clapping. Shouting loudly, cheering you . . . Does that mean anything to you, dear?"

I slowly turned my head. Her dark eyes watched me calmly.

"That's the past," I said.

It's recent," she said. "It's still there."

I didn't believe it. I didn't believe in fortune-tellers. I wondered if she had seen me before, on a racecourse or talking on television. She must have.

She bent her head again over the crystal, which she held on my hand, moving the glass gently over my skin.

"You have good health. You have vigor. You have great physical stamina . . . There is much to endure."

Her voice broke off, and she raised her head a little, frowning. I had a strong impression that what she had said had surprised her.

After a pause, she said, "I can't tell you any more."

"Why not?"

"I'm not used to the right hand."

"Tell me what you see," I said.

She shook her head slightly and raised the calm dark eyes.

"You will live a long time."

I glanced out through the plastic curtain. The trackers had moved off out of sight.

"How much do I owe you?" I asked. She told me, and I paid her, and went quietly over to the doorway.

"Take care, dear," she said. "Be careful."

I looked back. Her face was still calm but her voice had been urgent. I didn't want to believe in the conviction that looked out of her eyes. She might have felt the disturbance of my present problem with the trackers, but no more than that. I pushed the curtain gently aside and stepped from the dim world of hovering horrors into the bright May sunlight, where they might in truth lie in wait.

CHAPTER 11

THERE WAS NO longer any need to ask where the balloons were. No one could miss them. They were beginning to rise like gaudy monstrous mushrooms, humped on the ground, spread all over an enormous area of grassland beyond the actual showground. I had thought vaguely that there would be two or three balloons, or at most six, but there must have been twenty.

Among a whole stream of people going the same way, I went down to the gate and through into the far field, and realized that I had absolutely underestimated the task of finding John Viking.

There was a rope, for a start, and marshals telling the crowd to stand behind it. I ducked those obstacles at least, but found myself in a forest of half-inflated balloons, which billowed immensely all around and cut off any length of sight.

The first clump of people I came to were busy with a pink-and-purple monster into whose mouth they were blowing air by means of a large engine-driven fan. The balloon was attached by four fine nylon ropes to a basket, which lay on its side, with a young man in a red crash helmet peering anxiously into its depths.

"Excuse me," I said to a girl on the edge of the group. "Do you know where I can find John Viking?"

"Sorry."

The red crash helmet raised itself to reveal a pair of very blue eyes. "He's here somewhere," she said politely. "Flies a Stormcloud balloon. Now would you mind getting the hell out. We're busy."

I walked along the edge of things, trying to keep out of their way. Balloon races, it seemed, were a serious business and no occasion for light laughter and

social chat. The intent faces leaned over ropes and equipment, testing, checking, worriedly frowning. No balloons looked much like stormclouds. I risked
another question.

"John Viking? That bloody idiot. Yes, he's here. Flies a Stormcloud." He
turned away, busy and anxious.

"What color is it?" I said.

"Yellow and green. Look . . . go away, will you?"

There were balloons advertising whisky and marmalade and towns, and
even insurance companies. Balloons in brilliant primary colors and pink-and-
white pastels, balloons in the sunshine rising from the green grass in glorious
jumbled rainbows. On an ordinary day, a scene of delight, but to me, trying
to get round them to ask fruitlessly at the next clump gathered anxiously by
its basket, a frustrating silky maze.

I circled a soft billowing black-and-white monster and went deeper into
the center. As if at a signal, there arose in a chorus from all around a series of
deep-throated roars, caused by flames suddenly spurting from the large burners which were supported on frames above the baskets. The flames roared into
the open mouths of the half-inflated balloons, heating and expanding the air
already there and driving in more. The gleaming envelopes swelled and surged
with quickening life, growing from mushrooms to toadstools, the tops rising
slowly and magnificently toward the hazy blue sky.

"John Viking? Somewhere over there." A girl swung her arm vaguely.
"But he'll be as busy as we are."

As the balloons filled, they began to heave off the ground and sway in
great floating masses, bumping into each other, still billowing, still not full
enough to live with the birds. Under each balloon the flames roared, scarlet
and lusty, with the little clusters of helpers clinging to the baskets to prevent
them from escaping too soon.

With the balloons off the ground, I saw a yellow-and-green one quite easily: yellow and green in segments, like a grapefruit with a wide green band at
the bottom. There was one man already in the basket, with about three people
holding it down, and he, unlike everyone else in sight, wore not a crash helmet but a blue denim cap.

I ran in his direction, and even as I ran there was the sound of a starter's pistol. All around me the baskets were released, and began dragging and bumping
over the ground; and a great cheer went up from the watching crowd.

I reached the bunch of people I was aiming for and put my hand on the
basket.

"John Viking?"

No one listened. They were deep in a quarrel. A girl in a crash helmet, ski jacket, jeans, and boots stood on the ground, with the two helpers beside her looking glum and embarrassed.

"I'm not coming. You're a bloody madman."

"Get in, get in, dammit. The race has started."

He was very tall, very thin, very agitated.

"I'm not coming."

"You must." He made a grab at her and held her wrist in a sinewy grip. It looked almost as if he were going to haul her wholesale into the basket, and she certainly believed it. She tugged and panted and screamed at him. "Let go, John. Let go. I'm not coming."

"Are you John Viking?" I said loudly.

He swung his head and kept hold of the girl.

"Yes, I am, what do you want? I'm starting this race as soon as my passenger gets in."

"I'm not *going*," she screamed.

I looked around. The other baskets were mostly airborne, sweeping gently across the area a foot or two above the surface, and rising in a smooth, glorious crowd. Every basket, I saw, carried two people.

"If you want a passenger," I said, "I'll come."

He let go of the girl and looked me up and down.

"How much do you weigh?" And then, impatiently as he saw the other balloons getting a head start, "Oh, all right, get in. Get in."

I gripped hold of a stay, and jumped, and wriggled, and ended standing inside a rather small hamper under a very large cloud of balloon.

"Leave go," commanded the captain of the ship, and the helpers somewhat helplessly obeyed.

The basket momentarily stayed exactly where it was. Then John Viking reached above his head and flipped a lever which operated the burners, and there at close quarters, right above our heads, was the flame and the ear-filling roar.

The girl's face was still on a level with mine. "He's mad," she yelled. "And you're crazy."

The basket moved away, bumped, and rose quite suddenly to a height of six feet. The girl ran after it and delivered a parting encouragement. "And you haven't got a crash helmet."

What I did have, though, was a marvelous escape route from two purposeful thugs, and a crash helmet at that moment seemed superfluous, particularly as my companion hadn't one, either.

John Viking was staring about him in the remnants of fury, muttering under his breath, and operating the burner almost nonstop. His was the last balloon away. I looked down to where the applauding holiday crowd were watching the mass departure, and a small boy darted suddenly from under the restraining rope and ran into the now empty starting area, shouting and pointing. Pointing at John Viking's balloon, pointing excitedly at me.

My pal Mark, with his bright little eyes and his truthful tongue. My pal Mark, whom I'd have liked to strangle.

John Viking started cursing. I switched my attention from ground to air and saw that the reason for the resounding and imaginative obscenities floating to heaven was a belt of trees lying ahead which might prevent our going in the same direction. One balloon already lay in a tangle on the takeoff side, and another, scarlet and purple, seemed set on a collision course.

John Viking yelled at me over the continuing roar of the burner: "Hold on bloody tight with both hands. If the basket hits the tops of the trees, we don't want to be spilled right out."

The trees looked sixty feet high and a formidable obstacle, but most of the balloons had cleared them easily and were drifting away skyward, great bright pear-shaped fantasies hanging on the wind.

John Viking's basket closed with a rush toward the treetops, with the burner roaring over our heads like a demented dragon. The lift it should have provided seemed totally lacking.

"Turbulence," John Viking shrieked. "Bloody wind turbulence. Hold on. It's a long way down."

Frightfully jolly, I thought, being tipped out of a hamper sixty feet from the ground without a crash helmet. I grinned at him, and he caught the expression and looked startled.

The basket hit the treetop and tipped on its side, tumbling me from the vertical to the horizontal with no trouble at all. I grabbed right-handed at whatever I could to stop myself from falling right out, and I felt as much as saw that the majestically swelling envelope above us was carrying on with its journey regardless. It tugged the basket after it, crashing and bumping through the tops of the trees, flinging me about like a rag doll with at times most of my body hanging out in space. My host, made of sterner stuff, had one arm clamped like a vise round one of the metal struts that supported the burner, and the other twined into a black rubber strap. His legs were braced against the side of the basket, which was now the floor, and he changed his footholds as necessary, at one point planting one foot firmly on my stomach.

With a last sickening jolt and wrench, the basket tore itself free, and we swung to and fro under the wobbling balloon like a pendulum. I was by this maneuver wedged into a disorganized heap in the bottom of the basket, but John Viking still stood rather splendidly on his feet.

There really wasn't much room, I thought disentangling myself and straightening upward. The basket, still swaying and shaking, was only four feet square, and reached no higher than one's waist. Along two opposite sides stood eight gas cylinders, four each side, fastened to the wickerwork with rubber straps. The oblong space left was big enough for two men to stand in, but not overgenerous even for that: about two feet by two feet per person.

John Viking gave the burner a rest at last, and into the sudden silence said forcefully, "Why the hell didn't you hold on like I told you to? Don't you know you damned nearly fell out and got me into trouble?"

"Sorry," I said, amused. "Is it usual to go on burning when you're stuck on a tree?"

It got us clear, didn't it?" he demanded.

"It sure did."

"Don't complain, then. I didn't ask you to come."

He was of about my own age; perhaps a year or two younger. His face under his blue denim yachting cap was craggy, with a bone structure that might one day give him distinction, and his blue eyes shone with the brilliance of the true fanatic. John Viking the madman, I thought, and warmed to him.

"Check round the outsides, will you?" he said. "See if anything's come adrift."

It seemed he meant the outside of the basket, as he was himself looking outward, over the edge. I discovered that on my side, too, there were bundles on the outside of the basket, either strapped to it tight, or swinging on ropes.

One short rope, attached to the basket, had nothing on the end of it. I pulled it up and showed it to him.

"Damnation," he said explosively. "Lost in the trees, I suppose. Plastic water container. Hope you're not thirsty." He stretched up and gave the burner another long burst, and I listened in my mind to the echo of his Etonian drawl and totally understood why he was as he was.

"Do you have to finish first to win a balloon race?" I said.

He looked surprised. "Not this one. This is a two-and-a-half-hour race. The one who gets farthest in that time is the winner." He frowned. "Haven't you ever been in a balloon before?"

"No."

"My God," he said. "What chance have I got?"

"None at all, if I hadn't come," I said mildly.

"That's true." He looked down from somewhere like six feet four. "What's your name?"

"Sid," I said.

He looked as if Sid wasn't exactly the sort of name his friends had, but faced the fact manfully.

"Why wouldn't your girl come with you?" I said.

"Who? Oh, you mean Popsy. She's not my girl. I don't really know her. She was going to come because my usual passenger broke his leg, silly bugger, when we made a bit of a rough landing last week. Popsy wanted to bring some ruddy big handbag. Wouldn't come without it, wouldn't be parted from it. I ask you! Where is the room for a handbag? And it was heavy, as well. Every pound counts. Carry a pound less, you can go a mile farther."

"Where do you expect to come down?" I said.

"It depends on the wind." He looked up at the sky. "We're going roughly northeast at the moment, but I'm going higher. There's a front forecast from the west, and I guess there'll be some pretty useful activity high up. We might make it to Brighton."

"*Brighton.*" I had thought in terms of perhaps twenty miles, not a hundred. And he must be wrong, I thought; one couldn't go a hundred miles in a balloon in two and a half hours.

"If the wind's more from the northwest, we might reach the isle of Wight. Or France. Depends how much gas is left; we don't want to come down in the sea, not in this. Can you swim?"

I nodded. I supposed I still could: hadn't tried it one-handed. "I'd rather not," I said.

He laughed. "Don't worry. The balloon's too darned expensive for me to want to sink it."

Once free of the trees we had risen very fast, and now floated across country at a height from which cars on the roads looked like toys, though still recognizable as to size and color.

Noises came up clearly. One could hear the cars' engines, and dogs barking, and an occasional human shout. People looked up and waved to us as we passed. A world removed, I thought. I was in a child's world, idyllically drifting with the wind, sloughing off the dreary earthbound millstones, free and rising and filled with intense delight.

John Viking flipped the lever and the flame roared, shooting up into the green-and-yellow cavern, a scarlet-and-gold tongue of dragon fire. The burn endured for twenty seconds and we rose perceptibly in the sudden ensuing silence.

"What gas do you use?" I said.

"Propane."

He was looking over the side of the basket and around at the countryside, as if judging his position. "Look, get the map out, will you? It's in a pouch thing on your side. And for God's sake don't let it blow away."

I looked over the side and found what he meant. A satchel-like object strapped on through the wickerwork, its outward-facing flap fastened shut with a buckle. I undid the buckle, looked inside, took a fair grip of the large folded map, and delivered it safely to the captain.

He was looking fixedly at my left hand, which I'd used as a sort of counterweight on the edge of the basket while I leaned over. I let it fall by my side, and his gaze swept upward to my face.

"You're missing a hand," he said incredulously.

"That's right."

He waved his two arms in a fierce gesture of frustration. "How the *hell* am I going to win this race?"

I laughed.

He glanced at me. "It's not damned funny."

"Oh, yes it is. And I like winning races. . . . You won't lose it because of me."

He frowned disgustedly. "I suppose you can't be much more useless than Popsy," he said. "But at least they say she can read a map." He unfolded the sheet I'd given him, which proved to be a map designed for the navigation of aircraft, its surface covered with a plastic film, for writing on. "Look," he said. "We started from here." He pointed. "We're traveling roughly northeast. You take the map, and find out where we are." He paused. "Do you know the first bloody thing about using your watch as a compass, or about dead reckoning?"

I had a book about dead reckoning, which I hadn't read, in a pocket of the light cotton anarak I was wearing; and also, I thanked God, in another zippered compartment, a spare fully charged battery. "Give me the map," I said. "And let's see."

He handed it over with no confidence and started another burn. I worked out roughly where we should be, and looked over the side, and discovered straight away that the ground didn't look like the map. Where villages and roads were marked clearly on the map, they faded into the brown and green carpet of earth like patches of camouflage, the sunlight mottling them with shadows and dissolving them into ragged edges. The spread-out vistas all around all looked the same, defying me to recognize anything special, proving conclusively I was less use than Popsy.

Dammit, I thought. Start again.

We had set off at three o'clock, give a minute or two. We had been airborne for twelve minutes. On the ground the wind had been gentle and from the south, but we were now traveling slightly faster, and northeast. Say, fifteen knots. Twelve minutes at fifteen knots . . . about three nautical miles. I had been looking too far ahead. There should be, I thought, a river to cross; and in spite of gazing earnestly down I nearly missed it, because it was a firm blue line on the map and in reality a silvery reflecting thread that wound unobtrusively between a meadow and a wood. To the right of it, half hidden by a hill, lay a village, and beyond it, a railway line.

"We're there," I said, pointing to the map.

He squinted at the print and searched the ground beneath us.

"Fair enough," he said. "So we are. Right. You keep the map. We might as well know where we are, all the way."

He flipped the lever and gave it a long burn. The balloons ahead of us were also lower. We were definitely looking down on their tops. During the next patch of silence he consulted two instruments which were strapped onto the outside of the basket at his end, and grunted.

"What are those?" I said, nodding at the dials.

"Altimeter and rate-of-climb meter," he said. "We're at five thousand feet now, and rising at eight hundred feet a minute."

"Rising?"

"Yeah." He gave a sudden wolfish grin in which I read unmistakably the fierce unholy glee of the mischievous child. "That's why Popsy wouldn't come. Someone told her I would go high. She didn't want to."

"How high?" I said.

"I don't mess about," he said. "When I race, I race to win. They don't like it. They think you should never take risks. They're all safety conscious these days and getting softer. Ha!" His scorn was absolute. "In the old days, at the beginning of the century, when they had the Gordon Bennett races, they would fly for two days and do a thousand miles or more. But nowadays . . . safety bloody first." He glanced at me. "And if I didn't have to have a passenger, I wouldn't. Passengers always argue and complain."

He pulled a packet of cigarettes out of his pocket and lit one with a flick of a lighter. We were surrounded by cylinders of liquid gas. I thought about all the embargoes against naked flames near any sort of stored fuel, and kept my mouth shut.

The flock of balloons below us seemed to be veering away to the left; but then I realized that it was we who were going to the right. John Viking watched the changing direction with great satisfaction and started another long burn. We rose perceptibly faster, and the sun, instead of shining full on our backs, appeared on our starboard side.

In spite of the sunshine it was getting pretty cold. A look over the side showed the earth very far beneath, and one could now see a very long way, in all directions. I checked with the map, and kept an eye on where we were.

"What are you wearing?" he said.

"What you see, more or less."

"Huh."

During the burns, the flame over one's head was almost too hot, and there was always a certain amount of hot air escaping from the bottom of the balloon. There was no wind factor, as of course the balloon was traveling with the wind, at the wind's speed. It was sheer altitude that was making us cold.

"How high are we now?" I said.

He glanced at his instruments. "Eleven thousand feet."

"And still rising?"

He nodded. The other balloons, far below and to the left, were a cluster of distant bright blobs against the green earth.

"All that lot," he said, "will stay down at five thousand feet, because of staying under the airways." He gave me a sideways look. "You'll see on the map. The airways that the airlines use are marked, and so are the heights at which one is not allowed to fly through them."

"And one is not allowed to fly through an airway at eleven thousand feet in a balloon?"

"Sid," he said, grinning, "you're not bad."

He flicked the lever, and the burner roared, cutting off chat. I checked the ground against the map and nearly lost our position entirely, because we seemed suddenly to have traveled much faster, and quite definitely to the southeast. The other balloons, when I next looked, were out of sight.

In the next silence John Viking told me that the helpers of the other balloons would follow them on the ground, in cars, ready to retrieve them when they came down.

"What about you?" I asked. "Do we have someone following?"

Did we indeed have Peter Rammileese following, complete with thugs, ready to pounce again at the farther end? We were even, I thought fleetingly, doing him a favor with the general direction, taking him southeastward, home to Kent.

John Viking gave his wolfish smile, and said, "No car on earth could keep up with us today."

"Do you mean it?" I exclaimed.

He looked at the altimeter. "Fifteen thousand feet," he said. "We'll stay at that. I got a forecast from the air boys for this trip. Fifty-knot wind from two nine zero at fifteen thousand feet; that's what they said. You hang on, Sid, pal, and we'll get to Brighton."

I thought about the two of us standing in a waist-high four-foot-square wicker basket, supported by Dacron and hot air, fifteen thousand feet above the solid ground, traveling without any feeling of speed at fifty-seven miles an hour. Quite mad, I thought.

From the ground, we would be a black speck. On the ground, no car could keep up. I grinned back at John Viking with a satisfaction as great as his own, and he laughed aloud.

"Would you believe it?" he said. "At last I've got someone up here who's not puking with fright."

He lit another cigarette, and then he changed the supply line to the burner from one cylinder to the next. This involved switching off the empty tank, unscrewing the connecting nut, screwing it into the next cylinder, and switching on the new supply. There were two lines to the double burner, one for each set of four cylinders. He held the cigarette in his mouth throughout, and squinted through the smoke.

I had seen from the map that we were flying straight toward the airway that led in and out of Gatwick, where large airplanes thundered up and down not expecting to meet squashy balloons illegally in their path.

His appetite for taking risks was way out of my class. He made sitting on a horse over fences on the ground seem rather tame. Except, I thought with a jerk, that I no longer did it; I fooled around instead with men who threatened to shoot hands off . . . and I was safer up here with John Viking the madman, propane and cigarettes, midair collisions, and all.

"Right," he said. "We just stay as we are for an hour and a half and let the wind take us. If you feel odd, it's lack of oxygen." He took a pair of wool gloves from his pocket and put them on. "Are you cold?"

"Yes, a bit."

He grinned. "I've got long johns under my jeans, and two sweaters under my anorak. You'll just have to freeze."

"Thanks very much." I stood on the map and put my real hand deep into the pocket of my cotton anarak and he said at least the false hand couldn't get frostbite.

He operated the burner and looked at his watch and the ground and the altimeter, and seemed pleased with the way things were. Then he looked at me in slight puzzlement and I knew he was wondering, now that there was time, how I had happened to be where I was.

"I came to Highalane Park to see you," I said. "I mean you, John Viking, particularly."

He looked startled. "Do you read minds?"

"All the time." I pulled my hand out of one pocket and dipped into another, and brought out the paperback on navigation. "I came to ask you about this. It's got your name on the flyleaf."

He frowned at it, and opened the front cover. "Good Lord. I wondered where this had got to. How did you have it?"

"Did you lend it to anyone?"

"I don't think so."

"Um . . ." I said. "If I describe someone to you, will you say if you know him?"

"Fire away."

"A man of about twenty-eight," I said. "Dark hair, good looks, full of fun and jokes, easygoing, likes girls, great company, has a habit of carrying a knife strapped to his leg under his sock, and is very likely a crook."

"Oh, yes," he said, nodding. "He's my cousin."

CHAPTER 12

HIS COUSIN, NORRIS Abbott. What had he done this time? he demanded, and I asked, What had he done before?

"A trail of bouncing checks that his mother paid for."

Where did he live? I asked. John Viking didn't know. He saw him only when Norris turned up occasionally on his doorstep, usually broke and looking for free meals.

"A laugh a minute for a day or two. Then he's gone."

"Where does his mother live?"

"She's dead. He's alone now. No parents or brothers or sisters. No relatives except me." He peered at me, frowning. "Why do you ask all this?"

"A girl I know wants to find him." I shrugged. "It's nothing much."

He lost interest at once and flicked the lever for another burn. "We use twice the fuel up here as near the ground," he said afterward. "That's why I brought so much. That's how some Nosy Parker told Popsy I was planning to go high, and through the airways."

By my reckoning the airway was not that far off.

"Won't you get into trouble?" I said.

The wolf grin came and went. "They've got to see us first. We won't show up on radar. We're too small for the equipment they use. With a bit of luck, we'll sneak across and no one will be any the wiser."

I picked up the map and studied it. At fifteen thousand feet we would be illegal from when we entered controlled air space until we landed, all but the last two hundred feet. The airway over Brighton began at a thousand feet above sea level and the hills to the north were eight hundred feet high. Did John Viking know all that? Yes, he did.

When we had been flying for an hour and fifty minutes, he made a fuel line change from cylinder to cylinder that resulted in a thin jet of liquid gas spurting out from the connection like water out of a badly joined hose. The jet shot across the corner of the basket and hit a patch of wickerwork about six inches below the top rail.

John Viking was smoking at the time.

Liquid propane began trickling down the side of the basket in a stream. John Viking cursed and fiddled with the faulty connection, bending over it; and his glowing cigarette ignited the gas.

There was no ultimate and final explosion. The jet burned as jets do, and directed its flame in an organized manner at the patch of basket it was hitting. John Viking threw his cigarette over the side and snatched off his denim cap, and beat at the burning basket with great flailing motions of his arm, while I managed to stifle the jet at source by turning off the main switch on the cylinder.

When the flames and smoke and cursing died down, we had a hole six inches in diameter right through the basket, but no other damage.

"Baskets don't burn easily," he said calmly, as if nothing had happened. "Never known one to burn much more than this." He inspected his cap, which was scorched into black-edged lace, and gave me a manical four seconds from the bright blue eyes. "You can't put out a fire with a crash helmet," he said.

I laughed quite a lot

It was the altitude, I thought, that was making me giggle.

"Want some chocolate?" he said.

There were no signposts in the sky to tell us when we crossed the boundary of the airway. We saw an airplane or two some way off, but nothing near us. No one came buzzing around to direct us downward. We simply sailed straight on, blowing across the sky as fast as a train.

At ten past five he said it was time to go down, because if we didn't touch ground by five-thirty exactly he would be disqualified, and he didn't want that; he wanted to win. Winning was what it was all about.

"How would anyone know exactly when we touched down?" I said.

He gave me a pitying look and gently directed his toe at a small box strapped to the floor beside one of the corner cylinders.

"In here is a barograph, all stuck about with pompous red seals. The judges seal it before the start. It shows variation in air pressure. Highly sensitive. All our journey shows up like a row of peaks. When you're on the ground, the trace is flat and steady. It tells the judges just when you took off and when you landed. Right?"

"Right."

"O.K. Down we go, then."

He reached up and untied a red cord which was knotted to the burner frame, and pulled it. "It opens a panel at the top of the balloon," he said. "Lets the hot air out."

His idea of descent was all of a piece. The altimeter unwound like a broken clock and the rate-of-climb meter was pointing to a thousand feet a minute, downward. He seemed to be quite unaffected, but it made me queasy and hurt my eardrums. Swallowing made things a bit better, but not much. I concentrated, as an antidote, on checking with the map to see where we were going.

The Channel lay like a broad gray carpet to our right, and it was incredible, but whichever way I looked at it, it seemed that we were on a collision course with Beachy Head.

"Yeah," John Viking casually confirmed. "Guess we'll try not to get blown off those cliffs. Might be better to land on the beach farther on . . ." He checked his watch. "Ten minutes to go. We're still at six thousand feet. . . . That's all right. . . . Might be the edge of the sea."

"Not the sea," I said positively.

"Why not? We might have to."

"Well," I said, "this . . ." I lifted my left arm. "Inside this hand-shaped plastic there's actually a lot of fine engineering. Strong pincers inside the thumb and first two fingers. A lot of fine precision gears, and transistors and

printed electrical circuits. Dunking it in the sea would be like dunking a radio. A total ruin. And it would cost me two thousand quid to get a new one."

He was astonished. "You're joking."

"No."

"Better keep you dry, then. And anyway, now we're down here, I don't
think we'll get as far south as Beachy Head. Probably farther east." He paused
and looked at my left hand doubtfully. "It'll be a rough landing. The fuel's
cold from being so high . . . the burner doesn't function well on cold fuel. It
takes time to heat enough air to give us a softer touchdown."

A softer touchdown took time . . . too much time.

"Win the race," I said.

His face lit into sheer happiness. "Right," he said decisively. "What's that
town just ahead?"

I studied the map. "Eastbourne."

He looked at his watch. "Five minutes." He looked at the altimeter and
at Eastbourne, upon which we were rapidly descending. "Two thousand feet.
Bit dicey, hitting the roofs. There isn't much wind down here, is there? . . .
But if I burn, we might not get down in time. No; no burn."

A thousand feet a minute, I reckoned, was eleven or twelve miles an hour.
I had been used for years to hitting the ground at more than twice that
speed . . . though not in a basket, and not when the ground might turn out to
be fully inhabited by brick walls.

We were traveling sideways over the town, with houses below us. Descent
was very fast. "Three minutes," he said.

The sea lay ahead again, fringing the far side of the town, and for a moment it looked as if it was there we would have to come down after all. John
Viking, however, knew better.

"Hang on," he said. "This is it."

He hauled strongly on the red cord he held, which led upward into the
balloon. Somewhere above, the vent for the hot air widened dramatically, the
lifting power of the balloon fell away, and the solid edge of Eastbourne came
up with a rush.

We scraped the eaves of gray slate roofs, made a sharp diagonal descent
over a road and a patch of grass, and smashed down on a broad concrete walk
twenty yards from the waves.

"Don't get out. Don't get out," he yelled. The basket tipped on its side
and began to slither along the concrete, dragged by the still half-inflated
silken mass. "Without our weight, it could still fly away."

As I was again wedged among the cylinders, it was superfluous advice.

The basket rocked and tumbled a few more times and I with it, and John Viking cursed and hauled at his red cord and finally let out enough air for us to be still.

He looked at his watch, and his blue eyes blazed with triumph.

"We've made it. Five twenty-nine. That was a bloody good race. The best ever. What are you doing next Saturday?"

I WENT BACK to Aynsford by train, which took forever, with Charles picking me up from Oxford station not far short of midnight.

"You went on the balloon race," he repeated disbelievingly. "Did you enjoy it?"

"Very much."

"And your car's still at Highalane Park?"

"It can stay there until morning," I yawned. "Nicholas Ashe now has a name, by the way. He's someone called Norris Abbott. Same initials, silly man."

"Will you tell the police?"

"See if we can find him first."

He glanced at me sideways. "Jenny came back this evening, after you'd telephoned."

"Oh, no."

"I didn't know she was going to."

I supposed I believed him. I hoped she would have gone to bed before I arrived, but she hadn't. She was sitting on the gold brocade sofa in the drawing room, looking belligerent.

"I don't like you coming here so much," she said.

A knife to the heart of things from my pretty wife.

Charles said smoothly, "Sid is welcome here always."

"Discarded husbands should have more pride than to fawn on their fathers-in-law, who put up with it because they're sorry for them."

"You're jealous," I said, surprised.

She stood up fast, as angry as I'd ever seen her.

"How dare you!" she said. "He always takes your side. He thinks you're bloody marvelous. He doesn't know you like I do, all your stubborn little ways and your meanness and thinking you're always *right*."

"I'm going to bed." I said.

"And you're a coward as well," she said furiously. "Running away from a few straight truths."

"Good night, Charles," I said. "Good night, Jenny. Sleep well, my love, and pleasant dreams."

"You . . ." she said. "You . . . I hate you, Sid."

I went out of the drawing room without fuss and upstairs to the bedroom I thought of as mine, the one I always slept in nowadays at Aynsford.

You don't have to hate me, Jenny, I thought miserably: I hate myself.

CHARLES DROVE ME to Wiltshire in the morning to collect my car, which still stood where I'd left it, though surrounded now by acres of empty grass. There was no Pete Rammileese in sight, and no thugs waiting in ambush. All clear for an uneventful return to London.

"Sid," Charles said, as I unlocked the car door. "Don't pay any attention to Jenny."

"No."

"Come to Aynsford whenever you want."

I nodded.

"I mean it, Sid."

"Yeah."

"Damn Jenny," he said explosively.

"Oh, no. She's unhappy. She . . ." I paused. "I guess she needs comforting. A shoulder to cry on, and all that."

He said austerely, "I don't care for tears."

"No." I sighed and got into the car, waved goodbye, and drove over the bumpy grass to the gate. The help that Jenny needed, she wouldn't take from me; and her father didn't know how to give it. Just another of life's bloody muddles, another irony in the general mess.

I drove into the city and around in a few small circles, and ended up in the publishing offices of *Antiques for All*, which proved to be only one of a number of specialist magazines put out by a newspaper company. To the *Antiques* editor, a fair-haired, earnest young man in heavy-framed specs, I explained both the position and the need.

"Our mailing list?" he said doubtfully. "Mailing lists are strictly private, you know."

I explained all over again, and threw in a lot of pathos. My wife behind bars if I didn't find the con man, that sort of thing.

"Oh, very well," he said. "But it will be stored in a computer. You'll have to wait for a printout."

I waited patiently, and received in the end a stack of paper setting out fifty-three thousand names and addresses, give or take a few dead ones.

"And we want it back," he said severely. "Unmarked and complete."

"How did Norris Abbott get hold of it?" I asked.

He didn't know, and neither the name nor the description of Abbott/Ashe brought any glimmer of recognition.

"How about a copy of the magazine, for good measure?"

I got that too, and disappeared before he could regret all his generosity. Back in the car, I telephoned to Chico and got him to come to the flat. Meet me outside, I said. Carry my bag upstairs and earn your salary.

He was there when I pulled up at a vacant parking meter and we went upstairs together. The flat was empty, and quiet, and safe.

"A lot of legwork, my son," I said, taking the mailing list out of the package I had transported it in, and putting it on the table. "All your own."

He eyed it unenthusiastically. "And what about you?"

"Chester races," I said. "One of the syndicate horses runs there tomorrow. Meet me back here Thursday morning, ten o'clock. O.K.?"

"Yeah." He thought. "Suppose our Nicky hasn't got himself organized yet, and sends out his begging letters next week, after we've drawn a blank?"

"Mm . . . Better take some sticky labels with this address on, and ask them to send the letter here if they get them."

"We'll be lucky."

"You never know. No one likes being conned."

"May as well get started, then." He picked up the folder containing the magazine and mailing list, and looked ready to leave.

"Chico . . . Stay until I've repacked my bag. I think I'll start northward right now. Stay until I go."

He was puzzled. "If you like, but what for?"

"Er . . ."

"Come on, Sid. Out with it."

"Peter Rammileese and a couple of guys came looking for me yesterday at Aynsford. So I'd just like you around while I'm here."

"What sort of guys?" he said suspiciously.

I nodded. "Those sort. Hard eyes and boots."

"Guys who kick people half to death in Tunbridge Wells?"

"Maybe," I said.

"You dodged them, I see."

"In a balloon." I told him about the race while I put some things in a suitcase. He laughed at the story but afterward came quite seriously back to business.

"Those guys of yours don't sound like your ordinary run-of-the-mill rent-a-thug," he said. "Here, let me fold that jacket; you'll turn up at Chester all creased." He took my packing out of my hands and did it for me, quickly and

neatly. "Got all the spare batteries? There's one in the bathroom." I fetched it.
"Look, Sid, I don't like these syndicates." He snapped the locks shut and carried the case into the hall. "Let's tell Lucas Wainwright we're not doing
them."

"And who tells Peter Rammileese?"

"We do. We ring him up and tell him."

"You do it," I said. "Right now."

We stood and looked at each other. Then he shrugged and picked up the
suitcase. "Got everything?" he said. "Raincoat?" We went down to the car
and stowed my case in the boot. "Look, Sid, you just take care, will you? I
don't like hospital visiting, you know that."

"Don't lose that mailing list," I said. "Or the editor of *Antiques* will be
cross."

I BOOKED UNMOLESTED into a motel and spent the evening watching
television, and the following afternoon arrived without trouble at Chester
races.

All the usual crowd were there, standing around, making the usual conversations. It was my first time on a racecourse since the dreary week in Paris,
and it seemed to me when I walked in that the change in me must be clearly
visible. But no one, of course, noticed the blistering sense of shame I felt at the
sight of George Caspar outside the weighing room, or treated me any differently from usual. It was I alone who knew I didn't deserve the smiles and the
welcome. I was a fraud. I shrank inside. I hadn't known I would feel so bad.

The trainer from Newmarket who had offered me a ride with his string
was there, and repeated his offer.

"Sid, do come. Come this Friday, stay the night with us, and ride work on
Saturday morning."

There wasn't much, I reflected, that anyone could give me that I'd rather
accept: and besides, Peter Rammileese and his merry men would have a job
finding me there.

"Martin . . . Yes, I'd love to."

"Great." He seemed pleased. "Come for evening stables, Friday night."

He went on into the weighing room, and I wondered if he would have
asked me if he'd known how I'd spent Guineas day.

Bobby Unwin buttonholed me with inquisitive eyes. "Where have you
been?" he said. "I didn't see you at the Guineas."

"I didn't go."

"I thought you'd be bound to, after all your interest in Tri-Nitro."

"No."

"I reckon you had the smell of something going on there, Sid. All that interest in the Caspars, and about Gleaner and Zingaloo. Come clean, now: what do you know?"

"Nothing, Bobby."

"I don't believe you." He gave me a hard unforgiving stare and steered his beaky nose toward more fruitful copy in the shape of a top trainer enduring a losing streak. I would have trouble persuading him, I thought, if I should ever ask for his help again.

Rosemary Caspar, walking with a woman friend to whom she was chatting, almost bumped into me before either of us was aware of the other's being there. The look in her eyes made Bobby Unwin seem loving.

"Go away," she said violently. "Why are you here?"

The woman friend looked very surprised. I stepped out of the way without saying a word, which surprised her still further. Rosemary impatiently twitched her onward, and I heard her voice rising: "But surely, Rosemary, that was Sid Halley. . . ."

My face felt stiff. It's too bloody much, I thought. I couldn't have made their horse win if I'd stayed. *I couldn't*. . . . But I might have. I would always think I might have, if I'd tried. If I hadn't been scared out of my mind.

"Hello, Sid," a voice said at my side. "Lovely day, isn't it?"

"Oh, lovely."

Philip Friarly smiled and watched Rosemary's retreating back. "She's been snapping at everyone since that disaster last week. Poor Rosemary. Takes things so much to heart."

"You can't blame her," I said. "She said it would happen, and no one believed her."

"Did she tell you?" he said curiously.

I nodded.

"Ah," he said, in understanding. "Galling for you."

I took a deep loosening breath and made myself concentrate on something different.

"That horse of yours today," I said. "Are you just giving it a sharpener, running it here on the flat?"

"Yes," he said briefly. "And if you ask me how it will run, I'll have to tell you that it depends on who's giving the orders, and who's taking them."

"That's cynical."

"Have you found out anything for me?"

"Not very much. It's why I came here." I paused. "Do you know the name and address of the person who formed your syndicates?"

"Not offhand," he said. "I didn't deal with him myself, do you see? The syndicates were already well advanced when I was asked to join. The horses had already been bought, and most of the shares were sold."

"They used you," I said. "Used your name. A respectable front."

He nodded unhappily. "I'm afraid so."

"Do you know Peter Rammileese?"

"Who?" He shook his head. "Never heard of him."

"He buys and sells horses," I said. "Lucas Wainwright thinks it was he who formed your syndicates, and he who is operating them, and he's bad news to the Jockey Club and barred from most racecourses."

"Oh, dear." He sounded distressed. "If Lucas is looking into them . . . What do you think I should do, Sid?"

"From your point of view," I said, "I think you should sell your shares, or dissolve the syndicates entirely, and get your name out of them, as fast as possible."

"All right, I will. And, Sid . . . next time I'm tempted, I'll get you to check on the other people in the syndicate. The Security Service are supposed to have done these, and look at them!"

"Who's riding your horse today?" I said.

"Larry Server."

He waited for an opinion, but I didn't give it. Larry Server was middle ability, middle employed, rode mostly on the flat and sometimes over hurdles, and was to my mind in the market for unlawful bargains.

"Who chooses the jockey?" I said. "Larry Server doesn't ride all that often for your horse's trainer."

"I don't know," he said doubtfully. "I leave all that to the trainer, of course."

I made a small grimace.

"Don't you approve?" he said.

"If you like," I said, "I'll give you a list of jockeys for your jumpers that you can at least trust to be trying to win. Can't guarantee their ability, but you can't have everything."

"Now who's a cynic?" He smiled, and said with patent and piercing regret, "I wish you were still riding them, Sid."

"Yeah." I said with a smile, but he saw the flicker I hadn't managed to keep out of my eyes.

With a compassion I definitely didn't want, he said, "I'm so sorry."

"It was great while it lasted," I said lightly. "That's all that matters."

He shook his head, annoyed with himself for his clumsiness.

"Look," I said, "if you were *glad* I'm not still riding them, I'd feel a whole lot worse."

"We had some grand times, didn't we? Some exceptional days."

"Yes, we did."

There could be an understanding between an owner and a jockey, I thought, that was intensely intimate. In the small area where their lives touched, where the speed and the winning were all that mattered, there could be privately shared joy, like a secret, that endured like cement. I hadn't felt it often, nor with many of the people I had ridden for, but with Philip Friarly, nearly always.

A man detached himself from another group near us, and came toward us with a smiling face.

"Philip, Sid. Nice to see you."

We made the polite noises back, but with genuine pleasure, as Sir Thomas Ullaston, the reigning Senior Steward, head of the Jockey Club, head, more or less, of the whole racing industry, was a sensible man and a fair and open-minded administrator. A little severe at times, some thought, but it wasn't a job for a soft man. In the short time since he'd been put in charge of things, there had been some good new rules and a clearing out of injustices, and he was as decisive as his predecessor had been weak.

"How's it going, Sid?" he said. "Caught any good crooks lately?"

"Not lately," I said ruefully

He smiled to Philip Friarly. "Our Sid's putting the Security Service's nose out of joint, did you know? I had Eddy Keith along in my office on Monday complaining that we give Sid too free a hand, and asking that we shouldn't let him operate on the racecourse."

"Eddy Keith?" I said.

"Don't look so shocked, Sid," Sir Thomas said teasingly. "I told him that racing owed you a great deal, starting with the saving of Seabury racecourse itself and going right on from there, and that in no way would the Jockey Club ever interfere with you, unless you did something absolutely diabolical, which on past form I can't see you doing."

"Thank you," I said faintly.

"And you may take it," he said firmly, "that that is the official Jockey Club view, as well as my own."

"Why," I said slowly, "does Eddy Keith want me stopped?"

He shrugged. "Something about access to the Jockey Club files. Apparently you saw some, and he resented it. I told him he'd have to live with it, because I was certainly not in any way going to put restraints on what I consider a positive force for good in racing."

I felt grindingly undeserving of all that, but he gave me no time to protest.

"Why don't both of you come upstairs for a drink and a sandwich? Come along, Sid, Philip . . ." He turned, gesturing us to follow, leading the way.

We went up those stairs marked "Private" which on most racecourses lead to the civilized luxuries of the stewards' box, and into a carpeted glass-fronted room looking out to the white-railed track. There were several groups of people there already, and a manservant handing around drinks on a tray.

"I expect you know most people," Sir Thomas said, hospitably making introductions. "Madelaine, my dear"—to his wife—"do you know about Lord Friarly, and Sid Halley?" We shook her hand. "And oh, yes, Sid," he said, touching my arm to bring me around face to face with another of his guests. . . .

"Have you met Trevor Deansgate?"

CHAPTER 13

WE STARED AT each other, probably equally stunned.

I thought of how he had last seen me, on my back in the straw barn, spilling my guts out with fear. He'll see it still in my face, I thought. He knows what he's made of me. I can't just stand here without moving a muscle . . . and yet I must.

My head seemed to be floating somewhere above the rest of my body, and an awful lot of awfulness got condensed into four seconds.

"Do you know each other?" Sir Thomas said, slightly puzzled.

Trevor Deansgate said, "Yes. We've met."

There was at least no sneer in either his eyes or his voice. If it hadn't been impossible, I would have thought that what he looked was *wary*.

"Drink, Sid?" said Sir Thomas; and I found the man with the tray at my elbow. I took a tumbler with whisky-colored contents and tried to stop my fingers from trembling.

Sir Thomas said conversationally, "I've just been telling Sid how much the Jockey Club appreciates his successes, and it seems to have silenced him completely."

Neither Trevor Deansgate nor I said anything. Sir Thomas raised his eyebrows a fraction and tried again. "Well, Sid, tell us a good thing for the big race."

I dragged my scattered wits back into at least a pretense of life going uneventfully on.

"Oh . . . Winetaster, I should think."

My voice sounded strained to me, but Sir Thomas seemed not to notice. Trevor Deansgate looked down to the glass in his own well-manicured hand and swiveled the ice cubes round in the golden liquid. Another of the guests spoke to Sir Thomas, and he turned away, and Trevor Deansgate's gaze came immediately back to my face, filled with naked savage threat. His voice, quick and hard, spoke straight from the primitive underbelly, the world of violence and vengeance and no pity at all.

"If you break your assurance, I'll do what I said."

He held my eyes until he was sure I had received the message, and then he too turned away, and I could see the heavy muscles of his shoulders bunching formidably inside his coat.

"Sid," Philip Friarly said, appearing once more at my side. "Lady Ullaston wants to know . . . I say, are you feeling all right?"

I nodded.

"My dear chap, you took frightfully pale."

"I . . . er . . ." I took a vague grip on things. "What did you say?"

"Lady Ullaston wants to know . . ." He went on at some length, and I listened and answered with a feeling of complete unreality. One could literally be torn apart in spirit while standing with a glass in one's hand making social chitchat to the Senior Steward's lady. I couldn't remember, five minutes later, a word that was said. I couldn't feel my feet on the carpet. I'm a mess, I thought.

The afternoon went on. Winetaster got beaten in the big race by a glossy dark filly called Mrs. Hillman, and in the race after that Larry Server took Philip Friarly's syndicate horse to the back of the field, and stayed there. Nothing improved internally, and after the fifth I decided it was pointless staying any longer, since I couldn't even effectively think.

Outside the gate there was the usual gaggle of chauffeurs leaning against

cars, waiting for their employers; and also, with them, one of the jump jockeys whose license had been lost through taking bribes from Rammileese.

I nodded to him as I passed. "Jacksy."

"Sid."

I walked on to the car, and unlocked it, and slung my race glasses onto the
back seat. Got in. Started the engine. Paused for a bit, and reversed all the
way back to the gate.

"Jacksy?" I said. "Get in. I'm buying."

"Buying what?" He came over and opened the passenger door, and sat in
beside me. I fished my wallet out of my rear trouser pocket and tossed it into
his lap.

"Take all the money," I said. I drove forward through the car park and out
through the distant gate onto the public road.

"But you dropped me quite a lot not long ago," he said.

I gave him a fleeting sideways smile. "Yeah. Well . . . this is for services
about to be rendered."

He counted the notes. "All of it?" he said doubtfully.

"I want to know about Peter Rammileese."

"Oh, no." He made as if to open the door, but the car by then was going
too fast.

"Jacksy," I said, "no one's listening but me, and I'm not telling anyone
else. Just say how much he paid you and what for, and anything else you can
think of."

He was silent for a bit. Then he said, "It's more than my life's worth, Sid.
There's a whisper out that he's brought two pros down from Glasgow for a special job and anyone who gets in his way just now is liable to be stamped on."

"Have you seen these pros?" I said, thinking that I had.

"No. It just come through on the grapevine, like."

"Does the grapevine know what the special job is?"

He shook his head.

"Anything to do with syndicates?"

"Be your age, Sid. Everything to do with Rammileese is always to do with
syndicates. He runs about twenty. Maybe more."

Twenty, I thought, frowning. I said, "What's his rate for the job of doing
a Larry Server, like today?"

"Sid," he protested.

"How does he get someone like Larry Server onto a horse he wouldn't normally ride?"

"He asks the trainer nicely, with a fistful of dollars."

"He bribes the *trainers?*"

"It doesn't take much sometimes." He looked thoughtful for a while. "Don't you quote me, but there were races run last autumn where Rammileese was behind every horse in the field. He just carved them up as he liked."

"It's impossible," I said.

"No. All that dry weather we had, remember? Fields of four, five, or six runners sometimes, because the ground was so hard? I know of three races for sure when all the runners were his. The poor sodding bookies didn't know what had hit them."

Jacksy counted the money again. "Do you know how much you've got here?" he said.

"Just about."

I glanced at him briefly. He was twenty-five, an ex-apprentice grown too heavy for the flat and known to resent it. Jump jockeys on the whole earned less than the flat boys, and there were the bruises besides, and it wasn't everyone who, like me, found steeplechasing double the fun. Jacksy didn't; but he could ride pretty well, and I'd raced alongside him often enough to know he wouldn't put you over the rails for nothing at all. For a consideration, yes, but for nothing, no.

The money was troubling him. For ten or twenty he would have lied to me easily: but we had a host of shared memories of changing rooms and horses and wet days and mud and falls and trudging back over sodden turf in paper-thin racing boots, and it isn't so easy, if you're not a real villain, to rob someone you know as well as that.

"Funny," he said, "you taking to this detecting lark."

"Riotous."

"No, straight up. I mean, you don't come after the lads for little things."

"No," I agreed. Little things like taking bribes. My business, on the whole, was with the people who offered them.

"I kept all the newspapers," he said, "after that trial."

I shook my head resignedly. Too many people in the racing world had kept those papers, and the trial had been a trial for me in more ways than one. Defense counsel had reveled in deeply embarrassing the victim; and the prisoner, charged with causing grievous bodily harm with intent, contrary to Section 18 of the Offenses Against the Person Act 1861 (or in other words, bopping an ex-jockey's left hand with a poker), had been rewarded by four years in clink. It would be difficult to say who had enjoyed the proceedings less, the one in the witness box or the one in the dock.

Jacksy kept up his disconnected remarks, which I gathered were a form of time filling while he sorted himself out underneath.

"I'll get my license back for next season," he said.

"Great."

"Seabury's a good track. I'll be riding there in August. All the lads think it's fine the course is still going, even if . . ." He glanced at my hand. "Well . . . you couldn't race with it anyway, could you, as it was?"

"Jacksy," I said, exasperated. "Will you or won't you?"

He flipped through the notes again, and folded them, and put them in his pocket.

"Yes. All right. Here's your wallet."

"Put it in the glove box."

He did that, and looked out the window. "Where are you going?" he said.

"Anywhere you like."

"I got a lift to Chester. He'll have gone without me by now. Can you take me south, like, and I'll hitch the rest."

So I drove toward London, and Jacksy talked.

"Rammileese gave me ten times the regular fee, for riding a loser. Now listen, Sid, you swear this won't get back to him?"

"Not through me."

"Yeah. Well, I suppose I do trust you."

"Get on, then."

"He buys quite good horses. Horses that can win. Then he syndicates them. I reckon sometimes he makes five hundred percent profit on them, for a start. He bought one I knew of for six thousand and sold ten shares at three thousand each. He's got two pals who are O.K. registered owners, and he puts one of them in each syndicate, and they swing it so some fancy figurehead takes a share, so the whole thing looks right."

"Who are the two pals?"

He gulped a lot, but told me. One name meant nothing, but the other had appeared on all of Philip Friarly's syndicates.

"Right," I said. "On you go."

"The horses get trained by anyone who can turn them out looking nice for double the usual training fees and no questions asked. Then Rammileese works out what races they're going to run in, and they're all running way below their real class, see, so that when he says go, by Christ you're on a flier." He grinned. "Twenty times the riding fee, for a winner."

It sounded a lot more than it was.

"How often did you ride for him?"

"One or two, most weeks."

"Will you do it again, when you get your license back?"

He turned in his seat until his back was against the car's door and spent a long time studying the half he could see of my face. His silence itself was an answer, but when we had traveled fully three miles he sighed deeply and said, finally, "Yes."

As an act of trust, that was remarkable.

"Tell me about the horses," I said, and he did, at some length. The names of some of them were a great surprise, and the careers of all of them as straightforward as Nicholas Ashe.

"Tell me how you got your license suspended," I said.

He had been riding for one of the amenable trainers, he said, only the trainer hadn't had an amenable wife. "She had a bit of a spite on, so she shopped him with the Jockey Club. Wrote to Thomas Ullaston personally, I ask you. Of course the whole bleeding lot of stewards believed her, and suspended the lot of us—me, him, and the other jock who rides for him, poor sod, who never got a penny from Rammileese and wouldn't know a backhander if it smacked him in the face."

"How come," I asked casually, "that no one in the Jockey Club has found out about all these syndicates and done something positive about Rammileese?"

"Good question."

I glanced at him, hearing the doubt in his voice and seeing the frown. "Go on," I said.

"Yeah . . . This is strictly a whisper, see, not even a rumor hardly, just something I heard . . ." He paused, then he said, "I don't reckon it's true."

"Try me."

"One of the bookies . . . I was waiting about outside the gates at Kempton, see, and these two bookies came out, and one was saying that the bloke in the Security Service would smooth it over if the price was right." He stopped again, and went on. "One of the lads said I'd've never got suspended if that bitch of a trainer's wife had sent her letter to the Security Service and not to the big white chief himself."

"Which of the lads said that?"

"Yeah. Well, I can't remember. And don't look like that, Sid; I really can't. It was months ago. I mean, I didn't even think about it until I heard the bookies at Kempton. I don't reckon there could be anyone that bent in the Security Service, do you? I mean, not in the Jockey Club."

His faith was touching, I thought, considering his present troubles, but in days gone by I would have thought he was right. Once plant the doubt, though, and one could see there were a lot of dirty misdeeds that Eddy Keith might have ignored in return for a tax-free gain. He had passed the four Friarly syndicates, and he might have done all of the twenty or more. He might even have put Rammileese's two pals on the respectable owners' list, knowing they weren't. Somehow or other, I would have to find out.

"Sid," Jacksy said, "don't you get me in bad with the brass. I'm not repeating what I just told you, not to no stewards."

"I won't say you told me," I assured him. "Do you know those two bookies at Kempton?"

"Not a chance. I mean, I don't even know they were bookies. They just looked like them. I mean, I thought 'bookies' when I saw them."

So strong an impression was probably right, but not of much help; and Jacksy, altogether, had run dry. I dropped him where he wanted, at the outskirts of Watford, and the last thing he said was that if I was going after Rammileese, to keep him, Jacksy, strictly out of it, like I'd promised.

I STAYED IN a hotel in London instead of the flat, and felt overcautious. Chico, however, when I telephoned, said it made sense. Breakfast, I suggested, and he said he'd be there.

He came, but without much hooray. He had trudged around all day visiting the people on the mailing list, but no one had received a begging letter from Ashe within the last month.

"Tell you what, though," he said. "People beginning with A and B and right down to K have had wax in the past, so it'll be the P's and R's that get done next time, which narrows the legwork."

"Great," I said, meaning it.

"I left sticky labels everywhere with your address on, and some of them said they'd let us know if it came. But whether they'll bother . . ."

"It would only take one," I said.

"That's true."

"Feel like a spot of breaking and entering?"

"Don't see why not." He started on a huge order of scrambled eggs and sausages. "Where and what for?"

"Er . . ." I said. "This morning you do a recce. This evening, after office hours but before it gets dark, we drift along to Portman Square."

Chico stopped chewing in midmouthful, and then carefully swallowed before saying, "By Portman Square, do you mean the Jockey Club?"

"That's right."

"Haven't you noticed they let you in the front door?"

"I want a quiet look-see that they don't know about."

He shrugged. "All right, then. Meet you back here after the recce?"

I nodded. "The Admiral's coming here for lunch. He went down to the wax factory yesterday."

"That should put a shine in his eyes."

"Oh, very funny."

While he finished the eggs and attacked the toast, I told him most of what Jacksy had said about the syndicates, and also about rumors of kickbacks in high places.

"And that's what we're looking for? Turning out Eddy Keith's office to see what he didn't do when he should've?"

"You got it. Sir Thomas Ullaston—Senior Steward—says Eddy was along complaining to him about me seeing the files, and Lucas Wainwright can't let me see them without Eddy's secretary knowing, and she's loyal to Eddy. So if I want to look, it has to be quiet." And would breaking into the Jockey Club, I wondered, be considered "absolutely diabolical" if I was found out?

"O.K.," he said. "I got the judo today, don't forget."

"The little bleeders," I said, "are welcome."

CHARLES CAME AT twelve, sniffing the air of the unfamiliar surroundings like an unsettled dog.

"I got your message from Mrs. Cross," he said. "But why here? Why not the Cavendish, as usual?"

"There's someone I don't want to meet," I said. "He won't look for me here. Pink gin?"

"A double."

I ordered the drinks. He said, "Is that what it was, for those six days? Evasive action?"

I didn't reply.

He looked at me quizzically. "I see it still hurts you, whatever it was."

"Leave it, Charles."

He sighed and lit a cigar, sucking in smoke and eyeing me through the flame of the match. "So who don't you want to meet?"

"A man called Peter Rammileese. If anyone asks, you don't know where I am."

"I seldom do." He smoked with enjoyment, filling his lungs and inspecting the burning ash as if it were precious. "Going off in balloons . . ."

I smiled. "I got offered the post of regular copilot to a madman."

"It doesn't surprise me," he said dryly.

"How did you get on with the wax?"

He wouldn't tell me until after the drinks had come, and then he wasted a lot of time asking why I was drinking Perrier water and not whisky.

"To keep a clear head for burglary," I said truthfully, which he half believed and half didn't.

"The wax is made," he said finally, "in a sort of cottage industry flourishing next to a plant which processes honey."

"Beeswax!" I said incredulously.

He nodded. "Beeswax, paraffin wax, and turpentine, that's what's in that polish." He smoked luxuriously, taking his time. "A charming woman there was most obliging. We spent a long time going back over the order books. People seldom ordered as much at a time as Jenny had done, and very few stipulated that the tins should be packed in white boxes for posting." His eyes gleamed over the cigar. "Three people, all in the last year, to be exact."

"Three . . . Do you think . . . it was Nicholas Ashe three times?"

"Always about the same amount," he said, enjoying himself. "Different names and addresses, of course."

"Which you did bring away with you?"

"Which I did." He pulled a folded paper out of an inner pocket. "There you are."

"Got him," I said, with intense satisfaction. "He's a fool."

"There was a policeman there on the same errand," Charles said. "He came just after I'd written out those names. It seems they really are looking for Ashe themselves."

"Good. Er . . . did you tell them about the mailing list?"

"No, I didn't." He squinted at his glass, holding it up to the light, as if one pink gin were not the same as the next and he wanted to memorize the color. "I would like it to be you who finds him first."

"Hm." I thought about that. "If you think Jenny will be grateful, you'll be disappointed."

"But you'll have got her off the hook."

"She would prefer it to be the police." She might even be nicer to me, I thought, if she was sure I had failed; and it wasn't the sort of niceness I would want.

CHICO TELEPHONED THE hotel during the afternoon.

"What are you doing in your bedroom at this time of day?" he demanded.

"Watching Chester races on television."

"Stands to reason," he said resignedly. "Well, look, I've done the recce,

and we can get in all right, but you'll have to be through the main doors before four o'clock. I've scrubbed the little bleeders. Look, this is what you do.
You go in through the front door, right, as if you'd got pukka business. Now,
in the hall there's two lifts. One that goes to a couple of businesses that are on
the first and second floors, and as far as the third, which is all Jockey Club, as
you know."

"Yes," I said.

"When all the little workers and stewards and such have gone home, they
leave that lift at the third floor, with its doors open, so no one can use it.
There's a night porter, but after he's seen to the lift he doesn't do any rounds,
he just stays downstairs. And oh, yes, when he's fixed the lift he goes down
your actual stairs, locking a door across the stairway at each landing, which
makes three in all. Got it?"

"Yes."

"Right. Now, there's another lift, which goes to the top four floors of the
building, and up there there's eight flats, two on each floor, with people living in them. And between those floors and the Jockey Club below, there's
only one door locked across the stairway."

"I'm with you," I said.

"Right. Now, I reckon the porter in the hall, or whatever you call him, he
might just know you by sight, so he'd think it odd if you came after the offices were closed. So you'd better get there before, and go up in the lift to the
flats, go right up to the top, and I'll meet you there. It's O.K., there's a sort of
seat by a window; read a book or something."

"I'll see you," I said.

I went in a taxi, armed with a plausible reason for my visit if I should
meet anyone I knew in the hall; but in fact I saw no one, and stepped into the
lift to the flats without any trouble. At the top, as Chico had said, there was
a bench by a window, where I sat and thought unproductively for over an
hour. No one came or went from either of the two flats. No one came up in
the lift. The first time its door opened, it brought Chico.

Chico was dressed in white overalls and carried a bag of tools. I gave him
a sardonic head-to-foot inspection.

"Well, you got to look the part," he said defensively. "I came here like this
earlier, and when I left I told the chap I'd be back with spare parts. He just
nodded when I walked in just now. When we go, I'll keep him talking while
you gumshoe out."

"If it's the same chap."

"He goes off at eight. We better be finished before then."

"Was the Jockey Club lift still working?" I said.

"Yeah."

"Is the stairway door above the Jockey Club locked?"

"Yeah."

"Let's go down there, then, so we can hear when the porter brings the lift up and leaves it."

He nodded. We went through the door beside the lift, into the stairwell, which was utilitarian, not plushy, and lit by electric lights, and just inside there dumped the clinking bag of tools. Four floors down, we came to the locked door, and stood there, waiting.

The door was flat, made of some filling covered on the side on which we stood by a sheet of silvery metal. The keyhole proclaimed a mortice lock set into the depth of the door, the sort of barrier which it took Chico about three minutes, usually, to negotiate.

As usual on these excursions, we had brought gloves. I thought back to one of the first times, when Chico had said, "One good thing about that hand of yours, it can't leave any dabs." I wore a glove over it anyway, as being a lot less noticeable if we were ever casually seen where we shouldn't be.

I had never got entirely used to breaking in, not to the point of not feeling my heart beat faster or my breath go shallow. Chico, for all his longer experience at the same game, gave himself away always by smoothing out the laughter lines round his eyes as the skin tautened over his cheekbones. We stood there waiting, the physical signs of stress with us, knowing the risks.

We heard the lift come up and stop. Held our breaths to see if it would go down again, but it didn't. Instead, we were electrified by the noise of someone unlocking the door we were standing behind. I caught a flash of Chico's alarmed eyes as he leaped away from the lock and joined me on the hinge side, our backs pressed hard against the wall.

The door opened until it was touching my chest. The porter coughed and sniffed on the other side of the barrier, looking, I thought, up the stairs, checking that all was as it should be.

The door swung shut again, and the key clicked in the lock. I let a long-held breath out in a slow soundless whistle, and Chico gave me the sort of sick grin that came from semireleased tension.

We felt the faint thud through the fabric of the building as the door on the floor below us was shut and locked. Chico raised his eyebrows and I nodded, and he addressed his bunch of lock-pickers to the problem. There was a faint scraping noise as he sorted his way into the mechanism, and then the application of some muscle, and finally his clearing look of satisfaction as the metal tongue retracted into the door.

We went through, taking the keys but leaving the door unlocked, and found ourselves in the familiar headquarters of British racing. Acres of carpet, comfortable chairs, polished wood furniture, and the scent of extinct cigars.

The Security Service had its own corridor of smaller workaday offices, and down there without difficulty we eased into Eddy Keith's.

None of the internal doors seemed to be locked, and I supposed there was in fact little to steal, bar electric typewriters and other such trifles. Eddy Keith's filing cabinets all slid open easily, and so did the drawers in his desk.

In the strong evening sunlight we sat and read the reports on the extra syndicates that Jacksy had told me of. Eleven horses whose names I had written down, when he'd gone, so as not to forget them. Eleven syndicates apparently checked and accepted by Eddy, with Rammileese's two registered-owner pals appearing inexorably on all of them: and as with the previous four, headed by Philip Friarly, there was nothing in the files themselves to prove anything one way or the other. They were carefully, meticulously presented, openly ready for inspection.

There was one odd thing: the four Friarly files were all missing.

We looked through the desk. Eddy kept in it few personal objects: a battery razor, indigestion tablets, a comb, and about sixteen packs of book matches, all from gambling clubs. Otherwise there was simply stationery, pens, a pocket calculator, and a desk diary. His engagements, past and future, were merely down as the race meetings he was due to attend.

I looked at my watch. Seven forty-five. Chico nodded and began putting the files back nearly into their drawers. Frustrating, I thought. An absolute blank.

When we were ready to go, I took a quick look into a filing cabinet marked "Personnel," which contained slim factual files about everyone presently employed by the Jockey Club, and everyone receiving its pensions. I looked for a file headed "Mason," but someone had taken that too.

"Coming?" Chico said.

I nodded regretfully. We left Eddy's office as we'd found it and went back to the door to the stairway. Nothing stirred. The headquarters of British racing lay wide open to intruders, who were having to go empty away.

CHAPTER 14

ON FRIDAY AFTERNOON, depressed on many counts, I drove comparatively slowly to Newmarket.

The day itself was hot, the weather reportedly stoking up to the sort of intense heat wave one could get in May, promising a glorious summer that seldom materialized. I drove in shirtsleeves with the window open, and decided to go to Hawaii and lie on the beach for a while, like a thousand years.

Martin England was out in his stable yard when I got there, also in shirtsleeves and wiping his forehead with a handkerchief.

"Sid!" he said, seeming truly pleased. "Great. I'm just starting evening stables. You couldn't have timed it better."

We walked round the boxes together in the usual ritual, the trainer visiting every horse and checking its health, the guest admiring and complimenting and keeping his tongue off the flaws. Martin's horses were middling to good, like himself, like the majority of trainers, the sort that provided the bulk of all racing, and of all jockeys' incomes.

"A long time since you rode for me," he said, catching my thought.

"Ten years or more."

"What do you weigh now, Sid?"

"About ten stone, stripped." Thinner, in fact, than when I'd stopped racing.

"Pretty fit, are you?"

"Same as usual," I said. "I suppose."

He nodded, and we went from the fillies' side of the yard to the colts'. He had a good lot of two-year-olds, it seemed to me, and he was pleased when I said so.

"This is Flotilla," he said, going to the next box. "He's three. He runs in the Dante at York next Wednesday, and if that's O.K. he'll go for the Derby."

"He looks well," I said.

Martin gave a carrot to his hope of glory. There was pride in his kind, fiftyish face, not for himself but for the shining coat and quiet eyes and waiting muscles of the splendid four-legged creature. I ran my hand down the glossy neck, and patted the dark bay shoulder, and felt the slender, rock-hard forelegs.

"He's in grand shape," I said. "Should do you proud."

He nodded with the thoroughly normal hint of anxiety showing under the pride, and we continued down the line, patting and discussing, and feeling content. Perhaps this was what I really needed, I thought: forty horses and hard work and routine. Planning and administering and paper work. Pleasure enough in preparing a winner, sadness enough in seeing one lose. A busy, satisfying, out-of-doors life style, a businessman on the back of a horse.

I thought of what Chico and I had been doing for months. Chasing villains, big and small. Wiping up a few messy bits of the racing industry. Getting knocked about, now and then. Taking our wits into minefields and fooling with people with shotguns.

It would be no public disgrace if I gave it up and decided to train. A much more normal life for an ex-jockey, everyone would think. A sensible, orderly decision, looking forward to middle and old age. I alone—and Trevor Deansgate—would know why I'd done it. I could live for a long time, knowing it.

I didn't want to.

IN THE MORNING at seven-thirty I went down to the yard in jodhpurs and boots and a pull-on jersey shirt. Early as it was, the air was warm, and with the sounds and bustle and smell of the stables all around, my spirits rose from bedrock and hovered at somewhere about knee level.

Martin, standing with a list in his hand, shouted good morning, and I went down to join him to see what he'd given me to ride. There was a five-year-old, up to my weight, that he'd think just the job.

Flotilla's lad was leading him out of his box, and I watched him admiringly as I turned toward Martin.

"Go on, then," he said. There was amusement in his face, enjoyment in his eyes.

"What?" I said.

"Ride Flotilla."

I swung toward the horse, totally surprised. His best horse, his Derby horse, and I out of practice and with one hand.

"Don't you want to?" he said. "He'd've been yours ten years ago as of right. And my jockey's gone to Ireland to race at the Curragh. It's either you or one of my lads, and to be honest, I'd rather have you."

I didn't argue. One doesn't turn down a chunk of heaven. I thought he was a bit mad, but if that was what he wanted, so did I. He gave me a leg up, and I pulled the stirrup leathers to my own length, and felt like an exile coming home.

"Do you want a helmet?" he said, looking around vaguely as if expecting one to materialize out of the tarmac.

"Not for this."

He nodded. "You never have." And he himself was wearing his usual checked cloth cap, in spite of the heat. I had always preferred riding bareheaded except in races: something to do with liking the feel of lightness and moving air.

"What about a whip?" he said.

He knew that I'd always carried one automatically, because a jockey's whip was a great aid to keeping a horse balanced and running straight: a tap down the shoulder did the trick, and one pulled the stick through from hand to hand, as required. I looked at the two hands in front of me. I thought that if I took a whip and fumbled it, I might drop it: and I needed above all to be efficient.

I shook my head. "Not today."

"Right, then," he said. "Let's be off."

With me in its midst, the string pulled out of the yard and went right through Newmarket town on the horse walks along the back roads, out to the wide sweeping Limekilns gallops to the north. Martin, himself riding the quiet five-year-old, pulled up there beside me.

"Give him a sharpish warm-up canter for three furlongs, and then take him a mile up the trial ground, upsides with Gulliver. It's Flotilla's last workout before the Dante, so make it a good one. O.K.?"

"Yes," I said.

"Wait until I get up there"—he pointed—"to watch."

"Yep."

He rode away happily toward a vantage point more than half a mile distant, from where he could see the whole gallop. I wound the left-hand rein round my plastic fingers and longed to be able to feel the pull from the horse's mouth. It would be easy to be clumsy, to upset the lie of the bit and the whole balance of the horse, if I got the tension wrong. In my right hand, the reins felt alive, carrying messages, telling Flotilla, and Flotilla telling me, where we were going, and how, and how fast. A private language, shared, understood.

Let me not make a mess of it, I thought. Let me just be able to do what I'd done thousands of times in the past; let the old skill be there, one hand or no. I could lose him the Dante and Derby and any other race you cared to mention, if I got it really wrong.

The boy on Gulliver circled with me, waiting for the moment, answering my casual remarks in monosyllables and grunts. I wondered if he was the one who would have ridden Flotilla if I hadn't been there, and asked him, and he said, grumpily, yes. Too bad, I thought. Your turn will come.

Up the gallop, Martin waved. The boy on Gulliver kicked his mount in to a fast pace at once, not waiting to start evenly together. You little sod, I thought. You do what you damned well like, but I'm going to take Flotilla along at the right speeds for the occasion and distance, and to hell with your tantrums.

It was absolutely great, going up there. It suddenly came right, as natural as if there had been no interval, and no missing limb. I threaded the left rein through bad and good hands alike and felt the vibrations from both sides of the bit, and if it wasn't the most perfect style ever seen on the Heath, it at least got the job done.

Flotilla swept over the turf in a balanced working gallop and came upsides with Gulliver effortlessly. I stayed beside the other horse then for most of the way, but as Flotilla was easily the better, I took him on from six furlongs and finished the mile at a good pace that was still short of strain. He was fit, I thought, pulling him back to a canter. He would do well in the Dante. He'd given me a good feel.

I said so to Martin, when I rejoined him, walking back. He was pleased, and laughed. "You can still ride, can't you? You looked just the same."

I sighed internally. I had been let back for a brief moment into the life I'd lost, but I wasn't just the same. I might have managed one working gallop without making an ass of myself, but it wasn't the Gold Cup at Cheltenham.

"Thanks," I said, "for a terrific morning."

We walked back through the town to his stable, and to breakfast, and afterward I went with him in his Land-Rover to see his second lot work on the racecourse side. When we got back from that we sat in his office and drank coffee and talked for a bit, and with some regret I said it was time I was going.

The telephone rang. Martin answered it, and held out the receiver to me. "It's for you, Sid."

I thought it would be Chico, but it wasn't. It was, surprisingly, Henry Thrace, calling from his stud farm just outside the town.

"My girl assistant says she saw you riding work on the Heath," he said. "I didn't really believe her, but she was sure. Your head, without a helmet, unmistakable. With Martin England's horses, she said, so I rang on the off chance."

"What can I do for you?" I said.

"Actually it's the other way round," he said. "Or at least, I think so. I had a letter from the Jockey Club earlier this week, all very official and everything, asking me to let them know at once if Gleaner or Zingaloo died, and not to get rid of the carcass. Well, when I got that letter I rang Lucas Wainwright, who signed it, to ask what the hell it was all about, and he said it was really *you* who wanted to know if either of those horses died. He was telling me that in confidence, he said."

My mouth went as dry as vinegar.

"Are you still there?"

"Yes," I said.

"Then I'd better tell you that Gleaner has, in fact, just died."

"When?" I said, feeling stupid. "Er . . . how?" My heart rate had gone up to at least double. Talk about overreacting, I thought, and felt the fear stab through like toothache.

"A mare he was due to cover came into use, so we put him to her," he said, "this morning. An hour ago, maybe. He was sweating a lot, in this heat. It's hot in the breeding shed, with the sun on it. Anyway, he served her, and got down all right, and then he just staggered and fell, and died almost at once."

I unstuck my tongue. "Where is he now?"

"Still in the breeding shed. We're not using it again this morning, so I've left him there. I've tried to ring the Jockey Club, but it's Saturday and Lucas Wainwright isn't there, and anyway, as my girl said that you yourself were actually here in Newmarket . . ."

"Yes," I said. I took a shaky breath. "A post-mortem. You would agree, wouldn't you?"

"Essential, I'd say. Insurance, and all that."

"I'll try and get Ken Armadale," I said. "From the Equine Research Establishment. I know him . . . Would he do you?"

"Couldn't be better."

"I'll ring you back."

"Right," he said, and disconnected.

I stood with Martin's telephone in my hand and looked into far dark spaces. It's too soon, I thought. Much too soon.

"What's the matter?" Martin said.

"A horse I've been inquiring about has died." Oh, God almighty . . . "Can I use your phone?" I said.

"Help yourself."

Ken Armadale said he was gardening and would much rather cut up a dead horse. I'll pick you up, I said, and he said he'd be waiting. My hand, I saw remotely, was actually shaking.

I rang back to Henry Thrace, to confirm. Thanked Martin for his tremendous hospitality. Put my suitcase and myself in the car, and picked up Ken Armadale from his large modern house on the southern edge of Newmarket.

"What am I looking for?" he said.

"Heart, I think."

He nodded. He was a strong, dark-haired research vet in his middle thirties, a man I'd dealt with on similar jaunts before, to the extent that I felt easy with him and trusted him, and as far as I could tell, he felt the same about me. A professional friendship, extending to a drink in a pub but not to Christmas cards, the sort of relationship that remained unchanged and could be taken up and put down as need arose.

"Anything special?" he said.

"Yes . . . but I don't know what."

"That's cryptic."

"Let's see what you find."

Gleaner, I thought. If there were three horses I should definitely be doing nothing about, they were Gleaner and Zingaloo and Tri-Nitro. I wished I hadn't asked Lucas Wainwright to write those letters, one to Henry Thrace, the other to George Caspar. If those horses died, let me know . . . but not so soon, so appallingly soon.

I drove into Henry Thrace's stud farm and pulled up with a jerk. He came out of his house to meet us, and we walked across to the breeding shed. As with most such structures, its walls swept up to a height of ten feet, unbroken except for double entrance doors. Above that there was a row of windows, and above those, a roof. Very like Peter Rammileese's covered riding school, I thought, only smaller.

The day, which was hot outside, was very much hotter inside. The dead horse lay where he had fallen on the tan-covered floor, a sad brown hump with milky gray eyes.

"I rang the knackers," Ken said. "They'll be here pretty soon."

Henry Thrace nodded. It was impossible to do the post-mortem where the horse lay, as the smell of blood would linger for days and upset any other horse that came in there. We waited for not very long until the lorry arrived with its winch, and when the horse was loaded, we followed it down to the knackers' yard, where Newmarket's casualties were cut up for dog food. A small hygienic place; very clean.

Ken Armadale opened the bag he had brought and handed me a washable nylon boiler suit, like his own, to cover trousers and shirt. The horse lay in a square room with whitewashed walls and a concrete floor. In the floor, runnels and a drain. Ken turned on a tap so that water ran out of the hose beside the horse, and pulled on a pair of long rubber gloves.

"All set?" he said.

I nodded, and he made the first long incision. The smell, as on past occasions, was what I liked least about the next ten minutes, but Ken seemed not to notice it as he checked methodically through the contents. When the chest cavity had been opened, he removed its whole heart-lung mass and carried it over to the table which stood under the single window.

"This is odd," he said, after a pause.

"What is?"

"Take a look."

I went over beside him and looked where he was pointing, but I hadn't his knowledge behind my eyes, and all I saw was a blood-covered lump of tissue with tough-looking ridges of gristle in it.

"His heart?" I said.

"That's right. Look at these valves. . . ." He turned his head to me, frowning. "He died of something horses don't get." He thought it over. "It's a great pity we couldn't have had a blood sample before he died."

"There's another horse at Henry Thrace's with the same thing," I said. "You can get your blood sample from him."

He straightened up from bending over the heart, and stared at me.

"Sid," he said, "you'd better tell me what's up. And outside, don't you think, in some fresh air."

We went out, and it was a great deal better. He stood listening, with blood all over his gloves and down the front of his coveralls, while I wrestled with the horrors in the back of my mind and spoke with flat lack of emotion from the front.

"There are—or were—four of them," I said. "Four that I know of. They were all top star horses, favorites all winter for the guineas and the Derby. That class. The very top. They all came from the same stable. They all went out to race in Guineas week looking marvelous. They all started hot favorites, and they all totally flopped. They all suffered from a mild virus infection at about that time, but it didn't develop. They all were subsequently found to have heart murmurs."

Ken frowned heavily. "Go on."

"There was Bethesda, who ran in the One Thousand Guineas two years ago. She went to stud, and she died of heart failure this spring, while she was foaling."

Ken took a deep breath.

"There's this one," I said, pointing. "Gleaner. He was favorite for the Guineas last year. He then got a really bad heart, and also arthritis. The other horse at Henry Thrace's, Zingaloo, he went out fit to a race and afterwards could hardly stand from exhaustion."

Ken nodded. "And which is the fourth one?"

I looked up at the sky. Blue and clear. I'm killing myself, I thought. I looked back at him and said, "Tri-Nitro."

"Sid!" He was shocked. "Only ten days ago."

"So what is it?" I said. "What's the matter with them?"

"I'd have to do some tests to be certain," he said. "But the symptoms you've described are typical, and those heart valves are unmistakable. That horse died from swine erysipelas, which is a disease you get only in pigs."

KEN SAID, "WE need to keep that heart for evidence."

"Yes," I said.

Dear God . . .

"Get one of those bags, will you?" he said. "Hold it open." He put the heart inside. "We'd better go along to the research center later. I've been thinking. . . . I know I've got some reference papers there about erysipelas in horses. We could look them up, if you like."

"Yes," I said.

He peeled off his blood-spattered coveralls. "Heat and exertion," he said. "That's what did for this fellow. A deadly combination, with a heart in that state. He might have lived for years, otherwise."

Ironic, I thought bitterly.

He packed everything away, and we went back to Henry Thrace. A blood sample from Zingaloo? No problem, he said.

Ken took enough blood to flog a battleship, it seemed to me, but what was a liter to a horse, which had gallons? We accepted reviving Scotches from Henry with gratitude, and afterward took our trophies to the Equine Research Establishment, along the Bury Road.

Ken's office was a small extension to a large laboratory, where he took the bag containing Gleaner's heart over to the sink and told me he was washing out the remaining blood.

"Now come and look," he said.

This time I could see exactly what he meant. Along all the edges of the valves there were small knobbly growths, like baby cauliflowers, creamy white.

"That's vegetation," he said. "It prevents the valves from closing. Makes the heart as efficient as a leaking pump."

"I can see it would."

"I'll put this in the fridge, then we'll look through those veterinary journals for that paper."

I sat on a hard chair in his utilitarian office while he searched for what he wanted. I looked at my fingers. Curled and uncurled them. This can't all be happening, I thought. It's only three days since I saw Trevor Deansgate at Chester. *If you break your assurance, I'll do what I said.*

"Here it is," Ken exclaimed, flattening a paper open. "Shall I read you the relevant bits?"

I nodded.

" 'Swine erysipelas . . . in 1938 . . . occurred in a horse, with vegetative endocarditis . . . the chronic form of the illness in pigs.' " He looked up. "That's those cauliflower growths. Right?"

"Yes."

He read again from the paper. " 'During 1944 a mutant strain of erysipelas rhusiopathiae appeared suddenly in a laboratory specializing in antisera production and produced acute endocarditis in the serum horse.' "

"Translate," I said.

He smiled. "They used to use horses for producing vaccines. You inject the horse with pig disease, wait until it develops antibodies, draw off blood, and extract the serum. The serum, injected into healthy pigs, prevents them getting the disease. Same process as for all human vaccinations, smallpox and so on. Standard procedure."

"O.K.," I said. "Go on."

"What happened was that instead of growing antibodies as usual, the horses themselves got the disease."

"How could that happen?"

"It doesn't say here. You'd have to ask the pharmaceutical firm concerned, which I see is the Tierson vaccine lab along at Cambridge. They'd tell you, I should think, if you asked. I know someone there, if you want an introduction."

"It's a long time ago," I said.

"My dear fellow, germs don't die. They can live like time bombs, waiting for some fool to take stupid liberties. Some of these labs keep virulent strains around for decades. You'd be surprised."

He looked down again at the paper, and said, "You'd better read these next paragraphs yourself. They look pretty straightforward." He pushed the journal across to me, and I read the page where he pointed.

1. 24–48 hours after intramuscular injection of the pure culture, inflammation of one or more of the heart valves commences. At this time, apart from a slight rise in temperature and occasional palpitations, no other symptoms are seen unless the horse is subjected to severe exertion, when auricular fibrillation or interference with the blood supply to the lungs occurs; both occasion severe distress which only resolves after 2–3 hours rest.

2. Between the second and the sixth day, pyrexia (temperature rise) increases and white cell count of the blood increases and the horse is listless and off food. This could easily be loosely diagnosed as "the virus." However, examination by stethoscope reveals a progressively increasing heart murmur. After about ten days the temperature returns to normal and, unless subjected to more than walk or trot, the horse may appear to have recovered. The murmur is still present and it then becomes necessary to retire the horse from fast work since this induces respiratory distress.

3. Over the next few months vegetations grow on the heart valves, and arthritis in some joints, particularly of the limbs, may or may not appear. The condition is permanent and progressive and death may occur suddenly following exertion or during very hot weather, sometimes years after the original infection.

I looked up. "That's it, exactly, isn't it?" I said.

"Bang on the nose."

I said slowly, "Intramuscular injection of the pure culture could absolutely not have occurred accidentally."

"Absolutely not," he agreed.

I said, "George Caspar had his yard sewn up so tight this year with alarm bells and guards and dogs that no one could have got within screaming distance of Tri-Nitro with a syringeful of live germs."

He smiled. "You wouldn't need a syringeful. Come into the lab and I'll show you."

I followed him and we fetched up beside one of the cupboards with sliding doors that lined the whole of the wall. He opened the cupboard and pulled out a box, which proved to contain a large number of smallish plastic envelopes.

He tore open one of the envelopes and tipped the contents onto his hand: a hypodermic needle attached to a plastic capsule only the size of a pea. The whole thing looked like a tiny dart with a small round balloon at one end, about as long, altogether, as one's little finger.

He picked up the capsule and squeezed it. "Dip that into liquid, you draw up half a teaspoonful. You don't need that much pure culture to produce a disease."

"You could hold that in your hand, out of sight," I said.

He nodded. "Just slap the horse with it. Done in a flash. I use these sometimes for horses that shy away from a syringe." He showed me how, holding the capsule between thumb and index finger, so that the sharp end pointed down from his palm. "Shove the needle in and squeeze," he said.

"Could you spare one of these?"

"Sure," he said, giving me an envelope. "Anything you like."

I put it in my pocket. Dear God in heaven.

Ken said slowly, "You know, we might just be able to do something about Tri-Nitro."

"How do you mean?"

He pondered, looking at the large bottle of Zingaloo's blood, which stood on the draining board beside the sink.

"We might find an antibiotic which would cure the disease."

"Isn't it too late?" I said.

"Too late for Zingaloo. But I don't think those vegetations would start growing at once. If Tri-Nitro was infected, say . . ."

"Say two weeks ago, today, after his final working gallop."

He looked at me with amusement. "Say, two weeks ago, then. His heart will be in trouble, but the vegetation won't have started. If he gets the right antibiotic soon, he might make a full recovery."

"Do you mean . . . back to normal?"

"Don't see why not."

"What are you waiting for?" I said.

CHAPTER 15

I SPENT MOST of Sunday beside the sea, driving northeast from New-market to the wide deserted coast of Norfolk. Just for somewhere to go, some-thing to do, to pass the time.

Even though the sun shone, the wind off the North Sea was keeping the beaches almost empty: small groups were huddled into the shelter of flimsy canvas screens, and a few intrepid children built castles.

I sat in the sun in a hollow in a sand dune which was covered with coarse tufts of grass, and watched the waves come and go. I walked along the shore, kicking the worm casts. I stood looking out to sea, holding up my left upper arm for support, aware of the weight of the machinery lower down, which was not so very heavy, but always there.

I had often felt released and restored by lonely places, but not on that day. The demons came with me. The cost of pride . . . the price of safety. If you didn't expect so much of yourself, Charles had said once, you'd give yourself an easier time. It hadn't really made sense. One was as one was. Or at least, one was as one was until someone came along and broke you all up.

If you sneezed on the Limekilns, they said in Newmarket, it was heard two miles away on the racecourse. The news of my attendance at Gleaner's post-mortem would be given to George Caspar within a day. Trevor Deans-gate would hear of it; he was sure to.

I could still go away, I thought. It wasn't too late. Travel. Wander by other seas, under other skies. I could go away and keep very quiet. I could still escape from the terror he induced in me. I could still . . . run away.

I left the coast and drove numbly to Cambridge. Stayed in the University Arms Hotel and, in the morning, went to Tierson Pharmaceuticals Vaccine Laboratories. I asked for, and got, a Mr. Livingston, who was maybe sixty and grayishly thin. He made small nibbling movements with his mouth when he spoke. He looks a dried-up old cuss, Ken Armadale had said, but he's got a mind like a monkey.

"Mr. Halley, isn't it?" Livingston said, shaking hands in the entrance hall. "Mr. Armadale has been on the phone to me, explaining what you want. I think I can help you, yes, I do indeed. Come along, come along, this way."

He walked in small steps before me, looking back frequently to make sure I was following. It seemed to be a precaution born of losing people, because the place was a labyrinth of glass-walled passages with laboratories and gardens apparently intermixed at random.

"The place just grew," he said, when I remarked on it. "But here we are." He led the way into a large laboratory which looked through glass walls into the passage on one side, and a garden on another, and straight into another lab on the third.

"This is the experimental section," he said, his gesture embracing both rooms. "Most of the laboratories just manufacture the vaccines commercially, but in here we putter about inventing new ones."

"And resurrecting old ones?" I said.

He looked at me sharply. "Certainly not. I believe you came for information, not to accuse us of carelessness."

"Sorry," I said placatingly. "That's quite right."

"Well, then. Ask your question."

"Er . . . yes. How did the serum horses you were using in the 1940s get swine eryspielas?"

"Ah," he said. "Pertinent. Brief. To the point. We published a paper about it, didn't we? Before my time, of course. But I've heard about it. Yes. Well, it's possible. It happened. But it shouldn't have. Sheer carelessness, do you see? I hate carelessness. Hate it."

Just as well, I thought. In his line of business, carelessness might be fatal.

"Do you know anything about the production of erysipelas antiserum?" he said.

"You could write it on a thumbnail."

"Ah," he said. "Then I'll explain as to a child. Will that do?"

"Nicely," I said.

He gave me another sharp glance, in which there was this time amusement.

"You inject live erysipelas germs into a horse. Are you with me? I am talking about the past now, when they did use horses. We haven't used horses since the early 1950s, nor have Burroughs Wellcome, and Bayer in Germany. The past, do you see?"

"Yes," I said.

"The horse's blood produces antibodies to fight the germs, but the horse does not develop the disease, because it is a disease pigs get and horses don't."

"A child," I assured him, "would understand."

"Very well. Now, sometimes the standard strain of erysipelas becomes weakened, and in order to make it virulent again we pass it through pigeons."

"Pigeons?" I said, very politely.

He raised his eyebrows. "Customary practice. Pass a weak strain through pigeons to recover virulence."

"Oh, of course," I said.

He pounced on the satire in my voice. "Mr. Halley," he said severely. "Do you want to know all this or don't you?"

"Yes, please," I said meekly.

"Very well, then. The virulent strain was removed from the pigeons and subcultured onto blood agar plates." He broke off, looking at the blankness of my ignorance. "Let me put it this way. The live virulent germs were transferred from the pigeons onto dishes containing blood, where they then multiplied, thus producing a useful quality for injecting into the serum horses."

"That's fine," I said. "I do understand."

"All right." He nodded. "Now, the blood on the dishes was bull's blood. Bovine blood."

"Yes," I said.

"But owing to someone's stupid carelessness, the blood agar plates were prepared one day with horse blood. This produced a mutant strain of the disease." He paused. "Mutants are changes which occur suddenly and for no apparent reason throughout nature."

"Yes," I said again.

"No one realized what had happened," he said. "Until the mutant strain was injected into the serum horses and they all got erysipelas. The mutant strain proved remarkably constant. The incubation period was always twenty-four to forty-eight hours after inoculation, and endocarditis—that is, inflammation of the heart valves—was always the result."

A youngish man in a white coat, unbuttoned down the front, came into the room next door, and I watched him vaguely as he began puttering about.

"What became of this mutant strain?" I said.

Livingston nibbled a good deal with the lips, but finally said, "We could have kept some, I daresay, as a curiosity. But of course it would be weakened by now, and to restore it to full virulence, one would have to . . ."

"Yeah," I said. "Pass it through pigeons."

He didn't think it was funny. "Quite so," he said.

"And all this passing through pigeons and subculture on agar plates . . . how much skill does this take?"

He blinked. "I could do it, of course."

I couldn't. Any injections I'd handled had come in neat little ampules, packed in boxes.

The man in the next room was opening cupboards, looking for something.

I said, "Would there be any of this mutant strain anywhere else in the world, besides here? I mean, did this laboratory send any of it out to anywhere else?"

The lips pursed themselves and the eyebrows went up. "I've no idea," he said. He looked through the glass and gestured toward the man in the next room. "You could ask Barry Shummuck. He would know. Mutant strains are his specialty."

He pronounced "Shummuck" to rhyme with "hummock." I know the name, I thought. I . . . *Oh, my God.*

The shock of it fizzed through my brain and left me half breathless. I knew someone too well whose real name was Shummuck.

I swallowed and felt shivery. "Tell me more about your Mr. Shummuck," I said.

Livingston was a natural chatterer and saw no harm in it. He shrugged. "He came up the hard way. Still talks like it. He used to have a terrible chip on his shoulder. The world owed him a living, that sort of thing. Shades of student demos. He's settled down recently. He's good at his job."

"You don't care for him?" I said.

Livingston was startled. "I didn't say that."

He had, plainly, in his face and in his voice. I said only, "What sort of accent?"

"Northern. I don't know exactly. What does it matter?"

Barry Shummuck looked like no one I knew. I said slowly, hesitantly, "Do you know if he has . . . a brother?"

Livingston's face showed surprise. "Yes, he has. Funny thing, he's a bookmaker." He pondered. "Some name like Terry. Not Terry . . . Trevor, that's it. They come here together sometimes, the two of them. . . . Thick as thieves."

Barry Shummuck gave up his search and moved toward the door.

"Would you like to meet him?" Mr. Livingston said.

Speechlessly, I shook my head. The last thing I wanted, in a building full of virulent germs which he knew how to handle and I didn't, was to be introduced to the brother of Trevor Deansgate.

Shummuck went through the door and into the glass-walled corridor, and turned in our direction.

Oh, no, I thought.

He walked purposefully along and pushed open the door of the lab we were in. Head and shoulders leaned forward.

"Morning, Mr. Livingston," he said. "Have you seen my box of transparencies anywhere?"

The basic voice was the same, self-confident and slightly abrasive. Manchester accent, much stronger. I held my left arm out of sight half behind my back and willed him to go away.

"No," said Mr. Livingston, with just a shade of pleasure. "But, Barry, can you spare . . ."

Livingston and I were standing in front of a workbench which held various empty glass jars and a row of clamps. I turned leftward, with my arm still hidden, and clumsily, with my right hand, knocked over a clamp and two glass jars.

More clatter than breakage. Livingston gave a quick nibble of surprised annoyance, and righted the rolling jars. I gripped the clamp, which was metal and heavy, and would have to do.

I turned back toward the door.

The door was shutting. The back view of Barry Shummuck was striding away along the corridor, the front edges of his white coat flapping.

I let a shuddering breath out through my nose and carefully put the clamp back at the end of the row.

"He's gone," Mr. Livingston said. "What a pity."

I drove back to Newmarket, to the Equine Research Establishment and Ken Armadale.

I wondered how long it would take chatty Mr. Livingston to tell Barry Shummuck of the visit of a man called Halley who wanted to know about a pig disease in horses.

I felt faintly, and continuously, sick.

"IT'S BEEN MADE resistant to all ordinary antibiotics," Ken said. "A real neat little job."

"How do you mean?"

"If any old antibiotic would kill it, you couldn't be sure the horse wouldn't be given a shot as soon as he had a temperature, and never develop the disease."

I sighed. "So how do they make it resistant?"

"Feed it tiny doses of antibiotic until it becomes immune."

"All this is technically difficult, isn't it?"

"Yes, fairly."

"Have you ever heard of Barry Shummuck?"

He frowned. "No, I don't think so."

The craven inner voice told me urgently to shut up, to escape, to fly to safety . . . to Australia . . . to a desert.

"Do you have a cassette recorder here?" I said.

"Yes. I use it for making notes while I'm operating." He went out and fetched it and set it up for me on his desk, loaded with a new tape. "Just talk," he said. "It has a built-in microphone."

"Stay and listen," I said. "I want . . . a witness."

He regarded me slowly. "You look so strained. . . . It's no gentle game, is it, what you do?"

"Not always."

I switched on the recorder, and for introduction spoke my name, the place, and the date. Then I switched off again and sat looking at the fingers I needed for pressing the buttons.

"What is it, Sid?" Ken said.

I glanced at him and down again. "Nothing."

I had to do it, I thought. I absolutely had to. I was never in any way going to be whole again if I didn't.

If I had to choose, and it seemed to me that I did have to choose, I would have to settle for wholeness of mind, and put up with what it cost. Perhaps I could deal with physical fear. Perhaps I could deal with anything that happened to my body, and even with helplessness. What I could not forever deal with—and I saw it finally with clarity and certainty—was despising myself.

I pressed the "play" and "record" buttons together, and irrevocably broke my assurance to Trevor Deansgate.

CHAPTER 16

I TELEPHONED CHICO at lunchtime and told him what I'd found out about Rosemary's horses.

"What it amounts to," I said, "is that those four horses had bad hearts because they'd been given a pig disease. There's a lot of complicated info about how it was done, but that's now the stewards' headache."

"Pig disease?" Chico said disbelievingly.

"Yeah. That big bookmaker Trevor Deansgate has a brother who works in a place that produces vaccines for inoculating people against smallpox and diphtheria and so on, and they cooked up a plan to squirt pig germs into those red-hot favorites."

"Which duly lost," Chico said, "while the bookmaker raked in the lolly."

"Right," I said.

It felt very odd to put Trevor Deansgate's scheme into casual words and to be talking about him as if he were just one of our customary puzzles.

"How did you find out?" Chico said.

"Gleaner died at Harry Thrace's, and the pig disease turned up at the post-mortem. When I went to the vaccine lab I saw a man called Shummuck who deals in odd germs, and I remembered that Shummuck was Trevor Deansgate's real name. And Trevor Deansgate is very thick with George Caspar . . . and all the affected horses, that we know of, have come from George Caspar's stable."

"Circumstantial, isn't it?" Chico said.

"A bit, yes. But the Security Service can take it from there."

"Eddy Keith?" he said skeptically.

"He can't hush this one up; don't you worry."

"Have you told Rosemary?"

"Not yet."

"Bit of a laugh," Chico said.

"Mm."

"Well, Sid, mate," he said, "this is results day all round. We got a fix on Nicky Ashe."

Nicky Ashe, with a knife in his sock. A pushover, compared with . . . compared with . . .

"Hey," Chico's voice said aggrievedly through the receiver. "Aren't you pleased?"

"Yes, of course. What sort of fix?"

"He's been sending out some of those damnfool letters. I went to your place this morning, just to see, like, and there were two envelopes there with our sticky labels on."

"Great," I said.

"I opened them. They'd both been sent to us by people whose names start with *P.* All that legwork paid off."

"So we've got the begging letter?"

"We sure have. It's exactly the same as the ones your wife had, except for the address to send the money to, of course. Got a pencil?"

"Yeah."

He read out the address, which was in Clifton, Bristol. I looked at it thoughtfully. I could either give it straight to the police, or I could check it first myself. Checking it, in one certain way, had persuasive attraction.

"Chico," I said, "ring Jenny's flat in Oxford and ask for Louise McInnes. Ask her to ring me here at the Rutland Hotel in Newmarket."

"Scared of your missus, are you?"

"Will you do it?"

"Oh, sure." He laughed, and rang off. When the bell rang again, however, it was not Louise on the other end, but still Chico.

"She's left the flat," he said. "Your wife gave me her new number." He read it out. "Anything else?"

"Can you bring your cassette player to the Jockey Club, Portman Square, tomorrow afternoon at, say, four o'clock?"

"Like last time?"

"No," I said. "Front door, all the way."

LOUISE, TO MY relief, answered her telephone. When I told her what I wanted, she was incredulous.

"You've actually *found* him?"

"Well," I said, "probably. Will you come there and identify him?"

"Yes." No hesitation. "Where and when?"

"Someplace in Bristol." I paused, and said diffidently, "I'm in Newmarket now. I could pick you up in Oxford this afternoon, and we could go straight on. We might spot him this evening . . . or tomorrow morning."

There was a silence at the other end. Then she said, "I've moved out of Jenny's flat."

"Yes."

Another silence, and then her voice, quiet, and committed.

"All right."

She was waiting for me in Oxford, and she had brought an overnight bag.

"Hello," I said, getting out of the car.

"Hello."

We looked at each other. I kissed her cheek. She smiled with what I had to believe was enjoyment, and slung her case in the boot beside mine.

"You can always retreat," I said.

"So can you."

We sat in the car, however, and I drove to Bristol feeling contented and carefree. Trevor Deansgate wouldn't yet have started looking for me, and Peter Rammileese and his boys hadn't been in sight for a week, and no one except Chico knew where I was going. The shadowy future, I thought, was not going to spoil the satisfactory present. I decided not even to think of it, and for most of the time, I didn't.

We went first to an inn that someone had once told me of, high on the cliffs overlooking the Avon gorge, and geared to rich-American-tourist comfort.

"We'll never get in here," Louise said, eyeing the opulence.

"I telephoned."

"How organized! One room or two?"

"One."

She smiled as if that suited her well, and we were shown into a large wood-paneled room with stretches of carpet, antique polished furniture, and a huge fourposter bed decked with American-style white muslin frills.

"My God," Louise said. "And I expected a motel."

"I didn't know about the fourposter," I said a little weakly.

"Wow," she said, laughing. "This is more *fun*."

We parked the suitcases and freshened up in the modern bathroom tucked discreetly behind the paneling, and went back to the car; and Louise smiled to herself all the way to the new address of Nicholas Ashe.

It was a prosperous-looking house in a prosperous-looking street. A solid five- or six-bedroom affair, mellowed and white-painted and uniformative in the early evening sun.

I stopped the car on the same side of the road, pretty close, at a place from where we could see both the front door and the gate into the driveway. Nicky, Louise had said on the way down, often used to go out for a walk at about seven o'clock, after a hard day's typing. Maybe he would again, if he was there.

Maybe he wouldn't.

We had the car's windows open because of the warm air. I lit a cigarette, and the smoke floated in a quiet curl through lack of wind. Very peaceful, I thought, waiting there.

"Where do you come from?" Louise said.

I blew a smoke ring. "I'm the posthumous illegitimate son of a twenty-year-old window cleaner who fell off his ladder just before his wedding."

She laughed. "Very elegantly put."

"And you?"

"The legitimate daughter of the manager of a glass factory and a magistrate, both alive and living in Essex."

We consulted about brothers and sisters, of which I had none and she had two, one of each. About education, of which I'd had some and she a lot. About life in general, of which she'd seen a little, and I a bit more.

An hour passed in the quiet street. A few birds sang. Sporadic cars drove by. Men came home from work and turned into the driveways. Distant doors slammed. No one moved in the house we were watching.

"You're patient," Louise said.

"I spend hours doing this sometimes."

"Pretty unexciting."

I looked at her clear intelligent eyes. "Not this evening."

Seven o'clock came and went; and Nicky didn't.

"How long will we stay?"

"Until dark."

"I'm hungry."

Half an hour drifted by. I learned that she liked curry and paella and hated rhubarb. I learned that the thesis she was writing was giving her hell.

"I'm so far behind schedule," she said. "And . . . Oh, my goodness, *there he is.*"

Her eyes had opened very wide. I looked where she looked, and saw Nicholas Ashe.

Coming not from the front door, but from the side of the house. My age, or a bit younger. Taller, but of my own thin build. My coloring. Dark hair, slightly curly. Dark eyes. Narrow jaw. All the same.

He looked sufficiently like me for it to be a shock, but was nevertheless quite different. I took my baby camera out of my trouser pocket and pulled it open with my teeth as usual, and took his picture.

When he reached the gate he paused and looked back, and a woman ran after him, calling, "Ned, Ned, wait for me."

"Ned!" Louise said, sliding down in her seat. "If he comes this way, won't he see me?"

"Not if I kiss you."

"Well, do it," she said.

I took, however, another photograph.

The woman looked older, about forty; slim, pleasant, excited. She tucked her arm into his and looked up at his eyes, her own clearly, even from twenty feet away, full of adoration. He looked down and laughed delightfully, then he kissed her forehead and swung her in a little circle onto the pavement, and put his arm around her waist, and walked toward us with vivid gaiety and a bounce in his step.

I risked one more photograph from the shadows of the car, and leaned across and kissed Louise with enthusiasm.

Their footsteps went past. Abreast of us, they must have seen us, or at least my back, for they both suddenly giggled lightheartedly, lovers sharing their secret with lovers. They almost paused, then went on, their steps growing softer until they had gone.

I sat up reluctantly.

Louise said, "Whew!" but whether it was the result of the kiss, or the proximity of Ashe, I wasn't quite sure.

"He's just the same," she said.

"Casanova himself," I said dryly.

She glanced at me swiftly and I guessed she was wondering whether I was jealous of his success with Jenny, but in fact I was wondering whether Jenny had been attracted to him because he resembled me, or whether she had been attracted to me in the first place, and also to him, because we matched some internal picture she had of a sexually interesting male. I was more disturbed than I liked by the physical appearance of Nicholas Ashe.

"Well," I said, "that's that. Let's find some dinner."

I drove back to the hotel, and we went upstairs before we ate, Louise saying she wanted to change out of the blouse and skirt she had worn all day.

I took the battery charger out of my suitcase and plugged it in; took a spent battery from my pocket, and rolled up my shirtsleeve and snapped out the one from my pocket, and rolled up my shirtsleeve and snapped out the one from my arm, and put them both in the charger. Then I took a charged battery from my suitcase and inserted it in the empty socket in the arm. And Louise watched.

I said, "Are you . . . revolted?"

"No, of course not."

I pulled my sleeve down and buttoned the cuff.

"How long does a battery last?" she said.

"Six hours, if I use it a lot. About eight, usually."

She merely nodded, as if people with electric arms were as normal as people with blue eyes. We went down to dinner and ate sole and afterward strawberries, and if they'd tasted of seaweed I wouldn't have cared. It wasn't only because of Louise, but also because since that morning I had stopped tearing myself apart, and had slowly been growing back toward peace. I could feel it happening, and it was marvelous.

We sat side by side on a sofa in the hotel lounge, drinking small cups of coffee.

"Of course," she said, "now that we have seen Nicky, we don't really need to stay until tomorrow."

"Are you thinking of leaving?" I said.

"About as much as you are."

"Who is seducing whom?" I said.

"Mm," she said, smiling. "This whole thing is so unexpected."

She looked calmly at my left hand, which rested on the sofa between us. I couldn't tell what she was thinking, but I said on impulse, "Touch it."

She looked up at me quickly. "What?"

"Touch it. Feel it."

She tentatively moved her right hand until her fingers were touching the tough, lifeless, plastic skin. There was no drawing back, no flicker of revulsion in her face.

"It's metal, inside there," I said. "Gears and levers and electric circuits. Press harder, and you'll feel them."

She did as I said, and I saw her surprise as she discovered the shape of the inner realities.

"There's a switch inside there too," I said. "You can't see it from the outside, but it's just below the thumb. One can switch the hand off, if one wants."

"Why would you want to?"

"Very useful for carrying things, like a briefcase. You shut the fingers round the handle, and switch the current off, and the hand just stays shut without you having to do it all yourself."

I put my right hand over and pushed the switch off and on, to show her.

"It's like the push-through switch on a table lamp," I said. "Feel it. Push it."

She fumbled a bit because it wasn't all that easy to find if one didn't know, but in the end pushed it both ways, off and on. Nothing in her expression but concentration.

She felt some sort of tension relax in me, and looked up, accusingly.

"You were testing me," she said.

I smiled. "I suppose so."

"You're a pig."

I felt an unaccustomed uprush of mischief. "As a matter of fact," I said, holding my left hand in my right, "if I unscrew it firmly round this way several times, the whole hand will come right off at the wrist."

"Don't do it," she said, horrified.

I laughed with absolute enjoyment. I wouldn't have thought I would ever feel that way about that hand.

"Why does it come right off?" she said.

"Oh . . . servicing. Stuff like that."

"You look so different," she said.

I nodded. She was right. I said, "Let's go to bed."

"WHAT A WORLD of surprises," she said, a good while later. "Almost the last thing I would have expected you to be as a lover is gentle."

"Too gentle?"

"No. I liked it."

We lay in the dark, drowsily. She herself had been warmly receptive and generous, and had made it for me an intense sunburst of pleasure. It was a shame, I thought hazily, that the act of sex had got so cluttered up with taboos and techniques and therapists and sin and voyeurs and the whole commercial ballyhoo. Two people fitting together in the old design should be a private matter, and if you didn't expect too much, you'd get on better. One was as one was. Even if a girl wanted it, I could never have put on a pretense of being a rough, aggressive bull of a lover, because, I thought sardonically, I would have laughed at myself in the middle. And it had been all right, I thought, as it was.

"Louise," I said.

No reply.

I shifted a little for deeper comfort and drifted, like her, to sleep.

A while later, awake early as usual, I watched the daylight strengthen on her sleeping face. The fair hair lay tangled round her head in the way I had seen it first, and her skin looked soft and fresh. When she woke, even before she opened her eyes, she was smiling.

"Good morning," I said.

"Morning."

She moved toward me in the big bed, the white muslin frills on the canopy overhead surrounding us like a frame.

"Like sleeping in clouds," she said.

She came up against the hard shell of my left arm, and blinked from the awareness of it.

"You don't sleep in this when you're alone, do you?" she said.

"No."

"Take it off, then."

I said with a smile, "No."

She gave me a long considering inspection.

"Jenny's right about you being like flint," she said.

"Well, I'm not."

"She told me that at the exact moment some chap was smashing up your arm you were calmly working out how to defeat him."

I made a face.

"Is it true?" she said.

"In a way."

"Jenny said . . ."

"To be honest," I said, "I'd rather talk about you."

"I'm not interesting."

"That's a right come-on, that is," I said.

"What are you waiting for, then?"

"I do so like your retreating maidenly blushes."

I touched her lightly on her breast and it seemed to do for her what it did for me. Instant arousal, mutually pleasing.

"Clouds," she said contentedly. "What do you think of when you're doing it?"

"Sex?"

She nodded.

"I feel. It isn't thought."

"Sometimes I see roses . . . on trellises . . . scarlet and pink and gold. Sometimes spiky stairs. This time it will be white frilly muslin clouds."

I asked her, after.

"No. All bright sunlight. Quite blinding."

The sunlight, in truth, had flooded into the room, making the whole white canopy translucent and shimmering.

"Why didn't you want the curtains drawn last night?" she asked. "Don't you like the dark?"

"I don't like sleeping when my enemies are up and about."

I said it without thinking. The actual truth of it followed after, like a freezing shower.

"Like an animal," she said, and then, "What's the matter?"

Remember me, I thought, as I am. And I asked, "Like some breakfast?"

WE WENT BACK to Oxford. I took the film to be developed, and we had lunch at Les Quat' Saisons, where the delectable pâté de turbot and the superb quenelle de brochet soufflée kept the shadows at bay a while longer. With the coffee, though, came the unavoidable minute.

"I have to be in London at four o'clock," I said.

Louise said, "When are you going to the police about Nicky?"

"I'll come back here on Thursday, day after tomorrow, to pick up the photos. I'll do it then." I reflected. "Give that lady in Bristol two more happy days."

"Poor thing."

"Will I see you Thursday?" I said.

"Unless you're blind."

CHICO WAS PROPPING up the Portman Square building with a look of resignation, as if he'd been there for hours. He shifted his shoulder off the stonework at my on-foot approach and said, "Took your time, didn't you?"

"The car park was full."

From one hand he dangled the black cassette recorder we used occasionally, and he was otherwise wearing jeans and a sports shirt and no jacket. The hot weather, far from vanishing, had settled in on an almost stationary high pressure system, and I was also in shirtsleeves, though with a tie on, and a jacket over my arm. On the third floor all the windows were open, the street noises coming up sharply, and Sir Thomas Ullaston, sitting behind his big desk, had dealt with the day in pale blue shirting with white stripes.

"Come in, Sid," he said, seeing me appear in his open doorway. "I've been waiting for you."

"I'm sorry I'm late," I said, shaking hands. "This is Chico Barnes, who works with me."

He shook Chico's hand. "Right," he said. "Now you're here, we'll get Lucas Wainwright and the others along." He pressed an intercom button and spoke to his secretary. "And bring some more chairs, would you?"

The office slowly filled up with more people than I'd expected, but all of whom I knew at least to talk to. The top administrative brass in full force, about six of them, all urbane worldly men, the people who really ran racing. Chico looked at them slightly nervously, as if at an alien breed, and seemed to be relieved when a table was provided for him to put the recorder on. He sat with the table between himself and the room, like a barrier. I fished into my jacket for the cassette I'd brought, and gave it to him.

Lucas Wainwright came with Eddy Keith on his heels, Eddy looking coldly out of the genial face; big, bluff Eddy, whose warmth for me was slowly dying.

"Well, Sid," Sir Thomas said, "here we all are. Now, on the telephone yesterday you told me you had discovered how Tri-Nitro had been nobbled for the Guineas, and—as you see—we are all very interested." He smiled. "So fire away."

I made my own manner match theirs: calm and dispassionate, as if Trevor Deansgate's threat wasn't anywhere in my mind, instead of continually flashing through it like stabs.

"I've . . . er . . . put it all onto tape," I said. "You'll hear two voices. The other is Ken Armadale, from Equine Research. I asked him to clarify the veterinary details, which are his province, not mine."

The well-brushed heads nodded. Eddy Keith merely stared. I glanced at Chico, who pressed the start button, and my own voice, disembodied, spoke loudly into a wholly attentive silence.

"This is Sid Halley, at the Equine Research Establishment, on Monday, May fourteenth. . . ."

I listened to the flat sentences, spelling it out. The identical symptoms in four horses, the lost races, the bad hearts. My request, via Lucas Wainwright, to be informed if any of the three still alive should die. The post-mortem on Gleaner, with Ken Armadale repeating in greater details my own simpler account. His voice explaining, again after me, how horses had come to be infected by a disease of pigs. His voice saying, "I found active live germs in the lesions on Gleaner's heart valves, and also in the blood taken from Zingaloo . . ." and my voice continuing, "A mutant strain of the disease was produced at the Tierson Vaccine Laboratories at Cambridge in the following manner. . . ."

It wasn't the easiest of procedures to understand, but I watched the faces and saw that they did, particularly by the time Ken Armadale had gone through it all again, confirming what I'd said.

"As to motive and opportunity," my voice said, "we come to a man called Trevor Deansgate. . . ."

Sir Thomas's head snapped back from its forward, listening posture, and he stared at me bleakly from across the room. Remembering, no doubt, that he had entertained Trevor Deansgate in the steward's box at Chester. Remembering, perhaps, that he had brought me and Trevor Deansgate there face to face.

Among the other listeners the name had created an almost equal stir. All of them either knew him or knew of him: the big up-and-coming influence among bookmakers, the powerful man shouldering his way into top-rank social acceptance. They knew Trevor Deansgate, and their faces were shocked.

"The real name of Trevor Deansgate is Trevor Shummuck," my voice said.

"There is a research worker at the vaccine laboratory called Barry Shummuck, who is his brother. The two brothers, on friendly terms, have been seen together at the laboratories on several occasions. . . ."

Oh, God, I thought. My voice went on, and I listened in snatches. I've really done it. There's no going back.

"This is the laboratory where the mutant strain originally arose . . . unlikely after all this time for there to be any of it anywhere else. . . .

"Trevor Deansgate owns a horse which George Caspar trains. Trevor Deansgate is on good terms with Caspar . . . watches the morning gallops and goes to breakfast. Trevor Deansgate stood to make a fortune if he knew in advance that the over-winter favorites for the Guineas and the Derby couldn't win. Trevor Deansgate had the means—the disease; the motive—money; and the opportunity—entry into Caspar's well-guarded stable. It would seem, therefore, that there are grounds for investigating his activities further."

My voice stopped, and a few seconds later Chico switched off the recorder. Looking slightly dazed himself, he ejected the cassette and laid it carefully on the table.

"It's incredible," Sir Thomas said, but not as if he didn't believe it. "What do you think, Lucas?"

Lucas Wainwright cleared his throat. "I think we should congratulate Sid on an exceptional piece of work."

Except for Eddy Keith, they agreed with him and did so, to my embarrassment, and I thought it generous of him to have said it at all, considering the Security Service themselves had done negative dope tests and left it at that. But then the Security Service, I reflected, hadn't had Rosemary Caspar visiting them in false curls and hysteria; and they hadn't had the benefit of Trevor Deansgate's revealing himself to them as a villain before they even positively suspected him, threatening vile things if they didn't leave him alone.

As Chico had said, our successes had stirred up the enemy to the point where they were likely to clobber us before we knew why.

Eddy Keith sat with his head held very still, watching me. I looked back at him, probably with much the same deceptively blank outer expression. Whatever he was thinking, I couldn't read. What I thought about was breaking into his office, and if he could read that, he was clairvoyant.

Sir Thomas and the administrators, consulting among themselves, raised their heads to listen when Lucas Wainwright asked a question.

"Do you really think, Sid, that Deansgate infected those horses himself?" He seemed to think it unlikely. "Surely he couldn't produce a syringe anywhere near any of those horses, let alone all four."

"I did think," I said, "that it might have been someone else . . . like a work jockey, or even a vet." Inky Poole and Brothersmith, I thought, would have had me for slander if they could have heard. "But there's a way almost anyone could do it."

I dipped again into my jacket and produced the packet containing the needle attached to the pea-sized bladder. I gave the packet to Sir Thomas, who opened it, tipping the contents onto his desk.

They all looked. Understood. Were convinced.

"He'd be more likely to do it himself if he could," I said. "He wouldn't want to risk anyone else knowing, and perhaps having a hold over him."

"It amazes me," Sir Thomas said with apparent genuineness, "how you work these things out, Sid."

"But I . . ."

"Yes," he said, smiling. "We all know what you're going to say. At heart you're still a jockey."

There seemed to be a long pause. Then I said, "Sir, you're wrong. This"— I pointed to the cassette—"is what I am now. And from now on."

His face sobered into a long frowning look in which it seemed that he was reassessing his whole view of me, as so many others had recently done. It was to him, as to Rosemary, that I still appeared as a jockey, but to myself, no longer. When he spoke again his voice was an octave lower, and thoughtful.

"We've taken you too lightly." He paused. "I did mean what I said to you at Chester about being a positive force for good in racing, but I also see that I thought of it as something of an unexpected joke." He shook his head slowly. "I'm sorry."

Lucas Wainwright said briskly, "It's been increasingly clear what Sid has become." He was tired of the subject and waiting as usual to spur on to the next thing. "Do you have any plans, Sid, as to what to do next?"

"Talk to the Caspars," I said. "I thought I might drive up there tomorrow."

"Good idea," Lucas said. "You won't mind if I come? It's a matter for the Security Service now, of course."

"And for the police, in due course," said Sir Thomas, with a touch of gloom. He saw all public prosecutions for racing-based crimes as sources of disgrace to the whole industry, and was inclined to let people get away with things, if prosecuting them would involve a damaging scandal. I tended to agree with him, to the point of doing the same myself, but only if privately one could fix it so that the offense wouldn't be repeated.

"If you're coming, Commander," I said to Lucas Wainwright, "perhaps you could make an appointment with them. They may be going to York. I was simply going to turn up at Newmarket early and trust to luck, but you won't want to do that."

"Definitely not," he said crisply. "I'll telephone straight away."

He bustled off to his own office, and I put the cassette into its small plastic box and handed it to Sir Thomas.

"I put it on tape because it's complicated, and you might want to hear it again."

"You're so right, Sid," said one of the administrators, ruefully. "All that about pigeons . . . !"

Lucas Wainwright came back. "The Caspars are at York, but went by air taxi and are returning tonight. George Caspar wants to see his horses work in the morning before flying back to York. I told his secretary chap that it was of the utmost importance I see Caspar, so we're due there at eleven. Suit you, Sid?"

"Yes, fine."

"Pick me up here, then, at nine?"

I nodded. "O.K."

"I'll be up in my office, checking the mail."

Eddy Keith gave me a final blank stare and without a word removed himself from the room.

Sir Thomas and all the administrators shook my hand and also Chico's; and going down in the lift, Chico said, "They'll be kissing you next."

"It won't last."

We walked back to where I had left the Scimitar, which was where I shouldn't have. There was a parking ticket under the wiper blade. There would be.

"Are you going back to the flat?" Chico said, folding himself into the passenger's seat.

"No."

"You still think those boot men . . . ?"

"Trevor Deansgate," I said.

Chico's face melted into half-mocking comprehension.

"Afraid he'll duff you up?"

"He'll know by now . . . from his brother." I shivered internally from a strong flash of the persistent horrors.

"Yeah, I suppose so." It didn't worry him. "Look, I brought that begging letter for you. . . ." He dug into a trouser pocket and produced a much-folded and slightly grubby sheet of paper. I eyed it disgustedly, reading it through.

Exactly the same as the ones Jenny had sent, except signed with a flourish, "Elizabeth More," and headed with the Clifton address.

"Do you realize they may have to produce this filthy bit of paper in court?"

"Been in my pocket, hasn't it?" he said defensively.

"What else've you got in there? Potting compost?"

He took the letter from me and put it in the glove box, and let down the window.

"Hot, isn't it?"

"Mm."

I wound down my own side window, and started the car, and drove him back to his place in Finchley Road.

"I'll stay in the same hotel," I said. "And look . . . come to Newmarket with me tomorrow."

"Sure, if you want. What for?"

I shrugged, making light of it. "Bodyguard."

He was surprised. He said wonderingly, "You can't really be afraid of him—this Deansgate—are you?"

I shifted in my seat a bit, and sighed.

"I guess so," I said.

CHAPTER 17

I TALKED TO Ken Armadale in the early evening. He wanted to know how my session with the Jockey Club had gone, but more than that, he sounded smugly self-satisfied, and not without reason.

"That erysipelas strain has been made immune to practically every antibiotic in the book," he said. "Very thorough. But I reckon there's an obscure little bunch he won't have bothered with, because no one would think of pumping them into horses. Rare, they are, and expensive. All the signs I have here are that they would work. Anyway, I've tracked some down."

"Great," I said. "Where?"

"In London, at one of the teaching hospitals. I've talked with the pharmacist there, and he's promised to pack some in a box and leave it at the reception desk for you to collect. It will have 'Halley' on it."

"Ken, you're terrific."

"I've had to mortgage my soul to get it."

I picked up the parcel in the morning and arrived at Portman Square to find Chico again waiting on the doorstep. Lucas Wainwright came down from his office and said he would drive us in his car, if we liked, and I thought of all the touring around I'd been doing for the past fortnight, and accepted gratefully. We left the Scimitar in the car park which had been full the day before, a temporary open-air affair in a cleared building site, and set off to Newmarket in a large, air-conditioned Mercedes.

"It's too darned hot," Lucas said, switching on the refrigeration. "Wrong time of year."

He had come tidily dressed in a suit, which Chico and I hadn't: jeans and sports shirts and not a jacket between us.

"Nice car, this," Chico said admiringly.

"You used to have a Merc, Sid, didn't you?" Lucas said.

I said yes, and we talked about cars half the way to Suffolk. Lucas drove well but as impatiently as he did everything else. A pepper-and-salt man, I thought, sitting beside him. Brown-and-gray speckled hair, brownish-gray eyes, with flecks in the iris. Brown-and-gray checked shirt, with a nondescript tie. Pepper and salt in his manner, in his speech patterns, in all his behavior.

He said, as in the end he was bound to, "How are you getting on with the syndicates?"

Chico, sitting in the back seat, made a noise between a laugh and a snort.

"Er . . ." I said. "Pity you asked, really."

"Like that, is it?" Lucas said, frowning.

"Well," I said, "there is very clearly something going on, but we haven't come up with much more than rumor and hearsay." I paused. "Any chance of us collecting expenses?"

He was grimly amused. "I suppose I could put it under the heading of general assistance to the Jockey Club. Can't see the administrators quibbling, after yesterday."

Chico gave me a thumbs-up sign from behind Lucas's head, and I thought I would pile it on a bit while the climate was favorable, and recover what I'd paid to Jacksy.

"Do you want us to go on trying?" I said.

"Definitely." He nodded positively. "Very much so."

We reached Newmarket in good time and came to a smooth halt in George Caspar's well-tended driveway.

There were no other cars there: certainly not Trevor Deansgate's Jaguar. On that day he should, in the normal course of things, be at York, attending to his bookmaking business. I had no faith that he was.

George, expecting Lucas, was not at all pleased to see me, and Rosemary, coming downstairs and spotting me in the hall, charged across the parquet and rugs with shrill disapproval.

"Get out," she said. "How dare you come here?"

Two spots of color flamed in her cheeks, and she looked almost as if she was going to try to throw me out bodily.

"No, no, I say," Lucas Wainwright said, writhing as usual with naval embarrassment in the face of immodest female behavior. "George, make your wife *listen* to what we've come to tell you."

Rosemary was persuaded, with a ramrod-stiff back, to perch on a chair in her elegant drawing room, while Chico and I sat lazily in armchairs, and Lucas Wainwright did the talking, this time, about pig disease and bad hearts.

The Caspars listened in growing bewilderment and dismay, and when Lucas mentioned Trevor Deansgate, George stood up and began striding about in agitation.

"It isn't possible," he said. "Not Trevor. He's a friend."

"Did you let him near Tri-Nitro after that last training gallop?" I said.

George's face gave the answer.

"Sunday morning," Rosemary said, in a hard cold voice. "He came on the Sunday. He often does. He and George walked round the yard." She paused. "Trevor likes slapping horses. Slaps their rumps. Some people do that. Some people pat necks. Some people pull ears. Trevor slaps rumps."

Lucas said, "In due course, George, you'll have to give evidence in court."

"I'm going to looked a damned fool, aren't I?" he said sourly. "Filling my yard with guards and taking Deansgate in myself."

Rosemary looked at me stonily, unforgiving.

"I told you they were being nobbled. I told you. You didn't believe me."

Lucas looked surprised. "But I thought you understood, Mrs. Caspar. Sid did believe you. It was Sid who did all this investigating, not the Jockey Club."

Her mouth opened, and stayed open, speechlessly.

"Look," I said awkwardly, "I've brought you a present. Ken Armadale along at Equine Research has done a lot of work for you, and he thinks Tri-

Nitro can be cured, by a course of some rather rare antibiotics. I've brought them with me from London."

I stood up and took the box to Rosemary, put it into her hands, and kissed her cheek.

"I'm sorry, Rosemary, love, that it wasn't in time for the Guineas. Maybe the Derby . . . but anyway the Irish Derby and the Diamond Stakes, and the Arc de Triomphe. Tri-Nitro will be fine for those."

Rosemary Caspar, that tough lady, burst into tears.

WE DIDN'T GET back to London until nearly five, owing to Lucas's insisting on going to see Ken Armadale and Henry Thrace himself, face to face. The Director of Security to the Jockey Club was busy making everything official.

He was visibly relieved when Ken absolved the people who'd done blood tests on the horses after their disaster races.

"The germ makes straight for the heart valves, and in the acute stage you'd never find it loose in the blood, even if you were thinking of illness and not merely looking for dope. It's only later, sometimes, that it gets freed into the blood, as it had in Zingaloo when we took that sample."

"Do you mean," Lucas demanded, "that if you did a blood test on Tri-Nitro at this minute you couldn't prove he had the disease?"

Ken said, "You would only find antibodies."

Lucas wasn't happy. "Then how can we prove in court that he has got it?"

"Well," Ken said. "You could do an erysipelas antibody count today and another in a week's time. There would be a sharp rise in the number present, which would prove the horse must have the disease, because he's fighting it."

Lucas shook his head mournfully. "Juries won't like this."

"Stick to Gleaner," I said, and Ken agreed.

At one point Lucas disappeared into the Jockey Club rooms in the High Street and Chico and I drank in the White Hart and felt hot.

I changed the batteries. Routine. The day crawled.

"Let's go to Spain," I said.

"Spain?"

"Anywhere."

"I could just fancy a señorita."

"You're disgusting."

"Look who's talking."

We reordered and drank and still felt hot.

"How much do you reckon we'll get?" Chico said.

"More or less what we ask."

George Caspar had promised, if Tri-Nitro recovered, that the horse's owner would give us the earth.

"A fee will do," I'd said dryly.

Chico said, "What will you ask, then?"

"I don't know. Perhaps five percent of his prize money."

"He couldn't complain."

We set off southward, finally, in the cooling car, and listened on the radio to the Dante Stakes at York.

Flotilla, to my intense pleasure, won it.

Chico, in the back seat, went to sleep. Lucas drove as impatiently as on the way up; and I sat and thought of Rosemary, and Trevor Deansgate, and Nicholas Ashe, and Trevor Deansgate, and Louise, and Trevor Deansgate.

Stab. Stab. *"I'll do what I said."*

LUCAS DROPPED US at the entrance to the car park where I'd left the Scimitar. It would be like a furnace inside, I thought, sitting there all day in the sun. Chico and I walked over to it across the uneven stone-strewn ground.

Chico yawned.

A bath, I thought. A long drink. Dinner. Find a hotel room again . . . not the flat.

There was a Land-Rover with a two-horse trailer parked beside my car. Odd, I thought idly, to see them in central London. Chico, still yawning, walked between the trailer and my car to wait for me to unlock the doors.

"It'll be baking," I said, fishing down into my pocket for the keys, and looking downward into the car.

Chico made a choking sort of noise. I looked up, and thought confusedly how fast, how very fast, a slightly boring hot afternoon could turn to stone cold disaster.

A large man stood in the space between the trailer and my car with his left arm clamped around Chico, who was facing me. The man was more or less supporting Chico's weight, because Chico's head lolled forward.

In his right hand the man held a small pear-shaped black truncheon.

The second man was letting down the ramp at the rear of the trailer.

I had no difficulty in recognizing them. The last time I'd seen them I'd been with a fortune-teller who hadn't liked my chances.

"Get in the trailer, laddie," the one holding Chico said to me. "The right-hand stall, laddie. Nice and quick. Otherwise I'll give your friend another tap or two. On the eyes, laddie. Or the base of the brain."

Chico, on the far side of the Scimitar, mumbled vaguely and moved his head. The big man raised his truncheon and produced another short burst of uncompromising Scottish accent.

"Get in the trailer," he said. "Go right in, to the back."

Seething with fury, I walked round the back of my car and up the ramp into the trailer. The right-hand stall, as he'd said. To the back. The second man stood carefully out of hitting distance, and there was no one else in the car park.

I found I was still holding my car keys, and put them back automatically into my pocket. Keys, handkerchief, money . . . and in the left-hand pocket, only a discharged battery. No weapon of any sort. A knife in the sock, I thought. I should have learned from Nicholas Ashe.

The man holding Chico came round to the back of the trailer and half dragged, half carried Chico into the left-hand stall.

"You make a noise, laddie," he said, putting his head round to my side of the central partition, "and I'll hit your friend here. On the eyes, laddie, and the mouth. You try and get help by shouting, laddie, and your friend won't have much face to speak of. Get it?"

I thought of Mason in Tunbridge Wells. A vegetable, and blind.

I said nothing at all.

"I'm traveling in here with your friend, all the way," he said. "Just remember that, laddie."

The second man closed the ramp, shutting out the sunlight, creating instant night. Where many trailers were open at the top at the back, this one was not.

Numb, I suppose, is how I felt.

The engine of the Land-Rover started, and the trailer moved, backing out of the parking lot. The motion was enough to rock me against the trailer's side, enough to show I wasn't going very far standing up.

My eyes slowly adjusted to a darkness which wasn't totally black owing to various points where the ramp fitted less closely than others against the back of the trailer. In the end I could see clearly, as if it mattered, the variations that had been done to turn an ordinary trailer into an escape-proof transport. The extra piece at the back, closing the gap usually left open for air, and the extra piece inside, lengthways, raising the central partition from head height to the roof.

Basically, it was still a box built to withstand the weight and kicks of horses. I sat helplessly on the floor, which was bare of everything except muddy dust, and thought absolutely murderous thoughts.

After all that unpredictable traveling around, I had agreed to go with Lucas and had stupidly left my car in plain vulnerable view all day. They must have picked me up at the Jockey Club, I thought. Either yesterday, or this morning. Yesterday, I thought, there had been no room in the car park, and I'd left my car in the street and got a ticket. . . .

I hadn't been to my flat. I hadn't been back to Aynsford. I hadn't been to the Cavendish, or to any routine place.

I had, in the end, gone to the Jockey Club.

I sat and cursed and thought about Trevor Deansgate.

THE JOURNEY LASTED for well over an hour: a hot, jolting, depressing time which I spent mostly in consciously not wondering what lay at the end of it. After a while I could hear Chico talking through the partition, though not the words. The flat, heavy, Glaswegian voice made shorter replies, rumbling like thunder.

A couple of pros from Glasgow, Jacksy had said. The one in with Chico, I thought, was certainly that. Not an average bashing mindless thug, but a hard man with brain power and so much the worse.

Eventually the jolting stopped, and there were noises of the trailer being unhitched from the coupling; the Land-Rover drove away, and in the sudden quiet I could hear Chico plainly.

"What's happening?" he said, and sounded still groggy.

"You'll find out soon enough, laddie."

"Where's Sid?" he said.

"Be quiet, laddie."

There was no sound of a blow, but Chico was quiet.

The man who had raised the ramp came and lowered it, and six-thirty, Wednesday evening, flooded into the trailer.

"Out," he said.

He was backing away from the trailer as I got to my feet, and he held a pitchfork at the ready, the sharp tines pointing my way.

From deep in the trailer I looked out and saw where we were. The trailer itself, disconnected from the Land-Rover, was inside a building, and the building was the indoor riding school on Peter Rammileese's farm.

Timber-lined walls, windows in the roof, open because of the heat. No way that anyone could see in, casually, from outside.

"Out," he said again, jerking the fork.

"Do what he says laddie," said the threatening voice of the man with Chico. "At once."

I did what he said.

Walked down the ramp onto the quiet tan-colored riding school floor.

"Over there." He jerked the fork. "Against the wall." His voice was rougher, the accent stronger, than the man with Chico. For sheer bullying power, there wasn't much to choose.

I walked, feeling that my feet didn't belong to me.

"Back to the wall. Face this way."

I turned with my shoulders lightly touching the wood.

Behind the man with the pitchfork, standing where from in the trailer I hadn't been able to see him, was Peter Ramileese. His face bore a nasty mixture of satisfaction, sneer, and anticipation, quite unlike the careful intentness of the two Scots. He had driven the Land-Rover, I supposed, out of my sight.

The man with Chico brought Chico to the top of the ramp and held him there. Chico half stood and half lay against him, smiling slightly and hopelessly disorganized.

"Hello, Sid," he said.

The man holding him lifted the hand with the truncheon, and spoke to me.

"Now listen, laddie. You stand quite still. Don't move. If you move, I'll finish your friend so quick you won't see it happen. Get it?"

I made no response of any kind, but after a moment he nodded sharply to the one with the pitchfork.

He came toward me slowly; warily. Showing me the prongs.

I looked at Chico. At the truncheon. At damage I couldn't risk.

I stood . . . quite still.

The man with the pitchfork raised it from pointing at my stomach to pointing at my heart, and from there, still higher. Slowly, carefully one step at a time, he came forward until one of the prongs brushed my throat.

"Stand still," said the man with Chico, warningly.

I stood.

The prongs of the pitchfork slid past my neck, one each side below my chin, until they came to rest on the wooden surface behind me. Pushing my head back. Pinning me by the neck against the wall, unharmed. Better than through the skin, I thought dimly, but hardly a ball for one's self-respect.

When he'd got the fork aligned as he wanted it, he gave the handle a strong thrusting jerk, digging the sharp tines into the wood. After that he put his weight into pushing against the handle, so that I shouldn't dislodge what he'd done, and get myself free. I had seldom felt more futile or more foolish.

The man holding Chico moved suddenly as if released, carrying Chico bodily down the ramp and giving him a rough over-balancing shove at the bottom. As weak as a rag doll, Chico sprawled on the soft wood shavings, and the man strode over to me to feel for himself the force being applied in keeping me where I was.

He nodded to his partner. "And you keep your mind on your business," he said to him. "Never mind yon other laddie. I'll see to him."

I looked at their faces, to remember them forever.

The hard callous lines of cheekbone and mouth. The cold eyes, observant and unfeeling. The black hair and pale skin. The set of a small head on a thick neck, the ears flat. The heavy shape of a jaw blue with beard. Late thirties, I guessed. Both much alike, and both giving forth at great magnitude the methodical brutality of the experienced mercenary.

Peter Rammileese, approaching, seemed in comparison a matter of sponge. Despite his chums' disapproval, he too put a hand on the pitchfork handle and tried to give it a shake. It seemed to surprise him that he couldn't.

He said to me, "You'll keep your snotty nose out, after this."

I didn't bother to answer. Behind them, Chico got to his feet and for one surging moment I thought that he'd been fooling them a bit with the concussed act, and was awake and on the point of some effective judo.

It was only a moment. The kick he aimed at the man who had been holding him wouldn't have knocked over a house of cards. In sick and helpless fury I watched the truncheon land again on Chico's head, sending him down onto his knees, deepening the haze in his brain.

The man with the pitchfork was doing what he'd been told and concentrating on keeping up the pressure on the handle. I tugged and wrenched at it with desperation to get free, and altogether failed, and the big man with Chico unfastened his belt.

I saw with incredulity that what he'd worn round his waist was not a leather strap but a length of chain, thin and supple, like the stuff in grandfather clocks. At one end he had fixed some sort of handle, which he grasped; and he swung his arm so that the free end fizzed through the air and wrapped itself around Chico.

Chico's head snapped up and his eyes and mouth opened wide with astonishment, as if the new pain had cleared away the mists like a flamethrower. The man swung his arm again and the chain landed on Chico, and I could

hear myself shouting, "Bastards, bloody bastards . . ." and it made no difference at all.

Chico swayed to his feet and took some stumbling steps to get away, and
the man followed him, hitting him all over with unvarying ferocity, taking a
pride in his work.

I yelled incoherently . . . unconnected words, screaming at him to
stop . . . feeling anger and grief and an agony of responsibility. If I hadn't
taken Chico to Newmarket . . . if I hadn't been afraid of Trevor Deansgate . . .
It was because of my fear that Chico was there . . . on that day. God . . . Bastard. Stop it . . . Stop . . . Wrenched at the pitchfork and couldn't get free.

Chico lurched and stumbled and finally crawled in a wandering circle
round the riding school, and ended lying on his stomach not far away from
me. The thin cotton of his shirt twitched when the chain landed, and I saw
dotted red streaks of blood in the fabric here and there.

Chico . . . God . . .

It wasn't until he lay entirely still that the torment stopped. The man
stood over him, looking down judiciously, holding his chain in a relaxed
grasp.

Peter Rammileese looked if anything disconcerted and scared, and it was
he who had got us there, he who had arranged it.

The man holding the pitchfork stopped looking at me for the first time
and switched his attention to where Chico lay. It was only a partial shift of his
balance, but it made all the difference to the pressure on my neck. I wrenched
at the handle with a force he wasn't ready for, and finally got myself away and
off the wall; and it wasn't the man with Chico I sprang at in bloodlusting
rage, but Peter Rammileese himself, who was nearer.

I hit him on the side of the face with all my strength, and I hit him with
my hard left arm, two thousand quids' worth of delicate technology packed
into a built-in club.

He screeched and raised his arms round his head, and I said "Bastard!"
with savage intensity and hit him again, on the ribs.

The man with Chico turned his attention to me, and I discovered, as
Chico had, that one's first feeling was of astonishment. The sting was incredible: and after the lacerating impact, a continuing fire.

I turned on the man in a rage I wouldn't have thought I could feel, and it
was he who backed away from me.

I caught the next swing of his chain on my unfeeling arm. The free end
wrapped itself twice round the forearm, and I tugged with such fierceness
that he lost his grip on the handle. It swung down toward me, a stitched piece

of leather; and if there had been just the two of us I would have avenged Chico and fought our way out of there, because there was nothing about cold blood in the way I went for him.

I grasped the leather handle, and as the supple links unwound and fell off my arm I swung the chain in a circle above my head and hit him an almighty crack around the shoulders. From his wide-opening eyes and the outraged Scottish roar I guessed that he was learning for the first time just what he had inflicted on others.

The man with the pitchfork at that point brought up the reserves, and I might perhaps have managed one but it was hopeless against two.

He came charging straight at me with the wicked prongs, and though I dodged them like a bullfighter, the first man grabbed my right arm with both of his, intent on getting his chain back.

I swung round toward him in a sort of leap, and with the inside of my metal wrist hit him so hard on the ear and side of the head that the jolt shuddered up through my elbow and upper arm into my shoulder.

For a brief second I saw into his eyes at very close quarters: saw the measure of a hard fighting man, and knew he wasn't going to sit on the ramp of the trailer and wail, as Peter Rammileese was doing.

The crash on the head all the same loosened his grasp enough for me to wrench myself free, and I lunged away from him, still clutching his chain, and turned to look for the pitchfork. The pitchfork man, however, had thrown the fork away and was unfastening his own belt. I jumped toward him while he had both his hands at his waist and delivered to him too the realities of their chosen warfare.

In the half second in which both of the Scots were frozen with shock, I turned and ran for the door, where, somewhere outside, there had to be people and safety and help.

Running on wood shavings felt like running through treacle, and although I got to the door I didn't get through it, because it was a large affair like a chunk of wall which pushed to one side on rollers, and it was fastened shut by a bolt which let down into the floor.

The pitchfork man reached me there before I even got the bolt up, and I found that his belt wasn't leather either, nor grandfather clock innards, but more like the chain for tethering guard dogs. Less sting. More thud.

I still had the stinger, and I swung round low from trying to undo the bolt and wrapped it round his legs. He grunted and rushed at me, and I found the other man right at my back, both of them clutching, and unfortunately I did them no more damage after that, though not for want of trying.

He got his chain back because he was stronger than I was and banged my hand against the wall to loosen my grasp, the other one holding on to me at the same time, and I thought, Well, I'm damned well not going to make it easy for you and you'll have to work for what you want; and I ran round that place, and made them run, round the trailer, and round by the walls and down again to the door at the end.

I picked up the pitchfork and for a while held them off, and threw it at one of them, and missed; and because one can convert pain into many other things so as not to feel it, I felt little except rage and fury and anger, and concentrated on those feelings to make them a shield.

I ended as Chico had, stumbling and swaying and crawling and finally lying motionless on the soft floor. Not so far from the door . . . but a long way from help.

They'll stop now I'm still, I thought; they'll stop in a minute; and they did.

CHAPTER 18

I LAY WITH my face in the wood shavings and listened to them panting as they stood over me, both of them taking great gulps of breath after their exertions.

Peter Rammileese apparently came across to them because I heard his voice from quite close, loaded with spite, mumbling and indistinct.

"Kill him," he said. "Don't stop there. Kill him."

"Kill *him*?" said the man who'd been with Chico. "Are you crazy?" He coughed, dragging in air. "Yon laddie . . ."

"He's broken my jaw."

"Kill him yourself, then. We're not doing it."

"Why not? He's cut your ear half off."

"Grow up, mon." He coughed again. "We'd be grassed inside five minutes. We've been down here too long. Too many people've seen us. And this laddie, he's won money for every punter in Scotland. We'd be inside in a week."

"I want you to kill him," Peter Rammileese said, insisting.

"You're not paying," said the Scot flatly, still breathing heavily. "We've done what was ordered, and that's that. We'll go into your house now for a beer, and after dark we'll dump these two, as arranged, and then we're finished. And we'll go straight up north tonight; we've been down here too long."

They went away, and rolled the door open, and stepped out. I heard their feet on the gritty yard, and the door closing, and the metal grate of the outside bolt, which was to keep horses in, and would do for men.

I moved my head a bit to get my nose clear of the shavings, and looked idly at the color of them so close to my eyes, and simply lay where I was, feeling shapeless, feeling pulped, and stupid, and defeated.

Jelly. A living jelly. Red. On fire. Burning, in a furnace.

There was a lot of romantic rubbish written about fainting from pain, I thought. One absolutely tended not to, because there was no provision for it in nature. The mechanics were missing. There were no fail-safe cut-offs on sensory nerves: they went right on passing the message for as long as the message was there to pass. No other system had evolved, because through millennia it had been unnecessary. It was only man, the most savage of animals, who inflicted pain for its own sake on his fellows.

I thought, I did manage it once, for a short time, after very much too long. I thought, This isn't as bad as that, so I'm going to stay here awake, so I may as well find something to think about. If one couldn't stop the message passing, one could distract the receptors from paying much attention, as in acupuncture; and over the years I'd had a lot of practice.

I thought about a night I'd spent once where I could see a hospital clock. To distract myself from a high state of awfulness, I'd spent the time counting. If I shut my eyes and counted for five minutes, five minutes would be gone: and every time I opened my eyes to check, it was only four minutes; and it had been a very long night. I could do better than that nowadays.

I thought about John Viking in his balloon, and imagined him scudding across the sky, his blue eyes blazing with the glee of breaking safety regulations like bubbles. I thought about Flotilla on the gallops at Newmarket, and winning the Dante Stakes at York. I thought about races I'd ridden in, and won, and lost; and I thought about Louise, a good deal about Louise and four-poster beds.

Afterward I reckoned that Chico and I had laid there without moving for over an hour, though I hadn't any clear idea of it at the time. The first sharp intrusion of the uncomfortable present was the noise of the bolt clicking open on the outside of the door, and the grinding noise as the door itself rolled partially open. They were going to dump us, they'd said, after dark; but it wasn't yet dark.

Footsteps made no sound on that soft surface, so that the first thing I heard was a voice.

"Are you asleep?"

"No," I said.

I shifted my head back a bit and saw little Mark squatting there on his heels, in his pajamas, studying me with six-year-old concern. Beyond him, the door, open enough to let his small body through. On the other side of the door, out in the yard, the Land-Rover.

"Go and see if my friend's awake," I said.

"O.K."

He straightened his legs and went over to Chico, and I'd got myself up from flat to kneeling by the time he returned with his report.

"He's asleep," he said, looking at me anxiously. "Your face is all wet. Are you hot?"

"Does your dad know you're down here?" I said.

"No, he doesn't. I had to go to bed early, but I heard a lot of shouting. I was frightened, I think."

"Where's your dad now?" I said.

"He's in the sitting room with those friends. He's hurt his face and he's bloody angry."

I practically smiled. "Anything else?"

"Mum was saying what did he expect, and they were all having drinks." He thought a bit. "One of the friends said his eardrum was burst."

"If I were you," I said, "I'd go straight back to bed and not let them catch you out here. Otherwise your dad might be bloody angry with you too, and that wouldn't be much fun, I shouldn't think."

He shook his head.

"Goodnight, then," I said.

"Good night."

"And leave the door open," I said. "I'll shut it."

"All right."

He gave me a trusting and slightly conspiratorial smile, and crept out of the doorway to sneak back to bed.

I got to my feet and staggered around a bit, and made it to the door.

The Land-Rover stood there about ten feet away. If the keys were in it, I thought, why wait to be dumped?

Ten steps. Leaned against the gray-green bodywork, and looked through the glass.

Keys. In the ignition.

I went back into the riding school and over to Chico, and knelt beside him because it was a lot less demanding than bending.

"Come on," I said. "Wake up. Time to go."

He groaned.

"Chico, you've got to walk. I can't carry you."

He opened his eyes. Still confused, I thought, but a great deal better.

"Get up," I said urgently. "We can get out, if you'll try."

"Sid . . ."

"Yeah," I said. "Come on."

"Go away. I can't."

"Yes, you damned well can. You just say 'Sod the buggers,' and it comes easy."

It came harder than I'd thought, but I half lugged him to his feet and put my arm round his waist, and we meandered waveringly to the door like a pair of drunken lovers.

Through the door, and across to the Land-Rover. No furious yells of discovery from the house; and as the sitting room was at the far end of it, with a bit of luck they wouldn't even hear the engine start.

I shoveled Chico onto the front seat and shut the door quietly, and went round to the driving side.

Land-Rovers, I thought disgustedly, were made for left-handed people. All the controls, except the indicators, were on that side; and whether it was because I myself was weak, or the battery was flat, or I'd damaged the machinery by using it as a club, the fingers of my left hand would scarcely move.

I swore to myself and did everything with my right hand, which meant twisting, which would have hurt if I hadn't been in such a hurry.

Started the engine. Released the brake. Shoved the gear lever into first. Did the rest thankfully with my feet, and set off. Not the smoothest start ever, but enough. The Land-Rover rolled to the gate, and I turned out in the opposite direction from London, thinking instinctively that if they found we'd gone and chased after us, it would be toward London that they would go in pursuit.

The "sod the buggers" mentality lasted me well for two or three miles and through some dicey one-handed gear changing, but suffered a severe setback when I looked at the petrol gauge and found it pointing to nearly empty.

The question of where we were going had to be sorted out, and immediately; and before I'd decided, we came round a bend and found in front of us a large garage, still open, with attendants by the pumps. Hardly believing it,

I swerved untidily into the forecourt, and came to a jerking halt by the two-star.

Money in right-hand pocket, along with car keys and handkerchief. I pulled all of them out in a handful and separated the crumpled notes. Opened the window beside me. Gave the attendant who appeared the money and said I'd have that much petrol.

He was young, a school kid, and he looked at me curiously.

"You all right?"

"It's hot," I said, and wiped my face with the handkerchief. Some wood shavings fell out of my hair. I must indeed have looked odd.

The boy merely nodded, however, and stuck the petrol nozzle into the Land-Rover's filling place, which was right beside the driver's door. He looked across me to Chico, who was half lying on the front seat with his eyes open.

"What's wrong with him, then?"

"Drunk," I said.

He looked as if he thought we both were, but he simply finished the filling, and replaced the cap, and turned away to attend to the next customer. I went again through the tedious business of starting right-handedly, and pulled out onto the road. After a mile I turned off the main road into a side road, and went round a bend or two, and stopped.

"What's happening?" Chico said.

I looked at his still woozy eyes. Decide where to go, I thought. Decide for Chico. For myself, I already knew. I'd decided when I found I could drive without hitting things, and at the garage which had turned up so luckily, and when I'd had enough money for the petrol, and when I hadn't asked the boy to get us help in the shape of policemen and doctors.

Hospitals and bureaucracy and questions and being prodded about: all the things I most hated. I wasn't going near any of them, unless I had to for Chico.

"Where did we go today?" I said.

After a while he said, "Newmarket."

"What's twice eight?"

Pause. "Sixteen."

I sat in a weak sort of gratitude for his returning wits, waiting for strength to go on. The impetus which had got me into the Land-Rover and as far as that spot had ebbed away and left room for a return of fire and jelly. Power would come back, I thought, if I waited. Stamina and energy always came in cycles, so that what one couldn't do one minute, one could the next.

"I'm burning," Chico said.

"Mm."

"That was too much."

I didn't answer. He moved on the seat and tried to sit upright, and I saw the full awareness flood into his face. He shut his eyes tight and said "Jesus," and after a while he looked at me through slits, and said, "You too?"

"Mm."

The long hot day was drawing to dusk. If I didn't get started, I thought vaguely, I wouldn't get anywhere.

The chief practical difficulty was that driving a Land-Rover with one hand was risky, if not downright dangerous, as I had to let go of the steering wheel and lean to the left every time I changed gear: and the answer to that was to get the left-hand fingers to grip the knob just once, and tightly, so that I could switch off the current, and the hand would stay there on the gear lever, unmoving, until further notice.

I did that. Then I switched on the side lights, and the headlights, dipped. Then the engine. I'd give anything for a drink, I thought, and set off on the long drive home.

"Where are we going?" Chico said.

"To the Admiral's."

I had taken the southern route round Sevenoaks and Kingston and Colnbrook, and there was the M-4 motorway stretch to do, and the cross at Maidenhead to the M-40 motorway just north of Marlow, and then round the north Oxford ring road and the last leg to Aynsford.

Land-Rovers weren't built for comfort and jolted the passengers at the best of times. Chico groaned now and then, and cursed, and said he wasn't getting into a mess like that again, ever. I stopped twice briefly on the way from weakness and general misery, but there wasn't much traffic, and we rolled into Charles's drive in three and a half hours, not too bad for the course.

I switched the Land-Rover off and my left hand on, and couldn't get the fingers to move. That was all it needed, I thought despairingly, the final humiliation of that bloody evening, if I had to detach myself from the socket end and leave the electric part of me stuck to the gears. Why, *why*, couldn't I have two hands, like everyone else?

"Don't struggle," Chico said, "and you'll do it easy."

I gave a cough that was somewhere between a laugh and a sob, and the fingers opened a fraction, and the hand fell off the knob.

"Told you," he said.

I laid my right arm across the steering wheel and put my head down on that, and felt spent and depressed . . . and punished. And someone, somehow, had to raise the strength to go in to tell Charles we were there.

He solved that himself by coming out to us in his dressing gown, the light streaming out behind him from his open front door. The first I knew, he was standing by the window of the Land-Rover, looking in.

"Sid?" he said incredulously. "Is it you?"

I dragged my head off the steering wheel and opened my eyes, and said, "Yeah."

"It's after midnight," he said.

I got a smile at least into my voice. "You said I could come any time."

AN HOUR LATER, Chico was upstairs in bed and I sat sideways on the gold sofa, shoes off, feet up, as I often did.

Charles came into the drawing room and said the doctor had finished with Chico and was ready for me, and I said no, thanks very much, and tell him to go home.

"He'll give you some knockout stuff, like Chico."

"Yes, and that's exactly what I don't want, and I hope he was careful about Chico's concussion, with those drugs."

"You told him yourself about six times, when he came." He paused. "He's waiting for you."

"I mean it, Charles," I said. "I want to think. I want just to sit here and think, so would you please say goodbye to the doctor and go to bed?"

"No," he said. "You can't."

"I certainly can. In fact, I have to, while I still feel . . ." I stopped. While I still feel *flayed*, I thought: but one couldn't say that.

"It's not sensible."

"No. The whole thing isn't sensible. That's the point. So go away and let me work it out."

I had noticed before that sometimes when the body was injured the mind cleared sharply and worked for a while with acute perception. It was a time to use, if one wanted to; not to waste.

"Have you seen Chico's skin?" he said.

"Often," I said flippantly.

"Is yours in the same state?"

"I haven't looked."

"You're exasperating."

"Yeah," I said. "Go to bed."

WHEN HE'D GONE I sat there, deliberately and vividly remembering in mind and body the biting horror I'd worked so hard to blank out.

It had been too much, as Chico said.

Too much.

Why?

CHARLES CAME DOWNSTAIRS again at six o'clock, in his dressing gown, and with his most impassive expression.

"You're still there, then," he said.

"Yuh."

"Coffee?"

"Tea," I said.

He went and made it, and brought two big steaming mugs, naval fashion. He put mine on the table that stood along the back of the sofa, and sat with his in an armchair. The empty-looking eyes were switched steadily my way.

"Well?" he said.

I rubbed my forehead. "When you look at me . . ." I said, hesitatingly. "Usually, I mean. Not now. When you look at me, what do you see?"

"You know what I see."

"Do you see a lot of fears and self-doubts, and feelings of shame and uselessness and inadequacy?"

"Of course not." He seemed to find the question amusing, and then sipped the scalding tea, and said more seriously, "You never show feelings like that."

"No one does," I said. "Everyone has an outside and an inside, and the two can be quite different."

"Is that just a general observation?"

"No." I picked up the mug of tea, and blew across the steaming surface. "To myself, I'm a jumble of uncertainty and fear and stupidity. And to others . . . Well, what happened to Chico and me last evening was because of the way others see us." I took a tentative taste. As always when Charles made it, the tea was strong enough to rasp the fur off your tongue. I quite liked it, sometimes. I said, "We've been lucky, since we started this investigating thing. In other words, the jobs we've done have been comparatively easy, and we've been getting a reputation for being successful, and the reputation has been getting bigger than the reality."

"Which is, of course," Charles said dryly, "that you're a pair of dim-witted layabouts."

"You know what I mean."

"Yes, I do. Tom Ullaston rang me here yesterday morning, to arrange about stewards for Epsom, he said, but I gathered it was mostly to tell me what he thought about you, which was, roughly speaking, that if you had still been a jockey it would be a pity."

"It would be great," I said, sighing.

"So someone lammed into you and Chico yesterday to stop you chalking up another success?"

"Not exactly," I said.

I told him what I had spent the night sorting out; and his tea got cold.

When I'd finished he sat for quite a while in silence, simply staring at me in his best give-away-nothing manner.

Then he said, "It sounds as if yesterday evening was . . . terrible."

"Well, yes, it was."

More silence. Then, "So what next?"

"I was wondering," I said diffidently, "if you'd do one or two jobs for me today, because I . . . er . . ."

"Of course," he said. "What?"

"It's your day for London. Thursday. So could you bear to drive the Land Rover up instead of the Rolls, and swap it for my car?"

"If you like," he said, not looking enchanted.

"The battery charger's in it, in my suitcase," I said.

"Of course I'll go."

"Before that, in Oxford, could you pick up some photographs? They're of Nicholas Ashe."

"Sid!"

I nodded. "We found him. There's a letter in my car too, with his new address. A begging letter, same as before."

He shook his head at the foolishness of Nicholas Ashe. "Any more jobs?"

"Two, I'm afraid. The first's in London, and easy. But as for the other . . . would you go to Tunbridge Wells?"

When I told him why, he said he would, even though it meant canceling his afternoon's board meeting.

"And would you lend me your camera, because mine's in the car . . . and a clean shirt?"

"In that order?"

"Yes, please."

Wishing I didn't have to move for a couple of thousand years, I slowly unstuck myself from the sofa some time later and went upstairs, with Charles's
camera, to see Chico.

He was lying on his side, his eyes dull and staring vaguely into space, the
effect of the drugs wearing off. Sore enough to protest wearily when I told
him what I wanted to photograph.

"Sod off."

"Think about barmaids."

I peeled back the blanket and sheet covering him and took pictures of the
visible damage, front and back. Of the invisible damage there was no measure. I put the covers back again.

"Sorry," I said.

He didn't answer, and I wondered whether I was really apologizing for
disturbing him at that moment or more basically for having tangled his life
in mine, with such dire results. A hiding to nothing was what he'd said we
were on with those syndicates, and he'd been right.

I took the camera out onto the landing and gave it to Charles.

"Ask for blown-up prints by tomorrow morning," I said. "Tell him it's for
a police case."

"But you said no police . . ." Charles said.

"Yes, but if he thinks it's already for the police, he won't go trotting
round to them when he sees what he's printing."

"I suppose it's never occurred to you," Charles said, handing over a clean
shirt, "that it's your view of you that's wrong, and Thomas Ullaston's that's
right?"

I TELEPHONED TO Louise and told her I couldn't make it that day after all.
Something's come up, I said, in the classic evasive excuse, and she answered
with the disillusion it merited.

"Never mind, then."

"I do mind, actually," I said. "So how about a week tomorrow? What are
you doing after that for a few days?"

"Days?"

"And nights."

Her voice cheered up considerably. "Research for a thesis."

"What subject?"

"Clouds and roses and stars, their variations and frequency in the life of your average liberated female."

"Oh, Louise," I said, "I'll . . . er . . . help you all I can."

She laughed and hung up, and I went to my room and took off my dusty, stained, sweaty shirt. Looked at my reflection briefly in the mirror and got no joy from it. Put on Charles's smooth Sea Island cotton and lay on the bed. I lay on one side, like Chico, and felt what Chico felt; and at one point or other, went to sleep.

In the evening I went down and sat on the sofa, as before, to wait for Charles, but the first person who came was Jenny.

She walked in, saw me, and was immediately annoyed. Then she took a second look, and said, "Oh, no, not again."

I said merely, "Hello."

"What is it this time? Ribs again?"

"Nothing."

"I know you too well." She sat at the other end of the sofa, beyond my feet. "What are you doing here?"

"Waiting for your father."

She looked at me moodily. "I'm going to sell that flat in Oxford," she said.

"Are you?"

"I don't like it any more. Louise McInnes has left, and it reminds me too much of Nicky. . . ."

After a pause I said, "Do I remind you of Nicky?"

With a flash of surprise she said, "Of course not." And then, more slowly, "But he . . ." She stopped.

"I saw him," I said. "Three days ago, in Bristol. And he looks like me, a bit."

She was stunned, and speechless.

"Didn't you realize?" I said.

She shook her head.

"You were trying to go back," I said. "To what we had at the beginning."

"It's not true." But her voice said that she saw it was. She had even told me so, more or less, the evening I'd come to Aynsford to start finding Ashe.

"Where will you live?" I said.

"What do you care?"

I supposed I would always care, to some extent, which was my problem, not hers.

"How did you find him?" she said.

"He's a fool."

She didn't like that. The look of enmity showed where her instinctive preference still lay.

"He's living with another girl," I said.

She stood up furiously, and I remembered a bit late that I really didn't want her to touch me.

"Are you telling me that to be beastly?" she demanded.

"I'm telling you so you'll get him out of your system before he goes on trial and to jail. You're going to be damned unhappy if you don't."

"I hate you," she said.

"That's not hate, that's injured pride."

"How dare you!"

"Jenny," I said, "I'll tell you plainly, I'd do a lot for you. I've loved you a long time, and I do care what happens to you. It's no good finding Ashe and getting him convicted of fraud instead of you, if you don't wake up and see him for what he is. I want to make you angry with him. For your own sake."

"You won't manage it," she said fiercely.

"Go away," I said.

"What?"

"Go away. I'm tired."

She stood there looking as much bewildered as annoyed, and at that moment Charles came back.

"Hello," he said, taking a disapproving look at the general atmosphere. "Hello, Jenny."

She went over and kissed his cheek, from long habit.

"Has Sid told you he's found your friend Ashe?" he said.

"He couldn't wait."

Charles was carrying a large brown envelope. He opened it, pulled out the contents, and handed them to me: the three photographs of Ashe, which had come out well, and the new begging letter.

Jenny took two jerky strides and looked down at the uppermost photograph.

"Her name is Elizabeth More," I said slowly. "His real name is Norris Abbott. She calls him Ned."

The picture, the third one I'd taken, showed them laughing and entwined, looking into each other's eyes, the happiness in their faces sharply in focus.

Silently, I gave Jenny the letter. She opened it and looked at the signature at the bottom, and went very pale. I felt sorry for her, but she wouldn't have wanted me to say so.

She swallowed, and handed the letter to her father

"All right," she said after a pause. "All right. Give it to the police."

She sat down again on the sofa with a sort of emotional exhaustion slackening her limbs and curving her spine. Her eyes turned my way.

"Do you want me to thank you?" she said.

I shook my head.

"I suppose one day I will."

"There's no need."

With a flash of anger she said, "You're doing it again."

"Doing what?"

"Making me feel guilty. I know I'm pretty beastly to you sometimes. Because you make me feel guilty, and I want to get back at you for that."

"Guilty for what?" I said.

"For leaving you. For our marriage going wrong."

"But it wasn't your fault," I protested.

"No, it was yours. Your selfishness, your pigheadedness. Your bloody determination to win. You'll do anything to win. You always have to win. You're so hard. Hard on yourself. Ruthless to yourself. I couldn't live with it. No one could live with it. Girls want men who'll come to them for comfort. Who say, I need you, help me, comfort me, kiss away my troubles. But you . . . you can't do that. You always build a wall and deal with your own troubles in silence, like you're doing now. And don't tell me you aren't hurt, because I've seen it in you too often, and you can't disguise the way you hold your head, and this time it's very bad, I can see it. But you'd never say, would you, Jenny, hold me, help me, I want to cry?"

She stopped, and in the following silence made a sad little gesture with her hand.

"You see?" she said. "You can't say it, can you?"

After another long pause I said, "No."

"Well," she said, "I need a husband who's not so rigidly in control of himself. I want someone who's not afraid of emotion, someone uninhibited, someone weaker. I can't live in the sort of purgatory you make of life for yourself. I want someone who can break down. I want . . . an ordinary man."

She got up from the sofa and bent over and kissed my forehead.

"It's taken me a long time to see all that," she said. "And to say it. But I'm glad I have." She turned to her father. "Tell Mr. Quayle I'm cured of

Nicky, and I won't be obstructive from now on. I think I'll go back to the flat now. I feel a lot better."

She went with Charles toward the door, and then paused and looked back, and said, "Goodbye, Sid."

"Goodbye," I said; and I wanted to say, Jenny, hold me, help me, I want to cry; but I couldn't.

CHAPTER 19

CHARLES DROVE HIMSELF and me to London the following day in the Rolls, with me still in a fairly droopy state and Charles saying we should put it off until Monday.

"No," I said.

"But even for you this is daunting . . . and you're dreading it."

Dread, I thought, was something I felt for Trevor Deansgate, who wasn't going to hold off just because I had other troubles. Dread was too strong a word for the purpose of the present journey; and reluctance too weak. Aversion, perhaps.

"It's better done today," I said.

He didn't argue. He knew I was right, otherwise he wouldn't have been persuaded to drive me.

He dropped me at the door of the Jockey Club in Portman Square, and went and parked the car, and walked back again. I waited for him downstairs, and we went up in the lift together: he in his city suit, and I in trousers and a clean shirt, but no tie and no jacket. The weather was still hot. A whole week of it we'd had, and it seemed that everyone except me was bronzed and healthy.

There was a looking glass in the lift. My face stared out of it, grayish and hollow-eyed, with a red streak of a healing cut slanting across near the hairline on my forehead, and a blackish bruise on the side of my jaw. Apart from that I looked calmer, less damaged, and more normal than I felt, which was a relief. If I concentrated, I should be able to keep it that way.

We went straight to Sir Thomas Ullaston's office, where he was waiting for us. Shook hands, and all that.

To me he said, "Your father-in-law told me on the telephone yesterday that you have something disturbing to tell me. He wouldn't say what it was."

"No, not on the telephone," I agreed.

"Sit down, then. Charles . . . Sid . . ." He offered chairs, and himself perched on the edge of his big desk. "Very important, Charles said. So here I am, as requested. Fire away."

"It's about syndicates," I said. I began to tell him what I'd told Charles, but after a few minutes he stopped me.

"No. Look, Sid, this is not going to end here simply between me and you, is it? So I think we must have some of the others in, to hear what you're saying."

I would have preferred him not to, but he summoned the whole heavy mob; the Controller of the Secretariat, the Head of Administration, the Secretary to the Stewards, the Licensing Officer, who dealt with the registration of owners, and the Head of Rules Department, whose province was disciplinary action. They came into the room and filled up the chairs, and for the second time in four days turned their serious civilized faces my way, to listen to the outcome of an investigation.

It was because of Tuesday, I thought, that they would listen to me now. Trevor Deansgate had given me an authority I wouldn't otherwise have had, in that company, in that room.

I said, "I was asked by Lord Friarly, whom I used to ride for, to look into four syndicates, which he headed. The horses were running in his colors, and he wasn't happy about how they were doing. That wasn't surprising, as their starting prices were going up and down like yo-yos, with results to match. Lord Friarly felt he was being used as a front for some right wicked goings on, and he didn't like it."

I paused, knowing I was using a light form of words because the next bit was going to fall like lead.

"On the same day, at Kempton, Commander Wainwright asked me to look into the same four syndicates, which I must say had been manipulated so thoroughly that it was a wonder they weren't a public scandal already."

The smooth faces registered surprise. Sid Halley was not the natural person for Commander Wainwright to ask to look into syndicates, which were the normal business of the Security Service.

"Lucas Wainwright told me that all four syndicates had been vetted and O.K.'d by Eddy Keith, and he asked me to find out if there was any unwelcome significance in that."

For all that I put it at its least dramatic, the response from the cohorts was one of considerable shock. Racing might suffer from its attraction for knaves and rogues, as it always had, but corruption within the headquarters itself? Never.

I said, "I came here to Portman Square to make notes about the syndicates, which I took from Eddy Keith's files, without his knowledge. I wrote the notes in Lucas's office, and he told me about a man he'd sent out on the same errand as myself, six months ago. That man, Mason, had been attacked, and dumped in the streets of Tunbridge Wells, with appalling head injuries, caused by kicks. He was a vegetable, and blind. Lucas told me also that the man who had formed the syndicates, and who had been doing the manipulating, was a Peter Rammileese, who lived at Tunbridge Wells."

The faces were all frowningly intent.

"After that I . . . er . . . went away for a week, and I also lost the notes, so I had to come back here and do them again, and Eddy Keith discovered I'd been seeing his files, and complained to you, Sir Thomas, if you remember?"

"That's right. I told him not to fuss."

There were a few smiles all around, and a general loosening of tension. Inside me, a wilting fatigue.

"Go on, Sid," Sir Thomas said.

Go on, I thought. I wished I felt less weak, less shaky, less continuously sore. Had to go on, now I'd started. Get on with it. Go on.

I said, "Well, Chico Barnes, who was here with me on Tuesday"—they nodded—"Chico and I, we went down to Tunbridge Wells, to see Peter Rammileese. He was away, as it happened. His wife and little son were there, but the wife had fallen off a horse and Chico went to the hospital with her, taking the little boy, which left me, and an open house. So I . . . er . . . looked around."

Their faces said, "Tut-tut," but none of their voices.

"I looked for any possible direct tie-in with Eddy, but actually the whole place was abnormally tidy and looked suspiciously prepared for any searches any tax men might make."

They smiled slightly.

"Lucas warned me at the beginning that as what I was doing was unofficial, I couldn't be paid, but that he'd give me help instead, if I needed it. So I asked him to help me with the business of Trevor Deansgate, and he did."

"In what way, Sid?"

"I asked him to write to Henry Thrace, to make sure that the Jockey Club would hear at once if Gleaner died, or Zingaloo, and to tell me, so that I could get a really thorough post-mortem done."

They all nodded. They remembered.

"And then," I said, "I found Peter Rammileese on my heels with two very large men who looked just the sort to kick people's heads in and leave them blinded in Tunbridge Wells."

No smiles.

"I dodged them that time, and I spent the next week rolling around England in unpredictable directions so that no one could really have known where to find me, and during that time, when I was chiefly learning about Gleaner and heart valves and so on, I was also told that the two big men had been imported especially from Scotland for some particular job with Peter Rammileese's syndicates. There was also a rumor of someone high up in the Security Service who would fix things for crooks, if properly paid."

They were shocked again.

"Who told you that, Sid?" Sir Thomas asked.

"Someone reliable," I said, thinking that maybe they wouldn't think a suspended jockey like Jacksy as reliable as I did.

"Go on."

"I wasn't really making much progress with those syndicates, but Peter Rammileese apparently thought I was, because he and his two men laid an ambush for Chico and me, the day before yesterday."

Sir Thomas reflected. "I thought that was the day you were going to Newmarket with Lucas to see the Caspars. The day after you were here telling us about Trevor Deansgate."

"Yes, we did go to Newmarket. And I made the mistake of leaving my car in plain view near here all day. The two men were waiting beside it when we got back. And . . . er . . . Chico and I got abducted, and where we landed up was at Peter Rammileese's place at Tunbridge Wells."

Sir Thomas frowned. The others listened to the unemotional relating of what they must have realized had been a fairly violent occurrence with a calm understanding that such things could happen.

There had seldom been, I thought, a more silently attentive audience.

I said, "They gave Chico and me a pretty rough time, but we did get out of there, owing to Peter Rammileese's little boy opening a door for us by chance, and we didn't end up in Tunbridge Wells streets; we got to my father-in-law's house near Oxford."

They all looked at Charles, who nodded.

I took a deep breath. "At about that point," I said, "I . . . er . . . began to see things the other way round."

"How do you mean, Sid?"

"Until then, I thought the two Scotsmen were supposed to be preventing us from finding what we were looking for in those syndicates."

They nodded. Of course.

"But supposing it was exactly the reverse . . . Supposing I'd been pointed at those syndicates in order to be led to the ambush. Suppose the ambush itself was the whole aim of the exercise."

Silence.

I had come to the hard bit, and needed the reserves I didn't have, of staying power, of will. I was aware of Charles sitting steadfastly beside me, trying to give me his strength.

I could feel myself shaking. I kept my voice flat and cold, saying the things I didn't like saying, that had to be said.

"I was shown an enemy, who was Peter Rammileese. I was given a reason for being beaten up, which was the syndicates. I was fed the expectation of it, through the man Mason. I was being given a background to what was going to happen; a background I would accept."

Total silence and blank, uncomprehending expressions.

I said, "If someone had savagely attacked me out of the blue, I wouldn't have been satisfied until I had found out who and why. So I thought, supposing someone wanted to attack me, but it was imperative that I didn't find out who or why. If I was given a false who, and a false why, I would believe in those, and not look any further."

One or two very slight nods.

"I did believe in that who and that why for a while," I said. "But the attack, when it came, seemed out of all proportion . . . and from something one of our attackers said, I gathered it was not Peter Rammileese himself who was paying them, but someone else."

Silence.

"So after we had reached the Admiral's house, I began thinking, and I thought, if the attack itself was the point, and it was not Peter Rammileese who had arranged it, then who had? Once I saw it that way, there was only one possible who. The person who had laid the trail for me to follow."

The faces began to go stiff.

I said, "It was Lucas himself who set us up."

They broke up into loud, jumbled, collective protest, moving in their chairs with embarrassment, not meeting my eye, not wanting to look at someone who was so mistaken, so deluded, so pitiably ridiculous.

"No, Sid, really," Sir Thomas said. "We've a great regard for you"—the others looked as if the great regard was now definitely past tense—"but you can't say things like that."

"As a matter of fact," I said slowly, "I would much rather have stayed

away and not said it. I won't tell you any more, if you don't want to hear it."
I rubbed my fingers over my forehead from sheer lack of inner energy, and
Charles half made, and then stopped himself from making, a protective ges-
ture of support.

Sir Thomas looked at Charles and then at me, and whatever he saw was
enough to calm him from incredulity to puzzlement.

"All right," he said soberly. "We'll listen."

The others all looked as if they didn't want to, but if the Senior Steward
was willing, it was enough.

I said, with deep weariness and no satisfaction, "To understand the *why*
part, it's necessary to look at what's been happening during the past months;
during the time Chico and I have been doing . . . what we have. As you yourself said, Sir Thomas, we've been successful. Lucky . . . tackling pretty easy
problems . . . but mostly sorting them out. To the extent that a few villains
have tried to stop us dead as soon as we've appeared on the skyline."

The disbelief still showed like snow in July, but at least they seemed to
understand that too much success invited retaliation. The uncomfortable
shiftings in the chairs grew gradually still.

"We've been prepared for it, more or less," I said. "In some cases it's even
been useful, because it's shown us we're nearing the sensitive spot. . . . But
what we usually get is a couple of rent-a-thug bullies in or out of funny
masks, giving us a warning bash or two and telling us to lay off. Which advice," I added wryly, "we have never taken."

They had all begun looking at me again, even if sideways.

"So then people begin to stop thinking of me as a jockey, and gradually see that what Chico and I are doing isn't really the joke it seemed at first.
And we get what you might call the Jockey Club Seal of Approval, and all
of a sudden, to the really big crooks, we appear as a continuing, permanent
menace."

"Do you have proof of that, Sid?" Sir Thomas said.

Proof . . . Short of getting Trevor Deansgate in there to repeat his threat
before witnesses, I had no proof. I said, "I've had threats . . . only threats, before this."

A pause. No one said anything, so I went on.

"I understand on good authority," I said, with faint amusement, "that
there would be some reluctance to solve things by actually killing us, as
people who had won money in the past on my winners would rise up in wrath
and grass on the murderers."

Some tentative half smiles amid general dislike of such melodrama.

"Anyway, such a murder would tend to bring in its trail precisely the investigation it was designed to prevent."

They were happier with that.

"So the next best thing is an ultimate deterrent. One that would so sicken Chico and me that we'd go and sell brushes instead. Something to stop us investigating anything else, ever again."

It seemed all of a sudden as if they did understand what I was saying. The earlier, serious attention came right back. I thought it might be safe to mention Lucas again, and when I did there was none of the former vigorous reaction.

"If you could just imagine for a moment that there *is* someone in the Security Service who can be bribed, and that it is the Director himself, would you, if you were Lucas, be entirely pleased to see an independent investigator making progress in what had been exclusively your territory? Would you, if you were such a man, be pleased to see Sid Halley right here in the Jockey Club being congratulated by the Senior Steward and being given carte blanche to operate wherever he liked throughout racing?"

They stared.

"Would you, perhaps, be afraid that one of these days Sid Halley would stumble across something you couldn't afford for him to find out? And might you not, at that point, decide to remove the danger of it once and for all? Like putting weed-killer on a nettle before it stings you."

Charles cleared his throat. "A preemptive strike," he said smoothly, "might appeal to a retired commander."

They remembered Charles had been an admiral, and looked thoughtful.

"Lucas is only a man," I said. "The title Director of Security sounds pretty grand, but the Security Service isn't that big, is it? I mean, there are only about thirty people in it full time, aren't there, over the whole country?"

They nodded.

"I don't suppose the pay is a fortune. One hears about bent policemen from time to time, who've taken bribes from crooks. Well . . . Lucas is constantly in contact with people who might say, for instance, how about a quiet thousand in readies, Commander, to smother my little bit of trouble?"

The faces were shocked.

"It does happen, you know," I said mildly. "Backhanders are a flourishing industry. I agree that you wouldn't want the head of racing security to be shutting his eyes to skulduggery, but it's more a breach of trust than anything aggressively wicked."

What he'd done to Chico and me was indeed aggressively wicked, but that wasn't the point I wanted to make.

"What I'm saying," I said, "is that in the wider context of the everyday immoral world, Lucas's dishonesty is no great matter."

They looked doubtful, but that was better than negative shakes of the head. If they could be persuaded to think of Lucas as a smallish-scale sinner, they would believe more easily that he'd done what he had.

"If you start from the idea of a deterrent," I said, "you see everything from the other side." I stopped. The inner exhaustion didn't. I'd like to sleep for a week, I thought.

"Go on, Sid."

"Well . . ." I sighed. "Lucas had to take the slight risk of pointing me at something he was involved in, because he needed a background he could control. He must have been badly shocked when Lord Friarly said he'd asked me to look into those syndicates, but if he had already toyed with the idea of getting rid of me, I'd guess he saw at that point how to do it."

One or two of the heads nodded sharply in comprehension.

"Lucas must have been sure that a little surface digging wouldn't get me anywhere near him—which it didn't—but he minimized the risk by specifically directing my attention to Eddy Keith. It was safe to set me investigating Eddy's involvement with the shady side of the syndicates, because of course he wasn't involved. I could look forever, and find nothing." I paused. "I don't think I was supposed to have much time to find out anything at all. I think that catching us took much longer than was intended in the original plan."

Catching us . . . catching me. They'd have taken me alone, but both had been better for them . . . and far worse for me. . . .

"Took much longer? How do you mean?" Sir Thomas said.

Concentrate, I thought. Get on with it.

"From Lucas's point of view, I was very slow," I said. "I was working on the Gleaner thing, and I didn't do anything at all about the syndicates for a week after he asked me. Then directly I'd been told about Peter Rammileese and Mason, and could have been expected to go down to Tunbridge Wells, I went away somewhere else entirely, for another week; during which time Lucas rang Chico four times to ask him where I was."

Silent attention, as before.

"When I came back, I'd lost the notes, so I did them again in Lucas's office, and I told him Chico and I would go down to Peter Rammileese's place the following day, Saturday. I think it's likely that if we had done so, the . . .

er . . . deterring would have been done then, but in fact we went the same afternoon that I'd been talking to Lucas, on the Friday, and Peter Rammileese
wasn't there."

Weren't they all thirsty? I wondered. Where was the coffee? My mouth
was dry, and a good deal of me hurt.

"It was on that Friday morning that I asked Lucas to write to Henry
Thrace. I also asked him—entreated him, really—not to mention my name at
all in connection with Gleaner, as it might get me killed."

A lot of frowns awaited an explanation.

"Well . . . Trevor Deansgate had warned me in those sort of terms to stop
investigating those horses."

Sir Thomas managed to raise his eyebrows and imply a frown at one and
the same time.

"Are those the threats you mentioned before?" he said.

"Yes, and he repeated them when you . . . er . . . introduced us, in your
box at Chester."

"Good God."

"I wanted to get the investigation of Gleaner done by the Jockey Club so
that Trevor Deansgate wouldn't know it had anything to do with me."

"You did take those threats seriously," Sir Thomas said thoughtfully.

I swallowed. "They were . . . seriously given."

"I see," said Sir Thomas, although he didn't. "Go on."

"I didn't actually tell Lucas about the threats themselves," I said. "I just
begged him not to tie me in with Gleaner. And within days, he had told
Henry Thrace that it was I, not the Jockey Club, who really wanted to know
if Gleaner died. At the time I reckoned that he had just been careless or for-
getful, but now I think he did it on purpose. Anything which might get me
killed was to him a bonus, even if he didn't see how it could do."

They looked doubtful. Doubts were possible.

"So then Peter Rammileese—or Lucas—traced me to my father-in-law's
house, and on the Monday Peter Rammileese and the two Scots followed me
from there to a horse show, where they had a shot at abduction, which didn't
come off. After that I kept out of their way for eight more days, which must
have frustrated them no end."

The faces waited attentively.

"During that time I learned that Peter Rammileese was manipulating not
four, but nearer twenty syndicates, bribing trainers and jockeys wholesale. It
was then also that I learned about the bribable top man in the Security Ser-

vice who was turning a blind eye to the goings on, and I regret to say I thought it must be Eddy Keith."

"I suppose," Sir Thomas said, "that that was understandable."

"So anyway, on Tuesday Chico and I came here, and Lucas at last knew where I was. He asked to come to Newmarket with us on Wednesday, and he took us there in his own super four-liter air-conditioned highly expensive Mercedes, and although he's usually so keen to get on with the next thing, he wasted hours doing nothing in Newmarket, during which time I now think he was in fact arranging and waiting for the ambush to be properly set up, so that this time there should be no mistakes. Then he drove us to where the Scots were waiting for us, and we walked straight into it. The Scots did the special job they had been imported for, which was deterring Chico and me, and I heard one of them tell Peter Rammileese that now that they had done what was ordered, they were going north straight away, they'd been down in the south too long."

Sir Thomas was looking slightly strained.

"Is that all, Sid?"

"No. There's the matter of Mason."

Charles stirred beside me, uncrossing and recrossing his legs.

"I asked my father-in-law to go to Tunbridge Wells yesterday, to ask about Mason."

Charles said, in his most impressive drawl, "Sid asked me to see if Mason existed. I saw the police fellows in Tunbridge Wells. Very helpful, all of them. No one called Mason, or anything else for that matter, has been found kicked near to death and blinded in their streets, ever."

"Lucas told me about Mason's case in great detail," I said. "He was very convincing, and of course I believed him. But have any of you ever heard of anyone called Mason who was employed by the Security Service, that was so badly injured?"

They silently, bleakly, shook their heads. I didn't tell them that I'd finally had doubts about Mason because there was no file for him in "Personnel." Even in a good cause, our breaking and entering wouldn't please them.

A certain amount of gloom had settled on their faces, but there were also questions they wanted to ask. Sir Thomas put their doubts into words.

"There's one obvious flaw in your reverse view of things, Sid, and that is that this deterrent . . . hasn't deterred you."

After a pause I said, "I don't know that it hasn't. Neither Chico nor I could go on, if it meant . . . if we thought . . . anything like that would happen again."

"Like exactly what, Sid?"

I didn't reply. I could feel Charles glancing my way in his best noncommittal manner, and it was he, eventually, who got quietly to his feet, and walked across the room, and gave Sir Thomas the envelope which contained the pictures of Chico.

"It was a chain," I said matter-of-factly.

They passed the photographs around in silence. I didn't particularly look to see what they were thinking; I was just hoping they wouldn't ask what I knew they would; and Sir Thomas said it baldly. "Was this done to you as well?"

I reluctantly nodded.

"Will you take your shirt off, then, Sid?"

"Look," I said, "what does it matter? I'm not laying any charges of assault or grievous bodily harm, or anything like that. There's going to be no police, no court case, nothing. I've been through all that once, as you know, and I'm not, absolutely not, doing it again. This time there's to be no noise. All that's necessary is to tell Lucas I know what's been happening, and if you thought it right, to get him to resign. There's nothing to be gained by anything else. You don't want any public scandal. It would be harmful to racing as a whole."

"Yes, but . . ."

"There's Peter Rammileese," I said. "Perhaps Eddy Keith might really sort out those syndicates now. It would only get Rammileese deeper in if he boasted that he'd bribed Lucas, so I shouldn't think he would. I doubt if he'd talk about Chico and me, either."

Except perhaps, I thought sardonically, to complain that I'd hit him very hard.

"What about the two men from Glasgow?" Sir Thomas said. "Are they just to get away with it?"

"I'd rather that than go to court again as a victim," I said. I half smiled. "You might say that the business over my hand successfully deterred me from that sort of thing for the rest of my life."

A certain amount of urbane relief crept into both the faces and the general proceedings.

"However," Sir Thomas said, "the resignation of the Director of Security cannot be undertaken lightly. We must judge for ourselves whether or not what you have said is justified. The photographs of Mr. Barnes aren't enough. So please . . . take off your shirt."

Bugger it, I thought. I didn't want to. And from the distaste in their faces, they didn't want to see. I hated the whole damned thing. Hated what had happened to us. Detested it. I wished I hadn't come to Portman Square.

"Sid," Sir Thomas said seriously, "you must."

I undid the buttons and stood up and slid the shirt off. The only pink bit of me was the plastic arm, the rest being mottled black with dark red criss-crossed streaks. It looked, by that time, with all the bruising coming out, a lot worse than it felt. It looked, as I knew, appalling. It also looked, on that day, the worst it would. It was because of that that I'd insisted on going to Portman Square on that day. I hadn't wanted to show them the damage, yet I'd known they would insist, and I would have to: and if I had to, that day was the most convincing. The human mind was deviously ambivalent when it wanted to defeat its enemies.

In a week or so, most of the marks would have gone, and I doubted whether there would be a single permanent external scar. It had all been quite precisely a matter of outraging the sensitive nerves of the skin, transient, leaving no trace. With such a complete lack of lasting visible damage, the Scots would know that even if they were brought to trial, they would get off lightly. For a hand, all too visible, the sentence had been four years. The going rate for a few days' surface discomfort was probably three months. In long robbery-with-violence sentences it was always the robbery that stretched the time, not the violence.

"Turn round," Sir Thomas said.

I turned round, and after a while I turned back. No one said anything. Charles looked his most unruffled. Sir Thomas stood up and walked over to me, and inspected the scenery more closely. Then he picked up my shirt from the chair, and held it for me to put on again.

I said, "Thank you," and did up the buttons. Pushed the tails untidily into the top of my trousers. Sat down.

It seemed quite a long time before Sir Thomas lifted the interoffice telephone and said to his secretary, "Would you ask Commander Wainwright to come here, please?"

IF THE ADMINISTRATORS still had any doubts, Lucas himself dispelled them. He walked briskly and unsuspectingly into a roomful of silence, and when he saw me sitting there, he suddenly stopped moving, as if his brain had given up transmitting to his muscles.

The blood drained from his face, leaving the gray-brown eyes staring from a barren landscape. I had an idea that I must have looked like that to

Trevor Deansgate in the stewards' box at Chester. I thought that quite likely, at that moment, Lucas couldn't feel his feet on the carpet.

"Lucas," Sir Thomas said, pointing to a chair, "sit down."

Lucas fumbled his way into the chair with his gaze still fixedly on me, as if he couldn't believe I was there, as if by staring hard enough he would make me vanish.

Sir Thomas cleared his throat. "Lucas, Sid Halley, here, has been telling us certain things which require explanation."

Lucas was hardly listening. Lucas said to me, "You can't be here."

"Why not?" I said.

They waited for Lucas to answer, but he didn't.

Sir Thomas said eventually, "Sid has made serious charges. I'll put them before you, Lucas, and you can answer as you will."

He repeated more or less everything I'd told them, without emphasis and without mistake. The judicial mind, I thought, taking the heat out of things, reducing passion to probabilities. Lucas appeared to be listening, but he looked at me all the time.

"So you see," Sir Thomas said finally, "we are waiting for you to deny—or admit—that Sid's theories are true."

Lucas turned his head away from me and looked vaguely round the room.

"It's all rubbish, of course," he said.

"Carry on," said Sir Thomas.

"He's making it all up." He was thinking again, fast. The briskness in some measure returned to his manner. "I certainly didn't tell him to investigate any syndicates. I certainly didn't tell him I had doubts about Eddy. I never talked to him about this imaginary Mason. He's invented it all."

"With what purpose?" I asked.

"How should I know?"

"I didn't invent coming here twice to copy down notes of the syndicates," I said. "I didn't invent Eddy complaining because I'd seen those files. I didn't invent you telephoning Chico at my flat four times. I didn't invent you dropping us at the car park. I didn't invent Peter Rammileese, who might be persuaded to . . . er . . . talk. I could also find those two Scots, if I tried."

"How?" he asked.

I'd ask young Mark, I thought. He would have learned a lot about the friends in all that time: little Mark and his accurate ears.

I said, "Don't you mean, I invented the Scots?"

He glared at me.

"I could also," I said slowly, "start looking for the real reasons behind all this. Trace the rumors of corruption to their source. Find out who, besides Peter Rammileese, is keeping you in Mercedeses."

Lucas Wainwright was silent. I didn't know that I could do all I'd said, but he wouldn't want to bet I couldn't. If he hadn't thought me capable, he'd have seen no need to get rid of me in the first place. It was his own judgment I was invoking, not mine.

"Would you be prepared for that, Lucas?" Sir Thomas asked.

Lucas stared my way some more, and didn't answer.

"On the other hand," I said, "I think if you resigned, it would be the end of it."

He turned his head away from me and stated at the Senior Steward instead.

Sir Thomas nodded. "That's all, Lucas. Just your resignation, now, in writing. If we had that, I would see no reason to proceed any further."

It was the easiest let-off anyone could have had, but to Lucas, at that moment, it must have seemed bad enough. His face looked strained and pale, and there were tremors round his mouth.

Sir Thomas produced from his desk a sheet of paper, and from his pocket a gold ballpoint pen.

"Sit here, Lucas."

He rose and gestured to Lucas to sit by the desk.

Commander Wainwright walked over with stiff legs and shakily sat where he'd been told. He wrote a few words, which I read later. *I resign from the post of Director of Security to the Jockey Club. Lucas Wainwright.*

He looked around at the sober faces, at the people who had known him well, and trusted him, and had worked with him every day. He hadn't said a word, since he'd come into the office, of defense or appeal. I thought, How odd it must be for them all, facing such a shattering readjustment.

He stood up, the pepper-and-salt man, and walked toward the door.

As he came in to where I sat, he paused, and looked at me blankly, as if not understanding.

"What does it take," he asked, "to stop you?"

I didn't answer.

What it took rested casually on my knee. Four strong fingers, and a thumb, and independence.

CHAPTER 20

CHARLES DROVE US back to Aynsford. "You'll get a bellyful of courtrooms anyway," he said. "With Nicholas Ashe, and Trevor Deansgate."

"It's not so bad just being an ordinary witness."

"You've done it a good few times now."

"Yes," I said.

"What will Lucas Wainwright do after this, I wonder?"

"God knows."

Charles glanced at me. "Don't you feel the slightest desire to gloat?"

"Gloat?" I was astounded.

"Over the fallen enemy."

"Oh, yes?" I said. "And in your war at sea, what did you do when you saw an enemy drowning? Gloat? Push him under?"

"Take him prisoner," Charles said.

After a bit I said, "His life from now on will be prison enough."

Charles smiled his secret smile, and ten minutes farther on he said, "And do you forgive him, as well?"

"Don't ask such difficult questions."

Love thine enemy. Forgive. Forget. I was no sort of Christian, I thought. I could manage not to hate Lucas himself. I didn't think I could forgive; and I would never forget.

We rolled on to Aynsford, where Mrs. Cross, carrying a tray upstairs to her private sitting room, told me that Chico was up, and feeling better, and in the kitchen. I went along there and found him sitting alone at the table, looking at a mug of tea.

"Hello," I said.

"Hello."

There was no need, with him, to pretend anything. I filled a mug from the pot and sat opposite him.

"Bloody awful," he said, "wasn't it?"

"Yeah."

"And I was dazed, like."

"Mm."

"You weren't. Made it worse."

We sat for a while without talking. There was a sort of stark dullness in his eyes, and none of it, any longer, was concussion.

"Do you reckon," he said, "they let your head alone for that?"

"Don't know."

"They couldn've."

I nodded. We drank the tea, bit by bit.

"What did they say today?" he asked. "The brass."

"They listened. Lucas resigned. End of story."

"Not for us."

"No."

I moved stiffly on the chair.

"What'll we do?" he asked.

"Have to see."

"I couldn't . . ." He stopped. He looked tired and sore, and dispirited.

"No," I said. "Nor could I."

"Sid . . . I reckon . . . I've had enough."

"What, then?"

"Teach judo."

And I could make a living, I supposed, from equities, commodities, insurance, and capital gains. Some sort of living . . . not much of a life.

In depression we finished the tea, feeling battered and weak and sorry for ourselves. I couldn't go on if he didn't, I thought. He'd made the job seem worthwhile. His naturalness, his good nature, his cheerfulness: I needed them around me. In many ways I couldn't function without him. In many ways, I wouldn't bother to function if I didn't have him to consider.

After a while I said, "You'd be bored."

"What, with Wembley and not hurting, and the little bleeders?"

I rubbed my forehead, where the stray cut itched.

"Anyway," he said, "it was you, last week, who was going to give up."

"Well . . . I don't like being . . ." I stopped.

"Beaten," he said.

I took my hand away and looked at his eyes. There was the same thing there that had suddenly been in his voice. An awareness of the two meanings of the word. A glimmer of sardonic amusement. Life on its way back.

"Yeah." I smiled twistedly. "I don't like being beaten. Never did."

"Sod the buggers, then?" he said.

I nodded. "Sod 'em."

"All right."

We went on sitting there, but it was a lot better after that.

THREE DAYS LATER, on Monday evening, we went back to London, and Chico, humoring the fears he didn't take seriously, came with me to the flat.

The hot weather had gone back to normal, or in other words, warm-front drizzle. Road surfaces were slippery with the oily patina left by hot dry tires, and in west London every front garden was soggy with roses. Two weeks to the Derby . . . and perhaps Tri-Nitro would run in it, if the infection cleared up. He was fit enough, apart from that.

The flat was empty and quiet.

"Told you," Chico said, dumping my suitcase in the bedroom. "Want me to look in the cupboards?"

"As you're here."

He raised his eyebrows to heaven and did an inch-by-inch search.

"Only spiders," he said. "They've caught all the flies."

We went down to where I'd parked at the front and I drove him to his place.

"Friday," I said, "I'm going away for a few days."

"Oh, yes? Dirty weekend?"

"You never know. I'll call you when I get back."

"Just the nice gentle crooks from now on, right?"

"Throw all the big ones back," I said.

He grinned, waved, and went in, and I drove away, with lights going on everywhere in the dusk. Back at the flats, I went round to the lock-up garages to leave the car in the one I rented there, out of sight.

Unlocked the roll-up door, and pushed it high. Switched the light on. Drove the car in. Got out. Locked the car door. Put the keys in my pocket.

"Sid Halley," a voice said.

A voice. *His* voice.

Trevor Deansgate.

I stood facing the door I'd just locked, as still as stone.

"Sid Halley."

I had known it would happen, I supposed. Sometime, somewhere, as he'd said. He had made a serious threat. He had expected to be believed. I had believed him.

Oh, God, I thought. It's too soon. It's always too soon. Let him not see the terror I feel. Let him not know. Dear God . . . give me courage.

I turned slowly toward him.

He stood a step inside the garage, in the light, the thin drizzle like a dark gray-silver sheet behind him.

He held the shotgun, with the barrels pointing my way.

I had a brick wall on my left and another behind me, and the car on my right; and there were never many people about at the back of the flats, by the garages. If anyone came, they'd hardly dawdle around in the rain.

"I've been waiting for you," he said.

He was dressed, as ever, in city pin stripes. He brought, as always, the aura of power.

With eyes and gun facing unwaveringly my way, he stretched up behind him quickly with his left hand and found the bottom edge of the roll-up door. He gave it a sharp downward tug, and it rolled down nearly to the ground behind him, closing us in. Both hands, clean, manicured, surrounded by white cuffs, were back on the gun.

"I've been waiting for you, on and off, for days. Since last Thursday."

I didn't say anything.

"Last Thursday two policemen came to see me. George Caspar telephoned. The Jockey Club warned me they were going to take proceedings. My solicitor told me I'd lose my bookmaking license. I would be warned off from racing, and might well go to jail. Since last Thursday, I've been waiting for you."

His voice, as before, was a threat in itself, heavy with the raw realities of the urban jungle.

"The police have been to the lab. My brother is losing his job. His career. He worked hard for it."

"Let's all cry," I said. "You both gambled. You've lost. Too bloody bad."

His eyes narrowed and the gun barrels moved an inch or two as his body reacted.

"I came here to do what I said I would."

Gambled . . . lost. . . . So had I.

"I've been waiting in my car around these flats," he said. "I knew you'd come back, sometime or other. I knew you would. All I had to do was wait. I've spent most of my time here since last Thursday, waiting for you. So tonight you came back . . . with that friend. But I wanted you on your own. . . . I went on waiting. And you came back. I knew you'd come, in the end."

I said nothing.

"I came here to do what I promised. To blow your hand off." He paused. "Why don't you beg me not to? Why don't you go down on your bloody knees and beg me not to?"

I didn't answer. Didn't move.

He gave a short laugh that had no mirth in it at all. "It didn't stop you, did it, that threat? Not for long. I thought it would. I thought no one could risk losing both their hands. Not just to get me busted. Not for something small like that. You're a bloody fool, you are."

I agreed with him, on the whole. I was also trembling inside, and concerned that he shouldn't see it.

"You don't turn a hair, do you?" he said.

He's playing with me, I thought. He must know I'm frightened. No one could possibly, in these circumstances, not be frightened to death. He's making me sweat . . . wanting me to beg him . . . and I'm not . . . *not* . . . going to.

"I came here to do it," he said. "I've been sitting here for days, thinking about it. Thinking of you with no hands, with just stumps . . . with two plastic hooks."

Sod you, I thought.

"Today," he said, "I started thinking about myself. I shoot off Sid Halley's right hand, and what happens to me?" He stared at me with increased intensity. "I get the satisfaction of fixing you, making you a proper cripple instead of half a one. I get revenge . . . hideous, delightful revenge. And what else do I get? I get ten years, perhaps. You can get life for G.B.H., if it's bad enough. Both hands . . . that might be bad enough. That's what I've been sitting here today, thinking. And I've been thinking of the feeling there'd be against me in the slammer, for shooting your other hand off. Yours, of all people. I'd be better off killing you. That's what I thought."

I thought numbly that I wasn't so sure, either, that I wouldn't rather be dead.

"This evening," he said, "after you'd come back for ten minutes, and gone away again, I thought of rotting away in jail year after year wishing I'd had the bloody sense to leave you alone. I reckoned it wasn't worth years in jail, just to know I'd fixed you. Fixed you alive, or fixed you dead. So I decided, just before you came back, not to do that, but just to get you down on the ground squealing for me not to. I'd have my revenge that way. I'd remind you of it all your life. I'd tell people I'd had you crawling. Make them snigger."

Jesus, I thought.

"I'd forgotten," he said, "what you're like. You've no bloody nerves. But I'm not going to shoot you. Like I said, it's not worth it."

He turned abruptly, and stooped, putting one hand under the garage door. Heaved; rolled it upward and open.

The warm drizzle in the dark outside fell like shoals of silver minnows. The gentle air came softly into the garage.

He stood there for a moment, brooding, holding his gun; and then he gave me back what in the straw barn he'd taken away.

"Isn't there *anything*," he said bitterly, "that you're afraid of?"

COME TO GRIEF

CHAPTER 1

I HAD THIS friend, you see, that everyone loved.

(My name is Sid Halley.)

I had this friend that everyone loved, and I put him on trial.

The trouble with working as an investigator, as I had been doing for approaching five years, was that occasionally one turned up facts that surprised and appalled and smashed peaceful lives forever.

It had taken days of inner distress for me to decide to act on what I'd learned. Miserably, by then, I'd suffered through disbelief, through denial, through anger and at length through acceptance; all the stages of grief. I grieved for the man I'd known. For the man I *thought* I'd known, who had all along been a façade. I grieved for the loss of a friendship, for a man who still looked the same but was different, alien . . . despicable. I could much more easily have grieved for him dead.

The turmoil I'd felt in private had on public disclosure become universal. The press, jumping instinctively and strongly to his defense, had given me, as his accuser, a severely rough time. On racecourses, where I chiefly worked, long-time acquaintances had turned their backs. Love, support and comfort poured out towards my friend. Disbelief and denial and anger prevailed: acceptance lay a long way ahead. Meanwhile I, not he, was seen as the target for hatred. It would pass, I knew. One had simply to endure it, and wait.

On the morning set for the opening of his trial, my friend's mother killed herself.

The news was brought to the Law Courts in Reading, in Berkshire, where the presiding judge, enrobed, had already heard the opening statements and where I, a witness for the prosecution, waited alone in a soulless side room to be called. One of the court officials came to give me the suicide information and to say that the judge had adjourned the proceedings for the day, and I could go home.

"Poor woman," I exclaimed, truly horrified.

Even though he was supposed to be impartial, the official's own sympathies were still with the accused. He eyed me without favor and said I should return the following morning, ten o'clock sharp.

I left the room and walked slowly along the corridor towards the exit, fielded on the way by a senior lawyer who took me by the elbow and drew me aside.

"His mother took a room in a hotel and jumped from the sixteenth floor," he said without preamble. "She left a note saying she couldn't bear the future. What are your thoughts?"

I looked at the dark, intelligent eyes of Davis Tatum, a clumsy, fat man with a lean, agile brain.

"You know better than I do," I said.

"*Sid.*" A touch of exasperation. "Tell me your thoughts."

"Perhaps he'll change his plea."

He relaxed and half smiled. "You're in the wrong job."

I wryly shook my head. "I catch the fish. You guys gut them."

He amiably let go of my arm and I continued to the outside world to catch a train for the thirty-minute ride to the terminus in London, flagging down a taxi for the last mile or so home.

Ginnie Quint, I thought, traveling through London. Poor, poor Ginnie Quint, choosing death in preference to the everlasting agony of her son's disgrace. A lonely slamming exit. An end to tears. An end to grief.

The taxi stopped outside the house in Pont Square (off Cadogan Square), where I currently lived on the second floor, with a balcony overlooking the central leafy railed garden. As usual, the small, secluded square was quiet, with little passing traffic and only a few people on foot. A thin early-October wind shook the dying leaves on the lime trees, floating a few of them sporadically to the ground like soft yellow snowflakes.

I climbed out of the cab and paid the driver through his open window, and as I turned to cross the pavement and go up the few steps to the front door, a man who was apparently quietly walking past suddenly sprang at me in fury, raising a long black metal rod with which he tried to brain me.

I sensed rather than saw the first wicked slash and moved enough to catch the weight of it on my shoulder, not my head. He was screaming at me, half-demented, and I fielded a second brutal blow on a raised defensive forearm. After that I seized his wrist in a pincer grip and rolled the bulk of his body backward over the leg I pushed out rigidly behind his knees, and felled him, sprawling, iron bar and all, onto the hard ground. He yelled bitter words; cursing, half-incoherent, threatening to kill.

The taxi still stood there, diesel engine running, the driver staring wide-mouthed and speechless, a state of affairs that continued while I yanked open the black rear door and stumbled in again onto the seat. My heart thudded. Well, it would.

"*Drive*," I said urgently. "Drive on."

"But . . ."

"Just drive. Go *on*. Before he finds his feet and breaks your windows."

The driver closed his mouth fast and meshed his gears, and wavered at something above running pace along the road.

"Look," he said, protesting, half turning his head back to me, "I didn't see nothing. You're my last fare today, I've been on the go eight hours and I'm on my way home."

"Just drive," I said. Too little breath. Too many jumbled feelings.

"Well . . . but, drive where *to*?"

Good question. Think.

"He didn't look like no mugger," the taxi driver observed aggrievedly. "But you never can tell these days. D'you want me to drop you off at the police? He hit you something shocking. You could *hear* it. Like he broke your arm."

"Just drive, would you?"

The driver was large, fiftyish and a Londoner, but no John Bull, and I could see from his head movements and his repeated spiky glances at me in his rear-view mirror that he didn't want to get involved in my problems and couldn't wait for me to leave his cab.

Pulse eventually steadying, I could think of only one place to go. My only haven, in many past troubles.

"Paddington," I said. "Please."

"St. Mary's, d'you mean? The hospital?"

"No. The trains."

"But you've just come from there!" he protested.

"Yes, but please go back."

Cheering a little, he rocked round in a U-turn and set off for the return to Paddington Station, where he assured me again that he hadn't seen nothing, nor heard nothing neither, and he wasn't going to get involved, did I see?

I simply paid him and let him go, and if I memorized his cab-licensing number it was out of habit, not expectation.

As part of normal equipment I wore a mobile phone on my belt and, walking slowly into the high, airy terminus, I pressed the buttons to reach the man I trusted most in the world, my ex-wife's father, Rear Admiral Charles Roland, Royal Navy, retired, and to my distinct relief he answered at the second ring.

"Charles," I said. My voice cracked a bit, which I hadn't meant.

A pause, then, "Is that you, Sid?"

"May I . . . visit?"

"Of course. Where are you?"

"Paddington Station. I'll come by train and taxi."

He said calmly, "Use the side door. It's not locked," and put down his receiver.

I smiled, reassured as ever by his steadiness and his brevity with words. An unemotional, undemonstrative man, not paternal towards me and very far from indulgent, he gave me nevertheless a consciousness that he cared considerably about what happened to me and would proffer rocklike support if I needed it. Like I needed it at that moment, for several variously dire reasons.

Trains to Oxford being less frequent in the middle of the day, it was four in the afternoon by the time the country taxi, leaving Oxford well behind, arrived at Charles's vast old house at Aynsford and decanted me at the side door. I paid the driver clumsily owing to stiffening bruises, and walked with relief into the pile I really thought of as home, the one unchanging constant in a life that had tossed me about, rather, now and then.

Charles sat, as often, in the large leather armchair that I found too hard for comfort but that he, in his uncompromising way, felt appropriate to accommodate his narrow rump. I had sometime in the past moved one of the softer but still fairly formal old gold brocade armchairs from the drawing room into the smaller room, his "wardroom," as it was there we always sat when the two of us were alone. It was there that he kept his desk, his collection of flies for fishing, his nautical books, his racks of priceless old orchestral recordings and the gleaming marble-and-steel wonder of a custom-built, frictionless turntable on which he played them. It was there on the dark-green walls that he'd hung large photographs of the ships he'd commanded, and smaller photos of shipmates, and there, also, that he'd lately positioned a painting of me as a jockey riding over a fence at Cheltenham racecourse, a picture that summed up every ounce of vigor needed for race-riding, and which had hung for years less conspicuously in the dining room.

He had had a strip of lighting positioned along the top of the heavy gold frame, and when I got there that evening, it was lit.

He was reading. He put his book face down on his lap when I walked in, and gave me a bland, noncommittal inspection. There was nothing, as usual, to be read in his eyes: I could often see quite clearly into other people's minds, but seldom his.

"Hullo," I said.

I could hear him take a breath and trickle it out through his nose. He spent all of five seconds looking me over, then pointed to the tray of bottles and glasses which stood on the table below my picture.

"Drink," he said briefly. An order, not invitation.

"It's only four o'clock."

"Immaterial. What have you eaten today?"

I didn't say anything, which he took to be answer enough.

"Nothing," he said, nodding. "I thought so. You look thin. It's this *bloody* case. I thought you were supposed to be in court today."

"It was adjourned until tomorrow."

"Get a drink."

I walked obediently over to the table and looked assessingly at the bottles. In his old-fashioned way he kept brandy and sherry in decanters. Scotch— Famous Grouse, his favorite—remained in the screw-topped bottle. I would have to have scotch, I thought, and doubted if I could pour even that.

I glanced upward at my picture. In those days, six years ago, I'd had two hands. In those days I'd been British steeplechasing's champion jockey: whole, healthy and, I dared say, fanatical. A nightmare fall had resulted in a horse's sharp hoof half ripping off my left hand: the end of one career and the birth, if you could call it that, of another. Slow, lingering birth of a detective, while I spent two years pining for what I'd lost and drifted rudderless like a wreck that didn't quite sink but was unseaworthy all the same. I was ashamed of those two years. At the end of them a ruthless villain had smashed beyond mending the remains of the useless hand and had galvanized me into a resurrection of the spirit and the impetus to seek what I'd had since, a myoelectric false hand that worked on nerve impulses from my truncated forearm and looked and behaved so realistically that people often didn't notice its existence.

My present problem was that I couldn't move its thumb far enough from its fingers to grasp the large heavy cut-glass brandy decanter, and my right hand wasn't working too well, either. Rather than drop alcohol all over Charles's Persian rug, I gave up and sat in the gold armchair.

"What's the matter?" Charles asked abruptly. "Why did you come? Why don't you pour a drink?"

After a moment I said dully, knowing it would hurt him, "Ginnie Quint killed herself."

"*What?*"

"This morning," I said. "She jumped from sixteen floors up."

His fine-boned face went stiff and immediately looked much older. The bland eyes darkened, as if retreating into their sockets. Charles had known

Ginnie Quint for thirty or more years, and had been fond of her and had been a guest in her house often.

Powerful memories lived in my mind also. Memories of a friendly, rounded, motherly woman happy in her role as a big-house wife, inoffensively rich, working genuinely and generously for several charities and laughingly glowing in reflected glory from her famous, good-looking successful only child, the one that everyone loved.

Her son, Ellis, that I had put on trial.

The last time I'd seen Ginnie she'd glared at me with incredulous contempt, demanding to know how I could possibly seek to destroy the golden Ellis, who counted me his friend, who liked me, who'd done me favors, who would have trusted me with his life.

I'd let her molten rage poor over me, offering no defense. I knew exactly how she felt. Disbelief and denial and anger . . . The idea of what he'd done was so sickening to her that she rejected the guilt possibility absolutely, as almost everyone else had done, though in her case with anguish.

Most people believed I had got it all wrong, and had ruined *myself*, not Ellis. Even Charles, at first, had said doubtfully, "Sid, are you sure?"

I'd said I was certain. I'd hoped desperately for a way out . . . for *any* way out . . . as I knew what I'd be pulling down on myself if I went ahead. And it had been at least as bad as I'd feared, and in many ways worse. After the first bombshell solution—a proposed solution—to a crime that had had half the country baying for blood (but not *Ellis's* blood, no, *no*, it was *unthinkable*), there had been the first court appearance, the remand into custody (a *scandal*, he should *of course* be let out immediately on bail), and after that there had fallen a sudden press silence, while the sub judice law came into effect.

Under British sub judice law, no evidence might be publicly discussed between the remand and the trial. Much investigation and strategic trial planning could go on behind the scenes, but neither potential jurors nor John Doe in the street was allowed to know details. Uninformed public opinion had consequently stuck at the "Ellis is innocent" stage, and I'd had nearly three months, now, of obloquy.

Ellis, you see, was a Young Lochinvar in spades. Ellis Quint, once champion amateur jump jockey, had flashed onto television screens like a comet, a brilliant, laughing, able, funny performer, the draw for millions on sports quiz program, the ultimate chat-show host, the model held up to children, the glittering star that regularly raised the nation's happiness level, to whom everyone, from tiara to baseball cap worn backwards, responded.

Manufacturers fell over themselves to tempt him to endorse their products, and half the kids in England strode about with machismo in glamorized
jockey-type riding boots over their jeans. And it was this man, this *paragon*,
that I sought to eradicate.

No one seemed to blame the tabloid columnist who'd written, "The once-
revered Sid Halley, green with envy, tries to tear down a talent he hasn't a
prayer of matching. . . ." There had been inches about "a spiteful little man
trying to compensate for his own inadequacies." I hadn't shown any of it to
Charles, but others had.

The telephone at my waist buzzed suddenly, and I answered its summons.
"Sid . . . Sid . . ."

The woman on the other end was crying. I'd heard her crying often.

"Are you at home?" I asked.

"No . . . In the hospital."

"Tell me the number and I'll phone straight back."

I heard murmuring in the background; then another voice came on, efficient, controlled, reading out a number, repeating it slowly. I tapped the dig-
its onto my mobile so that they appeared on the small display screen.

"Right," I said, reading the number back. "Put down your receiver." To
Charles I said, "May I use your phone?"

He waved a hand permissively towards his desk, and I pressed the button
on his phone to get back to where I'd been.

The efficient voice answered immediately.

"Is Mrs. Ferns still there?" I said. "It's Sid Halley."

"Hang on."

Linda Ferns was trying not to cry. "Sid . . . Rachel's worse. She's asking
for you. Can you come? Please."

"How bad is she?"

"Her temperature keeps going up." A sob stopped her. "Talk to Sister
Grant."

I talked to the efficient voice, Sister Grant. "How bad is Rachel?"

"She's asking for you all the time," she said. "How soon can you come?"

"Tomorrow."

"Can you come this evening?"

I said, "Is it that bad?"

I listened to a moment of silence, in which she couldn't say what she
meant because Linda was beside her.

"Come this evening," she repeated.

This evening. Dear God. Nine-year-old Rachel Ferns lay in a hospital in Kent a hundred and fifty miles away. Ill to death, this time, it sounded like.

"Promise her," I said, "that I'll come tomorrow." I explained where I was. "I have to be in court tomorrow morning, in Reading, but I'll come to see Rachel as soon as I get out. Promise her. Tell her I'm going to be there. Tell her I'll bring six wigs and an angel fish."

The efficient voice said, "I'll tell her," and then added. "is it true that Ellis Quint's mother has killed herself? Mrs. Ferns says someone heard it on the radio news and repeated it to her. She wants to know if it's true."

"It's true."

"Come as soon as you can," the nurse said, and disconnected.

I put down the receiver. Charles said, "The child?"

"It sounds as if she's dying."

"You knew it was inevitable."

"It doesn't make it any easier for the parents." I sat down again slowly in the gold armchair. "I would go tonight if it would save her life, but I . . ." I stopped, not knowing what to say, how to explain that I wouldn't go. Couldn't go. Not except to save her life, which no one could do however much they ached to.

Charles said briefly, "You've only just got here."

"Yeah."

"And what else is there, that you haven't told me?"

I looked at him.

"I know you too well, Sid," he said. "You didn't come all this way just because of Ginnie. You could have told me about her on the telephone." He paused. "From the look of you, you came for the oldest of reasons." He paused again, but I didn't say anything. "For sanctuary," he said.

I shifted in the chair. "Am I so transparent?"

"Sanctuary from what?" he asked "What is so sudden . . . and urgent?"

I sighed. I said with as little heat as possible, "Gordon Quint tried to kill me."

Gordon Quint was Ginnie's husband. Ellis was their son.

It struck Charles silent, open-mouthed: and it took a great deal to do that.

After a while I said, "When they adjourned the trial I went home by train and taxi. Gordon Quint was waiting there in Pont Square for me. God knows how long he'd been there, how long he would have waited, but anyway, he was there, with an iron bar." I swallowed. "He aimed it at my head, but I sort of ducked, and it hit my shoulder. He tried again . . . Well, this mechanical hand has its uses. I closed it on his wrist and put into practice some of the judo I've spent so many hours learning, and I tumbled him onto his back . . . and he was screaming at me all the time that I'd killed Ginnie . . . I'd killed her."

"*Sid.*"

"He was half-mad . . . raving, really . . . He said I'd destroyed his whole family. I'd destroyed all their lives . . . he swore I would die for it . . . that he would get me . . . get me . . . I don't think he knew what he was saying, it just poured out of him."

Charles said dazedly, "So what did you do?"

"The taxi driver was still there, looking stunned, so . . . er . . . I got back into the taxi."

"You got back . . . ? But . . . what about Gordon?"

"I left him there. Lying on the pavement. Screaming revenge . . . starting to stand up . . . waving the iron bar. I . . . er . . . I don't think I'll go home tonight, if I can stay here."

Charles said faintly, "Of course you can stay. It's taken for granted. You told me once that this was your home."

"Yeah."

"Then believe it."

I did believe it, or I wouldn't have gone there. Charles and his certainties had in the past saved me from inner disintegration, and my reliance on him had oddly been strengthened, not evaporated, by the collapse of my marriage to his daughter Jenny, and our divorce.

Aynsford offered respite. I would go back soon enough to defuse Gordon Quint; I would swear an oath in court and tear a man to shreds; I would hug Linda Ferns and, if I were in time, make Rachel laugh; but for this one night I would sleep soundly in Charles's house in my own accustomed room—and let the dry well of mental stamina refill.

Charles said, "Did Gordon . . . er . . . hurt you, with his bar?"

"A bruise or two."

"I know your sort of bruises."

I sighed again. "I think . . . um . . . he's cracked a bone. In my arm."

His gaze flew instantly to the left arm, the plastic job.

"No," I said, "the other one."

Aghast, he said, "Your *right* arm?"

"Well, yeah. But only the ulna, which goes from the little-finger side of the wrist up to the elbow. Not the radius as well, luckily. The radius will act as a natural splint."

"But, *Sid* . . ."

"Better than my skull. I had the choice."

"How can you *laugh* about it?"

"A bloody bore, isn't it?" I smiled without stress. "Don't *worry* so, Charles. It'll heal. I broke the same bone worse once before, when I was racing."

"But you had two hands then."

"Yes, so I did. So would you mind picking up that damned heavy brandy decanter and sloshing half a pint of anesthetic into a glass?"

Wordlessly he got to his feet and complied. I thanked him. He nodded. End of transaction.

When he was again sitting down he said, "So the taxi driver was a witness."

"The taxi driver is a 'don't-get-involved' man."

"But if he *saw* . . . He must have heard . . ."

"Blind and deaf, he insisted he was." I drank fiery, neat liquid gratefully. "Anyway, that suits me fine."

"But, Sid . . ."

"Look," I said reasonably, "what would you have me do? Complain? Prosecute? Gordon Quint is normally a level-headed, worthy sixtyish citizen. He's not your average murderer. Besides, he's your own personal longtime friend, and I, too, have eaten in his house. But he already hates me for attacking Ellis, the light of his life, and he'd not long learned that Ginnie, his adored wife, had killed herself because she couldn't bear what lies ahead. So how do you think Gordon feels?" I paused. "I'm just glad he didn't succeed in smashing my brains in. And, if you can believe it. I'm almost as glad for *his* sake that he didn't, as for my own."

Charles shook his head resignedly.

"Grief can be dangerous," I said.

He couldn't dispute it. Deadly revenge was as old as time.

We sat companionably in silence. I drank brandy and felt marginally saner. Knots of tension relaxed in my stomach. I made various resolutions to give up chasing the deadlier crooks—but I'd made resolutions like that before, and hadn't kept them.

I'd stopped asking myself why I did it. There were hundreds of other ways of passing the time and earning one's keep. Other ex-jockeys became trainers or commentators or worked in racing in official capacities, and only I, it seemed, felt impelled to swim around the hidden fringes, attempting to sort out doubts and worries for people who for any reason didn't want to bother the police or the racing authorities.

There was a need for me and what I could do, or I would have sat around idle, twiddling my thumbs. Instead, even in the present general climate of ostracism, I had more offers of work than I could accept.

Most jobs took me less than a week, particularly those that involved looking into someone's credit and credibility rating: bookmakers asked me to do that frequently, before taking on new account customers, and trainers paid me fees to assure them that if they bought expensive two-year-olds for new owners at the Sales, they wouldn't be left with broken promises and a mountain of debt. I'd checked on all sorts of proposed business plans and saved a lot of people from confidence tricksters, and I'd uncovered absconding debtors, and thieves of all sorts, and had proved a confounded nuisance to imaginative felons.

People had sobbed on my shoulders from joy and deliverance: others had threatened and battered to make me quit: Linda Ferns would hug me and Gordon Quint hate me; and I also had two more investigations in hand that I'd spent too little time on. So why didn't I give it up and change to a life of quiet, safe financial management, which I wasn't bad at, either? I felt the effects of the iron bar from neck to fingers . . . and didn't know the answer.

The mobile phone on my belt buzzed and I answered it as before, finding on the line the senior lawyer I'd talked to in the corridor in the law courts.

"Sid, this is Davis Tatum. I've news for you," he said.

"Give me your number and I'll call you back."

"Oh? Oh, OK." He read off his number, which I copied as before, and also as before I borrowed Charles's phone on the desk to get back to square one.

"Sid," said Tatum, coming as usual straight to the point, "Ellis Quint is changing his plea from not guilty to guilty by reason of diminished responsibility. It seems his mother's powerful statement of no confidence in his innocence has had a laxative effect on the bowels of the counsel for the defense."

"Jeez," I said.

Tatum chuckled. I imagined his double chin wobbling. He said, "The trial will now be adjourned for a week to allow expert psychiatric witnesses to be briefed. In other words, you don't have to turn up tomorrow."

"Good."

"But I hope you will."

"How do you mean?"

"There's a job for you."

"What sort of job?"

"Investigating, of course. What else? I'd like to meet you somewhere privately."

"All right," I said, "but sometime tomorrow I have to go to Kent to see the child, Rachel Ferns. She's back in the hospital and it doesn't sound good."

"Hell."

"Yeah."

"Where are you?" he asked. "The press are looking for you."

"They can wait a day."

"I told the people from *The Pump* that after the mauling they've given you they haven't a prayer of you talking to them."

"I appreciate that," I said, smiling.

He chuckled. "About tomorrow . . ."

"I'll go to Kent in the morning," I said. "I don't know how long I'll stay, it depends on Rachel. How about five o'clock in London? Would that do you? The end of your business day."

"Right. Where? Not in my office. How about your place? No, perhaps not, if *The Pump*'s after you."

"How about, say, the upstairs bar of Le Meridien restaurant in Piccadilly?"

"I don't know it."

"All the better."

"If I need to change it," he said, "can I still get you on your mobile phone?"

"Always."

"Good. See you tomorrow."

I replaced Charles's receiver and sat on the gold armchair as before. Charles looked at the mobile instrument I'd laid this time on the table beside my glass and asked the obvious question.

"Why do you ring them back? Why don't you just talk?"

"Well," I said, "someone is listening to this gadget."

"Listening?"

I explained about the insecurity of open radio transmission, that allowed anyone clever and expert to hear what they shouldn't.

Charles said, "How do you know someone's listening to you?"

"A lot of small things people have recently learned that I haven't told them."

"Who is it?"

"I don't actually know. Someone has also accessed my computer over the phone lines. I don't know who did that, either. It's disgustingly easy nowadays—but again, only if you're expert—to suss out people's private passwords and read their secret files."

He said with slight impatience, "Computers are beyond me."

"I've had to learn," I said, grinning briefly. "A bit different from scudding over hurdles at Plumpton on a wet day."

"Everything you do astounds me."

"I wish I was still racing."

"Yes, I know. But if you were, you'd anyway be coming to the end of it soon, wouldn't you? How old are you now? Thirty-four?"

I nodded. Thirty-five loomed.

"Not many top jump jockeys go on much after that."

"You put things so delightfully bluntly, Charles."

"You're of more use to more people the way you are.

Charles tended to give me pep talks when he thought I needed them. I could never work out how he knew. He'd said something once about my looking like a brick wall: that when I shut out the world and retreated into myself, things were bad. Maybe he was right. Retreat inward meant for me not retreating outwardly, and I supposed I'd learned the technique almost from birth.

Jenny, my loved and lost wife, had said she couldn't live with it. She'd wanted me to give up race-riding and become a softer-shelled person, and when I wouldn't—or couldn't—we had shaken acridly apart. She had recently remarried, and this time she'd tied herself not to a thin, dark-haired, risk-taking bundle of complexes, but to a man to fit her needs, a safe, graying, sweet-natured uncomplicated fellow with a knighthood. Jenny, the warring unhappy Mrs. Halley, was now serenely Lady Wingham. A photograph of her with her handsome, beaming Sir Anthony stood in a silver frame next to the telephone on Charles's desk.

"How's Jenny?" I asked politely.

"Fine," Charles answered without expression.

"Good."

"He's a bore, after you," Charles observed.

"You can't say such things."

"I can say what I bloody well like in my own house."

In harmony and mutual regard we passed a peaceful evening, disturbed only by five more calls on my mobile phone, all demanding to know, with varying degrees of peremptoriness, where they could find Sid Halley.

I said each time, "This is an answering service. Leave your number and we'll pass on your message."

All of the callers, it seemed, worked for newspapers, a fact that particularly left me frowning.

"I don't know where they all got this number from," I told Charles. "It's not in any directory. I give it only to people I'm working for, so they can reach me day or night, and only to others whose calls I wouldn't want to miss. I tell them it's a private line for their use only. I don't hand this number out on printed cards, and I don't have it on my writing paper. Quite often I reroute calls to this phone from my phone in the flat, but I didn't today because of Gordon Quint bashing away outside and preventing me from going in. So how do half the newspapers in London know it?"

"How will you find out?" Charles asked.

"Um . . . engage Sid Halley to look into it, I daresay."

Charles laughed. I felt uneasy all the same. Someone had been listening on that number, and now someone had broadcast it. It wasn't that my phone conversations were excessively secret—and I'd started the semi-exclusive number anyway solely so that the machine didn't buzz unnecessarily at awkward moments—but now I had a sense that someone was deliberately crowding me. Tapping into my computer—which wouldn't get anyone far, as I knew a lot of defenses. Assaulting me electronically. *Stalking.*

Enough was enough. Five newspapers were too much. Sid Halley, as I'd said, would have to investigate his own case.

Charles's long-time live-in housekeeper, Mrs. Cross, all dimples and delight, cooked us a simple supper and fussed over me comfortably like a hen. I guiltily found her a bit smothering sometimes, but always sent her a card for her birthday.

I went to bed early and found that, as usual, Mrs. Cross had left warm welcoming lights on in my room and had put out fresh pajamas and fluffy towels.

A pity the day's troubles couldn't be as easily cosseted into oblivion.

I undressed and brushed my teeth and eased off the artificial hand. My left arm ended uselessly four inches below the elbow; a familiar punctuation, but still a sort of bereavement.

My right arm now twinged violently at every use.

Damn the lot, I thought.

CHAPTER 2

THE MORNING BROUGHT little improvement.

I sometimes used a private chauffeur-driven car-hire firm based in London to ferry around people and things I wanted to keep away from prying eyes and consequently, waking to a couple of faulty arms, I telephoned from Charles's secure number and talked to my friends at Teledrive.

"Bob?" I said. "I need to get from northwest of Oxford to Kent, Canterbury. There'll be a couple of short stops on the journey. And, sometime this afternoon, a return to London. Can anyone do it at such short notice?"

"Give me the address," he said briefly. "We're on our way."

I breakfasted with Charles. That is to say, we sat in the dining room where Mrs. Cross, in her old-fashioned way, had set out toast, coffee and cereals and a warming dish of scrambled eggs.

Charles thought mornings hadn't begun without scrambled eggs. He ate his on toast and eyed me drinking coffee left-handedly. From long acquaintance with my preference for no fuss, he made no comment on the consequences of iron bars.

He was reading a broad-sheet newspaper which, as he showed me, was making a good-taste meal of Ginnie Quint's death. Her pleasant, smiling face inappropriately spread across two columns. I shut out of my mind any image of what she might look like sixteen floors down.

Charles said, reading aloud, "'Friends say she appeared depressed about her son's forthcoming trial. Her husband, Gordon, was unavailable for comment.' In other words, the press couldn't find him."

Ordeal by newsprint, I thought; the latter-day torture.

"Seriously, Sid," Charles said in his most calm, civilized voice, "was Gordon's rage at you transient or . . . er . . . obsessive?"

"Seriously," I echoed him, "I don't know." I sighed. "I should think it's too soon to tell. Gordon himself probably doesn't know."

"Do take care, Sid."

"Sure." I sorted through the flurry of impressions I'd gathered in the brief seconds of violence in Pont Square. "I don't know where Ginnie was when she jumped," I said, "but I don't think Gordon was with her. I mean, when he leaped at me he was wearing country clothes. Work-day clothes: mud on his boots, corduroy trousers, old tweed jacket, open-necked blue shirt. He hadn't been staying in any sixteen-story hotel. And the metal bar he hit me with . . . it wasn't a smooth rod, it was a five-foot piece of angle iron, the sort you thread wire through for fencing. I saw the holes in it."

Charles stared.

I said, "I'd say he was at home in Berkshire when he was told about Ginnie. I think if I'd loitered around to search, I would have found Gordon's Land-Rover parked near Pont Square."

Gordon Quint, though a landowner, was a hands-on custodian of his multiple acres. He drove tractors, scythed weeds to clear streams, worked alongside his men to repair his boundaries, re-fence his sheep fields and thin out his woodlands, enjoying both the physical labor and the satisfaction of a job most competently done.

I knew him also as self-admiring and as expecting—and receiving—deference from everyone, including Ginnie. It pleased him to be a generous host while leaving his guests in no doubt of his superior worth.

The man I'd seen in Pont Square, all "squire" manner stripped away, had been a raw, hurt, *outraged* and oddly more genuine person than the Gordon I'd known before: but until I learned for sure which way the explosively tossed-up bricks of his nature would come down, I would keep away from fencing posts and any other agricultural hardware he might be traveling with.

I told Charles I'd engaged Teledrive to come and pick me up. To his raised eyebrows I explained I would put the cost against expenses. Whose expenses? General running expenses, I said.

"Is Mrs. Ferns paying you?" Charles neutrally asked.

"Not anymore."

"Who is, exactly?" He liked me to make a profit. I did, but he seldom believed it.

"I don't starve," I said, drinking my coffee. "Have you ever tried three or four eggs whipped up in mushroom soup? Instant mushroom omelette, not at all bad."

"Disgusting," Charles said.

"You get a different perspective, living alone."

"You need a new wife," Charles said. "What about that girl who used to share a flat with Jenny in Oxford?"

"Louise McInnes?"

"Yes. I thought you and she were having an affair."

No one had affairs anymore. Charles's words were half a century out of date. But though the terms might now be different, the meaning was eternal.

"A summer picnic," I said. "The frosts of winter killed it off."

"Why?"

"What she felt for me was more curiosity than love."

He understood that completely. Jenny had talked about me so long and intimately to her friend Louise, mostly to my detriment, that I recognized—in retrospect—that the friend had chiefly been fascinated in checking out the information personally. It had been a lighthearted passage from mating to parting. Nice while it lasted, but no roots.

When the car came for me I thanked Charles for sanctuary.

"Anytime," he said, nodding.

We parted as usual without physically touching. Eye contact said it all.

Getting the driver to thread his way back and forth through the maze of shopping dead ends in the town of Kingston in Surrey, I acquired six dressing-up party wigs from a carnival store and an angel fish in a plastic tub from a pet shop; and, thus armed, arrived eventually at the children's cancer ward that held Rachel Ferns.

Linda greeted my arrival with glittering tears, but her daughter still lived. Indeed, in one of those unpredictable quirks that made leukemia such a roller coaster of hope and despair, Rachel was marginally better. She was awake, semi-sitting up in bed and pleased at my arrival.

"Did you bring the angel fish?" she demanded by way of greeting.

I held up the plastic bucket, which swung from my plastic wrist. Linda took it and removed the watertight lid, showing her daughter the shining black and silver fish that swam vigorously inside.

Rachel relaxed. "I'm going to call him Sid," she said.

She'd been a lively, blond, pretty child once, according to her photographs: now she seemed all huge eyes in a bald head. Lassitude and anemia had made her frighteningly frail.

When her mother had first called me in to investigate an attack on Rachel's pony, the illness had been in remission, the dragon temporarily sleeping. Rachel had become someone special to me and I'd given her a fish tank complete with lights, aeration, water plants, Gothic castle arches, sand and brilliant tropical swimming inhabitants. Linda had wept. Rachel had spent hours getting to know her new friends' habits; the ones that skulked in corners, the one who bossed all the rest. Half of the fish were called Sid.

The fish tank stood in the Fernses' sitting room at home and it seemed uncertain now whether Rachel would see the new Sid among his mates.

It was there, in the comfortable middle-sized room furnished with unaggressively expensive modern sofas, with glass-topped end tables and stained-glass Tiffany lamps, that I had first met my clients, Linda and Rachel Ferns.

There were no books in the room, only a few magazines; dress fashions and horses. Shiny striped curtains in crimson and cream; geometrically patterned carpet in merging fawn and gray; flower prints on pale pink walls. Overall the impression was a degree of lack of coordination which probably indicated impulsive inhabitants without strongly formed characters. The Fernses weren't "old" money, I concluded, but there appeared to be plenty of it.

Linda Ferns, on the telephone, had begged me to come. Five or six ponies in the district had been attacked by vandals, and one of the ponies belonged to her daughter, Rachel. The police hadn't found out who the vandals were and now months had gone by, and her daughter was still very distressed and would I *please, please*, come and see if I could help.

"I've heard you're my only hope. I'll pay you, of course. I'll pay you *anything* if you help Rachel. She has these terrible nightmares. *Please.*"

I mentioned my fee.

"Anything," she said.

She hadn't told me, before I arrived in the far-flung village beyond Canterbury, that Rachel was ill unto death.

When I met the huge-eyed bald-headed slender child she shook hands with me gravely.

"Are you really Sid Halley?" she asked.

I nodded.

"Mum said you would come. Daddy said you didn't work for kids."

"I do sometimes."

"My hair is growing," she said; and I could see the thin fine blond fuzz just showing over the pale scalp.

"I'm glad."

She nodded. "Quite often I wear a wig, but they itch. Do you mind if I don't?"

"Not in the least."

"I have leukemia," she said calmly.

"I see."

She studied my face, a child old beyond her age, as I'd found all sick young people to be.

"You will find out who killed Silverboy, won't you?"

"I'll try," I said. "How did he die?"

"No, no," Linda interrupted. "Don't ask her. I'll tell you. It upsets her. Just say you'll sort them out, those *pigs*. And, Rachel, you take Pegotty out into the garden and push him round so that he can see the flowers."

Pegotty, it transpired, was a contented-looking baby strapped into a buggy. Rachel without demur pushed him out into the garden and could presently be seen through the window giving him a close-up acquaintance with an azalea.

Linda Ferns watched and wept the first of many tears.

"She needs a bone-marrow transplant," she said, trying to suppress sobs. "You'd think it would be simple, but no one so far can find a match to her, not even in the international register set up by the Anthony Nolan Trust."

I said inadequately, "I'm sorry."

"Her father and I are divorced," Linda said. "We divorced five years ago, and he's married again." She spoke without bitterness. "These things happen."

"Yes," I said.

I was at the Ferns house early in a June of languorous days and sweet-smelling roses, a time for the lotus, not horrors.

"A bunch of vandals," Linda said with a fury that set her whole body trembling, "they maimed a lot of ponies in Kent . . . in this area particularly . . . so that poor loving kids went out into their paddocks and found their much loved ponies *mutilated.* What sick, sick mind would *blind* a poor, inoffensive pony that had never done anyone any harm? Three ponies round here were blinded and others had had knives stuck up their back passages." She blinked on her tears. "Rachel was terribly upset. All the children for miles were crying inconsolably. And the police couldn't find who'd done any of it."

"Was Silverboy blinded?" I asked.

"No . . . No . . . It was worse . . . For Rachel, it was worse. She found him, you see . . . out in the paddock . . ." Linda openly sobbed. "Rachel wanted to sleep in a makeshift stable . . . a lean-to shed, really. She wanted to sleep there at nights with Silverboy tied up there beside her, and I wouldn't let her. She's been ill for nearly three years. It's such a *dreadful* disease, and I feel so helpless. . . ." She wiped her eyes, plucking a tissue from a half-empty box. "She keeps saying it wasn't my fault, but I know she thinks Silverboy would be alive if I'd let her sleep out there."

"What happened to him?" I asked neutrally.

Linda shook her head miserably, unable still to tell me. She was a pretty woman in a conventional thirty-something way: trim figure, well-washed short fair hair, all the health and beauty magazine tips come to admirable life. Only the dullness in the eyes and the intermittent vibrations in many of her muscles spoke plainly of the long strain of emotional buffeting still assailing her.

"She went out," she said eventually, "even though it was bitter cold, and beginning to rain . . . February . . . she always went to see that his water trough was filled and clean and not frozen over . . . and I'd made her put on warm clothes and gloves and a scarf and a real thick woolly hat . . . and she came back running, and screaming . . . *screaming* . . ."

I waited through Linda's unbearable memories.

She said starkly, "Rachel found his *foot*."

There was a moment of utter stillness, an echo of the stunned disbelief of that dreadful morning.

"It was in all the papers," Linda said.

I moved and nodded. I'd read—months ago—about the blinded Kent ponies. I'd been busy, inattentive: hadn't absorbed names or details, hadn't realized that one of the ponies had lost a foot.

"I've found out since you telephoned," I said, "that round the country, not just here in Kent, there have been another half a dozen or so scattered vandalizing attacks on ponies and horses in fields."

She said unhappily, "I did see a paragraph about a horse in Lancashire, but I threw the paper away so that Rachel wouldn't read it. Every time anything reminds her of Silverboy she has a whole week of nightmares. She wakes up sobbing. She comes into my bed, shivering, crying. Please, please find out why . . . find out *who* . . . She's so ill . . . and although she's in remission just now and able to live fairly normally, it almost certainly won't last. The doctors say she needs the transplant."

I said, "Does Rachel know any of the other children whose ponies were attacked?"

Linda shook her head. "Most of them belonged to the Pony Club, I think, but Rachel didn't feel well enough to join the club. She loved Silverboy—her father gave him to her—but all she could do was sit in the saddle while we led her round. He was a nice, quiet pony, a very nice-looking gray with a darker, smoky-colored mane. Rachel called him Silverboy, but he had a long pedigree name, really. She needed something to love, you see, and she wanted a pony so *much*."

I asked, "Did you keep any of the newspaper accounts of Silverboy and the other local ponies being attacked? If you did, can I see them?"

"Yes," she answered doubtfully, "but I don't see how they could help. They didn't help the police."

"They'd be a start" I said.

"All right, then." She left the room and after a while returned with a small blue suitcase, the size for stowing under the seats of aircraft. "Everything's in here," she said, passing me the case, "including a tape of a program a television company made. Rachel and I are in it. You won't lose it, will you? We never show it, but I wouldn't want to lose it." She blinked against tears. "It was actually the only good thing that happened. Ellis Quint came to see the children and he was utterly sweet with them. Rachel loved him. He was so *kind*."

"I know him quite well," I said. "If anyone could comfort the children, he could."

"A really *nice* man," Linda said.

I took the blue suitcase with its burden of many small tragedies back with me to London and spent indignant hours reading muted accounts of a degree of vandalism that must have been mind-destroying when fresh and bloody and discovered by loving children.

The twenty-minute videotape showed Ellis Quint at his best: the gentle, sympathetic healer of unbearable sorrows; the sensible, caring commentator urging the police to treat these crimes with the seriousness given to murders. How good he was, I thought, at pitching his responses exactly right. He put his arms around Rachel and talked to her without sentimentality, not mentioning, until right at the end of the program, when the children were off the screen, that for Rachel Ferns the loss of her pony was just one more intolerable blow in a life already full of burdens.

For that program, Rachel had chosen to wear the pretty blond wig that gave her back her prechemotherapy looks. Ellis, as a final dramatic impact, had shown for a few seconds a photo of Rachel bald and vulnerable: an ending poignant to devastation.

I hadn't seen the program when it had been broadcast: judging from the March date on the tape, I knew I'd been away in America trying to find an absconding owner who'd left a monstrous training account unpaid. There were, anyway, many of Ellis's programs I hadn't seen: he presented his twenty-minute twice-weekly journalistic segments as part of an hour-long sports news medley, and was too often on the screen for any one appearance to be especially fanfared.

Meeting Ellis, as I often did at the races, I told him about Linda Ferns calling me in, and asked him if he'd learned any more on the subject of who had mutilated the Kent ponies.

"My dear old Sid," he said, smiling, "all of that was months ago, wasn't it?"

"The ponies were vandalized in January and February and your program was aired in March."

"And it's now June, right?" He shook his head, neither distressed nor

surprised. "You know what my life's like, I have *researchers* digging out stories
for me. Television is insatiably hungry. Of course if there were any more dis-
coveries about these ponies, I would have been told, and I would have done a
follow-up, but I've heard nothing."

I said, "Rachel Ferns, who has leukemia, still has nightmares."

"Poor little kid."

"She said you were very kind."

"Well . . ." he made a ducking, self-deprecating movement of his head,
". . . it isn't so very difficult. Actually that program did marvels for my ratings." He paused. "Sid, do you know anything about this bookmaker kick-
back scandal I'm supposed to be doing an exposé on next week?"

"Nothing at all," I regretted. "But, Ellis, going back to the mutilations,
did you chase up those other scattered cases of foals and two-year-old thoroughbreds that suffered from vandalism?"

He frowned lightly, shaking his head. "The researchers didn't think them
worth more than a mention or two. It was copycat stuff. I mean, there wasn't
anything as strong as that story about the children." He grinned. "There were
no heartstrings attached to the others."

"You're a cynic," I said.

"Aren't we all?"

We had been close friends for years, Ellis and I. We had ridden against
each other in races, he as a charismatic amateur, I as a dedicated pro, but both
with the inner fire that made hurtling over large jumps on semi-wild half-ton
horses at thirty miles an hour seem a wholly reasonable way of passing as
many afternoons as possible.

Thinking, after three or four months of no results from the police or the
Ellis Quint program, that I would probably fail also in the search for vandals,
I nevertheless did my best to earn my fee by approaching the problem crab-
wise, from the side, by asking questions not of the owners of the ponies, but
of the newspapermen who had written the columns in the papers.

I did it methodically on the telephone, starting with the local Kent papers, then chasing up the by-line reporters in the London dailies. Most of the
replies were the same: the story had originated from a news agency that supplied all papers with condensed factual information. Follow-ups and interpretation were the business of the papers themselves.

Among the newspapers Linda Ferns had given me, *The Pump* had stirred
up the most disgust, and after about six phone calls I ran to earth the man
who'd practically burned holes in the page with the heat of his prose: Kevin
Mills, *The Pump*'s chief bleeding-hearts reporter.

"A jar?" he said, to my invitation. "Don't see why not."

He met me in a pub (nice anonymous surroundings) and he told me he'd personally been down to Kent on that story. He'd interviewed all the children and their parents and also a fierce lady who ran one of the branches of the Pony Club, and he'd pestered the police until they'd thrown him out.

"Zilch," he said, downing a double gin and tonic. "No one saw a thing. All those ponies were out in fields and all of them were attacked sometime between sunset and dawn, which in January and February gave the vandals hours and hours to do the job and vamoose."

"All dark, though," I said.

He shook his head. "They were all done over on fine nights, near the full moon in each month."

"How many, do you remember?"

"Four altogether in January. Two of them were blinded. Two were mares with torn knife wounds up their . . . well, *birth passages*, as our squeamish editor had me put it."

"And February?"

"One blinded, two more chopped-up mares, one cut-off foot. A poor little girl found the foot near the water trough where her pony used to drink. Ellis Quint did a brilliant TV program about it. Didn't you see it?"

"I was in America, but I've heard about it since."

"There were trailers of that program all week. Almost the whole nation watched it. It made a hell of an impact. That pony was the last one in Kent, as far as I know. The police think it was a bunch of local thugs who got the wind up when there was so much fuss. And people stopped turning ponies out into unguarded fields, see?"

I ordered him another double. He was middle aged, half-bald, doing nicely as to paunch. He wiped an untidy mustache on the back of his hand and said that in his career he'd interviewed so many parents of raped and murdered girls that the ponies had been almost a relief.

I asked him about the later copycat attacks on thoroughbreds in other places, not Kent.

"Copycat?" he repeated. "So they say."

"But?" I prompted.

He drank, thought it over, confided.

"All the others," he said, "are not in bunches, like Kent. As far as I know—and there may be still others—there were about five very young horses, foals and yearlings, that had things done to them, bad enough mostly for them to have to be put down, but none of them was blinded. One had his

muzzle hacked off. None of them were mares. But . . ." He hesitated; sure of
his facts, I thought, but not of how I would react to them.

"Go on."

"See, three others were two-year-olds, and all of those had a foot off."

I felt the same revulsion that I saw in his face.

"One in March," he said. "One in April. One last month."

"Not," I said slowly, "at the full moon?"

"Not precisely. Just on moonlit nights."

"But why haven't you written about it?"

"I got sent to major disasters," he said patiently. "Air crashes, multiple
deaths, dozens of accidents and murders. Some nutter driving around chop-
ping off a horse's foot now and again—it's not my absolute priority, but
maybe I'll get round to it. The news agency hasn't picked up on it, but I tend
to read provincial papers. Old habit. There has been just a para or two here
and there about animal vandals. It's always happening. Horses, sheep, dogs—
weirdos get their mucky hands on them. Come to think of it, though, if
there's another one this month I'll insist on giving it the both-barrel treatment. And now, don't you go feeding this to other papers. I want my scoop."

"Silence," I promised, "if . . ."

He asked suspiciously, "If what?"

"If you could give me a list of the people whose thoroughbreds have been
damaged."

He said cautiously, "It'll cost you."

"Done," I said, and we agreed both on a fee and on my giving him first
chance at any story I might come up with.

He fulfilled his commitment that same afternoon by sending a motorbike
courier bearing a sealed brown envelope containing photocopies of several inconspicuous small paragraphs culled from provincial papers in Liverpool,
Reading, Shrewsbury, Manchester, Birmingham and York. All the papers
gave the names and vague addresses of the owners of vandalized thoroughbreds, so I set off by car and visited them.

Four days later, when I returned to Linda Ferns's house in Kent, I had
heard enough about man's inhumanity to horses to last me for life. The injuries inflicted, from the hacked-off muzzle onwards, were truly beyond comprehension but, compared with three two-year-olds, were all random and
without pattern. It was the severed feet that were connected.

"I came across his foot by the water trough in the field," one woman said,
her eyes screwing up at the memory. "I couldn't *believe* it. Just a *foot.* Tell you
the truth, I brought up my breakfast. He was a really nice two-year-old colt."

She swallowed. "He wasn't standing anywhere near his foot. The off-fore, it was. He'd wandered away on three legs and he was eating grass. Just *eating*, as if nothing had happened. He didn't seem to feel any pain."

"What did you do?" I asked.

"I called the vet. He came . . . He gave *me* a tranquilizer. He said I needed it more than the colt did. He looked after everything for me."

"Was the colt insured?" I asked.

She took no offense at the question. I guessed it had been asked a dozen times already. She said there had been no insurance. They had bred the two-year-old themselves. They had been going to race him later in the year. They had been to Cheltenham races and had backed the winner of the Gold Cup, a great day, and the very next morning . . .

I asked her for the vet's name and address, and I went to see him at his home.

"How was the foot taken off?" I asked.

He wrinkled his forehead. "I don't rightly know. It was neat. The colt had bled very little. There was a small pool of blood on the grass about a yard away from the foot, and that was all. The colt himself let me walk right up to him. He looked calm and normal, except that his off-fore ended at the fetlock."

"Was it done with an axe?"

He hesitated. "I'd say more like a machete. Just the one cut, fast and clean. Whoever did it knew just where to aim for, unless he was simply lucky."

"Did you tell the police?"

"Sure. A detective sergeant came out. He vomited, too. Then I called the knackers and put the colt down. Bloody vandals! I'd like to cut off *their* foot, see if they liked life with a stump." He remembered suddenly about my own sliced-off hand, and reddened, looking confused and embarrassed. There had been a much publicized court case about my hand. Everyone knew what had happened. I had finally stopped wincing visibly when people referred to it.

"It's all right," I said mildly.

"I'm sorry. My big mouth . . ."

"Do you think the colt's amputation was done by a vet? By any sort of surgical expert? Was it done with a scalpel? Was the colt given a local anesthetic?"

He said, disturbed, "I don't know the answers. I'd just say that whoever did it was used to handling horses. That colt was loose in the field, though wearing a head collar."

I went to see the detective sergeant, who looked as if he might throw up again at the memory.

"I see a lot of injured people. Dead bodies, too," he said, "but that was different. Mindless. Fair turned my stomach."

The police had found no culprit. It had been an isolated event, not part of a pattern. The only report they'd had was of the presence of a blue Land-Rover driving away along the lane from the colt's field; and Land-Rovers were two a penny in the countryside. Case not closed, but also not being actively investigated. The colt and his hoof had long gone to the glue factory.

"Are there any photographs?" I asked.

The sergeant said that the photographs were a police matter, not open to the general public.

"I do know who you are," he said, not abrasively, "but to us you're the general public. Sorry."

The colt's owner, consulted, said she had been too upset to want photographs.

I drove onwards, northwards to Lancashire, into a gale of anger. Big, blustery and impressively furious, a hard competent large-scale farmer let loose his roaring sense of injustice, yelling in my face, spraying me with spittle, jabbing the air with a rigid forefinger, pushing his chin forward in a classic animal gesture of aggression.

"Best colt I ever owned," he bellowed. "He cost me a packet, but he was a good 'un. Breeding, conformation, the lot. And he was *fast*, I'll tell you. He was going to Newmarket the next week." He mentioned a prestigious trainer who I knew wouldn't have accepted rubbish. "A good 'un," the farmer repeated. "And then the sodding police asked if I'd killed him for the insurance. I ask you! He wasn't insured, I told them. They said I couldn't *prove* he wasn't insured. Did you know that? Did you know you can prove something *is* insured, but you can't prove it *isn't*? Did you know that?"

I said I'd heard it was so.

"I told them to bugger off. They weren't interested in finding who took my colt's foot off, only in proving I did it myself. They made me that *angry*. . . ." His words failed him. I'd met many people unjustly accused of setting fires, battering children, stealing and taking bribes, and by then I knew the vocal vibrations of truly outraged innocence. The angry farmer, I would have staked all on it, had not taken the foot off his own colt, and I told him so. Some of his anger abated into surprise. "So you *believe* me?"

"I sure do." I nodded. "The point is, who knew you'd bought a fine fast colt that you had at your farm in a field?"

"Who knew?" He suddenly looked guilty, as if he'd already had to face an unpalatable fact. "I'd blown my mouth off a bit. Half the county knew. And I'd been boasting about him at Aintree, the day before the Grand National. I was at one of those sponsors' lunch things—Topline Foods, it was—and the colt was fine that night. I saw him in the morning. And it was the next night, after the National, that he was got at."

He had taken his own color photographs (out of distrust of the police) and he showed them to me readily.

"The off-fore," he said, pointing to a close-up of the severed foot. "He was cut just below the fetlock. Almost through the joint. You can see the white ends of the bones."

The photographs jolted. It didn't help that I'd seen my own left wrist in much the same condition. I said, "What was your vet's opinion?"

"Same as mine."

I went to see the vet. One chop, he said. Only one. No missed shots. Straight through at the leg's most vulnerable point.

"What weapon?"

He didn't know.

I pressed onwards to Yorkshire, where, barely a month earlier, at the time of the York Spring Meeting, a dark-brown two-year-old colt had been deprived of his off-fore foot on a moonlit night. One chop. No insurance. Sick and angry owners. No clues.

These owners were a stiff-upper-lip couple with elderly manners and ancient immutable values who were as deeply bewildered as repelled by the level of evil that would for no clear reason destroy a thing of beauty; in this case the fluid excellence of a fleet, glossy equine princeling.

"*Why?*" they asked me insistently. "*Why* would anyone do such a pointlessly wicked thing?"

I had no answer. I prompted them only to talk, to let out their pain and deprivation. I got them to talk, and I listened.

The wife said, "We had such a lovely week. Every year we have people to stay for the York Spring Meeting . . . because, as you can see, this is quite a large house . . . so we have six or eight friends staying, and we get in extra staff and have a party—such fun, you see—and this year the weather was perfect and we all had a great time."

"Successful, don't you know," said her husband, nodding.

"Dear Ellis Quint was one of our guests," the hostess said with a smile, "and he lifted everyone's spirits in that easy way of his so that it seemed we spent the whole week laughing. He was filming for one of his television programs at York races, so we were all invited behind the scenes and enjoyed it all so much. And then . . . then . . . the very night after all our guests had left . . . well . . ."

"Jenkins came and told us—Jenkins is our groom—he told us while we were sitting at breakfast, that our colt . . . our colt . . ."

"We have three brood-mares," his wife said. "We love to see the foals and yearlings out in the fields, running free, you know . . . and usually we sell the yearlings, but that colt was so beautiful that we kept him, and he was going into training soon. . . . All our guests had admired him."

"Jenkins had made a splendid job of breaking him in."

"Jenkins was in *tears*," the wife said. "Jenkins! A tough, leathery old man. In *tears*."

The husband said with difficulty, "Jenkins found the foot by the gate, beside the water trough."

His wife went on. "Jenkins told us that Ellis had done a program a few months ago about a pony's foot being cut off and the children being so devastated. So we wrote to Ellis about our colt and Ellis telephoned at once to say how *awful* for us. He couldn't have been nicer. Dear Ellis. But there wasn't anything he could do, of course, except sympathize."

"No," I agreed, and I felt only the faintest twitch of surprise that Ellis hadn't mentioned the York colt when I'd been talking to him less than a week earlier about Rachel Ferns.

CHAPTER 3

BACK IN LONDON I met Kevin Mills, the journalist from *The Pump*, at lunchtime in the same pub as before.

"It's time for both barrels," I said.

He swigged the double gin. "What have you discovered?"

I outlined the rest of the pattern, beyond what he'd told me about two-year-old colts on moonlit nights. One chop from something like a machete. Always the off-fore fool. Always near a water trough. No insurance. And always just after a major local race meeting: the Gold Cup Festival at Cheltenham; the Grand National at Liverpool; the Spring Meeting at York.

"And this Saturday, two days from now," I said levelly, "we have the Derby."

He put his glass down slowly, and after a full silent minute said, "What about the kid's pony?"

I shrugged resignedly. "It was the first that we know of."

"And it doesn't fit the pattern. Not a two-year-old colt, was he? And no major race meeting, was there?"

"The severed foot was by the water trough. The off-fore foot. Moon in the right quarter. One chop. No insurance."

He frowned, thinking. "Tell you what," he said eventually, "it's worth a *warning.* I'm not a sports writer, as you know, but I'll get the message into the paper somewhere. 'Don't leave your two-year-old colts unguarded in open fields during and after the Epsom meeting.' I don't think I can do more than that."

"It might be enough."

"Yeah. *If* all the owners of colts read *The Pump.*"

"It will be the talk of the racecourse. I'll arrange that."

"On Derby Day?" He looked skeptical. "Still, it will be better than nothing." He drank again. "What we really need to do is catch the bugger red-handed."

We gloomily contemplated that impossibility. Roughly fifteen thousand thoroughbred foals were born each year in the British Isles. Half would be colts. Many of those at two would already be in training for flat racing, tucked away safely in stables; but that still left a host unattended out of doors. By June, also, yearling colts, growing fast, could be mistaken at night for two-year-olds.

Nothing was safe from a determined vandal.

Kevin Mills went away to write his column and I traveled on to Kent to report to my clients.

"Have you found out *who?*" Linda demanded.

"Not yet."

We sat by the sitting-room window again, watching Rachel push Pegotty in his buggy around the lawn, and I told her about the three colts and their shattered owners.

"Three more," Linda repeated numbly. "In March, April and May? And Silverboy in February?"

"That's right."

"And what about *now?* This month . . . *June?*"

I explained about the warning to be printed in *The Pump.*

"I'm not going to tell Rachel about the other three," Linda said. "She wakes up screaming as it is."

"I inquired into other injured horses all over England," I said, "but they were all hurt differently from each other. I think . . . well . . . that there are several different people involved. And I don't think the thugs that blinded and cut the ponies round here had anything to do with Silverboy."

Linda protested. "But they must have done! There couldn't be *two* lots of vandals."

"I think there were."

She watched Rachel and Pegotty, the habitual tears not far away. Rachel was tickling the baby to make him laugh.

"I'd do anything to save my daughter," Linda said. "The doctor said that if only she'd had several sisters, one of them might have had the right tissue type. Joe—Rachel's father—is half Asian. It seems harder to find a match. So I had the baby. I had Pegotty five months ago." She wiped her eyes. "Joe has his new wife and he wouldn't sleep with me again, not even for Rachel. So he donated sperm and I had artificial insemination, and it worked at once. It seemed an omen . . . and I had the baby . . . but he doesn't match Rachel. . . . There was only ever one chance in four that he would have the same tissue type and antigens. . . . I hoped and prayed . . . but he *doesn't*." She gulped, her throat closing. "So I have Pegotty . . . he's Peter, really, but we call him Pegotty . . . but Joe won't bond with him . . . and we still can't find a match anywhere for Rachel, and there isn't much time for me to try with another baby . . . and Joe *won't*, anyway. His wife objects . . . and he didn't want to do it the first time."

"I'm so sorry," I said.

"Joe's wife goes on and on about Joe having to pay child support for Pegotty . . . and now she's pregnant herself."

Life, I thought, brought unlimited and complicated cruelties.

"Joe isn't mean," Linda said. "He loves Rachel and he bought her the pony and he keeps us comfortable, but his wife says I could have *six* children without getting a match . . . ." Her voice wavered and stopped, and after a while she said, "I don't know why I burdened you with all that. You're so easy to talk to."

"And interested."

She nodded, sniffing and blowing her nose. "Go out and talk to Rachel. I told her you were coming back today. She liked you."

Obediently I went out into the garden and gravely shook hands with Rachel, and we sat side by side on a garden bench like two old buddies.

Though still warm, the golden days of early June were graying and growing damp: good for roses, perhaps, but not for the Derby.

I apologized that I hadn't yet found out who had attacked Silverboy.

"But you will in the end, won't you?"

"I hope so," I said.

She nodded. "I told Daddy yesterday that I was sure you would."

"Did you?"

"Yes. He took me out in his car. He does that sometimes, when Didi goes to London to do shopping."

"Is Didi his wife?"

Rachel's nose wrinkled in a grimace, but she made no audible judgment. She said, "Daddy says someone chopped your hand off, just like Silverboy."

She regarded me gravely, awaiting confirmation.

"Er," I said, unnerved, "not exactly like Silverboy."

"Daddy says the man who did it was sent to prison, but he's out again now on parole."

"Do you know what 'on, parole' means?" I asked curiously.

"Yes. Daddy told me."

"Your daddy knows a lot."

"Yes, but is it *true* that someone chopped your hand off?"

"Does it matter to you?"

"Yes, it does," she said. "I was thinking about it in bed last night. I have awful dreams. I tried to stay awake because I didn't want to go to sleep and dream about you having your hand chopped off."

She was trying to be grown up and calm, but I could feel screaming hysteria too near the surface; so, stifling my own permanent reluctance to talk about it, I gave her an abbreviated account of what had happened.

"I was a jockey," I began.

"Yes, I know. Daddy said you were the champion for years."

"Well, one day my horse fell in a race, and while I was on the ground another horse landed over a jump straight onto my wrist and . . . um . . . tore it apart. It got stitched up, but I couldn't use my hand much. I had to stop being a jockey, and I started doing what I do now, which is finding out things, like who hurt Silverboy."

She nodded.

"Well, I found out something that an extremely nasty man didn't want me to know, and he . . . er . . . he hit my bad wrist and broke it again, and that time the doctor couldn't stitch it up, so they decided that I'd be better off with a useful plastic hand instead of the useless old one."

"So he didn't really . . . not *really* chop it off. Not like with an axe or anything?"

"No. So don't waste dreams on it."

She smiled with quiet relief and, as she was sitting on my left, put her right hand down delicately but without hesitation on the replacement parts. She stroked the tough plastic, unfeeling skin and looked up with surprise at my eyes.

"It isn't *warm*," she said.

"Well, it isn't cold, either."

She laughed with uncomplicated fun. "How does it work?"

"I tell it what to do," I said simply. "I send a message from my brain down my arm saying open thumb from fingers, or close thumb to fingers, to grip things, and the messages reach very sensitive terminals called electrodes, which are inside the plastic and against my skin." I paused, but she didn't say she didn't understand. I said, "My real arm ends about there"—I pointed—"and the plastic arm goes up round my elbow. The electrodes are up in my forearm, there, against my skin. They feel my muscles trying to move. That's how they work."

"Is the plastic arm tied on or anything?"

"No. It just fits tightly and stays on by itself. It was specially made to fit me."

Like all children she took marvels for granted, although to me, even though by then I'd had the false arm for nearly three years, the concept of nerve messages moving machinery was still extraordinary.

"There are three electrodes," I said. "One for opening the hand, one for closing, and one for turning the wrist."

"Do electrodes work on electricity?" It puzzled her. "I mean, you're not plugged into the wall, or anything?"

"You're a clever girl," I told her. "It works on a special sort of battery which slots into the outside above where I wear my watch. I charge up the batteries on a charger which is plugged into the wall."

She looked at me assessingly. "It must be pretty useful to have that hand."

"It's brilliant," I agreed.

"Daddy says Ellis Quint told him that you can't tell you have a plastic hand unless you touch it."

I asked, surprised, "Does your daddy know Ellis Quint?"

She nodded composedly. "They go to the same place to play squash. He helped Daddy buy Silverboy. He was really really sorry when he found out it was Silverboy himself that he was making his program about."

"Yes, he would be."

"I wish . . . ," she began, looking down at my hand, "I do wish Silverboy could have had a new foot . . . with electrodes and a battery."

I said prosaically, "He might have been able to have a false foot fitted, but he wouldn't have been able to trot or canter, or jump. He wouldn't have been happy just limping around."

She rubbed her own fingers over the plastic ones, not convinced.

I said, "Where did you keep Silverboy?"

"The other side of that fence at the end of the garden." She pointed. "You can't see it from here because of those trees. We have to go through the house and out and down the lane."

"Will you show me?"

There was a moment of drawing back, then she said, "I'll take you if I can hold your hand on the way."

"Of course." I stood up and held out my real, warm, normal arm.

"No . . ." She shook her head, standing up also. "I mean, can I hold this hand that you can't feel?"

It seemed to matter to her that I wasn't whole; that I would understand someone ill, without hair.

I said lightly, "You can hold which hand you like."

She nodded, then pushed Pegotty into the house, and matter-of-factly told Linda she was taking me down to the field to show me where Silverboy had lived. Linda gave me a wild look but let us go, so the bald-headed child and the one-handed man walked in odd companionship down a short lane and leaned against a five-barred gate across the end.

The field was a lush paddock of little more than an acre, the grass growing strongly, uneaten. A nearby standing pipe with an ordinary tap on it stood ready to fill an ordinary galvanized water trough. The ground around the trough was churned up, the grass growing more sparsely, as always happened around troughs in fields.

"I don't want to go in," Rachel said, turning her head away.

"We don't need to."

"His foot was by the trough," she said jerkily, "I mean . . . you could see *blood* . . . and white bones."

"Don't talk about it." I pulled her with me and walked back along the lane, afraid I should never have asked her to show me.

She gripped my unfeeling hand in both of hers, slowing me down.

"It's all right," she said. "It was a long time ago. It's all right now when I'm awake."

"Good."

"I don't like going to sleep."

The desperation of that statement was an open appeal, and had to be addressed.

I stopped walking before we reached the door of the house. I said, "I don't usually tell anyone this, but I'll tell you. I still sometimes have bad dreams about my hand. I dream I can clap with two hands. I dream I'm still a jockey. I dream about my smashed wrist. Rotten dreams can't be helped. They're awful when they happen. I don't know how to stop them. But one does wake up."

"And then you have leukemia . . . or a plastic arm."

"Life's a bugger," I said.

She put her hand over her mouth and, in a fast release of tension, she giggled. "Mum won't let me say that."

"Say it into your pillow."

"Do you?"

"Pretty often."

We went on into the house and Rachel again pushed Pegotty into the garden. I stayed in the sitting room with Linda and watched through the window.

"Was she all right?" Linda asked anxiously.

"She's a very brave child."

Linda wept.

I said, "Did you hear anything at all the night Silverboy was attacked?"

"Everyone asks that. I'd have said if I had."

"No car engines?"

"The police said they must have stopped the car in the road and walked down the lane. My bedroom window doesn't face the lane, nor does Rachel's. But that lane doesn't go anywhere except to the field. As you saw, it's only a track really, it ends at the gate."

"Could anyone see Silverboy from the road?"

"Yes, the police asked that. You could see him come to drink. You can see the water trough from the road, if you know where to look. The police say the thugs must have been out all over this part of Kent looking for unguarded ponies like Silverboy. Whatever you say about two-year-olds, Silverboy *must* have been done by thugs. Why don't you ask the police?"

"If you wholeheartedly believed the police, you wouldn't have asked me for help."

"Joe just telephoned," she confessed, wailing, "and he says that calling you in to help is a waste of money."

"Ah."

"I don't know what to think."

I said, "You're paying me by the day, plus expenses. I can stop right now, if you like."

"No. Yes. I don't *know*." She wiped her eyes, undecided, and said, "Rachel dreams that Silverboy is standing in the field and he's glowing bright and beautiful in the moonlight. He's *shining*, she says. And there's a dark mass of monsters oozing down the lane . . . 'oozing' is what she says . . . and they are shapeless and devils and they're going to kill Silverboy. She says she is trying to run fast to warn him, and she can't get through the monsters, they clutch at her like cobwebs. She can't get through them and they reach Silverboy and smother his light, and all his hair falls out, and she wakes up and screams. It's always the same nightmare. I thought if you could find out who cut the poor thing's foot off, the monsters would have names and faces and would be in the papers, and Rachel would know who they were and stop thinking they're lumps that ooze without eyes and won't let her through."

After a pause, I said, "Give me another week."

She turned away from me sharply and, crossing to a desk, wrote me a check. "For two weeks, one gone, one ahead."

I looked at the amount. "That's more than we agreed on."

"Whatever Joe says, I want you to go on trying."

I gave her tentatively a small kiss on the cheek. She smiled, her eyes still dark and wet. "I'll pay anything for Rachel," she said.

I drove slowly back to London thinking of the cynical old ex-policeman who had taught me the basics of investigation. "There are two cardinal rules in this trade," he said. "One. Never believe everything a client tells you, and always believe they could have told you more if you'd asked the right questions. And two. Never, never get emotionally involved with your client."

Which was all very well, except when your client was a bright, truthful nine-year-old fighting a losing battle against a rising tide of lympboblasts.

I BOUGHT A take-out curry on the way home and ate it before spending the evening on overdue paperwork.

I much preferred the active side of the job, but clients wanted, and deserved, and paid for, detailed accounts of what I'd done on their behalf, preferably with results they liked. With the typed recital of work done, I sent also my final bill, adding a list of itemized expenses supported by receipts. I almost always played fair, even with clients I didn't like: investigators had been known to charge for seven days' work when, with a little application, they could have finished the job in three. I didn't want that sort of reputation. Speed succeeded in my new occupation as essentially as in my old.

Besides bathroom and kitchen, my pleasant (and frankly, expensive) apartment consisted of three rooms: bedroom, big sunny sitting room and a third, smaller room that I used as an office. I had no secretary or helper; no one read the secrets I uncovered except the client and me, and whatever the client did with the information he'd paid for was normally his or her own business. Privacy was what drove many people to consult me, and privacy was what they got.

I listened to some unexciting messages on my answering machine, typed a report on my secure word processor, printed it and put it ready for mailing. For reports and anything personal I used a computer system that wasn't connected to any phone line. No one could in consequence tap into it and, as a precaution against thieves, I used unbreakable passwords. It was my second system that could theoretically be accessed; the one connected by modem to the big wide world of universal information. Any snooper was welcome to anything found there.

On the subject of the management of secrecy, my cynical mentor had said, "Never, ever tell your right hand what your left hand is doing. Er . . . ," he added, "whoops. Sorry, Sid."

"It'll cost you a pint."

"And," he went on later, drinking, "keep back-up copies of completed sensitive inquiries in a bank vault, and wipe the information from any computer systems in your office. If you use random passwords, and change them weekly, you should be safe enough while you're actually working on something, but once you've finished, get the back-up to the bank and wipe the office computer, like I said."

"All right."

"Never forget," he told me, "that the people you are investigating may go to violent lengths to stop you."

He had been right about that.

"Never forget that you don't have the same protection as the police do. You have to make your own protection. You have to be careful."

"Maybe I should look for another job."

"No, Sid," he said earnestly, "you have a gift for this. You listen to what I tell you and you'll do fine."

He had taught me for the two years I'd spent doing little but drift in the old Radnor detection agency after the end of my racing life and, for nearly three years since, I'd lived mostly by his precepts. But he was dead now, and

Radnor himself also, and I had to look inward for wisdom, which could be a variable process, not always ultraproductive.

I could try to comfort Rachel by telling her I had bad dreams also, but I could never have told her how vivid and liquefying they could be. That night, after I'd eased off the arm and showered and gone peacefully to bed, I fell asleep thinking of her, and descended after midnight into a familiar dungeon.

It was always the same.

I dreamed I was in a big dark space, and some people were coming to cut off both my hands.

Both.

They were making me wait, but they would come. There would be agony and humiliation and helplessness . . . and no way out.

I semi-awoke in shaking, sweating, heart-thudding terror and then realized with flooding relief that it wasn't true, I was safe in my own bed—and then remembered that it had already half happened in fact, and also that I'd come within a fraction once of a villain's shooting the remaining hand off. As soon as I was awake enough to be clear about the present actual not-too-bad state of affairs I slid back reassured into sleep, and that night the whole appalling nightmare cycled again . . . and again.

I forced myself to wake up properly, to sit up and get out of bed and make full consciousness take over. I stood under the shower again and let cool water run through my hair and down my body. I put on a terry cloth bathrobe and poured a glass of milk, and sat in an armchair in the sitting room with all the lights on.

I looked at the space where a left hand had once been, and I looked at the strong whole right hand that held a glass, and I acknowledged that often, both waking as well as sleeping, I felt, and could not repress, stabs of savage, petrifying fear that one day it would indeed be both. The trick was not to let the fear show, nor to let it conquer, nor rule, my life.

It was pointless to reflect that I'd brought the terrors on myself. I had chosen to be a jockey. I had chosen to go after violent crooks. I was at that moment actively seeking out someone who knew how to cut off a horse's foot with one chop.

My own equivalent of the off-fore held a glass of milk.

I had to be mentally deranged.

But then there were people like Rachel Ferns.

In one way or another I had survived many torments, and much could have been avoided but for my own obstinate nature. I knew by then that whatever came along, I would deal with it. But that child had had her hair fall out and had found her beloved pony's foot, and none of that was her fault. No nine year-old mind could sleep sweetly under such assaults.

Oh God, Rachel, I thought I would dream your nightmares for you if I could.

IN THE MORNING I made a working analysis in five columns of the Ferns pony and the three two-year-olds. The analysis took the form of a simple graph, ruled in boxes. Across the top of the page I wrote: Factors, Ferns, Cheltenham, Aintree, York, and down the left-hand column, Factors, I entered "date," "name of owner," "racing program," "motive" and finally, "who knew of victim's availability?" I found that although I could *think* of answers to that last question, I hadn't the wish to write them in, and after a bit of indecision I phoned Kevin Mills at *The Pump* and, by persistence, reached him.

"Sid," he said heartily, "the warning will be in the paper tomorrow. You've done your best. Stop agitating."

"Great," I said, "but could you do something else? Something that could come innocently from *The Pump*, but would raise all sorts of reverberations if I asked directly myself."

"Such as what?"

"Such as ask Topline Foods for a list of the guests they entertained at a sponsors' lunch at Aintree the day before the National."

"What the *hell* for?"

"Will you do it?"

He said, "What are you up to?"

"The scoop is still yours. Exclusive."

"I don't know why I trust you."

"It pays off," I said, smiling.

"It had better." He put down his receiver with a crash, but I knew he would do what I asked.

It was Friday morning. At Epsom that day they would be running the Coronation Cup and also the Oaks, the fillies' equivalent of the Derby. It was also lightly raining: a weak warm front, it seemed, was slowly blighting southern England.

Racecourses still drew me as if I were tethered to them with bungee elastic, but before setting out I telephoned the woman whose colt's foot had been amputated during the night after the Cheltenham Gold Cup.

"I'm sorry to bother you again, but would you mind a few more questions?"

"Not if you can catch the bastards."

"Well . . . was the two-year-old alone in his field?"

"Yes he was. It was only a paddock. Railed, of course. We kept him in the paddock nearest to the house, that's what is so infuriating. We had two old hacks turned out in the field beyond him, but the vandals left them untouched."

"And," I said neutrally, "how many people knew the colt was accessible? And how accessible was he?"

"Sid," she exclaimed, "don't think we haven't racked our brains. The trouble is, all our friends knew about him. We were excited about his prospects. And then, at the Cheltenham meeting, we had been talking to people about *trainers.* Old Gunners, who used to train for us in the past, has died, of course, and we don't like that uppity assistant of his that's taken over the stable, so we were asking around, you see."

"Yeah. And did you decide on a trainer?"

"We did, but, of course . . ."

"Such a bloody shame," I sympathized. "Who did you decide on?"

She mentioned a first-class man. "Several people said that with him we couldn't go wrong."

"No." I mentally sighed, and asked obliquely, "What did you especially enjoy about the festival meeting?"

"The Queen came," she said promptly. "I had thick, warm boots on, and I nearly fell over them, curtseying." She laughed. "And oh, also, I suppose you do know you're in the Hall of Fame there?"

"It's an honor," I said. "They gave me an engraved glass goblet that I can see across the room right now from where I'm sitting."

"Well, we were standing in front of that big exhibit they've put together of your life, and we were reading the captions, and dear Ellis Quint stopped beside us and put his arm round my shoulders and said that our Sid was a pretty great guy, all in all."

Oh *shit*, I thought.

Her warm smile was audible down the line. "We've known Ellis for years, of course. He used to ride our horses in amateur races. So he called in at our house for a drink on his way home after the Gold Cup. Such a *lovely* day." She sighed. "And then those *bastards* . . . You will catch them, won't you, Sid?"

"If I can," I said.

I left a whole lot of the boxes empty on my chart, and drove to Epsom Downs, spirits as gray as the skies. The bars were crowded. Umbrellas dripped. The brave colors of June dresses hid under drabber raincoats, and only the geraniums looked happy.

I walked damply to the parade ring before the two-year-old colts' six-furlong race and thoughtfully watched all the off-fore feet plink down light-heartedly. The young, spindly bones of those forelegs thrust thousand-pound bodies forward at sprinting speeds near forty miles an hour. I had mostly raced on the older, mature horses of steeplechasing, half a ton in weight, slightly slower, capable of four miles and thirty jumps from start to finish, but still on legs scarcely thicker than a big man's wrist.

The anatomy of a horse's foreleg consisted, from the shoulder down, of forearm, knee, cannon bone, fetlock joint (also known as the ankle), pastern bone, and hoof. The angry Lancashire farmer's colored photograph had shown the amputation to have been effected straight through the narrowest part of the whole leg, just at the base of the fetlock joint, where the pastern emerged from it. In effect, the whole pastern and the hoof had been cut off.

Horses had very fast instincts for danger and were easily scared. Young horses seldom stood still. Yet one single chop had done the job each time. *Why* had all those poor animals stood quietly while the deed was done? None of them had squealed loud enough to alert his owner.

I went up on the stands and watched the two-year-olds set off from the spur away to the left at the top of the hill; watched them swoop down like a flock of starlings round Tattenham Corner, and sort themselves out into win-ner and losers along the straight with its deceptively difficult camber that could tilt a horse towards the rails if his jockey was inexperienced.

I watched, and I sighed. Five long years had passed since I'd ridden my last race. Would regret, I wondered, ever fade?

"Why so pensive, Sid lad?" asked an elderly trainer, grasping my elbow. "A scotch and water for your thoughts!" He steered me around towards the nearest bar and I went with him unprotestingly, as custom came my way quite often in that casual manner. He was great with horses and famously mean with his money.

"I hear you're damned expensive," he began inoffensively, handing me a glass. "What will you charge me for a day's work?"

I told him.

"Too damned much. Do it for nothing, for old times' sake."

I added, smiling, "How many horses do you train for nothing?"

"That's different."

"How many races would you have asked me to ride for nothing?"

"Oh, all *right*, then. I'll pay your damned fee. The fact is, I think I'm being *had*, and I want you to find out."

It seemed he had received a glowing testimonial from the present employer of a chauffeur/houseman/handyman who'd applied for a job he'd advertised. He wanted to know if it was worth bringing the man up for an interview.

"She," he said, "his employer is a woman. I phoned her when I got the letter, to check the reference, you see. She couldn't have been more complimentary about the man if she'd tried, but . . . I don't know . . . She was *too* complimentary, if you see what I mean."

"You mean you think she might be glad to see the back of him?"

"You don't hang about, Sid. That's exactly what I mean."

He gave me the testimonial letter of fluorescent praise.

"No problem," I said, reading it. "One day's fee, plus travel expenses. I'll phone you, then send you a written report."

"You still *look* like a jockey," he complained. "You're a damned sight more expensive on your feet."

I smiled, put the letter away in a pocket, drank his scotch and applauded the string of winners he'd had recently, cheering him up before separating him from his cash.

I drifted around pleasurably but unprofitably for the rest of the day, slept thankfully without nightmares and found on a dry and sunny Derby Day morning that my friendly *Pump* reporter had really done his stuff.

"Lock up your colts," he directed in the paper. "You've heard of foot fetishists? This is one beyond belief."

He outlined in succinct paragraphs the similarities in "the affair of the four severed fetlocks" and pointed out that on that very night after the Derby—the biggest race of all—there would be moonlight enough at three A.M. for flashlights to be unnecessary. All two-year-old colts should, like Cinderella, be safe indoors by midnight. "And if . . . ," he finished with a flourish, ". . . you should spy anyone creeping through the fields armed with a machete, phone ex-jockey turned gumshoe Sid Halley, who provided the information gathered here and can be reached via *The Pump*'s special hotline. Phone *The Pump!* Save the colts! Halley to the rescue!"

I COULDN'T IMAGINE how he had got that last bit—including a telephone number—past any editor, but I needn't have worried about spreading the message on the rarecourse. No one spoke to me about anything else all afternoon.

I phoned *The Pump* myself and reached someone eventually who told me that Kevin Mills had gone to a train crash; sorry.

"Damn," I said. "So how are you rerouting calls about colts to me? I didn't arrange this. How will it work?"

"Hold on."

I held on. A different voice came back.

"As Kevin isn't available, we're rerouting all Halley hotline calls to this number," he said, and he read out my own Pont Square number.

"Where's your bloody Mills? I'll wring his neck."

"Gone to the train crash. Before he left he gave us this number for reaching you. He said you would want to know at once about any colts."

That was true enough—but hell's bloody bells, I thought, I could have set it up better if he'd warned me.

I watched the Derby with inattention. An outsider won.

Ellis teased me about the piece in *The Pump*.

"Hotline Halley," he said, laughing and clapping me on the shoulder, tall and deeply friendly and wiping out in a flash the incredulous doubts I'd been having about him. "Its an extraordinary coincidence, Sid, but I actually saw one of those colts. Alive, of course. I was staying with some chums from York, and after we'd gone home someone vandalized their colt. Such fun people. They didn't deserve anything like that."

"No one does."

"True."

"The really puzzling thing is motive," I said. "I went to see all the owners. None of the colts was insured. Nor was Rachel Ferns's pony, of course."

He said interestedly, "Did you think it was an insurance scam?"

"It jumps to mind, doesn't it? Theoretically it's possible to insure a horse and collect the lucre without the owner knowing anything about it. It's been done. But if that's what this is all about, perhaps someone in an insurance company somewhere will see the piece in *The Pump* and connect a couple of things. Come to think of it," I finished slowly, "I might send a copy to every likely insurance company's board of directors, asking, and warning them."

"Good idea," he said. "Does insurance and so on really take the place of racing? It sounds a pretty dull life for you, after what we used to do."

"Does television replace it for you?"

"Not a hope." He laughed. "Danger is addictive, wouldn't you say? The only dangerous job in television is reporting wars and—have you noticed?—the same few war reporters get out there all the time, talking with their earnest, committed faces about this or that month's little dust-up, while bullets fly and chip off bits of stone in the background to prove how brave they are."

"You're jealous." I smiled.

"I get sodding bored sometimes with being a chat-show celebrity, even if it's nice being liked. Don't you ache for speed?"

"Every day," I said.

"You're about the only person who understands me. No one else can see that fame's no substitute for danger."

"It depends what you risk."

Hands, I thought. One could risk hands.

"Good luck, Hotline," Ellis said.

It was the owners of two-year-old colts that had the good luck. My telephone jammed and rang nonstop all evening and all night when I got home after the Derby, but the calls were all from people enjoying their shivers and jumping at shadows. The moonlight shone on quiet fields, and no animal, whether colt or two-year-old thoughbred or children's pony, lost a foot.

In the days that followed, interest and expectation dimmed and died. It was twelve days after the Derby, on the last night of the Royal Ascot meeting, that the screaming heebie-jeebies re-awoke.

CHAPTER 4

ON THE MONDAY after the Derby, I trailed off on the one-day dig into the overblown reference and, without talking to the lady-employer herself (which would clearly have been counterproductive) I uncovered enough to phone the tight-fisted trainer with sound advice.

"She wants to get rid of him without risk of being accused of unfair dismissal," I said. "He steals small things from her house which pass through a couple of hands and turn up in the local antique shop. She can't prove they were hers. The antique shop owner is whining about his innocence. The lady has apparently said she won't try to prosecute her houseman if he gets the heck out. Her testimonial is part of the bargain. The houseman is a regular in the local betting shop, and gambles heavily on horses. Do you want to employ him?"

"Like hell."

"The report I'll write and send to you," I told him, "will say only, 'Work done on recruitment of staff.' You can claim tax relief on it."

He laughed dryly. "Anytime you want a reference," he said, pleased, "I'll write you an affidavit."

"You never know," I said, "and thanks."

I had phoned the report from the car park of a motorway service station on my way home late in the dusky evening, but it was when I reached Pont Square that the day grew doubly dark. There was a two-page fax waiting on my machine and I read it standing in the sitting room with all thoughts of a friendly glass of scotch evaporating into disbelief and the onset of misery.

The pages were from Kevin Mills. "I don't know why you want this list of the great and good," he wrote, "but for what it's worth and because I promised, here is a list of the guests entertained by Topline Foods at lunch at Aintree on the day before the Grand National."

The list contained the name of the angry Lancashire farmer, as was expected, but it was the top of the list that did the psychological damage.

"Guest of Honor," it announced, "Ellis Quint."

All the doubts I'd banished came roaring back with double vigor. Back too came self-ridicule and every defense mechanism under the sun.

I couldn't, didn't, *couldn't* believe that Ellis could maim—and effectively kill—a child's pony and three young racehorses. Not Ellis! No! It was *impossible.*

There had to be *dozens* of other people who could have learned where to find all four of those vulnerable, unguarded animals. It was *stupid* to give any weight to an unreliable coincidence. All the same, I pulled my box chart out of a drawer, and in very small letters, as if in that way I could physically diminish the implication, I wrote in each "Who knew of victim's availability" space the unthinkable words, Ellis Quint.

The "motive" boxes had also remained empty. There was no apparent rational motive. Why did people poke out the eyes of ponies? Why did they stalk strangers and write poison-pen letters? Why did they torture and kill children and tape-record their screams?

I wrote "self-gratification," but it seemed too weak. Insanity? Psychosis? The irresistible primordial upsurge of a hunger for pointless, violent destruction?

It didn't fit the Ellis I knew. Not the man I'd raced against and laughed with and had deemed a close friend for years. One couldn't know someone that well, and yet not know them at all.

Could one?

No.

Relentless thoughts kept me awake all night, and in the morning I sent Linda Ferns's check back to her, uncashed.

"I've got no further," I wrote. "I'm exceedingly sorry."

Two days later the same check returned.

"Dear Sid," Linda replied, "Keep the money. I know you'll find the thugs one day. I don't know what you said to Rachel but she's much happier and she hasn't had any bad dreams since you came last week. For that alone I would pay you double. Affectionately, Linda Ferns."

I put the check in a pending file, caught up with paperwork and attended my usual judo training session.

The judo I practiced was the subtle art of self-defense, the shifting of balance that used an attacker's own momentum to overcome him. Judo was rhythm, leverage and speed; a matter sometimes of applying pressure to nerves and always, in the way I learned, a quiet discipline. The yells and the kicks of karate, the arms slapped down on the padded mat to emphasize aggression, they were neither in my nature nor what I needed. I didn't seek physical domination. I didn't by choice start fights. With the built-in drawbacks of half an arm, a light frame and a height of about five feet seven, my overall requirement was survival.

I went through the routines absentmindedly. They were at best a mental crutch. A great many dangers couldn't be wiped out by an ability to throw an assailant over one's shoulder.

Ellis wouldn't leave my thoughts.

I was wrong. Of *course* I was wrong.

His face was universally known. He wouldn't risk being seen sneaking around fields at night armed with anything like a machete.

But he was bored with celebrity. Fame was no substitute for danger, he'd said. Everything he had was not enough.

All the same . . . *he couldn't.*

IN THE SECOND week after the Derby I went to the four days of the Royal Ascot meeting, drifting around in a morning suit, admiring the gleaming coats of the horses and the women's extravagant hats. I should have enjoyed it, as I usually did. Instead, I felt as if the whole thing were a charade taking illusory place over an abyss.

Ellis, of course, was there every day: and, of course, he sought me out.

"How's it going, Hotline?"

"The hotline is silent."

"There you are, then," Ellis said with friendly irony, "you've frightened your foot merchant off."

"Forever, I hope."

"What if he can't help it?" Ellis said.

"I turned my head: looked at his eyes. "I'll catch him," I said.

He smiled and looked away. "Everyone knows you're a whiz at that sort of thing, but I'll bet you—"

"Don't," I interrupted. "Don't bet on it. It's bad luck."

Someone came up to his other elbow, claiming his attention. He patted my shoulder, said with the usual affection, "See you, Sid," and was drawn away; and I couldn't believe, I *couldn't*, that he had told me *why*, even if not how.

"What if he can't help it?"

Could compulsion lead to cruel, senseless acts?

No . . .

Yes, it could, and yes, it often did.

But not in Ellis. No, *not* in Ellis.

Alibis, I thought, seeking for a rational way out. I would find out—some-how—exactly where Ellis had been on the nights the horses had been at-tacked. I would prove to my own satisfaction that it couldn't have been Ellis, and I would return with relief to the beginning and admit I had no pointers at all and would never find the thugs for Linda, and would quite happily chalk up a failure.

At five-thirty in the morning on the day after the Ascot Gold Cup, I sleepily awoke and answered my ringing telephone to hear a high agitated fe-male voice saying, "I want to reach Sid Halley."

"You have," I said, pushing myself up to sitting and squinting at the clock.

"What?"

"You are talking to Sid Halley." I stifled a yawn. Five-bloody-thirty.

"But I phoned *The Pump* and asked for the hotline!"

I said patiently, "They reroute the hotline calls direct to me. This is Sid Halley you're talking to. How can I help you?"

"Christ," she said, sounding totally disorganized. "We have a colt with a foot off."

After a breath-catching second I said, "Where are you?"

"At home. Oh, I see, Berkshire."

"Where, exactly?"

"Combe Bassett, south of Hungerford."

"And . . . um . . ." I thought of asking, "What's the state of play?" and discarded it as less than tactful. "What is . . . happening?"

"We're all up. Everyone's yelling and crying."

"And the vet?"

"I just phoned him. He's coming."

"And the police?"

"They're sending someone. Then we decided we'd better call you."

"Yes," I replied. "I'll come now, if you like."

"That's why I phoned you."

"What's your name, then? Address?"

She gave them—"Betty Bracken, Manor House, Combe Bassett"— stumbling on the words as if she couldn't remember.

"Please," I said, "ask the vet not to send the colt or his foot off to the knackers until I get there."

"I'll try," she said jerkily. "For God's sakes, *why*? Why our colt?"

"I'll be there in an hour," I said.

What if he can't help it . . .

But it took such planning. Such stealth. So many crazy risks. Someone, sometime, would see him.

Let it not be Ellis, I thought. Let the compulsion be some other poor bastard's ravening subconscious. Ellis would be able to control such a vicious appetite, even if he felt it.

Let it not be Ellis.

Whoever it was, he had to be stopped: and I would stop him, if I could.

I shaved in the car (a Mercedes), clasping the battery-driven razor in the battery-driven hand, and I covered the eighty miles to southwest Berkshire in a time down the comparatively empty M4 that had the speedometer needle quivering where it had seldom been before. The radar speed traps slept. Just as well.

It was a lovely high June morning, fine and fresh. I curled through the gates of Combe Bassett Manor, cruised to a stop in the drive and at six-thirty walked into a house where open doors led to movement, loud voices and a general gnashing of teeth.

The woman who'd phoned rushed over when she saw me, her hands flapping in the air, her whole demeanor in an out-of-control state of fluster.

"Sid Halley? Thank God. Punch some sense into this lot."

This lot consisted of two uniformed policemen and a crowd of what later proved to be family members, neighbors, ramblers and half a dozen dogs.

"Where's the colt?" I asked. "And where's his foot?"

"Out in the field. The vet's there. I told him what you wanted but he's an opinionated Scot. God knows if he'll wait, he's a cantankerous old devil. He—"

"Show me where," I said abruptly, cutting into the flow.

She blinked. "What? Oh, yes. This way."

She set off fast, leading me through big-house, unevenly painted hinterland passages reminiscent of those of Aynsford, of those of any house built with servants in mind. We passed a gun room, flower room and mud room (ranks of green wellies) and emerged at last through a rear door into a yard inhabited by trash cans. From there, through a green wooden garden door, she led the way fast down a hedge-bordered grass path and through a metal-railing gate at the far end of it. I'd begun to think we were off to limbo when suddenly, there before us, was a lane full of vehicles and about ten people leaning on paddock fencing.

My guide was tall, thin, fluttery, at a guess about fifty, dressed in old cord trousers and a drab olive sweater. Her graying hair flopped, unbrushed, over a high forehead. She had been, and still was, beyond caring how she looked, but I had a powerful impression that she was a woman to whom looks mattered little anyway.

She was deferred to. The man leaning on the paddock rails straightened and all but touched their forelocks. "Morning, Mrs. Bracken."

She nodded automatically and ushered me through the wide metal gate that one of the men swung open for her.

Inside the field, at a distance of perhaps thirty paces, stood two more men, also a masculine-looking woman and a passive colt with three feet. All, except the colt, showed the facial and body language of impatience.

One of the men, tall, white-haired, wearing black-rimmed glasses, took two steps forward to meet us.

"Now, Mrs. Bracken, I've done what you asked, but it's past time to put your poor boy out of his misery. And you'll be Sid Halley, I suppose," he said, peering down as from a mountaintop. "There's little you can do." He shook hands briefly as if it were a custom he disapproved of.

He had a strong Scottish accent and the manner of one accustomed to command. The man behind him, unremarkably built, self-effacing in manner, remained throughout a silent watcher on the fringe.

I walked over to the colt and found him wearing a head collar, with a rope halter held familiarly by the woman. The young horse watched me with calm, bright eyes, unafraid. I stroked my hand down his nose, talking to him quietly. He moved his head upward against the pressure and down again as if nodding, saying hello. I let him whiffle his black lips across my knuckles. I stroked his neck and patted him. His skin was dry: no pain, no fear, no distress.

"Is he drugged?" I asked.

"I'd have to run a blood test," the Scotsman said.

"Which you are doing, of course?"

"Of course."

One could tell from the faces of the other man and the woman that no blood test had so far been considered.

I moved around the colt's head and squatted down for a close look at his off-fore, running my hand down the back of his leg, feeling only a soft area of no resistance where normally there would be the tough bowstring tautness of the leg's main tendon. Pathetically, the fetlock was tidy, not bleeding. I bent up the colt's knee and looked at the severed end. It had been done neatly, sliced through, unsplintered ends of bone showing white, the skin cleanly cut as if a practiced chef had used a disjointing knife.

The colt jerked his knee, freeing himself from my grasp.

I stood up.

"Well?" the Scotsman challenged.

"Where's his foot?"

"Over yon, out of sight behind the water trough." He paused, then, as I turned away from him, suddenly added, "It wasn't found there. I put it there, out of sight. It was they ramblers that came to it first."

"Ramblers?"

"Aye."

Mrs. Bracken, who had joined us, explained. "One Saturday every year in June, all the local rambling clubs turn out in force to walk the footpaths in this part of the country, to keep them legally open for the public."

"If they'd stay on the footpaths," the Scot said forbiddingly, "they'd be within their rights."

Mrs. Bracken agreed. "They bring their children and their dogs and their picnics, and act as if they own the place."

"But . . . what on earth time did they find your colt's foot?"

"They set off soon after dawn," Mrs. Bracken observed morosely. "In the middle of June, that's four-thirty in the morning, more or less. They gather before five o'clock, while it is still cool, and set off across my land first, and they were hammering on my door by five-fifteen. Three of the children were in full-blown hysteria, and a man with a beard and a pony-tail was screaming that he blamed the elite. What elite? One of the ramblers phoned the press and then someone fanatical in animal rights, and a carload of activists arrived with 'ban horse racing' banners." She rolled her eyes. "I *despair*," she said. "It's bad enough losing my glorious colt. These people are turning it into a *circus*."

Hold on to the real tragedy at the heart of the farce, I thought briefly, and walked over to the water trough to look at the foot that lay behind it. There were horsefeed nuts scattered everywhere around. Without expecting much emotion, I bent and picked the foot up.

I hadn't seen the other severed feet. I'd actually thought some of the re-ported reactions excessive. But the reality of that poor, unexpected, curiously lonely lump of bone, gristle and torn ends of blood vessels, that wasted mira-cle of anatomical elegance, moved me close to the fury and grief of all the owners.

There was a shoe on the hoof; the sort of small, light shoe fitted to young-sters to protect their forefeet out in the field. There were ten small nails tack-ing the shoe to the hoof. The presence of the shoe brought its own powerful message: civilization had offered care to the colt's foot, barbarity had hacked it off.

I'd loved horses always: it was hard to explain the intimacy that grew be-tween horses and those who tended or rode them. Horses lived in a parallel world, spoke a parallel language, were a mass of instincts, lacked human per-ceptions of kindness or guilt, and allowed a merging on an untamed, untam-able mysterious level of spirit. The Great God Pan lived in racehorses. One cut off his foot at one's peril.

On a more prosaic level I put the hoof back on the ground, unclipped the mobile phone I wore on my belt and, consulting a small diary/notebook for the number, connected myself to a veterinary friend who worked as a surgeon in an equine hospital in Lambourn.

"Bill?" I said. "This is Sid Halley."

"Go to sleep," he said.

"Wake up. It's six-fifty and I'm in Berkshire with the severed off-fore hoof of a two-year-old colt."

"Jesus." He woke up fast.

"I want you to look at it. What do you advise?"

"How long has it been off? Any chance of sewing it back on?"

"It's been off at least three hours, I'd say. Probably more. There's no sign of the Achilles tendon. It's contracted up inside the leg. The amputation is through the fetlock joint itself."

"One blow, like the others?"

I hesitated. "I didn't see the others."

"But something's worrying you?"

"I want you to look at it," I said.

Bill Ruskin and I had worked on other, earlier puzzles, and got along together in a trusting, undemanding friendship that remained unaltered by periods of noncontact.

"What shape is the colt in, generally?" he asked.

"Quiet. No visible pain."

"Is the owner rich?"

"It looks like it."

"See if he'll have the colt—and his foot, of course—shipped over here."

"She," I said. "I'll ask her."

Mrs. Bracken gaped at me mesmerized when I relayed the suggestion, and said "Yes" faintly.

Bill said, "Find a sterile surgical dressing for the leg. Wrap the foot in another dressing and a plastic bag and pack it in a bucket of ice cubes. Is it clean?"

"Some early-morning ramblers found it."

He groaned. "I'll send a horse ambulance," he said. "Where to?"

I explained where I was, and added, "There's a Scots vet here that's urging to put the colt down at once. Use honey-tongued diplomacy."

"Put him on."

I returned to where the colt still stood and, explaining who he would be talking to, handed my phone to the vet. The Scot scowled. Mrs. Bracken said, "Anything, anything," over and over again. Bill talked.

"Very well," the Scot said frostily, finally, "but you do understand, don't you, Mrs. Bracken, that the colt won't be able to race, even if they do succeed in reattaching his foot, which is very, very doubtful."

She said simply, "I don't want to lose him. It's worth a try."

The Scot, to give him his due, set about enclosing the raw leg efficiently in a dressing from his surgical bag and in wrapping the foot in a businesslike bundle. The row of men leaning on the fence watched with interest. The masculine-looking woman holding the head collar wiped a few tears from her weather-beaten cheeks while crooning to her charge, and eventually Mrs. Bracken and I returned to the house, which still rang with noise. The ramblers, making the most of the drama, seemed to be rambling all over the ground floor and were to be seen assessing their chances of penetrating upstairs. Mrs. Bracken clutched her head in distraction and said, "Please, will everyone leave," but without enough volume to be heard.

I begged one of the policemen, "Shoo the lot out, can't you?" and finally most of the crowd left, the ebb revealing a large basically formal pale green and gold drawing room inhabited by five or six humans, three dogs and a clutter of plastic cups engraving wet rings on ancient polished surfaces. Mrs. Bracken, like a somnambulist, drifted around picking up cups from one place only to put them down in another. Ever tidy minded, I couldn't stop myself twitching up a wastepaper basket and following her, taking the cups from her fingers and collecting them all together.

She looked at me vaguely. She said, "I paid a quarter of a million for that colt."

"Is he insured?"

"No. I don't insure my jewelry, either."

"Or your health?"

"No, of course not."

She looked unseeingly around the room. Five people now sat on easy chairs, offering no help or succor.

"Would someone make a cup of tea?" she asked.

No one moved.

She said to me, as if it explained everything, "Esther doesn't start work until eight."

"Mm," I said. "Well . . . er . . . who is everybody?"

"Goodness, yes. Rude of me. That's my husband." Her gaze fell affectionately on an old bald man who looked as if he had no comprehension of anything. "He's deaf, the dear man."

"I see."

"And that's my aunt, who mostly lives here."

The aunt was also old and proved unhelpful and selfish.

"Our tenants." Mrs. Bracken indicated a stolid couple. "They live in part of the house. And my nephew."

Even her normal good manners couldn't keep the irritation from either her voice or her face at this last identification. The nephew was a teenager with a loose mouth and an attitude problem.

None of this hopeless bunch looked like an accomplice in a spite attack on a harmless animal, not even the unsatisfactory boy, who was staring at me intensely as if demanding to be noticed: almost, I thought fleetingly, as if he wanted to tell me something by telepathy. It was more than an interested inspection, but also held neither disapproval nor fear, as far as I could see.

I said to Mrs. Bracken, "If you tell me where the kitchen is, I'll make you some tea."

"But you've only one hand."

I said reassuringly, "I can't climb Everest but I can sure make tea."

A streak of humor began to banish the morning's shocks from her eyes. "I'll come with you," she said.

The kitchen, like the whole house, had been built on a grand scale for a cast of dozens. Without difficulties we made tea in a pot and sat at the well-scrubbed old wooden central table to drink it from mugs.

"You're not what I expected," she said. "You're *cozy.*"

I liked her, couldn't help it.

She went on, "You're not like my brother said. I'm afraid I didn't explain that it is my brother who is out in the field with the vet. It was he who said I should phone you. He didn't say you were cozy, he said you were flint. I should have introduced you to him, but you can see how things are. . . . Anyway, I rely on him dreadfully. He lives in the next village. He came at once when I woke him."

"Is he," I asked neutrally, "your nephew's father?"

"Goodness, no. My nephew . . . Jonathan . . ." She stopped, shaking her head. "You don't want to hear about Jonathan."

"Try me."

"He's our sister's son. Fifteen. He got into trouble, expelled from school . . . on probation . . . his step-father can't stand him. My sister was at her wits' end so I said he could come here for a bit. It's not working out, though. I can't get through to him." She looked suddenly aghast. "You don't think he had anything to do with the colt?"

"No, no. What trouble did he get into? Drugs?"

She sighed, shaking her head. "He was with two other boys. They stole a car and crashed it. Jonathan was in the back seat. The boy driving was also fifteen and broke his neck. Paralyzed. Joy-riding, they called it. Some joy! Stealing, that's what it was. And Jonathan isn't repentant. Really, he can be a pig. But not the colt . . . not that."

"No," I assured her, "positively not." I drank hot tea and asked, "Is it well known hereabouts that you have this great colt in that field?"

She nodded. "Eva, who looks after him, she talks of nothing else. All the village knows. That's why there are so many people here. Half the men from the village, as well as the ramblers. Even so early in the morning."

"And your friends?" I prompted.

She nodded gloomily. "Everyone. I bought him at the Premium Yearling Sales last October. His breeding is a dream. He was a late foal—end of April—he's . . . he *was* going into training next week. Oh *dear.*"

"I'm so sorry," I said. I screwed myself unhappily to ask the unavoidable question, "Who, among your friends, came here in person to admire the colt?"

She was far from stupid, and also vehement. "No one who came here could *possibly* have done this! People like Lord and Lady Dexter? Of course not! Gordon and Ginnie Quint and darling Ellis? Don't be silly. Though I suppose," she went on doubtfully, "they could have mentioned him to other people. He wasn't a *secret*. Anyone since the Sales would know he was here, like I told you."

"Of course," I said.

Ellis.

We finished the tea and went back to the drawing room. Jonathan, the nephew, stared at me again unwaveringly, and after a moment, to test my own impression, I jerked my head in the direction of the door, walking that way; and, with hardly a hesitation, he stood up and followed.

I went out of the drawing room, across the hall and through the still-wide-open front door onto the drive.

"Sid Halley," he said behind me.

I turned. He stopped four paces away, still not wholly committed. His accent and general appearance spoke of expensive schools, money and privilege. His mouth and his manner said slob.

"What is it that you know?" I asked.

"Hey! Look here! What do you mean?"

I said without pressure, "You want to tell me something, don't you?"

"I don't know. Why do you think so?"

I'd seen that intense bursting-at-the-seams expression too often by then to mistake it. He knew something that he ought to tell: it was only his own contrary rebelliousness that had kept him silent so far.

I made no appeal to a better nature that I wasn't sure he had.

I said, guessing, "Were you awake before four o'clock?"

He glared but didn't answer.

I tried again, "You hate to be helpful, is that it? No one is going to catch you behaving well—that sort of thing? Tell me what you know. I'll give you as bad a press as you want. Your obstructive reputation will remain intact."

"Sod you," he said.

I waited.

"She'd kill me," he said. "Worse, she'd pack me off home."

"Mrs. Bracken?"

He nodded. "My Aunt Betty."

"What have you done?"

He used a few old Anglo-Saxon words: bluster to impress me with his virility, I supposed. Pathetic, really. Sad.

"She has these effing stupid rules," he said. "Be back in the house at night by eleven-thirty."

"And last night," I suggested, "you weren't?"

"I got probation," he said. "Did she tell you?"

"Yeah."

He took two more steps towards me, into normal talking distance.

"If she knew I went out again," he said, "I could get youth custody."

"If she shopped you, you mean?"

He nodded. "But . . . sod it . . . to cut a foot off a horse . . ."

Perhaps the better nature was somewhere there after all. Stealing cars was OK, maiming racehorses wasn't. He wouldn't have blinded those ponies: he wasn't that sort of lout.

"If I fix it with your aunt, will you tell me?" I asked.

"Make her promise not to tell Archie. He's worse."

"Er," I said, "who is Archie?"

"My uncle. Aunt Betty's brother. He's Establishment, man. He's the flogging classes."

I made no promises. I said, "Just spill the beans."

"In three weeks I'll be sixteen." He looked at me intently for reaction, but all he'd caused in me was puzzlement. I thought the cut-off age for crime to be considered "juvenile" was two years older. He wouldn't be sent to an adult jail.

Jonathan saw my lack of understanding. He said impatiently, "You can't be underage for sex if you're a man, only if you're a girl."

"Are you sure?"

"*She* says so."

"Your Aunt Betty?" I felt lost.

"No, stupid. The woman in the village."

"Oh . . . ah."

"Her old man's a long-distance truck driver. He's away for nights on end. He'd kill me. Youth custody would be apple pie."

"Difficult," I said.

"She *wants* it, see? I'd never done it before. I bought her a gin in the pub." Which, at fifteen, was definitely illegal to start with.

"So . . . um . . . ," I said, "last night you were coming back from the village . . . When, exactly?"

"It was dark. Just before dawn. There had been more moonlight earlier, but I'd left it late. I was *running*. She—Aunt Betty—she wakes with the cocks. She lets the dogs out before six." His agitation, I thought, was producing what sounded like truth.

I thought and asked, "Did you see any ramblers?"

"No. It was earlier than them."

I held my breath. I had to ask the next question, and dreaded the answer. "So, who was it that you saw?"

"It wasn't a 'who,' it was a 'what.'" He paused and reassessed his position. "I didn't go to the village," he said. "I'll deny it."

I nodded. "You were restless. Unable to sleep. You went for a walk."

He said, "Yeah, that's it," with relief.

"And you saw?"

"A Land-Rover."

Not a who. A what. I said, partly relieved, partly disappointed, "That's not so extraordinary, in the country."

"No, but it wasn't Aunt Betty's Land-Rover. It was much newer, and blue, not green. It was standing in the lane not far from the gate into the field. There was no one in it. I didn't think much of it. There's a path up to the house from the lane. I always go out and in that way. It's miles from Aunt Betty's bedroom."

"Through the yard with all the trash cans?" I asked.

He was comically astounded. I didn't explain that his aunt had taken me out that way. I said, "Couldn't it have been a rambler's Land-Rover?"

He said sullenly, "I don't know why I bothered to tell you."

I asked, "What else did you notice about the Land-Rover, except for its color?"

"Nothing. I told you, I was more interested in getting back into the house without anyone spotting me."

I thought a bit and said, "How close did you get to it?"

"I touched it. I didn't see it until I was almost on top of it. Like I told you, I was running along the lane. I was mostly looking at the ground, and it was still almost dark."

"Was it facing you, or did you run into the back of it?"

"Facing. There was still enough moonlight to reflect off the windshield. That's what I saw first, the reflection."

"What part of it did you touch?"

"The hood." Then he added, as if surprised by the extent of his memory, "It was quite hot."

"Did you see a number plate?"

"Not a chance. I wasn't hanging about for things like that."

"What else did you see?"

"Nothing."

"How did you know there was no one in the cab? There might have been a couple lying in there snogging."

"Well, there wasn't. I looked through the window."

"Open or shut window?"

"Open." He surprised himself again. "I looked in fast, on the way past. No people, just a load of machinery behind the front seats."

"What sort of machinery?"

"How the eff do I know? It had handles sticking up. Like a lawn mower. I didn't look. I was in a hurry. I didn't want to be seen."

"No," I agreed. "How about an ignition key?"

"Hey?" It was a protest of hurt feelings. "I didn't drive it away."

"Why not?"

"I don't take every car I see. Not alone, ever."

"There's no fun in it if you're alone?"

"Not so much."

"So there *was* a key in the ignition?"

"I suppose so. Yeah."

"Was there one key, or a bunch?"

"Don't know."

"Was there a key ring?"

"You don't ask much!"

"Think, then."

He said unwillingly, "See, I *notice* ignition keys."

"Yes."

"It was a bunch of keys, then. They had a silver horseshoe dangling from them on a little chain. A little horseshoe. Just an ordinary key ring."

We stared at each other briefly.

He said, "I didn't think anything of it."

"No." I agreed. "You wouldn't. Well, go back a bit. When you put your hand on the hood, were you looking at the windshield?"

"I must have been."

"What was on it?"

"Nothing. What do you mean?"

"Did it have a tax disk?"

"It must have done, mustn't it?" he said.

"Well . . . did it have anything else? Like, say, a sticker saying 'Save the Tigers'?"

"No, it didn't."

"Shut your eyes and think," I urged him. "You're running. You don't want to be seen. You nearly collide with a Land-Rover. Your face is quite near the windshield—"

"There was a red dragon," he interrupted. "A red circle with a dragon thing in it. Not very big. One of those sort of transparent transfers that stick to glass."

"Great," I said. "Anything else?"

For the first time he gave it concentrated thought, but came up with nothing more.

"I'm nothing to do with the police," I said, "and I won't spoil your probation and I won't give you away to your aunt, but I'd like to write down what you've told me, and if you agree that I've got it right, will you sign it?"

"Hey. I don't know. I don't know why I told you."

"It might matter a lot. It might not matter at all. But I'd like to find this bugger. . . ." God help me, I thought. I have to.

"So would I." He meant it. Perhaps there was hope for him yet.

He turned on his heel and went rapidly alone into the house, not wanting to be seen in even semi-reputable company, I assumed. I followed more slowly. Jonathan had not returned to the drawing room, where the tenants still sat stolidly, the difficult old aunt complained about being woken early, the deaf husband said, "Eh?" mechanically at frequent intervals and Betty Bracken sat looking into space. Only the three dogs, now lying down and resting their heads on their front paws, seemed fully sane.

I said to Mrs. Bracken, "Do you by any chance have a typewriter?"

She said incuriously, "There's one in the office."

"Er . . ."

"I'll show you." She rose and led me to a small, tidy back room containing the bones of communication but an impression of under-use.

"I don't know how anything works," Betty Bracken said frankly. "We have a part-time secretary, once a week. Help yourself."

She left, nodding, and I thanked her, and I found an electric typewriter under a fitted dust cover, plugged ready into the current.

I wrote:

Finding it difficult to sleep, I went for a short walk in the grounds of Combe Bassett Manor at about three-thirty in the morning. {I inserted the date.} In the lane near to the gate of the home paddock I passed a Land-Rover that was

parked there. The vehicle was blue. I did not look at the number plate. The en-
gine was still hot when I touched the hood in passing. There was a key in the
ignition. It was one of a bunch of keys on a key ring which had a silver horse-
shoe on a chain. There was no one in the vehicle. There was some sort of equip-
ment behind the front seat, but I did not take a close look. On the inside of the
windshield I observed a small transfer of a red dragon in a red circle. I went
past the vehicle and returned to the house.

Under another fitted cover I located a copier, so I left the little office with three sheets of paper and went in search of Jonathan, running him to earth eating a haphazard breakfast in the kitchen. He paused over his cereal, spoon in air, while he read what I'd written. Wordlessly, I produced a ball-point pen and held it out to him.

He hesitated, shrugged and signed the first of the papers with loops and a flourish.

"Why *three?*" he asked suspiciously, pushing the copies away.

"One for you," I said calmly. "One for my records. One for the on-going file of bits and pieces which may eventually catch our villain."

"Oh." He considered. "All right, then." He signed the other two sheets and I gave him one to keep. He seemed quite pleased with his civic-mindedness. He was rereading his edited deposition over his flakes as I left.

Back in the drawing room, looking for her, I asked where Mrs. Bracken had gone. The aunt, the tenants and the deaf husband made no reply.

Negotiating the hinterland passage and the dustbin yard again, I arrived back at the field to see Mrs. Bracken herself, the fence-leaners, the Scots vet and her brother watching the horse ambulance drive into the field and draw up conveniently close to the colt.

The horse ambulance consisted of a narrow, low-slung trailer pulled by a Land-Rover. There was a driver and a groom used to handling sick and in-jured horses and, with crooning noises from the solicitous Eva, the poor young colt made a painful-looking, head-bobbing stagger up a gentle ramp into the waiting stall.

"Oh *dear*, oh *dear*," Mrs. Bracken whispered beside me. "My dear, dear young fellow . . . how *could* they?"

I shook my head. Rachel Ferns's pony and four prized colts . . . How could *anyone?*

The colt was shut into the trailer, the bucket containing the foot was loaded, and the pathetic twelve-mile journey to Lambourn began.

The Scots vet patted Betty Bracken sympathetically on the arm, gave her his best wishes for the colt, claimed his car from the line of vehicles in the lane and drove away.

I unclipped my mobile phone and got through to *The Pump*, who forwarded my call to an irate newspaperman at his home in Surrey.

Kevin Mills yelled, "Where the hell are you? They say all anyone gets on the hotline now is your answering machine, saying you'll call back. About fifty people have phoned. They're all rambling."

"Ramblers," I said.

"What?"

I explained.

"It's supposed to be my day off," he grumbled. "Can you meet me in the pub? What time? Five o'clock?"

"Make it seven," I suggested.

"It's no longer a *Pump* exclusive, I suppose you realize?" he demanded. "But save yourself for me alone, will you, buddy? Give me the inside edge?"

"It's yours."

I closed my phone and warned Betty Bracken to expect the media on her doorstep.

"Oh, no!"

"Your colt is one too many."

"Archie!" She turned to her brother for help with a beseeching gesture of the hand and, as if for the thousandth time in their lives, he responded with comfort and competent solutions.

"My dear Betty," he said, "if you can't bear to face the press, simply don't be here."

"But . . . ," she wavered.

"I shouldn't waste time," I said.

The brother gave me an appraising glance. He himself was of medium height, lean of body, gray in color, a man to get lost in a crowd. His eyes alone were notable: brown, bright and *aware*. I had an uncomfortable feeling that, far beyond having his sister phone me, he knew a good deal about me.

"We haven't actually met," he said to me civilly. "I'm Betty's brother. I'm Archie Kirk."

I said, "How do you do," and I shook his hand.

CHAPTER 5

BETTY BRACKEN, ARCHIE Kirk and I returned to the house, again circumnavigating the trash cans. Archie Kirk's car was parked outside the manor's front door, not far from my own.

The lady of the manor refusing to leave without her husband, the uncomprehending old man, still saying "Eh?" was helped with great solicitude across the hall, through the front door and into an ancient Daimler, an Establishment-type conservative-minded political statement if ever I saw one.

My own Mercedes, milk-coffee colored, stood beyond: and what, I thought astringently, was it saying about *me*? Rich enough, sober enough, preferring reliability to flash? All spot on, particularly the last. And speed, of course.

Betty spooned her beloved into the back seat of the Daimler and folded herself in beside him, patting him gently. Touch, I supposed, had replaced speech as their means of communication. Archie Kirk took his place behind the wheel as natural commander-in-chief and drove away, leaving for me the single short parting remark, "Let me know."

I nodded automatically. Let him know *what*? Whatever I learned, I presumed.

I returned to the drawing room. The stolid tenants, on their feet, were deciding to return to their own wing of the house. The dogs snoozed. The cross aunt crossly demanded Esther's presence. Esther, on duty at eight and not a moment before, come ramblers, police or whatever, appeared forbiddingly in the doorway, a small, frizzy-haired worker, clear about her "rights."

I left the two quarrelsome women pitching into each other and went in search of Jonathan. What a household! The media were welcome to it. I looked but couldn't find Jonathan, so I just had to trust that his boorishness would keep him well away from inquisitive reporters with microphones. The Land-Rover he'd seen might have brought the machete to the colt, and I wanted, if I could, to find it before its driver learned there was a need for rapid concealment.

The first thing in my mind was the colt himself. I started the car and set off north to Lambourn, driving thoughtfully, wondering what was best to do concerning the police. I had had varying experiences with the force some good, some rotten. They did not, in general, approve of freelance investigators like myself, and could be downright obstructive if I appeared to be working on something they felt belonged to them alone. Sometimes, though, I'd found them willing to take over if I'd come across criminal activity that couldn't go unprosecuted. I stepped gingerly around their sensitive areas, and also those of racing's own security services run by the Jockey Club and the British Horseracing Board. I was careful always not to claim credit for clearing up three-pipe problems. Not even one-pipe problems, hardly worthy of Sherlock Holmes.

Where the Jockey Club itself was concerned, I fluctuated in their view between flavor of the month and anathema, according as to who currently reigned as Senior Steward. With the police, collaboration depended very much on which individual policeman I reached and his private-life stress level at the moment of contact.

The rules governing evidence, moreover, were growing ever stickier. Juries no longer without question believed the police. For an object to be admitted for consideration in a trial it had to be ticketed, docketed and continuously accounted for. One couldn't, for instance, flourish a machete and say, "I found it in X's Land-Rover, therefore it was X who cut off a colt's foot." To get even within miles of conviction one needed a specific search warrant before one could even *look* in the Land-Rover for a machete, and search warrants weren't granted to Sid Halleys, and sometimes not to the police.

The police force as a whole was divided into autonomous districts, like the Thames Valley Police, who solved crimes in their own area but might not take much notice outside. A maimed colt in Lancashire might not have been heard of in Yorkshire. Serial rapists had gone for years uncaught because of the slow flow of information. A serial horse maimer might have no central file.

Dawdling along up the last hill before Lambourn, I became aware of a knocking in the car and pulled over to the side with gloomy thoughts of broken shock absorbers and misplaced trust in reliability, but after the car stopped the knocking continued. With awakening awareness, I climbed out, went around to the back and with difficulty opened the trunk. There was something wrong with the lock.

Jonathan lay curled in the space for luggage. He had one shoe off, with which he was assaulting my milk-coffee bodywork. When I lifted the lid he stopped banging and looked at me challengingly.

"What the hell are you doing there?" I demanded.

Silly question. He looked at his shoe. I rephrased it. "Get out."

He maneuvered himself out onto the road and calmly replaced his shoe with no attempt at apology. I slammed the trunk lid shut at the second try and returned to the driver's seat. He walked to the passenger side, found the door there locked and tapped on the window to draw my attention to it. I started the engine, lowered the electrically controlled window a little and shouted to him, "It's only three miles to Lambourn."

"No. Hey! You can't leave me here!"

Want to bet, I thought, and set off along the deserted downland road. I saw him, in the rear-view mirror, running after me determinedly. I drove slowly, but faster than he could run. He went on running, nevertheless.

After nearly a mile a curve in the road took me out of his sight. I braked and stopped. He came around the bend, saw my car and put on a spurt, racing this time up to the driver's side. I'd locked the door but lowered the window three or four inches.

"What's all that for?" he demanded.

"What's all what for?"

"Making me run."

"You've broken the lock on my trunk."

"What?" He looked baffled. "I only gave it a clout. I didn't have a key." No key; a clout. Obvious, his manner said.

"Who's going to pay to get it mended?" I asked.

He said impatiently, as if he couldn't understand such small-mindedness, "What's that got to do with it?"

"With what?"

"With the colt."

Resignedly I leaned across and pulled up the locking knob on the front passenger door. He went around there and climbed in beside me. I noted with interest that he was hardly out of breath.

Jonathan's haircut, I thought as he settled into his seat and neglected to buckle the seat belt, shouted an indication of his adolescent insecurity, of his desire to shock or at least to be *noticed.* He had, I thought, bleached inexpert haphazard streaks into his hair with a comb dipped in something like hydrogen peroxide. Straight and thick, the mop was parted in the center with a wing on each side curving down to his cheek, making a curtain beside his eye. From one ear backwards, and around to the other ear, the hair had been sliced off in a straight line. Below the line, his scalp was shaved. To my eyes it looked ugly, but then I wasn't fifteen.

Making a statement through hairstyle was universal, after all. Men with bald crowns above pigtails, men with plaited beards, women with severely scraped-back pinnings, all were saying "This is *me*, and I'm *different.*" In the days of Charles I, when long male hair was normal, rebellious sons had cut off their curls to have roundheads. Archie Kirk's gray hair had been short, neat and controlled. My own dark hair would have curled girlishly if allowed to grow. A haircut was still the most unmistakable give-away of the person inside.

Conversely, a wig could change all that.

I asked Jonathan, "Have you remembered something else?"

"No, not really."

"Then why did you stow away?"

"Come on, man, give me a break. What am I supposed to do all day in that graveyard of a house? The aunt's whining drives me insane and even Karl Marx would have throttled Esther."

He did, I supposed, have a point.

I thoughtfully coasted down the last hill towards Lambourn.

"Tell me about your uncle, Archie Kirk," I said.

"What about him?"

"You tell me. For starters, what does he do?"

"He works for the government."

"What as?"

"Some sort of civil servant. Dead boring."

Boring, I reflected, was the last adjective I would have applied to what I'd seen in Archie Kirk's eyes.

"Where does he live?" I asked.

"Back in Shelley Green, a couple of miles from Aunt Betty. She can't climb a ladder unless he's holding it."

Reaching Lambourn itself, I took the turn that led to the equine hospital. Slowly though I had made the journey, the horse ambulance had been slower. They were still unloading the colt.

From Jonathan's agog expression, I guessed it was in fact the first view he'd had of a shorn-off leg, even if all he could now see was a surgical dressing.

I said to him, "If you want to wait half an hour for me, fine. Otherwise, you're on your own. But if you try stealing a car, I'll personally see you lose your probation."

"Hey. Give us a break."

"You've had your share of good breaks. Half an hour. OK?"

He glowered at me without words. I went across to where Bill Ruskin, in a white coat, was watching his patient's arrival. He said, "Hello, Sid," absentmindedly, then collected the bucket containing the foot and, with me following, led the way into a small laboratory full of weighing and measuring equipment and microscopes.

Unwrapping the foot, he stood it on the bench and looked at it assessingly. "A good, clean job," he said.

"There's nothing good about it."

"Probably the colt hardly felt it."

"How was it done?" I asked.

"Hm." He considered. "There's no other point on the leg that you could amputate a foot without using a saw to cut through the bone. I doubt if a single swipe with a heavy knife would achieve this precision. And achieve it several times, on different animals, right?"

I nodded.

"Yes, well, I think we might be looking at game shears."

"*Game shears?*" I exclaimed. "Do you mean those sort of heavy scissors that will cut up duck and pheasant?"

"Something along those lines, yes."

"But those shears aren't anywhere near big enough for this."

He pursed his mouth. "How about a gralloching knife, then? The sort used for disemboweling deer out on the mountains?"

"Jeez."

"There are signs of *compression*, though. On balance, I'd hazard heavy game shears. How did he get the colt to stand still?"

"There were horse nuts on the ground."

He nodded morosely. "Slimeball."

"There aren't any words for it."

He peered closely at the raw red and white end of the pastern. "Even if I can reattach the foot, the colt will never race."

"His owner knows that. She wants to save his life."

"Better to collect the insurance."

"No insurance. A quarter of a million down the drain. But it's not the money she's grieving over. What she's feeling is guilt."

He understood. He saw it often.

Eventually he said, "I'll give it a try. I don't hold out much hope."

"You'll photograph this as it is?"

He looked at the foot. "Oh, sure. Photos, X rays, blood tests on the colt, micro-stitching, every luxury. I'll get on with anesthetizing the colt as soon as possible. The foot's been off too long . . ." He shook his head. "I'll try."

"Phone my mobile." I gave him the number. "Anytime."

"See you, Sid. And catch the bugger."

He bustled away, taking the foot with him, and I returned to my car to find Jonathan not only still there but jogging around with excitement.

"What's up?" I asked.

"That Land-Rover that pulled the trailer that brought the colt . . ."

"What about it?"

"It's got a red dragon on the windshield!"

"What? But you said a *blue*—"

"Yeah, yeah, it wasn't the vet's Land-Rover I saw in the lane, but it's got a red dragon transfer on it. Not exactly the same, I don't think, but definitely a red dragon."

I looked around, but the horse ambulance was no longer in sight.

"They drove it off," Jonathan said, "but I saw the transfer close to, and it has *letters* in it." His voice held triumph, which I allowed was justified.

"Go on, then," I said. "What letters?"

"Aren't you going to say 'well done'?"

"Well done. What letters?"

"E.S.M. They were cut out of the red circle. Gaps, not printed letters." He wasn't sure I understood.

"I do see," I assured him.

I returned to the hospital to find Bill and asked him when he'd bought his Land-Rover.

"Our local garage got it for us from a firm in Oxford."

"What does E.S.M. stand for?"

"God knows."

"I can't ask God. What's the name of the Land-Rover firm in Oxford?"

He laughed and thought briefly. "English Sporting Motors. E.S.M. Good Lord."

"Can you give me the name of someone there? Who did you actually deal with?"

With impatience he said, "Look, Sid, I'm trying to scrub up to see what I can do about sticking the colt's foot back on."

"And I'm trying to catch the bugger that took it off. And it's possible he traveled in a Land-Rover sold by English Sporting Motors."

He said "Christ" wide-eyed and headed for what proved to be the hospital's record office, populated by filing cabinets. Without much waste of time he flourished a copy of a receipted account, but shook his head.

"Ted James in the village might help you. I paid *him.* He dealt direct with Oxford. You'd have to ask Ted James."

I thanked him, collected Jonathan, drove into the small town of Lambourn and located Ted James, who would do a lot for a good customer like Bill Ruskin, it seemed.

"No problem," he assured me. "Ask for Roger Brook in Oxford. Do you want me to phone him?"

"Yes, please."

"Right on." He spoke briefly on the phone and reported back. "He's busy. Saturday's always a busy sales day. He'll help you if it doesn't take long."

The morning seemed to have been going on forever, but it was still before eleven o'clock when I talked to Roger Brook, tubby, smooth and self-important in the carpeted sales office of English Sporting Motors.

Roger Brook pursed his lips and shook his head; not the firm's policy to give out information about its customers.

I said ruefully, "I don't want to bother the police. . . ."

"Well . . ."

"And, of course, there would be a fee for your trouble."

A fee was respectable where a bribe wasn't. In the course of life I disbursed a lot of fees.

It helpfully appeared that the red-dragon transparent transfers were slightly differently designed each year: *improved* as time went on, did I see?

I fetched Jonathan in from outside for Roger Brook to show him the past and present dragon logos, and Jonathan with certainty picked the one that had been, Brook said, that of the year before last.

"Great," I said with satisfaction. "How many blue Land-Rovers did you sell in that year? I mean, what are the names of the actual buyers, not the middlemen like Ted James?"

An open-mouthed silence proved amenable to a larger fee. "Our Miss Denver" helped with a computer printout. Our Miss Denver got a kiss from me. Roger Brook with dignity took his reward in readies, and Jonathan and I returned to the Mercedes with the names and addresses of 211 purchasers of blue Land-Rovers a little back in time.

Jonathan wanted to read the list when I'd finished. I handed it over, reckoning he'd deserved it. He looked disappointed when he reached the end, and I didn't point out to him the name that had made my gut contract.

One of the Land-Rovers had been delivered to Twyford Lower Farms Ltd.

I had been to Twyford Lower Farms to lunch. It was owned by Gordon Quint.

Noon, Saturday. I sat in my parked car outside English Sporting Motors, while Jonathan fidgeted beside me, demanding, "What next?"

I said, "Go and eat a hamburger for your lunch and be back here in twenty minutes."

He had no money. I gave him some. "Twenty minutes."

He promised nothing, but returned with three minutes to spare. I spent his absence thinking highly unwelcome thoughts and deciding what to do, and when he slid in beside me smelling of raw onions and french fries I set off southwards again, on the roads back to Combe Bassett.

"Where are we going?"

"To see your Aunt Betty."

"But hey! She's not at home. She's at Archie's."

"Then we'll go to Archie's. You can show me the way."

He didn't like it, but he made no attempt to jump ship when we were stopped by traffic lights three times on the way out of Oxford. We arrived together in due course outside a house an eighth the size of Combe Bassett Manor; a house, moreover, that was frankly modern and not at all what I'd expected.

I said doubtfully, "Are you sure this is the place?"

"The lair of the wolf. No mistake. He won't want to see me."

I got out of the car and pressed the thoroughly modern doorbell beside a glassed-in front porch. The woman who came to answer the summons was small and wrinkled like a drying apple, and wore a sleeveless sundress in blue and mauve.

"Er . . . ," I said to her inquiring face, "Archie Kirk?"

Her gaze lengthened beyond me to include Jonathan in my car, a sight that pinched her mouth and jumped her to an instant wrong conclusion. She whirled away and returned with Archie, who said repressively, "What is *he* doing here?"

"Can you spare me half an hour?" I asked.

"What's Jonathan done?"

"He's been extraordinarily helpful. I'd like to ask your advice."

"Helpful!"

"Yes. Could you hold your disapproval in abeyance for half an hour while I explain?"

He gave me an intense inspection, the brown eyes sharp and knowing, as before. Decision arrived there plainly.

"Come in," he said, holding his front door wide.

"Jonathan's afraid of you," I told him. "He wouldn't admit it but he is. Could I ask you not to give him the normal tongue-lashing? Will you invite him in and leave him alone?"

"You don't know what you're asking."

"I do," I said.

"No one speaks to me like this." He was, however, only mildly affronted.

I smiled at his eyes. "That's because they know you. But I met you only this morning."

"And," he said, "I've heard about your lightning judgments."

I felt, as on other occasions with people of his sort, a deep thrust of mental satisfaction. Also, more immediately, I knew I had come to the right place.

Archie Kirk stepped out from his door, took the three paces to my car, and said through the window, "Jonathan, please come into the house."

Jonathan looked past him to me. I jerked my head, as before, to suggest that he complied, and he left the safe shelter and walked to the house, even if reluctantly and frozen faced.

Archie Kirk led the way across a modest hallway into a middle-sized sitting room where Betty Bracken, her husband and the small woman who'd answered my ring were sitting in armchairs drinking cups of coffee.

The room's overall impression was of old oak and books, a room for dark winter evenings and lamps and log fires, not fitted to the dazzle of June. None of the three faces turned towards us could have looked welcoming to the difficult boy.

The small woman, introducing herself as Archie's wife, stood up slowly and offered me coffee. "And . . . er . . . Jonathan . . . Coca-Cola?"

Jonathan, as if reprieved, followed her out to the next-door kitchen, and I told Betty Bracken that her colt was at that moment being operated on, and that there should be news of him soon. She was pathetically pleased: too pleased, I was afraid.

I said casually to Archie, "Can I talk to you in private?" and without question he said, "This way," and transferred us to a small adjacent room, again all dark oak and books, that he called his study.

"What is it?" he asked.

"I need a policeman," I said.

He gave me a long, level glance and waved me to one of the two hard oak chairs, himself sitting in the other, beside a paper-strewn desk.

I told him about Jonathan's night walk (harmless version) and about our tracing the Land-Rover to the suppliers at Oxford. I said that I knew where the Land-Rover might now be, but that I couldn't get a search warrant to examine it. For a successful prosecution, I mentioned, there had to be integrity of evidence; no chance of tampering or substitution. So I needed a policeman, but one that would listen and cooperate, not one that would either brush me off altogether or one that would do the police work sloppily.

"I thought you might know someone," I finished. "I don't know who else to ask, as at the moment this whole thing depends on crawling up to the machine-gun nest on one's belly, so to speak."

He sat back in his chair staring at me vacantly while the data got processed.

At length he said, "Betty called in the local police this morning early, but . . . ," he hesitated, "they hadn't the clout you need." He thought some more, then picked up an address book; he leafed through it for a number and made a phone call.

"Norman, this is Archie Kirk."

Whoever Norman was, it seemed he was unwilling.

"It's extremely important," Archie said.

Norman apparently capitulated, but with protest, giving directions.

"You had better be right," Archie said to me, disconnecting. "I've just called in about a dozen favors he owed me."

"Who is he?"

"Detective Inspector Norman Picton, Thames Valley Police."

"Brilliant," I said.

"He's off duty. He's on the gravel pit lake. He's a clever and ambitious young man. And I," he added with a glimmer, "am a magistrate, and I may sign a search warrant myself, if he can clear it with his superintendent."

He rendered me speechless, which quietly amused him.

"You didn't know?" he asked.

I shook my head and found my voice. "Jonathan said you were a civil servant."

"That, too," he agreed. "How did you get that boorish young man to talk?"

"Er . . . ," I said. "What is Inspector Picton doing on the gravel pit lake?"

"Water skiing," Archie said.

THERE WERE SPEEDBOATS, children, wet-suits, picnics. There was a clubhouse in a sea of scrubby grass and people sliding over the shining water pulled by strings.

Archie parked his Daimler at the end of a row of cars, and I, with Jonathan beside me, parked my Mercedes alongside. We had agreed to bring both cars so that I could go on eventually to London, with Archie ferrying Jonathan back to pick up the Brackens and take them all home to Combe Bassett. Jonathan hadn't warmed to the plan, but had ungraciously accompanied me as being a lesser horror than spending the afternoon mooching aimlessly around Archie's aunt-infested house.

Having got as far as the lake, he began looking at the harmless physical

activity all around him, not with a sneer but with something approaching interest. On the shortish journey from Archie's house he had asked three moody
questions, two of which I answered.

First: "This is the best day for a long time. How come you get so much
done so quickly?"

No answer possible.

And second: "Did you ever steal anything?"

"Chocolate bars," I said.

And third: "Do you mind having only one hand?"

I said coldly, "Yes."

He glanced with surprise at my face and I saw that he'd expected me to
say no. I supposed he wasn't old enough to know it was a question one
shouldn't ask; but then, perhaps he would have asked it anyway.

When we climbed out of the car at the water-ski club I said, "Can you
swim?"

"Do me a favor."

"Then go jump in the lake."

"Sod you," he said, and actually laughed.

Archie had meanwhile discovered that one of the scudding figures on the
water was the man we'd come to see. We waited a fair while until a large presence in a blue wet-suit with scarlet stripes down arms and legs let go of the
rope pulling him and skied free and gracefully to a sloping landing place on
the edge of the water. He stepped off his skis grinning, knowing he'd shown
off his considerable skill, and wetly shook Archie's hand.

"Sorry to keep you waiting," he said, "but I reckoned once you got here
I'd have had it for the day."

His voice, with its touch of Berkshire accent, held self-confidence and
easy authority.

Archie said formally, "Norman, this is Sid Halley." I shook the offered
hand, which was cold besides wet. I received the sort of slow, searching inspection I'd had from Archie himself: and I had no idea what the policeman
thought.

"Well," he said finally, stirring, "I'll get dressed."

We watched him walk away, squelching, gingerly barefooted, carrying
his skis. He was back within five minutes, clad now in jeans, sneakers, open-
necked shirt and sweater, his dark hair still wet and spiky, uncombed.

"Right," he said to me. "Give."

"Er . . ." I hesitated. "Would it be possible for Mr. Kirk's nephew
Jonathan to go for a ride in a speedboat?"

Both he and Archie looked over to where Jonathan, not far away, lolled unprepossessingly against my car. Jonathan did himself no favors, I thought; self-destruction rampant in every bolshie tilt of the anti-authority haircut.

"He doesn't deserve any ride in a speedboat," Archie objected.

"I don't want him to overhear what I'm saying."

"That's different," Norman Picton decided. "I'll fix it."

Jonathan ungraciously allowed himself to be driven around the lake by Norman Picton's wife in Norman Picton's boat, accompanied by Norman Picton's son. We watched the boat race past with a roar, Jonathan's streaky mop blown back in the wind.

"He's on the fence," I said mildly to Archie. "There's a lot of good in him."

"You're the only one who thinks so."

"He's looking for a way back without losing face."

Both men gave me the slow assessment and shook their heads.

I said, bringing Jonathan's signed statement from my pocket, "Try this on for size."

They both read it, Picton first, Archie after.

Archie said in disbelief, "He never talks. He wouldn't have said all this."

"I asked him questions," I explained. "Those are his answers. He came with me to the Land-Rover central dealers in Oxford who put that red-dragon transfer on the windshield of every vehicle they sell. And we wouldn't know of the Land-Rover's presence in the lane, or its probable owner and whereabouts now, except for Jonathan. So I really do think he's earned his ride on the lake."

"What exactly do you want the search warrant *for?*" Picton asked. "One can't get search warrants unless one can come up with a good reason—or at least a convincing possibility or probability of finding something material to a case."

"Well," I said, "Jonathan put his hand on the hood of the vehicle standing right beside the gate to the field where Betty Bracken's colt lost his foot. If you search a certain Land-Rover and find Jonathan's hand-print on the hood, would that be proof enough that you'd found the right wheels?"

Picton said, "Yes."

"So," I went on without emphasis, "if we leave Jonathan here by the lake while your people fingerprint the Land-Rover, there could be no question of his having touched it this afternoon, and not last night."

"I've heard about you," Picton said.

"I think," I said, "that it would be a good idea to fingerprint that hood before it rains, don't you? Or before anyone puts it through a car-wash?"

"Where is it?" Picton asked tersely.

I produced the English Sporting Motors' print-out, and pointed. "There," I said. "That one."

Picton read it silently; Archie aloud.

"But I know the place. You're quite *wrong*. I've been a guest there. They're friends of Betty's."

"And of mine," I said.

He listened to the bleakness I could hear in my own voice.

"Who are we talking about?" Picton asked.

"Gordon Quint," Archie said. "It's rubbish."

"Who is Gordon Quint?" Picton asked again.

"The father of Ellis Quint," Archie said. "And you must have heard of *him*."

Picton nodded. He had indeed.

"I suppose it's possible," I suggested tentatively, "that someone *borrowed* the Land-Rover for the night."

"But you don't believe it," Picton remarked.

"I wish I did."

"But where's the connection?" Picton asked. "There has to be *more*. The fact that Twyford Lower Farms Limited owned a blue Land-Rover of the relevant year isn't enough on its own. We cannot search that vehicle for handprints unless we have good reason to believe that it was that one and no other that we are looking for."

Archie said thoughtfully, "Search warrants have been issued on flimsier grounds before now."

He and Picton walked away from me, the professionals putting their distance between themselves and Sid Public. I thought that if they refused to follow the trail it would be a relief, on the whole. It would let me off the squirming hook. But there could be another month and another colt . . . and an obsession feeding and fattening on success.

They came back, asking why I should link the Quint name to the deed. I described my box chart. Not conclusive, Archie said judiciously, and I agreed, no.

Picton repeated what I'd just said: "Rachel's pony was bought by her father, Joe, on the advice of Ellis Quint?"

I said, "Ellis did a broadcast about Rachel's pony losing his foot."

"I saw it," Picton said.

They didn't want to believe it any more than I did. There was a fairly long, indeterminate silence.

Jonathan came back looking uncomplicatedly happy from his fast laps around the lake, and Norman Picton abruptly went into the clubhouse, re-turning with a can of Coke, which he put into Jonathan's hands. Jonathan held it in his left hand to open it and his right hand to drink. Norman took the empty can from him casually but carefully by the rim, and asked if he would like to try the skiing itself, not just a ride in the boat.

Jonathan, on the point of enthusiastically saying, "*Yes*," remembered his cultivated disagreeableness and said, "I don't mind. If you insist, I suppose I'll have to."

"That's right," Picton said cheerfully. "My wife will drive. My son will watch the rope. We'll find you some swimming trunks and a wet-suit."

He led Jonathan away. Archie watched inscrutably.

"Give him a chance," I murmured. "Give him a challenge."

"Pack him off to the colonies to make a man of him?"

"Scoff," I said with a smile. "But long ago it often worked. He's bright and he's bored and he's not yet a totally confirmed delinquent."

"You'd make a soft and rotten magistrate."

"I expect you're right."

Picton returned, saying, "The boy will stay here until I get back, so we'd better get started. We'll take two cars, mine and Mr. Halley's. In that way he can go on to London when he wants. We'll leave your car here, Archie. Is that all right?"

Archie said he didn't trust Jonathan not to steal it.

"He doesn't think stealing's much fun without his pals," I said.

Archie stared. "That boy never says *anything*."

"Find him a dangerous job."

Picton, listening, said, "Like what?"

"Like," I said, unprepared, "like . . . well . . . on an oil rig. Two years of that. Tell him to keep a diary. Tell him to write."

"Good God," Archie said, shaking his head, "he'd have the place in flames."

He locked his car and put the keys in his pocket, climbing into the front passenger seat beside me as we followed Norman Picton into Newbury, to his official place of work.

I sat in my car outside the police station while Archie and Picton, inside, arranged the back-ups: the photographer, the fingerprinter, the detective con-stable to be Inspector Picton's note-taking assistant.

I sat with the afternoon sun falling through the windshield and wished I were anywhere else, engaged on any other mission.

All the villains I'd caught before hadn't been people I knew. Or people—one had to face it—people I'd thought I'd known. I'd felt mostly satisfaction, sometimes relief, occasionally even regret, but never anything approaching this intensity of entrapped despair.

Ellis was loved. I was going to be hated.

Hatred was inevitable.

Could I bear it?

There was no choice, really.

Archie and Picton came out of the police station followed by their purposeful troop.

Archie, sliding in beside me, said the search warrant was signed, the Superintendent had given the expedition his blessing, and off we could go to the Twyford Lower Farms.

I sat without moving, without starting the car.

"What's the matter?" Archie demanded, looking at my face.

I said with pain, "Ellis is my friend."

CHAPTER 6

GINNIE QUINT WAS gardening in a large straw hat, businesslike gloves and gray overall dungarees, waging a losing war on weeds in flower beds in front of the comfortable main house of Twyford Lower Farms.

"Hello, dear Sid!" She greeted me warmly, standing up, holding the dirty gloves wide and putting her soft cheek forward for a kiss of greeting. "What a nice surprise. But Ellis isn't here, you know. He went to the races, then he was going up to the Regents Park apartment. That's where you'll find him, dear."

She looked in perplexity over my shoulder to where the Norman Picton contingent were erupting from their transport.

Ginnie said uncertainly, "Who are your friends, dear?" Her face cleared momentarily in relief, and she exclaimed, "Why, it's Archie Kirk! My dear man. How nice to see you."

Norman Picton, carrying none of Archie's or my social-history baggage, came rather brutally to the point.

"I'm Detective Inspector Picton, madam, of the Thames Valley Police. I've reason to believe you own a blue Land-Rover, and I have a warrant to inspect it."

Ginnie said in bewilderment, "It's no secret we have a Land-Rover. Of course we have. You'd better talk to my husband. Sid . . . Archie . . . what's all this about?"

"It's possible," I said unhappily, "that someone borrowed your Land-Rover last night and . . . er . . . committed a crime."

"Could I see the Land-Rover, please, madam?" Picton insisted.

"It will be in the farmyard," Ginnie said. "I'll get my husband to show you."

The scene inexorably unwound. Gordon, steaming out of the house to take charge, could do nothing but protest in the face of a properly executed search warrant. The various policemen went about their business, photographing, fingerprinting and collecting specimens of dusty earth from the tire treads. Every stage was carefully documented by the assisting constable.

The warrant apparently covered the machinery and anything else behind the front seat. The two sticking-up handles that had looked to Jonathan like those of a lawn mower were, in fact, the handles of a lawn mower—a light electric model. There were also a dozen or so angle iron posts for fencing, also a coil of fencing wire and the tools needed for fastening the wire through the posts. There was an opened bag of horse-feed nuts. There was a rolled leather apron, like those used by farriers. There were two spades, a heavy four-pronged fork and a large knife like a machete wrapped in sacking.

The knife was clean, sharp and oiled.

Gordon, questioned, growled impatiently that a good workman looked after his tools. He picked up a rag and a can of oil, to prove his point. What was the knife for? Clearing ditches, thinning woodland, a hundred small jobs around the fields.

There was a second, longer bundle of sacking lying beneath the fencing posts. I pointed to it noncommittally, and Norman Picton drew it out and unwrapped it.

Inside there were two once-varnished wooden handles a good meter in length, with, at the business end, a heavy arrangement of metal.

"Lopping shears," Gordon pronounced. "For lopping off small branches of trees in the woods. Have to keep young trees pruned, you know, or you get a useless tangle where nothing will grow."

He took the shears from Picton's hands to show him how they worked. The act of parting the handles widely away from each other opened heavy metal jaws at the far end; sharp, clean and oiled jaws with an opening wide enough to grip a branch three inches thick. Gordon, with a strong, quick motion, pulled the handles towards each other, and the metal jaws closed with a snap.

"Very useful," Gordon said, nodding, and rewrapped the shears in their sacking.

Archie, Picton and I said nothing.

I felt faintly sick.

Archie walked away speechlessly and Gordon, not understanding, laid the sacking parcel back in the Land-Rover and walked after him, saying, puzzled, "Archie! What is it?"

Picton said to me, "Well?"

"Well," I said, swallowing, "what if you took those shears apart? They look clean, but in the jaws . . . in that hinge . . . just one drop of blood . . . or one hair . . . that would do, wouldn't it?"

"So these shears fit the bill?"

I nodded faintly. "Mr. Kirk saw the colt's leg, like I did. And he saw the foot." I swallowed again. "*Lopping* shears. Oh, Christ."

"It was only a *horse*," he protested.

"Some people love their horses like they do their children," I said. "Suppose someone lopped off your son's foot?"

He stared. I said wryly, "Betty Bracken is the fifth bereaved owner I've met in the last three weeks. Their grief gets to you."

"My son," he said slowly, "had a dog that got run over. He worried us sick . . . wouldn't eat properly . . ." He stopped, then said, "You and Archie Kirk are too close to this."

"And the Great British public," I reminded him, "poured their hearts out to those cavalry horses maimed by terrorists in Hyde Park."

He was old enough to remember the carnage that had given rise to the daily bulletins and to medals and hero status bestowed on Sefton, the wonderful survivor of heartless bombs set off specifically to kill harmless horses used by the army solely as a spectacle in plumed parades.

This time the Great British public would vilify the deed, but wouldn't, and couldn't, believe a national idol guilty. Terrorists, yes. Vandals, yes. Idol . . . *no.*

Picton and I walked in the wake of Archie and Gordon, returning to Ginnie in front of the house.

"I don't understand," Ginnie was saying plaintively. "When you say the Land-Rover may have been taken and used in a crime . . . what crime do you mean?"

Gordon jumped in without waiting for Picton to explain.

"It's always for robbery," he said confidently.

"Where did the thieves take it?"

Instead of answering, Norman Picton asked if it was Gordon Quint's habit to leave the ignition key in the Land-Rover.

"Of course not," Gordon said, affronted. "Though a little thing like no ignition key never stops a practiced thief."

"If you did by any chance leave the key available—which I'm sure you didn't, sir, please don't get angry—but if anyone could have found and used your key, would it have been on a key ring with a silver chain and a silver horseshoe?"

"Oh, no," Ginnie interrupted, utterly guilelessly. "That's Ellis's key ring. And it's not a silver horseshoe, it's white gold. I had it made especially for him last Christmas."

I DROVE ARCHIE Kirk back to Newbury. The unmarked car ahead of us carried the four policemen and a variety of bagged, docketed, documented objects for which receipts had been given to Gordon Quint.

Lopping shears in sacking. Machete, the same. Oily rag and oil can. Sample of horse-feed nuts. Instant photos of red-dragon logo. Careful containers of many lifted fingerprints, including one sharply defined right full hand-print from the Land-Rover's hood that, on first inspection, matched exactly the right hand-print from the Coke can held by Jonathan at the lake.

"There's no doubt that it was the Quint Land-Rover in my sister's lane," Archie said. "There's no doubt Ellis's keys were in the ignition. But there's no proof that Ellis himself was anywhere near."

"No," I agreed. "No one saw him."

"Did Norman ask you to write a report?"

"Yes."

"He'll give your report and Jonathan's statement to the Crown Prosecution Service, along with his own findings. After that, it's up to them."

"Mm."

After a silence, as if searching for words of comfort, Archie said, "You've done wonders."

"I hate it."

"But it doesn't stop you."

What if he can't help it . . . ? What if I couldn't help it, either?

At the police station, saying good-bye, Archie said, "Sid . . . you don't mind if I call you Sid? And I'm Archie, of course, as you know . . . I do have some idea of what you're facing. I just wanted you to know."

"I . . . er . . . thanks," I said. "If you wait a minute, I'll phone the equine hospital and find out how the colt is doing."

His face lightened but the news was moderate.

"I've reattached the tendon," Bill reported. "I grafted a couple of blood vessels so there's now an adequate blood supply to the foot. Nerves are always difficult. I've done my absolute best and, bar infection, the foot could technically stay in place. The whole leg is now in a cast. The colt is semiconscious. We have him in slings. But you know how unpredictable this all is. Horses don't recover as easily as humans. There'll be no question of racing, of course, but breeding . . . I understand he's got the bloodlines of champions. Absolutely no promises, mind."

"You're brilliant," I said.

"It's nice," he chuckled, "to be appreciated."

I said, "A policeman will come and collect some of the colt's hair and blood."

"Good. Catch the bugger," he said.

I DROVE WILLY-NILLY without haste in heavy traffic to London. By the time I reached the pub I was half an hour late for my appointment with Kevin Mills of *The Pump* and he wasn't there. No balding head, no paunch, no drooping beer-frothed mustache, no cynical world-weariness.

Without regret I mooched tiredly to the bar, bought some whisky and poured into it enough London tap water to give the distiller fits.

All I wanted was to finish my mild tranquilizer, go home, find something to eat, and sleep. Sleep, I thought, yawning, had overall priority.

A woman's voice at my side upset those plans.

"Are you Sid Halley?" it said.

I turned reluctantly. She had shining black shoulder-length hair, bright light-blue eyes and dark-red lipstick, sharply edged. Naturally unblemished skin had been given a matte porcelain powdering. Black eyebrows and eyelashes gave her face strong definition, an impression her manner reinforced. She wore black clothes in June. I found it impossible to guess her age, within ten years, from her face, but her manicured red-nailed hands said no more than thirty.

"I'm from *The Pump*," she said. "My colleague, Kevin Mills, has been called away to a rape."

I said, "Oh," vaguely.

"I'm India Cathcart," she said.

I said "Oh" again, just as vaguely, but I knew her by her name, by her

reputation and by her writing. She was a major columnist, a ruthless inter-
viewer, a deconstructing nemesis, a pitiless exposer of pathetic human secrets.
They said she kept a penknife handy for sharpening her ball-points. She was
also funny, and I, like every *Pump* addict, avidly read her stuff and laughed
even as I winced.

I did not, however, aim to be either her current or future quarry.

"I came to pick up our exclusive," she said.

"Ah. 'Fraid there isn't one."

"But you *said*."

"I hoped," I agreed.

"And you haven't answered your phone all day."

I unclipped my mobile phone and looked at it as if puzzled, which I
wasn't. I said, making a discovery, "It's switched off."

She said, disillusioned, "I was warned you weren't dumb."

There seemed to be no answer to that, so I didn't attempt one.

"We tried to reach you. Where have you been?"

"Just with friends," I said.

"I went to Combe Bassett. What did I find? No colt, with or without feet.
No Sid Halley. No sobbing colt owner. I find some batty old fusspot who says
everyone went to Archie's house."

I gazed at her with a benign expression. I could do a benign expression
rather well.

"So," continued India Cathcart with visible disgust, "I go to the house of
a Mr. Archibald Kirk in the village of Shelley Green, and what do I find *there*?"

"What?"

"I find about five other newspapermen, sundry photographers, a Mrs.
Archibald Kirk and a deaf old gent saying 'Eh?' "

"So then what?"

"Mrs. Kirk is lying, all wide-eyed and helpful. She's saying she doesn't
know where anyone is. After three hours of that, I went back to Combe Bassett to look for ramblers."

"Did you find any?"

"They had rambled twenty miles and had climbed a stile into a field with
a resident bull. A bunch of ramblers crashed out in panic through a hedge
backwards and the rest are discussing suing the farmer for letting a dangerous animal loose near a public footpath. A man with a pony-tail says he's also
suing Mrs. Bracken for not keeping her colt in a stable, thus preventing an
amputation that gave his daughter hysterics."

"Life's one long farce," I said.

A mistake. She pounced on it. "Is that your comment on the maltreatment of animals?"

"No."

"Your opinion of ramblers?"

"Footpaths are important," I said.

She looked past me to the bartender. "Sparkling mineral water, ice and lemon, please."

She paid for her own drink as a matter of course. I wondered how much of her challenging air was unconscious and habitual, or whether she volume-adjusted it according to who she was talking to. I often learned useful things about people's characters by watching them talk to others than myself, and comparing the response.

"You're not playing fair," she said, judging me over the wedge of lemon bestriding the rim of her glass. "It was *The Pump*'s hotline that sent you to Combe Bassett. Kevin says you pay your debts. So pay."

"The hotline was his own idea. Not a bad one, except for about a hundred false alarms. But there's nothing I can tell you this evening."

"Not can't. Won't."

"It's often the same thing."

"Spare me the philosophy!"

"I enjoy reading your page every week," I said.

"But you don't want to figure in it?"

"That's up to you."

She raised her chin. "Strong men *beg* me not to print what I know."

I didn't want to antagonize her completely and I could forgo the passing pleasure of banter, so I gave her the benign expression and made no comment.

She said abruptly, "Are you married?"

"Divorced."

"Children?"

I shook my head. "How about you?"

She was more used to asking questions than answering. There was perceptible hesitation before she said, "The same."

I drank my scotch. I said, "Tell Kevin I'm very sorry I can't give him his inside edge. Tell him I'll talk to him on Monday."

"Not good enough."

"No, well . . . I can't do more."

"Is someone *paying* you?" she demanded. "Another paper?"

I shook my head. "Maybe Monday," I said. I put my empty glass on the bar. "Good-bye."

"Wait!" She gave me a straight stare, not overtly or aggressively feminist, but one that saw no need to make points in a battle that had been won by the generation before her. I thought that perhaps India Cathcart wouldn't have made it a condition of continued marriage that I should give up the best skill I possessed. I'd married a loving and gentle girl and turned her bitter: the worst, the most miserable failure of my life.

India Cathcart said, "Are you hungry? I've had nothing to eat all day. My expense account would run to two dinners."

There were many worse fates. I did a quick survey of the possibility of being deconstructed all over page fifteen, and decided as usual that playing safe had its limits. Take risks with caution: a great motto.

"Your restaurant or mine?" I said, smiling, and was warned by the merest flash of triumph in her eyes that she thought the tarpon hooked and as good as landed.

We ate in a noisy, brightly lit, large and crowded black-mirrored restaurant that was clearly the in-place for the in-crowd. India's choice. India's habitat. A few sycophantic hands shot out to make contact with her as we followed a lisping young greeter to a central, noteworthy table. India Cathcart acknowledged the plaudits and trailed me behind her like a comet's tail (Halley's?) while introducing me to no one.

The menu set out to amaze, but from long habit I ordered fairly simple things that could reasonably be dealt with one-handed: watercress mousse, then duck curry with sliced baked plantains. India chose baby eggplants with oil and pesto, followed by a large mound of crisped frogs' legs that she ate uninhibitedly with her fingers.

The best thing about the restaurant was that the decibel level made private conversation impossible: everything anyone said could be overheard by those at the next table.

"So," India raised her voice, teeth gleaming over a herb-dusted *cuisse*, "was Betty Bracken in tears?"

"I didn't see any tears."

"How much was the colt worth?"

I ate some plantain and decided they'd overdone the caramel. "No one knows," I said.

"Kevin told me it cost a quarter of a million. You're simply being evasive."

"What it cost and what it was worth are different. It might have won the Derby. It might have been worth millions. No one knows."

"Do you always play word games?"

"Quite often." I nodded. "Like you do."

"Where did you go to school?"

"Ask Kevin," I said, smiling.

"Kevin's told me things about you that you wouldn't want me to know."

"Like what?"

"Like it's easy to be taken in by your peaceful front. Like you having tungsten where other people have nerves. Like you being touchy about losing a hand. That's for starters."

I would throttle Kevin, I thought. I said, "How are the frogs' legs?"

"Muscular."

"Never mind," I said. "You have sharp teeth."

Her mind quite visibly changed gears from patronizing to uncertain, and I began to like her.

Risky to like her, of course.

After the curry and the frogs we drank plain black coffee and spent a pause or two in eye-contact appraisal. I expected she saw me in terms of adjectives and paragraphs. I saw her with appeased curiosity. I now knew what the serial reputation-slasher looked like at dinner.

In the way one does, I wondered what she looked like in bed; and in the way that one doesn't cuddle up to a potential cobra, I made no flicker of an attempt to find out.

She seemed to take this passivity for granted. She paid for our meal with a *Pump* business credit card, as promised, and crisply expected I would kick in my share on Monday as an exclusive for Kevin.

I promised what I knew I wouldn't be able to deliver, and offered her a lift home.

"But you don't know where I live!"

"Wherever," I said.

"Thanks. But there's a bus."

I didn't press it. We parted on the sidewalk outside the restaurant. No kiss. No handshake. A nod from her. Then she turned and walked away, not looking back: and I had no faith at all in her mercy.

ON SUNDAY MORNING I reopened the small blue suitcase Linda had lent me, and read again through all the clippings that had to do with the maimed Kent ponies.

I played again the videotape of the twenty-minute program Ellis had made of the child owners, and watched it from a different, and sickened, perspective.

There on the screen he looked just as friendly, just as charismatic, just as expert. His arms went around Rachel in sympathy. His good-looking face filled with compassion and outrage. Blinding ponies, cutting off a pony's foot, he said, those were crimes akin to murder.

Ellis, I thought in wretchedness, how *could* you?

What if he can't help it?

I played the tape a second time, taking in more details and attentively listening to what he had actually said.

His instinct for staging was infallible. In the shot where he'd commiserated with the children all together, he had had them sitting around on hay bales in a tack room, the children dressed in riding breeches, two or three wearing black riding hats. He himself had sat on the floor among them, casual in a dark open-necked jogging suit, a peaked cap pushed back on his head, sunglasses in pocket. Several of the children had been in tears. He'd given them his handkerchief and helped them cope with grief.

There were phrases he had used when talking straight to the camera that had brought the children's horrors sharply to disturbingly visual life: "pierced empty sockets, their eyesight running down their cheeks," and "a pure-bred silver pony, proud and shining in the moonlight."

His caring tone of voice alone had made the word pictures bearable.

"A silver pony shining in the moonlight." The basis of Rachel's nightmare.

"In the moonlight." He had *seen* the pony in the moonlight.

I played the tape a third time, listening with my eyes shut, undistracted by the familiar face, or by Rachel in his comforting hug.

He said, "A silver pony trotting trustfully across the field lured by a handful of horse nuts."

He shouldn't have known that.

He could have known it if any of the Fernses had suggested it.

But the Fernses themselves wouldn't have said it. They hadn't fed Silverboy on nuts. The agent of destruction that had come by night had brought the nuts.

Ellis would say, of course, that he had made it up, and the fact that it might be true was simply a coincidence. I rewound the tape and stared for a while into space. Ellis would have an answer to everything. Ellis would be believed.

In the afternoon I wrote a long, detailed report for Norman Picton: not a joyous occupation.

Early Monday morning, as he had particularly requested it, I drove to the police station in Newbury and personally delivered the package into the Detective Inspector's own hands.

"Did you talk about this to anybody?" he asked.

"No."

"Especially not to Quint?"

"Especially not. But . . . ," I hesitated, "they're a close family. It's more than likely that on Saturday evening or yesterday, Ginnie and Gordon told Ellis that you and I and Archie were sniffing round the Land-Rover and that you took away the shears. I think you must consider that Ellis knows the hunt is on."

He nodded disgustedly. "And as Ellis Quint officially lives in the Metropolitan area, we in the Thames Valley district cannot pursue our inquiries as freely as we could have."

"You mean, you can't haul him down to the local Regents Park nick and ask him awkward questions, like what was he doing at three A.M. on Saturday?"

"We can ask him ourselves if the Met agrees."

"I thought these divisions were being done away with."

"Cooperation is improving all the time."

I left him to sort out his problems and set off to drive to Kent. On the way, wanting to give Rachel Ferns a cheering-up present, I detoured into the maze of Kingston and, having parked, walked around the precincts looking for inspiration in the shops.

A windowful of tumbling puppies made me pause; perhaps Rachel needed an animal to love, to replace the pony. And perhaps Linda would *not* be pleased at having to house-train a growing nuisance that molted and chewed the furniture. I went into the pet shop, however, and that's how I came to arrive at Linda Ferns's house with my car full of fish tank, water weeds, miniature ruined castle walls, electric pump, lights, fish food, instructions, and three large lidded buckets of tropical fish.

Rachel was waiting by the gate for my arrival.

"You're half an hour late," she accused. "You said you'd be here by twelve."

"Have you heard of the M25?"

"*Everyone* makes that motorway an excuse."

"Well, sorry."

Her bald head was still a shock. Apart from that, she looked well, her cheeks full and rounded by steroids. She wore a loose sundress and clumpy sneakers on sticklike legs. It was crazy to love someone else's child so comprehensively, yet for the first time ever, I felt the idea of fatherhood take a grip.

Jenny had refused to have children on the grounds that any racing day could leave her a widow, and at the time I hadn't cared one way or another. If ever I married again, I thought, following Rachel into the house, I would long for a daughter.

Linda gave me a bright, bright smile, a pecking kiss and the offer of a gin and tonic while she threw together some pasta for our lunch. The table was laid. She set out steaming dishes.

"Rachel was out waiting for you two hours ago!" she said. "I don't know what you've done to the child."

"How are things?"

"Happy." She turned away abruptly, tears as ever near the surface. "Have some more gin. You said you'd got news for me."

"Later. After lunch. And I've brought Rachel a present."

The fish tank after lunch was the ultimate success. Rachel was enthralled, Linda interested and helpful. "Thank goodness you didn't give her a dog," she said. "I can't stand animals under my feet. I wouldn't let Joe give her a dog. That's why she wanted a pony."

The vivid fish swam healthily through the Gothic ruins, the water weeds rose and swelled, the lights and bubbles did their stuff. Rachel sprinkled fish food and watched her new friends eat. The pet shop owner had persuaded me to take a bigger tank than I'd thought best, and he had undoubtedly been right. Rachel's pale face glowed. Pegotty, in a baby-bouncer, sat wide-eyed and open-mouthed beside the glass. Linda came with me into the garden.

"Any news about a transplant?" I asked.

"It would have been the first thing I'd told you."

We sat on the bench. The roses bloomed. It was a beautiful day, heart-breaking.

Linda said wretchedly, "In acute lymphoblastic leukemia, which is what Rachel's got, chemotherapy causes remission almost always. More than ninety percent of the time. In seven out of ten children, the remission lasts forever, and after five years they can be thought of as cured for life. And girls have a better chance than boys, isn't that odd? But in thirty percent of children, the disease comes back."

She stopped.

"And it has come back in Rachel?"

"Oh, Sid!"

"Tell me."

She tried, the tears trickling while she spoke. "The disease came back in Rachel after less than two years, and that's not good. Her hair was beginning to grow, but it came out again with the drugs. They re-established her again in remission, and they're so good, it isn't so easy the second time. But I know from their faces—and they don't suggest transplants unless they have to, because only about half of bone-marrow transplants are successful. I always talk as if a transplant will definitely save her, but it only *might*. If they found a tissue match they'd kill all her own bone marrow with radiation, which makes the children terribly nauseous and wretched, and then when the marrow's all dead they transfuse new liquid marrow into the veins and hope it will migrate into the bones and start making leukemia-free blood there, and quite often it *works* . . . and sometimes a child can be born with one blood group and be transfused with another. It's extraordinary. Rachel now has type A blood, but she might end up with type O, or something else. They can do so *much* nowadays. One day they may cure *everybody*. But oh . . . oh . . ."

I put my arm around her shoulders while she sobbed. So many disasters were forever. So many Edens lost.

I waited until the weeping fit passed, and then I told her I'd discovered who had maimed and destroyed Silverboy.

"You're not going to like it," I said, "and it might be best if you can prevent Rachel from finding out. Does she ever read the newspapers?"

"Only Peanuts."

"And the television news?"

"She doesn't like news of starving children." Linda looked at me fearfully. "I've *wanted* her to know who killed Silverboy. That's what I'm paying you for."

I took out of my pocket and put into her hands an envelope containing her much-traveled check, torn now into four pieces.

"I don't like what I found, and I don't want your money. Linda . . . I'm so very sorry . . . but it was Ellis Quint himself who cut off Silverboy's foot."

She sprang in revulsion to her feet, immediate anger filling her, the shock hard and physical, the enormity of what I'd said making her literally shake.

I should have broken it more slowly, I thought, but the words had had to be said.

"How can you say such a thing?" she demanded. "How *can* you? You've got it all wrong. He couldn't possibly! You're *crazy* to say such a thing."

I stood up also. "Linda . . ."

"Don't say anything. I won't listen. I *won't*. He is so *nice*. You're *truly* crazy. And of course I'm not going to tell Rachel what you've accused him of, because it would upset her, and you're *wrong*. And I know you've been kind to her . . . and to me . . . but I wouldn't have asked you here if I'd thought you could do so much awful harm. So please . . . *go*. Go. Just *go*."

I shrugged a fraction. Her reaction was extreme, but her emotions were always at full stretch. I understood her, but that didn't much help.

I said persuasively, "Linda, *listen*."

"No!"

I said, "Ellis has been my own friend for years. This is terrible for me, too."

She put her hands over her ears and turned her back, screaming, "Go away. Go away."

I said uncomfortably, "Phone me, then," and got no reply.

I touched her shoulder. She jerked away from me and ran a good way down the lawn, and after a minute I turned and went back into the house.

"Is Mummy crying?" Rachel asked, looking out of the window. "I heard her shout."

"She's upset." I smiled, though not feeling happy. "She'll be all right. How are the fish?"

"Cool." She went down on her knees, peering into the wet little world.

"I have to go now," I said.

"Good-bye." She seemed sure I would come back. It was a temporary farewell, between friends. She looked at the fishes, not turning her head.

"'Bye," I said, and drove ruefully to London, knowing that Linda's rejection was only the first: the beginning of the disbelief.

In Pont Square the telephone was ringing when I opened my front door, and continued to ring while I poured water and ice from a jug in the refrigerator, and continued to ring while I drank thirstily after the hot afternoon, and continued to ring while I changed the battery in my left arm.

In the end, I picked up the receiver.

"Where the bloody hell have you *been*?"

The Berkshire voice filled my ear, delivering not contumely, but information. Norman Picton, Detective Inspector, Thames Valley Police.

"You've heard the news, of course."

"What news?" I asked.

"Do you live with your head in the sand? Don't you own a radio?"

"What's happened?"

"Ellis Quint is in custody," he said.

"He's *what*?"

"Yes, well, hold on, he's sort of in custody. He's in hospital, under guard."

"Norman," I said, disoriented. "Start at the beginning."

"Right." He sounded over-patient, as if talking to a child. "This morning two plainclothes officers of the Metropolitan Police went to Ellis Quint's flat overlooking Regents Park intending to interview him harmlessly about his whereabouts early Saturday morning. He came out of the building before they reached the main entrance, so, knowing him by sight, they approached him, identifying themselves and showing him their badges. At which point"—Picton cleared his throat but didn't seem able to clear his account of pedestrian police phraseology—"at which point Mr. Ellis Quint pushed one of the officers away so forcefully that the officer overbalanced into the roadway and was struck by a passing car. Mr. Quint himself then ran into the path of traffic as he attempted to cross the road to put distance between himself and the police officers. Mr. Quint caused a bus to swerve. The bus struck Mr. Quint a glancing blow, throwing him to the ground. Mr. Quint was dazed and bruised. He was taken to hospital, where he is now in a secure room while investigations proceed."

I said, "Are you reading that from a written account?"

"That's so."

"How about an interpretation in your own earthy words?"

"I'm at work. I'm not alone."

"OK," I said. "Did Ellis panic or did he think he was being mugged?"

Picton half laughed. "I'd say the first. His lawyers will say the second. But, d'you know what? When they emptied his pockets at the hospital, they found a thick packet of cash—and his passport."

"No!"

"It isn't illegal."

"What does he say?"

"He hasn't said anything yet."

"How's the officer he pushed?"

"Broken leg. He was lucky."

"And . . . when Ellis's daze wears off?"

"It'll be up to the Met. They can routinely hold him for one day while they frame a charge. I'd say that's a toss-up. With the clout he can muster, he'll be out in hours."

"What did you do with my report?"

"It went to the proper authorities."

Authorities was such a vague word. Who ever described their occupation as "an authority"?

"Thanks for phoning," I said.

"Keep in touch." An order, it sounded like.

I put down the receiver and found a handwritten scrawl from Kevin Mills on *Pump* letterhead paper in my fax.

He'd come straight to the point.

"Sid, you're a shit."

CHAPTER 7

THE WEEK GOT worse, slightly alleviated only by a letter from Linda on Thursday morning.

Variably slanting handwriting. Jerky. A personality torn this way and that.

> *Dear Sid.*
>
> *I'm sorry I talked to you the way I did. I still cannot believe that Ellis Quint would cut off Silverboy's foot, but I remember thinking when he came here to do the TV program that he already knew a lot about what had happened. I mean things that hadn't been in the papers, like Silverboy liking horse nuts, which we never gave him, so how did he know, we didn't know ourselves, and I did wonder who had told him, but of course Joe asked Ellis who to buy a pony from, so of course I thought Ellis knew things about him from way back, like Silverboy being fed on horse nuts before he came to us.*
>
> *Anyway, I can see how you got it wrong about Ellis, and it was very nice of you to bring the fish tank for Rachel, I can't tear her away from it. She keeps asking when you will come back and I don't like to tell her you won't, not as things are, so if you'll visit us again I will not say any more about your being wrong about Ellis. I ask you for Rachel.*
>
> *We are both glad Ellis wasn't hurt today by that horrid bus.*
>
> *Yours sincerely,*
> *Linda Ferns.*

I wrote back thanking her for her letter, accepting her invitation and saying I would phone her soon.

ON TUESDAY ELLIS was charged with "actual bodily harm" for having inadvertently and without intention pushed "an assailant" into the path of potential danger (under the wheels of a speeding motor) and was set free "pending inquiries."

Norman Picton disillusionedly reported, "The only approximately good thing is that they confiscated his passport. His lawyers are pointing their fingers up any police nose they can confront, screeching that it's a scandal."

"Where's Ellis now?"

"Look to your back. Your report is with the Crown Prosecution Service, along with mine."

"Do you mean you don't know where he is?"

"He's probably in Britain or anywhere he can get to where he doesn't need a passport. He told the magistrates in court that he'd decided to do a sports program in Australia, and he had to have his passport with him because he needed it to get a visa for Australia."

"Never underestimate his wits," I said.

"And he'd better look out for yours."

"He and I know each other too well."

ON WEDNESDAY AFTERNOON Ellis turned up at his regular television studio as if life were entirely normal and, on completion of an audience-attended recording of a sports quiz, was quietly arrested by three uniformed police officers. Ellis spent the night in custody, and on Thursday morning was charged with severing the foot of a colt: to be exact, the off-fore foot of an expensive two-year-old thoroughbred owned by Mrs. Elizabeth Bracken of Combe Bassett Manor, Berkshire. To the vociferous fury of most of the nation, the magistrates remanded him in custody for another seven days, a preliminary precaution usually applied to those accused of murder.

Norman Picton phoned me privately on my home number.

"I'm not telling you this," he said. "Understand?"

"I've got cloth ears."

"It would mean my job."

"I hear you," I said. "I won't talk."

"No," he said, "that, I believe."

"Norman?"

"Word gets around. I looked up the transcript of the trial of that man that smashed off your hand. You didn't tell *him* what he wanted to know, did you?"

"No . . . well . . . everyone's a fool sometimes."

"Some fool. Anyway, pin back the cloth ears. The reason why Ellis Quint is remanded for seven days is because after his arrest he tried to hang himself in his cell with his tie."

"He *didn't*!"

"No one took his belt or tie away, because of who he was. No one in the station *believed* in the charge. There's all hell going on now. The top brass are passing the parcel like a children's party. No one's telling anyone outside anything on pain of death, so, Sid . . ."

"I promise," I said.

"They'll remand him next week for another seven days, partly to stop him committing suicide and partly because . . ." He faltered on the brink of utter trust, his whole career at risk.

"I *promise*," I said again. "And if I know what it is you want kept quiet, then I'll know what not to guess at publicly, won't I?"

"God," he said, half the anxiety evaporating, "then . . . there's horse blood in the hinges of the shears, and horse blood and hairs on the oily rag, and horse blood and hairs in the sacking. They've taken samples from the colt in the hospital at Lambourn, and everything's gone away for DNA testing. The results will be back next week."

"Does Ellis know?"

"I imagine that's why he tried the quick way out. It was a Hermès tie, incidentally, with a design of horseshoes. The simple knot he tied slid undone because the tie was pure smooth silk."

"For God's sake . . ."

"I keep forgetting he's your friend. Anyway, his lawyers have got to him. They're six deep. He's now playing the lighthearted celebrity, and he's sorrowful about *you*, Sid, for having got him all wrong. His lawyers are demanding proof that Ellis himself was ever at Combe Bassett by night, and we are asking for proof that he wasn't. His lawyers know we would have to drop the case if they can come up with a trustable alibi for any of the other amputations, but so far they haven't managed it. It's early days, though. They'll dig and dig, you can bet on it."

"Yeah."

"None of the Land-Rover evidence will get into the papers because the sub judice rule kicked in the minute they remanded him. Mostly that helps us, but you, as Sid Halley, won't be able to justify yourself in print until after the trial."

"Even if I can then."

"Juries are unpredictable."

"And the law is, frequently, an ass."

"People in the force are already saying you're off your rocker. They say Ellis is too well known. They say that wherever he went he would be recognized, therefore if no one recognized him, that in itself is proof he wasn't there."

"Mm," I said. "I've been thinking about that. Do you have time off at the weekend?"

"Not this weekend, no. Monday do you?"

"I'll see if I can fix something up with Archie . . . and Jonathan."

"And there's another thing," Norman said, "the Land-Rover's presence at Combe Bassett is solid in itself, but Jonathan, if he gets as far as the witness box, will be a *meal* for Ellis's lawyers. On probation for stealing cars! What sort of a witness is that?"

"I understood the jury isn't allowed to know anything about a witness. I was at a trial once in the Central Law Courts—the Old Bailey—when a beautifully dressed and blow-dried twenty-six-year-old glamour boy gave evidence—all lies—and the jury weren't allowed to know that he was already serving a sentence for confidence tricks and had come to court straight from jail, via the barber and the wardrobe room. The jury thought him a *lovely* young man. So much for juries."

"Don't you believe in the jury system?"

"I would believe in it if they were told more. How can a jury come to a prison-or-freedom decision if half the facts are withheld? There should be *no* inadmissible evidence."

"You're naive."

"I'm Sid Public, remember? The law bends over backwards to give the accused the benefit of the slightest doubt. The *victim* of murder is never there to give evidence. The colt in Lambourn can't talk. It's safer to kill animals. I'm sorry, but I can't stand what Ellis has become."

He said flatly, "Emotion works against you in the witness box."

"Don't worry. In court, I'm a block of ice."

"So I've heard."

"You've heard too damned much."

He laughed. "There's an old-boy internet," he said. "All you need is the password and a whole new world opens up."

"What's the password?"

"I can't tell you."

"Don't bugger me about. What's the password?"

"Archie," he said.

I was silent for all of ten seconds, remembering Archie's eyes the first time I met him, remembering the *awareness*, the message of knowledge. Archie knew more about me than I knew about him.

I asked, "What exactly does Archie do in the çivil service?"

"I reckon," Norman said, amused, "that he's very like you, Sid. What he don't want you to know, he don't tell you."

"Where can I reach you on Monday?"

"Police station. Say you're John Paul Jones."

KEVIN MILLS DOMINATED the front page of *The Pump* on Friday—a respite from the sexual indiscretions of cabinet ministers but a demolition job on me. "*The Pump*," he reminded readers, "had set up a hotline to Sid Halley to report attacks on colts. Owners had been advised to lock their stable doors, and to great effect had done so after the Derby. *The Pump* disclaimed all responsibility for Sid Halley's now ludicrously fingering Ellis Quint as the demon responsible for torturing defenseless horses. Ellis Quint, whose devotion to thoroughbreds stretches back to his own starry career as the country's top amateur race-rider, the popular hero who braved all perils in the ancient tradition of gentlemen sportsmen . . ."

More of the same.

"See also 'Analysis,' on page ten, and India Cathcart, page fifteen."

I supposed one had to know the worst. I read the leader column: "Should an ex-jockey be allowed free rein as pseudo sleuth? (Answer: no, of course not.)" and then dredging deep for steel, I finally turned to India Cathcart's piece.

> *Sid Halley, smugly accustomed to acclaim as a champion, in short time lost his career, his wife and his left hand, and then weakly watched his friend soar to super-celebrity and national-star status, all the things that he considered should be his. Who does this pathetic little man think he's kidding? He's no Ellis Quint. He's a has-been with an ego problem, out to ruin what he envies.*

That was for starters. The next section pitilessly but not accurately dissected the impulse that led one to compete at speed (ignoring the fact that presumably Ellis himself had felt the same power-hungry inferiority complex).

My ruthless will to win, India Cathcart had written, had destroyed everything good in my own life. The same will to win now aimed to destroy my friend Ellis Quint. This was ambition gone mad.

The Pump would not let it happen. Sid Halley was a beetle ripe for squashing. *The Pump* would exterminate. The Halley myth was curtains.

DAMN, AND BLAST her, I thought, and, for the first time in eighteen years, got drunk.

ON SATURDAY MORNING, groaning around the apartment with a headache, I found a message in my fax machine.

Handwritten scrawl, *Pump*-headed paper same as before . . . Kevin Mills.

> *Sid, sorry, but you asked for it.*
>   *You're still a shit.*

Most of Sunday I listened to voices on my answering machine delivering the same opinion.

Two calls relieved the gloom.

One from Charles Roland, my ex–father-in-law. "Sid, if you're in trouble, there's always Aynsford," and a second from Archie Kirk, "I'm at home. Norman Picton says you want me."

Two similar men, I thought gratefully. Two men with cool, dispassionate minds who would listen before condemning.

I phoned back to Charles, who seemed relieved I sounded sane.

"I'm all right," I said.

"Ellis is a knight in shining armor, though."

"Yeah."

"Are you *sure*, Sid?"

"Positive."

"But Ginnie . . . and Gordon . . . they're *friends*."

"Well," I said, "if *I* cut the foot off a horse, what would you do?"

"But you *wouldn't*."

"No."

I sighed. That was the trouble. No one could believe it of Ellis.

"Sid, come, anytime," Charles said.

"You're my rock," I said, trying to make it sound light. "I'll come if I need to."

"Good."

I phoned Archie and asked if Jonathan was still staying with Betty Bracken.

Archie said, "I've been talking to Norman. Jonathan is now addicted to water skiing and spends every day at the lake. Betty is paying hundreds and says it's worth it to get him out of the house. He'll be at the lake tomorrow. Shall we all meet there?"

We agreed on a time, and met.

When we arrived, Jonathan was out on the water.

"That's him." Norman said, pointing.

The flying figure in a scarlet wet-suit went up a ramp, flew, turned a somersault in the air and landed smoothly on two skis.

"*That*," Archie said in disbelief, "is *Jonathan*?"

"He's a natural," Norman said. "I've been out here for a bit most days. Not only does he know his spatial balance and attitude by instinct, but he's fearless."

Archie and I silently watched Jonathan approach the shore, drop the rope and ski confidently up the sloping landing place with almost as much panache as Norman himself.

Jonathan grinned. Jonathan's streaky hair blew wetly back from his forehead. Jonathan, changed, looked blazingly *happy*.

A good deal of the joy dimmed with apprehension as he looked at Archie's stunned and expressionless face. I took a soft sports bag out of my car and held it out to him, asking him to take it with him to the dressing rooms.

"Hi," he said. "OK." He took the bag and walked off barefooted, carrying his skis.

"Incredible," Archie said, "but he can't ski through life."

"It's a start," Norman said.

After we'd stood around for a few minutes discussing Ellis we were approached by a figure in a dark-blue tracksuit also wearing black running shoes, a navy baseball cap and sunglasses and carrying a sheet of paper. He came to within fifteen feet of us and stopped.

"Yes?" Norman asked, puzzled, as to a stranger. "Do you want something?"

I said, "Take off the cap and the glasses."

He took them off. Jonathan's streaky hair shook forward into its normal startling shape and his eyes stared at my face. I gave him a slight jerk of the head, and he came the last few paces and handed the paper to Norman.

Archie for once looked wholly disconcerted. Norman read aloud what I'd written on the paper.

" 'Jonathan, this is an experiment. Please put on the clothes you'll find in this bag. Put on the baseball cap, peak forward, hiding your face. Wear the sunglasses. Bring this paper. Walk towards me, stop a few feet away, and don't speak. OK? Thanks, Sid.' "

Norman lowered the paper, looked at Jonathan and said blankly, "Bloody hell."

"Is that the lot?" Jonathan asked me.

"Brilliant," I said.

"Shall I get dressed now?"

I nodded, and he walked nonchalantly away.

"He looked totally different," Archie commented, still amazed. "I didn't know him at all."

I said to Norman, "Did you look at the tape of Ellis's program, that one I put in with my report?"

"The tape covered with stickers saying it was the property of Mrs. Linda Ferns? Yes, I did."

"When Ellis was sitting on the floor with those children," I said, "he was wearing a dark tracksuit, open at the neck. He had a peaked cap pushed back on his head. He looked young. Boyish. The children responded to him . . . touched him . . . *loved* him. He had a pair of sunglasses tucked into a breast pocket.

After a silence Norman said, "But he *wouldn't*. He wouldn't wear those clothes on television if he'd worn them to mutilate the Ferns pony."

"Oh yes he would. It would deeply amuse him. There's nothing gives him more buzz than taking risks."

"A baseball cap," Archie said thoughtfully, "entirely changes the shape of someone's head."

I nodded. "A baseball cap and a pair of running shorts can reduce any man of stature to anonymity."

"We'll never prove it," Norman said.

Jonathan slouched back in his own clothes and with his habitual half-sneering expression firmly in place. Archie's exasperation with him sharply returned.

"This is not the road to Damascus," I murmured.

"Damn you, Sid." Archie glared, and then laughed.

"What are you talking about?" Norman asked.

"Saint Paul's conversion on the road to Damascus happened like a thunderclap," Archie explained. "Sid's telling me not to look for instant miracles by the gravel pit lake."

Jonathan, not listening, handed me the bag. "Cool idea," he said. "No one knew me."

"They would, close to."

"It was still a risk," Norman objected.

"I told you," I said, "the risk is the point."

"It doesn't make sense."

"Cutting off a horse's foot doesn't make sense. Half of human actions don't make sense. Sense is in the eye of the beholder."

I DROVE BACK to London.

My answering machine had answered so many calls that it had run out of recording tape.

Among the general abuse, three separate calls were eloquent about the trouble I'd stirred up. All three of the owners of the other colt victims echoed Linda Ferns's immovable conviction.

The lady from Cheltenham: "I can't believe you can be so misguided. Ellis is absolutely innocent. I wouldn't have thought of you as being jealous of him, but all the papers say so. I'm sorry, Sid, but you're not welcome here anymore."

The angry Lancashire farmer. "You're a moron, do you know that? Ellis Quint! You're stupid. You were all right as a jockey. You should give up this pretense of being Sherlock Holmes. You're pitiful, lad."

The lady from York: "How *can* you? Dear Ellis! He's worth ten of you, I have to say."

I switched off the critical voices, but they went on reverberating in my brain.

The press had more or less uniformly followed *The Pump*'s lead. Pictures of Ellis at his most handsome smiled confidently from newsstands everywhere. Trial by media found Ellis Quint the wronged and innocent hero, Sid Halley the twisted, jealous cur snapping at his heels.

I'd known it would be bad: so why the urge to bang my head against the wall? Because I was human, and didn't have tungsten nerves, whatever anyone thought. I sat with my eyes shut, ostrich fashion.

Tuesday was much the same. I still didn't bang my head. Close-run thing.

On Wednesday Ellis appeared again before magistrates, who that time set him free on bail.

Norman phoned.

"Cloth ears?" he said. "Same as before?"

"Deaf," I assured him

"It was fixed beforehand. Two minutes in court. Different time than posted. The press arrived after it was over. Ellis greeted them, free, smiling broadly."

"Shit."

Norman said, "His lawyers have done their stuff. It's rubbish to think the well-balanced personality intended to kill himself—his tie got caught somehow but he managed to free it. The policeman he pushed failed to identify himself adequately and is now walking about comfortably in a cast. The colt Ellis is accused of attacking is alive and recovering well. As bail is granted in cases of manslaughter, it is unnecessary to detain Ellis Quint any longer on far lesser charges. So . . . he's walked."

"Is he still to be tried?"

"So far. His lawyers have asked for an early trial date so that he can put this unpleasantness behind him. He will plead not guilty, of course. His lawyers are already patting each other on the back. And . . . I think there's a heavyweight maneuvering somewhere in this case."

"A heavyweight? Who?"

"Don't know. It's just a feeling."

"Could it be Ellis's father?"

"No, no. Quite different. It's just . . . since our reports, yours and mine, reached the Crown Prosecution Service, there's been a new factor. Political, perhaps. It's difficult to describe. It's not exactly a cover-up. There's already been too much publicity, it's more a sort of redirection. Even officially, and not just to the press, someone with muscle is trying to get you thoroughly and, I'm afraid I must say, *malignantly* discredited."

"Thanks a bunch."

"Sid, seriously, look out for yourself."

I FELT AS prepared as one could be for some sort of catastrophic pulverization to come my way, but in the event the process was subtler and long drawn out.

As if nothing had happened, Ellis resumed his television program and began making jokes about Sid Halley—"Sid Halley? That friend of mine! Have you heard that he comes from Halifax? Halley facts—he makes them up."

And "I like halibut—I eat it." And the old ones that I was used to, "halitosis" and "Hallelujah."

Hilarious.

When I went to the races, which I didn't do as often as earlier, people either turned their backs or *laughed*, and I wasn't sure which I disliked more.

I took to going only to jumping meetings, knowing Ellis's style took him to the most fashionable meetings on the flat. I acknowledged unhappily to myself that in my avoidance of him there was an element of cringe. I despised myself for it. All the same, I shrank from a confrontation with him and truly didn't know whether it was because of an ever-deepening aversion to what he had done, or because of the fear—the certainty—that he would publicly mock me.

He behaved as if there were never going to be a trial; as if awkward details like Land-Rovers, lopping shears and confirmed matching DNA tests tying the shears to the Bracken colt were never going to surface once the sub judice silence ended.

Norman, Archie and also Charles Roland worried that, for all the procedural care we had taken, Ellis's lawyers would somehow get the Land-Rover disallowed. Ellis's lawyers, Norman said, backed by the heavy unseen presence that was motivating them and possibly even paying the mounting fees, now included a defense counsel whose loss rate for the previous seven years was nil.

Surprisingly, despite the continuing barrage of ignominy, I went on being offered work. True, the approach was often tentative and apologetic— "Whether you're right or pigheaded about Ellis Quint . . ." and "Even if you've got Ellis Quint all wrong . . ."—but the nitty gritty seemed to be that they needed me and there was no one else.

Well hooray for that. I cleaned up minor mysteries, checked credit ratings, ditto characters, found stolen horses, caught sundry thieves, all the usual stuff.

July came in with a deluge that flooded rivers and ruined the shoes of racegoers, and no colt was attacked at the time of the full moon, perhaps because the nights were wet and windy and black, dark with clouds.

The press finally lost interest in the daily trashing of Sid Halley and Ellis Quint's show wrapped up for the summer break. I went down to Kent a couple of times, taking new fish for Rachel, sitting on the floor with her, playing checkers. Neither Linda nor I mentioned Ellis. She hugged me good-bye each time and asked when I would be coming back. Rachel, she said, had had no more nightmares. They were a thing of the past.

August came quietly and left in the same manner. No colts were attacked. The hotline went cold. India Cathcart busied herself with a cabinet member's mistress but still had a routinely vindictive jab at me each Friday. I went to America for two short weeks and rode horses up the Grand Tetons in Wyoming, letting the wide skies and the forests work their peace.

In September, one dew-laden early-fall English Saturday morning after a calm moonlit night, a colt was discovered with a foot off.

Nauseated, I heard the announcement on the radio in the kitchen while I made coffee.

Listeners would remember, the cool newsreader said, that in June Ellis Quint had been notoriously accused by ex-jockey Sid Halley of a similar attack. Quint was laughing off this latest incident, affirming his total ignorance on the matter.

There were no hotline calls from *The Pump*, but Norman Picton scorched the wires.

"Have you heard?" he demanded.

"Yes. But no details."

"It was a yearling colt this time. Apparently there aren't many two-year-olds in the fields just now, but there are hundreds of yearlings."

"Yes," I agreed. "The yearling sales are starting."

"The yearling in question belonged to some people near Northampton. They're frantic. Their vet put the colt out of his misery. But get this. Ellis Quint's lawyers have already claimed he has an alibi."

I stood in silence in my sitting room, looking out to the unthreatening garden.

"Sid?"

"Mm."

"You'll have to break that alibi. Otherwise, it will break *you*."

"Mm."

"Say something else, dammit."

"The police can do it. Your lot."

"Face it. They're not going to try very hard. They're going to believe in his alibi, if it's anything like solid."

"Do you think, do you *really* think," I asked numbly, "that an ultra-respected barrister would connive with his client to mutilate . . . to kill . . . a colt—or pay someone else to do it—to cast doubt on the prosecution's case in the matter of a *different* colt?"

"Put like that, no."

"Nor do I."

"So Ellis Quint has set it up himself, and what he has set up, you can knock down."

"He's had weeks—more than two months—to plan it."

"Sid," he said, "it's not like you to sound defeated."

If he, I thought, had been on the receiving end of a long, pitiless barrage of systematic denigration, he might feel as I did, which, if not comprehensively defeated, was at least battle weary before I began.

"The police at Northampton," I said, "are not going to welcome me with open arms."

"That's never stopped you before."

I sighed. "Can you find out from the Northampton police what his alibi actually is?"

"Piece of cake. I'll phone you back."

I put down the receiver and went over to the window. The little square looked peaceful and safe, the railed garden green and grassy, a tree-dappled haven where generations of privileged children had run and played while their nursemaids gossiped. I'd spent my own childhood in Liverpool's back streets, my father dead and my mother fighting cancer. I in no way regretted the contrast in origins. I had learned self-sufficiency and survival there. Perhaps because of the back streets I now valued the little garden more. I wondered how the children who'd grown up in that garden would deal with Ellis Quint. Perhaps I could learn from them. Ellis had been that sort of child.

Norman phoned back later in the morning.

"Your friend," he said, "reportedly spent the night at a private dance in Shropshire, roughly a hundred miles to the northwest of the colt. Endless friends will testify to his presence, including his hostess, a duchess. It was a dance given to celebrate the twenty-first birthday of the heir."

"Damn."

"He could hardly have chosen a more conspicuous or more watertight alibi."

"And some poor bitch will swear she lay down for him at dawn."

"Why dawn?"

"It's when it happens."

"How do you know?"

"Never you mind," I said.

"You're a bad boy, Sid."

Long ago, I thought. Before Jenny. Summer dances, dew, wet grass, giggles and passion. Long ago and innocent.

Life's a bugger, I thought.

"Sid," Norman's voice said, "do you realize the trial is due to start two weeks on Monday?"

"I do realize."

"Then get a move on with this alibi."

"Yes, sir, Detective Inspector."

He laughed. "Put the bugger back behind bars."

ON TUESDAY I went to see the Shropshire duchess, for whom I had ridden winners in that former life. She even had a painting of me on her favorite horse, but I was no longer her favorite jockey.

"Yes, of *course* Ellis was here all night," she confirmed. Short, thin, and at first unwelcoming, she led me through the armor-dotted entrance hall of her drafty old house to the sitting room, where she had been watching the jump racing on television when I arrived.

Her front door had been opened to me by an arthritic old manservant who had hobbled away to see if Her Grace was in. Her Grace had come into the hall clearly anxious to get rid of me as soon as possible, and had then relented, her old kindness towards me resurfacing like a lost but familiar habit.

A three-mile steeplechase was just finishing, the jockeys kicking side by side to the finish line, the horses tired and straining, the race going in the end to the one carrying less weight.

The duchess turned down the volume, the better to talk.

"I cannot *believe*, Sid," she said, "that you've accused dear Ellis of something so *disgusting*. I know you and Ellis have been friends for years. Everyone knows that. I do think he's been a bit unkind about you on television, but you did *ask* for it, you know."

"But he *was* here . . . ?" I asked.

"Of course. All night. It was five or later when everyone started to leave. The band was playing still . . . we'd all had breakfast . . ."

"When did the dance start?" I asked.

"*Start*? The invitations were for ten. But you know how people are. It was eleven or midnight before most people came. We had the fireworks at three-thirty because rain was forcast for later, but it was fine all night, thank goodness."

"Did Ellis say good night when he left?"

"My dear Sid, there were over three hundred people here last Friday night. A succès fou, if I say it myself."

"So you don't actually remember when Ellis left?"

"The last I saw of him he was dancing an eightsome with that gawky Raven girl. Do drop it, Sid. I'm seeing you now for old times' sake, but you're not doing yourself any good, are you?"

"Probably not."

She patted my hand. "I'll always *know* you, at the races and so on."

"Thank you," I said.

"Yes. Be a dear and find your own way out. Poor old Stone has such bad arthritis these days."

She turned up the volume in preparation for the next race, and I left.

THE GAWKY RAVEN girl who had danced an eightsome reel with Ellis turned out to be the third daughter of an earl. She herself had gone off to Greece to join someone's yacht, but her sister (the second daughter) insisted that Ellis had danced with dozens of people after that, and wasn't I, Sid Halley, being a teeny-weeny *twit*?

I WENT TO see Miss Richardson and Mrs. Bethany, joint owners of the Windward Stud Farm, home of the latest colt victim: and to my dismay found Ginnie Quint there as well.

All three women were in the stud farm's office, a building separate from the rambling one-story dwelling house. A groom long-reining a yearling had directed me incuriously and I drew up outside the pinkish brick new-looking structure without relish for my mission, but not expecting a tornado.

I knocked and entered, as one does with such offices, and found myself in the normal clutter of desks, computers, copiers, wall charts and endless piles of paper.

I'd done a certain amount of homework before I went there, so it was easy to identify Miss Richardson as the tall, bulky, dominant figure in tweed jacket, worn cord trousers and wiry gray short-cropped curls. Fifty, I thought; despises men. Mrs. Bethany, a smaller, less powerful version of Miss Richardson, was reputedly the one who stayed up at night when the mares were foaling, the one on whose empathy with horses the whole enterprise floated.

The women didn't own the farm's two stallions (they belonged to syndicates) nor any of the mares: Windward Stud was a cross between a livery stable and a maternity ward. They couldn't afford the bad publicity of the victimized yearling.

Ginnie Quint, sitting behind one of the desks, leaped furiously to her feet the instant I appeared in the doorway and poured over me an accumulated concentration of verbal volcanic lava, scalding shriveling, sticking my feet to the ground and my tongue in dryness to the roof of my mouth.

"He *trusted* you. He would have *died* for you."

I sensed Miss Richardson and Mrs. Bethany listening in astonishment, not knowing who I was nor what I'd done to deserve such an onslaught; but I had eyes only for Ginnie, whose long fondness for me had fermented to hate.

"You're going to go into court and try to send your best friend to prison . . . to destroy him . . . pull him down . . . ruin him. You're going to *betray* him. You're not fit to live."

Emotion twisted her gentle features into ugliness. Her words came out spitting.

It was her own son who had done this. Her golden, idolized son. He had made of me finally the traitor that would deliver the kiss.

I SAID ABSOLUTELY nothing.

I felt more intensely than ever, the by now accustomed and bitter awareness of the futility of rebellion. Gagged by sub judice, I'd been unable all along to put up any defense, especially because the press had tended to pounce on my indignant protests and label them as "whining" and "diddums," and "please, Teacher, he hit me . . ." and "it's not fair, I hit him first."

A quick check with a lawyer had confirmed that though trying to sue one paper for libel might have been possible, suing the whole lot was not practical. Ellis's jokes were not actionable and, unfortunately, the fact that I was still profitably employed in my chosen occupation meant that I couldn't prove the criticism had damaged me financially.

"Grit your teeth and take it," he'd advised cheerfully, and I'd paid him for an opinion I gave myself free every day.

As there was no hope of Ginnie's listening to anything I might say, I unhappily but pragmatically turned to retreat, intending to return another day to talk to Miss Richardson and Mrs. Bethany, and found my way barred by two new burly arrivals, known already to the stud owners as policemen.

"Sergeant Smith reporting, madam," one said to Miss Richardson.

She nodded. "Yes, Sergeant?"

"We've found an object hidden in one of the hedges round the field where your horse was done in."

No one objected to my presence, so I remained in the office, quiet and riveted.

Sergeant Smith carried a long, narrow bundle which he laid on one of the desks. "Could you tell us, madam, if this belongs to *you*?"

His manner was almost hostile, accusatory. He seemed to expect the answer to be yes.

"What is it?" Miss Richardson asked, very far from guilty perturbation.

"This, madam," the sergeant said with a note of triumph, and lifted back folds of filthy cloth to reveal their contents, which were two long wooden handles topped by heavy metal clippers.

A pair of lopping shears.

Miss Richardson and Mrs. Bethany stared at them unmoved. It was Ginnie Quint who turned slowly white and fainted.

CHAPTER 8

SO HERE WE were in October, with the leaves weeping yellowly from the trees.

Here I was, perching on the end of Rachel Ferns's bed, wearing a huge, fluffy orange clown wig and a red bulbous nose, making sick children laugh while feeling far from merry inside.

"Have you hurt your arm?" Rachel asked conversationally.

"Banged it," I said.

She nodded. Linda looked surprised. Rachel said, "When things hurt it shows in people's eyes."

She knew too much about pain for a nine-year-old. I said, "I'd better go before I tire you."

She smiled, not demurring. She, like the children wearing the other wigs I'd brought, all had very short bursts of stamina. Visiting was down to ten minutes maximum.

I took off the clown wig and kissed Rachel's forehead. "'Bye," I said.

"You'll come back?"

"Of course."

She sighed contentedly, knowing I would. Linda walked with me from the ward to the hospital door.

"It's . . . *awful*," she said, forlorn, on the exit steps. Cold air. The chill to come.

I put my arms around her. Both arms. Hugged her.

"Rachel asks for you all the time," she said. "Joe cuddles her and cries. She cuddles *him*, trying to comfort him. She's her daddy's little girl. She loves him. But you . . . you're her *friend*. You make her laugh, not cry. It's you she asks for all the time—not Joe."

"I'll always come if I can."

She sobbed quietly on my shoulder and gulped, "Poor Mrs. Quint."

"Mm," I said.

"I haven't told Rachel about Ellis . . ."

"No. Don't," I said.

"I've been beastly to you."

"No, far from it."

"The papers have said such *dreadful* things about you." Linda shook in my arms. "I knew you weren't like that . . . I told Joe I have to believe you about Ellis Quint and he thinks I'm stupid."

"Look after Rachel, nothing else matters."

She went back into the hospital and I rode dispiritedly back to London in the Teledrive car.

Even though I'd returned with more than an hour to spare, I decided against Pont Square and took the sharp memory of Gordon Quint's attack straight to the restaurant in Piccadilly, where I'd agreed to meet the lawyer Davis Tatum.

With a smile worth millions, the French lady in charge of the restaurant arranged for me to have coffee and a sandwich in the tiny bar while I waited for my friend. The bar, in fact, looked as if it had been wholly designed as a meeting place for those about to lunch. There were no more than six tables, a bartender who brought drinks to one's elbow, and a calm atmosphere. The restaurant itself was full of daylight, with huge windows and green plants, and was sufficiently hidden from the busy artery of Mayfair downstairs as to give peace and privacy and no noisy passing trade.

I sat at a bar table in the corner with my back to the entrance, though in fact few were arriving: more were leaving after long hours of talk and lunch. I took some ibuprofen, and waited without impatience. I spent hours in my job, sometimes, waiting for predators to pop out of their holes.

Davis Tatum arrived late and out of breath from having apparently walked up the stairs instead of waiting for the elevator. He wheezed briefly behind my back, then came around into view and lowered his six-feet-three-inch bulk into the chair opposite.

He leaned forward and held out his hand for a shake. I gave him a limp approximation, which raised his eyebrows but no comment.

He was a case of an extremely agile mind in a totally unsuitable body. There were large cheeks, double chins, fat lidded eyes and a small mouth. Dark, smooth hair had neither receded nor grayed. He had flat ears, a neck like a weight lifter, and a charcoal pin-striped suit straining over a copious belly. He might have difficulty, I thought, in catching sight of certain parts of his own body. Except in the brain-box, nature had dealt him a sad hand.

"First of all," he said, "I have some bad news, and I possibly shouldn't be here talking to you at all, according to how you read *Archbold*."

"*Archbold* being the dos and don'ts manual for trial lawyers?"

"More or less."

"What's the bad news, then?" I asked. There hadn't been much that was good.

"Ellis Quint has retracted his 'guilty' plea, and has gone back to 'not guilty.'"

"*Retracted?*" I exclaimed. "How can one retract a confession?"

"Very easily." He sighed. "Quint says he was upset yesterday about his mother's death, and what he said about feeling guilty was misinterpreted. In other words, his lawyers have got over the shock and have had a rethink. They apparently know you have so far not been able to break Ellis Quint's alibi for the night that last colt was attacked in Northamptonshire, and they think they can therefore get the Bracken colt charge dismissed, despite the Land-Rover and circumstantial evidence, so they are aiming for a complete acquittal, not psychiatric treatment, and, I regret to tell you, they are likely to succeed."

He didn't have to tell me that my own reputation would never recover if Ellis emerged with his intact.

"And *Archbold*?"

"If I were the Crown Prosecuting counsel in this case I could be struck off for talking to you, a witness. As you know, I am the senior barrister in the chambers where the man prosecuting Ellis Quint works. I have seen his brief and discussed the case with him. I can absolutely properly talk to you, though perhaps some people might not think it prudent."

I smiled. "'Bye-'bye, then."

"I may not discuss with you a case in which I may be examining you as a witness. But of course I will not be examining you. Also, we can talk about anything else. Like, for instance, golf."

"I don't play golf."

"Don't be obtuse, my dear fellow. Your perceptions are acute."

"Are we talking about angles?"

His eyes glimmered behind the folds of fat. "I saw the report package that you sent to the CPS."

"The Crown Prosecution Service?"

"The same. I happened to be talking to a friend. I said your report had surprised me, both by its thoroughness and by your deductions and conclusions. He said I shouldn't be surprised. He said you'd had the whole top echelon of the Jockey Club hanging on your every word. He said that, about a year ago, you'd cleared up two major racing messes at the same time. They've never forgotten it."

"A year last May," I said. "Is that what he meant?"

"I expect so. He said you had an assistant then that isn't seen around anymore. The job I'd like you to do might need an assistant for the leg-work. Don't you have your assistant nowadays?"

"Chico Barnes?"

He nodded. "A name like that."

"He got married," I said briefly. "His wife doesn't like what I do, so he's given it up. He teaches judo. I still see him—he gives me a judo lesson most weeks, but I can't ask him for any other sort of help."

"Pity."

"Yes. He was good. Great company and bright."

"And he got *deterred*. That's why he gave it up."

I went, internally, very still. I said, "What do you mean?"

"I heard," he said, his gaze steady on my face, "that he got beaten with some sort of thin chain to deter him from helping you. To deter him from all detection. And it worked."

"He got married," I said.

Davis Tatum leaned back in his chair, which creaked under his weight.

"I heard," he said, "that the same treatment was doled out to you, and in the course of things the Jockey Club mandarins made you take your shirt off. They said they had never seen anything like it. The whole of your upper body, arms included, was black with bruising, and there were vicious red weals all over you. And with your shirt hiding all that you'd calmly explained to them how and why you'd been attacked and how one of their number, who had arranged it, was a villain. You got one of the big shots chucked out."

"Who told you all that?"

"One hears things."

I thought in unprintable curses. The six men who'd seen me that day with my shirt off had stated their intention of never talking about it. They'd wanted to keep to themselves the villainy I'd found within their own walls; and nothing had been more welcome to me than that silence. It had been bad enough at the time. I didn't want continually to be reminded.

"Where does one hear such things?" I asked.

"Be your age, Sid. In the clubs . . . Bucks, the Turf, the RAC, the Garrick . . . these things get mentioned."

"How often . . . do they get mentioned? How often have you heard that story?"

He paused as if checking with an inner authority, and then said, "Once."

"Who told you?"

"I gave my word."

"One of the Jockey Club?"

"I gave my word. If you'd given your word, would *you* tell *me*?"

"No."

He nodded. "I asked around about you. And that's what I was told. Told in confidence. If it matters to you, I've heard it from no one else."

"It matters."

"It reflects to your credit," he protested. "It obviously didn't stop you."

"It could give other villains ideas."

"And do villains regularly attack you?"

"Well, no," I said. "Physically no one's laid a finger on me since that time." Not until yesterday, I thought. "If you're talking about nonphysical assaults . . . Have you read the papers?"

"Scurrilous." Davis Tatum twisted in his seat until he could call the barman. "Tanqueray, and tonic, please—and for you, Sid?"

"Scotch. A lot of water."

The barman brought the glasses, setting them out on little round white mats.

"Health," Davis Tatum toasted, raising his gin.

"Survival," I responded, and drank to both.

He put down his glass and came finally to the point.

"I need someone," he said, "who is clever, unafraid and able to think fast in a crisis."

"No one's like that."

"What about you?"

I smiled. "I'm stupid, scared silly a good deal of the time and I have nightmares. What you think you see is not what you get."

"I get the man who wrote the Quint report."

I looked benignly at my glass and not at his civilized face. "If you're going to do something to a small child that you know he won't like," I said, "such as sticking a needle into him, you *first* tell him what a brave little boy he is—in the hope that he'll then let you make a pincushion of him without complaint."

There was a palpable silence, then he chuckled, the low, rich timbre filling the air. There was embarrassment in there somewhere; a ploy exposed.

I said prosaically, "What's the job?"

He waited while four businessmen arrived, arranged their drinks and sank into monetary conversation at the table farthest from where we sat.

"Do you know who I mean by Owen Yorkshire?" Tatum asked, looking idly at the newcomers, not at me.

"Owen Yorkshire." I rolled the name around in memory and came up with only doubts. "Does he own a horse or two?"

"He does. He also owns Topline Foods."

"Topline . . . as in sponsored race at Aintree? As in Ellis Quint, guest of honor at the Topline Foods lunch the day before the Grand National?"

"That's the fellow."

"And the inquiry?"

"Find out if he's manipulating the Quint case to his own private advantage."

I said thoughtfully, "I did hear that there's a heavy-weight abroad."

"Find out who it is, and why."

"What about poor old Archbold? He'd turn in his grave."

"So you'll do it!"

"I'll try. But why me? Why not the police? Why not the old-boy internet?"

He looked at me straightly. "Because you include silence in what you sell."

"And I'm expensive," I said.

"Retainer and refreshers," he promised.

"Who's paying?"

"The fees will come through me."

"And it's agreed," I said, "that the results, if any, are yours. Prosecution or otherwise will normally be your choice."

He nodded.

"In case you're wondering," I said, "when it comes to Ellis Quint, I gave the client's money back, in order to be able to stop him myself. The client didn't at first believe in what he'd done. I made my own choice. I have to tell you that you'd run that risk."

He leaned forward and extended his pudgy hand.

"We'll shake on it," he said, and grasped my palm with a firmness that sent a shock wave fizzing clear up to my jaw.

"What's the matter?" he said, sensing it.

"Nothing."

He wasn't getting much of a deal, I thought. I had a reputation already in tatters, a cracked ulna playing up, and the prospect of being chewed to further shreds by Ellis's defense counsel. He'd have done as well to engage my pal Jonathan of the streaky hair.

"Mr. Tatum," I began

"Davis. My name's Davis."

"Will you give me your *assurance* that you won't speak of that Jockey Club business around the clubs?"

"Assurance?"

"Yes."

"But I told you . . . it's to your credit."

"It's a private thing. I don't like *fuss*."

He looked at me thoughtfully. He said, "You have my assurance." And I wanted to believe in it, but I wasn't sure that I did. He was too intensely a club man, a filler of large armchairs in dark paneled rooms full of old exploded reputations and fruitily repeated secrets: "Won't say a word, old boy."

"Sid."

"Mm?"

"Whatever the papers say, where it really counts, you are respected."

"Where's that?"

"The clubs are good for gossip, but these days that's not where the power lies."

"Power wanders round like the magnetic North Pole."

"Who said that?"

"I just did," I said.

"No. I mean, did you make it up?"

"I've no idea."

"Power, these days, is fragmented," he said.

I added, "And where the power is at any one time is not necessarily where one would want to be."

He beamed proprietorially as if he'd invented me himself.

There was a quick rustle of clothes beside my ear and a drift of flowery scent and a young woman tweaked a chair around to join our table and sat in it, looking triumphant.

"Well, well, well," she said. "Mr. Davis Tatum and Sid Halley! What a surprise!"

I said, to Davis Tatum's mystified face, "This is Miss India Cathcart, who writes for *The Pump*. If you say nothing you'll find yourself quoted repeating things you never thought, and if you say anything at all, you'll wish you hadn't."

"Sid," she said mock-sorrowfully, "can't you take a bit of kicking around?"

Tatum opened his mouth indignantly and, as I was afraid he might try to defend me, I shook my head. He stared at me, then with a complete change of manner said in smooth, lawyerly detachment, "Miss Cathcart, why are you here?"

"Why? To see you, of course."

"But why?"

She looked from him to me and back again, her appearance just as I remembered it: flawless porcelain skin, light-blue eyes, cleanly outlined mouth, black shining hair. She wore brown and red, with amber beads.

She said, "Isn't it improper for a colleague of the Crown Prosecutor to be seen talking to one of the witnesses?"

"No, it isn't," Tatum said, and asked me, "Did you tell her we were meeting here?"

"Of course not."

"Then how . . . why, Miss Cathcart, are you here?"

"I told you. It's a story."

"Does *The Pump* know you're here?" I asked.

A shade crossly she said, "I'm not a child. I'm allowed out on my own, you know. And anyway, the paper sent me."

"*The Pump* told you we'd be here?" Tatum asked.

"My editor said to come and see. And he was right!"

Tatum said, "Sid?"

"Mm," I said. "Interesting."

India said to me, "Kevin says you went to school in Liverpool."

Tatum, puzzled, asked, "What did you say?"

She explained, "Sid wouldn't tell me where he went to school, so I found out." She looked at me accusingly. "You don't sound like Liverpool."

"Don't I?"

"You sound more like Eton. How come?"

"I'm a mimic," I said.

If she really wanted to, she could find out also that between the ages of sixteen and twenty-one I'd been more or less adopted by a Newmarket trainer (who *had* been to Eton) who made me into a good jockey and by his example changed my speech and taught me how to live and how to behave and how to manage the money I earned. He'd been already old then, and he died. I often thought of him. He opened doors for me still.

"Kevin told me you were a slum child," India said.

"Slum is an attitude, not a place."

"Prickly, are we?"

Damn, I thought. I will *not* let her goad me. I smiled, which she didn't like.

Tatum, listening with disapproval, said, "Who is Kevin?"

"He works for *The Pump*," I told him.

India said, "Kevin Mills is *The Pump*'s chief reporter. He did favors for Halley and got kicked in the teeth."

"Painful," Tatum commented dryly.

"This conversation's getting nowhere," I said. "India, Mr. Tatum is not the prosecutor in any case where I am a witness, and we may talk about anything we care to, including, as just now before you came, golf."

"You can't play golf with one hand."

It was Tatum who winced, not I. I said, "You can watch golf on television without arms, legs or ears. Where did your editor get the idea that you might find us here?"

"He didn't say. It doesn't matter."

"It is of the essence," Tatum said.

"It's interesting," I said, "because to begin with, it was *The Pump* that worked up the greatest head of steam about the ponies mutilated in Kent. That was why I got in touch with Kevin Mills. Between us we set up a hot-line, as a 'Save the *Tussilago farfara*' sort of thing."

India demanded, "What did you say?"

"*Tussilago farfara*," Tatum repeated, amused. "It's the botanical name of the wildflower coltsfoot."

"How did you know that?" she asked me fiercely.

"I looked it up."

"Oh."

"Anyway, the minute I linked Ellis Quint, even tentatively, to the colts, and to Rachel Ferns's pony, *The Pump* abruptly changed direction and started tearing me apart with crusading claws. I can surely ask, India, why do you write about me so ferociously? Is it just your way? Is it that you do so many hatchet jobs that you can't do anything else? I didn't expect kindness, but you are . . . every week . . . extreme."

She looked uncomfortable. She did what she had one week called me "diddums" for doing: she defended herself.

"My editor gives me guidelines." She almost tossed her head.

"You mean he tells you what to write?"

"Yes. No."

"Which?"

She looked from me to Tatum and back.

She said, "He subs my piece to align it with overall policy."

I said nothing. Tatum said nothing. India, a shade desperately, said, "Only saints get themselves burned at the stake."

Tatum said with gravitas, "If I read any lies or innuendos about my having improperly talked to Sid Halley about the forthcoming Quint trial, I will sue you personally for defamation, Miss Cathcart, and I will ask for punitive damages. So choose your stake. Flames seem inevitable."

I felt almost sorry for her. She stood up blankly, her eyes wide.

"Say we weren't here," I said.

I couldn't read her frozen expression. She walked away from us and headed for the stairs.

"A confused young woman," Tatum said. "But how did she—or her paper—know we would be here?"

I asked, "Do you feed your appointments into a computer?"

He frowned. "I don't do it personally. My secretary does it. We have a system which can tell where all the partners are, if there's a crisis. It tells where each of us can be found. I did tell my secretary I was coming here, but not who I was going to meet. That still doesn't explain . . ."

I sighed. "Yesterday evening you phoned my mobile number."

"Yes, and you phoned me back."

"Someone's been listening on my mobile phone's frequency. Someone heard you call me."

"Hell! But you called me back. They heard almost nothing."

"You gave your name . . . How secure is your office computer?"

"We change passwords every three months."

"And you use passwords that everyone can remember easily?"

"Well . . ."

"There are people who crack passwords just for the fun of it. And others hack into secrets. You wouldn't believe how *careless* some firms are with their most private information. Someone has recently accessed my own on-line computer—during the past month. I have a detector program that tells me. Much good it will do any hacker, as I never keep anything personal there. But a combination of my mobile phone and your office computer must have come up with the *possibility* that your appointment was with me. Someone in *The Pump* did it. So they sent India along to find out . . . and here we are. And because they succeeded, we now know they tried."

"It's incredible."

"Who runs *The Pump*? Who sets the policy?"

Tatum said thoughtfully, "The editor is George Godbar. The proprietor's Lord Tilepit."

"Any connection with Ellis Quint?"

He considered the question and shook his head. "Not that I know of."

"Does Lord Tilepit have an interest in the television company that puts on Ellis Quint's program? I think I'd better find out."

Davis Tatum smiled.

REFLECTING THAT, AS about thirty hours had passed since Gordon Quint had jumped me in Pont Square, he was unlikely still to be hanging about there with murderous feelings and his fencing post (not least because with Ginnie dead he would have her inquest to distract him), and also feeling that one could take self-preservation to shaming lengths, I left the Piccadilly restaurant in a taxi and got the driver to make two reconnoitering passes around the railed central garden.

All seemed quiet. I paid the driver, walked without incident up the steps to the front door, used my key, went up to the next floor and let myself into the haven of home.

No ambush. No creaks. Silence.

I retrieved a few envelopes from the wire basket clipped inside the letter box and found a page in my fax. It seemed a long time since I'd left, but it had been only the previous morning.

My cracked arm hurt. Well, it would. I'd ridden races—and winners—now and then with cracks: disguising them, of course, because the betting public deserved healthy riders to carry their money. The odd thing was that in the heat of a race one didn't feel an injury. It was in the cooler ebbing of excitement that the discomfort returned.

The best way, always, to minimize woes was to concentrate on something else. I looked up a number and phoned the handy acquaintance who had set up my computer for me.

"Doug," I said, when his wife had fetched him in from an oil change, "tell me about listening in to mobile phones."

"I'm covered in grease," he complained. "Won't this do another time?"

"Someone is listening to my mobile."

"Oh." He sniffed. "So you want to know how to stop it?"

"You're dead right."

He sniffed again. "I've got a cold," he said, "my wife's mother is coming to dinner and my sump is filthy."

I laughed; couldn't help it. "Please, Doug."

He relented. "I suppose you've got an analog mobile. They have radio signals that can be listened to. It's difficult, though. Your average bloke in the pub couldn't do it."

"Could you?"

"I'm not your average bloke in the pub. I'm a walking midlife crisis halfway through an oil change. I could do it if I had the right gear."

"How do I deal with it?"

"Blindingly simple." He sneezed and sniffed heavily. "I need a tissue." There was a sudden silence on the line, then the distant sound of a nose being vigorously blown, then the hoarse voice of wisdom in my ear.

"OK," he said. "You ditch the analog, and get a digital."

"I do?"

"Sid, being a jockey does not equip the modern man to live in tomorrow's world."

"I do see that."

"Everyone," he sniffed, "if they had any sense, would go digital."

"Teach me."

"The digital system," he said, "is based on two numbers, zero and one. Zero and one have been with us from the dawn of computers, and no one has ever invented anything better."

"They haven't?"

He detected my mild note of irony. "Has anyone," he asked, "reinvented the wheel?"

"Er, no."

"Quite. One cannot improve on an immaculate conception."

"That's blasphemous." I enjoyed him always.

"Certainly not," he said. "Some things are perfect to begin with. $E=mc^2$, and all that."

"I grant that. How about my mobile?"

"The signal sent to a digital telephone," he said, "is not one signal, as in analog, but is eight simultaneous signals, each transmitting one-eighth of what you hear."

"Is that so?" I asked dryly.

"You may bloody snigger," he said, "but I'm giving you the goods. A digital phone receives eight simultaneous signals, and it is *impossible* for anyone to decode them except the receiving mobile. Now, because the signal arrives in eight pieces, the reception isn't always perfect. You don't get the crackle or the fading in and out that you get on analog phones, but you do sometimes get bits of words missing. Still, *no one* can listen in. Even the police can never tap a digital mobile number."

"So," I said, fascinated, "where do I get one?"

"Try Harrods," he said.

"Harrods?"

"Harrods is just round the corner from where you live, isn't it?"

"More or less."

"Try there, then. Or anywhere else that sells phones. You can use the same number that you have now. You just need to tell your service provider. And of course you'll need an SIM card. You have one, of course?"

I said meekly, "No."

"Sid!" he protested. He sneezed again. "Sorry. An SIM card is a Subscriber's Identity Module. You can't live without one."

"I can't?"

"Sid, I despair of you. Wake up to technology."

"I'm better at knowing what a horse thinks."

Patiently he enlightened me, "An SIM card is like a credit card. It actually *is* a credit card. Included on it are your name and mobile phone number and other details, and you can slot it into any mobile that will take it. For instance, if you are someone's guest in Athens and he has a mobile that accepts an SIM card, you can slot *your* card into *his* phone and the charge will appear on your account, not his."

"Are you serious?" I asked:

"With my problems, would I joke?"

"Where do I get an SIM card?"

"Ask Harrods." He sneezed. "Ask anyone who travels for a living. Your service provider will provide." He sniffed. "So long, Sid."

Amused and grateful, I opened my mail and read the fax. The fax being most accessible got looked at first.

Handwritten, it scrawled simply, "Phone me," and gave a long number.

The writing was Kevin Mills's, but the fax machine he'd sent it from was anonymously not *The Pump*'s.

I phoned the number given, which would have connected me to a mobile, and got only the infuriating instruction, "Please try later."

There were a dozen messages I didn't much want on my answering machine and a piece of information I *definitely* didn't want in a large brown envelope from Shropshire.

The envelope contained a copy of a glossy county magazine, one I'd sent for as I'd been told it included lengthy coverage of the heir-to-the-dukedom's coming-of-age dance. There were, indeed, four pages of pictures, mostly in color, accompanied by prose gush about the proceedings and a complete guest list.

A spectacular burst of fireworks filled half a page, and there in a group of heaven-gazing spectators, there in white tuxedo and all his photogenic glory, there unmistakably stood Ellis Quint.

My heart sank. The fireworks had started at three-thirty. At three-thirty, when the moon was high, Ellis had been a hundred miles northwest of the Windward Stud's yearling.

There were many pictures of the dancing, and a page of black and white shots of the guests, names attached. Ellis had been dancing. Ellis smiled twice from the guests' page, carefree, having a good time.

Damn it to hell, I thought. He had to have taken the colt's foot off early. Say by one o'clock. He could then have arrived for the fireworks by three-thirty. I'd found no one who'd seen him *arrive*, but several who swore to his presence after five-fifteen. At five-fifteen he had helped the heir to climb onto a table to make a drunken speech. The heir had poured a bottle of champagne over Ellis's head. Everyone remembered *that*. Ellis could not have driven back to Northampton before dawn.

For two whole days the previous week I'd traipsed around Shropshire, and next-door Cheshire, handed on from grand house to grander, asking much the same two questions (according to sex): Did you dance with Ellis Quint, or did you drink/eat with him? The answers at first had been freely given, but as time went on, news of my mission spread before me until I was progressively met by hostile faces and frankly closed doors. Shropshire was solid Ellis country. They'd have stood on their heads to prove him unjustly accused. They were not going to say that they didn't know when he'd arrived.

In the end I returned to the duchess's front gates, and from there drove as fast as prudence allowed to the Windward Stud Farm, timing the journey at two hours and five minutes. On empty roads at night, Northampton to the duchess might have taken ten minutes less. I'd proved nothing except that Ellis had had time.

Enough time was not enough.

As always before gathering at such dances, the guests had given and attended dinner parties both locally and farther away. No one that I'd asked had entertained Ellis to dinner.

No dinner was not enough.

I went through the guest list crossing off the people I'd seen. There were still far more than half unconsulted, most of whom I'd never heard of.

Where was Chico? I needed him often. I hadn't the time or, to be frank, the appetite to locate and question all the guests, even if they would answer. There must have been people—local people—helping with the parking of cars that night. Chico would have chatted people up in the local pubs and found out if any of the car-parkers remembered Ellis's arrival. Chico was good at pubs, and I wasn't in his class.

The police might have done it, but they wouldn't. The death of a colt still didn't count like murder.

The police.

I phoned Norman Picton's police station number and gave my name as John Paul Jones.

He came on the line in a good humor and listened to me without protest.

"Let me get this straight," he said. "You want me to ask favors of the Northamptonshire police? What do I offer in return?"

"Blood in the hinges of lopping shears."

"They'll have made their own tests."

"Yes, and that Northamptonshire colt is dead and gone to the glue factory. An error, wouldn't you say? Might they not do you a favor in exchange for commiseration?"

"You'll have my head off. What is it you actually *want*?"

"Er . . . ," I began, "I was there when the police found the lopping shears in the hedge."

"Yes, you told me."

"Well, I've been thinking. Those shears weren't wrapped in sacking, like the ones we took from the Quints."

"No, and the shears weren't the same, either. The ones at Northampton are a slightly newer model. They're on sale everywhere in garden centers. The problem is that Ellis Quint hasn't been reported as buying any, not in the Northamptonshire police district, nor ours."

"Is there any chance," I asked, "of my looking again at the material used for wrapping the shears?"

"If there are horse hairs in it, there's nothing left to match them to, same as the blood."

"All the same, the cloth might tell us where the shears came from. *Which* garden center, do you see?"

"I'll see if they've done that already."

"Thanks, Norman."

"Thank Archie. He drives me to help you."

"Does he?"

He heard my surprise. "Archie has *influence*," he said, "and I do what the magistrate tells me."

When he'd gone off the line I tried Kevin Mills again and reached the same electronic voice: "Please try later."

After that I sat in an armchair while the daylight faded and the lights came on in the peaceful square. We were past the equinox, back in winter thoughts, the year dying ahead. Fall for me had for almost half my life meant the longed-for resurgence of major jump racing, the time of big winners and speed and urgency in the blood. Winter now brought only nostalgia and heating bills. At thirty-four I was growing old.

I sat thinking of Ellis and the wasteland he had made of my year. I thought of Rachel Ferns and Silverboy, and lymphoblasts. I thought of the press, and especially *The Pump* and India Cathcart and the orchestrated months of vilification. I thought of Ellis's relentless jokes.

I thought for a long time about Archie Kirk, who had drawn me to Combe Bassett and given me Norman Picton. I wondered if it had been from Archie that Norman had developed a belief in a heavy presence behind the scenes. I wondered if it could possibly be Archie who had prompted Davis Tatum to engage me to find that heavyweight. I wondered if it could possibly have been Archie who told Davis Tatum about my run-in with the bad hat at the Jockey Club, and if so, how did *he* know?

I trusted Archie. He could pull my strings, I thought, as long as I was willing to go where he pointed, and as long as I was sure no one was pulling *his*.

I thought about Gordon Quint's uncontrollable rage and the practical difficulties his fencing post had inflicted. I thought of Ginnie Quint and despair and sixteen floors down.

I thought of the colts and their chopped-off feet.

When I went to bed I dreamed the same old nightmare.

Agony. Humiliation. Both hands.

I awoke sweating.

Damn it all to hell.

CHAPTER 9

IN THE MORNING, when I'd failed yet again to get an answer from Kevin Mills, I shunted by subway across central London and emerged not far from Companies House at 55 City Road, E.C.

Companies House, often my friend, contained the records of all public and private limited companies active in England, including the audited annual balance sheets, investment capital, fixed assets and the names of major shareholders and the directors of the boards.

Topline Foods, I soon learned, was an old company recently taken over by a few new big investors and a bustling new management. The chief shareholder and managing director was listed as Owen Cliff Yorkshire. There were fifteen non-executive directors, of whom one was Lord Tilepit.

The premises at which business was carried out were located at Frodsham, Cheshire. The registered office was at the same address.

The product of the company was foodstuffs for animals.

After Topline I looked up Village Pump Newspapers (they'd dropped the "Village" in about 1900, but retained the idea of a central meeting place for gossip) and found interesting items, and after Village Pump Newspapers I looked up the TV company that aired Ellis's sports program, but found no sign of Tilepit or Owen Yorkshire in its operations.

I traveled home (safely) and phoned Archie, who was, his wife reported, at work.

"Can I reach him at work?" I asked.

"Oh, no, Sid. He wouldn't like it. I'll give him a message when he gets back."

Please try later.

I tried Kevin Mills later and this time nearly got my eardrums perforated. "At last!"

"I've tried you a dozen times," I said.

"I've been in an old people's home."

"Well, bully for you."

"A nurse hastened three harpies into the hereafter."

"Poor old sods."

"If you're in Pont Square," he said, "can I call round and see you? I'm in my car not far away."

"I thought I was *The Pump*'s number one all-time shit."

"Yeah. Can I come?"

"I suppose so."

"Great." He clicked off before I could change my mind and he was at my door in less than ten minutes.

"This is *nice*," he said appreciatively, looking around my sitting room. "Not what I expected."

There was a Sheraton writing desk and buttoned brocade chairs and a couple of modern exotic wood inlaid tables by Mark Boddington. The overall colors were grayish-blue, soft and restful. The only brash intruder was an ancient slot machine that worked on tokens.

Kevin Mills made straight towards it, as most visitors did. I always left a few tokens haphazardly on the floor, with a bowl of them nearby on a table. Kevin picked a token from the carpet, fed it into the slot and pulled the handle. The wheels clattered and clunked. He got two cherries and a lemon. He picked up another token and tried again.

"What wins the jackpot?" he asked, achieving an orange, a lemon and a banana.

"Three horses with jockeys jumping fences."

He looked at me sharply.

"It used to be the bells," I said. "That was boring, so I changed it."

"And do the three horses ever come up?"

I nodded. "You get a fountain of tokens all over the floor."

The machine was addictive. It was my equivalent of the psychiatrist's couch. Kevin played throughout our conversation but the nearest he came was two horses and a pear.

"The trial has started, Sid," he said, "so give us the scoop."

"The trial's only technically started. I can't tell you a thing. When the adjournment's over, you can go to court and listen."

"That's not exclusive," he complained.

"You know damned well I can't tell you."

"I gave you the story to begin with."

"I sought you out," I said. "Why did *The Pump* stop helping the colt owners and shaft me instead?"

He concentrated hard on the machine. Two bananas and a blackberry.

"Why?" I said.

"Policy."

"Whose policy?"

"The public wants demolition, they gobble up spite."

"Yes, but—"

"Look, Sid, we get the word from on high. And don't ask *who* on high, I don't know. I don't like it. None of us likes it. But we have the choice: go along with overall policy or go somewhere else where we feel more in tune. And do you know where that gets you? I work for *The Pump* because it's a good paper with, on the whole, fair comment. OK, so reputations topple. Like I said, that's what Mrs. Public wants. Now and then we get a *request*, such as 'lean hard on Sid Halley.' I did it without qualms, as you'd clammed up on me."

He looked all the time at the machine, playing fast.

"And India Cathcart?" I asked.

He pulled the lever and waited until two lemons and a jumping horse came to rest in a row.

"India . . . ," he said slowly. "For some reason she didn't want to trash you. She said she'd enjoyed her dinner with you and you were quiet and kind. Kind! I ask you! Her editor had to squeeze the poison out of her drop by drop for that first long piece. In the end he wrote most of her page himself. She was furious the next day when she read it, but it was out on the streets by then and she couldn't do anything about it."

I was more pleased than I would have expected, but I wasn't going to let Kevin see it. I said, "What about the continued stab wounds almost every week?"

"I guess she goes along with the policy. Like I said, she has to eat."

"Is it George Godbar's policy?"

"The big white chief himself? Yes, you could say the editor of the paper has the final say."

"And Lord Tilepit?"

He gave me an amused glance. Two pears and a lemon. "He's not a hands-on proprietor of the old school. Not a Beaverbrook or a Harmsworth. We hardly know he's alive."

"Does he give the overall policy to George Godbar?"

"Probably." A horse, a lemon and some cherries. "Why do I get the idea that *you* are interviewing *me*, instead of the other way round?"

"I cannot imagine. What do you know about Owen Cliff Yorkshire?"

"Bugger all. Who is he?"

"Quite likely a friend of Lord Tilepit."

"Sid," he protested, "I do my job. Rapes, murders, little old ladies smothered in their sleep. I do not chew off the fingernails of my paycheck."

He banged the slot machine frustratedly. "The bloody thing hates me."

"It has no soul," I said. I fed in a stray token myself with my plastic fingers and pulled the handle. Three horses. Fountains of love. Life's little irony.

Kevin Mills took his paunch, his mustache and his disgusted disgruntlement off to his word processor, and I again phoned Norman as John Paul Jones.

"My colleagues now think John Paul Jones is a snitch," he said.

"Fine."

"What is it this time?"

"Do you still have any of those horse nuts I collected from Betty Bracken's field, and those others we took from the Land-Rover?"

"Yes, we do. And as you know, they're identical in composition."

"Then could you find out if they were manufactured by Topline Foods Limited, of Frodsham in Cheshire?"

After a short silence he said cautiously, "It could be done, but is it necessary?"

"If you could let me have some of the nuts I could do it myself."

"I can't let you have any. They are bagged and counted."

"Shit." And I could so easily have kept some in my own pocket. Careless. Couldn't be helped.

"Why does it matter where they came from?" Norman asked.

"Um . . . You know you told me you thought there might be a heavy-weight somewhere behind the scenes? Well, I've been asked to find out."

"Jeez," he said. "Who asked you?"

"Can't tell you. Client confidentiality and all that."

"Is it Archie Kirk?"

"Not so far as I know."

"Huh!" He sounded unconvinced. "I'll go this far. If you get me some authenticated Topline nuts I'll see if I can run a check on them to find out if they match the ones we have. That's the best I can do, and that's stretching it, and you wouldn't have a prayer if you hadn't been the designer of our whole prosecution—and you can *not* quote me on that."

"I'm truly grateful. I'll get some Topline nuts, but they probably won't match the ones you have."

"Why not?"

"The grains—the balance of ingredients—will have changed since those were manufactured. Every batch must have its own profile, so to speak."

He well knew what I meant, as an analysis of ingredients could reveal their origins as reliably as grooves on a bullet.

"What interests you in Topline Foods?" Norman asked.

"My client."

"Bugger your client. Tell me." I didn't answer and he sighed heavily. "All right. You can't tell me now. I hate amateur detectives. I've got you a strip off that dirty Northampton material. At least, it's promised for later today. What are you going to do about it and have you cracked Ellis Quint's alibi yet?"

"You're *brilliant*," I said. "Where can I meet you? And no, I haven't cracked the alibi."

"Try harder."

"I'm only an amateur."

"Yeah, yeah. Come to the lake at five o'clock. I'm picking up the boat to take it home for winter storage. OK?"

"I'll be there."

"See you."

I phoned the hospital in Canterbury. Rachel, the ward sister told me, was "resting comfortably."

"What does that mean?"

"She's no worse than yesterday, Mr. Halley. When can you return?"

"Sometime soon."

"Good."

I spent the afternoon exchanging my old vulnerable analog mobile cellular telephone for a digital mobile receiving eight splintered transmissions that would baffle even the Thames Valley stalwarts, let alone *The Pump*.

From my apartment I then phoned Miss Richardson of Northamptonshire, who said vehemently that *no*, I certainly might *not* call on her again. Ginnie and Gordon Quint were her dear friends and it was *unthinkable* that Ellis could harm horses, and I was foul and *wicked* even to think it. Ginnie had told her about it. Ginnie had been very distressed. It was all my fault that she had killed herself.

I persevered with two questions, however, and did get answers of sorts.

"Did your vet say how long he thought the foot had been off when the colt was found at seven o'clock?"

"No, he didn't."

"Could you give me his name and phone number?"

"No."

As I had over the years accumulated a whole shelfful of area telephone directories, it was not so difficult via the Northamptonshire Yellow Pages to find and talk to Miss Richardson's vet. He would, he said, have been helpful if he could. All he could with confidence say was that neither the colt's leg nor the severed foot had shown signs of recent bleeding. Miss Richardson herself had insisted he put the colt out of his misery immediately, and, as it was also his own judgment, he had done so.

He had been unable to suggest to the police any particular time for the attack; earlier rather than later was as far as he could go. The wound had been clean: one chop. The vet said he was surprised a yearling would have stood up long enough for shears to be applied. Yes, he confirmed, the colt had been lightly shod, and yes, there had been horse nuts scattered around, but Miss Richardson often gave her horses nuts as a supplement to grass.

He'd been helpful, but no help.

After that I had to decide how to get to the lake, as the normal taken-for-granted act of driving now had complications. I had a knob fixed on the steering wheel of my Mercedes which gave me a good grip for one-(right)handed operation. With my left, unfeeling hand I shifted the automatic-gear lever.

I experimentally flexed and clenched my right hand. Sharp protests. Boring. With irritation I resorted to ibuprofen and drove to the lake wishing Chico were around to do it.

Norman had winched his boat halfway onto its trailer. Big, competent and observant, he watched my slow emergence to upright and frowned.

"What hurts?" he asked.

"Self-esteem."

He laughed. "Give me a hand with the boat, will you? Pull when I lift."

I looked at the job and said briefly that I couldn't.

"You only need one hand for pulling."

I told him unemotionally that Gordon Quint had aimed for my head and done lesser but inconvenient damage. "I'm telling you, in case he tries again and succeeds. He was slightly out of his mind over Ginnie."

Norman predictably said I should make an official complaint.

"No," I said. "This is unofficial, and ends right here."

He went off to fetch a friend to help him with the boat, and then busied himself with wrapping and stowing his powerful outboard engine.

I said, "What first gave you the feeling that there was some heavyweight meandering behind the scenes?"

"First?" he went on working while he thought. "It's months ago. I talked it over with Archie. I expect it was because one minute I was putting together an ordinary case—even if Ellis Quint's fame made it newsworthy—and the next I was being leaned on by the superintendent to find some reason to drop it, and when I showed him the strength of the evidence, he said the Chief Constable was unhappy, and the reason for the Chief Constable's unhappiness was always the same, which was political pressure from outside."

"What sort of political?"

Norman shrugged. "Not party politics especially. A pressure group. Lobbying. A bargain struck somewhere, along the lines of 'get the Quint prosecution aborted and such-and-such a good thing will come your way!'"

"But not a direct cash advantage?"

"Sid!"

"Well, sorry."

"I should frigging well hope so." He wrapped thick twine around the shrouded engine. "I'm not asking cash for a strip of rag from Northamptonshire.

"I grovel," I said.

He grinned. "That'll be the day." He climbed into his boat and secured various bits of equipment against movement en route.

"No one has entirely given in to the pressure," he pointed out. "The case against Ellis Quint has not been dropped. True, it's now in a ropy state. You yourself have been relentlessly discredited to the point where you're almost a liability to the prosecution, and even though that's brutally unfair, it's a fact."

"Mm."

In effect, I thought, I'd been commissioned by Davis Tatum to find out who had campaigned to defeat me. It wasn't the first time I'd faced campaigns to enforce my inactivity, but it was the first time I'd been offered a fee to save myself. To save myself, in this instance, meant to defeat Ellis Quint: so I was being paid for *that*, in the first place. And for what *else*?

Norman backed his car up to the boat trailer and hitched them together. Then he leaned through the open front passenger window of the car, unlocked the glove compartment there and drew out and handed to me a plastic bag.

"One strip of dirty rag," he said cheerfully. "Cost to you, six grovels before breakfast for a week."

I took the bag gratefully. Inside, the filthy strip, about three inches wide, had been loosely folded until it was several layers thick.

"It's about a meter long," Norman said. "It was all they would let me have. I had to sign for it."

"Good."

"What are you going to do with it?"

"Clean it, for a start."

Norman said doubtfully, "It's got some sort of pattern in it but there wasn't any printing on the whole wrapping. Nothing to say where it came from. No garden center name, or anything."

"I don't have high hopes," I said, "but frankly, just now every straw's worth clutching."

Norman stood with his legs apart and his hands on his hips. He looked a pillar of every possible police strength but what he was actually feeling turned out to be indecision.

"How far can I trust you?" he asked.

"For silence?"

He nodded.

"I thought we'd discussed this already."

"Yes, but that was months ago."

"Nothing's changed," I said.

He made a decision, stuck his head into his car again and this time brought out a business-sized brown envelope which he held out to me.

"It's a copy of the analysis done on the horse nuts," he said. "So read it and shred it."

"OK. And thanks."

I held the envelope and plastic bag together and knew I couldn't take such trust lightly. He must be very sure of me, I thought, and felt not complimented but apprehensive.

"I've been thinking," I said, "do you remember, way back in June, when we took those things out of Gordon Quint's Land-Rover?"

"Of course I remember."

"There was a farrier's apron in the Land-Rover. Rolled up. We didn't take that, did we?"

He frowned. "I don't remember it, but no, it's not among the things we took. What's significant about it?"

I said, "I've always thought it odd that the colts should stand still long enough for the shears to close round the ankle, even with head collars and those nuts. But horses have an acute sense of smell . . . and all those colts had shoes on—I checked with their vets—and they would have known the smell of a blacksmith's apron. I think Ellis might have worn that apron to reassure the colts. They may have thought he was the man who shod them. They would have *trusted* him. He could have lifted an ankle and gripped it with the shears."

He stared.

"What do you think?" I asked.

"It's you who knows horses."

"It's how I might get a two-year-old to let me near his legs."

"As far as I'm concerned," he said, "that's how it was done."

He held out his hand automatically to say good-bye, then remembered Gordon Quint's handiwork, shrugged, grinned and said instead, "If there's anything interesting about that strip of rag, you'll let me know?"

"Of course."

"See you."

He drove off with a wave, trailing his boat, and I returned to my car, stowed away the bag and the envelope and made a short journey to Shelley Green, the home of Archie Kirk.

He had returned from work. He took me into his sitting room while his smiling wife cooked in the kitchen.

"How's things?" Archie asked. "Whisky?"

I nodded. "A lot of water . . ."

He indicated chairs, and we sat. The dark room looked right in October: imitation flames burned imitation coals in the fireplace, giving the room a life that the sun of June hadn't achieved.

I hadn't seen Archie since then. I absorbed again the probably deliberate grayness of his general appearance, and I saw again the whole internet in the dark eyes.

He said casually, "You've been having a bit of a rough time."

"Does it show?"

"Yes."

"Never mind," I said. "Will you answer some questions?"

"It depends what they are."

I drank some of his undistinguished whisky and let my muscles relax into the ultimate of nonaggressive, noncombative postures.

"For a start, what do you do?" I said.

"I'm a civil servant."

"That's not . . . well . . . specific."

"Start at the other end," he said.

I smiled. I said, "It's a wise man who knows who's paying him."

He paused with his own glass halfway to his lips.

"Go on," he said.

"Then . . . do you know Davis Tatum?"

After a pause he answered, "Yes."

It seemed to me he was growing wary; that he, as I did, had to sort through a minefield of facts one could not or should not reveal that one knew. The old dilemma—does he know I know he knows—sometimes seemed like child's play.

I said, "How's Jonathan?"

He laughed. "I hear you play chess," he said. "I hear you're a whiz at misdirection. Your opponents think they're winning, and then . . . wham."

I played chess only with Charles at Aynsford, and not very often.

"Do you know my father-in-law?" I asked. "Ex–father-in-law, Charles Roland?"

With a glimmer he said, "I've talked to him on the telephone."

At least he hadn't lied to me, I thought; and, if he hadn't lied he'd given me a fairly firm path to follow. I asked about Jonathan, and about his sister, Betty Bracken.

"That wretched boy is still at Combe Bassett, and now that the waterskiing season is over he is driving everyone *mad*. You are the only person who sees any good in him."

"Norman does."

"Norman sees a talented water-skier with criminal tendencies."

"Has Jonathan any money?"

Archie shook his head. "Only the very little we give him for toothpaste and so on. He's still on probation. He's a mess." He paused. "Betty has been paying for the water skiing. She's the only one in our family with real money. She married straight out of school. Bobby's thirty years older—he was rich when they married and he's richer than ever now. As you saw, she's still devoted to him. Always has been. They had no children; she couldn't. Very sad. If Jonathan had any sense he would be *nice* to Betty."

"I don't think he's that devious. Or not yet, anyway."

"Do you like him?" Archie asked curiously.

"Not much, but I hate to see people go to waste."

"Stupid boy."

"I checked on the colt," I said. "The foot stayed on."

Archie nodded. "Betty's delighted. The colt is permanently lame, but they're going to see if, with his breeding, he's any good for stud. Betty's offering him free next year to good mares."

Archie's sweet wife came in and asked if I would stay to dinner; she could easily cook extra. I thanked her but stood up to go. Archie shook my hand. I winced through not concentrating, but he made no comment. He came out to my car with me as the last shreds of daylight waned to dark.

He said, "In the civil service I work in a small unacknowledged off-shoot department which was set up some time ago to foretell the probable outcome of any high political appointment. We also predict the future inevitable consequences of pieces of proposed legislation." He paused and went on wryly,

"We call ourselves the Cassandra outfit. We see what will happen and no one believes us. We are always on the lookout for exceptional independent investigators with no allegiances. They're hard to find. We think you are one."

I stood beside my car in the dying light, looking into the extraordinary eyes. An extraordinary man of unimaginable insights. I said, "Archie, I'll work for you to the limit as long as I'm sure you're not sending me into a danger that you know exists but are not telling me about."

He took a deep breath but gave no undertaking.

"Good night," I said mildly.

"Sid."

"I'll phone you." It was as firm a promise, I thought, as "let's do lunch."

He was still standing on his gravel as I drove out through his gates. A true civil servant, I thought ruefully. No positive assurances could ever be given because the rules could at any time be changed under one's feet. I drove north across Oxfordshire to Aynsford and rang the bell of the side entrance of Charles's house. Mrs. Cross came in answer to the summons, her inquiring expression melting to welcome as she saw who had arrived.

"The Admiral's in the wardroom," she assured me when I asked if he was at home, and she bustled along before me to give Charles the news.

He made no reference to the fact that it was the second time in three days that I had sought his sanctuary. He merely pointed to the gold brocade chair and poured brandy into a tumbler without asking.

I sat and drank and looked gratefully at the austerity and restraint of this thin man who'd commanded ships and was now my only anchor.

"How's the arm?" he asked briefly, and I said lightly, "Sore."

He nodded and waited.

"Can I stay?" I said.

"Of course."

After a longish pause, I said, "Do you know a man called Archibald Kirk?"

"No, I don't think so."

"He says he talked to you on the telephone. It was months ago, I think. He's a civil servant and a magistrate. He lives near Hungerford, and I've come here from his house. Can you remember? Way back. I think he may have been asking you about *me.* Like sort of checking up, like a reference. You probably told him that I play chess."

He thought about it, searching for the memory.

"I would always give you a good reference," he said. "Is there any reason why you'd prefer I didn't?"

"No, definitely not."

"I've been asked several times about your character and ability. I always say if they're looking for an investigator they couldn't do better."

"You're . . . very kind."

"Kind, my foot. Why do you ask about this Archibald Church?"

"Kirk."

"Kirk, then."

I drank some brandy and said, "Do you remember that day you came with me to the Jockey Club? The day we got the head of the security section sacked?"

"I could hardly forget it, could I?"

"You didn't tell Archie Kirk about it, did you?"

"Of course not. I *never* talk about it. I gave you my word I wouldn't."

"Someone has," I said morosely.

"The Jockey Club didn't actually swear an oath of silence."

"I know." I thought a bit and asked, "Do you know a barrister called Davis Tatum? He's the head of chambers of the prosecuting counsel at Ellis's trial."

"I know *of* him. Never met him."

"You'd like him. You'd like Archie, too." I paused, and went on, "They both know about that day at the Jockey Club."

"But, Sid . . . does it really matter? I mean, you did the Jockey Club a tremendous favor, getting rid of their villain."

"Davis Tatum and, I'm sure, Archie, have engaged me to find out who is moving behind the scenes to get the Quint trial quashed. And I'm not telling you that."

He smiled. "Client confidentiality?"

"Right. Well, Davis Tatum made a point of telling me that he knew all about the mandarins insisting I take off my shirt, and why. I think he and Archie are trying to reassure themselves that if they ask me to do something dangerous, I'll do it."

He gave me a long, slow look, his features still and expressionless.

Finally he said, "And will you?"

I sighed. "Probably."

"What sort of danger?"

"I don't think they know. But realistically, if someone has an overwhelming reason for preventing Ellis's trial from ever starting, who is the person standing chiefly in the way?"

"*Sid!*"

"Yes. So they're asking me to find out if anyone might be motivated enough to ensure my permanent removal from the scene. They want me to find out *if* and *who* and *why*."

"God, Sid."

From a man who never blasphemed, those were strong words.

"So . . . ," I sighed, "Davis Tatum gave me a name, Owen Yorkshire, and told me he owned a firm called Topline Foods. Now Topline Foods gave a sponsored lunch at Aintree on the day before the Grand National. Ellis Quint was guest of honor. Also among the guests was a man called Lord Tilepit, who is both on the board of Topline Foods and the proprietor of *The Pump*, which has been busy mocking me for months."

He sat as if frozen.

"So," I said, "I'll go and see what Owen Yorkshire and Lord Tilepit are up to, and if I don't come back you can kick up a stink."

When he'd organized his breath, he said, "Don't do it, Sid."

"No . . . but if I don't, Ellis will walk out laughing, and my standing in the world will be down the tubes forever, if you see what I mean."

He saw.

After a while he said, "I do vaguely remember talking to this Archie fellow. He asked about your *brains*. He said he knew about your physical resilience. Odd choice of words—I remember them. I told him you played a wily game of chess. And it's true, you do. But it was a long time ago. Before all this happened."

I nodded. "He already knew a lot about me when he got his sister to phone at five-thirty in the morning to tell me she had a colt with his foot off."

"So that's who he is? Mrs. Bracken's brother?"

"Yeah." I drank brandy and said, "If you're ever talking to Sir Thomas Ullaston, would you mind asking him—and don't make a drama of it—if he told Archie Kirk or Davis Tatum about that morning in the Jockey Club?"

Sir Thomas Ullaston had been Senior Steward at the time, and had conducted the proceedings which led to the removal of the head of the security section who had arranged for Chico and me to be thoroughly deterred from investigating anything ever again. As far as I was concerned it was all past history, and I most emphatically wanted it to remain so.

Charles said he would ask Sir Thomas.

"Ask him not to let *The Pump* get hold of it."

Charles contemplated that possibility with about as much horror as I did myself.

The bell of the side door rang distantly, and Charles frowned at his watch.

"Who can that be? It's almost eight o'clock."

We soon found out. An ultrafamiliar voice called "Daddy?" across the hall outside, and an ultrafamiliar figure appeared in the doorway. Jenny . . . Charles's younger daughter . . . my sometime wife. My still embittered wife, whose tongue had barbs.

Smothering piercing dismay, I stood up, and Charles also.

"Jenny," Charles said, advancing to greet her. "What a lovely surprise."

She turned her cheek coolly, as always. and said, "We were passing. It seemed impossible not to call in." She looked at me without much emotion and said, "We didn't know *you* were here until I saw your car outside."

I took the few steps between us and gave her the sort of cheek-to-cheek salutation she'd bestowed on Charles. She accepted the politeness, as always, as the civilized acknowledgment of adversaries after battle.

"You took thin," she observed, not with concern but with criticism, from habit.

She, I thought, looked as beautiful as always, but there was nothing to be gained by saying so. I didn't want her to sneer at me. To begin with, it turned the sweet curve of her mouth. She could hurt me with words whenever she tried, and she'd tried often. My only defense had been—and still was—silence.

Her handsome new husband had followed her into the room, shaking hands with Charles and apologizing for having appeared without warning.

"My dear fellow, anytime," Charles assured him.

Anthony Wingham turned my way and with self-conscious affability said, "Sid . . . ," and held out his hand.

It was extraordinary, I thought, enduring his hearty, embarrassed grasp, how often one regularly shook hands in the course of a day. I'd never really noticed it before.

Charles poured drinks and suggested dinner. Anthony Wingham waffled a grateful refusal. Jenny gave me a cool look and sat in the gold brocade chair.

Charles made small talk with Anthony until they'd exhausted the weather. I stood with them but looked at Jenny, and she at me. Into a sudden silence she said, "Well, Sid, I don't suppose you want me to say it, but you've got yourself into a proper mess this time."

"No."

"No what?"

"No, I don't want you to say it."

"Ellis Quint! Biting off more than you can chew. And back in the summer the papers pestered me, too. I suppose you know?"

I unwillingly nodded.

"That reporter from *The Pump*," Jenny complained. "India Cathcart, I couldn't get rid of her. She wanted to know all about you and about our divorce. Do you know what she wrote? She wrote that I'd told her that quite apart from being crippled, you weren't man enough for me."

"I read it," I said briefly.

"Did you? And did you like it? Did you like that, Sid?"

I didn't reply. It was Charles who fiercely protested. "*Jenny!* Don't."

Her face suddenly softened, all the spite dissolving and revealing the gentle girl I'd married. The transformation happened in a flash, like prison bars falling away. Her liberation, I thought, had dramatically come at last.

"I didn't say that," she told me, as if bewildered. "I really didn't. She made it up."

I swallowed. I found the reemergence of the old Jenny harder to handle than her scorn.

"What *did* you say?" I said.

"Well . . . I . . . I . . ."

"*Jenny*," Charles said again.

"I told her," Jenny said to him, "that I couldn't live in Sid's hard world. I told her that whatever she wrote she wouldn't smash him or disintegrate him because no one had ever managed it. I told her that he never showed his feelings and that steel was putty compared to him, and that I couldn't live with it."

Charles and I had heard her say much the same thing before. It was Anthony who looked surprised. He inspected my harmless-looking self from his superior height and obviously thought she had got me wrong.

"India Cathcart didn't believe Jenny, either," I told him soothingly.

"*What?*"

"He reads minds, too," Jenny said, putting down her glass and rising to her feet. "Anthony, darling, we'll go now. OK?" To her father she said, "Sorry it's such a short visit," and to me, "India Cathcart is a bitch."

I kissed Jenny's cheek.

"I still love you," I said.

She looked briefly into my eyes. "I couldn't live with it. I told her the truth."

"I know."

"Don't let her break you."

"No."

"Well," she said brightly, loudly, smiling, "when birds fly out of cages they sing and rejoice. So . . . good-bye, Sid."

She looked happy. She laughed. I ached for the days when we'd met, when she looked like that always; but one could never go back.

"Good-bye, Jenny," I said.

Charles, uncomprehending, went with them to see them off and came back frowning.

"I simply don't understand my daughter," he said. "Do you?"

"Oh, yes."

"She tears you to pieces. *I* can't stand it, even if you can. Why don't you ever fight back?"

"Look what I did to her."

"She knew what she was marrying."

"I don't think she did. It isn't always easy, being married to a jockey."

"You forgive her too much! And then, do you know what she said just now, when she was leaving? I don't understand her. She gave me a hug—a hug—not a dutiful peck on the cheek, and she said, 'Take care of Sid.'"

I felt instantly liquefied inside: too close to tears.

"Sid . . ."

I shook my head, as much to retain composure as anything else.

"We've made our peace," I said.

"When?"

"Just now. The old Jenny came back. She's free of me. She felt free quite suddenly . . . so she'll have no more need to . . . to tear me to pieces, as you put it. I think that all that destructive anger has finally gone. Like she said, she's flown out of the cage."

He said, "I do hope so," but looked unconvinced. "I need a drink."

I smiled and joined him, but I discovered, as we later ate companionably together, that even though his daughter might no longer despise or torment me, what I perversely felt wasn't relief, but loss.

CHAPTER 10

LEAVING AYNSFORD EARLY, I drove back to London on Thursday morning and left the car, as I normally did, in a large public underground car park near Pont Square. From there I walked to the laundry where I usually took my shirts and waited while they fed my strip of rag from Northampton twice through the dry-cleaning cycle.

What emerged was a stringy-looking object, basically light turquoise in color, with a non-geometric pattern on it of green, brown and salmon pink. There were also black irregular stains that had stayed obstinately in place.

I persuaded the cleaners to iron it, with the only result that I had a flat strip instead of a wrinkled one.

"What if I wash it with detergent and water?" I asked the burly, half-interested dry cleaner.

"You couldn't exactly *harm* it," he said sarcastically.

So I washed it and ironed it and ended as before: turquoise strip, wandering indeterminate pattern, stubborn black stain.

With the help of the Yellow Pages I visited the wholesale showrooms of a well-known fabric designer. An infinitely polite old man there explained that my fabric pattern was *woven*, while theirs—the wholesaler's—was *printed*. Different market, he said. The wholesaler aimed at the upper end of the middle-class market. I, he said, needed to consult an interior decorator, and with kindness he wrote for me a short list of firms.

The first two saw no profit in answering questions. At the third address I happened on an underworked twenty-year-old who ran pale long fingers through clean shoulder-length curls while he looked with interest at my offering. He pulled out a turquoise thread and held it up to the light.

"This is silk," he said.

"Real silk?"

"No possible doubt. This was expensive fabric. The pattern is woven in. See." He turned the piece over to show me the back "This is remarkable. Where did you get it? It looks like a very old lampas. Beautiful. The colors are organic, not mineral."

I looked at his obvious youth and asked if he could perhaps seek a second opinion.

"Because I'm straight out of design school?" he guessed without umbrage. "But I studied *fabrics*. That's why they took me on here. I *know* them. The designers don't weave them, they use them."

"Then tell me what I've got."

He fingered the turquoise strip and held it to his lips and his cheek and seemed to commune with it as if it were a crystal ball.

"It's a modern copy," he said. "It's very skillfully done. It is lampas, woven on a Jacquard loom. There isn't enough of it to be sure, but I think it's a copy of a silk hanging made by Philippe de Lasalle in about 1760. But the original hadn't a blue-green background, it was cream with this design of ropes and leaves in greens and red and gold."

I was impressed. "Are you sure?"

"I've just spent three years learning this sort of thing."

"Well . . . who makes it now? Do I have to go to France?"

"You could try one or two English firms but you know what—"

He was brusquely interrupted by a severe-looking woman in a black dress and huge Aztec-type necklace who swept in and came to rest by the counter on which lay the unprepossessing rag.

"What are you doing?" she asked. "I asked you to catalog the new shipment of passementerie."

"Yes, Mrs. Lane."

"Then please get on with it. Run along now."

"Yes, Mrs. Lane."

"Do you want help?" she asked me briskly.

"Only the names of some weavers."

On his way to the passementerie my source of knowledge spoke briefly over his shoulder. "It looks like a solitary weaver, not a firm. Try Saul Marcus."

"Where?" I called.

"London."

He went out of sight. Under Mrs. Lane's inhospitable gaze I picked up my rag, smiled placatingly and departed.

I found Saul Marcus first in the telephone directory and then in white-bearded person in an airy artist's studio near Chiswick, West London, where he created fabric patterns.

He looked with interest at my rag but shook his head.

I urged him to search the far universe.

"It might be Patricia Huxford's work," he said at length, dubiously. "You could try her. She does—or did—work like this sometimes. I don't know of anyone else."

"Where would I find her?"

"Surrey, Sussex. Somewhere like that."

"Thank you very much."

Returning to Pont Square, I looked for Patricia Huxford in every phone book I possessed for Surrey and Sussex and, for good measure, the bordering southern counties of Hampshire and Kent. Of the few Huxfords listed, none turned out to be Patricia, a weaver.

I really *needed* an assistant, I thought, saying good-bye to Mrs. Paul Huxford, wife of a double-glazing salesman. This sort of search could take hours. Damn Chico, and his dolly-bird protective missus.

With no easy success from the directories I started on directory inquiries, the central computerized number-finder. As always, to get a number one had to give an address, but the computer system contemptuously spat out Patricia Huxford, Surrey, as being altogether too vague.

I tried Patricia Huxford, Guildford (Guildford being Surrey's county town), but learned only of the two listed P. Huxfords that I'd already tried. Kingston, Surrey: same lack of results. I systematically tried all the other main areas; Sutton, Epsom, Leatherhead, Dorking . . . Surrey might be a small county in square-mile size, but large in population. I drew a uniform blank.

Huxfords were fortunately rare. A good job she wasn't called Smith.

Sussex, then. There was East Sussex (county town Brighton) and West Sussex (Chichester). I flipped a mental coin and chose Chichester, and could hardly believe my lucky ears.

An impersonal voice told me that the number of Patricia Huxford was ex-directory and could be accessed only by the police, in an emergency. It was not even in the C.O. grade-one class of ex-directory, where one could sweet-talk the operator into phoning the number on one's behalf (C.O. stood for calls offered). Patricia Huxford valued absolute grade-two privacy and couldn't be reached that way.

In the highest, third-grade, category, there were the numbers that weren't on any list at all, that the exchanges and operators might not know even existed; numbers for government affairs, the Royal Family and spies.

I yawned, stretched and ate cornflakes for lunch.

While I was still unenthusiastically thinking of driving to Chichester, roughly seventy more miles of arm-ache, Charles phoned from Aynsford.

"So glad to catch you in," he said. "I've been talking to Thomas Ullaston, I thought you'd like to know."

"Yes," I agreed with interest. "What did he say?"

"You know, of course, that he's no longer Senior Steward of the Jockey Club? His term of office ended."

"Yes, I know."

I also regretted it. The new Senior Steward was apt to think me a light-weight nuisance. I supposed he had a point, but it never helped to be discounted by the top man if I asked for anything at all from the department heads in current power. No one was any longer thanking me for ridding them of their villain: according to them, the whole embarrassing incident was best forgotten, and with that I agreed, but I wouldn't have minded residual warmth.

"Thomas was dumbfounded by your question," Charles said. "He protested that he'd meant you no harm."

"Ah!" I said.

"Yes. He didn't deny that he'd told someone about that morning, but he assured me that it had been only *one* person, and that person was someone of utterly good standing, a man of the utmost probity. I asked if it was Archibald Kirk, and he *gasped*, Sid. He said it was early in the summer when Archie Kirk sought him out to ask about you. Archie Kirk told him he'd heard you were a good investigator and he wanted to know *how* good. It seems Archie Kirk's branch of the civil service occasionally likes to employ independent investigators quietly, but that it's hard to find good ones they can trust. Thomas Ullaston told him to trust *you*. Archie Kirk apparently asked more and more questions, until Thomas found himself telling about that chain and those awful marks . . . I mean, sorry, Sid."

"Yeah," I said, "go on."

"Thomas told Archie Kirk that with your jockey constitution and physical resilience—he said physical resilience, Thomas did, so that's exactly where Kirk got that phrase from—with your natural inborn physical resilience you'd shaken off the whole thing as if it had never happened."

"Yes," I said, which wasn't entirely true. One couldn't ever forget. One could, however, ignore. And it was odd, I thought, that I never had nightmares about whippy chains.

Charles chuckled. "Thomas said he wouldn't want young master Halley on his tail if he'd been a crook."

Young master Halley found himself pleased.

Charles asked, "Is there anything else I can do for you, Sid?"

"You've been great."

"Be careful."

I smiled as I assured him I would. Be careful was hopeless advice to a jockey, and at heart I was as much out to win as ever.

On my way to the car I bought some robust adhesive bandage and, with my right forearm firmly strapped and a sufficient application of ibuprofen, drove to Chichester in West Sussex, about seven miles inland from the English Channel.

It was a fine spirits-lifting afternoon. My milk-coffee Mercedes swooped over the rolling South Downs and sped the last flat mile to the cathedral city of Chichester, wheels satisfyingly fast but still not as fulfilling as a horse.

I sought out the public library and asked to see the electoral roll.

There were masses of it: all the names and addresses of registered voters in the county, divided into electoral districts.

Where was Chico, blast him?

Resigned to a long search that could take two or three hours, I found Patricia Huxford within a short fifteen minutes. A record. I hated electoral rolls: the small print made me squint.

Huxford, Patricia Helen, Bravo House, Lowell.

Hallelujah.

I followed my road map and asked for directions in the village of Lowell, and found Bravo House, a small converted church with a herd of cars and vans outside. It didn't look like the reclusive lair of an ex-directory hermit.

As people seemed to be walking in and out of the high, heavy open west door, I walked in, too. I had arrived, it was soon clear, towards the end of a photographic session for a glossy magazine.

I said to a young woman hugging a clipboard, "Patricia Huxford?"

The young woman gave me a radiant smile. "Isn't she *wonderful?*" she said.

I followed the direction of her gaze. A small woman in an astonishing dress was descending from a sort of throne that had been built on a platform situated where the old transepts crossed the nave. There were bright theatrical spotlights that began to be switched off, and there were photographers unscrewing and dismantling and wrapping cables into hanks. There were effusive thanks in the air and satisfied excitement and the overall glow of a job done well.

I waited, looking about me, discovering the changes from church to modern house. The window glass, high up, was clear, not colored. The stone-flagged nave had rugs, no pews, comfortable modern sofas pushed back against the wall to accommodate the crowd, and a large-screen television set.

A white-painted partition behind the throne platform cut off the view of what had been the altar area, but nothing had been done to spoil the sweep of the vaulted ceiling, built with soaring stone arches to the glory of God.

One would have to have a very secure personality, I thought, to choose to live in that place.

The media flock drifted down the nave and left with undiminished goodwill. Patricia Huxford waved to them and closed her heavy door and, turning, was surprised to find me still inside.

"So sorry," she said, and began to open the door again.

"I'm not with the photographers," I said. "I came to ask you about something else."

"I'm tired," she said. "I must ask you to go."

"You look beautiful," I told her, "and it will only take a minute." I brought my scrap of rag out and showed it to her. "If you are Patricia Huxford, did you weave this?"

"Trish," she said absently. "I'm called Trish."

She looked at the strip of silk and then at my face.

"What's your name?" she asked.

"John."

"John what?"

"John Sidney."

John Sidney were my real two first names, the ones my young mother had habitually used. "John Sidney, give us a kiss." "John Sidney, wash your face." "John Sidney, have you been fighting again?"

I often used John Sidney in my job: whenever, in fact, I didn't want to be known to be Sid Halley. After the past months of all-too-public drubbing I wasn't sure that Sid Halley would get me anything anywhere but a swift heave-ho.

Trish Huxford, somewhere, I would have guessed, in the middle to late forties, was pretty, blond (natural?), small-framed and cheerful. Bright, observant eyes looked over my gray business suit, white shirt, unobtrusive tie, brown shoes, dark hair, dark eyes, unthreatening manner: my usual working confidence-inspiring exterior.

She was still on a high from the photo session. She needed someone to help her unwind, and I looked—and was—safe. Thankfully I saw her relax.

The amazing dress she had worn for the photographs was utterly simple in cut, hanging heavy and straight from her shoulders, floor length and sleeveless with a soft ruffled frill around her neck. It was the cloth of the dress that staggered: it was blue and red and silver and gold, and it *shimmered.*

"Did you weave your dress?" I asked

"Of course."

"I've never seen anything like it."

"No, you wouldn't, not nowadays. Can I do anything for you? Where did you come from?"

"London. Saul Marcus suggested you might know who wove my strip of silk."

"Saul! How is he?"

"He has a white beard," I said. "He seemed fine."

"I haven't seen him for years. Will you make me some tea? I don't want marks on this dress."

I smiled. "I'm quite good at tea."

She led the way past the throne and around the white-painted screen. There were choir stalls beyond, old and untouched, and an altar table covered by a cloth that brought me to a halt. It was of a brilliant royal blue with shining gold Greek motifs woven into its deep hem. On the table, in the place of a religious altar, stood an antique spinning wheel, good enough for Sleeping Beauty. Above the table, arched clear glass windows rose to the roof.

"This way," Patricia Huxford commanded, and, leading me past the choir stalls, turned abruptly through a narrow doorway which opened onto what had once probably been a vestry and was now a small modern kitchen with a bathroom beside it.

"My bed is in the south transept," she told me, "and my looms are in the north. You might expect us to be going to drink China tea with lemon out of a silver teapot, but in fact I don't have enough time for that sort of thing, so the tea bags and mugs are on that shelf."

I half filled her electric kettle and plugged it in, and she spent the time walking around watching the miraculous colors move and mingle in her dress.

Intrigued, waiting for the water to boil, I asked, "What is it made of?"

"What do you think?"

"Er, it looks like . . . well . . . gold."

She laughed. "Quite right. Gold, silver thread and silk."

I rather clumsily filled the mugs.

"Milk?" she suggested.

"No, thank you."

"That's lucky. The crowd that's just left finished it off." She gave me a brilliant smile, picked up a mug by its handle and returned to the throne, where she sat neatly on the vast red velvet chair and rested a thin arm delicately along gilt carving. The dress fell into sculptured folds over her slender thighs.

"The photographs," she said, "are for a magazine about a festival of the arts that Chichester is staging all next summer."

I stood before her like some medieval page: stood chiefly because there was no chair nearby to sit on.

"I suppose," she said, "that you think me madly eccentric?"

"Not madly."

She grinned happily. "Normally I wear jeans and an old smock." She drank some tea. "Usually I work. Today is play-acting."

"And magnificent."

She nodded. "No one, these days, makes cloth of gold."

"The Field of the Cloth of Gold," I exclaimed.

"That's right. What do you know of it?"

"Only that phrase."

"The field was the meeting place at Guines, France, in June 1520, of Henry the Eighth of England and Francis the First of France. They were supposed to be making peace between England and France but they hated each other and tried to outdo each other in splendor. So all their courtiers wore cloth woven out of gold and they gave each other gifts you'd never see today. And I thought it would be historic to weave some cloth of gold for the festival . . . so I did. And this dress weighs a ton, I may tell you. Today is the only time I've worn it and I can't bear to take it off."

"It's breathtaking," I said.

She poured out her knowledge. "In 1476 the Duke of Burgundy left behind a hundred and sixty gold cloths when he fled from battle against the Swiss. You make gold cloth—like I made this—by supporting the soft gold on threads of silk, and you can recover the gold by burning the cloth. So when I was making this dress, that's what I did with the pieces I cut out to make the neck and armholes. I burnt them and collected the melted gold."

"Beautiful."

"You know something?" she said. "You're the only person who's seen this dress who hasn't asked how much it cost."

"I did wonder."

"And I'm not telling. Give me your strip of silk."

I took her empty mug and tucked it under my left arm, and in my right hand held out the rag, which she took; and I found her looking with concentration at my left hand. She raised her eyes to meet my gaze.

"Is it . . . ?" she said.

"Worth its weight in gold," I said flippantly. "Yes."

I carried the mugs back to the kitchen and returned to find her standing and smoothing her fingers over the piece of rag.

"An interior decorator," I said, "told me it was probably a modern copy of a hanging made in 1760 by . . . um . . . I think Philippe de Lasalle."

"How clever. Yes, it is. I made quite a lot of it at one time." She paused, then said abruptly, "Come along," and dived off again, leaving me to follow.

We went this time through a door in another white-painted partition and found ourselves in the north transept, her workroom.

There were three looms of varying construction, all bearing work in progress. There was also a business section with filing cabinets and a good deal of office paraphernalia, and another area devoted to measuring, cutting and packing.

"I make fabrics you can't buy anywhere else," she said. "Most of it goes to the Middle East." She walked towards the largest of the three looms, a monster that rose in steps to double our height

"This is a Jacquard loom," she said. "I made your sample on this."

"I was told this piece was . . . a lampas? What's a lampas?"

She nodded. "A lampas is a compound weave with extra warps and wefts which put patterns and colors on the face of the fabric only, and are tucked into the back." She showed me how the design of ropes and branches of leaves gleamed on one side of the turquoise silk but hardly showed on the reverse. "It takes ages to set up," she said. "Nowadays almost no one outside the Middle East thinks the beauty is worth the expense, but once I used to sell quite a lot of it to castles and great houses in England, and all sorts of private people. I only make it to order."

I said neutrally, "Would you know who you made this piece for?"

"My dear man. No, I can't remember. But I probably still have the records. Why do you want to know? Is it important?"

"I don't know if it is important. I was given the strip and asked to find its origin."

She shrugged "Let's find it then. You never know, I might get an order for some more."

She opened cupboard doors to reveal many ranks of box files, and ran her fingers along the labels on the spines until she came to one that her expression announced as possible. She lifted the box file from the shelf and opened it on a table.

Inside were stiff pages with samples of fabric stapled to them with full details of fibers, dates, amount made, names of purchasers and receipts.

She turned the stiff pages slowly, holding my strip in one hand for comparison. She came to several versions of the same design, but all in the wrong color.

"That's it!" she exclaimed suddenly. "That's the one. I see I wove it almost thirty years ago. How time flies. I was so young then. It was a hanging for a four-poster bed. I see I supplied it with gold tassels made of gimp."

I asked without much expectation, "Who to?"

"It says here a Mrs. Gordon Quint."

I said, ". . . Er . . ." meaninglessly, my breath literally taken away. Ginnie? *Ginnie* had owned the material?

"I don't remember her or anything about it," Trish Huxford said. "But all the colors match. It must have been this one commission. I don't think I made these colors for anyone else." She looked at the black stains disfiguring the strip I'd brought. "What a pity! I think of my fabrics as going on forever. They could easily last two hundred years. I love the idea of leaving something beautiful in the world. I expect you think I'm a sentimental old bag."

"I think you're splendid," I said truthfully, and asked, "Why are you ex-directory, with a business to run?"

She laughed. "I hate being interrupted when I'm setting up a design. It takes vast concentration. I have a mobile phone for friends—I can switch it off—and I have an agent in the Middle East, who gets orders for me. Why am I telling you all this?"

"I'm interested."

She closed the file and put it back on the shelf, asking, "Does Mrs. Quint want some more fabric to replace this damaged bit, do you think?"

Mrs. Quint was sixteen floors dead.

"I don't know," I said.

ON THE DRIVE back to London I pulled off the road to phone Davis Tatum at the number he'd given me, his home.

He was in and, it seemed, glad to hear from me, wanting to know what I'd done for him so far.

"Tomorrow," I said, "I'll give Topline Foods a visit. Who did you get Owen Yorkshire's name from?"

He said, stalling, "I beg your pardon?"

"Davis," I said mildly, "you want me to take a look at Owen Yorkshire and his company, so why? Why *him*?"

"I can't tell you."

"Do you mean you promised not to, or you don't know?"

"I mean . . . just go and take a look."

I said, "Sir Thomas Ullaston, Senior Steward last year of the Jockey Club, told Archie Kirk about that little matter of the chains, and Archie Kirk told *you*. So did the name Owen Yorkshire come to you from Archie Kirk?"

"Hell," he said.

"I like to know what I'm getting into."

After a pause he said, "Owen Yorkshire has been seen twice in the board-room of *The Pump*. We don't know why."

"Thank you," I said.

"Is that enough?"

"To be going on with. Oh, and my mobile phone is now safe. No more leaks. See you later."

I drove on to London, parked in the underground garage and walked along the alleyway between tall houses that led into the opposite side of the square from my flat.

I was going quietly and cautiously in any case, and came to a dead stop when I saw that the streetlight almost directly outside my window was not lit.

Boys sometimes threw stones at it to break the glass. Normally its dark-ness wouldn't have sent shudders up my spine and made my right arm re-member Gordon Quint from fingers to neck. Normally I might have crossed the square figuratively whistling while intending to phone in the morning to get the light fixed.

Things were not normal.

There were two locked gates into the central garden, one opposite the path I was on, and one on the far side, opposite my house. Standing in shadow, I sorted out the resident-allocated garden key, went quietly across the circling roadway and unlocked the near gate.

Nothing moved. I eased the gate open, slid through and closed it behind me. No squeaks. I moved slowly from patch to patch of shaded cover, the half-lit tree branches moving in a light breeze, yellow leaves drifting down like ghosts.

Near the far side I stopped and waited.

There could be no one there. I was foolishly afraid over nothing.

The streetlight was out.

It had been out at other times. . . .

I stood with my back to a tree, waiting for alarm to subside to the point where I would unlock the second gate and cross the road to my front steps. The sounds of the city were distant. No cars drove into the cul-de-sac square.

I couldn't stand there all night, I thought . . . *and then I saw him.*

He was in a car parked by one of the few meters. His head—unmistak-ably Gordon Quint's head—moved behind the window. He was looking straight ahead, waiting for me to arrive by road or pavement.

I stood immobile as if stuck to the tree. It had to be obsession with him, I thought. The burning fury of Monday had settled down not into grief but revenge. I hadn't been in my flat for about thirty hours. How long had he been sitting there waiting? I'd had a villain wait almost a week for me once, before I'd walked unsuspectingly into his trap.

Obsession—fixation—was the most frightening of enemies and the hardest to escape.

I retreated, frankly scared, expecting him to see my movement, but he hadn't thought of an approach by garden. From tree to tree, around the patches of open grass, I regained the far gate, eased through it, crossed the road and drifted up the alleyway, cravenly expecting a bellow and a chase and, as he was a farmer, perhaps a shotgun.

Nothing happened. My shoes, soled and heeled for silence, made no sound. I walked back to my underground car and sat in it, not exactly trembling but nonetheless stirred up.

So much, I thought, for Davis Tatum's myth of a clever, unafraid investigator.

I kept always in the car an overnight bag containing the personality-change clothes I'd got Jonathan to wear: dark two-piece tracksuit (trousers and zip-up jacket), navy blue sneakers, and a baseball cap. The bag also contained a long-sleeved open-necked shirt, two or three charged-up batteries for my arm, and a battery charger, to make sure. Habitually around my waist I wore a belt with a zipped pocket big enough for a credit card and money.

I had no weapons or defenses like mace. In America I might have carried both.

I sat in the car considering the matter of distance and ulnas. It was well over two hundred miles from my Landon home to Liverpool, city of my birth. Frodsham, the base town of Topline Foods, wasn't quite as far as Liverpool, but still over two hundred miles. I had already, that day, steered a hundred and fifty—Chichester and back. I'd never missed Chico so much.

I considered trains. Too inflexible. Airline? Ditto. Teledrive? I lingered over the comfort of Teledrive but decided against, and resignedly set off northwards.

It was an easy drive normally; a journey on wide fast motorways taking at most three hours. I drove for only one hour, then stopped at a motel to eat and sleep, and at seven o'clock in the morning wheeled on again, trying to ignore both the obstinately slow-mending fracture and India Cathcart's column that I'd bought from the motel's newsstand.

Friday mornings had been a trial since June. Page fifteen in *The Pump*—trial by the long knives of journalism, the blades that ripped the gut.

She hadn't mentioned at all seeing Tatum and me in the Le Meridien bar. Perhaps she'd taken my advice and pretended we hadn't been there. What her column said about me was mostly factually true but spitefully wrong. I wondered how she could do it? Had she no sense of humanity?

Most of her page concerned yet another politician caught with his trousers at half-mast, but the far-right column said.

> *Sid Halley, illegitimate by-blow of a nineteen-year-old window cleaner and a packer in a biscuit factory, ran amok as a brat in the slums of Liverpool. Home was a roach-infested council flat. Nothing wrong with that! But this same Sid Halley now puts on airs of middle-class gentility. A flat in Chelsea? Sheraton furniture? Posh accent? Go back to your roots, lad. No wonder Ellis Quint thinks you funny. Funny pathetic!*
>
> *The slum background clearly explains the Halley envy. Halley's chip on the shoulder grows more obvious every day. Now we know why!*
>
> *The Halley polish is all a sham, just like his plastic left hand.*

Christ, I thought, how much more? Why did it so bloody hurt?

My father had been killed in a fall eight months before my birth and a few days before he was due to marry my eighteen-year-old mother. She'd done her best as a single parent in hopeless surroundings. "Give us a kiss, John Sidney . . ."

I hadn't ever run amok. I'd been a quiet child, mostly. "Have you been fighting again, John Sidney . . . ?" She hadn't liked me fighting, though one had to sometimes, or be bullied.

And when she knew she was dying she'd taken me to Newmarket, because I'd been short for my age, and had left me with the king of trainers to be made into a jockey, as I'd always wanted.

I couldn't possibly go back to my Liverpool "roots." I had no sense of ever having grown any there.

I had never envied Ellis Quint. I'd always liked him. I'd been a better jockey than he, and we'd both known it. If anything, the envy had been the other way around. But it was useless to protest, as it had been all along. Protests were used regularly to prove *The Pump*'s theories of my pitiable inadequacy.

My mobile phone buzzed. I answered it.

"Kevin Mills," a familiar voice said. "Where are you? I tried your apartment. Have you seen today's *Pump* yet?"

"Yes."

"India didn't write it," he said. "I gave her the info, but she wouldn't use it. She filled that space with some pars on sexual stress and her editor subbed them out."

Half of my muscles unknotted, and I hadn't realized they'd been tense. I forced unconcern into my voice even as I thought of hundreds of thousands of readers sniggering about me over their breakfast toast.

"Then you wrote it yourself," I said. "So who's a shit now? You're the only person on *The Pump* who's seen my Sheraton desk."

"Blast you. Where are you?"

"Going back to Liverpool. Where else?"

"Sid, look, I'm sorry."

"Policy?"

He didn't answer.

I asked, "Why did you phone to tell me India didn't write today's bit of demolition?"

"I'm getting soft."

"No one's listening to this phone anymore. You can say what you like."

"Jeez." He laughed. "That didn't take you long." He paused. "You might not believe it, but most of us on *The Pump* don't any more like what we've been doing to you."

"Rise up and rebel," I suggested dryly.

"We have to eat. And you're a tough bugger. You can take it."

You just try it, I thought.

"Listen," he said, "the paper's received a lot of letters from readers complaining that we're not giving you a fair deal."

"How many is a lot?"

"Two hundred or so. Believe me, that's a *lot*. But we're not allowed to print any."

I said with interest, "Who says so?"

"That's just it. The ed, Godbar himself, says so, and he doesn't like it, either, but the policy is coming from the very top."

"Tilepit?"

"Are you *sure* this phone's not bugged?"

"You're safe."

"You've had a bloody raw mauling, and you don't deserve it. I know that. We all know it. I'm sorry for my part in it. I'm sorry I wrote today's venom, especially that bit about your hand. Yes, it's Tilepit. The proprietor himself."

"Well . . . thanks."

He said, "Did Ellis Quint *really* cut off those feet?"

I smiled ruefully. "The jury will decide."

"Sid, look here," he protested, "you *owe* me!"

"Life's a bugger," I said.

CHAPTER 11

NINE O'CLOCK FRIDAY morning I drove into the town of Frodsham and asked for Topline Foods.

Not far from the river, I was told. Near the river; the Mersey.

The historic docks of Liverpool's Mersey waterfront had long been silent, the armies of tall cranes dismantled, the warehouses converted or pulled down. Part of the city's heart had stopped beating. There had been bypass surgery of sorts, but past muscle would never return. The city had a vast red-brick cathedral, but faith, as in much of Britain, had dimmed.

For years I'd been to Liverpool only to ride there on Aintree racecourse. The road I'd once lived in lay somewhere under a shopping mall. Liverpool was a place, but not home.

At Frodsham there was a "Mersey View" vantage point with, away to the distant north, some still-working docks at Runcorn on the Manchester Ship Canal. One of those docks, I'd seen earlier, was occupied by Topline Foods. A ship lying alongside bearing the flag and insignia of Canada had been unloading Topline grain.

I'd stopped the car from where I could see the sweep of river with the seagulls swooping and the stiff breeze tautening flags at the horizontal. I stood in the cold open air, leaning on the car, smelling the salt and the mud and hearing the drone of traffic on the roads below.

Were these roots? I'd always loved wide skies, but it was the wide sky of Newmarket Heath that I thought of as home. When I'd been a boy there'd been no wide skies, only narrow streets, the walk to school, and rain. "John Sidney, wash your face. Give us a kiss."

The day after my mother died I'd ridden my first winner, and that evening I'd got drunk for the first and only time until the arrest of Ellis Quint.

Soberly, realistically, in the Mersey wind I looked at the man I had become: a jumble of self-doubt, ability, fear and difficult pride. I had grown as I was from the inside out. Liverpool and Newmarket weren't to blame.

Stirring and getting back into the car, I wondered where to find all those tungsten nerves I was supposed to have.

I didn't know what I was getting into. I could still at that point retreat and leave the field to Ellis. I could—and I couldn't. I would have myself to live with, if I did.

I'd better simply get on with it, I thought.

I drove down from the vantage point, located the Topline Foods factory and passed through its twelve-feet-high but hospitably open wire-mesh gates. There was a guard in a gatehouse who paid me no attention.

Inside there were many cars tidily parked in ranks. I added myself to the end of one row and decided on a clothing compromise of suit trousers, zipped-up tracksuit top, white shirt, no tie, ordinary shoes. I neatly combed my hair forward into a young-looking style and looked no threat to anybody.

The factory, built around three sides of the big central area, consisted of loading bays, a vast main building and a new-looking office block. Loading and unloading took place under cover, with articulated semi-trailers backing into the bays. In the one bay I could see into clearly, the cab section had been disconnected and removed; heavy sacks that looked as if they might contain grain were being unloaded from a long container by two large men who slung the sacks onto a moving conveyer belt of rollers.

The big building had a row of windows high up: there was no chance of looking in from outside.

I ambled across to the office building and shouldered open a heavy glass door that led into a large but mostly bare entrance hall, and found there the reason for the unguarded front gates. The security arrangements were all inside.

Behind a desk sat a purposeful-looking middle-aged woman in a green jumper. Flanking her were two men in navy blue security-guard suits with Topline Foods insignia on their breast pockets.

"Name, please," said the green jumper. "State your business. All parcels, carriers and handbags must be left here at the desk."

She had a distinct Liverpool accent. With the same inflection in my own voice, I told her that, as she could see, I had no bag, carrier or handbag with me.

She took the accent for granted and unsmilingly asked again for my name.

"John Sidney."

"Business?"

"Well," I said, as if perplexed by the reception I was getting, "I was asked to come here to see if you made some horse nuts." I paused. "Like," I lamely finished, dredging up the idiom.

"Of course, we make horse nuts. It's our business."

"Yes," I told her earnestly, "but this farmer, like, he asked me to come in, as I was passing this way, to see if it was you that made some horse nuts that someone had given him, that were very good for his young horse, like, but he was given them loose and not in a bag and all he has is a list of what's in the nuts and he wanted to know if you made them, see?" I half pulled a sheet of paper from an inside pocket and pushed it back.

She was bored by the rigmarole.

"If I could just *talk* to someone," I pleaded. "See, I owe this farmer a favor and it wouldn't take no more than a minute, if I could talk to someone. Because this farmer, he'll be a big customer if these are the nuts he's looking for."

She gave in, lifted a telephone and repeated a shortened version of my improbable tale.

She inspected me from head to foot. "Couldn't hurt a fly," she reported.

I kept the suitably feeble half-anxious smile in place.

She put down the receiver. "Miss Rowse will be down to help you. Raise your hands."

"Eh?"

"Raise your hands . . . please."

Surprised, I did as I was told. One of the security guards patted me all over in the classic way of their job, body and legs. He missed the false hand and the cracked bone. "Keys and mobile phone," he reported. "Clean."

Green jumper wrote "John Sidney" onto a clip-on identity card and I clipped it dutifully on.

"Wait by the elevator," she said.

I waited.

The doors finally parted to reveal a teenage girl with wispy fair hair who said she was Miss Rowse. "Mr. Sidney? This way, please."

I stepped into the elevator with her and rode to the third floor.

She smiled with bright inexperienced encouragement and led me down a newly carpeted passage to an office conspicuously labeled Customer Relations on its open door.

"Come in," Miss Rowse said proudly. "Please sit down."

I sat in a Scandinavian-inspired chair of blond wood with arms, simple lines, blue cushioning and considerable comfort.

"I'm afraid I didn't really understand your problem," Miss Rowse said trustingly. "If you'll explain again, I can get the right person to talk to you."

I looked around her pleasant office, which showed almost no sign of work in progress.

"Have you been here long?" I asked. (Guileless Liverpool accent, just like hers.) "Nice office. They must think a lot of you here."

She was pleased, but still honest. "I'm new this week. I started on Monday—and you're my second inquiry."

No wonder, I thought, that she'd let me in.

I said, "Are all the offices as plush as this?"

"Yes," she said enthusiastically. "Mr. Yorkshire, he likes things nice."

"Is he the boss?"

"The chief executive officer." She nodded. The words sounded stiff and unfamiliar, as if she'd only newly learned them.

"Nice to work for, is he?" I suggested.

She confessed, "I haven't met him yet. I know what he looks like, of course, but . . . I'm new here, like I said."

I smiled sympathetically and asked what Owen Yorkshire looked like.

She was happy to tell me, "He's ever so *big*. He's got a big head and a lovely lot of hair, wavy like."

"Mustache?" I suggested. "Beard?"

"No," she giggled. "And he's not *old*. Not a granddad. Everyone gets out of his way."

Do they indeed, I thought.

She went on, "I mean, Mrs. Dove, she's my boss really, she's the office manager, she says not to make him angry, whatever I do. She says just to do my job. She has a lovely office. It used to be Mr. Yorkshire's own, she says."

Miss Rowse, shaped like a woman, chattered like a child.

"Topline Foods must be doing all right to have rich new offices like these," I said admiringly.

"They've got the TV cameras coming tomorrow to set up for Monday. They brought dozens of potted plants round this morning. Ever so keen on publicity, Mrs. Dove says Mr. Yorkshire is."

"The plants do make it nice and homey," I said. "Which TV company, do you know?"

She shook her head, "All the Liverpool big noises are coming to a huge reception on Monday. The TV cameras are going all over the factory. Of course, although they're going to have all the machines running, they won't really make any nuts on Monday. It will all be pretend."

"Why's that?"

"Security. They have to be security mad, Mrs. Dove says. Mr. Yorkshire worries about people putting things in the feed, she says."

"What things?"

"I don't know. Nails and safety pins and such. Mrs. Dove says all the searching at the entrance is Mr. Yorkshire's idea."

"Very sensible," I said.

An older and more cautious woman came into the office, revealing herself to be the fount of wisdom, Mrs. Dove. Middle-aged and personally secure, I thought. Status, ability and experience all combining in priceless efficiency.

"Can I help you?" she said to me civilly, and to the girl, "Marsha dear, I thought we'd agreed you would always come to me for advice."

"Miss Rowse has been really helpful," I said. "She's going to find someone to answer my question. Perhaps you could yourself?"

Mrs. Dove (gray hair pinned high under a flat black bow, high heels, customer-relations neat satin shirt, cinched waist and black tights) listened with slowly glazing eyes to my expanding tale of the nutty farmer.

"You need our Willy Parrott," she said when she could insert a comment. "Come with me."

I waggled conspiratorial fingers at Marsha Rowse and followed Mrs. Dove's busy back view along the expensive passage with little partitioned but mostly empty offices on each side. She continued through a thick fire door at the end, to emerge on a gallery around an atrium in the main factory building, where the nuts came from.

Rising from the ground, level almost to the gallery, were huge mixing vats, all with paddles circulating, activated from machinery stretching down from above. The sounds were an amalgam of whir, rattle and slurp: the air bore fine particles of cereal dust and it looked like a brewery, I thought. It smelled rather the same also, but without the fermentation.

Mrs. Dove passed me thankfully on to a man in brown overalls who inspected my dark clothes and asked if I wanted to be covered in fall-out.

"Not particularly."

He raised patient eyebrows and gestured to me to follow him, which I did, to find myself on an iron staircase descending one floor, along another gallery and ending in a much-used battered little cubby-hole of an office, with a sliding glass door that he closed behind us.

I commented on the contrast from the office building.

"Fancy fiddle-faddle," he said. "That's for the cameras. This is where the work is done."

"I can see that," I told him admiringly.

"Now, lad," he said, looking me up and down, unimpressed, "what is it you want?"

He wasn't going to be taken in very far by the farmer twaddle. I explained in a shorter version and produced the folded paper bearing the analysis of the nuts from Combe Bassett and the Land-Rover, and asked if it was a Topline formula.

He read the list that by then I knew by heart.

Wheat, oat feed, ryegrass, straw, barley, corn, molasses, salt, linseed
Vitamins, selenium, copper, other substances and probably the antioxidant
Ethoxyquin.

"Where did you get this?" he asked.

"From a farmer, like I told you."

"This list isn't complete," he said.

"No . . . but is it enough?"

"It doesn't give percentages. I can't possibly match it to any of our products." He folded the paper and gave it back. "Your cubes might be our supplement feed for horses out at grass. Do you know anything about horses?"

"A little."

"Then, the more oats you give them, the more energy they expend. Racehorses need more oats. I can't tell you for sure if these cubes were for racehorses in training unless I know the proportion of oats."

"They weren't racehorses in training."

"Then your farmer friend couldn't do better than our Sweetfield mix. They do contain everything on your list."

"Are other people's cubes much different?"

"There aren't very many manufacturers. We're perhaps fourth on the league table but after this advertisement campaign we expect that to zoom up. The new management aims for the top."

"But . . . um . . . do you have enough space?"

"Capacity?"

I nodded.

He smiled. "Owen Yorkshire has plans. He talks to us man to man." His face and voice were full of approval. "He's brought the old place back to life."

I said inoffensively, "Mrs. Dove seems in awe of his anger."

Willy Parrott laughed and gave me a male chauvinist–type wink. "He has a flaming temper, has our Owen Yorkshire. And the more a man for that."

I looked vaguely at some charts taped to a wall. "Where does he come from?" I asked.

"Haven't a clue," Willy told me cheerfully. "He knows bugger all about nutrition. He's a salesman, and *that's* what we needed. We have a couple of nerds in white coats working on what we put in all the vats."

He was scornful of scientists as well as women. I turned back from the wall charts and thanked him for his time. Very interesting job, I told him. Obviously he ran the department that mattered most.

He took the compliment as his due and saved me the trouble of asking by offering to let me tag along with him while he went to his next task, which was to check a new shipment of wheat. I accepted with an enthusiasm that pleased him. A man good at his job often enjoyed an audience, and so did Willy Parrott.

He gave me a set of over-large brown overalls and told me to clip the identity card on the outside, like his own.

"Security is vital," he said to me. "Owen's stepped it all up. He lectures us on not letting strangers near the mixing vats. I can't let you any nearer than this. Our competitors wouldn't be above adding foreign substances that would put us out of business."

"D'you mean it?" I said, looking avid.

"You have to be specially careful with horse feed," he assured me, sliding open his door when I was ready. "You can't mix cattle feed in the same vats, for instance. You can put things in cattle feed that are prohibited for race-horses. You ran get traces of prohibited substances in the horse cubes just by using the same equipment, even if you think you've cleaned everything thoroughly."

There had been a famous example in racing of a trainer getting into trouble by unknowingly giving his runners contaminated nuts.

"Fancy," I said.

I thought I might have overdone the impressed look I gave him, but he accepted it easily.

"We do nothing else except horse cubes here," Willy said. "Owen says when we expand we'll do cattle feed and chicken pellets and all sorts of other muck, but I'll be staying here, Owen says, in charge of the equine branch."

"A top job," I said with admiration.

He nodded. "The best."

We walked along the gallery and came to another fire door, which he lugged open.

"All these internal doors are locked at night now, and there's a watchman with a dog. Very thorough, is Owen." He looked back to make sure I was following, then stopped at a place from which we could see bags marked with red maple leaves traveling upward on an endless belt of bag-sized ledges, only to be tumbled off the top and be manhandled by two smoothly swinging muscular workers.

"I expect you saw those two security men in the entrance hall?" Willy Parrott said, the question of security not yet exhausted.

"They frisked me." I grinned. "Going a bit far, I thought."

"They're Owen's private bodyguards," Willy Parrott said with a mixture of awe and approval. "They're real hard men from Liverpool. Owen says he needs them in case the competitors try to get rid of him the old-fashioned way."

I frowned disbelievingly. "Competitors don't kill people."

"Owen says he's taking no risks because he definitely is trying to put other firms out of business, if you look at it that way."

"So you think he's right to need bodyguards?"

Willy Parrott turned to face me and said, "It's not the world I was brought up in, lad. But we have to live in this new one, Owen says."

"I suppose so."

"You won't get far with that attitude, lad." He pointed to the rising bags. "That's this year's wheat straight from the prairie. Only the best is good enough, Owen says, in trade wars."

He led the way down some nearby concrete stairs and through another heavy door, and I realized we were on ground level, just off the central atrium. With a smile of satisfaction he pushed through one more door and we found ourselves amid the vast mixing vats, pygmies surrounded by giants.

He enjoyed my expression.

"Awesome," I said.

"You don't need to go back upstairs to get out," he said. "There's a door out to the yard just down here."

I thanked him for his advice about the nuts for the farmer, and for showing me around. I'd been with him for half an hour and couldn't reasonably stretch it further, but while I was in midsentence he looked over my shoulder and his face changed completely from man-in-charge to subservient subject.

I turned to see what had caused this transformation and found it not to be a Royal Person but a large man in white overalls accompanied by several anxious blue-clad attendants who were practically walking backwards.

"Morning, Willy," said the man in white. "Everything going well?"

"Yes, Owen. Fine."

"Good. Has the Canadian wheat come up from the docks?"

"They're unloading it now, Owen."

"Good. We should have a talk about future plans. Come up to my new office at four this afternoon. You know where it is? Top floor, turn right from the lift, like my old office."

"Yes, Owen."

"Good."

The eyes of the businessman glanced my way briefly and incuriously, and passed on. I was wearing brown overalls and an identity card, after all, and looked like an employee. Not an employee of much worth, either, with my over-big overalls wrinkling around my ankles and drooping down my arms to the fingers. Willy didn't attempt to explain my presence, for which I was grateful. Willy was almost on his knees in reverence.

Owen Yorkshire was, without doubt, impressive. Easily over six feet tall, he was simply large, but not fat. There was a lot of heavy muscle in the shoulders, and a trim, sturdy belly. Luxuriant closely waving hair spilled over his collar, with the beginnings of gray in the lacquered wings sweeping back from above his ears. It was a hairstyle that in its way made as emphatic a statement as Jonathan's. Owen Yorkshire intended not only to rule but to be remembered.

His accent was not quite Liverpool and not at all London, but powerful and positive. His voice was unmistakably an instrument of dominance. One could imagine that his rages might in fact shake the building. One could have sympathy with his yes-men.

Willy said "Yes, Owen," several more times.

The man-to-man relationship that Willy Parrott prized so much extended, I thought, not much further than the use of first names. True, Owen Yorkshire's manner to Willy was of the "we're all in this together" type of management technique, and seemed to be drawing the best out of a good man; but I could imagine the boss also finding ways of getting rid of his Willy Parrott, if it pleased him, with sad shrugs and "you know how it is these days, we no longer *need* a production manager just for horse cubes; your job is computerized and phased out. Severance pay? Of course. See my secretary. No hard feelings."

I hoped it wouldn't happen to Willy.

Owen Yorkshire and his satellites swept onwards. Willy Parrott looked after him with pride tinged very faintly with anxiety.

"Do you work tomorrow?" I asked. "Is the factory open on Saturdays?"

He reluctantly removed his gaze from the Yorkshire back view and began to think I'd been there too long.

"We're opening on Saturdays from next week," he said. "Tomorrow they're making more advertising films. There will be cameras all over the place, and on Monday, too. We won't get anything useful done until Tuesday." He was full of disapproval, but he would repress all that, it was clear, for man-to-man Owen. "Off you go then, lad. Go back to the entrance and leave the overalls and identity tag there."

I thanked him again and this time went out into the central yard, which since my own arrival had become clogged with vans and truckloads of television and advertising people. The television contingent were from Liverpool. The advertisement makers, according to the identification on their vans, were from Intramind Imaging (Manchester) Ltd.

One of the Intramind drivers, in the unthinking way of his kind, had braked and parked at an angle to all the other vehicles. I walked across to where he still sat in his cab and asked him to straighten up his van.

"Who says so?" he demanded belligerently.

"I just work here," I said, still in the brown overalls that, in spite of Willy Parrott's instructions, I was not going to return. "I was sent out to ask you. Big artics have to get in here." I pointed to the unloading bays.

The driver grunted, started his engine, straightened his vehicle, switched off and jumped down to the ground beside me.

"Will that do?" he asked sarcastically.

"You must have an exciting job," I said enviously. "Do you see all those film stars?"

He sneered. "We make *advertising* films, mate. Sure, sometimes we get big names, but mostly they're endorsing things."

"What sort-of things?"

"Sports gear, often. Shoes, golf clubs."

"And horse cubes?"

He had time to waste while others unloaded equipment. He didn't mind a bit of showing off.

He said, "They've got a lot of top jockeys lined up to endorse the horse nuts."

"Have they?" I asked interestedly. "Why not trainers?"

"It's the jockeys the public know by their faces. That's what I'm told. I'm a football man myself."

He didn't, I was grateful to observe, even begin to recognize my own face, that in years gone by had fairly often taken up space on the nation's sports pages.

Someone in his team called him away and I walked off, sliding into my own car and making an uneventful exit through the tall unchecked outward gates. Odd, I thought, that the security-paranoid Owen Yorkshire didn't have a gate bristling with electronic barriers and ominous name gatherers; and the only reason I could think of for such laxity was that he didn't always want name takers to record everyone's visits.

Blind-eye country, I thought, like the private backstairs of the great before the India Cathcarts of the world floodlit the secretive comings and goings, and rewarded promiscuity with taint.

Perhaps Owen Yorkshire's backstairs was the elevator to the fifth floor. Perhaps Mrs. Green Jumper and the bouncers in blue knew who to admit without searching.

Perhaps this, perhaps that. I'd seen the general layout and been near the power running the business, but basically I'd done little there but reconnoiter.

I stopped in a public car park, took off the brown overalls and decided to go to Manchester.

THE JOURNEY WAS quite short, but it took me almost as long again to find Intramind Imaging (Manchester) Ltd., which, although in a back street, proved to be a much bigger outfit than I'd pictured; I shed the tracksuit top and the Liverpool accent and approached the reception desk in suit, tie, and business aura.

"I've come from Topline Foods," I said. "I'd like to talk to whoever is in charge of their account."

Did I have an appointment?

No, it was a private matter.

If one pretended sufficient authority, I'd found, doors got opened, and so it was at Intramind Imaging. A Mr. Gross would see me. An electric door latch buzzed and I walked from the entrance lobby into an inner hallway, where cream paint had been used sparingly and there was no carpet underfoot. Ostentation was out.

Mr. Gross was "third door on the left." Mr. Gross's door had his name and a message on it: Nick Gross. What the F Do You Want?

Nick Gross looked me up and down. "Who the hell are *you*? You're not Topline Foods top brass, and you're over-dressed."

He himself wore a black satin shirt, long hair and a gold earring. Forty-five disintegrating to fifty, I thought, and stuck in a time warp of departing youth. Forceful, though. Strong lines in his old-young face. Authority.

"You're making advertising film for Topline," I said.

"So what? And if you're another of their whining accountants sent to beg for better terms, the answer is up yours, mate. It isn't our fault you haven't been able to use those films you spent millions on. They're all brilliant stuff, the best. So you creep back to your Mr. Owen effing Yorkshire and tell him there's no deal. Off you trot, then. If he wants his jockey series at the same price as before he has to send us a check every week. *Every week* or we yank the series, got it?"

I nodded.

Nick Gross said, "And tell him not to forget that in ads the magic is in the *cutting*, and the cutting comes *last*. No check, no cutting. No cutting, no magic. No magic, no message. No message, we might as well stop right now. Have you got it?"

I nodded again.

"Then you scurry right back to Topline and tell them no check, no cutting. And that means no campaign. Got it?"

"Yes."

"Right. Bugger off."

I meekly removed myself but, seeing no urgent reason to leave altogether, I turned the wrong way out of his office and walked as if I belonged there down a passage between increasingly technical departments.

I came to an open door through which one could see a screen showing startlingly familiar pieces of an ad campaign currently collecting critical acclaim as well as phenomenally boosting sales. There were bursts of pictures as short as three seconds followed by longer intervals of black. Three seconds of fast action. Ten of black.

I stopped, watching, and a man walked into my sight and saw me standing there.

"Yes?" he said. "Do you want something?"

"Is that," I said, nodding towards the screen, "one of the mountain bike ads?"

"It will be when I cut it together."

"Marvelous," I said. I took half a step unthreateningly over his threshold. "Can I watch you for a bit?"

"Who are you, exactly?"

"From Topline Foods. I came to see Nick Gross."

"Ah." There was a world of comprehension in the monosyllable: comprehension that I immediately aimed to transfer from his brain to mine.

He was younger than Nick Gross and not so mock-rock-star in dress. His certainty shouted from the zany speed of his three-second flashes and the wit crackling in their juxtaposition: he had no need for earrings.

I said, quoting the bike campaign's slogan, "Every kid under fifty wants a mountain bike for Christmas."

He fiddled with reels of film and said cheerfully, "There'll be hell to pay if they don't."

"Did you work on the Topline ads?" I asked neutrally.

No, thank Christ. A colleague did. Eight months of award-worthy brilliant work sitting idle in cans on the shelves. No prizes for us, and your top man's shitting himself, isn't he? All that cabbage spent and bugger all back. And all because some twisted little pipsqueak gets the star attraction arrested for something he didn't do."

I held my breath, but he had no flicker of an idea what the pipsqueak looked like. I said I'd better be going and he nodded vaguely without looking up from his problems.

I persevered past his domain until I came to two big doors, one saying Sound Stage Keep Out and one, opening outward with a push-bar, marked Backlot. I pushed that door half-open and saw outside in the open air a huge yellow crane dangling a red sports car by a rear axle. Film cameras and crews were busy around it. Work in progress.

I retreated. No one paid me any attention on the way out. This was not, after all, a bank vault, but a dream factory. No one could steal dreams.

The reception lobby, as I hadn't noticed on my way in, bore posters around the walls of past and current purse-openers, all prestigious prize-winning campaigns. Ad campaigns. I'd heard, were now considered an OK step on the career ladder for both directors and actors. Sell cornflakes one day, play Hamlet the next. Intramind Imaging could speed you on your way.

I drove into the center of Manchester and anonymously booked into a spacious restful room in the Crown Plaza Hotel. Davis Tatum might have a fit over the expense but if necessary I would pay for it myself. I wanted a shower, room service and cosseting, and hang the price.

I phoned Tatum's home number and got an answering machine. I asked him to call back to my mobile number and repeated it, and then sat in an armchair watching racing on television—flat racing at Ascot.

There was no sight of Ellis on the course. The commentator mentioned that his "ludicrous" trial was due to resume in three days' time, on Monday.

Sid Halley, he said, was sensibly keeping his head down as half Ellis's fan club was baying for his blood.

This little tid-bit came from a commentator who'd called me a wizard and a force for good not long ago. Times changed: did they ever. There were smiling closeups of Ellis's face, and of mine, both helmetless but in racing colors, side by side. "They used to be the closest of friends," said the commentator sadly. "Now they slash and gore each other like bulls."

Sod him, I thought.

I also hoped that none of Mrs. Green Jumper, Marsha Rowse, Mrs. Dove, Willy Parrott, the Intramind van driver, Nick Gross and the film cutter had switched on to watch racing at Ascot. I didn't think Owen Yorkshire's sliding glance across my overalls would have left an imprint but the others would remember me for a day or two. It was a familiar risk, sometimes lucky, sometimes not.

When the racing ended I phoned Intramind Imaging and asked a few general questions that I hadn't thought of in my brief career on the spot as a Topline Foods employee.

Were advertising campaigns originally recorded on film or on disks or on tape, I wanted to know, and could the public buy copies. I was answered helpfully: Intramind usually used film, especially for high-budget location-based ads, and no, the public could *not* buy copies. The finished film would eventually be transferred onto broadcast-quality videotape, known as Betacam. These tapes then belonged to the clients, who paid television companies for airtime. Intramind did not act as an agent.

"Thanks very much," I said politely, grateful always for knowledge.

Davis Tatum phoned soon after.

"Sid," he said, "where are you?"

"Manchester, city of rain."

It was sunny that day.

"Er . . . ," Davis said. "Any progress?"

"Some," I said.

"And, er . . ." He hesitated again. "Did you read India Cathcart this morning?"

"She didn't write that she'd seen us at Le Meridien," I said.

"No. She took your excellent advice. But as to the rest . . . !"

I said, "Kevin Mills phoned especially to tell me that she didn't write the rest. He did it himself. Policy. Pressure from above. Same old thing."

"But wicked."

"He apologized. Big advance."

"You take it so lightly," Davis said.

I didn't disillusion him. I said, "Tomorrow evening—would you be able to go to Archie Kirk's house?"

"I should think so, if it's important. What time?"

"Could you arrange that with him? About six o'clock, I should think. I'll arrive there sometime myself. Don't know when."

With a touch of complaint he said, "It sounds a bit vague."

I thought I'd better not tell him that with burglary, times tended to be approximate.

CHAPTER 12

I PHONED *THE PUMP,* asking for India Cathcart. Silly me.

Number one, she was never in the office on Fridays.

Number two, *The Pump* never gave private numbers to unknown callers.

"Tell her Sid Halley would like to talk to her," I said, and gave the switchboard operator my mobile number, asking him to repeat it so I could make sure he had written it down right.

No promises, he said.

I sat for a good while thinking about what I'd seen and learned, and planning what I would do the next day. Such plans got altered by events as often as not, but I'd found that no plan at all invited nil results. If all else failed, try Plan B. Plan B, in my battle strategy, was to escape with skin intact. Plan B had let me down a couple of times, but disasters were like falls in racing; you never thought they'd happen until you were nose down to the turf.

I had some food sent up and thought some more, and at ten-fifteen my mobile buzzed.

"Sid?" India said nervously.

"Hello."

"Don't say anything! I'll cry if you say anything." After a pause she said, "Sid! Are you there?"

"Yes. But I don't want you to cry so I'm not saying anything."

"Oh, God." It was half a choke, half a laugh. "How can you be so . . . so *civilized*?"

"With enormous difficulty," I said. "Are you busy on Sunday evening? Your restaurant or mine?"

She said disbelievingly, "Are you asking me out to dinner?"

"Well," I said, "it's not a proposal of marriage. And no knife through the ribs. Just food."

"How, can you *laugh*?"

"Why are you called India?" I asked.

"I was conceived there. What has that got to do with anything?"

"I just wondered," I said.

"Are you *drunk*?"

"Unfortunately not. I'm sifting soberly in an armchair contemplating the state of the universe, which is C minus, or thereabouts."

"Where? I mean, where is the armchair?"

"On the floor," I said.

"You don't trust me!"

"No," I sighed, "I don't. But I do want to have dinner with you."

"Sid," she was almost pleading, "be sensible."

Rotten advice, I'd always thought. But then if I'd been sensible I would have two hands and fewer scars, and I reckoned one had to be *born* sensible, which didn't seem to have happened in my case.

I said. "Your proprietor—Lord Tilepit—have you met him?"

"Yes." She sounded a bit bewildered. "He comes to the office party at Christmas. He shakes everyone's hand."

"What's he like?"

"Do you mean to look at?"

"For a start."

"He's fairly tall. Light-brown hair."

"That's not much," I said when she stopped.

"He's not part of my day-to-day life."

"Except that he burns saints," I said.

A brief silence, then, "Your restaurant, this time."

I smiled. Her quick mind could reel in a tarpon where her red mouth couldn't. "Does Lord Tilepit," I asked, "wear an obvious cloak of power? Are you aware of his power when you're in a room with him?"

"Actually . . . no."

"Is anyone . . . *Could* anyone be physically in awe of him?"

"No." It was clear from her voice that she thought the idea laughable.

"So his leverage," I said, "is all economic?"

"I suppose so."

"Is there anyone that *he* is in awe of?"

"I don't know. Why do you ask?"

"That man," I said, "has spent four months directing his newspaper to . . . well . . . ruin me. You must allow, I have an interest."

"But you aren't ruined. You don't sound in the least ruined. And anyway, your ex-wife said it was impossible."

"She said *what* was impossible?"

"To . . . to . . ."

"Say it."

"To reduce you to rubble. To make you beg."

She silenced me.

She said, "Your ex-wife's still in love with you."

"No, not anymore."

"I'm an expert on ex-wives," India said. "Wronged wives, dumped mistresses, women curdled with spite, women angling for money. Women wanting revenge, women breaking their hearts. I know the scenery. Your Jenny said she couldn't live in your purgatory, but when I suggested you were a selfish brute she defended you like a tigress."

Oh *God*, I thought. After nearly six years apart the same old dagger could pierce us both.

"Sid?"

"Mm."

"Do you still love *her*?"

I found a calm voice. "We can't go back, and we don't want to," I said. "I regret a lot, but it's now finally over. She has a better husband, and she's happy."

"I met her new man," India said. "He's sweet."

"Yes." I paused. "What about your own ex?"

"I fell for his looks. It turned out he wanted an admiration machine in an apron. End of story."

"Is his name Cathcart?"

"No," she said. "Patterson."

Smiling to myself. I said, "Will you give me your phone number?"

She said, "Yes," and did so.

"Kensington Place restaurant. Eight o'clock."

"I'll be there."

WHEN I WAS alone, which was usual nowadays, since Louise McInnes and I had parted, I took off my false arm at bedtime and replaced it after a shower in the morning. I couldn't wear it in showers, as water wrecked the works. Taking it off after a long day was often a pest, as it fitted tightly and tended to cling to my skin. Putting it on was a matter of talcum powder, getting the angle right and pushing hard.

The arm might be worth its weight in gold, as I'd told Trish Huxford, but even after three years, whatever lighthearted front I might now achieve in public, in private the management of amputation still took me a positive effort of the "get on with it" ethos. I didn't know why I continued to feel vulnerable and sensitive. Too much pride, no doubt.

I'd charged up the two batteries in the charger overnight, so I started the new day, Saturday, with a fresh battery in the arm and a spare in my pocket.

It was by then five days since Gordon Quint had cracked my ulna, and the twinges had become less acute and less frequent. Partly it was because one naturally found the least painful way of performing any action, and partly because the ends of bone were beginning to knit. Soft tissue grew on the site of the break, and on the eighth day it would normally begin hardening, the whole healing process being complete within the next week. Only splintered, displaced ends caused serious trouble, which hadn't occurred in this case.

When I'd been a jockey the feel of a simple fracture had been an almost twice-yearly familiarity. One tended in jump racing to fall on one's shoulder, quite often at thirty miles an hour, and in my time I'd cracked my collarbones six times each side: only once had it been distinctly bad.

Some jockeys had stronger bones than others, but I didn't know anyone who'd completed a top career unscathed. Anyway, by Saturday morning, Monday's crack was no real problem.

Into my overnight bag I packed the battery charger, washing things, pajamas, spare shirt, business suit and shoes. I wore both pieces of the tracksuit, white shirt, no tie and the dark sneakers. In my belt I carried money and a credit card, and in my pocket a bunch of six keys on a single ring, which bore also a miniature flashlight. Three of the keys were variously for my car and the entry doors of my flat. The other three, looking misleadingly simple, would between them open any ordinary lock, regardless of the wishes of the owners.

My old teacher had had me practice until I was quick at it. He'd shown me also how to open the simple combination locks on suitcases; the method used by airport thieves.

I checked out of the hotel and found the way back to Frodsham, parking by the curb within sight of Topline Foods' wire-mesh gates.

As before, the gates were wide open and, as before, no one going in and out was challenged by the gatekeeper. No one, in fact, seemed to have urgent

business in either direction and there were far fewer cars in the central area
than on the day before. It wasn't until nearly eleven o'clock that the promised
film crews arrived in force.

When getting on for twenty assorted vans and private cars had come to a
ragged halt all over the place, disgorging film cameras (Intramind Imaging),
a television camera (local station) and dozens of people looking purposeful
with heavy equipment and chest-hugged clipboards, I got out of my car and
put on the ill-fitting brown overalls, complete with identity badge. Into the
trunk I locked my bag and also the mobile phone, first taking the SIM card
out of it and stowing it in my belt. "Get into the habit of removing the SIM
card," my supplier had advised. "Then if someone steals your phone, too bad,
they won't be able to use it."

"Great," I'd said.

I started the car, drove unhesitatingly through the gates, steered a course
around the assorted vans and stopped just beyond them, nearest to the unloading bays. Saturday or not, a few other brown overall hands were busy on
the rollers and the shelf escalator, and I simply walked straight in past them,
saying "Morning" as if I belonged.

They didn't answer, didn't look up, took me for granted.

Inside, I walked up the stairs I'd come down with Willy Parrott and, when
I reached the right level, ambled along the gallery until I came to his office.

The sliding glass door was closed and locked and there was no one inside.

The paddles were silent in the vats. None of the day before's hum and activity remained, and almost none of the smells. Instead, there were cameras
being positioned below, with Owen Yorkshire himself directing the director,
his authoritative voice telling the experts their job.

He was too busy to look up. I went on along the gallery, coming to the
fire door up the flight of metal stairs. The fire doors were locked at night,
Willy had said. By day, they were open. Thankful, I reached in the end the
plush carpet of the offices.

There was a bunch of three media people in there, measuring angles and
moving potted plants. Office work, I gathered, was due for immortality on
Monday. Cursing internally at their presence, I walked on towards the elevator, passing the open door of Customer Relations. No Marsha Rowse.

To the right of the elevator there was a door announcing Office Manager,
A. Dove, fastened with businesslike locks.

Looking back, I saw the measuring group taking their damned time. I
needed them out of there and they infuriatingly dawdled.

I didn't like to hover. I returned to the elevator and, to fill in time, opened a nearby door which proved to enclose fire stairs, as I'd hoped.

Down a floor, and through the fire door there, I found an expanse of open space, unfurnished and undecorated, the same in area as the office suite above. Up two stories, above the offices, there was similar quiet, undivided, clean-swept space. Owen Yorkshire had already built for expansion, I gathered.

Cautiously, I went on upward to the fifth floor, lair of the boss.

Trusting that he was still down among the vats, I opened the fire door enough to put my head through.

More camera people moved around. Veritable banks of potted plants blazed red and gold. To the left, open, opulently gleaming double doors led into an entertaining and boardroom area impressive enough for a major in-dustry of self-importance. On the right, more double doors led to Yorkshire's own new office; not, from what I could see, a place of paperwork. Polished wood gleamed. Plants galore. A tray of bottles and glasses.

I retreated down the unvarnished nitty-gritty fire stairs until I was back on the working-office floor, standing there indecisively, wondering if the mea-surers still barred my purpose.

I heard voices, growing louder and stopping on the other side of the door. I was prepared to go into a busy-employee routine, but it appeared they pre-ferred the elevator to the stairs. The lifting machinery whirred on the other side of the stairwell, the voices moved into the elevator and diminished to zero. I couldn't tell whether they'd gone up or down, and I was concerned only that they'd *all* gone and not left one behind.

There was no point in waiting. I opened the fire door, stepped onto the carpet and right towards Mrs. Dove's domain.

I had the whole office floor to myself.

Great.

Mrs. Dove's door was locked twice: an old-looking mortise and a new knob with a keyhole in the center. These were locks I liked. There could be no nasty surprises like bolts or chains or wedges on the inside: also the emphatic statement of two locks probably meant that there were things of worth to guard.

The mortise lock took a whole minute, with the ghost of my old master breathing disapprovingly down my neck. The modern lock took twenty sec-onds of delicate probing. One had to "feel" one's way through. False fingers for that, as for much else, were useless.

Once inside Mrs. Dove's office, I spent time relocking the door so that anyone outside trying it for security would find it as it should be. If anyone came in with keys, I would have warning enough to hide.

Mrs. Dove's cote was large and comfortable, with a wide desk, several of the Scandinavian-design armchairs and grainy blow-up black and white photographs of racing horses around the walls. Along one side there were the routine office machines—fax, copier, and large printout calculator, and, on the desk, a computer, shrouded for the weekend in a fitted cover. There were multiple filing cabinets and a tall white-painted and—as I discovered—locked cupboard.

Mrs. Dove had a window with louvered blinds and a distant view of the Mersey. Mrs. Dove's office was managing director stuff.

I had only a vague idea of what I was looking for. The audited accounts I'd seen in Companies House seemed not to match the actual state of affairs at Frodsham. The audit did, of course, refer to a year gone by, to the first with Owen Yorkshire in charge, but the fragile bottom-line profit, as shown, would not suggest or justify expensive publicity campaigns or televised receptions for the notables of Liverpool.

The old French adage "look for the lady" was a century out of date, my old teacher had said. In modern times it should be "look for the money," and shortly before he died, he had amended that to "follow the paper." Shady or doubtful transactions, he said, always left a paper trail. Even in the age of computers, he'd insisted that paper showed the way; and over and over again I'd proved him right.

The paper in Mrs. Dove's office was all tidied away in the many filing cabinets, which were locked.

Most filing cabinets, like these, locked all drawers simultaneously with a notched vertical rod out of sight within the right-hand front corner, operated by a single key at the top. Turning the key raised the rod, allowing all the drawers to open. I wasn't bad at opening filing cabinets.

The trouble was that Topline Foods had little to hide, or at least not at first sight. Pounds of paper referred to orders and invoices for incoming supplies; pounds more to sales, pounds more to the expenses of running an industry, from insurance to wages, to electricity to general maintenance.

The filing cabinets took too long and were a waste of time. What they offered was the entirely respectable basis of next year's audit.

I locked them all again and, after investigating the desk drawers themselves, which held only stationery, took the cover off the computer and switched it on, pressing the buttons for List Files, and Enter. Scrolls of file names appeared and I tried one at random: "Aintree."

Onto the screen came details of the lunch given the day before the Grand National, the guest list, the menu, a summary of the speeches and a list of the coverage given to the occasion in the press.

Nothing I could find seemed any more secret. I switched it off, replaced the cover and turned my lock pickers to the tall white cupboard.

The feeling of time running out, however irrational, shortened my breath and made me hurry. I always envied the supersleuths in films who put their hands on the right papers in the first ten seconds and, this time, I didn't know if the right paper even existed.

It turned out to be primarily not a paper but a second computer.

Inside the white cupboard, inside a drop-down desk arrangement in there, I came across a second keyboard and a second screen. I switched the computer on and nothing happened, which wasn't astounding as I found an electric lead lying alongside, disconnected. I plugged it into the computer and tried again, and with a grumble or two the machine became ready for business.

I pressed List Files again, and this time found myself looking not at individual subjects, but at Directories, each of which contained file names such as "Formula A."

What I had come across were the more private records, the electronic files, some very secret, some not.

in quick succession I highlighted the "Directories" and brought them to the screen until one baldly listed "Quint": but no amount of button pressing got me any further.

Think.

The reason I couldn't get the Quint information onto the screen must be because it wasn't in the computer.

OK? OK. So where was it?

On the shelf above the computer stood a row of box files, numbered 1 to 9, but not one labeled Quint.

I lifted down number 1 and looked inside. There were several letters filed in there, also a blue computer floppy disk in a clear cover. According to the letters, box file number 1 referred to loans made to Topline Foods, loans not repaid on the due date. There was also a mention of "sweeteners" and "quid pro quos." I fed the floppy disk into the drive slot in the computer body and got no further than a single, unhelpful word on the screen: PASSWORD?

Password? Heaven knew. I looked into the box files one by one and came to Quint in number 6. There were three floppies in there, not one.

I fed in the first.

PASSWORD?

Second and third disks—PASSWORD?

Bugger, I thought.

Searching for anything helpful, I lifted down a heavy white cardboard box, like a double-height shoebox, that lined the rest of the box-file shelf. In there was a row of big black high-impact plastic protective coverings. I picked out one and unlatched its fastenings, and found inside it a videotape, but a tape of double the ordinary width. A label on the tape said Broadcast Quality Videotape. Underneath that was a single word, Betacam. Under that was the legend "Quint Series. 15 × 30 secs."

I closed the thick black case and tried another one. Same thing. Quint series. 15 × 30 secs. All of the cases held the same.

These double-size tapes needed a special tape player not available in Mrs. Dove's office. To see what was on these expensive tapes meant taking one with me.

I could, of course, simply put one of them inside my tracksuit jacket and walk out with it. I could take all the "password" disks. If I did I was (a) stealing, (b) in danger of being found carrying the goods, and (c) making it impossible for any information they held to be used in any later legal inquiry. I would steal the information itself, if I could, but not the software.

Think.

As I'd told Charles at Aynsford, I'd had to learn a good deal about computers just to keep a grip on the accelerating world, but the future became the present so fast that I could never get ahead.

Someone tried to open the door.

There was no time to restore the room to normal. I could only speed across the carpet and stand where I would be hidden by the door when it swung inward. Plan B meant simply running—and I was wearing running shoes.

The knob turned again and rattled, but nothing else happened. Whoever was outside had presumably been either keyless or reassured: in either case it played havoc with my breathing.

Oddly, the pumping adrenaline brought me my computer answer, which was, if I couldn't bring the contents of a floppy disk to the screen, I could transfer it whole to another computer, one that would give me all the time I needed to crack the password, or to get help from people who could.

Alongside the unconnected electric cable there had been a telephone cable, also unattached. I snapped it into the telephone socket on the computer, thereby connecting Mrs. Dove's modem to the world-wide Internet.

It needed a false start or two while I desperately tried to remember half-learned techniques, but finally I was rewarded by the screen prompting: "Enter telephone number."

I tapped in my own home number in the apartment in Pont Square, and pressed Enter and the screen announced nonchalantly "Dialing in progress," then "Call accepted," then "Transfer," and finally "Transfer complete."

Whatever was on the first guarded "Quint" disk was now in my own computer in London. I transferred the other two "Quint" floppies in the same way, and then the disk from box-file number 1, and for good measure another from box 3, identified as "Tilepit."

There was no way that I knew of transferring the Betacam tapes. Regretfully I left them alone. I looked through the paper pages in the "Quint" box and made a photocopy of one page—a list of unusual racecourses—folding it and hiding it within the zipped pocket of my belt.

Finally I disconnected the electric and telephone cables again, closed the computer compartment, checked that the box files and Betacam tapes were as they should be, relocked the white cupboard, then unlocked and gently opened the door to the passage.

Silence.

Breathing out with relief, I relocked Mrs. Dove's door and walked along through the row of cubby-hole offices and came to the first setback: the fire door leading to brown-overalls territory was not merely locked but had a red light shining above it.

Shining red lights often meant alarm systems switched on with depressingly loud sirens ready to screech.

I'd been too long in Mrs. Dove's office. I retreated towards her door again and went down the fire stairs beside the elevator, emerging into the ground-floor entrance hall with its glass doors to the parking area beyond.

One step into the lobby proved to be one step too far. Something hit my head rather hard, and one of the beefy bodyguards in blue flung a sort of strap around my body and effectively pinned my upper arms to my sides.

I plunged about a bit and got another crack on the head, which left me unable to help myself and barely able to think. I was aware of being in the elevator, but wasn't quite sure how I'd got there. I was aware of having my ankles strapped together and of being dragged ignominiously over some carpet and dropped in a chair.

Regulation Scandinavian chair with wooden arms, like all the others.

"Tie him up," a voice said, and a third strap tightened across my chest, so that when the temporary mist cleared I woke to a state of near physical immobility and a mind full of curses.

The voice belonged to Owen Yorkshire. He said, "Right. Good. Well done. Leave the wrench on the desk. Go back downstairs and don't let anyone up here."

"Yes, sir."

"Wait," Yorkshire commanded, sounding uncertain. "Are you sure you've got the right man?"

"Yes, sir. He's wearing the identity badge we issued to him yesterday. He was supposed to return it when he left, but he didn't."

"All right Thanks. Off you go."

The door closed behind the bodyguards and Owen Yorkshire plucked the identity badge from my overalls, read the name and flung it down on his desk.

We were in his fifth-floor office. The chair I sat in was surrounded by carpet. Marooned on a desert island, feeling dim and stupid.

The man-to-man, all-pals-together act was in abeyance. The Owen Yorkshire confronting me was very angry, disbelieving and, I would have said, *frightened.*

"What are you doing here?" he demanded, bellowing.

His voice echoed and reverberated in the quiet room. His big body loomed over me, his big head close to mine. All his features, I thought, were slightly oversized: big nose, big eyes, wide forehead, large flat cheeks, square jaw, big mouth. The collar-length black wavy hair with its gray-touched wings seemed to vibrate with vigor. I would have put his age at forty; maybe a year or two younger.

"Answer," he yelled. "What are you doing here?"

I didn't reply. He snatched up from his desk a heavy fifteen-inch-long silvery wrench and made as if to hit my head with it. If that was what his boys-in-blue had used on me, and I gathered it was, then connecting it again with my skull was unlikely to produce any answer at all. The same thought seemed to occur to him, because he threw the wrench down disgustedly onto the desk again, where it bounced slightly under its own weight.

The straps around my chest and ankles were the sort of fawn close-woven webbing often used around suitcases to prevent them from bursting open. There was no elasticity in them, no stretch. Several more lay on the desk.

I felt a ridiculous desire to chatter, a tendency I'd noticed in the past in mild concussions after racing falls, and sometimes on waking up from anesthetics. I'd learned how to suppress the garrulous impulse, but it was still an effort, and in this case, essential.

Owen Yorkshire was wearing man-to-man togs; that is to say, no jacket, a man-made-fiber shirt (almost white with vertical stripes made of interlock-

ing beige-colored horseshoes), no tie, several buttons undone, unmissable view
of manly hairy chest, gold chain and medallion.

I concentrated on the horseshoe stripes. If I could count the number of
horseshoes from shoulder to waist I would not have any thoughts that might
dribble out incautiously. The boss was talking. I blanked him out and
counted horseshoes and managed to say nothing.

He went abruptly out of the room, leaving me sitting there looking foolish.
When he returned he brought two people with him: they had been along in the
reception area, it seemed, working out table placements for Monday's lunch.

They were a woman and a man; Mrs. Dove and a stranger. Both exclaimed
in surprise at the sight of my trussed self. I shrank into the chair and looked
mostly at their waists.

"Do you know who this is?" Yorkshire demanded of them furiously.

The man shook his head, mystified. Mrs. Dove, frowning, said to me,
"Weren't you here yesterday? Something about a farmer?"

"This," Yorkshire said with scorn, "is Sid Halley."

The man's face stiffened, his mouth forming an O.

"*This*, Verney," Yorkshire went on with biting sarcasm "is the feeble creature you've spent months thundering on about. This! And Ellis said he was
dangerous! Just look at him! All those big guns to frighten a mouse."

Verney *Tilepit*. I'd looked him up in *Burke's Peerage*. Verney Tilepit, Third
Baron, aged forty-two, a director of Topline Foods, proprietor—by inheritance—of *The Pump*.

Verney Tilepit's grandfather, created a baron for devoted allegiance to the
then prime minister, had been one of the old roistering, powerful opinion
makers who'd had governments dancing to their tune. The first Verney
Tilepit had put his shoulder to history and given it a shove. The third had
surfaced after years of quiescence, primarily, it seemed, to discredit a minor
investigator. Policy! His bewildered grandfather would have been speechless.

He was fairly tall, as India had said, and he had brown hair. The flicking
glance I gave him took in also a large expanse of face with small features
bunched in the middle: small nose, small mouth, small sandy mustache,
small eyes behind large, light-framed glasses. Nothing about him seemed
physically threatening. Perhaps I felt the same disappointment in my adver-
sary as he plainly did about me.

"How do you know he's Sid Halley?" Mrs. Dove asked.

Owen Yorkshire said disgustedly, "One of the TV crew knew him. He
swore there was no mistake. He'd filmed him often. He *knows* him."

Bugger, I thought.

Mrs. Dove pulled up the long left sleeve of my brown overalls, and looked at my left hand. "Yes. It must be Sid Halley. Not much of a champion now, is he?"

Owen Yorkshire picked up the telephone, pressed numbers, waited and forcefully spoke.

"Get over here quickly," he said. "We have a crisis. Come to my new office." He listened briefly. "No," he said, "just get over here." He slammed down the receiver and stared at me balefully. "What the sod are you doing here?"

The almost overwhelming urge to tell him got as far as my tongue and was over-ridden only by clamped-shut teeth. One could understand why people confessed. The itch to unburden outweighed the certainty of retribution.

"Answer," yelled Yorkshire. He picked up the wrench again. "Answer, you little cuss."

I did manage an answer of sorts.

I spoke to Verney Tilepit directly in a weak, mock-respectful tone. "I came to see you . . . sir."

"My lord," Yorkshire told me. "Call him 'my lord.'"

"My lord," I said.

Tilepit said, "What for?" and "What made you think I would be here?"

"Someone told me you were a director of Topline Foods, my lord, so I came here to ask you to stop and I don't know why I've been dragged up here and tied up like this." The last twenty words just dribbled out. Be *careful*, I thought. *Shut up.*

"To stop *what*?" Tilepit demanded.

"To stop your paper telling lies about me." Better.

Tilepit didn't know how to answer such naïveté. Yorkshire properly considered it barely credible. He spoke to Mrs. Dove, who was dressed for Saturday morning, not in office black and white, but in bright red with gold buttons.

"Go down and make sure he hasn't been in your office."

"I locked it when I left last night, Owen."

Mrs. Dove's manner towards her boss was interestingly like Willy Parrott's. All-equals-together; up to a point.

"Go and look," he said. "And check that cupboard."

"No one's opened that cupboard since you moved offices up here this week. And you have the only key."

"Go and check anyway," he said.

She had no difficulty with obeying him. I remembered Marsha Rowse's ingenuous statement—"Mrs. Dove says never to make Mr. Yorkshire angry."

Mrs. Dove, self-contained, confident, was taking her own advice. She was not, I saw, in love with the man, nor was she truly afraid of him. His temper, I would have thought, was to her more of a nuisance than life—or even job—threatening.

As things stood, or rather as I sat, I saw the wisdom of following Mrs. Dove's example for as long as I could.

She was gone a fair time, during which I worried more and more anxiously that I'd left something slightly out of place in that office, that she would know by some sixth sense that someone had been in there, that I'd left some odor in the air despite never using aftershave, that I'd closed the filing cabinets incorrectly, that I'd left visible fingerprints on a shiny surface, that I'd done *anything* that she knew she hadn't.

I breathed slowly, trying not to sweat.

When she finally came back she said, "The TV crews are leaving. Everything's ready for Monday. The florists are bringing the Lady Mayoress's bouquet at ten o'clock. The red-carpet people are downstairs now measuring the lobby. And, oh, the man from Intramind Imaging says they want a check."

"What about the office?"

"The office? Oh, the office is all right." She was unconcerned. "It was all locked. Just as I left it."

"And the cupboard?" Yorkshire insisted.

"Locked." She thought he was over-reacting. I was concerned only to show no relief.

"What are you going to do with *him*?" she asked, indicating me. "You can't keep him here, can you? The TV crew downstairs were talking about him being here. They want to interview him. What shall I say?"

Yorkshire with black humor said, "Tell them he's all tied up."

She wasn't amused. She said, "I'll say he went out the back way. And I'll be off, too. I'll be here by eight, Monday morning." She looked at me calmly and spoke to Yorkshire. "Let him go," she said unemotionally. "What harm can he do? He's pathetic."

Yorkshire, undecided, said, "Pathetic? Why pathetic?"

She paused composedly half-way through the door, and dropped a pearl beyond price.

"It says so in *The Pump*."

NEITHER OF THESE two men, I thought, listening to them, was a full-blown criminal. Not yet. Yorkshire was too near the brink.

He still held the heavy adjustable wrench, slapping its head occasionally against his palm, as if it helped his thoughts.

"Please untie me," I said. At least I found the fatal loquaciousness had abated. I no longer wanted to gabble, but just to talk my way out.

Tilepit himself might have done it. He clearly was unused to—and disturbed by—even this level of violence. His power base was his grandfather's name. His muscle was his hire-and-fire clout. There were only so many top editorships in the British press, and George Godbar, editor of *The Pump*, wasn't going to lose his hide to save mine. Matters of principle were all too often an unaffordable luxury, and I didn't believe that in George Godbar's place, or even in Kevin Mills's or India's, I would have done differently.

Yorkshire said, "We wait."

He opened a drawer in his desk and drew out what looked bizarrely like a jar of pickles. Dumping the wrench temporarily, he unscrewed the lid, put the jar on the desk, pulled out a green finger and bit it, crunching it with large white teeth.

"Pickle?" he offered Tilepit.

The third baron averted his nose.

Yorkshire, shrugging, chewed uninhibitedly and went back to slapping his palm with the wrench.

"I'll be missed," I said mildly, "if you keep me much longer."

"Let him go," Tilepit said with a touch of impatience. "He's right, we can't keep him here indefinitely."

"We wait," Yorkshire said heavily, fishing out another pickle, and to the accompaniment of noisy munching, we waited.

I could smell the vinegar.

The door opened finally behind me and both Yorkshire and Tilepit looked welcoming and relieved.

I didn't. The newcomer, who came around in front of me blankly, was Ellis Quint.

Ellis, in open-necked white shirt; Ellis, handsome, macho, vibrating with showmanship; Ellis, the nation's darling, farcically accused. I hadn't seen him since the Ascot races, and none of his radiance had waned.

"What's *Halley* doing here?" he demanded, sounding alarmed. "What has he learned?"

"He was wandering about," Yorkshire said, pointing a pickle at me. "I had him brought up here. He can't have learned a thing."

Tilepit announced, "Halley says he came to ask me to stop *The Pump*'s campaign against him."

Ellis said positively, "He wouldn't have done that."

"Why not?" Yorkshire asked. "Look at him. He's a wimp."

"A *wimp*!"

Despite my precarious position I smiled involuntarily at the depth of incredulity in his voice. I even grinned at him sideways from below half-lowered eyelids, and saw the same private smile on his face: the acknowledgment of brotherhood, of secrecy, of shared esoteric experience, of cold winter afternoons, perils embraced, disappointments and injuries taken lightly, of indescribable triumphs. We had hugged each other standing in our stirrups, ecstatic after winning posts. We had trusted, bonded and twinned.

Whatever we were now, we had once been more than brothers. The past—our past—remained. The intense and mutual memories could not be erased.

The smiles died. Ellis said, "This *wimp* comes up on your inside and beats you in the last stride. This wimp could ruin us all if we neglect our inside rail. This wimp was champion jockey for five or six years and might have been still, and we'd be fools to forget it." He put his face close to mine. "Still the same old Sid, aren't you? Cunning. Nerveless. Win at all costs."

There was nothing to say.

Yorkshire bit into a pickle. "What do we do with him, then?"

"First we find out why he's here."

Tilepit said, "He came to get *The Pump* to stop—"

"Balls," Ellis interrupted. "He's lying."

"How can you tell?" Tilepit protested.

"I know him." He said it with authority, and it was true.

"What, then?" Yorkshire asked.

Ellis said to me, "You'll not get me into court, Sid. Not Monday. Not ever. You haven't been able to break my Shropshire alibi, and my lawyers say that without that the prosecution won't have a chance. They'll withdraw the charge. Understand? I know you *do* understand. You'll have destroyed your own reputation, not mine. What's more, my father's going to kill you."

Yorkshire and Tilepit showed, respectively, pleasure and shock.

"Before Monday?" I asked.

The flippancy fell like lead. Ellis strode around behind me and yanked back the right front of my brown overalls, and the tracksuit beneath. He tore a couple of buttons off my shirt, pulling that back after, then he pressed down strongly with his fingers.

"Gordon says he broke your collarbone," he said.

"Well, he didn't."

Ellis would see the remains of bruising and he could feel the bumps of calluses formed by earlier breaks, but it was obvious to him that his father had been wrong.

"Gordon will kill you," he repeated. "Don't you care?"

Another unanswerable question.

It seemed to me as if the cruel hidden side of Ellis suddenly took over, banishing the friend and becoming the threatened star who had everything to lose. He roughly threw my clothes together and continued around behind me until he stood on my left side.

"You won't defeat me," he said. "You've cost me half a million. You've cost me lawyers. You've cost me *sleep*."

He might insist that I couldn't defeat him, but we both knew I would in the end, if I tried, because he was guilty.

"You'll pay for it," he said.

He put his hands on the hard shell of my left forearm and raised it until my elbow formed a right angle. The tight strap around my upper arms and chest prevented me from doing anything to stop him. Whatever strength that remained in my upper left arm (and it was, in fact, quite a lot) was held in uselessness by that strap.

Ellis peeled back the brown sleeve, and the blue one underneath. He tore open my shirt cuff and pulled that sleeve back also. He looked at the plastic skin underneath.

"I know something about that arm," he said. "I got a brochure on purpose. That skin is a sort of glove, and it comes off."

He felt up my arm until, by the elbow, he came to the top of the glove. He rolled it down as far as the wrist and then, with concentration, pulled it off finger by finger, exposing the mechanics in all their detail.

The close-fitting textured glove gave the hand an appearance of life, with knuckles, veins and shapes like fingernails. The works inside were gears, springs and wiring. The bared forearm was bright pink, hard and shiny.

Ellis smiled.

He put his own strong right hand on my electrical left and pressed and twisted with knowledge and then, when the works clicked free, unscrewed the hand in several turns until it came right off.

Ellis looked into my eyes as at a feast "Well?" he said.

"You *shit*."

He smiled. He opened his fingers and let the unscrewed hand fall onto the carpet.

CHAPTER 13

TILEPIT LOOKED SHOCKED enough to vomit, but not Yorkshire: in fact, he laughed.

Ellis said to him sharply, "This man is not funny. Everything that has gone wrong is because of *him*, and don't you forget it. It's this Sid Halley that's going to ruin you, and if you think he doesn't care about what I've just done"—he put his toe against the fallen hand and moved it a few inches—"if you think it's something to laugh at, I'll tell you that for *him* it's almost unbearable . . . but *not* unbearable, is it, Sid?" He turned to ask me, and told Yorkshire at the same time, "No one yet has invented anything you've found actually unbearable, have they, Sid?"

I didn't answer.

Yorkshire protested, "But he's only—"

"Don't say *only*," Ellis interrupted, his voice hard and loud. "Don't you understand it yet? What do you think he's doing here? How did he get here? What does he know? He's not going to tell you. His nickname's 'Tungsten Carbide'—that's the hardest of all metals and it saws through steel. I *know* him. I've almost loved him. You have no idea what you're dealing with, and we've got to decide what to do with him. How many people know he's here?"

"My bodyguards," Yorkshire said. "They brought him up."

It was Lord Tilepit who gave him the real bad news. "It was a TV crew who told Owen that Sid Halley was in the building."

"*A TV crew!*"

"They wanted to interview him. Mrs. Dove said she would tell them he'd gone."

"*Mrs. Dove!*"

If Ellis had met Mrs. Dove he would know, as I did, that she wouldn't lie for Yorkshire. Mrs. Dove had seen me, and she would say so.

Ellis asked furiously, "Did Mrs. Dove see him tied in that chair?"

"Yes," Tilepit said faintly.

"You *stupid* . . ." Words failed Ellis, but for only a few short seconds. "Then," he said flatly, "you can't kill him here."

"*Kill* him?" Tilepit couldn't believe what he'd heard. His whole large face blushed pink. "I'm not . . . are you talking about *murder*?"

"Oh yes, my lord," I said dryly, "they are. They're thinking of putting Your Lordship behind bars as an accessory. You'll love it in the slammer."

I'd meant only to get Tilepit to see the enormity of what Ellis was proposing, but in doing so I'd made the mistake of unleashing Yorkshire's rage.

He took two paces and kicked my unscrewed hand with such force that it flew across the room and crashed against the wall. Then he realized the wrench was still in his hand and swung it at my head.

I saw the blow coming but couldn't get my head back far enough to avoid it altogether. The wrench's heavy screw connected with my moving cheekbone and tore the skin, but didn't this time knock me silly.

In Owen Yorkshire, the half-slipping brakes came wholly off. Perhaps the very sight of me, left-handless and bleeding and unable to retaliate, was all it took. He raised his arm and the wrench again, and I saw the spite in his face and the implacably murderous intention and I thought of nothing much at all, which afterwards seemed odd.

It was Ellis who stopped him. Ellis caught the descending arm and yanked Owen Yorkshire around sideways, so that although the heavy weapon swept on downwards, it missed me altogether.

"You're *brainless*," Ellis shouted. "I said *not in here*. You're a raving lunatic. Too many people know he came here. Do you want to splatter his blood and brains all over your new carpet? You might as well go and shout from the rooftops. Get a grip on that frigging temper and find a tissue."

"A what?"

"Something to stop him bleeding. Are you terminally insane? When he doesn't turn up wherever he's expected, you're going to get the police in here looking for him. TV crew! Mrs. Dove! The whole frigging county! You get one drop of his blood on anything in here, you're looking at twenty-five years."

Yorkshire, bewildered by Ellis's attack and turning sullen, said there weren't any tissues. Verney Tilepit tentatively produced a handkerchief; white, clean and embroidered with a coronet. Ellis snatched it from him and slapped it on my cheek, and I wondered if ever, in any circumstances, I could, to save myself, deliberately kill *him*, and didn't think so.

Ellis took the handkerchief away briefly, looked at the scarlet staining the white, and put it back, pressing.

Yorkshire strode about, waving the wrench as if jerked by strings. Tilepit looked extremely unhappy. I considered my probable future with gloom and Ellis, taking the handkerchief away again and watching my cheek critically, declared that the worst of the bleeding had stopped.

He gave the handkerchief back to Tilepit, who put it squeamishly in his pocket, and he snatched the wrench away from Yorkshire and told him to cool down and *plan.*

Planning took them both out of the office, the door closing behind them. Verney Tilepit didn't in the least appreciate being left alone with me and went to look out of the window, to look anywhere except at me.

"Untie me," I said with force.

No chance. He didn't even show he'd heard.

I asked, "How did you get yourself into this mess?"

No answer.

I tried again. I said, "If I walk out of here free, I'll forget I ever saw you."

He turned around, but he had his back to the light and I couldn't see his eyes clearly behind the spectacles.

"You really are in deep trouble," I said.

"Nothing will happen."

I wished I believed him. I said, "It must have seemed pretty harmless to you, just to use your paper to ridicule someone week after week. What did Yorkshire tell you? To save Ellis at all costs. Well, it *is* going to cost you."

"You don't understand. Ellis is blameless."

"I understand that you're up to your noble neck in shit."

"I can't do anything." He was worried, unhappy and congenitally helpless.

"Untie me," I said again, with urgency.

"It wouldn't help. I couldn't get you out."

"Untie me," I said. "I'll do the rest."

He dithered. If he had been capable of reasoned decisions he wouldn't have let himself be used by Yorkshire, but he wasn't the first or last rich man to stumble blindly into a quagmire. He couldn't make up his mind to attempt saving himself by letting me free and, inevitably, the opportunity passed.

Ellis and Yorkshire came back, and neither of them would meet my eyes. Bad sign.

Ellis, looking at his watch, said, "We wait."

"What for?" Tilepit asked uncertainly.

Yorkshire answered, to Ellis's irritation, "The TV people are on the point of leaving. Everyone will be gone in fifteen minutes."

Tilepit looked at me, his anxieties showing plainly. "Let Halley go," he begged.

Ellis said comfortingly, "Sure, in a while."

Yorkshire smiled. His anger was preferable, on the whole.

Verney Tilepit wanted desperately to be reassured, but even he could see that if freeing me was the intention, why did we have to wait?

Ellis still held the wrench. He wouldn't get it wrong, I thought. He wouldn't spill my blood. I would probably not know much about it. I might not consciously learn the reciprocal answer to my self-searching question: Could *he* personally kill *me*, to save himself? How deep did friendship go? Did it ever have absolute taboos? Had I already, by accusing him of evil, melted his innermost restraints? He wanted to get even. He would wound me any way he could. But *kill* . . . I didn't know.

He walked around behind me.

Time, in a way, stood still. It was a moment in which to plead, but I couldn't. The decision, whatever I said, would be *his*.

He came eventually around to my right-hand side and murmured, "Tungsten," under his breath.

Water, I thought, I had water in my veins.

He reached down suddenly and clamped his hand around my right wrist, pulling fiercely upward.

I jerked my wrist out of his grasp and without warning he bashed the wrench across my knuckles. In the moment of utter numbness that resulted he slid the open jaws of the wrench onto my wrist and tightened the screw. Tightened it further, until the jaws grasped immovably, until they squeezed the upper and lower sides of my wrist together, compressing blood vessels, nerves and ligaments, bearing down on the bones inside.

The wrench was heavy. He balanced its handle on the arm of the chair I was sitting in and held it steady so that my wrist was up at the same level. He had two strong hands. He persevered with the screw.

I said, "Ellis," in protest, not from anger or even fear, but in disbelief that he could do what he was doing: in a lament for the old Ellis, in a sort of passionate sorrow.

For the few seconds that he looked into my face, his expression was flooded with awareness . . . and shame. Then the feelings passed, and he returned in deep concentration to an atrocious pleasure.

It was extraordinary. He seemed to go into a kind of trance, as if the office and Yorkshire and Tilepit didn't exist, as if there were only one reality, which was the clench of forged steel jaws on a wrist and the extent to which he could intensify it.

I thought: if the wrench had been lopping shears, if its jaws had been knives instead of flat steel, the whole devastating nightmare would have come true. I shut my mind to it: made it cold. Sweated, all the same.

I thought: what I see in his face is the full-blown addiction; not the cruel satisfaction he could get from unscrewing a false hand, but the sinful fulfillment of cutting off a live hoof.

I glanced very briefly at Yorkshire and Tilepit and saw their frozen, bottomless astonishment, and I realized that until that moment of revelation they hadn't wholly believed in Ellis's guilt.

My wrist hurt. Somewhere up my arm the ulna grumbled.

I said, *"Ellis"* sharply, to wake him up.

He got the screw to tighten another notch.

I yelled at him, *"Ellis,"* and again, *"Ellis."*

He straightened, looking vaguely down at fifteen inches of heavy stainless steel wrench incongruously sticking out sideways from its task. He tied it to the arm of the chair with another strap from the desk and went over to the window, not speaking, but not rational, either.

I tried to dislodge myself from the wrench but my hand was too numb and the grip too tight. I found it difficult to think. My hand was pale blue and gray. Thought was a crushed wrist and an abysmal shattering fear that if the damage went on too long, it would be permanent. Hands could be lost.

Both hands . . . Oh, God. Oh, *God.*

"Ellis," I said yet again, but in a lower voice this time: a plea for him to return to the old self, that was there all the time, somewhere.

I waited. Acute discomfort and the terrible anxiety continued. Ellis's thoughts seemed far out in space. Tilepit cleared his throat in embarrassment and Yorkshire, as if in unconscious humor, crunched a pickle.

Minutes passed.

I said. "Ellis . . ."

I closed my eyes. Opened them again. More or less prayed.

Time and nightmare fused. One became the other. The future was a void.

Elba left the window and crossed with bouncing steps to the chair where I sat. He looked into my face and enjoyed what he could undoubtedly see there. Then he unscrewed and untied the wrench with violent jerks and dropped the abominable ratchet from a height onto the desk.

No one said anything. Ellis seemed euphoric, high, full of good spirits, striding around the room as if unable to contain his exhilaration.

I got stabbing pins and needles in my fingers, and thanked the fates for it. My hand felt dreadful but turned slowly yellowish pink.

Thought came back from outer space and lodged again earthily in my brain.

Ellis, coming down very slightly, looked at his watch. He plucked from the desk the cosmetic glove from my false arm, came to my right side, shoved the glove inside my shirt against my chest and, with a theatrical flourish, zipped up the front of my blue tracksuit to keep his gift from falling out.

He looked at his watch again. Then he went across the room, picked up the unscrewed hand, returned to my side and slapped the dead mechanism into my living palm. There was a powerful impression all around that he was busy making sure no trace of Sid Halley remained in the room.

He went around behind me and undid the strap fastening me into the chair. Then he undid the second strap that held my upper arms against my body.

"Screw the hand back on," he instructed.

Perhaps because they had bent from being kicked around, or perhaps because my real hand was eighty percent useless, the screw threads wouldn't mesh smoothly, and after three half turns they stuck. The hand looked reattached, but wouldn't work.

"Stand up," Ellis said.

I stood, swaying, my ankles still tied together.

"You're letting him go," Tilepit exclaimed, with grateful relief.

"Of course," Ellis said.

Yorkshire was smiling.

"Put your hands behind your back," Ellis told me.

I did so, and he strapped my wrists tight together.

Last, he undid my ankles.

"This way." He pulled me by the arm over to the door and through into the passage. I walked like an automaton.

Looking back, I saw Yorkshire put his hand on the telephone. Beyond him, Tilepit was happy with foolish faith.

Ellis pressed the call button for the elevator, and the door opened immediately.

"Get in," he said.

I looked briefly at his now unsmiling face. Expressionless. That made two of us, I thought, two of us thinking the same thing and not saying it.

I stepped into the elevator and he leaned in quickly and pressed the button for the ground floor, then jumped back. The door closed between us. The elevator began its short journey down.

To tie together the wrists of a man who could unscrew one of them was an exercise in futility. All the same, the crossed threads and my fumbling fingers gave me trouble and some severe moments of panic before the hand slipped free. The elevator had already reached its destination by the time I'd shed the tying strap, leaving no chance to emerge from the opening door with everything anywhere near normal.

I put the mechanical hand deep into my right-hand tracksuit trousers pocket. Surreal, I grimly thought. The long sleeve of brown overall covered the void where it belonged.

Ellis had given me a chance. Not much of one, probably, but at least I did have the answer to my question, which was no, he wouldn't personally kill me. Yorkshire definitely would.

The two blue-clad bodyguards were missing from the lobby.

The telephone on the desk was ringing, but the bodyguards were outside, busily positioning a Topline Foods van. One guard was descending from the driver's seat. The other was opening the rear doors.

A van, I understood, for abduction. For a journey to an unmarked grave. A bog job, the Irish called it. How much, I wondered, were they being paid?

Ellis's timing had given me thirty seconds. He'd sent me down too soon. In the lobby I had no future. Out in the open air . . . some.

Taking a couple of deep breaths, I shot out through the doors as fast as I could, and sprinted—and I ran not to the right, towards my own car, but veered left around the van towards the open gates.

There was a shout from one of the blue figures, a yell from the second, and I thought for a moment that I could avoid them, but to my dismay the gate-keeper himself came to unwelcome life, emerging from his kiosk and barring my exit. Big man in another blue uniform, overconfident.

I ran straight at him. He stood solidly, legs apart, his weight evenly balanced. He wasn't prepared for or expecting my left foot to knock aside the inside of his knee or for my back to bend and curl like a cannonball into his stomach: he fell over backwards and I was on my way before he struggled to his knees. The other two, though, had gained ground.

The sort of judo Chico had taught me was in part the stylized advances and throws of a regulated sport and in part an individual style for a one-handed victim. For a start, I never wore, in my private sessions with him, the loose white judogi uniform. I never fought in bare feet but always in ordinary shoes or sneakers. The judo I'd learned was how to save my life, not how to earn a black belt.

Ordinary judo needed two hands. Myoelectric hands had a slow response time, a measurable pause between instruction and action. Chico and I had scrapped all grappling techniques for that hand and substituted clubbing; and I used all his lessons at Frodsham as if they were as familiar as walking.

We hadn't exactly envisaged no useful hands at all, but it was amazing what one could do if one wanted to live. It was the same as it had been in races: win now, pay later.

My opponents were straight musclemen with none of the subtlety of the Japanese understanding of lift and leverage and speed. Chico could throw me every time, but Yorkshire's watchdogs couldn't.

The names of the movements clicked like a litany in my brain—*shintai, randori, tai-sabaki.* Fighting literally to live, I stretched every technique I knew and adapted others, using falling feints that involved my twice lying on the ground and sticking a foot into a belly to fly its owner over my head. It ended with one blue uniform lying dazed on his back, one complaining I'd broken his nose, and one haring off to the office building with the bad news.

I stumbled out onto the road, feeling that if I went back for my car the two men I'd left on the ground would think of getting up again and closing the gates.

In one direction lay houses, so I staggered that way. Better cover. I needed cover before anyone chased me in the Topline Foods van.

The houses, when I reached them, were too regular, the gardens too tidy and small. I chose one house with no life showing, walked unsteadily up the garden path, kept on going, found myself in the back garden with another row of houses over the back fence.

The fence was too high to jump or vault, but there was an empty crate lying there, a gift from the gods.

No one came out of any of the houses to ask me what I thought I was doing. I emerged into the next street and began to think about where I was going and what I looked like.

Brown overalls. Yorkshire would be looking for brown overalls.

I took them off and dumped them in one of the houses' brown-looking beech hedges.

Taking off the overalls revealed the nonexistence of a left hand.

Damn it, I thought astringently. Things are never easy, so cope.

I put the pink exposed end of arm, with its bare electrical contacts, into my left-hand jacket pocket, and walked, not ran, up the street. I wanted to run, but hadn't the strength. Weak . . . Stamina a memory, a laugh.

There was a boy in the distance roller-blading, coming toward me and wearing not the ubiquitous baseball cap but a striped woolen hat. That would do, I thought. I fumbled some money out of the zip pocket in my belt and stood in his way.

He tried to avoid me, swerved, overbalanced and called me filthy names until his gaze fell on the money in my hand.

"Sell me your hat," I suggested.

"Yer wha?"

"Your hat," I said, "for the money."

"You've got blood on your face," he said.

He snatched the money and aimed to roller-blade away. I stuck out a foot and knocked him off his skates. He gave me a bitter look and a choice of swear words, but also the hat, sweeping it off and throwing it at me.

It was warm from his head and I put it on, hoping he didn't have lice. I wiped my face gingerly on my sleeve and slouched along towards the road with traffic that crossed the end of the residential street . . . and saw the Topline Foods van roll past.

Whatever they were looking for, it didn't seem to be a navy tracksuit with a striped woolen hat.

Plan B—run away. OK.

Plan C—where to?

I reached the end of the houses and turned left into what might once have been a shopping street, but which now seemed to offer only realtors, building societies and banks. Marooned in this unhelpful landscape were only two possible refuges: a betting shop and a place selling ice cream.

I chose the ice cream. I was barely through the door when outside the window my own Mercedes went past.

Ellis was driving.

I still had its keys in my pocket. Jonathan, it seemed, wasn't alone in his car-stealing skill.

"What do you want?" a female voice said behind me.

She was asking about ice cream: a thin young woman, bored.

"Er . . . that one," I said, pointing at random.

"Cup or cone? Large or small?"

"Cone. Small." I felt disoriented, far from reality. I paid for the ice cream and licked it, and it tasted of almonds.

"You've cut your face," she said.

"I ran into a tree."

There were four or five tables with people sitting at them, mostly adolescent groups. I sat at a table away from the window and within ten minutes saw the Topline van pass twice more and my own car, once.

Tremors ran in my muscles. Fear, or over-exertion, or both.

There was a door marked Men's Room at the back of the shop. I went in there when I'd finished the ice cream and looked at my reflection in the small mirror over the sink.

The cut along my left cheekbone had congealed into a blackening line, thick and all too visible. Dampening a paper towel, I dabbed gently at the mess, trying to remove the clotted blood without starting new bleeding, but making only a partial improvement.

Locked in a cubicle, I had another try at screwing my wandering hand into place, and this time at length got it properly aligned and fastened, but it still wouldn't work. Wretchedly depressed, I fished out the long covering glove and with difficulty, because of no talcum powder and an enfeebled right hand, pulled that too into the semblance of reality.

Damn Ellis, I thought mordantly. He'd been right about some things being near to unbearable.

Never mind. Get on with it.

I emerged from the cubicle and tried my cheek again with another paper towel, making the cut paler, fading it into skin color.

Not too bad.

The face below the unfamiliar woolen hat looked strained. Hardly a surprise.

I went out through the ice cream shop and walked along the street. The Topline Foods van rolled past quite slowly, driven by one of the blue-clad guards, who was intently scanning the other side of the road. That bodyguard meant, I thought, that Yorkshire himself might be out looking for me in a car I couldn't recognize.

Perhaps all I had to do was go up to some sensible-looking motorist and say, "Excuse me, some people are trying to kill me. Please will you drive me to the police station?" And then, "Who are these people?" "The managing director of Topline Foods, and Ellis Quint." "Oh *yes*? And *you* are . . . ?"

I did go as far as asking someone the way to the police station—"Round there, straight on, turn left—about a mile"—and for want of anything better I started walking that way; but what I came to first was a bus shelter with several people standing in a line, waiting. I added myself to the patient half dozen and stood with my back to the road, and a woman with two children soon came up behind me, hiding me well.

Five long minutes later my Mercedes pulled up on the far side of the road with a white Rolls-Royce behind it. Ellis stepped out of my car and Yorkshire out of the Rolls. They conferred together, furiously stabbing the air, pointing up and down the street while I bent my head down to the children and prayed to remain unspotted.

The bus came while the cars were still there.

Four people got off. The waiting line, me included, surged on. I resisted the temptation to look out of the window until the bus was traveling again, and then saw with relief that the two men were still talking.

I had no idea where the bus was going.

Who cared? Distance was all I needed. I'd paid to go to the end of the line, wherever that was.

Peaceful Frodsham in Cheshire, sometime Saturday, people going shopping in the afternoon. I felt disconnected from that sort of life; and I didn't know what the time was, as the elastic metal bracelet watch I normally wore on my left wrist had come off in Yorkshire's office and was still there, I supposed.

The bus slowly filled at subsequent stops. Shopping baskets. Chatter. Where was I going?

The end of the line proved to be the railway depot in Runcorn, halfway to Liverpool, going north when I needed to go south.

I got off the bus and went to the depot. There was no Mercedes, no Rolls-Royce, no Topline Foods van in sight, which didn't mean they wouldn't think of buses and trains eventually. Runcorn railway depot didn't feel safe. There was a train to Liverpool due in four minutes, I learned, so I bought a ticket and caught it.

The feeling of unreality continued, also the familiar aversion to asking for help from the local police. They didn't approve of outside investigators. If I ever got into messes, besides, I considered it my own responsibility to get myself out. Norman Pictons were rare. In Liverpool, moreover, I was probably counted a local boy who'd been disloyal to his "roots."

At the Liverpool railway depot I read the well-displayed timetable for trains going south.

An express to London, I thought; then backtrack to Reading and get a taxi to Shelley Green, Archie Kirk's house.

No express for hours. What else, then?

The incredible words took a time to penetrate: Liverpool to Bournemouth, departing at 3:10 p.m. A slow train, meandering southwards across England, right down to the Channel, with many stops on the way . . . and one of the stops was *Reading*.

I sprinted, using the last shreds of strength. It was already, according to the big depot clock, ticking away at 3:07. Whistles were blowing when I stumbled into the last car in the long train. A guard helped thrust me in and closed the door. The wheels rolled. I had no ticket and little breath, but a marvelous feeling of escape. That feeling lasted only until the first of the many stops, which I discovered with horror to be *Runcorn*.

Square one: where I'd started. All fear came flooding back. I sat stiff and immobile, as if movement itself would give me away.

Nothing happened. The train quietly rolled onwards. Out on the platform a blue-clad Topline Foods security guard was speaking into a hand-held telephone and shaking his head.

CREWE, STAFFORD, WOLVERHAMPTON, Birmingham, Coventry, Leamington Spa, Banbury, Oxford, Didcot, Reading.

It took four hours. Slowly, in that time, the screwed-tight wires of tension slackened to manageable if not to ease. At every stop, however illogical I might tell myself it was, dread resurfaced. Oversize wrenches could kill when one wasn't looking. . . . Don't be a fool, I thought. I'd bought a ticket from the train conductor between Runcorn and Crewe, but every subsequent appearance of his dark uniform as he checked his customers bumped my heart muscles.

It grew dark. The train clanked and swayed into realms of night. Life felt suspended.

There were prosaically plenty of taxis at Reading. I traveled safely to Shelley Green and rang Archie Kirk's bell.

He came himself to open the door.

"Hello," I said.

He stood there staring, then said awkwardly, "We'd almost given you up." He led the way into his sitting room. "He's here," he said.

There were four of them. Davis Tatum, Norman Picton, Archie himself, and Charles.

I paused inside the doorway. I had no idea what I looked like, but what I saw on their faces was shock.

"Sid," Charles said, recovering first and standing up. "Good. Great. Come and sit down."

The extent of his solicitude always measured the depth of his alarm. He insisted I take his place in a comfortable chair and himself perched on a hard one. He asked Archie if he had any brandy and secured for me a half-tumblerful of a raw-tasting own brand from a supermarket.

"Drink it," he commanded, holding out the glass.

"Charles . . ."

"Drink it. Talk after."

I gave in, drank a couple of mouthfuls and put the glass on a table beside me. He was a firm believer in the life-restoring properties of distilled wine, and I'd proved him right oftener than enough.

I remembered that I still wore the soft, stripey hat, and took it off; and its removal seemed to make my appearance more normal to them, and less disturbing.

"I went to Topline Foods," I said.

I thought: I don't feel well; what's wrong with me?

"You've cut your face," Norman Picton said.

I also ached more or less all over from the desperate exertions of the judo. My head felt heavy and my hand was swollen and sore from Ellis's idea of entertainment. On the bright side, I was alive and home, safe . . . and reaction was all very well but I was *not* at this point going to faint.

"Sid!" Charles said sharply, putting out a hand.

"Oh . . . yes. Well, I went to Topline Foods."

I drank some brandy. The weak feeling of sickness abated a bit. I shifted in my chair and took a grip on things.

Archie said, "Take your time," but sounded as if he didn't mean it.

I smiled. I said, "Owen Yorkshire was there. So was Lord Tilepit. So was Ellis Quint."

"Quint!" Davis Tatum exclaimed.

"Mm. Well . . . you asked me to find out if there was a heavyweight lumbering about behind the Quint business, and the answer is yes, but it is Ellis Quint himself."

"But he's a playboy," Davis Tatum protested. "What about the big man, Yorkshire?" Tatum's own bulk quivered. "He's getting known. One hears his name."

I nodded. "Owen Cliff Yorkshire is a heavyweight in the making."

"What do you mean?"

I ached. I hadn't really noticed the wear and tear until then. Win now, pay later.

"Megalomania," I said. "Yorkshire's on the edge. He has a violent, unpredictable temper and an uncontrolled desire to be a tycoon. I'd call it incipient megalomania because he's spending far beyond sanity on self-aggrandizement. He's built an office block fit for a major industry—and it's mostly empty—before building the industry first. He's publicity mad—he's holding a reception for half of Liverpool on Monday. He has plans—a *desire*—to take over the whole horse-feed nuts industry. He employs at least two bodyguards who will murder to order because he fears his competitors will assassinate him . . . which is paranoia."

I paused, then said, "It's difficult to describe the impression he gives. Half the time he sounds reasonable, and half the time you can see that he will simply get rid of anyone who stands in his way. And he is desperate . . . *desperate* . . . to save Ellis Quint's reputation."

Archie asked "Why?" slowly.

"Because," I said, "he has spent a colossal amount of money on an advertising campaign featuring Ellis, and if Ellis is found guilty of cutting off a horse's foot, that campaign can't be shown."

"But a few advertisements can't have cost that much," Archie objected.

"With megalomania," I said, "you don't make a few economically priced advertisements. You really go to town. You engage an expensive, highly prestigious firm—in this case, Intramind Imaging of Manchester—and you travel the world."

With clumsy fingers I took from my belt the folded copy of the paper in the "Quint" box file in Mrs. Dove's office.

"This is a list of racecourses," I said. "These racecourses are where they filmed the commercials. A thirty-second commercial gleaned from each place at phenomenal expense."

Archie scanned the list uncomprehendingly and passed it to Charles, who read it aloud.

"Flemington, Germiston, Sha Tin, Churchill Downs, Woodbine, Longchamps, K. L., Fuchu . . ."

There were fifteen altogether. Archie looked lost.

"Flemington," I said, "is where they run the Melbourne Cup in Australia. Germiston is outside Johannesburg. Sha Tin is in Hong Kong. Churchill Downs is where they hold the Kentucky Derby. K. L. is Kuala Lumpur in Malaysia, Woodbine is in Canada. Longchamps is in Paris, Fuchu is where the Japan Cup is run in Tokyo."

They all understood.

"Those commercials are reported to be brilliant," I said, "and Ellis himself wants them shown as much as Yorkshire does."

"Have you seen them?" Davis asked.

I explained about the box of Betacam tapes. "Making those special broadcast-quality tapes themselves must have been fearfully expensive—and they need special playing equipment, which I didn't find at Topline Foods, so no, I haven't seen them."

Norman Picton, with his policeman's mind, asked, "Where did you see the tapes? Where did you get that list of racecourses?"

I said without emotion, "In an office at Topline Foods."

He gave me a narrow inspection.

"My car," I told him, "is still somewhere in Frodsham. Could you get your pals up there to look out for it?" I gave him its registration number, which he wrote down.

"Why did you leave it?" he asked.

"Er . . . I was running away at the time." For all that I tried to say it lightly, the grim reality reached them.

"Well," I sighed, "I'd invaded Yorkshire's territory. He found me there. It gave him the opportunity to get rid of the person most likely to send Ellis to jail. I accepted that possibility when I went there but, like you, I wanted to know what was causing terrible trouble behind the scenes. And it is the millions spent on those ads." I paused, and went on, "Yorkshire and Ellis set out originally, months ago, not to kill me but to discredit me so that nothing I said would get Ellis convicted. They used a figurehead, Topline Foods director Lord Tilepit, because he owned *The Pump*. They persuaded Tilepit that Ellis was innocent and that I was all that *The Pump* has maintained. I don't think Tilepit believed Ellis guilty until today. I don't think *The Pump* will say a word against me from now on." I smiled briefly. "Lord Tilepit was duped by Ellis, and so, also, to some extent, was Owen Yorkshire himself."

"How, Sid?" Davis asked.

"I think Yorkshire, too, believed in Ellis. Ellis dazzles people. Knowing Ellis, to Yorkshire, was a step up the ladder. Today they planned together to . . . er . . . wipe me out of the way. Yorkshire would have done it himself in reckless anger. Ellis stopped him, but left it to chance that the bodyguards might do it . . . but I escaped them. Yorkshire now knows Ellis is guilty, but he doesn't care. He cares only to be able to show that brilliant ad campaign, and make himself king of the horse nuts. And of course it's not just horse nuts that it's all about. They're a stepping-stone. It's about being the Big Man with the power to bring mayors to his doorstep. If Yorkshire isn't stopped you'll find him manipulating more than *The Pump*. He's the sort of man you get in the kitchens of political clout."

After a moment, Archie asked, "So how do we stop him?"

I shifted wearily in the chair and drank some brandy, and said, "I can, possibly, give you the tools."

"What tools?"

"His secret files. His financial maneuverings. His debts. Details of bribes,

I'd guess. Bargains struck. You scratch my back, I'll scratch yours. Evidence of leverage. Details of all his dealings with Ellis, and all his dealings with Tilepit. I'll give you the files. You can take it from there."

"But," Archie said blankly, "where are these files?"

"In my computer in London."

I explained the Internet transfer and the need for password cracking. I couldn't decide whether they were gladdened or horrified by what I'd done. A bit of both, I thought.

Charles looked the most shocked, Archie the least.

Archie said, "If I ask you, will you work for me another time?"

I looked into the knowing eyes, and smiled, and nodded.

"Good," he said.

CHAPTER 14

I WENT HOME to Aynsford with Charles.

It had been a long evening in Archie's house. Archie, Davis, Norman and Charles had all wanted details, which I found as intolerable to describe as to live through. I skipped a lot.

I didn't tell them about Ellis's games with my hands. I didn't know how to explain to them that, for a jockey, his hands were at the heart of his existence . . . of his skill. One knew a horse by the feet of the bit on the reins, one listened to the messages, one interpreted the vibrations, one *talked* to a horse through one's hands. Ellis understood more than most people what the loss of a hand had meant to me, and that day he'd been busy punishing me in the severest way he could think of for trying to strip him of what he himself now valued most, his universal acclaim.

I didn't know how to make them understand that to Ellis the severing of a horse's foot had become a drug more addictive than any substance invented, that the risk and the power were intoxicating; that I'd been lucky he'd had only a wrench to use on me.

I didn't know how near he had come in his own mind to irrevocably destroying my right hand. I only knew that to me it had seemed possible that he would. I couldn't tell them that I'd intensely lived my own nightmare and still shook from fear inside.

I told them only that an adjustable wrench in Yorkshire's hands had cut my face.

I told them a little about the escape by judo, and all about the boy on Rollerblades and the ice cream cone and catching the bus within sight of Yorkshire and Ellis. I made it sound almost funny.

Archie understood that there was a lot I hadn't said, but he didn't press it. Charles, puzzled, asked, "But did they *hurt* you, Sid?" and I half laughed and told him part of the truth. "They scared me witless."

Davis asked about Ellis's Shropshire alibi. His colleague, the Crown Prosecutor, was increasingly concerned, he said, that Ellis's powerful lawyers would prevent the trial from resuming.

I explained that I hadn't had time to find out at what hour Ellis had arrived at the dance.

"Someone must know," I said. "It's a matter of asking the local people, the people who helped to park the cars." I looked at Norman. "Any chance of the police doing it?"

"Not much," he said.

"Round the pubs," I suggested.

Norman shook his head.

"There isn't much time," Davis pointed out. "Sid, couldn't you do it tomorrow?"

Tomorrow, Sunday. On Monday, the trial.

Archie said firmly, "No, Sid can't. There's a limit . . . I'll try and find someone else."

"Chico would have done it," Charles said.

Chico had undisputedly saved my pathetic skin that day. One could hardly ask more.

Archie's wife, before she'd driven over to spend the evening with her sister-in-law Betty Bracken, had, it appeared, made a mound of sandwiches. Archie offered them diffidently. I found the tastes of cheese and of chicken strange, as if I'd come upon them new from another world. It was weird the difference that danger and the perception of mortality made to familiar things. Unreality persisted even as I accepted a paper napkin to wipe my fingers.

Archie's doorbell rang. Archie went again to the summons and came back with a pinched, displeased expression, and he was followed by a boy that I saw with surprise to be Jonathan.

The rebel wings of hair were much shorter. The yellow streaks had all but grown out. There were no shaven areas of scalp.

"Hi," he said, looking around the room and fastening his attention on my face. "I came over to see you. The aunts said you were here. Hey, man, you look different."

"Three months older." I nodded. "So do you."

Jonathan helped himself to a sandwich, disregarding Archie's disapproval.

"Hi," he add nonchalantly to Norman. "How's the boat?"

"Laid up for winter storage."

Jonathan chewed and told me, "They won't take me on an oil rig until I'm eighteen. They won't take me in the navy. I've got good pecs. What do I do with them?"

"Pecs?" Charles asked, mystified.

"Pectoral muscles," Norman explained. "He's strong from weeks of water-skiing."

"Oh."

I said to Jonathan, "How did you get here from Combe Bassett?"

"Ran."

He'd walked into Archie's house not in the least out of breath.

"Can you ride a motorbike," I asked, "now that you're sixteen?"

"Do me a favor!"

"He hasn't got one," Archie said.

"He can hire one."

"But . . . what for?"

"To go to Shropshire," I said.

I was predictably drowned by protests. I explained to Jonathan what was needed. "Find someone—anyone—who saw Ellis Quint arrive at the dance. Find the people who parked the cars."

"He can't go round the pubs," Norman insisted. "He's under-age."

Jonathan gave me a dark look, which I steadfastly returned. At fifteen he'd bought gin for a truck driver's wife.

"Hey," he said. "Where do I go?"

I told him in detail. His uncle and everyone else disapproved. I took all the money I had left out of my belt and gave it to him. "I want receipts," I said. "Bring me paper. A signed statement from a witness. It's all got to be solid."

"Is this," he asked slowly, "some sort of test?"

"Yes."

"OK."

"Don't stay longer than a day," I said. "Don't forget, you may be asked to give evidence this week at the trial."

"As if I could forget."

He took a bunch of sandwiches, gave me a wide smile, and without more words departed.

"You *can't*," Archie said to me emphatically.

"What do *you* propose to do with him?"

"But . . . he's . . ."

"He's bright," I said. "He's observant. He's athletic. Let's see how he does in Shropshire."

"He's only *sixteen*."

"I need a new Chico."

"But Jonathan steals cars."

"He hasn't stolen one all summer, has he?"

"That doesn't mean . . ."

"An ability to steal cars," I said with humor, "is in my eyes an asset. Let's see how he does tomorrow, with this alibi."

Archie, still looking affronted, gave in.

"Too much depends on it," Davis said heavily, shaking his head.

I said, "If Jonathan learns nothing, I'll go myself on Monday."

"That will be too late," Davis said.

"Not if you get your colleague to ask for one more day's adjournment. Invent flu or something."

Davis said doubtfully, "Are you totally committed to this trial? *The Pump*—or Ellis Quint—they haven't got to you in any way, have they? I mean . . . the hate campaign . . . do you want to back out?"

Charles was offended on my behalf. "Of course he doesn't," he said.

Such faith! I said plainly to Davis, "Don't let your colleague back down. That's the real danger. Tell him to insist on prosecuting, alibi or no alibi. Tell the prosecution service to dredge up some guts."

"Sid!" He was taken aback. "They're realists."

"They're shit-scared of Ellis's lawyers. Well, I'm not. Ellis took the foot off Betty Bracken's colt. I wish like hell that he hadn't, but he did. He has no alibi for that night. You get your colleague to tell Ellis's lawyers that the Northampton colt was a copycat crime. If we can't break Ellis's alibi, copycat is our story and we're sticking to it, and if you have any influence over your colleague the prosecutor, you make sure he gives me a chance in court to say so."

Davis said faintly, "I must not instruct him to do anything like that."

"Just manage to get it dripped into his mind."

"So there you are, Davis," Archie said dryly, "our boy shows no sign of the hate campaign having been successful. Rather the opposite, wouldn't you say?"

"Our boy" stood up, feeling a shade fragile. It seemed to have been a long day. Archie came out into the hall with Charles and me and offered his hand in farewell. Charles shook warmly. Archie lifted my wrist and looked at the swelling and the deep bruising that was already crimson and black.

He said, "You've had difficulty holding your glass all evening."

I shrugged a fraction, long resigned to occupational damage. My hand was still a hand, and that was all that mattered.

"No explanation?" Archie asked.

I shook my head.

"Stone walls tell more," Charles informed him calmly.

Archie, releasing my wrist, said to me, "The British Horseracing Board wants you to double-check some of their own members for loyalty. Ultra-secret digging."

"They wouldn't ask *me*." I shook my head. "I'm not the new people's idea of reliable."

"They asked *me*," he said, the eyes blazing with amusement. "I said it would be you or nobody."

"Nobody," I said.

He laughed. "You start as soon as the Quint thing is over."

The trouble, I thought, as I sat quietly beside Charles as he drove to Aynsford, was that for me the Quint thing would never be over. Ellis might or might not go to jail . . . but that wouldn't be the end for either of us. Gordon's obsession might deepen. Ellis might maim more than horses. In both of them lay a compulsive disregard of natural law.

No one could ever be comprehensively protected from obsession. One simply had to live as best one could and disregard the feral threat lying in wait—and I would somehow have to shake Gordon loose from staking out my Pont Square door.

Charles said, "Do you consider that transferring Yorkshire's secret files to your own computer was at all immoral? Was it . . . theft?"

He spoke without censure, but censure was implied. I remembered a discussion we'd had once along the lines of what was honorable and what was not. He'd said I had a vision of honor that made my life a purgatory and I'd said he was wrong, and that purgatory was abandoning your vision of honor and knowing you'd done it. "Only for you, Sid," he'd said. "The rest of the world has no difficulty at all."

It seemed he was applying to me my own rash judgment. Was stealing knowledge ever justified, or was it not?

I said without self-excuse, "It was theft, and dishonorable, and I would do it again."

"And purgatory can wait?"

I said with amusement, "Have you read *The Pump*?"

After about five miles he said, "That's specious."

"Mm."

"*The Pump*'s a different sort of purgatory."

I nodded and said idly, "The anteroom to hell."

He frowned, glancing across in distaste. "Has hell arrived, then?" He hated excess emotion. I cooled it.

I said, "No. Sorry. It's been a long day."

He drove another mile, then asked, "How *did* you hurt your hand?"

I sighed. "I don't want a fuss. Don't *fuss*, Charles, if I tell you."

"No. All right. No fuss."

"Then . . . Ellis had a go at it."

"*Ellis?*"

"Mm. Lord Tilepit and Owen Yorkshire watched Ellis enjoy it. That's how they now know he's guilty as charged with the colts. If Ellis had had shears instead of a wrench to use on my wrist, I would now have no hands— and for God's sake, Charles, keep your eyes on the road."

"But, *Sid* . . ."

"No fuss. You promised. There'll be no lasting harm." I paused. "If he'd wanted to kill me today, he could have done it, but instead he gave me a chance to escape. He wanted . . ." I swallowed. "He wanted to make me pay for defeating him . . . and he did make me pay . . . and on Monday in court I'll try to disgrace him forever . . . and I *loathe* it."

He drove to Aynsford in a silence I understood to be at least empty of condemnation. Braking outside the door, he said regretfully, "If you and Ellis hadn't been such good friends . . . no wonder poor Ginnie couldn't stand it."

Charles saw the muscles stiffen in my face.

"What is it, Sid?" he asked.

"I . . . I may have made a wrong assumption."

"What assumption?"

"Mm?" I add vaguely. "Have to think."

"Then think in bed," he said lightly. "It's late."

I thought for half the night. Ellis's revenge brutally throbbed in my fingers. Ellis had tied my wrists and given me thirty seconds . . . I would be dead, I thought, if we hadn't been friends.

AT AYNSFORD I kept duplicates of all the things I'd lost in my car—battery charger, razor, clothes and so on—all except the mobile phone. I did have the SIM card, but nothing to use it in.

The no-car situation was solved again by Teledrive, which came to pick me up on Sunday morning.

To Charles's restrained suggestion that I pass the day resting with him—"A game of chess, perhaps?"—I replied that I was going to see Rachel Ferns. Charles nodded.

"Come back," he said, "if you need to."

"Always."

"Take care of yourself, Sid."

RACHEL, LINDA TOLD me on the telephone, was home from the hospital for the day.

"Oh, do come," she begged. "Rachel *needs* you."

I went empty-handed with no new fish or wigs, but it didn't seem to matter.

Rachel herself looked bloodless, a white wisp of a child in the foothills of a far country. In the five days since I'd seen her, the bluish shadows under her eyes had deepened, and she had lost weight so that the round cheeks of the steroids under the bald head and the big shadowed eyes gave her the look of an exotic little bird, unlike life.

Linda hugged me and cried on my shoulder in the kitchen.

"It's good news, really," she said, sobbing. "They've found a donor."

"But that's *marvelous.*" Like a sunburst of hope, I thought, but Linda still wept.

"He's a Swiss," she said. "He's coming from Switzerland. He's coming on Wednesday. Joe is paying his airfare and the hotel bills. Joe says money's no object for his little girl."

"Then stop crying."

"Yes . . . but it may not work."

"And it *may,*" I said positively. "Where's the gin?"

She laughed shakily. She poured two glasses. I still didn't much care for gin but it was all she liked. We clinked to the future and she began talking about paella for lunch.

Rachel was half sitting, half lying, on a small sofa that had been repositioned in the sitting room so that she could look straight and closely into the fish tank. I sat beside her and asked how she felt.

"Did my mum tell you about the transplant?" she said.

"Terrific news."

"I might be able to run again."

Running, it was clear from her pervading lassitude, must have seemed at that point as distant as the moon.

Rachel said, "I begged to come home to see the fishes. I have to go back tonight, though. I hoped you would come. I begged God."

"You knew I would come."

"I meant *today*, while I'm home."

"I've been busy since I saw you on Tuesday."

"I know. Mummy said so. The nurses tell me when you phone every day."

Pegotty was crawling all around the floor, growing in size and agility and putting everything unsuitable in his mouth; making his sister laugh.

"He's so *funny*," she said. "They won't let him come to the hospital. I begged to see him and the fishes. They told me the transplant is going to make me feel sick, so I wanted to come home first."

"Yes," I said.

Linda produced steamy rice with bits of chicken and shrimps, which we all ate with spoons.

"What's wrong with your hand?" Linda asked. "In places it's almost black."

"It's only a bruise. It got a bit squashed."

"You've got sausage fingers," Rachel said.

"They'll be all right tomorrow."

Linda returned to the only important subject. "The Swiss donor," she said, "is older than I am! He has three children of his own. He's a schoolteacher . . . he sounds a nice man, and they say he's so pleased to be going to give Rachel some of his bone marrow."

Rachel said, "I wish it had been Sid's bone marrow."

I'd had myself tested, right at the beginning, but I'd been about as far from a match as one could get. Neither Linda nor Joe had been more than fifty percent compatible.

"They say he's a ninety percent match," Linda said. "You never get a hundred percent, even from siblings. Ninety percent is great."

She was trying hard to be positive. I didn't know enough to put a bet on ninety percent. It sounded fine to me; and no one was going to kill off Rachel's own defective bone marrow if they didn't believe they could replace it.

"They're going to put me into a bubble," Rachel said. "It's a sort of plastic tent over my bed. I won't be able to touch the Swiss man, except through the plastic. And he doesn't speak English, even. He speaks German. *Danke schoen.* I've learned that, to say to him. Thank you very much."

"He's a lucky man," I said.

Linda, clearing the plates and offering ice cream for dessert, asked if I would stay with Rachel while she took Pegotty out for a short walk in fresh air.

"Of course."

"I won't be long."

When she'd gone, Rachel and I sat on the sofa and watched the fish.

"You see that one?" Rachel pointed. "That's the one you brought on Tuesday. Look how fast he swims! He's faster than all the others."

The black and silver angel fish flashed through the tank, fins waving with vigor.

"He's you," Rachel said. "He's Sid."

I teased her, "I thought half of them were Sid."

"Sid is always the fastest one. That's Sid." She pointed. "The others aren't Sid anymore."

"Poor fellows."

She giggled. "I wish I could have the fishes in the hospital. Mummy asked, but they said no."

"Pity."

She sat loosely cuddled by my right arm but held my other hand, the plastic one, pulling it across towards her. That hand still wasn't working properly, though a fresh battery and a bit of tinkering had restored it to half-life.

After a long, silent pause, she said, "Are you afraid of dying?"

Another pause. "Sometimes," I said.

Her voice was quiet, almost murmuring. It was a conversation all in a low key, without haste.

She said, "Daddy says when you were a jockey you were never afraid of anything."

"Are you afraid?" I asked.

"Yes, but I can't tell Mummy. I don't like her crying."

"Are you afraid of the transplant?"

Rachel nodded.

"You will die without it." I said matter-of-factly. "I know you know that."

"What's dying like?"

"I don't know. No one knows. Like going to sleep, I should think." If you were lucky, of course.

"It's funny to think of not being here." Rachel said. "I mean, to think of being a *space*."

"The transplant will work."

"Everyone says so."

"Then believe it. You'll be running by Christmas."

She smoothed her fingers over my hand. I could feel the faint vibrations distantly in my forearm. Nothing, I thought, was ever entirely lost.

She said, "Do you know what I'll be thinking, lying there in the bubble feeling awfully sick?"

"What?"

"Life's a bugger."

I hugged her, but gently. "You'll do fine."

"Yes, but tell me."

"Tell you what?"

"How to be brave."

What a question, I thought. I said, "When you're feeling awfully sick, think about something you like doing. You won't feel as bad if you don't think about how bad you feel."

She thought it over. "Is that all?"

"It's quite a lot. Think about fishes. Think about Pegotty pulling off his socks and putting them in his mouth. Think about things you've enjoyed."

"Is that what *you* do?"

"It's what I do if something hurts, yes. It does work."

"What if nothing hurts yet, but you're going into something scary?"

"Well . . . it's all right to be frightened. No one can help it. You just don't have to let being frightened stop you."

"Are you ever frightened?" she asked.

"Yes." Too often, I thought.

She said lazily, but with certainty, "I bet you've never been so frightened you didn't do something. I bet you're always brave."

I was startled. "No . . . I'm not."

"But Daddy said . . ."

"I wasn't afraid of riding in races," I agreed. "Try me in a pit full of snakes, though, and I wouldn't be so sure."

"What about a bubble?"

"I'd go in there promising myself I'd come out running."

She smoothed my hand. "Will you come and see me?"

"In the bubble?" I asked. "Yes, if you like."

"You'll make me brave."

I shook my head. "It will come from inside you. You'll see."

We went on watching the fish. My namesake flashed his fins and seemed to have endless stamina.

"I'm going into the bubble tomorrow," Rachel murmured. "I don't want to cry when they put me in there."

"Courage is lonely," I said.

She looked up into my face. "What does that mean?"

It was too strong a concept, I saw, for someone of nine. I tried to make things simpler.

"You'll be alone in the bubble," I said, "so make it your own palace. The bubble is to keep you safe from infection—safe from dragons. You won't cry."

She snuggled against me; happier, I hoped. I loved her incredibly. The transplant had a fifty-fifty chance of success. Rachel would run again. She *had* to.

Linda and Pegotty came back laughing from their walk and Linda built towers of bright plastic building blocks for Pegotty to knock down, a game of endless enjoyment for the baby. Rachel and I sat on the floor, playing checkers.

"You always let me be white," Rachel complained, "and then you sneak up with the black counters when I'm not looking."

"You can play black, then."

"It's disgusting," she said, five minutes later. "You're cheating."

Linda looked up and said, astounded, "Are you two *quarreling*?"

"He always wins," Rachel objected.

"Then don't play with him," Linda said reasonably.

Rachel set up the white pieces as her own. I neglected to take one of them halfway through the game, and with glee she huffed me, and won.

"Did you *let* me win?" she demanded.

"Winning's more fun."

"I hate you." She swept all the pieces petulantly from the board and Pegotty put two of them in his mouth.

Rachel, laughing, picked them out again and dried them and set up the board again, with herself again as white, and peacefully we achieved a couple of close finishes until, suddenly as usual, she tired.

Linda produced tiny chocolate cakes for tea and talked happily of the Swiss donor and how everything was going to be *all right*. Rachel was convinced, I was convinced, Pegotty smeared chocolate all over his face. Whatever the next week might bring to all of us, I thought, that afternoon of hope and ordinariness was an anchor in reality, an affirmation that small lives mattered.

It wasn't until after she'd fastened both children into the back of her car to drive to the hospital that Linda mentioned Ellis Quint.

"That trial is on again tomorrow, isn't it?" she asked.

We stood in the chilly air a few paces from her car. I nodded. "Don't let Rachel know."

"She doesn't. It hasn't been hard to keep it all away from her. She never talks about Silverboy anymore. Being so ill . . . she hasn't much interest in anything else."

"She's terrific."

"Will Ellis Quint go to prison?"

How could I say "I hope so"? And *did* I hope so? Yet I had to stop him, to goad him, to make him fundamentally wake up.

I said, dodging it "It will be for the judge to decide."

Linda hugged me. No tears. "Come and see Rachel in her bubble?"

"You couldn't keep me away."

"God . . . I hope . . ."

"She'll be all right," I said. "So will you."

PATIENT TELEDRIVE TOOK me back to London and, because of the fixed hour of Linda's departure to the hospital, I again had time to spare before meeting India for dinner.

I again ducked being dropped in Pont Square in the dark evening, and damned Gordon for his vigilance. He had to sleep *sometime* . . . but when?

The restaurant called Kensington Place was near the northern end of Church Street, the famous road of endless antique shops, stretching from Kensington High Street, in the south, up to Notting Hill Gate, north. Teledrive left me and my overnight bag on the northwest corner of Church Street, where I dawdled awhile looking in the brightly lit windows of Waterstone's bookshop, wondering if Rachel would be able to hear the store's advertised children's audio tapes in her bubble. She enjoyed the subversive Just William stories. Pegotty, she thought, would grow up to be like him.

A large number of young Japanese people were milling around on the corner, all armed with cameras, taking flash pictures of one another. I paid not much attention beyond noticing that they all had straight black hair, short padded jackets, and jeans. As far as one could tell, they were happy. They also surged between me and Waterstone's windows.

They bowed to me politely, I bowed unenthusiastically in return.

They seemed to be waiting, as I was, for some prearranged event to occur. I gradually realized from their quiet chatter, of which I understood not a word, that half of them were men, and half young women.

We all waited. They bowed some more. At length, one of the young women shyly produced a photograph that she held out to me. I took it politely and found I was looking at a wedding. At a mass wedding of about ten happy couples wearing formal suits and Western bridal gowns. Raising my head from the photo, I was met by twenty smiles.

I smiled back. The shy young woman retrieved her photo, nodded her head towards her companions and clearly told me that they were all on their honeymoon. More smiles all around. More bows. One of the men held out his camera to me and asked—I gathered—if I would photograph them all as a group.

I took the camera and put my bag at my feet, and they arranged themselves in pairs neatly, as if they were used to it.

Click. Flash. The film wound on, quietly whirring.

All the newlyweds beamed.

I was presented, one by one, with nine more cameras. Nine more bows. I took nine more photos. Flash. Flash. Group euphoria.

What was it about me, I wondered, that encouraged such trust? Even without language there seemed to be no doubt on their part of my willingness to give pleasure. I mentally shrugged. I had the time, so what the hell. I took their pictures and bowed, and waited for eight o'clock.

I left the happy couples on Waterstone's corner and, carrying my bag, walked fifty yards down Church Street towards the restaurant. There was a narrow side street beside it, and opposite, on the other side of Church Street, one of those quirks of London life, a small recessed area of sidewalk with a patch of scrubby grass and a park bench, installed by philanthropists for the comfort of footsore shoppers and other vagrants. I would sit there, I decided, and watch for India. The restaurant doors were straight opposite the bench. A green-painted bench made of horizontal slats.

I crossed Church Street to reach it. The traffic on Sunday evening was sporadic to nonexistent. I could see a brass plate on the back of the bench: the name of the benefactor who'd paid for it.

I was turning to sit when at the same time I heard a bang and felt a searing flash of pain across my back and into my right upper arm. The impact knocked me over and around so that I ended sprawling on the bench, half lying, half sitting, facing the road.

I thought incredulously, I've been *shot*.

I'd been shot once before. I couldn't mistake the *thud*. Also I couldn't mistake the shudder of outrage that my invaded body produced. Also . . . there was a great deal of blood.

I'd been shot by Gordon Quint.

He walked out of the shadows of the side street opposite and came towards me across Church Street. He carried a handgun with its black, round mouth pointing my way. He was coming inexorably to finish what he'd started, and he appeared not to care if anyone saw him.

I didn't seem to have the strength to get up and run away.

There was nowhere to run to.

Gordon looked like a farmer from Berkshire, not an obsessed murderer. He wore a checked shirt and a tie and a tweed jacket. He was a middle-aged pillar of the community, a judge and jury and a hangman . . . a raw, primitive walking act of revenge.

There was none of the screaming out-of-control obscenity with which he'd attacked me the previous Monday. This killer was cold and determined and *reckless*.

He stopped in front of me and aimed at my chest.

"This is for Ginnie," he said.

I don't know what he expected. He seemed to be waiting for something. For me to protest, perhaps. To plead.

His voice was hoarse.

"For Ginnie," he repeated.

I was silent. I wanted to stand. Couldn't manage it.

"Say something!" he shouted in sudden fury. The gun wavered in his hand, but he was too close to miss. "Don't you *understand*?"

I looked not at his gun but at his eyes. Not the best view, I thought inconsequentially, for my last on earth.

Gordon's purpose didn't waver. I might deny him any enjoyment of my fear, but that wasn't going to stop him. He stared at my face. He didn't blink. No hesitancy there. No withdrawal or doubt. None.

Now, I thought frozenly. It's going to be *now*.

A voice was shouting in the road, urgent, frantic, coming nearer, far too late.

The voice shouted one despairing word.

"Dad."

Ellis . . . *Ellis* . . . Running across the road waving a five-foot piece of black angle-iron fencing and shouting in frenzy at his father, *"Dad . . . Dad . . . Don't . . . Don't do it."*

I could see him running. Nothing seemed very clear. Gordon could hear Ellis shouting but it wasn't going to stop him. The demented hatred simply hardened in his face. His arm straightened until his gun was a bare yard from my chest.

Perhaps I won't feel it, I thought.

Ellis swung the iron fencing post with two hands and all his strength and *hit his father on the side of the head.*

The gun went off. The bullet hissed past my ear and slammed into a shop window behind me. There were razor splinters of glass and flashes of light and shouting and confusion everywhere.

Gordon fell silently unconscious, face down on the scrubby patch of grass, his right hand with the gun underneath him. My blood ran into a scarlet and widening pool below the slats of the bench. Ellis stood for an eternity of seconds holding the fencing post and staring at my eyes as if he could see into my soul, as if he would show me his.

For an unmeasurable hiatus blink of time it seemed there was between us a fusing of psyche, an insight of total understanding. It could have been a hallucination, a result of too much stress, but it was unmistakably the same for him.

Then he dropped the fencing post beside his father, and turned, and went away at a slow run, across Church Street and down the side road, loping, not sprinting, until he was swallowed by shadow.

I was suddenly surrounded by Japanese faces all asking unintelligible questions. They had worried eyes. They watched me bleed.

The gunshots brought more people, but cautiously. Gordon's attack, that to me had seemed to happen in slow motion, had in reality passed to others with bewildering speed. No one had tried to stop Ellis. People thought he was going to bring help.

I lost further account of time. A police car arrived busily, lights flashing, the first manifestation of all that I most detested—questions, hospitals, forms, noise, bright lights in my eyes, clanging and banging and being shoved around. There wasn't a hope of being quietly stitched up and left alone.

I told a policeman that Gordon, though unconscious at present, was lying over a loaded gun.

He wanted to know if Gordon had fired the shots in self-defense.

I couldn't be bothered to answer.

The crowd grew bigger and an ambulance made an entrance.

A young woman pushed the uniforms aside, yelling that she was from the press. India . . . India . . . come to dinner.

"Sorry," I said.

"*Sid* . . ." Horror in her voice and a sort of despair.

"Tell Kevin Mills . . . ," I said. My mouth was dry from loss of blood. I tried again. She beat her head down to mine to hear above the hubbub.

With humor I said, "Those Japanese people took a load of photos . . . I saw the flashes . . . so tell Kevin to get moving . . . Get those photos . . . and he can have . . . his exclusive."

CHAPTER 15

INDIA WASN'T A newspaperwoman for nothing. The front page of Monday's *Pump* bore the moderately accurate headline "Shot in the Back," with, underneath, a picture taken of Gordon Quint aiming his gun unequivocally at my heart.

Gordon's half–back view was slightly out of focus. My own face was sharp and clear, with an expression that looked rather like polite interest, not the fatalistic terror I'd actually felt.

Kevin and *The Pump* had gone to town. *The Pump* acknowledged that its long campaign of denigration of Sid Halley had been a mistake.

Policy, I saw cynically, had done a one-eighty U-turn. Lord Tilepit had come to such senses as he possessed and was putting what distance he could between himself and Ellis Quint.

There had been twenty eyewitnesses to the shooting of J. S. Halley. Kevin, arming himself with a Japanese interpreter, had listened intently, sorted out what he'd been told, and got it right. Throughout his piece there was an undercurrent of awe that no one was going to be able to dispute the facts. He hadn't once said, "It is *alleged*."

Gordon Quint, though still unconscious, would in due course be "helping the police with their inquiries." Kevin observed that Ellis Quint's whereabouts were unknown.

Inside the paper there were more pictures. One showed Ellis, arms and fence post raised, on the point of striking his father. The Japanese collectively, and that one photographer in particular, had not known who Ellis Quint was. Ellis didn't appear on the TV screens in Japan.

Why had there been so much photo coverage? Because Mr. Halley, Kevin said, had been kind to the honeymooners, and many of them had been watching him as he walked away down Church Street.

I read *The Pump* while sitting upright in a high bed in a small white side room in Hammersmith hospital, thankfully alone except for a constant stream of doctors, nurses, policemen and people with clipboards.

The surgeon who'd dealt with my punctures came to see me at nine in the morning, before he went off duty for the day. He looked a lot worse for wear by then than I did, I thought.

"How are you doing?" he asked, coming in wearily in a sweat-stained green gown.

"As you see . . . fine, thanks to you."

He looked at the newspaper lying on the bed. "Your bullet," he said, "plowed along a rib and in and out of your arm. It tore a hole in the brachial artery, which is why you bled so much. We repaired that and transfused you with three units of blood and saline, though you may need more later. We'll see how you go. There's some muscle damage but with physiotherapy you should be almost as good as new. You seem to have been sideways on when he shot you."

"I was turning. I was lucky."

"You could put it like that," he said dryly. "I suppose you do know you've also got a half-mended fracture of the forearm? And some fairly deep trauma to the wrist?"

I nodded.

"And we've put a few stitches in your face."

"Great."

"I watched you race," he said. "I know how fast jockeys heal. Ex-jockeys, too, no doubt. You can leave here when you feel ready."

I said "Thanks" sincerely, and he smiled exhaustedly and went away.

I could definitely move the fingers of my right hand, even though only marginally at present. There had been a private moment of sheer cowardice in the night when I'd woken gradually from anesthesia and been unable to feel anything in my arm from the shoulder down. I didn't care to confess or remember the abject dread in which I'd forced myself to *look*. I'd awoken once before to a stump. This time the recurrent nightmare of helplessness and humiliation and no hands had drifted horrifyingly in and out, but when I did finally look, there was no spirit-pulverizing void but a long white-wrapped bundle that discernibly ended in fingernails. Even so, they didn't seem to be connected to me. I had lain for a grim while, trying to consider paralysis, and when at length pain had roared back it had been an enormous relief: only whole healthy nerves felt like that. I had an arm . . . and a hand . . . and a life.

Given those, nothing else mattered.

In the afternoon Archie Kirk and Norman Picton argued themselves past the No Visitors sign on the door, and sat in a couple of chairs bringing good news and bad.

"The Frodsham police found your car," Norman said, "but I'm afraid it's been stripped. It's up on bricks—no wheels."

"Contents?" I asked resignedly.

"No. Nothing."

"Engine?"

"Most of it's there. No battery, of course. Everything movable's missing."

Poor old car. It had been insured, though, for a fortune.

Archie said, "Charles sends his regards."

"Tell him thanks."

"He said you would be looking as though nothing much had happened. I didn't believe him. Why aren't you lying down?"

"It's more comfortable sitting up."

Archie frowned.

I amplified mildly. "There's a bullet burn across somewhere below my shoulder blade."

Archie said, "Oh."

They both looked at the tall contraption standing beside the bed with a tube leading from a high bag to my elbow. I explained that, too.

"It's one of those 'painkiller on demand' things," I said. "If I get a twinge I press a button, and bingo, it goes away."

Archie picked up the copy of *The Pump*. "All of a sudden," he commented, "you're Saint Sid who can do no wrong."

I said, "It's enough to make Ellis's lawyers weep."

"But you don't think, do you," Archie said doubtfully, "that Ellis's lawyers *connived* at the hate-Halley campaign?"

"Because they are ethical people?" I asked.

"Yes."

I shrugged and left it.

"Is there any news of Ellis?" I asked. "Or of Gordon?"

"Gordon Quint," Norman said in a policeman's voice, "was, as of an hour ago, still unconscious in a secure police facility and suffering from a depressed skull fracture. He is to have an operation to relieve the pressure on his brain. No one is predicting when he'll wake up or what mental state he'll be in, but as soon as he can understand, he'll be formally charged with attempted murder. As you know, there's a whole flock of eyewitnesses."

"And Ellis?" I asked.

Archie said, "No one knows where he is."

"It's very difficult," I said, "for him to go anywhere without being recognized."

Norman nodded. "Someone may be sheltering him. But we'll find him, don't worry."

"What happened this morning," I asked, "about the trial?"

"Adjourned. Ellis Quint's bail is rescinded as he didn't turn up, and also he'll be charged with grievous bodily harm to his father. A warrant for his arrest has been issued."

"He wanted to prevent his father from murdering," I said. "He can't have meant to hurt him seriously."

Archie nodded. "It's a tangle."

"And Jonathan," I asked. "Did he go to Shropshire?"

Both of them looked depressed

"Well," I said, "didn't he go?"

"Oh yes, he went," Norman said heavily. "And he found the car parkers."

"Good boy." I said.

"It's *not* so good." Archie, like a proper civil servant, had brought with him a briefcase, from which he now produced a paper that he brought over to the bed. I pinned it down with the weight of my still-sluggish left hand and took in its general meaning

The car parkers had signed a statement saying that Ellis Quint had dined with media colleagues and had brought several of them with him to the dance at about eleven-thirty. The parkers remembered him—of course—not only because of who he was (there had been plenty of other well-known people at the party, starting with members of the Royal Family) but chiefly because he had given them a tip and offered them his autograph. They knew it was before midnight, because their employment as car parkers had ended then. People who arrived later had found only one car parker—a friend of those who'd gone off duty.

Media colleagues! Dammit, I thought. I hadn't checked those with the duchess.

"It's an unbreakably solid alibi," Norman observed gloomily. "He was in Shropshire when the yearling was attacked."

"Mm."

"You don't seem disappointed, Sid." Archie said, puzzled.

"No."

"But why not?"

"I think," I said, "that you should phone Davis Tatum. Will he be in his office right now?"

"He might be. What do you want him for?"

"I want him to make sure the prosecutors don't give up on the trial."

"You told him that on Saturday." He was humoring me, I thought.

"I'm not light-headed from bullets, Archie, if that's what you think. Since Saturday I've worked a few things out, and they are not as they may seem."

"What things?"

"Ellis's alibi, for one."

"But, Sid—"

"Listen," I said. "This isn't all that easy to say, so don't look at me, look at your hands or something." They showed no sign of doing so, so I looked at my own instead. I said, "I have to explain that *I* am not as I seem. When people in general look at me they see a harmless person, youngish, not big, not tall, no threat to anyone. Self-effacing. I'm not complaining about that. In fact, I choose to be like that because people then *talk* to me, which is necessary in my job. They tend to think I'm cozy, as your sister Betty told me, Archie. Owen Yorkshire considers me a wimp. He said so. Only . . . I'm not really like that."

"A *wimp*!" Archie exclaimed.

"I can look it, that's the point. But Ellis knows me better. Ellis calls me cunning and ruthless, and I probably am. It was he who years ago gave me the nickname of Tungsten Carbide because I wasn't easy to . . . er . . . intimidate. He thinks I can't be terrified, either, though he's wrong about that. But I don't mind him thinking it. Anyway, unlikely though it may seem, all this past summer, Ellis has been afraid of me. That's why he made jokes about me on television and got Tilepit to set his paper onto me. He wanted to defeat me by ridicule."

I paused. Neither of them said a word.

I went on. "Ellis is not what he seems, either. Davis Tatum thinks him a playboy. Ellis is tall, good-looking, outgoing, charming and *loved*. Everyone thinks him a delightful entertainer with a knack for television. But he's not only that. He's a strong, purposeful and powerful man with enormous skills of manipulation. People underestimate both of us for various and different reasons—I look weak and he looks frivolous—but we don't underestimate each other. On the surface, the easy surface, we've been friends for years. But in our time we rode dozens of races against each other, and racing, believe me, strips your soul bare. Ellis and I know each other's minds on a deep level that has nothing to do with afternoon banter or chit-chat. We've been friends on that level, too. You and Davis can't believe that it is Ellis himself who is the heavyweight, not Yorkshire, but Ellis and I both know it. Ellis has manipulated everyone—Yorkshire, Tilepit, *The Pump*, public opinion, and also those so-smart lawyers of his who think they're dictating the pace."

"And you, Sid?" Norman asked. "Has he pulled your strings, too?"

I smiled ruefully, not looking at him. "He's had a go."

"I'd think it was impossible," Archie said. "He would have to put you underground to stop you."

"You've learned a lot about me, Archie," I said lazily, "I do like to win."

He said, "So why aren't you disappointed that Ellis's Shropshire alibi can't be broken?"

"Because Ellis set it up that way."

"How do you mean?"

"Ever since the Northampton yearling was attacked, Ellis's lawyers have been putting it about that if Ellis had an unbreakable alibi for that night, which I bet he assured them he had, it would invalidate the whole Combe Bassett case. They put pressure on the Crown Prosecution Service to withdraw, which they've been tottering on the brink of doing. Never mind that the two attacks were separate, the strong supposition arose that if Ellis couldn't have done one, then he hadn't done the other."

"Of course," Norman said.

"No," I contradicted. "He made for himself a positively unbreakable alibi in Shropshire, and he got someone else to go to Northampton."

"But no one *would*."

"One person would. And did."

"But *who*, Sid?" Archie asked.

"Gordon. His father."

Archie and Norman both stiffened as if turned to pillars of salt.

The nerves in my right arm woke up. I pressed the magic button and they went slowly back to sleep. Brilliant. A lot better than in days gone by.

"He *couldn't* have done," Archie said in revulsion.

"He did."

"You're just *guessing*. And you're *wrong*."

"No."

"But, *Sid* . . ."

"I know," I sighed. "You, Charles and I have all been guests in his house. But he shot me last night. See it in *The Pump*."

Archie said weakly, "But that doesn't mean . . ."

"I'll explain," I said. "Give me a moment."

My skin was sweating. It came and went a bit, now and then. An affronted body, letting me know.

"A moment?"

"I'm not made of iron."

Archie breathed on a smile. "I thought it was tungsten?"

"Mm."

They waited. I said, "Gordon and Ginnie Quint gloried in their wonderful son, their only child. I accused him of a crime that revolted them. Ginnie steadfastly believed in his innocence; an act of faith. Gordon, however reluctantly, faced with all the evidence we gathered from his Land-Rover, must have come to acknowledge to himself that the unthinkable was true."

Archie nodded.

I went on. "Ellis's wretched persecution of me didn't really work. Sure, I hated it, but I was still *there*, and meanwhile the time of the trial was drawing nearer and nearer. Whatever odium I drew onto myself by doing it, I was going to describe in court, with all the press and public listening, just how Ellis could have cut off the foot of Betty's colt. The outcome of the trial—whether or not the jury found Ellis guilty, and whether or not the judge sent him to jail—that wasn't the prime point. The trial itself, and all that evidence, would have convinced enough of the population of his guilt to destroy forever the shining-knight persona. Topline Foods couldn't have—and, in fact, won't be able to—use those diamond-plated round-the-world ads."

I took a deep couple of lungfuls of air. I was talking too much. Not enough oxygen, not enough blood.

I said, "The idea of the Shropshire alibi probably came about gradually, and heaven knows to which of them first. Ellis received an invitation to the dance. The plan must have started from that. They saw it as the one effective way to stop the trial from taking place."

Hell, I thought, I don't feel well. I'm getting old.

I said, "You have to remember that Gordon is a farmer. He's used to the idea of the death of animals being profitable. I dare say that the death of one insignificant yearling was as nothing to him when set beside the saving of his son. And he knew where to find such a victim. He would have to have long replaced the shears taken by the police. It must have seemed quite easy, and in fact he carried out the plan without difficulty."

Archie and Norman listened as if not breathing.

I started again. "Ellis is many things, but he's not a murderer. If he had been, perhaps he would have been a serial killer of humans, not horses. That urge to do evil—I don't understand it, but it *happens.* Wings off butterflies and so on." I swallowed. "Ellis has given me a hard time, but in spite of several opportunities he hasn't let me be killed. He stopped Yorkshire doing it. He stopped his father last night."

"People can hate until they make themselves ill," Archie nodded. "Very few actually murder."

"Gordon Quint tried it," Norman pointed out, "and all but succeeded."

"Yes," I agreed, "but that wasn't to help Ellis."

"What was it, then?"

"Have to go back a bit."

I'm too tired, I thought, but I'd better finish it.

I said to Norman, "You remember that piece of rag you gave me?"

"Yes. Did you do anything with it?"

I nodded.

"What rag?" Archie asked.

Norman outlined for him the discovery at Northampton of the lopping shears wrapped in dirty material.

"The local police found the shears hidden in a hedge," I said, "and they brought them into the stud farm's office while I was there. The stud farm's owners, Miss Richardson and Mrs. Bethany, were there, and so was Ginnie Quint, who was a friend of theirs and who had gone there to comfort them and sympathize. Ginnie forcibly said how much she despised me for falsely accusing her paragon of a son. For accusing my *friend.* She more or less called me Judas."

"Sid!"

"Well, that's how it seemed. Then she watched the policeman unwrap the shears that had cut off the yearling's foot and, quite slowly, she went white . . . and fainted."

"The sight of the shears," Norman said, nodding.

"It was much more than that. It was the sight of the *material.*"

"How do you mean?"

"I spent a whole day . . . last Thursday, it seems a lifetime away . . . I chased all over London with that little piece of cloth, and I finished up in a village near Chichester."

"Why Chichester?" Archie asked.

"Because that filthy old cloth had once been part of some bed hangings. They were woven as a special order by a Mrs. Patricia Huxford, who's a doll of the first rank. She has looms in Lowell, near Chichester. She looked up her records and found that that fabric had been made nearly thirty years ago especially—and exclusively—for a Mrs. Gordon Quint."

Archie and Norman both stared.

"Ginnie recognized the material," I said. "She'd just been giving me the most frightful tongue-lashing for believing Ellis capable of maiming horses, and she suddenly saw, because that material was wrapped round shears, that I'd been right. Not only that, she knew that Ellis had been in Shropshire the night Miss Richardson's colt was done. She knew the importance of his alibi . . . and she saw—she understood—that the only other person who could or would have wrapped lopping shears in that unique fabric was Gordon. Gordon wouldn't have thought twice about snatching up any old rag to wrap his shears in—and I'd guess he decided to dump them because we might have checked Quint's shears again for horse DNA if he'd taken them home. Ginnie saw that *Gordon* had maimed the yearling. It was too big a shock . . . and she fainted."

Archie and Norman, too, looked shocked.

I sighed. "I didn't understand that then, of course. I didn't understand it until the night before last, when everything sort of *clicked.* But now . . . I think it wasn't just because of Ellis's terrible guilt that Ginnie killed herself last Monday, but because it was Gordon's guilt and reputation as well . . . and then the trial was starting in spite of everything . . . and it was all too much . . . too much to bear."

I paused briefly and went on, "Ginnie's suicide sent Gordon berserk. He'd set out to help his son. He'd caused his wife's death. He blamed me for it, for having destroyed his family. He tried to smash my brains in the morning she'd died. He lay in wait for me outside my apartment . . . he was screaming that I'd killed her. Then, last night, in the actual moment that the picture in *The Pump* was taken, he was telling me the bullets were for Ginnie . . . it was my life for hers. He meant . . . he meant to do it."

I stopped talking.

The white room was silent.

LATER IN THE day I phoned the hospital in Canterbury and spoke to the ward sister.

"How is Rachel?" I asked.

"Mr. Halley! But I thought . . . I mean, we've all read *The Pump.*"

"But you didn't tell Rachel, did you?" I asked anxiously

"No . . . Linda—Mrs. Ferns—said not to."

"Good."

"But are you—"

"I'm absolutely OK," I assured her. "I'm in Hammersmith hospital. Du Cane Road."

"The best!" she exclaimed.

"I won't argue. How's Rachel?"

"You know that she's a very sick little girl, but we're all hopeful of the transplant."

"Did she go into the bubble?"

"Yes, very bravely. She says it's her palace and she's its queen."

"Give her my love."

"How soon . . . oh, dear, I shouldn't ask."

"I'll make it by Thursday."

"I'll tell her."

KEVIN MILLS AND India came to visit before ten o'clock the following morning, on their way to work.

I was again sitting up in the high bed but by then felt much healthier. In spite of my protests, my shot and mending arm was still held immobile in a swaddle of splint and bandages. Give it another day's rest, I'd been told, and just practice wiggling your fingers: which was all very well, except that the nurses had been too busy with an emergency that morning to reunite me with my left hand, which lay on the locker beside me. For all that it didn't work properly, I felt naked without it, and could do nothing for myself, not even scratch my nose.

Kevin and India both came in looking embarrassed by life in general and said far too brightly how glad they were to see me awake and recovering.

I smiled at their feelings. "My dear children," I said, "I'm not a complete fool."

"Look, mate . . ." Kevin's voice faded. He wouldn't meet my eyes.

I said, "Who told Gordon Quint where to find me?"

Neither of them answered.

"India," I pointed out, "you were the only person who knew I would turn up at Kensington Place at eight o'clock on Sunday evening."

"Sid!" She was anguished, as she had been in Church Street when she'd found me shot; and she wouldn't look at my face, either.

Kevin smoothed his mustache. "It wasn't her fault."

"Yours, then?"

"You're right about your not being a fool," Kevin said. "You've guessed what happened, otherwise you'd be flinging us out of here right now."

"Correct."

"The turmoil started Saturday evening," Kevin said, feeling secure enough to sit down. "Of course, as there's no daily *Pump* on Sundays there was hardly anyone in the office. George Godbar wasn't. No one was. Saturday is our night off. The shit really hit the fan on Sunday morning at the editorial meeting. You know editorial meetings . . . well, perhaps you don't. All the department editors—news, sport, gossip, features, whatever, and the senior reporters—meet to decide what stories will be run in the next day's paper, and there was George Godbar in a positive *lather* about reversing policy on S. Halley. I mean, Sid mate, you should've heard him swear. I never knew so many orifices and sphincters existed."

"The boss had leaned on him?"

"*Leaned!* There was a panic. Our lord the proprietor wanted you *bought off.*"

"How nice," I said.

"He'd suggested ten thousand smackers, George said. Try ten million, I said. George called for copies for everyone of the complete file of everything *The Pump* has published about you since June, nearly all of it in India's column on Fridays. I suppose you've kept all those pieces?"

I hadn't. I didn't say so.

"Such *poison*," Kevin said. "Seeing it all together like that. I mean, it silenced the whole meeting, and it takes a lot to do that."

"I wasn't there," India said. "I don't go to those meetings."

"Be fair to India," Kevin told me "she didn't write most of it. I wrote some. You know I did. Six different people wrote it."

India still wouldn't meet my eyes and still wouldn't sit in the one empty chair. I knew about "policy" and being burned at the stake and all that, yet week after week I'd dreaded her byline. Try as I would, I still felt sore from that savaging.

"Sit down," I said mildly.

She perched uneasily.

"If we make another dinner date," I said, "don't tell anyone."

"Oh, Sid."

"She didn't mean to get you *shot*, for Chrissakes," Kevin protested. "The Tilepit wanted you found. Wanted! He was shitting himself, George said. *The Pump*'s lawyer had passed each piece week by week as being just on the safe side of actionable, but at the meeting, when he read the whole file at once, he was *sweating*, Sid. He says *The Pump* should settle out of court for whatever you ask."

"And I suppose you're not supposed to be telling me that?"

"No," Kevin confessed, "but you did give me the exclusive of the decade."

"How did Gordon Quint find me?" I asked again.

"George said our noble lord was babbling on about you promising not to send him to jail if you walked out free from somewhere or other, and you *had* walked out free, and he wanted to keep you to your promise. George didn't know what he was talking about, but Tilepit made it crystal that George's job depended on finding you within the next five minutes, if not sooner. So George begged us all to find you, to say *The Pump* would confer sainthood immediately and fatten your bank balance, and I phoned India on the off chance, and she said not to worry, she would tell you herself . . . and I asked her how . . . and where. There didn't seem to be any harm in it."

"And you told George Godbar?" I said.

Kevin nodded.

"And he," I said, "told Lord Tilepit? And *he* told Ellis, I suppose . . . because Ellis turned up, too."

"George Godbar phoned Ellis's father's house, looking for Ellis. He got an answering machine telling him to try a mobile number, and he reached Gordon Quint in a car somewhere . . . and he told Gordon where you would be, if Ellis wanted to find you."

Round and round in circles, and the bullets come out *here*.

I sighed again. I was lucky to be alive. I would settle for that. I also wondered how much I would screw out of *The Pump*. Only enough, I decided, to keep His Lordship grateful.

Kevin, the confession over, got restlessly to his feet and walked around the room, stopping when he reached the locker on my left side.

He looked a little blankly at the prosthesis lying there and, after a moment, picked it up. I wished he wouldn't.

He said, surprised, "It's bigger than I pictured. And heavier. And *hard*."

"All the better to club you with," I said.

"Really?" he asked interestedly. "Straight up?"

"It's been known," I said, and after a moment he put the arm down.

"It's true what they say of you, isn't it? You may not look it, but you're one tough bugger, Sid mate, like I told you before."

I said, "Not many people look the way they are inside."

India said, "I'll write a piece about that."

"There you are then, Sid." Kevin was ready to go. "I've got a rape waiting. Thanks for those Japs. Makes us even, right?"

"Even." I nodded.

India stood up as if to follow him. "Stay a bit," I suggested.

She hesitated. Kevin said, "Stay and hold his bloody hand. Oh, shit. Well . . . sorry, mate. *Sorry.*"

"Get out of here," I said.

India watched him go.

"I'm really sorry," she said helplessly, "about getting you shot."

"I'm alive," I pointed out, "so forget it."

Her face looked softer. At that hour in the morning she hadn't yet put on the sharply outlined lipstick nor the matte porcelain makeup. Her eyebrows were as dark and positive, and her eyes as light-blue and clear, but this was the essential India I was seeing, not the worldly package. How different, I wondered, was the inner spirit from the cutting brain of her column?

She, too, as if compelled, came over to my left side and looked at the plastic arm.

"How does it work?" she asked.

I explained about the electrodes, as I had for Rachel.

She picked up the arm and put her fingers inside, touching the electrodes. Nothing happened. No movement in the thumb.

I swallowed. I said, "It probably needs a fresh battery."

"Battery?"

"It clips into the side. That boxlike thing"—I nodded towards the locker—"that's a battery charger. There's a recharged battery in there. Change them over."

She did so, but slowly, because of the unfamiliarity. When she touched the electrodes again, the hand obeyed the signals.

"Oh," she said.

She put the hand down and looked at me.

"Do you," she said, "have a steel rod up your backbone? I've never seen anyone more tense. And your forehead's sweating."

She picked up the box of tissues lying beside the battery charger and offered it to me.

I shook my head. She looked at the immobilized right arm and at the left one on the locker, and a wave of understanding seemed to leave her without breath.

I said nothing. She pulled a tissue out of the box and jerkily dabbed at a dribble of sweat that ran down my temple.

"Why don't you put this arm on?" she demanded. "You'd be better with it on, obviously."

"A nurse will do it." I explained about the emergency. "She'll come when she can."

"Let *me* do it." India said.

"No."

"Why not?"

"Because."

"Because you're too bloody *proud.*"

Because it's too private, I thought.

I was wearing one of those dreadful hospital gowns like a barber's smock that fastened at the back of the neck and shapelessly covered the body. A white flap covered my left shoulder, upper arm, elbow and what remained below. Tentatively India lifted and turned back the flap so that we both could see my elbow and the short piece of forearm.

"You hate it, don't you?" India said.

"Yes."

"I would hate it, too."

I can't bear this, I thought. I can bear Ellis unscrewing my hand and mocking me. I can't bear love.

India picked up the electric arm.

"What do I do?" she asked.

I said with difficulty, nodding again at the locker, "Talcum powder."

"Oh." She picked up the white tinful of comfort for babies. "In the arm, or on you?"

"On me."

She sprinkled powder on my forearm. "Is this right? More?"

"Mm."

She smoothed the powder all over my skin. Her touch sent a shiver right down to my toes.

"And now?"

"Now hold it so that I can put my arm into it."

She concentrated. I put my forearm into the socket, but the angle was wrong.

"What do I do?" she asked anxiously.

"Turn the thumb towards you a bit. Not too far. That's right. Now push up while I push down. That top bit will slide over my elbow and grip—and keep the hand on."

"Like that?" She was trembling.

"Like that," I said. The arm gripped where it was designed to.

I sent the messages. We both watched the hand open and close.

India abruptly left my side and walked over to where she'd left her purse, picking it up and crossing to the door.

"Don't go," I said.

"If I don't go, I'll cry."

I thought that might make two of us. The touch of her fingers on the skin of my forearm had been a caress more intimate than any act of sex. I felt shaky. I felt more moved than ever in my life.

"Come back," I said.

"I'm supposed to be in the office."

"India," I said, "Please . . ." Why was it always so impossible to plead? "Please . . ." I looked down at my left hand. "Please don't *write* about this."

"Don't *write* about it?"

"No."

"Well, I won't, but why not?"

"Because I don't like pity.'"

She came halfway back to my side with tears in her eyes.

"Your Jenny," she said, "told me that you were so afraid of being pitied that you would never ask for help."

"She told you too much."

"Pity," India said, coming a step nearer, "is actually about as far from what I feel for you as it's possible to get."

I stretched out my left arm and fastened the hand on her wrist.

She looked at it. I tugged, and she took the last step to my side.

"You're strong," she said, surprised.

"Usually."

I pulled her nearer. She saw quite clearly what I intended, and bent her head and put her mouth on mine as if it were not the first time, as if it were natural.

A pact, I thought.

A beginning.

TIME DRIFTED WHEN she'd gone.

Time drifted to the midday news.

A nurse burst into my quiet room. "Don't you have your television on? You're on it."

She switched on knobs, and there was my face on the screen, with a newsreader's unemotional voice saying, "Sid Halley is recovering in hospital." There was a widening picture of me looking young and in racing colors: a piece of old film taken years ago of me weighing in after winning the Grand National. I was holding my saddle in two hands and my eyes were full of the mystical wonder of having been presented with the equivalent of the Holy Grail.

The news slid to drought and intractable famine.

The nurse said, "Wait," and twiddled more knobs, and another channel opened with the news item and covered the story in its entirety.

A woman announcer whose lugubrious voice I had long disliked put on her portentous-solemn face and intoned: "Police today found the body of Ellis Quint in his car, deep in the New Forest in Hampshire. . . ."

Frozen, I heard her saying, as if from a distance, "Foul play is not suspected. It is understood that the popular broadcaster left a note for his father, still unconscious after an accidental blow to the head on Sunday night. Now over to our reporter in Hampshire, Buddy Bowes."

Buddy Bowes, microphone in hand, filled the foreground of the screen with, slightly out of focus in the distance behind him, woodland and activity and a rear view of a white car.

"This is a sad ending," Buddy Bowes said, appearing at least to show genuine regret, "to a fairy-tale life. Ellis Quint, thirty-eight, who gave pleasure to millions with his appearances on television, will also be remembered as the dashing champion amateur steeplechase jockey whose courage and gallantry inspired a whole generation to get out there and *achieve*. In recent months he has been troubled by accusations of cruelty to animals from his long-time colleague and supposed friend, Sid Halley, ex-professional top jockey. Quint was due to appear in court yesterday to refute those charges."

There was a montage of Ellis winning races, striding about in macho riding boots, wowing a chat-show audience, looking glowingly alive and handsome.

"Ellis will be mourned by millions," Buddy Bowes finished. "And now back to the studio . . ."

The nurse indignantly switched off the set. "They didn't say anything about your being shot."

"Never mind."

She went away crossly. The reputation Ellis had manufactured for me couldn't be reversed in a night, whatever *The Pump* might now say. Slowly perhaps. Perhaps never.

Ellis was dead.

I sat in the quiet white room.

Ellis was *dead*.

AN HOUR LATER a hospital porter brought me a letter that he said had been left by hand on the counter of the hospital's main reception desk and overlooked until now.

"Overlooked since when?"

Since yesterday, he thought.

When he'd gone I held the envelope in the pincer fingers and tore it open with my teeth.

The two-page letter was from Ellis, his handwriting strong with life. It said:

Sid, I know where you are. I followed the ambulance. If you are reading this, you are alive and I am dead. I didn't think you would catch me. I should have known you would.

If you're wondering why I cut off those feet, don't you ever want to break out? I was tired of goody-goody. I wanted the dark side. I wanted to smash. To explode. To mutilate. I wanted to laugh at the fools who fawned on me. I hugged myself. I mocked the proles.

And that scrunch.

I did that old pony to make a good program. The kid had leukemia. Sob-stuff story, terrific. I needed a good one. My ratings were slipping.

Then I lusted to do it again. The danger. The risk, the difficulty. And that scrunch. I can't describe it. It gives me an ecstasy like nothing else. Co-caine is for kids. Sex is nothing. I've had every woman I ever wanted. The scrunch of bones is a million-volt orgasm.

And then there's you. The only one I've ever envied. I wanted to corrupt you, too. No one should be unbendable.

I know all you fear is helplessness. I know you. I wanted to make you helpless in Owen Yorkshire's office but all you did was sit there watching your hand turn blue. I could feel you willing me to be my real self but my real self wanted to hear your wrist bones crunch to dust. I wanted to prove that no one was good. I wanted you to crumble. To be like me.

And then, you'll think I'm crazy, I was suddenly glad you weren't sob-bing and whining and I was proud of you that you really were how you are, and I felt happy and higher than a kite. And I didn't want you to die, not like that, not for nothing. Not because of me.

I see now what I've done. What infinite damage.

My father did that last colt. I talked him into it.

It's cost my mother's life. If my father lives they'll lock him up for trying to kill you. They should have let me hang, back in June, when I tried with my tie.

They say people want to be caught. They go on and on sinning until someone stops them.

The letter ended there except for three words much lower down the page:

You win, Sid.

The two sheets of paper lay on the white bedclothes. No one else would see them, I thought.

I remembered Rachel saying how odd it would be to be dead. To be a *space*. The whole white room was a space.

Good and evil, he had been my friend. An enemy: but finally a friend.

The sour, cruel underside of him receded.

I had the win, but there was no one standing in the stirrups to share it with.

Regret, loss, acceptance and relief; I felt them all.

I grieved for Ellis Quint.